HEART
&
SHADOW

ALSO BY AMANDA HOCKING

Switched
Torn
Ascend
Wake
Lullaby
Tidal
Elegy
Frostfire
Ice Kissed
Crystal Kingdom
Freeks

Heart
&
Shadow

Amanda Hocking

WEDNESDAY BOOKS
NEW YORK

HEART & SHADOW: BETWEEN THE BLADE AND THE HEART. Copyright © 2017 by Amanda Hocking. FROM THE EARTH TO THE SHADOWS. Copyright © 2018 by Amanda Hocking. All rights reserved. Printed in the United States of America. For information, address St. Martin's Press, 175 Fifth Avenue, New York, N.Y. 10010.

www.wednesdaybooks.com
www.stmartins.com

Designed by Devan Norman

The Library of Congress Cataloging-in-Publication Data is available upon request.

ISBN 978-1-250-30819-1 (trade paperback)

Our books may be purchased in bulk for promotional, educational, or business use. Please contact your local bookseller or the Macmillan Corporate and Premium Sales Department at 1-800-221-7945, extension 5442, or by email at MacmillanSpecialMarkets@macmillan.com.

First Edition: March 2019

10 9 8 7 6 5 4 3 2 1

BETWEEN
THE
BLADE
AND THE
HEART

For Mike & Gavin—for all your love and support

ACKNOWLEDGMENTS

———•◆•———

This will be the twenty-second book I've published, and while the process of writing books has gotten easier for me, writing acknowledgments is always hard. It's not because I'm not grateful or because I don't have people to thank—rather, it's the opposite. I worry that I can't properly express my gratitude, but I want to try, so here goes.

As always, first and foremost, I need to thank the readers. I am constantly moved and amazed by the responses I get from all of you—whether it be a message, a tweet, or an Instagram pic. I still can't believe that so many of you choose to spend your time with my imaginary friends, and that you love them just as much as I do. (Some of you, I think, maybe love them even more than I do.)

I still see the occasional article about me, referencing my start in self-publishing years ago, and they usually mention how I did it all on my own. But I didn't do any of this on my own. Without the amazing support from my friends, family, and readers like you propelling me forward, I would not be here writing these words today.

I want to thank my husband, Mike, and my stepson, Gavin, for understanding my long and sometimes frantic work hours, indulging all my odd obsessions, and lifting me up when I am down. Mike, in particular, does the hard work of reminding me that I'm capable of so much more than I think I am. I have a propensity to catastrophize and dramatize everything, but Mike and Gavin are both such literal people, they've made me so much more grounded and responsible. Without them both, I would be a much less happy and much less productive person, and they make even my worst days better.

My mom remains one of my strongest supporters, as does my aunt Cindy (who may be my biggest fan). My whole family in general is insanely wonderful and supportive, and I could write a whole book thanking them all. I want you to know that I love each and every one of you, and I'm so grateful for all of you.

My acknowledgments and my life would not be complete without thanking my best friend/cheerleader/former assistant, Eric. He may not work for me anymore, but he remains in my Top 5 Favorite People Ever. He's still always there to listen, offer advice on my life and my books, and make me laugh when I need it.

Of course, I have to thank all my friends who still remain unbelievably wonderful and loving, despite the fact that adult life has gotten in the way of all of us seeing each other as much as we'd like. Thank you to Fifi, Valerie, Gregg, Pete, Matthew, Josh, Gels, Mark, Lucas, Amelia, and now Baby Isabelle, Sofia, and Oliver.

I also want to give a special thank-you to my longtime editor, Rose Hilliard. She's worked with me the entire time I've been with St. Martin's, and together we've worked on twelve books and five short stories. I am a better writer now than I was five years ago, and that's in large part because of her encouragement and criticisms. She has now moved on to a different path, so this is the last book she worked on with me, but she has left an indelible mark on my life and my writing.

I want to thank the entire team at St. Martin's/Wednesday Books, including my new editor, Eileen Rothschild. Everyone there does an amazing job making my books so much better than I could do on my own, and the team always creates ridiculously beautiful covers. I am grateful to have all of them championing my books.

And finally, I have to thank my dogs, Isley and Sawyer. They are by my side constantly, which means that on days when I spend long hours in my office, they're in here, too. (As I write this, Isley is snoring softly as she sleeps by my feet, while Sawyer chews on a bone two feet away.) They might not work hard, but they make my days much happier, which definitely makes my job easier.

Valkyrie: *noun /val-ˈkir-ē/ from Old Norse valkyrja, literally "chooser of the slain," referring to any of the maidens of Odin who choose the immortals to be slain and conduct them to the afterlife.*

IN THE TIME BEFORE . . .

———◆———

In the vast emptiness of space, the gods grew restless, and so they created the heavens above and the worlds below. They filled the earth with every creature imaginable, from the smallest fish in the sea to the largest dragon in the sky.

Their creations fell into two groups:

Immortals, which could be divine beings such as angels and fairies, or impious humanoids like demons and vampires, and even beasts like dragons or centaurs. They could roam the earth forever if nothing stood in their way, and rarely were mortals able to. But with the gift was one sharp restriction: They did as they were made. Evil begat evil, and good begat good, and they all acted accordingly.

Mortals, which were either humans who lacked the gifts of the gods, or animals like birds and rabbits. Their life spans were short, over in the blink of a god's eye, but unlike the immortals, they had free will. They could act as good or evil as they chose.

While many of the immortals thought of themselves as gods and goddesses and often donned the title, the only real true gods were known as the Vanir gods—a council of supreme immortal beings that ruled over the cosmos. Unlike the immortals, the Vanir gods did not live on earth, and they had no power to create or destroy life at will.

The Vanir gods had agreed to watch from above and not interfere with the squabbles among the beings, but Odin could not be swayed by the pledge he'd made to the other Vanir gods. Despite his best intentions, he'd grown very fond of the humans.

Their joys, their determination, their unwavering belief in their own prestige—Odin relished it all. But he saw they were small and frail compared to the immortal creatures that stomped over them, trampling the humans despite their conviction of their own greatness. Angel and demon alike had taken over, claiming the world for their own, and soon the humans would be all but extinct.

To protect the fragile humans he'd grown so fond of, Odin created the Valkyries. They were mortal women he bestowed with supernatural powers and weapons, passed on from mother to daughter, and they were able to slay the immortals, keeping their powers in check.

The other gods cried out, saying that Odin was playing favorites if the humans could kill the immortals at will. So an intermediary was put in place—the Eralim, angelic beings who would take orders from the gods about what immortal should be slain and when. The Eralim would give the orders to the Valkyries, so that the humans never interacted directly with the gods.

A balance descended on the world, where the supernatural lived alongside the humans. For several millennia, this balance helped create an uneasy peace, one that the Valkyries would do anything to protect.

But one misstep, even the smallest lapse in duty, could send it all into a tailspin. . . .

That is not dead which can eternal lie.
And with strange aeons even death may die.

—H. P. LOVECRAFT

ONE

———— ◆ ————

The air reeked of fermented fish and rotten fruit, thanks to the overflowing dumpster from the restaurant behind us. The polluted alley felt narrow and claustrophobic, sandwiched between skyscrapers.

In the city, it was never quiet or peaceful, even at three in the morning. There were more than thirty million humans and supernatural beings coexisting, living on top of each other. It was the only life I'd ever really known, but the noise of the congestion grated on me tonight.

My eyes were locked on the flickering neon lights of the gambling parlor across the street. The *u* in *Shibuya* had gone out, so the sign flashed SHIB YA at me.

The sword sheathed at my side felt heavy, and my body felt restless and electric. I couldn't keep from fidgeting and cracked my knuckles.

"He'll be here soon," my mother, Marlow, assured me. She leaned back against the brick wall beside me, casually eating large jackfruit seeds from a brown paper sack. *Always bring a snack on a stakeout* was one of her first lessons, but I was far too nervous and excited to eat.

The thick cowl of her frayed black sweater had been pulled up like a hood, covering her cropped blond hair from the icy mist that fell on us. Her tall leather boots only went to her calf, thanks to her long legs. Her style tended to be monochromatic—black on black on black—aside from the shock of dark red lipstick.

My mother was only a few years shy of her fiftieth birthday, with almost thirty years of experience working as a Valkyrie, and she was still as strong and vital as ever. On her hip, her sword Mördare glowed a dull red through its sheath.

The sword of the Valkyries was one that appeared as if it had been broken in half—its blade only a foot long before stopping at a sharp angle. Mördare's blade was several thousand years old, forged in fires to look like red glass that would glow when the time was nigh.

My sword was called Sigrún, a present on my eighteenth birthday from Marlow. It was a bit shorter than Mördare, with a thicker blade, so it appeared stubby and fat. The handle was black utilitarian, a replacement that my mom had had custom-made from an army supply store, to match her own.

The ancient blade appeared almost black, but as it grew closer to its target, it would glow a vibrant purple. For the past hour that we'd been waiting on our stakeout, Sigrún had been glowing dully on my hip.

The mist grew heavier, soaking my long black hair. I kept the left side of my head shaved, parting my hair over to the right, and my scalp should've been freezing from the cold, but I didn't feel it. I didn't feel anything.

It had begun—the instinct of the Valkyrie, pushing aside my humanity to become a weapon. When the Valkyrie in me took over, I was little more than a scythe for the Grim Reaper of the gods.

"He's coming," Marlow said behind me, but I already knew.

The world fell into hyperfocus, and I could see every droplet of rain as it splashed toward the ground. Every sound echoed through me, from the bird flapping its wings a block away, to the club door as it groaned open.

Eleazar Bélanger stumbled out, his heavy feet clomping in the puddles. He was chubby and short, barely over four feet tall, and he would've appeared to be an average middle-aged man if it wasn't for the two knobby horns that stuck out on either side of his forehead. Graying tufts of black hair stuck out from under a bright red cap, and as he walked ahead, he had a noticeable limp favoring his right leg.

He was a Trasgu, a troublemaking goblin, and his appearance belied the strength and cunning that lurked within him. He was over three hundred years old, and today would be the day he died.

I waited in the shadows of the alley for him to cross the street. A coughing fit caused him to double over, and he braced himself against the brick wall.

I approached him quietly—this all went easier when they didn't have time to prepare. He took off his hat to use it to wipe the snot from his nose, and when he looked up at me, his green eyes flashed with understanding.

"It's you," Eleazar said in a weak, craggy voice. We'd never met, and I doubt he'd ever seen me before, but he recognized me, the way they all did when their time was up.

"Eleazar Bélanger, you have been chosen to die," I said, reciting my script, the words automatic and cold on my lips. "It is my duty to return you to the darkness from whence you came."

"No, wait!" He held up his pudgy hands at me. "I have money. I can pay you. We can work this out."

"This is not my decision to make," I said as I pulled the sword from my sheath.

His eyes widened as he realized I couldn't be bargained with. For a moment I thought he might just accept his fate, but they rarely did. He bowed his head and ran at me like a goat. He was stronger than he looked and caused me to stumble back a step, but he didn't have anywhere to go.

My mother stood blocking the mouth of the alley, in case I needed her. Eleazar tried to run toward the other end, but his leg slowed him, and I easily overtook him. Using the handle of my sword, I cracked him on the back of the skull, and he fell to the ground on his knees.

Sigrún glowed brightly, with light shining out from it and causing the air to glow purple around us. Eleazar mumbled a prayer to the Vanir gods. I held the sword with both hands, and I struck it across his neck, decapitating him.

And then, finally, the electricity that had filled my body, making my muscles quiver and my bones ache, left me, and I breathed in deeply. The corpse of an immortal goblin lay in a puddle at my feet, and I felt nothing but relief.

"It was a good return," my mother said, and put her hand on my shoulder. "You did well, Malin."

TWO

The crimson of the early morning sun glittered off the windows of the skyscrapers that towered above, making the glass look like fragmented rubies. In the heart of the city, dwarfed by all the buildings around it, sat the Evig Riksdag—the eternal parliament. Colloquially referred to as the Riks by Valkyries, it was where we all reported and got our orders from the Eralim.

The building's design made it similar to a concrete mushroom, with the lower twenty floors narrow and almost windowless, while the top ten floors extended far past the base, held up by metal beams. It was a feat of engineering that the top-heavy building didn't topple over. The austere appearance lent itself more to a government prison than to a place of celestial intervention.

A small computer screen was posted next to the front door, and I placed my hand on it. A beam of light flashed hotly over my hand, analyzing it, then the screen flashed green. The thick steel doors slowly slid open, and Marlow and I walked inside.

The lobby was deserted, save for the half dozen armed guards that were posted around the doors. Their black uniforms all had the same insignia on their shoulders—an eagle with the three horns of Odin. It was the symbol of the Vörðr, the powerful police force of the Evig Riksdag, mostly made up of sons of Valkyries.

The solid concrete walls enclosing the lobby gave the room a bunkerlike feel, but the black marble floors swirling with copper added a touch of elegance. Two bronze statues—men brandishing long swords, hunched under the shroud of their massive wings—were the only décor in the entire space.

But the Riksdag wasn't the kind of place that encouraged loitering or visitors of any kind. Security was of the highest priority. There had been many attacks by immortals against the Riks, some that resulted in deaths of the Eralim and Valkyries that ran it, which was why the Vörðr needed to be the most elite police force in the world.

Many immortals took umbrage with the idea of being "returned," which was the vernacular the Riks used for killing. We weren't murderers—we were simply returning the immortals back to a world where they belonged.

Marlow and I took the elevator to the twenty-ninth floor, where we were greeted with a retinal scan before we could exit. A long corridor stretched out before us—more black marble floors and copper walls closing in on us. At the very end was a massive bronze door, and on either side stood Samael's personal bodyguards.

Godfrey Wright was the larger of the two, but both were hulking. Godfrey stood well over seven feet tall, with bulging arms and a shaved cranium. But what people usually noticed first was that he was a cyclops, with a solitary large eye above his nose.

The smaller and younger guard was Atlas Malosi. With light brown skin and cropped black hair, he had an open face and glittering dark eyes that made him appear much too friendly to be a guard.

He was the son of a Valkyrie, so he had the strength and height of one, but none of the supernatural ability that would make it possible for him to slay immortals. Only daughters could wield such power.

"How are you ladies doing this lovely morning?" Atlas asked, with a broad grin to match his broad shoulders.

"Just finished the job," I replied.

"I assume that it all went well for you." Atlas continued grinning.

"Is Samael in?" Marlow asked, cutting Atlas's chatter.

The smile finally fell from Atlas's face. "You know Samael. He's always in."

Godfrey was a man of few words, so he merely let out a grunt of agreement and gestured toward the door.

"Thank you." I smiled politely at the guards, but Marlow was already opening the door and heading into Samael's spacious office.

Samael had been assigned as my Eralim, because he'd been my mother's before me. His office was sparsely furnished—a large desk in front of the glass wall that overlooked the city, a few art deco chairs and a sofa, and objets d'art he'd collected over the centuries displayed on the shelves that lined the walls.

Samael himself was sprawled out on the black velvet sofa, absently reading something on his electronic tablet, but he broke out in a smile when he spotted us. While Samael was well over three hundred years old, he didn't look a day over twenty-five.

Lounging in black slacks and a dress shirt with the sleeves rolled up, he looked more like a college kid playing at grown-up than an experienced supervisor. Adding to that, he was incredibly handsome, with warm umber skin, bright aqua eyes beneath a strong brow, and a mass of shoulder-length chestnut curls with natural blond highlights coursing through.

His full lips always seemed on the edge of a smirk, one that even my stoic mother couldn't resist. As he walked over to greet us, Marlow pushed down her cowled hood and smiled brazenly at him.

"How is it that you always manage to look so beautiful, even this early in the morning?" Samael mused, his eyes locked on my mother.

I rolled my eyes and sat in one of the several uncomfortable three-legged armchairs. I leaned back, propping my black moto boots up on the glass table to wait out Marlow and Samael's flirtation.

"You know work always brings out the best in me." Marlow smiled demurely at Samael, then turned and sauntered away from him, toward his desk.

He kept a crystal bowl on his desk, perpetually filled with treats like red bean paste covered in gold leaf or baby scorpions dipped in chocolate. As Samael turned his attention to me, Marlow grabbed a handful of whatever delicacy he had today, and as he spoke, she absently munched on it.

"So, Malin, how did it go?" Samael asked me.

I looked past him to my mother, searching her expression for clues as to how she thought it went, but she just stared down impassively at the morsels in her hand.

"He's dead, so I think it went about as well as it could have," I said finally.

"*Returned*," Samael corrected me, then cast his eyes toward the ceiling, as if someone upstairs cared enough to eavesdrop on us. "He's returned, not dead."

The immortals weren't killed—they merely shed their mortal coil in a way that meant they could never walk the earth again.

That was one of the basic tenets of the world we lived in, and one of the first things we were taught in grade school. The gods had given us dominion over the earth, where humans, animals, and supernatural beings were all supposed to live in harmony as much as we could.

Valkyries were instated to return immortals to another realm—to an underworld called Kurnugia—and they could not come back.

Mortals couldn't return from the dead, either, but that was mostly because we had no afterworld.

That was how things were kept "fair." Immortals returned to Kurnugia, but mortals could not. When we died, we were left to rot in the dirt.

The dead must stay dead. That which is dead cannot rise.

"If you're going to be a Valkyrie, you'll have to get the lingo down," Samael went on.

"I *am* a Valkyrie," I replied pointedly.

"It may be in your blood, but it's not your job title yet," Samael said, sitting back down on the sofa across from me. "You know how the folks upstairs love paperwork and procedure."

"That they do," Marlow snorted in agreement, but I already had plenty of experience with the bureaucracy of the Evig Riksdag.

My training in their protocol had begun shortly after my eighteenth birthday, with classes at Ravenswood Academy, and it had still taken almost a year before I was able to start apprenticing alongside my mother. Then it had been another six months of testing and training and red tape before I had finally gotten a permit and been allowed to make kills, as long as it was under the close supervision of Marlow.

Since then I had killed—or, rather, *returned*—four immortals. Eleazar Bélanger had been my fifth.

"How are you taking to it, then?" Samael leaned forward, resting his arms on his knees, and something in the softness of his voice led me to believe what he was really asking was how I was coping.

There had been an entire course at Ravenswood Academy called Guilt and How to Handle It, and we discussed how some Valkyries couldn't deal with it. The responsibility of being an executioner was too much.

But I'd never felt guilt. I'd never felt anything but purpose. My body was made to do this, and when there was too much time between jobs, I began to *crave* it. The way the electricity felt coursing through me, the buzzing around my heart, the way the pressure felt growing inside of me that wouldn't stop until I completed my mission.

It was all relief and release.

"I can't imagine doing anything else," I admitted.

Samael looked back over his shoulder at my mother. "You think she's doing well enough to go on her own soon?"

"She's ready to go now." Marlow absently brushed at the crumbs on her black pants. "I know the Riksdag wants her to have seven returns under her belt, so I'll be happy to shadow for the next two, but she doesn't need me."

Samael looked back at me, grinning. "Well, it sounds like you'll be a Valkyrie *very* soon."

My mother looked up, pride flashing momentarily in her dark gray eyes. "She was born for it."

THREE

———◆———

The city had outgrown the land, and a century or so ago it had expanded out onto the lake. I'm sure the engineer behind the New Edgewater development had visions of romantic architecture with canal streets, like Venice or St. Petersburg, but the reality had become something much different.

The water had become polluted, and it smelled of gasoline and dead fish, and the wealthy elites had fled. The condominiums and apartments that towered around me, scraping the clouds overhead, had become run-down and decrepit. Broken windows and rusty fire escapes, with clotheslines running from building to building.

Vehicles sped by on the canals, splashing filthy water onto the sidewalks. It was all old yellow taxis, hovercrafts, and luftfahrrads—motorcycles that hovered a few inches above the surface of the water.

Somewhere a baby was crying. In New Edgewater, there was always a baby crying somewhere within earshot. There was a large population of pontianaks here, and they lured victims with the sound of a crying infant.

It was getting late, but I walked slowly down the crowded sidewalks away from my apartment. As much as I loved working as a Valkyrie, it always took something out of me, and I crashed for hours after.

The garage would be closed by the time I got there, but the stack of silvery blue bills in my pocket would open the doors. Samael always paid me with freshly minted money, and I often wondered what became of the old worn dollars. Did the Riks shred them and constantly print their own money?

Above me, the overcast sky rumbled ominously. The lights from the city made the clouds glow orange and red, and I quickened my pace. I had only a block left to go when the sky opened up with angry, cold raindrops.

Galel's Garage was right on the edge of where dry land met the lake, and I jogged over to it. The plate-glass window proudly proclaimed that Galel's Garage had been serving the New Edgewater community for over 125 years, but that kind of thing was easier to do when you were immortal.

"We're closed!" a voice boomed from the garage as I stepped into the front lobby.

"I thought you might make an exception for your favorite customer," I said hopefully, and a few moments later Jude Locklear came in through the garage door, bowing his head slightly so his horns wouldn't hit the frame, as he dried his hands on a frayed towel.

His oil-stained overalls were rolled down to his hips, and his white tank top stretched taut over his chest and stood out sharply against his dark olive skin. Jude towered over me, with broad shoulders and biceps the size of tree trunks. His black hair fell in waves that landed just above his shoulders, and his dark eyebrows were always perfectly arched in a look of suggestive amusement.

At first glance, he looked like an ordinary guy—albeit a very muscular and very tall guy—in his early twenties. It was only the two massive ram's horns that curled out from the side of his head that revealed his true heritage as a Cambion, the son of a demon.

His father, Galel, was an incubus, to be precise, and someday his name might show up on Samael's orders to me. But Jude's never would, since he was mortal like his mother. Jude had only inherited his horns and his undeniable sex appeal from his father.

Well, that and his ability to fix nearly any vehicle in a short amount of time for a reasonable price.

"You're late." Jude grinned slowly at me, and there was an irresistible sparkle in his dark brown eyes every time he smiled.

"I overslept, and then I got caught in the rain." I motioned to the rain pounding against the glass behind me.

His eyes flitted over my body, at the clothes sticking wet to my skin, and I arched my back slightly, pushing out my chest. He smiled approvingly before tossing the towel at me.

"Dry yourself off, then I'll show you what I did with your luft." He turned, and I followed him into the garage as I ran the towel through my hair.

My luftfahrrad was a Frankenstein of a hoverbike, with parts from all kinds of old bikes and vehicles pieced together to somehow make a working luft, including a chrome skull between the handlebars. Jude himself had been the one to do most of the work, following my requests to get it done as cheaply as possible. It was actually a credit to his skill that the damned thing ever ran.

"You know, I don't mind seeing you every few weeks to duct-tape some new problem you have," Jude said as he finished explaining all the new adjustments he'd made to keep it afloat. "But I'd be a shitty mechanic if I didn't point out that it would be cheaper just to buy a new luft than to keep getting this one fixed up."

I pulled my cash out of my pocket and ignored his suggestion, the way I did every time he made it. "How much do I owe you this time?"

He rubbed the back of his neck and glanced over at the clock hanging on the wall. "It's getting late. Why don't we go out and get a drink, and we can settle up later?"

I smiled. "If that's what you want, it sounds fun to me."

"Just let me change, and we'll get out of here."

FOUR

———◆———

On the chipped-paint sign above the door, the name CARPE NOCTEM was barely legible. The brick façade was cracked and crumbling, and the large front window had been boarded up, with *yes, we're open* spray-painted across it.

Everything about the exterior looked ancient, except for the sign on the door, declaring that they served liliplum here. And even that had faded to lavender from bright purple, since it had been five years since liliplum was legalized.

Barstools were held together with duct tape, and broken glass littered the sticky floor. Despite the subpar décor and angry thumping of music through the stereo, the bar was always packed.

The clientele were mostly regulars, or at least it seemed to me that I always saw the same folks when I came here with Jude. Mostly big, burly, and male, wearing tattered leather and denim. Some were obviously craven, with horns and fangs and monstrous appendages, but others were just regular humans looking to escape the monotony of the nearby slums.

A place like this one might expect to smell like cheap beer and body odor—and it did, but only slightly, buried deep beneath the sweet floral and clove scent of the liliplum. In the corner of the bar, behind a curtain of beads, was the hookah bar, where patrons smoked the liliplum, and its dark violet smoke filled the room.

Jude found two open seats at the bar, and a waitress with large raven's wings growing from her back and a septum piercing came over to glare at us. He gruffly ordered a bottle of the cheapest beer, and when she set her angry-bird eyes on me, I ordered the same.

"How is work?" Jude asked, after the waitress had rolled her eyes and left us to retrieve our beer.

"It's good," I replied carefully.

Jude knew what I did, and he claimed he didn't care. But many others didn't think so highly of Valkyries, particularly immortal cravens like the kind that frequented this bar. After all, someday in the future, I might be the one to kill them.

"That'll be fifteen bucks," the waitress said, sounding both bored and pissed off as she set two lukewarm bottles of Dante's Lager in front of us. I put a twenty down on the bar, but the waitress had already sauntered off to be irritated by some other customer.

Jude took a long drink of his beer, grimacing as he swallowed it down. I followed suit, drinking down the tepid alcohol. It tasted like old socks but with a heat at the end that made my eyes water. Jude laughed and patted me heartily on the back, his massive hand feeling warm and powerful even through my jacket.

"Dante's Lager is an acquired taste," Jude admitted.

I wiped my mouth with the back of my arm. "Well, it is not a taste I wish to acquire." He laughed again, a warm rumble that seemed to permeate everything.

Jude motioned to the crisp twenty-dollar bill that the waitress had yet to collect. "I take it that you were working last night?"

I nodded, and despite the burning in my throat, I ventured taking another drink, gulping it down quickly.

"Anyone I know?" Jude asked. He was smiling, but there was a twisting at the corner of his lips and his eyes were downcast.

When people found out I was a Valkyrie, they usually reacted in three ways: anger, disgust, or curiosity. Sometimes it started out as one, then turned into another.

But I was already used to hearing the same questions over and over again.

Have you killed anyone?

What's it like to kill?

Don't you feel bad about it?

And then: *Would you kill me?*

So I tried to avoid the questions as much as possible, because nobody ever liked the answer to each.

Yes.

Like sex, only better.

No.

Yes, I would. And I will, if your name shows up on my orders.

"You know I don't like talking about work," I reminded Jude. We'd been friendly for a while, so this wasn't the first time it had come up.

Jude held his hand up in a gesture of peace. "Hey, I'm not one to judge. I don't care how people live their lives and make their money."

"I don't do it for the money," I replied quickly, maybe too quickly.

I was no mercenary, and I hated that people made that assumption. Yes, I got paid for my services, but it wasn't enough to make my rent, and most Valkyries had to have a second job. The paycheck just offset some of our costs, but the truth was that we'd all do it whether we got paid or not.

We were compelled to do it. We needed to do it the same way we needed to breathe.

"My old man always said that if you love what you do, you'll never work a day in your life," Jude said, breaking the uncomfortable silence that had settled over us. "But then again, my dad's also an incubus who works on the side banging women to steal their souls and valuables."

"It sounds like he's got life figured out, then," I muttered.

Jude chugged the last of his beer, then slammed the empty bottle on the bar. "That was shite. Wanna get some liliplum?"

He'd barely gotten the words out before I was already hopping off the barstool and chirping, "Yes, please."

Jude laughed and followed me back through the beaded curtains into the cloud of purple. People were sitting around on overstuffed couches, with the hookahs on tables in the center. The hookahs looked like tall, slender vases, with two hoses coming out of the glass base of each, and everyone was talking and laughing between drags on the hoses.

There wasn't a lot of room, and Jude took up a lot of space, so I sat on the arm of the couch beside him. He took a drag first before handing me the hose, and I inhaled deeply. It was like breathing in a campfire and a bouquet of flowers.

And then already I was feeling it and I sank back on the couch. It was like two shots of vodka, without the burning in the throat or the hangover. It was just lightness and calm, and it wrapped itself around me like a warm blanket.

Back here, the anger of the demonic metal band was replaced with something more melodic and velvety: the voice of a woman, sultry and slow, and the way her words went through me, softening the beating of my heart, made me wonder if she was a siren.

"Come on, Malin, you're not usually a lightweight." Jude's voice rumbled in my ear as he chuckled. His horn brushed against me, cold and hard on my temple, and I closed my eyes and leaned against him. His arm wrapped around me, steadying me. "I've seen you drink ogres under the table before."

"The lili hits me harder," I told him honestly. I usually only saved it for special occasions, and maybe tonight felt special because of my work this morning, or maybe I just didn't want to talk to Jude about it anymore, or maybe I just didn't want to talk.

I just wanted to fall into his arms, the way he would let me, and I knew he would carry me back to his place and do the things that only he seemed to know how to do.

I opened my eyes, preparing to yield to the temptation, to invite myself to his place, when the beaded curtains parted in front of us, and *she* walked in.

FIVE

Quinn Evelyn Devane.

A Valkyrie with long hair dyed silver, so it shimmered and danced in the light, except where her roots grew in black. Her mouth was slightly lopsided, and on other people that might look silly or strange, but on her it just looked like she had a wonderful secret and she was daring you to find out what it was.

She was tall, taller than me, even, with powerful legs that went on for days. Across her collarbone ran a dark red scar, and below that she revealed more than a hint of her ample cleavage.

Around her neck she wore a silver amulet inscribed with the Vegvisir—the Norse symbol of protection.

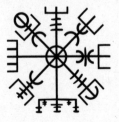

In the very center was a solitary red garnet that seemed to follow me everywhere I looked.

I was hoping she wouldn't see me, as if somehow, even though she was standing right in front of me, I would be able to disappear completely into Jude's arms. But then her eyes landed on me—bright green eyes, like a meadow in spring—and my breath caught in my throat.

"Malin," Quinn said, smiling her asymmetric smile. Her voice was low and husky, but it managed to carry over the music, and she sat down on the table across from me. "I haven't seen you since . . ."

She trailed off, and my heart pounded in my chest. Inside my head I was screaming, *Don't say it. Please don't say it. Please don't say "since we broke up."*

It was not because I was ashamed or I didn't want Jude to know—I didn't really care what he'd think, but I also knew he wouldn't care at all.

I just wasn't ready to talk about it. It had only been six months since we'd broken up, and I still didn't know how I felt about any of that.

"How do you two know each other?" Jude asked, probably since it seemed like I might not say anything ever again. He pulled his arm from around my waist so he could lean forward, and when Quinn crossed her legs, her foot brushed against mine, so I sat up straighter.

"I'm a Valkyrie," Quinn explained, not lowering her voice when she said that, the way I always did when I was in mixed company like this. "I was licensed a few years ago, so I was helping show Malin the ropes."

"Is Malin any good?" Jude asked, teasing.

Quinn's eyes were on me, sparkling underneath the veil of her dark lashes. "She's very good."

"It was nice seeing you, but I think we were just heading out." I stumbled to my feet. The heady intoxication from the liliplum was mixing with the muddled exhilaration I felt whenever I was around Quinn, and I couldn't handle the combination anymore.

Quinn was on her feet in a flash, blocking my path. "I was hoping we could talk."

"Not today." I shook my head. "I can't today."

"When?" she pressed as I walked around her.

"Later," I called back over my shoulder, and I'd taken Jude's hand so I could pull him through the bar and out into the street.

It wasn't until we were outside, in the pouring rain, that I felt like I could breathe again. The cold helped push away some of the haze, sobering me up.

"So what's with you and that Valkyrie back there?" Jude asked. "You were acting like she was a monster or an ex-girlfriend or something."

"She *is* my ex-girlfriend," I muttered.

"Oh. Well, that explains that, then." He stood beside me for a second, not saying anything. "Do you want to get out of this rain and come back to my place?"

"I would be happy to go anywhere with you, as long as it's not here."

Jude laughed as we started walking in the rain toward his apartment over the garage. "That's the kind of thing every guy can't wait to hear."

SIX

◆

My phone pulsated on the nightstand. The table was made out of bones—Jude claimed they were bones from his own ancestors—with a plate of glass on top, and the screen of my phone made the skulls glow blue.

I picked up my phone to see about a dozen text messages from my best friend/roommate Oona Warren.

Are you coming home tonight?

Where are you even?

I'm guessing you're not coming home tonight, so I went ahead and fed Bowie. I'm assuming that you went home with Jude again.

Just so I know you're not murdered or dead in the lake, you should text me and let me know.

Seriously, Mal. It's morning now. What are you doing?

You have class this morning.

Malin. Text me so I can stop worrying.

"Shit." I groaned, and, pushing the fog of sleep and a burgeoning hangover aside, I got out of bed.

In the darkness of Jude's bedroom, I scrambled to pull on my pants. I'd just gotten my bra on when Jude began to rouse in the bed.

"Where are you going so early?" Jude suppressed a yawn.

I sat on the edge of his bed, yanking on my moto boots and brushing back the tangles of long hair from my face. "It's not early. It's a quarter past eight, and I'm gonna be late for class."

"Class?" Jude asked, sounding more alert. "Wait, you aren't in high school, are you?"

"College," I replied, but Ravenswood Academy was much more of a trade school than a university. It was only for kids studying to work for the Evig Riksdag or other government agencies that dealt with the supernatural elements of our world.

I stood up and grabbed my jacket from the floor. "I still have to get my luft out of the shop."

"Just go in and tell my dad that I sent you to get it."

"Thanks." I dug in my jacket pocket and pulled out a small handful of twenties, and I set it on the nightstand. "I'm leaving the money here for you."

"Damn, Malin, you really know how to make a guy feel like a prostitute," Jude said with his rumbling laughter, but I was already on my way out the door, hurriedly texting Oona before she gave herself a heart attack worrying about me.

At the garage, Jude's dad wasn't so keen on letting me just run off with the luft, but after a quick call to Jude, he grudgingly let me go. The luft started hard, grumbling angrily at me, before kicking out a plume of mist and exhaust, and the wheel-like propulsion fans glowed a dull blue beneath the carriage.

Finally, it levitated off the ground, just above the six inches it would need to be street-legal. I throttled it back and flew down the road toward the academy. At this time of day, traffic could get locked up in the Ravenswood District, but with my luft I was able to swerve around a stalled-out bus and go up on the curb.

The sidewalks were crowded with merchants selling their wares, along with patrons and pedestrians just trying to get by. I narrowly slid past a woman selling brightly colored rainbow snakes out of tubs, claiming they were the mystical descendants of the Wagyl.

I managed to hit the brakes just before crashing into a food cart with a man selling sambusa. Sambusa were fried triangular pastry filled with delicious lentils and potatoes, and even though I was running late, my stomach warned me that I needed to eat something.

"I'll take one," I said as I rummaged in my pocket for money.

The man stood there glaring at me for a moment, but finally he took my money and handed me a sambusa, before muttering, "*Sharmoto.*"

"If you're gonna call me names, then give me my tip back." I held my hand out to him.

"You almost killed me, you crazy woman!" He waved his hands wildly at me. "Get out of here with your stupid bike!"

I didn't really have time to argue, and he was right, so maybe I should've tipped him more. I held the sambusa in my mouth, offered the merchant a small wave, then revved up my luft and sped off down the road to Ravenswood.

The whole area around Ravenswood was high-rise low-income apartment complexes, with a few offices and shops on the lower levels. And there was the Ravenswood Academy. It was an Elizabethan Prodigy house—a massive Tudor-style mansion that looked more like it belonged in the English countryside than in the slums of the city.

While the exterior was all the original architecture, meticulously maintained, the interior was more high-tech. Starting with the underground garage, where I had to pass through a blue wall of light to be certain I wasn't carrying any unapproved weapons, and then scan my school ID to get into the garage, and then scan my retinas to get into the building.

The hallway was relatively empty, and despite the high enrollment of the academy it always felt strangely quiet. The flooring was a mosaic inlay of black and white marble, and the walls were stark white with garishly bright crystal light fixtures in the ceiling.

Paintings and artwork adorned the walls, mostly from previous students and alumni, depicting some aspect of life they might be working toward here at Ravenswood, like careers or the beings they might serve.

There were several I always passed on my way up from the parking garage. One was a hanging mobile, looking a bit like a natural chandelier. Birch branches hung down, with horses carved into the white bark. According to the plaque on the wall beneath it, it was created as an offering for Bai-Ülgen.

Another was a large statue made of marble, titled *Ereshkigal of the Netherworld*. It showed a regal woman elegantly perched on a throne made of bones. The bones and the fabric that draped her body were stark white, while her skin was a darker veined gray. Her mouth was curved slightly into a smile, and even though she was made of stone, it felt like her eyes followed me whenever I walked by.

The final picture in the long hall, before I turned off to go toward my class, always made me pause. It depicted a woman in a chainmail bikini, her body rippling with muscles and strength, and her hands covered in blood. Her hair blew out behind her, and she stared up at the sky with a smile on her face as a single red tear slid down her cheek.

The plaque on the bottom read:

"The Desire of the Valkyrie"
Painted by Marlow Krigare during her senior year

My mother had painted it.

I made it to Intro to Divinity and Immortality only five minutes late, which really didn't seem that bad, considering. Fortunately, I'd had my messenger bag with me when I went to Jude's last night, which had my e-reader with my textbooks in it and my laptop for taking notes.

I opened the door as quietly as possible, but a girl—an alchemy major named Sloane Kothari—still turned to glare at me. As the daughter of a Deva, she took her divine disposition very seriously, and unfortunately I had three courses with her this semester.

The professor, Cashel Wu, paused in his lecture to watch me take my seat at a long stainless steel table in the back. He stood in front of the classroom, with the large screen at the front displaying a huge photo of a hieroglyph.

I mouthed, *Sorry*, and got situated as quickly and quietly as I possibly could. By now plenty of other students had turned to look at me. Most of them were human, but a few obviously had more exotic parentage, with wings and tails and horns.

But even those with more prestigious pedigrees came from some sort of mixed background, for them to be accepted into Ravenswood Academy, with usually one parent being human. Almost all offspring of immortals—even from the commingling of two different types of immortals—were mere mortals, with little or none of their parents' powers.

Ravenswood was designed to educate and train mortals for

careers in handling the supernatural, which made it the go-to school for mortal children who had no hope of following in their immortal parents' more elite footsteps.

Sloane Kothari didn't have any obvious signs of her parentage, other than the cold smile and the contempt in her dark eyes whenever she looked at me.

"As we were discussing last week," Professor Wu began once I was settled in, "immortality doesn't make one divine or superior, the same way that mortality doesn't make one weak or inferior.

"In past societies, those with longer life spans or different appearances than humans were often either revered as gods or feared as monsters and forced into exile," Professor Wu continued, and as he spoke, he clicked through photos on the screen.

The pictures changed to a depiction of men bent forward, worshipping feline-headed Bastet; then to the multi-armed Vishnu, adorned in gold and jewels; to the wolf-humanoid Lobishomen, with massive fangs, being stabbed with bloody spears; and the birdlike witch Baba Yaga, being burned alive as she cried out.

"But now, in our civilized society, that is not the case. We realize immortality is no more divine than having brown eyes or a short stature." He looked back at the screen, his gaze lingering on the intense agony in Baba Yaga's face, and he frowned.

"We will be looking back through history," Professor Wu continued. "Learning the mistakes that our ancestors made when confronted with immortality, so that we don't make the mistakes ourselves."

SEVEN

M alin Krigare?" Professor Wu called out, stopping me as I attempted to make my escape out of the classroom. "Can I speak to you for a moment?"

The other students continued their shuffle out of the room, and Sloane snickered at me as she walked out. I took a deep breath and trudged toward the front of class, to where Professor Wu was hunched over his desk making a few notes on his tablet.

"Sorry I was late. I missed my alarm, but I hurried as fast as I could," I began my apology.

"I understand that you're close to getting your license," the professor said, finally looking up at me.

Professor Wu appeared to be in his early thirties, and his well-tailored suits made him one of the more dapper members of the teaching staff here. His black hair was cropped short, and his Vandyke goatee added an additional air of nobility.

"Yeah, it should be soon." I picked absently at my chipped indigo nail polish before adding, "Hopefully."

"Actually, I saw that your Eralim sent a glowing message to the headmaster yesterday." Professor Wu leaned back and folded his arms over his chest. "He thinks your performance is absolutely exemplary."

"That's great," I said, smiling a little, but there was something about Wu's tone that made me worry there was a "but" coming.

"*But*," Wu said, and I grimaced inwardly, "you've been late to my class three times, and school's only been in session for a few weeks."

"I know. I've just been having trouble with my luft—"

"There's always public transportation," Wu cut me off. "But that's not even the point. I've seen plenty of good kids like you, excellent students with bright futures ahead of them, who lose sight of the goal."

I shook my head. "I don't think I'm losing sight of anything."

"I checked. Your grades have been slipping this semester," Wu said, and I lowered my eyes. "You know that even if you get your preliminary license now, it will be revoked if you don't graduate."

Sighing, I nodded. "I know."

"And the Valkyrie program isn't like some of the others here at Ravenswood. You need to pass with high marks or you don't pass at all," Wu lectured. "You still have a whole year left of your courses here. I would just hate for you to lose your career over a bout of senioritis."

"You're right," I said, hating that he was. "I'll start applying myself more and taking my attendance more seriously."

Wu smiled. "That's all I ask for as your professor, Malin."

After I left, I spent my next three classes sucking up, since I knew Wu wouldn't be the only one noticing my recent flakiness, and ended up working on an extracurricular project down in the stacks. Somehow, I'd gotten suckered into annotating a book on medieval demigods, but finally a reprieve came in the form of a text from Oona.

Bowie's out of food. That was all she wrote, but the time on my phone flashing 5:47 P.M. meant that I had been at school long enough for one day.

As quickly as I could without literally running, I rushed down to the parking garage—which was now fairly deserted—got on my luft, and raced out onto the street. The sky was overcast, the way it always seemed to be these days, and the air was cold, but nothing ever felt as good as the wind blowing in my hair as I drove through the city.

I pulled into the cramped parking lot outside Dillinger's Corner Market & Apothecary, and my luft dropped unceremoniously to the pavement. Jude hadn't quite gotten the bug out of the dismount yet.

The market's door beeped as I stepped inside, and Oona looked up at me from where she sat behind the counter. An ancient textbook was spread out before her, which was typical for her, since she usually tried to get as much studying done at work as she could.

"So I guess I can call the search off," Oona replied dryly. Her thick brows were arched downward in an attempt to look angry, but her lips were already curving up into a smile.

I offered her an apologetic smile. "Sorry for worrying you."

She shrugged her slender shoulders, and an easy grin lit up her face, making her eyes sparkle. "I just get bored when you're gone for too long." To emphasize her point, she ran her hand through her new haircut.

The last time I'd seen her—which had been yesterday morning—her jet-black hair had been a little longer, but now it had been cut into a jagged pixie cut, with the curls straightened out. Oona always planned to grow her hair out, but inevitably she'd get impatient or bored and cut it all off again.

"It looks good," I said, but her hair always looked good.

Oona may have been just a human—though she took great exception to the word *just*—but she was one of the most beautiful people I'd ever seen. Her flawless complexion was creamy brown, with high cheekbones above full lips, and her eyes were the color of black walnut. Even under the unforgiving cheap fluorescent lighting she was undeniably gorgeous.

"Thanks." She beamed at me, and the light glinted off her piercings. She had two small metal studs—one on either side of her mouth, just above her lips—colloquially known as Angelbites.

We'd been best friends since the fourth grade, when her family moved down the street from me. While we'd never had a ton in common, we always made each other laugh, and I knew that I could count on her no matter what.

Since Oona was just barely over five feet tall, I liked to joke that she'd stopped growing the day we met, so I grew twice as much for her.

"How was school?" Oona asked.

"Same old, same old," I said with a sigh.

I grabbed a basket and began strolling the cramped aisles of the tiny bodega. Despite the colorful addition of *Apothecary* in the name, the market mostly stocked overpriced food and toiletries, but there was a shelf in the back with crystals, amulets, and various enchanted herbs and potions.

"How about you?" I asked, grabbing a bag of carrots for Bowie.

Bowie was my six-year-old wolpertinger, which basically meant that he was a chubby fawn-colored rabbit with large wings and a tiny pair of antlers between his big ears. Some wolpertingers could fly, but Bowie had always been too fat and preferred doing as little as possible.

She groaned. "I had a pop quiz in Laws of Intercession, which I'm fairly certain I bombed."

Oona was a thaumaturgy major with the goal of a being a great sorceress someday. Even though she went to Ravenswood, we didn't have any classes together. Her area of study tended to be more mystical, while mine was more practical.

"So, anyway, you never did tell me where you were last night," Oona reminded me.

"Just with Jude," I replied, and I didn't need to look up to know that her eyebrows were arched suggestively.

Instead, I pretended to be focused on the bag of Ēostre's Lagomorph Chow, which was alleged to be perfectly formulated for the health needs of jackalopes, wolpertingers, rabbits, pikas, and colugos, before dropping it into my basket.

"That makes it twice in a month, doesn't it?" Oona asked.

"I only see him when my luft breaks down, and it just so happens that my luft kinda sucks." I grabbed a couple packets of ramen noodles and an energy drink that claimed to be infused with the elixir of the sun, whatever the hell that meant.

"I just don't see what the big deal is, Mal," Oona said as I made my way toward the counter. "If you like this guy, what's so bad about making him your boyfriend?"

"It's just not like that." I held up the energy drink. "What do you know about this?"

"I know there's this Nephilim chick in my class, and she swears by it, but I think it's mostly mango juice." Oona shrugged. "Don't change the subject, though. I just don't know why you're so opposed to officially dating someone. I mean, Quinn was your girlfriend before."

"Yeah, and you know how that worked out," I muttered. "Valkyries—"

"—don't fall in love," Oona finished for me with a dramatic eye roll and began ringing up my purchases. "Yeah, yeah, yeah, I know. The great Malin is impervious to the desires of us mere mortals. You may have the libido of a teenage boy. . . ."

I scowled at her, which only made her laugh. "Thanks."

"You know, I've heard you say that thing about Valkyries and love at least a hundred times, but I was reading in a textbook about

Valkyries the other day, and it didn't say anything about that," Oona commented.

"Did it say anything about Valkyries' personal lives at all?" I asked.

She frowned. "Well, no. Not really."

The subject wasn't something I'd really encountered in books, either. There was usually a line or two about Valkyries being loners and isolated, since our job didn't exactly make us popular with the supernatural beings. If it was a real in-depth book, it might offer a tip or two on how to handle those that were prejudiced against us, but that was about it.

Because of the nature of our jobs—which involved occasionally killing our neighbors—we tended to be a lonely people and rather nomadic, with few connections and relationships in this world. Not being able to love made it easier on us, and we were more likely to complete our assignments if there wasn't a risk of us getting attached to them.

Or at least that's what my mom had taught me. Over and over again, since I was very young, usually when I was upset about one thing or another, Marlow would lecture me about how I needed to toughen up, and remind me that we were made of something stronger, so we didn't need love. We didn't need anything.

"I think our inability to really love is one of those things that's common knowledge for Valkyries, but it isn't really talked about outside of the circle," I told Oona with a resigned shrug of my shoulders.

As I paid for my stuff and loaded it up into my messenger bag, Oona informed me that she'd be working for another few hours, so I'd have the place to myself, which gave me time to catch up on my schoolwork.

Oona worked at the market because it was only a couple blocks from our place, and I made it to our apartment complex in record time, parking my luft in the narrow gated alleyway. As I was locking up the luft, the dumpster beside me started shaking and snarling.

I waited a beat, reaching for the asp baton I always carried in my bag, and a Dobhar-chú climbed out, with a mouthful of rotten eggs and lettuce. The Dobhar-chú looked like a cross between an otter and salamander, except with patches of scales mixed in with its slick fur and a row of angry-looking fangs in its mouth.

It stared at me with its small round ears lying flat back against its head, and its gills fanned out as it growled, as if I wanted to steal the garbage from it.

"Go on. I won't bother you," I tried to assure the water hound, but it turned tail and ran out to the canal, where it dove in and disappeared.

The Dobhar-chú and other water creatures like it were part of the reason why complexes like mine—once billed as luxury—had fallen into disrepair. The canals brought along too many pests, smells, and corrosion.

The sign across the building that read TANNHAUSER TOWERS had once been shiny gold and lit up, but all the lights had burned out and the metal began to oxidize and rust. When a strong wind blew by, the letters would groan and shake, and it really was only a matter of time before one of them fell off.

The apartment I shared with Oona was on the sixty-seventh floor, and it had once been a penthouse suite before being cut up and converted into six microscopic apartments. Ours was a dingy two-bedroom, with my room being just barely large enough for a bed and a dresser.

The front door opened into the small living room/kitchen combo, with concrete floors covered in a few worn rugs and cold metal walls that we'd attempted to warm up with a couple posters and a wall tapestry. The only really nice thing about the flat was the rather large window that took up an entire wall and overlooked the canal below.

When I came in, I expected Bowie to greet me, the way he usually did when I got home, but instead of him excitedly hopping across the floor toward me, I was met with silence. Eerie and palpable, and my body instinctively tensed.

I hadn't yet turned the light on, but thanks to all the light pollution from advertising and vehicles, the room was fairly well lit, changing from neon blue to red and back again with the billboard across the canal.

"Bowie?" I called, setting down my messenger bag on the small pile of jackets and shoes Oona and I left by the door.

Then finally I spotted him, huddled underneath the kitchen table in the corner. He stomped his foot loudly on the floor, warning me of danger, but really, I hadn't needed it. I stepped toward Bowie, wanting to get to him and protect him from whatever threat was making the hair on the back of my neck stand up.

But by then it was already too late. I saw a flash of movement in the corner of my eye, and then arms were around me, with a hand over my mouth, blocking my screams.

EIGHT

———◆———

I bucked against my attacker, kicking back and sending him flying across the room. He slammed hard into the metal door of my bedroom, but he was up quickly. When he charged at me, I swung at him, but he grabbed my fist.

I faltered for a moment, caught off guard, and he took that opportunity to pin me to the floor. He held my hands out to either side, his large hands enveloping my wrists, and he straddled me, using his weight to hold me in place.

I could've fought back, but at the moment I was too stunned, trying to figure out how in the hell someone had gotten me on my back so quickly.

Thanks to my Valkyrie blood, I was almost six feet tall and endowed with a preternatural strength. That meant I could best any human I tangled with, be they man or woman, and supernatural beings stood even less of a chance against me.

Not only was I unnaturally strong, but I made immortals *weaker*. My blood was immortal kryptonite.

But this guy, he had stopped my fist like it was no big thing. I could have pushed through, but it would've taken all my strength, and that was alarming.

"What are you?" I asked, staring up at him in the shifting glow from the billboard.

He looked human, at least—black hair cropped short, dark blue eyes, a shadow of beard, a distressed jacket clinging to his broad shoulders.

His eyes narrowed, and his dark eyebrows pinched together. "How old are you?"

"How old am I?" I gaped up at him. "You pinned me to the floor to ask me how old I am?"

"You don't look a day past eighteen," he said, sounding annoyed, as if I had misled him somehow.

"Nineteen," I corrected him. "And what are you? Twenty-one? Why so judgy?" I shot back. "Who are you and what do you want?"

He tilted his head, looking toward the window, and blinked. I'd grown sick of this game, so I lifted my leg and kneed him in the tailbone. He let out a pained groan, but loosened his grip enough that I could easily push him off.

I turned my back to him so I could rush toward the kitchen counter. His footsteps scrambled on the floor behind me, and I kicked back at him. My foot collided firmly with his chest, slamming him back against the wall, just as I grabbed a butcher knife from the counter.

I whirled on him, holding him against the wall and pressing the knife to his throat. Standing like this, I realized I had underestimated him a bit. He may have been human, but he was a few inches taller than me and muscular, with a T-shirt pulled taut over his barrel chest. He could pack a punch.

"Who are you and what do you want?" I demanded.

He pursed his lips before letting out an irritated breath. "I'm looking for the Krigare Valkyrie."

I pushed the knife harder against his throat, as a warning. "That's me."

"No, it's not," he replied, with so much certainty that for a moment I didn't know how to respond.

"Why don't you believe me?" I asked.

"You're too young," he said, but there seemed to be a confused sadness dampening his insistence, and already I felt his body relaxing against me.

"I know my own name," I assured him. "What I don't know is who you are or what the hell you're doing in my apartment."

Finally his shoulders slackened as he relented, and his eyes met mine. The neon lights outside made the blue in his eyes glow, then darkened them red, as he spoke. "My name is Asher Värja. My mother was a Valkyrie."

I relaxed slightly—but only slightly—since I now had an explanation for his strength. He might not have the same kind of abilities I had, but sons of Valkyries had their own strength unique to them.

"Okay," I said finally. "But that doesn't explain why you're here."

He licked his lips and lowered his eyes, looking embarrassed. "Can you lower your knife so we can talk?"

"You're the one that ambushed me, remember?"

"I know. I made a mistake," he said in a voice thick with apology. "I'm sorry. I was just afraid you wouldn't talk to me if I knocked on your door."

"Well, maybe you should try knocking first, and only move on to assault as a last resort."

"I've just been looking for a long time, and I was overzealous," he admitted wearily.

"Fine." I took a step back from him, giving him some space, but I kept the knife in my hand. "You said I was too young, and your mom is a Valkyrie. What does that have to do with me?"

The light outside abruptly changed, as the billboards switched over to brand-new advertisements that glowed blinding white, and the apartment was suddenly flooded with light. In the brightness, I was able to get a better look at this Asher Värja, and I realized that my original assessment of his age may have been off.

He looked around my age, maybe a couple years older, but there was something about him that made him seem so much older. A world-weariness in his face, pulling all the lines down into tired angles.

But mostly it was his dark eyes that seemed to contradict his youthful appearance. He had the eyes of someone who had seen a great deal.

"Your sword came up on a search because it was recently registered," he explained, rubbing at his eyes with the palm of his hand. "I thought you were an older, experienced Valkyrie who was just relicensing it. You're the only M. Krigare I've been able to find, so I just assumed you were who I'd been searching for."

That did explain his confusion over my age, since both my mother and I were listed as M. Krigare in our records. We were assigned numbers that helped differentiate us in our personal files, but for someone just gathering info, it would be easy to mistake Malin for Marlow without more context.

He cleared his throat, looking at me with a desperately hopeful look in his eyes. "Is there any chance that your mother is named M. Krigare?"

"What do you want with her?" I asked carefully, rubbing my

thumb absently on the handle of the knife in my hand. "Is she an old friend of your mom's?"

"Not exactly." He glanced out the window, and hoarsely he replied, "I'm looking for Krigare Valkyrie." Then he turned back to look at me. "Because she killed my mother."

NINE

————— ◆ —————

Vengeance was an occupational hazard of being a Valkyrie. Most immortals didn't like the idea of being returned (although a few did welcome it with open arms). Those who resisted us were known for performing preemptive attacks on Valkyries, as if killing one of us would stop another from coming in our place.

And there were reports of loved ones retaliating after a Valkyrie had taken someone out. Just like everyone else, immortals had friends and families that didn't like being left behind.

While unfortunate and problematic, this reaction was normal. It was something we'd been taught to deal with. But vengeance from *another Valkyrie*? That didn't make any sense.

"You must be mistaken," I said after a long silence while I tried to absorb what Asher was saying. He stood in the center of the room, his arms hanging at his sides and his eyes locked on me with an odd expression of defeated determination.

"I'm not mistaken," he replied. His words were soft but blunt, and the deep rumbling of his voice conveyed absolute conviction.

"A Valkyrie *cannot* kill another Valkyrie," I insisted, but my words sounded weak, even to me.

Because that wasn't exactly true. It wasn't impossible—just incredibly difficult, thanks to how evenly matched we were.

"I may have been oversimplifying," Asher admitted, keeping his eyes locked on mine. "Your mother didn't kill my mother herself, but her actions led directly to her death."

A wave of relief washed over me, and I let out a shaky breath. "So you're blaming my mom for some kind of accident?"

I hadn't wanted to believe that Marlow had done what Asher accused her of, but the brutal truth was that I wouldn't have been able to put it past her, either. She was strong-willed and stubborn, and my mother did hold the rather unfortunate belief that violence was the solution to most problems.

"Three years ago my mother Adela was killed. She was left burnt beyond recognition." He spoke slowly and deliberately, as if the words were getting caught in his throat and he had to force them out.

"I'm sorry," I said simply.

Asher shook his head, brushing off my apology. He reached for the front of pocket of his moto jacket, then stopped himself. "Is it all right if I show you something?"

"As long it's not a weapon," I allowed.

"Of course." He gave me a brief, grateful smile before pulling out a small electronic tablet. "Here's an article about it—the *only* article, actually."

He held the screen out toward me, and I stepped closer to get a better look. It opened with a rather disturbing black-and-white photograph of an ashen skeleton. Below followed three quick sentences.

An unidentified woman was found dead in the alley behind a Huitaca-owned discothèque in Ou'helstad, Panama. Coroners say the woman died from smoke inhalation. Investigators are still looking into the incident, and Huitaca's representatives could not be reached for comment.

"So?" I asked, looking up at Asher, since there didn't seem to be even the slightest connection to me or Marlow.

"This was the only thing that was ever said about it." Asher tapped the screen, and I was about to repeat the word *so* when he added, "When was the last time you remember a Valkyrie getting killed?"

"Ten years ago?" I shrugged, but it suddenly came back to me.

Shortly after my eighth birthday, a Valkyrie was murdered by an angry widower. For weeks after, I was worried something like that would happen to my own mother. I remember begging Marlow not to leave, not to go out on jobs, and I'd thrown such a tantrum once, crying and fighting to get her to stay, that she'd finally locked me in my bedroom to keep me from chasing after her.

"Eleven years ago," I corrected myself.

"It was all over the news," Asher said. "The billboards downtown replayed endless interviews with witnesses and crime scene footage."

Valkyries were notoriously hard to kill, earning us the nickname of "cockroaches" by some of the more colorful immortals. We also provided a sense of order and safety to the world—at least from humankind's perspective. So whenever one was killed, it was a huge story.

"So why wasn't this all over the place?" Asher asked, pointing to the article on his tablet.

"It didn't say anything about her being a Valkyrie," I said. "That's probably why no one picked up on it."

"Exactly!" he said, sounding triumphant that I seemed to be catching on to what he was laying down. "They suppressed it."

"Who's they?" I asked.

"I don't know. The Evig Riksdag, maybe?" He shook his head. "After my mother was killed, my grandma and I started looking—"

Startled, I couldn't help but interrupt him to ask, "You know your grandmother?"

"Yeah, of course I do," Asher replied, giving me an odd look.

I'd never met mine, and Marlow told me that she'd never met hers, either. The only other Valkyrie I knew well in terms of a personal relationship was Quinn Devane, and she all but refused to talk about her family. As far as I knew, no Valkyries had relationships with their extended family.

"Never mind." I brushed it off. "Go on."

"Anyway, my grandma and I went to Ou'helstad and started looking into it, and no one would give us any answers about what happened to my mother," Asher explained. "It didn't seem like any kind of investigation had been done."

"You're telling me that a Valkyrie was killed and no one cared?" I asked.

"No. I'm telling you that a Valkyrie was killed and someone covered it up," Asher corrected me.

"You know you sound super-paranoid, right?" I asked.

"I know how it sounds, but look at the facts." He pointed to the article on his tablet again. "A Valkyrie is killed outside of a club owned by Huitaca, and no one reports on it?"

Huitaca was an immortal known as much for her beauty as she was for her partying. Her reputation for hooking up with celebrities and getting arrested had led to the media crowning her queen Celebutant for the past quarter of a century.

"So you think Huitaca killed your mom?" I asked.

"No, I know who killed her," Asher assured me. "I'm just saying the media covers every scandal Huitaca is involved in, but somehow ignored this one."

He had a point, but I was too distracted by the fact that he claimed he'd already found the murderer, so I asked, "Who killed her?"

"My grandma and I started our own investigation, since no one else seemed to care about my mother's murder," Asher expounded. "It was a lot of knocking on doors, bribery, and threats of violence, but we were finally able to come up with a name: Tamerlane Fayette.

"Everything we found pointed to him," Asher went on. "From what we gathered, Adela had gone to Huitaca's club on orders to return another immortal—a Laka—so it was no big deal."

Lakas were peaceful flower goddesses renowned for being among the easiest to deal with, and they almost always welcomed death and thanked the Valkyrie.

"The Laka even turned herself in to the Evig Riksdag two days later, where she was promptly returned," Asher elaborated. "So she had no reason to kill Adela. But while Adela was there, Tamerlane got a whiff of a Valkyrie in the club, and he lost it. Witnesses saw them arguing until a bouncer made them take it outside, and that's the last time anyone saw Adela."

"So who is this Tamerlane Fayette?" I asked.

"He's a Petro Loa," Asher said.

A Petro Loa was essentially a fiery angel. They were divine, which meant that they usually didn't cause much trouble, but a fiery angel would explain Adela's burnt corpse.

"Great. So you got your guy."

Asher looked at me somberly. "I *never* found him. Every avenue I tried was a total dead end. He'd completely disappeared. And then, a few months ago, I figured out why."

He quickly scrolled through his tablet until he found a screenshot of a form I knew very well.

PERSONAL DATA	LAST NAME FIRST NAME **FAYETTE TAMERLANE**			IMMORTAL NUMBER **PL87653422**		SOCIAL SECURITY NUMBER ▓▓▓▓		
	SPECIES **PETRO LOA**		BRANCH **DIVINE**	GRADE **7C**	D.O.B.	DATE **08**	MONTH **MAR**	YEAR **03**
	CITIZEN ☒ YES ☐ NO	PLACE OF BIRTH **CAP-HAÏTIEN HAITI**			D.O.T.	DATE **22**	MONTH **JAN**	YEAR **33**
DATA	VALKYRIE NUMBER **2S VL MK 91**	ASSIGNED VALKYRIE **M. KRIGARE**				DATE ASSIGNED **20**	**JAN**	**33**
TRANSFER OR DISCHARGE DATA	TYPE OF TRANSFER OR DISPATCH **RETURN**		STATION OF ASSIGNMENT **NEW EDGEWATER**					
	AUTHORITY **SAMAEL**			SERVICE DATE ▓▓▓▓				
	MAJOR AUTHORITY ▓▓▓▓		AUTHORITY GRANTED ON THE CONDION OF ▓▓▓▓					

"Where'd you get this?" I asked.

"Like I told you, we used a lot of bribery and threats of violence," he replied vaguely. "But even all that couldn't get me an entirely unredacted version."

"But you can't just get this," I insisted, as a sick feeling grew inside. "The Riksdag won't just hand out this kind of information. These forms are supposed to be top-secret."

"It took me over *two* years to get this," he said.

"Even if I believe this is authentic—and I don't know that I do—it doesn't mean anything," I said. "This says my mom was sent to kill Tamerlane Fayette, so I'm sure she did."

That's what I said, but that's not what I felt. A cold anxious feeling had settled inside me, working its way deep into the pit of my stomach, making my organs twist and my heart race.

Asher tapped the numbers beside the D.O.T.—the date of transfer, which was how the Riks coded returns on forms. "The date she was assigned to kill Tamerlane was over a year before my mother was killed."

"Maybe they put in the wrong date. It's much more likely this was a clerical error than that my mom didn't do her job." I kept asserting this, that none of this meant anything, but my words felt empty and left a metallic taste in my mouth.

He laughed darkly, and the raw pain in it cut through me like a knife. I realized he wasn't lying. He might be wrong about things—maybe even everything—but he *believed* everything he'd told me.

"Your mother failed in her duties and did not kill Tamerlane Fayette, and because of that, my mother is dead," Asher said, looking me directly in the eyes. "And I need to know why. You can help me. I'd like it if you did, actually. But whether you do or not, I'm going to find the truth."

TEN

———◆———

With the blinds closed, the only light in the apartment came from my laptop screen. Bowie sat curled up beside me, content now that the threat of Asher had gone. He cooed when he slept, sounding like a sleepy pigeon, and I absently scratched at the soft fur between his antlers.

After Asher had made his request for help, there hadn't been much more to discuss. He had already told me everything he knew, so it was then that I asked him to leave. Just before he did, he offered me his business card, and I took it quickly to hide the embarrassing trembling of my hands.

"In case you change your mind," he'd told me, then he turned and left my apartment.

I didn't plan on changing my mind, but I couldn't seem to stop glancing over at the card where it sat discarded on the arm of the couch beside me.

It was a tiny little screen, no bigger and no thicker than a playing card. It was black now, but when I reached over and touched it, it slowly faded to white. His name, job title—private investigator—and his number were in bold, beneath an animation of an eye looking around, a play on the term *private eye*, I assumed.

Once he'd left, I fed Bowie, closed my blinds, double-locked the door, and then immediately got on my computer. In the time since Asher had been gone, I'd done nothing but search online, looking for anything to destroy his story.

Unfortunately, I had yet to find it.

There was very little online about his mother, but that was typical for a Valkyrie. The only thing I could find tagged with her name was her obituary, which was deliberately sparse. I did manage to find the article that Asher had shown me with the burnt corpse in Ou'helstad, and the date of the murder did match up with her obit.

Tamerlane Fayette, on the other hand, had plenty written about him. After all, he had been alive for 230 years. That was more than enough time to make the news.

Most of what I found on him seemed positive and in line with what I knew about Petro Loas. He traveled a lot, working on foundations to help orphaned children. While he'd been born in Haiti, he spent the last fifty years living exclusively in the States.

Since he'd been here, he'd gotten married to a mortal woman and had three children. The pictures of his family I found in his sister-in-law's social media showed a happy family—all bright smiles, like they were doing an advert for toothpaste.

Then, four years ago, he'd disappeared. There was no trace of him, other than a few posts online of people inquiring where he went. According to official posts on the site for the orphanage he ran, he'd simply stopped showing up to work one day, and after a few months they'd had no choice but to replace him.

And then, six months later, his entire family was murdered. His wife and all three children. Well, *murder* wasn't exactly the right term. The agents investigating the crime were divided on whether it was a criminal act or simply an animal attack. The bodies had been shredded, so many were convinced it was an errant dragon or other wild beast that got them.

Some speculated that he'd show up for the funeral, but there was no sign of him. He'd simply vanished.

That is, of course, until he popped up to kill Adela Värja four months later, assuming that I believed Asher's story.

The locks on the door clicked, and I nearly jumped out of my skin. Bowie'd already had a rough night, so he squawked, flapped his wings, and then dashed under the table to hide. Oona walked into the apartment and flicked on the light.

"Why are you always sitting in the dark like some kind of weirdo, Mal?" Oona asked through a mouthful of food.

She had a small paper sack filled with fat round pastries in her hand. Based on the smell of clove and onion, I guessed it was kibbeh—a deep-fried croquette stuffed with mushrooms, onions, and pine nuts that a friendly marid sold at the street corner near our apartment.

"I'm not a weirdo." I closed my laptop and stood up to stretch. "It's just been a long night."

She held out the kibbeh toward me, offering me some, but I shook my head. I hadn't eaten tonight, but my stomach felt too queasy to put anything in it. My encounter with Asher left everything feeling . . . off.

"Were you working on something for school?" Oona asked as she flopped back on the couch.

Asher's business card had been sitting precariously on the arm, and it fell forward toward Oona, causing the screen to flash on.

"Who's Asher Värja?" Oona asked, picking up the card. "And why is this here?"

I poured myself a big of glass of water and took a deep breath before launching into the long story about Asher and everything he'd told me, and then about everything I'd found online.

"I thought that Draugrs were just urban legends," Oona said once I finished.

"Draugrs?" I asked.

"Yeah. You know, immortals that skip their death by Valkyrie, and become *really* immortal," she elaborated. "They walk the earth long after they're supposed to be gone."

"I've never heard that term in school," I said.

"Maybe that's because they've been trying to convince you that they don't exist, so you don't try to make one yourself," Oona supposed.

"Maybe," I allowed.

"But the rest of the story doesn't make any sense," Oona said.

"I know." I sat on the couch beside her with my legs crossed underneath me. "None of it does."

"Do you believe him?" Oona asked.

"I mean, no." I rubbed my temple and looked at Oona out of the corner of my eye. "Do you think I should?"

"There's parts of his story that seem like they add up, but then there's other parts that I just can't wrap my head around. I know I don't know your mom that well—"

"Join the club," I snorted.

"—but I just can't imagine her letting anyone go," Oona went on. "Not without good reason."

"So you're saying that I should talk to her about it?" I asked with a heavy sigh.

Growing up, I'd thought that Marlow was a pretty good mom. Not that I really had anything to compare her to, but she always made sure I had food, clothes, and a roof over my head. She just wasn't the kind of mom who tucked me in at night or read me bedtime stories or talked about my feelings. Hell, I'd been calling her "Marlow" instead of "mom" since grade school, and she preferred it that way.

In retrospect, she was more like a gruff aunt who really, really believed in self-reliance. And most of the time, that wasn't a bad thing.

But at times like this, I couldn't imagine her reacting well to me asking her if she'd ever failed at the one thing she prided herself on more than anything.

"That would be a start," Oona suggested. "Or if you're afraid of Marlow shutting you out, you could talk to somebody that's an expert on Valkyries. I honestly don't know enough about what you do to know if what Asher is suggesting is even possible."

I laid my head back on the couch and reached over to grab the last kibbeh out of Oona's bag. "First I eat, then I sleep. I can't ever come up with good ideas when I'm hungry and exhausted."

"So you're gonna talk to Marlow?" Oona asked with wide eyes.

"I'm gonna start small. I'll talk to Professor Wu first."

ELEVEN

Even though I made it to Intro to Divinity and Immortality ten minutes early, there were already a few students in their seats, including a busybody vampire talking to Professor Wu about bringing up his grade.

"So you're saying that if I do a report on an important figure in the netherworld, it will help my grade?" the vampire was asking.

"I'm saying that we're going to be covering Kurnugia in a few weeks, so having a knowledge of important figures would be helpful," Professor Wu replied carefully. "Researching immortals like Ereshkigal, Osiris, and Anguta would definitely be beneficial for you."

Since a moment alone to talk to Wu about Asher's claims was out of the question, I resigned myself to sitting in the back row and using the extra time to bone up on my coursework. I'd only just taken my seat when Sloane Kothari came into the classroom.

Her brown eyes widened, and then she narrowed them and grimaced, as if resenting the fact that I'd gotten here before her. Her perfectly coiled black curls bounced as she stomped to her spot.

"Nice outfit," Sloane sneered, taking her seat in the row in front of me.

Because of my muscular build, most clothes built for the average human woman did not fit me. Thankfully, Oona's mother was a seamstress by trade, and either she or Oona modified a lot of my clothes to make them work. Since we'd moved in together, Oona had even begun taking it upon herself to make me a few pieces herself, in exchange for me kicking in a bit extra when rent was due.

What I wore now was an ombre maxi skirt with a slit down the side—an Oona creation specifically for me—with a cropped black bralette and a frayed smoky open-knit sweater over the top. I actually really liked my outfit, especially in comparison to the prim and proper schoolgirl number that Sloane had on today.

I'd also added a leather garter around my thigh, where I'd sheathed a dagger, because my run-in with Asher last night had made me jumpy. I moved my leg so the slit would fall open and expose the dagger.

"If you wanna compare fashion tips, we can go outside after class and have a little chat," I suggested, deliberately aiming the garter so she'd be able to see it.

She glanced back at me, and when she noticed my dagger, she scoffed. "Must you always be so crude, Malin?"

"You just seem to bring out the worst in me," I admitted.

"So many early birds here today," Professor Wu commented, stopping whatever snide comment Sloane had right on her lips, and she turned back to face him. "Is everyone getting antsy about the midterms?"

"I just like to stay on top of things," Sloane said in her saccharine voice.

Wu sat on the corner of his desk and crossed his arms over his chest. "Well, you all should be a little worried. We had a staff meeting this morning, and I know for a fact that many of your midterm exams are going to be incredibly difficult."

A few of the students groaned, including myself. That's just what I needed on top of everything else right now. Impossibly hard tests.

"Is there anything that any of you have questions about that you'd like me to explore more in depth?" Wu asked.

No one said anything, and the class was still kinda empty, so I took a deep breath and decided to go for it. "What if, um, Valkyries didn't kill—or, *return*—someone?" I asked carefully.

"The biggest problem would be overpopulation," Wu explained. "We're already facing population growths that are causing major problems all over the world, and if you added the hundreds upon hundreds of thousands of immortals that *never* died into the mix, we'd all risk extinction from oversourcing the earth."

"No, I mean, what would happen if just *one* Valkyrie didn't kill *one* immortal?" I asked. "I would never, ever do that, but I was just curious. What would happen exactly?"

"It would be catastrophic," Wu intoned ominously. "The system we have in place is a perfect equation written by the gods and the Eralim. You've heard of the butterfly effect."

"It is the phenomenon whereby a minute localized change in a complex system can have large effects elsewhere," Sloane supplied to a question that Wu hadn't even asked.

"A butterfly flaps its wings in Brazil, and that causes a tsunami in Japan," Wu simplified. "And we don't know how one immortal living longer than he was intended to can affect everything else."

He grabbed a marker and began diagramming on the whiteboard, drawing symbols and numbers until they filled up the entire space.

"This is the basic formula—what's known as the Mortal Equation," Wu explained, gesturing to the board. Supposedly, it was math, but it looked like an alien language to me. "I'm not an expert on this, but essentially it explains every decision the Eralim ever pass down. Are you taking Devil's Abacus: An Advanced Course on Mathematics and Existence with Professor Lovelace?"

"I am," Sloane chirped, but I just shook my head. I was taking basic algebra for my math credit, and I'd barely scored high enough to even get into that class.

Wu waved his hand, attempting to cover up his mild disappointment. "Anyway, Professor Lovelace can explain this all better to you than I ever could, so that's where you should go if you have any more questions about the Mortal Equation.

"But to answer your question, it would be horrific if a Valkyrie failed to kill an immortal," Wu finished. "Our whole world could collapse on itself."

"Thanks," I mumbled, looking down at my tablet.

Which meant that if there was any truth to what Asher Värja had said, we would all be in serious trouble.

TWELVE

---◆---

As soon as my last class of the day had finished, I got on my luft and made the half-hour trek across the city to the Tesla Park borough. When I put my mind to it, I could make the trip in as little as fifteen minutes, but today I was in no hurry.

Marlow lived in a tiny fourth-floor walk-up apartment in a narrow brownstone. Even though I'd shared it with her until I moved out on my own over a year ago, the place never really felt like home. Still, it always felt strange coming back and knocking on my old front door.

It took her nearly five minutes to answer, and when she finally did, she was blurry-eyed and her short bleached-blond hair stuck up at odd angles. Her lips were permanently stained a shade of red from her lipstick, but the rest of her face was pale, other than the dark circles under her eyes.

"Malin?" Marlow asked, squinting at me. "What are you doing here? Did you have a job today?"

"No. I just wanted to visit," I explained lamely and offered a smile that I hoped didn't look as sick as it felt.

Marlow continued to stare at me, blinking a few times, as if the concept of visiting with your child was completely foreign to her, but then she stepped back and motioned me inside. "Come on in, then."

The apartment had always been rather cramped, but since I'd moved out, it seemed that Marlow had become a bit of a hoarder. Empty cardboard boxes were piled up on one wall, blocking the only window into the living room, and her new purchases were stacked on every available surface.

Except for the lumpy old couch, but based on the blankets and pillows on it, I guessed that for some reason Marlow had taken to sleeping on the couch instead of in her bedroom.

"I'm still half asleep. I was working last night," Marlow explained as she walked into her tiny kitchenette. She worked nights at a call center helping people in emergencies.

"It's okay," I said, absently picking up an olive-green bayonet that Mom had stacked on an end table. Glancing around the room, it seemed like most of her new stuff was army surplus. Other than the sealed plastic tubs labeled *brown rice* and *lentils* stacked up beside her TV, which glowed dully with an old black-and-white movie.

Marlow had apparently become some kind of prepper.

"Do you want anything?" Marlow asked, moving aside take-out containers to make herself a cup of coffee.

I shook my head. "No, I'm good."

"Suit yourself." She topped off her mug of coffee with a half-empty bottle of vodka, then she leaned back against the counter and turned to face me. "So, to what do I owe this visit?"

"I just wanted to see how you were doing," I lied.

Marlow took a long drink of her coffee and shrugged. "Well, as you can see, I'm fine."

I barely managed to suppress the scoff in my throat. Marlow did not look *fine*, but I couldn't say that to her. So I just lowered my eyes and pulled out a kitchen chair from the table, one of the only clean spaces in the apartment.

"Now, do you want to tell me what you're really doing here?" Marlow asked, cutting straight through the bullshit. She'd never had time for small talk.

"Actually, I wanted to talk to you about something weird that happened last night." I stared down at my hands, fiddling with the multiple rings I wore. "This guy broke into my apartment."

"Was he trying to rob you?" Marlow asked without a hint of worry.

I suppose she knew that I could handle myself, and she could see that I was fine, but it still would've been nice if she'd feigned a little bit of motherly concern.

"No, he just wanted to talk, and he apparently thought breaking in was the best way to do that," I said, trying to ignore the growing ball of dread in the pit of my stomach. "He told me about his mom, Adela Värja. She was a Valkyrie, and she was killed three years ago."

Marlow furrowed her brow, but didn't show any signs of recognition. "Why did he think you would care about that?"

"Well, he had this whole long story about what happened," I tried to explain as nonchalantly as I could, like I'd never even considered the possibility that he might be right. "He said an immortal had killed Adela because a different Valkyrie had failed to kill that same immortal."

I waited a beat, watching Marlow's blank expression before saying, "The immortal's name was Tamerlane Fayette."

She coughed then, choking on her coffee. She turned her back to me and leaned over the sink, coughing hard for a moment, and I felt like I might throw up.

Even though I knew—I knew the moment she gagged on her coffee—I pushed on ahead. I had to hear her admit it. I had to know her side of the story.

"He said that you were supposed to kill Tamerlane, but that you didn't," I went on. "Did that happen? Did you not follow your orders?"

Marlow leaned with her hands against the sink and her shoulders slumped. "How could you even ask me that?"

"Marlow, I just need to know," I pressed. "I have to know if what he said was true."

She cleared her throat, then wiped her mouth with the back of her arm. "Do you know how many immortals I've killed in my career?"

"No, I—"

"Over seven hundred immortals," she said and turned back to face me. "I've been doing this since I was eighteen years old, so that averages out to twenty-five a year."

"That's an impressive number," I said, since I had no idea what kind of response she was hoping to elicit.

"I have been an excellent Valkyrie," she insisted. "I did what I was told, when I was told, and I killed seven hundred immortals. Some of them fought me. Some of them went out quietly. A few even thanked me.

"But most of them . . ." She took a deep breath and closed her eyes. "Most of them just cried and begged for me to spare their lives. And I would tell them all the same thing: 'It's not my decision.'"

Marlow opened her eyes. "But that was a lie. Do you know that?"

I shook my head emphatically. "It's not *our* decision. It comes down from the Eralim."

"But we have a choice, Malin!" Marlow snapped at me. "We are living, breathing humans. We might have different powers and skills than most other mortals, but we have free will just like the rest of them. We don't have to just follow orders!"

"Right, you can quit!" I shot back. "If you don't want to be a Valkyrie, then don't be one. Valkyries quit or retire all the time. A girl in my class last semester flunked out because she couldn't hack it."

She laughed bitterly. "Oh, Malin, it's not that simple."

"Yes, it is," I persisted. "That's your choice as a human—you can work as a Valkyrie or not. But if you choose to be a Valkyrie, you must follow orders! All of life on earth depends on it!"

Marlow rolled her eyes. "You are so melodramatic sometimes." Then she pulled out a kitchen chair, knocking a stack of boxes to the floor as she did, and sat down across from me. "You want me to tell you about Tamerlane Fayette?"

No. I didn't want to know. It would be so much easier if I never knew the truth, but I couldn't seem to stop myself from saying, "Yes. Please."

"After Samael gave me my assignment, I tracked down Tamerlane and I followed him, the way I always do when I get a job," Marlow explained. "And you know what he did in the days that I stalked him? He bought his wife flowers. He took his kids to school. He raised money for orphans. Once, I saw him rescue a mangy dog on the street."

"He sounds like a real saint, Marlow," I said dryly. "But he can't have been the first saint you killed."

"No, he wasn't," Marlow admitted, barely blinking back tears. "But he was *good*, Malin. He helped so many people! Why would the world be better without him? How could it?"

"Oh, holy hell, Marlow." I bowed my head and rubbed my temples, desperately fighting to keep the bile from rising in my throat. "He was *supposed* to die! Don't you understand what you've done?"

Marlow stood up quickly, pushing her chair back so hard it clattered to the floor. "No, I know what they've told me. But I just couldn't believe it, with him. I went to kill him, but when I looked into his eyes, I only saw his light and goodness. He promised me he'd make the world even better if he lived."

"Well, obviously he lied!" I shouted. "Because he killed a Valkyrie!"

Marlow shook her head. "That's what they told you. Doesn't make it true."

I stood up. "Do you know what happened to Tamerlane's family? They're all dead. They were all brutally killed six months after he was supposed to die."

Her face paled even further. "What? Why?"

"I don't know. Maybe Tamerlane killed them." I shrugged. "Or maybe you're just not supposed to fuck with the order, and now everything is out of balance, and who the hell knows who is going to die next?"

She pressed her lips together tightly, trying to stop them from trembling, and shook her head fiercely. "No. He was good." Her breath caught in her throat, and when she spoke again, her words were barely audible. "I wanted to do something good, for once."

"You *do* do something good!" I yelled in disbelief. "Don't you get it? The world will fall apart without Valkyries."

My phone started ringing in my bag, an impatient demand, and I didn't want to argue anymore, so I turned my back to Marlow and dug it out. Samael's name flashed brightly across the screen.

"It's Samael," I told my mom.

"Go," she said in a blank voice. "Take it. He probably has a job for you, and we don't have anything more to talk about."

I left without saying anything else to her, and I didn't answer the phone. I needed to compose myself before speaking to someone like Samael. I hopped on my luft and sped across the city, fighting back nausea and feeling like I'd just learned that everything I believed in was a lie.

THIRTEEN

---◆---

Atlas greeted me with a warm smile at the end of the long copper corridor, but Godfrey just stared ahead with his solitary bulbous eye. My footfalls seemed to echo off the marble floors louder than normal, and the distance to Samael's office had never felt farther before.

"You're on your own today, Malin?" Atlas grinned down cheerily as I finally reached him.

I attempted to return his smile, but I couldn't shake the sick feeling I had, so I was sure it came out crooked and tense. "Yeah. Just me."

"I think this is the first time I've seen you here without your mother," Atlas commented. "You must be doing well, then. It won't be much longer until you're licensed to go solo."

"Yeah, something like that." I laughed uneasily and rubbed the back of my neck. "Is Samael ready to see me?"

"He should be," Godfrey muttered in a few gruff syllables.

"Go on in," Atlas said and pushed against the massive bronze door, holding it open for me.

Samael sat behind his desk, studying something intently on his computer monitor. With his curls tucked up in a messy bun paired with the tailored dress shirt he wore, he appeared even more like a college kid playing dress-up.

He lifted his head and smiled at the sound of the door opening. As soon as he realized it was just me, standing alone in his spacious office, his smile fell away.

"Where's Marlow?" Samael asked, slowly getting to his feet.

Behind him, rain pattered against the large window. A flash of lightning glared off the buildings that surrounded us, and the glass trembled for a second.

"She's, uh, she's at home," I replied, gulping back my nerves. "She thought I would be able to handle this on my own."

"Well." He stared off for a moment, drumming his fingers against the dark stone of his desk, and then he cleared his throat. "I'm sure you can." He smiled at me, but it felt flatter than usual.

When I'd finally returned Samael's phone call, he'd told me to come in for another assignment. He hadn't specifically requested that Marlow come with me, but he hadn't needed to. Protocol was that I wasn't supposed to attend meetings or go on any assignments on my own until I was licensed.

But after what Marlow had told me today, I didn't trust myself to act normally around her. It was hard enough acting normal *without* her presence. Besides, it didn't seem like Marlow cared as much about the rules as I once believed she had.

"Anyway." Samael picked up his e-tablet and came around his desk toward me. "I've got another assignment for you."

"So soon?" I asked.

Last year, when I had first started apprenticing with Marlow, she was getting two or maybe three assignments a month, and my own assignments were usually much, much fewer and farther apart. But my last one had been completed early Tuesday morning, and today was just Thursday.

"We've been busier lately," Samael answered vaguely as he scrolled through his tablet and took a seat on the couch.

"I thought it would be more consistent, like a job every two or three weeks," I said and sat down beside him.

"The birth and death rate isn't an exact constant, not for humans or immortals. Right now we must be having a rise in births, which would explain the compensation in the other direction," he explained, but he didn't sound entirely confident in his answer.

He stopped, staring off into space again. There was a subtle twitching at the corner of his eyes, like he was trying to figure something out.

"Samael?" I asked at length, when it felt like he'd been lost in thought too long.

He snapped back to life, offering me an apologetic smile. "Sorry about that." He rubbed the palm of his hand against his eyes. "It's been a long week."

"It's okay," I said, but I was beginning to fear that it actually was not okay. That nothing might be okay ever again.

"Anyway, your new assignment." Samael tilted the tablet toward me so I'd be able to see the screen. "All of this info has been uploaded to your secure Riksdag drop box, just like always, but it's still important for me to go over it with you, especially since you're still new to the job."

The picture showed a beautiful woman onstage for what appeared to be a high-class burlesque show. Her features were so perfect—flawless alabaster skin, flowing black hair, and wide brown eyes.

"Her name is Amaryllis Mori," Samael explained as he scrolled through a few more pictures, before stopping at a screen with all her pertinent info. "She's a Jorogumo. Have you ever dealt with one of those before?"

I shook my head. "No, but I've heard of them."

Samael brushed this off with an easy smile. "They're not too hard to deal with. A little more difficult than a Trasgu, but most things are."

Her profile said that she had been born in Japan 349 years ago. Sometimes, seeing a number on the screen like that, it hit me about all that she'd seen, all that she'd done, and now it was all coming to an end. And there was nothing she could do, even with all her experience and power.

"She's been working at a gentleman's club called Nysa in the Gold Coast District, which thankfully is only about an hour from here," Samael said. He lowered the tablet, then spoke more conversationally. "You know, I've sent Marlow on assignments as far away as Tanzania."

I remembered. When I was ten, I'd spent two weeks with Oona and her mom while Marlow took care of business on the other side of the world. She didn't call or write the entire time she was gone, and I'd had nightmares that she died.

"I went with her that trip. Didn't seem safe for her to go that far alone," Samael explained, but there was something wistful in his eyes. Then he shook his head, clearing it of the memories. "But this business with Amaryllis should be no problem."

"I'm sure it'll be fine," I said, even though I no longer had such confidence in myself or in the job. Marlow's confession had shaken everything I thought I knew.

Samael locked the screen and tilted his body to face me more directly. "So, do you have other questions or concerns?"

In my head, I wanted to tell him about Marlow and Tamerlane Fayette and Adela Värja's death. But I couldn't. While I knew that Samael was fond of my mother, I knew also that if the Evig Riksdag found out what she'd done—or rather, *hadn't* done—it would be very, very bad news for her.

So instead I just forced a smile and said, "Nope. I think I got it."

I stood up, preparing to leave, when Samael stopped me. "Is Marlow okay?"

"Yeah, of course," I replied quickly. "Why wouldn't she be?"

"I've just never known her to miss a meeting like this," Samael said.

"Yeah, um, yeah, I think she was just feeling a bit under the weather, and she thinks that I'm ready for more responsibility," I explained lamely.

Samael stood up slowly. "If Marlow is busy, we could maybe look into getting you a new mentor."

I swallowed back my unease. "I'm not sure what Marlow's schedule is like right now. You'd have to talk to her about that."

"Hmm." He rubbed his chin absently as he thought. "Maybe I could talk to Quinn Devane . . ." He trailed off, glancing back over at the couch behind us.

That's where Quinn had been sitting the first time I met her just over a year ago. Her hair had been dark then, a vibrant midnight-blue that cascaded down over her shoulders, and she'd been wearing a minidress that showed off her long, sinewy legs.

When she smiled at me—her lopsided smile filled with secrets and wishes—time seemed to slow for a moment. I could hear the sound of my heart beating, and the air suddenly felt too thin in the room.

Then she was standing and walking over to me, and my thoughts were scrambling—had I ever seen anyone as beautiful as her before, why did my hands feel so clammy, did I look as dumb as I felt, what would I say to her, and how could I speak?

"You must be Malin Krigare," she said, her eyes fluttering over my body in a way that made my skin flush. "I'm Quinn Devane. Samael thought I could help you."

"Why, uh, why would you do that?" I fumbled over my words, my tongue thick and clumsy. I tried to play it off all cool but I knew everything was coming out wrong.

"Because I'm a Valkyrie." Her smile broadened, looking amused. "I have more experience, so I can show you around."

I couldn't tell if that was an innuendo, or if I was just hoping it was one. The playful look in her green eyes and the mischievous twitch of her slender lips made me question this, and I could feel my cheeks reddening. I'd dated plenty before Quinn, both guys and girls, but I'd never felt so tongue-tied and flustered before.

"That should be very educational," I replied, trying much too hard to seem nonchalant and cool.

"I'm the finest teacher," she assured me.

I lowered my eyes, struggling to calm the racing heart and the growing swirl of butterflies inside me. My gaze happened to land on her chest—just above the crescent of her décolletage a dark red scar ran across, connecting her collarbones.

"An ennedi," Quinn said, startling me into looking back up at her.

"What?" I asked dumbly.

"Well, I assumed you were either staring at my tits or my scar," she said, still smirking playfully at me, but now my cheeks were burning with shame. "If it's my tits, I ought to point out that it's not polite to stare, though I suppose that works for the scar too."

"I didn't—I wasn't—I'm sorry," I stammered.

Quinn ignored my apology and ran her slender fingers across the scar. "It's from the scratch of an ennedi, which is sorta like a saber-toothed tiger. I returned it a few weeks ago, but not before it left me this nice permanent gift to remember him by."

"See? She's already teaching you something," Samael had said brightly and put his hand on Quinn's shoulder, attempting to diffuse the tension, but honestly, I'd forgotten he was there. As soon as Quinn had smiled at me, everything else had fallen away.

Back in the present, Samael cleared his throat and scratched his head. "Though, I suppose it wouldn't be appropriate for you two to work together, given the nature of your relationship."

"Since we've broken up, I would rather not be teamed up with her again," I admitted.

"That's understandable." He walked with me toward the door, seeing me out, with his hands in his pockets. "I'll look into other options for the future. But how is school going? Everything on track?"

"Yeah, it's all going great," I lied. "I'm working on a project for school, and I've been kind of learning about the Mortal Equation."

His blue eyes widened in surprise. "Are you a math major?"

"No, I'm horrible at math, actually, but my professor was talking about it, and I just got kind of curious to know more. Do you know the Mortal Equation?"

"I know some," he allowed, choosing his words carefully. "But I don't work on it myself. That's for the higher-ups." He motioned toward the ceiling. "I just interpret the orders for Valkyries like you."

"That makes sense, but . . ." I paused, trying to figure out how to phrase the question burning on my tongue. "Math can be difficult. I make mistakes all the time, and I know that the bosses upstairs are way smarter than I can even comprehend, but . . . do they ever make mistakes? They forget to carry the two, and the whole equation is off?"

Samael chuckled. "No, they don't make mistakes. That's not how they work. Everyone they send the Valkyries to return was meant to be returned."

"But what does that mean?" I pressed. "How can anyone be 'meant' to die? Unless everything is preordained, and if it's all preordained, then how can we ever veer off course?"

"You can't," Samael said firmly. "But the concepts of free will and predestination are rather lofty. If you're really interested in learning more, I suggest you talk to your professor. I'm certain he'd be able to explain everything far better than I ever could."

"Right, thank you. I will." I forced a smile at him. "I should get going. I have homework and all that."

Samael opened the door for me, telling me to call him if I had any problems. I promised that I would, but I didn't know if I meant it.

FOURTEEN

———— ◆ ————

Oona and I sat in the booth in the back corner of the restaurant. Aprazivel was a dark little hole in the wall that happened to serve some of the tastiest, cheapest Brazilian cuisine in the city, and it also happened to be only a few blocks from our apartment.

"So?" Oona asked. She sat across from me, sipping her cachaça—a liquor distilled from sugarcane—and stared at me expectantly with her big dark eyes. "How did it go with Marlow?"

On the wall behind Oona, the head of a tamanduá chifres had been mounted. The Brazilian great horned anteater. It was huge, roughly the size of a moose, with massive antlers to match and a long gray snout with its slender tongue poking out. Its two black eyes stared down at me, and for a moment I felt almost as if it were looking straight through me.

"I don't know," I said finally.

"You did go see her today, right?" Oona pressed on, undeterred by my apathy. This was the first chance I'd had all day to tell her about my visit with Marlow, but I wasn't ready to just dive into the topic.

As soon as I'd gotten home from meeting with Samael, Oona had demanded that we go out and get something to eat. I'd hardly eaten anything all day, and she claimed I was looking pale. Her solution to most problems in life seemed to involve food.

"Yeah, I saw her," I replied, looking down at the table, and then I noticed her hands. "What's that?"

Her dark skin was covered in elaborate white henna designs from her wrists down to her fingers, stopping just before her long fingernails, which were shaped to a point and painted a matte gray.

"What?" She glanced down, then waved me off dramatically. "It was just something I did for class today. Don't change the subject, Mal."

I gulped down the rest of my beer, then I put my arms on the table and leaned forward. The lighting in Aprazivel was dim and low, and it was crowded enough that the noise from the other customers should keep our conversation private. But still, I felt edgy about someone overhearing, and the unblinking gaze of the tamanduá chifres did nothing to ease my nerves.

"He was right," I whispered.

"What?" Oona leaned forward to hear me better.

"Asher Värja," I said, and it was at that moment the waiter appeared with our food, and I nearly jumped out of my skin.

"For the lovely lady." The waiter smiled, putting a bowl of rice, beans, and curded cheese in front Oona. "And the palmito for you."

Another day, I would've made a comment about his lack of a descriptor for me when he put my plate in front of me, but today I couldn't focus enough to come up with something to say.

"What do you mean?" Oona asked after the waiter had gone.

"I mean . . . she didn't do it," I explained in a hushed voice.

Oona had taken a bite of her food, and she stared at me for a moment, her mouth full, not chewing. Finally, she swallowed and asked, "Marlow didn't do her job?"

"No." I shook my head. "She had one thing to do, and she didn't do it."

"But Marlow loves her job, and it's a *really* important job," Oona said. "Why wouldn't she do it?"

I leaned back in the booth, and the warped plastic seat groaned underneath me. "She said she thought he could do more good alive than he would dead."

Oona put her hand to the side of her face, as if she just couldn't believe what she was hearing. "That's not how your job works, right? The people that are chosen to die are chosen for a reason. Leaving them can only do harm."

"That's pretty much exactly how it works," I said.

"Oh crap." She took a long drink of her cachaça, then motioned to me with her fork. "Eat your food. Starving to death won't help anything."

I sat up straighter and did as she commanded, cutting into my baked heart of palm. It was normally one of my favorite meals, but today it just felt tasteless and empty.

"So what's the plan?" Oona asked.

"What plan?" I shook my head. "Everything is totally messed up, and I don't know how anything can ever be made right."

"For starters, finishing the job that Marlow left undone would be good," Oona suggested.

"But he's already killed someone. Asher only knows about his mother, but that doesn't mean there aren't others," I realized. "He might have a whole trail of dead behind him. The damage is already done."

"The longer he's left alive, the more damage he can do," Oona countered.

"Probably," I conceded. "But I have no idea how to find him. Asher's been looking for him for *years*, and he has no clue."

"But he was looking on his own before," Oona persisted between bites of food. "He didn't have you or the connections you have."

I snorted. "What connections?"

Oona held up her hand, raising her fingers as she went down her list. "Samael. Your professors at school. Other Valkyries."

I shook my head adamantly. "I can't tell any of them what's going on or they'll string up Marlow." I paused as I came to a dark realization. "That's probably what she deserves, but I can't be a party to that. She's still my mom."

Oona's expression softened and her voice was gentler when she spoke. "No one is suggesting that you turn Marlow in. But maybe if you team up with Asher and pool your resources, you two could figure something out. Without dragging the authorities into it."

"Maybe," I admitted grudgingly.

"Look, you can't undo what Marlow did, but you can do what she wouldn't."

I laughed sourly. "That doesn't really make sense."

"No, it does," she insisted. "You're just overthinking it."

"But that Asher guy seemed too unstable," I reminded her.

"Breaking into our apartment was extreme, but just imagine how pissed you'd be if you were him. I mean, when he broke in, he thought you were Marlow," Oona reasoned.

"I *am* pissed at Marlow, and I haven't even lost what he lost," I agreed.

But that wasn't exactly true. My mom hadn't died, but I had lost the idea I had of her.

When I was growing up, she'd been cold at times—well, most of the time—but she was also strong and infallible. I'd always thought of her as a lighthouse, guiding the immortals safely to the end of their journey so they didn't go crashing into the shore.

But that wasn't her. She wasn't a hero or a savior. She had managed to become the villain in her own story.

"He left his business card, right?" Oona asked, drawing me from my thoughts. "You can give him a call tomorrow."

I picked emptily at my food. "Maybe I should wait until Monday. It's the Feast of the Dead this weekend, and it's gonna be crazy."

"Malin," Oona said firmly, causing me to look up at her. "Don't make excuses. You're going to have to deal with this, and it's better sooner rather than later."

"You're right," I said with a heavy sigh. "I'll call him tomorrow."

"Excellent." She beamed at me. "Now eat your food and order another beer."

"I don't see how that will help."

"Alcohol and food may not fix everything, but I've yet to encounter a problem they haven't at least helped with," Oona assured me.

FIFTEEN

———◆———

Most of the historical texts had been transferred onto digital formats for ease of reading, but not all of them. Ravenswood Academy had a whole wing dedicated to books that weren't permitted to ever be transferred into digital.

Those who oversaw Ravenswood Academy—a joint effort between an elite board of education and the Evig Riksdag—believed that some texts contained information too valuable and dangerous to be distributed en masse to the population, and they feared that digital media was rife for pirating.

The "sacred texts" were all carefully locked up behind secure doors in the Sacrorum Wing. As an added level of security, several Sinaa roamed the halls, guarding the books and chasing out troublemakers. The Sinaa looked just like jaguars, except some of their spots were actually additional eyes, so they could see everything, and they were obsessed with preserving knowledge at all costs.

Two dozen bomb-shelter-like rooms filled the wing, and each had shelves filled floor-to-ceiling with books. Some of the books dated back centuries, worn tomes bound with leather made from human flesh, and others were brand-new, with hardly a crack in the binding.

Once, between classes, Quinn had shown up and taken me down here, under the guise of studying, which for some reason I had believed. Leading me by the hand, she had chosen the room titled PLANTAE VITAM AETERNAM.

As soon as we'd gone in, she'd thrown me up against a bookcase—so hard it nearly toppled it over—and began kissing me roughly on the mouth.

"We shouldn't be doing this," I protested as her hands slid underneath my shirt. "What if someone comes in?"

"These are all books on immortal plants. Nobody wants to read these," she assured me between kisses, but it had only been a few more minutes before a Sinaa caught us.

A dozen tiny dark eyes locked on us, staring up from the spotted camouflage, and the Sinaa let out a low growl. We'd raced out of the room, Quinn laughing all the way as the beast chased us down the hall and out of the sacred library.

What I remember most about that afternoon was the way my heart had been pounding—terrified the Sinaa would maul us if it caught us, and also terrified I might get kicked out of school. Quinn had ignored all my fears, and then, after, once I was certain we were safe, I'd been so exhilarated and relieved. I told Quinn that I never wanted to do that again, but she'd only laughed and silenced me with kisses.

Today I had an hour-long break between my first and second class, so I headed down to the Sacrorum Wing to see what more I could find out about the situation with Marlow and Tamerlane Fayette.

The search took me to a room marked by a plaque above the door that read ET VIRGINES IN MORTE. My Latin wasn't as good as

Oona's, but I deciphered it out to be DEATH AND THE MAIDENS. The Valkyrie room.

Last night, after dinner, Oona and I had proceeded to get drunk on cheap beer, but that hadn't done anything to help the situation. Before I left for class this morning, she'd reminded me to call Asher, but I thought it might be better if I did some research on my own first.

It would be easier for me to be able to just ask my professors or Samael about things, but that would only raise a lot of red flags. I mean, I was a Valkyrie in training, and if I kept asking what happens if a Valkyrie doesn't kill her mark, people were liable to think either I was plotting something or that I had already screwed up.

And I definitely didn't need that added scrutiny.

I'd just sat down, leaning back against a shelf with a small stack of books on my lap, when my phone started ringing in my messenger bag. I scrambled to answer it, before one of the Sinaa came in and chased me out, because the last thing I needed was a supernatural jaguar angry with me.

"Hello?" I whispered into the phone, glancing around to make sure nobody was around.

"Malin, it's Marlow," she said wearily, sounding irritated that I had disrupted her, when she had been the one to call *me*.

"I'm kinda busy—"

"I've been looking into that Värja boy's claims," Marlow interrupted me. "And it seems like something went wrong."

That something being her failure to do her job, but I couldn't say that to her. So I just waited for her to explain what she meant.

"Mistakes were made," Marlow said, still skirting any culpability. "But I want to help make things right. Before things get worse. Do you know how to contact the Värja boy?"

"Yes," I replied cautiously.

"I'd like you to arrange a meeting with him," Marlow instructed me. "Today, if possible. I'm free this afternoon, so that would be best."

"You want to meet him?" I asked, so shocked I forgot to keep my voice down.

"Yes, I feel that we should talk," she elaborated. "There's a nice coffee shop near where I work—Kahvaltı. That should be good. See if you can get him to meet there, and let me know what time."

"Yeah, okay," I said. "I'll see what I can do."

And that was it. She hung up without thanking me or saying goodbye. Which was just as well, because a Sinaa poked his head into the room, his ears back flat, and let out a low rumbling growl before stalking off to quiet someone else.

I sat in a stunned silence for a few minutes, then I decided that I ought to text Asher before I lost my nerve. His business card was in my bag, so I pulled it out and quickly entered it into my phone.

Hi Asher—this is Malin Krigare. I've spoken to my mother, and she wants to meet today to talk to you. Would that be possible?

Roughly twenty seconds later, he replied back with, **Yes. Of course. Where/when?**

I gave him a time and the place, then forwarded his response to Marlow. Then I turned my phone off and shoved it way in the bottom of my bag. I couldn't handle dealing with anyone else.

I finally opened the book on my lap, and then I buried my hands in my hair and stared down blankly at the words. My mind was still reeling and I barely noticed the sound of footsteps until it was too late.

"What are you doing here?" Sloane demanded, like she'd caught me digging through her underwear drawer instead of reading a book in the library.

"What does it look like I'm doing?" I shot back.

She stood over me, glowering down at me with her arms crossed over her chest. Her plaid skirt was short enough that I would've been able to see her underwear, if it weren't for the opaque nylons she wore.

"Sucking up and doing an extra-credit project for History of Supernatural Professions and Their Modern Applications," Sloane said.

"Yes . . . that is what I am doing," I said, since that sounded much better than telling her I was trying to figure out how to save my mother and the world.

Sloane rolled her eyes. "I should've known you'd pick Valkyrie. It's so obvious."

"Why wouldn't I pick something that's relevant to me?" I asked, growing irritated about a fictional problem that I didn't even care about. But if Sloane Kothari was going to accuse me of something, I was damn sure going to defend myself. "Why did you pick it?"

"I'm trying to broaden my horizons and stretch out of my comfort zone." Sloane pursed her lips and shifted her weight from one foot to the other. "My career adviser said it would be good for me."

"Sounds great," I said, hoping that would be the end of that.

She narrowed her eyes at me. "Well, what are you doing? Maybe I can approach it from a different angle."

"I doubt it—" I tried to deflect her, but she was already bent over and lifting up the cover of the book to see the title.

"*Predestination and Divinity*?" Sloane asked, wrinkling her nose. "That doesn't have anything to do with the history of your job."

"Yeah, it does," I insisted, mostly because I didn't want to raise her suspicion. "I've just been thinking, and . . . do you think we have free will?"

She arched an eyebrow and stared down at me over her sharp nose. "What are you going on about?"

"Did I choose to be a Valkyrie, or did it choose me?" I wondered.

"You were born into it," Sloane reminded me. "I can't be a Valkyrie. Ninety percent of the beings on this planet could never be a Valkyrie. So, yeah, I would say it chose you."

"But I could've said no. Lots of people aren't cut out for it," I said.

"Then say no." She shrugged. "Are you rethinking your career? Because I've never really thought you were cut out for it."

"Thanks," I muttered, slamming my book closed, and got to my feet. "I'm looking for help, and you kick me when I'm down. Nice."

I started walking away, but Sloane sighed and called after me. "Sorry. I didn't realize you were actually having a genuine existential crisis."

I stopped to look back at her. "Well, I am."

"All the Valkyries I've ever known have been dumb jocks," Sloane explained, as if that would somehow make me feel better. "I'm working on trying to get over my own prejudices, and it's unfair of me to stereotype you like that."

"Thank you," I replied cautiously.

She took a deep breath, relaxing her stance slightly, and seemed to start over.

"To answer your question about free will . . . I used to believe in it. I still do, to some degree. Or at least, I'd like to believe that *I* chose to wear my hair up today." She pulled at one of her black curls, causing it to bounce back into the ponytail when she let go.

"I know some people find comfort in the idea that gods are watching over every little detail, helping them decide everything from what color underwear to put on to who they're going to marry," Sloane went on. "But I'm not one of those people."

"Neither am I," I agreed.

"I like to believe I make my own decisions. That I'm in control of my own fate. But . . ." She drew in a shaky breath. "My father is a Deva. He's inherently honest and good, because he was born that way. He has a great difficulty lying, which leads to some awkward situations sometimes."

"That can be helpful, too," I piped in.

She narrowed her eyes. "I'm not asking for your approval on my dad," she said in a haughty voice thick with venom, but then she apparently remembered that she was trying to be nice, and she forced a smile. "Sorry. It's just not about my dad."

"Okay. What is it about, then?" I asked.

"He's good, not because he wants to be, but because he was made that way," Sloane explained. "Sure, he still chooses how he likes his coffee or what color tie he's going to wear, and that might seem like free will, but it isn't."

Her expression changed again, slackening a bit. Her mouth turned down in a frown, and sadness darkened her eyes. "And one day, you'll kill him."

"Sloane—" I began, but she held her hand to silence me.

"If not you, then someone like you," she went on. "But his time will come, and that will be that. He didn't choose to be born. He didn't choose to be good in life. And he won't choose his death. Where is the free will in that?"

I let her words sink in, then softly said, "There isn't."

"So that's my answer," she replied.

"But what if he could?" I asked. "What if he changed the way he lived and went rogue and started lying and being bad?"

Sloane laughed. "You show me an angel that breaks bad, and I'll show you a devil in disguise."

"You think we can only be bad because we were made that way?" I asked. "Then we're all just behaving as we were made to, filling our role as good little cogs in the machine, and we can't choose to get off the tracks."

"Exactly. Then something else is the one in control of it all," she said. "If I don't believe in free will, the unfortunate logical conclusion is fate. If we're not choosing things for ourselves, then someone must be choosing it for us. They're the ones deciding our destiny."

Her words hit me like a slap across the face. If Sloane was right—and her theory made sense—there were only two conclusions about what Marlow had done.

The first assumed that Marlow was supposed to kill Tamerlane, and she didn't. That meant she somehow managed to bust free off her preordained track, and the whole thing would break down without her cog there rotating in its place.

The second assumed that this was actually Marlow's destiny the whole time. She did exactly as she was always meant to by shirking her duties in killing Tamerlane. But if she was only running her true course, who was the one plotting her path?

SIXTEEN

———◆———

Marlow sat closest to the window, amber sunlight spilling in through the wooden slats of the blinds. Hot black coffee filled the mugs before us, each rim stained with our own particular shade of lipstick. Hers was a sharper blood-red, while mine was more of a matte merlot—aptly called Velvet Vampire.

A spread of tasting food dubbed the Turkish Delight sat untouched on the table before us. Bowls of olives and Beyaz peynir cheese, a platter of cucumbers and tomatoes, a basket of katmer flat bread, and several tiny bowls of rose jam and fig marmalade. We had ordered this as a nicety and as a distraction, giving us all something to munch on.

The reason Marlow had chosen Kahvaltı to meet wasn't the food anyway—although the food was fairly good. It was the long, slender cigarillo she held between her fingers with its pungent bouquet of smoke hovering over us. Kahvaltı was one of the only places in the city that still allowed smoking tobacco.

"If I'd known he was going to be so late, I would've taken the time to touch up my hair," Marlow said.

Her bleached-blond hair had begun to grow out a bit, leaving a sliver of black roots along her scalp, but it had been styled well, hiding most of that flaw. Marlow had really done herself up today. Her makeup was a bit heavier than normal, with thicker eyeliner and false lashes, and her form-fitting black dress had long sleeves and a short hem.

Marlow exhaled smoke from the corner of her mouth and cast her scrutinizing gaze on me. She reached out, running her fingers through the thick stubble on the shaved side of my head.

"If you're going to insist on this ridiculous haircut, you ought to keep up with the shaving," she chastised. I leaned away from her touch, so she let her hand fall away. "It's getting long."

I dug through my messenger bag, searching for my phone so I could text Asher and find out what the holdup was. He was already twenty minutes late.

We were poised at a table right by the front entrance, and when the door opened, I looked up to see Asher. He'd cleaned up some since I'd seen him last, appearing a little less grizzled and a bit more rested.

I smiled and waved toward him, then realized that might not be the appropriate response for this meeting. His eyes met mine—as hard and dark as the ocean during a storm—and he nodded once, so I let my hand fall awkwardly back to my lap.

He turned, speaking quietly to a woman who had followed him in. Her jumpsuit was perfectly tailored for her tall frame, and a sarong was draped elegantly over her shoulders. With her glacial white hair meticulously styled and oversized black sunglasses covering most of her face, she looked stunningly regal.

Pursing her lips, she lowered her sunglasses to look at Marlow and me, and I could almost feel the daggers she was shooting piercing into me.

"Who is that woman?" Marlow leaned over and asked me.

"I don't know," I whispered, but they were already on the way toward us, and I suddenly felt so nervous that I wasn't sure I could do this.

Marlow set her cigarillo in the ashtray and stood up as they reached our table. "Hello," she said, flashing her most winning smile. "I'm Marlow Krigare."

I realized belatedly that I should've stood, but now my mother was leaning over to shake Asher's hand, and it felt too forced.

"I'm Asher Värja," he said, casting an uneasy glance down at me as he shook Marlow's hand. "This is my grandmother, Teodora Värja."

Marlow extended her hand to Teodora, but she just sniffed and sat down, ignoring Marlow's offering. My mother cleared her throat uncomfortably and took her seat across from Teodora.

"So, my daughter told me that you were looking for me," Marlow said, her eyes bouncing between Asher and his grandmother.

"You could say that," Teodora said with a weary sigh. She took off her sunglasses, and they clacked loudly when she set them on the table. "You really sodded things up, didn't you?"

"Beg pardon?" Marlow asked, and her plaster smile began to waver.

"*Amma*," Asher said, using the old Norse word for *grandmother*. "They invited us here. We should hear them out."

"He's right," I said, desperate to diffuse the growing tension between Teodora and Marlow. "We thought maybe if we could meet and exchange ideas, we might be able to track down Tamerlane."

"We did just want to be of help," Marlow replied, but her words came out stiff and robotic. She held her head and shoulders so high and straight, it looked painful.

"Oh, please." Teodora leaned back in her chair and gave a dry laugh. "How old are you?"

"I don't see what that has to do with anything," Marlow replied tightly.

Teodora rolled her eyes. "Fine, play that game. I turned seventy-five last May. I worked as a Valkyrie for almost fifty years before I retired." She leaned forward, resting her arms on the table and staring directly at my mother. "And do you know how many of my assignments I failed to return?"

I looked helplessly over to Asher, and his panic-stricken expression nearly mirrored my own. We were powerless to get our matriarchs to behave.

Marlow's lips twisted into a bitter smile. "You think I asked you here to listen to this shit? I thought I could help you."

"Yes, you're a real saint, aren't you?" Teodora continued with a nasty smile. "Inviting the family of your victim here to commiserate."

"My *victim*? I never even met your daughter."

"She wouldn't be dead if it weren't for your failed actions," Teodora countered.

"You don't know that," Marlow insisted coolly. "Maybe she was always meant to die. Only the gods know the true plan."

I actually winced when she said that.

"So that's why you called us here?" Teodora asked. "So you could convince yourself that you did nothing wrong?"

"I wanted to try to make things right. I wanted to help you. But now I see that you don't want my help. You just want to spew all your anger and hate out at me, and I won't let you." Marlow pushed her chair back and stood up. "I am not your punching bag."

"We're all emotional," Asher said, his voice taking on the same pained tone as it had when he was in my apartment. "Let's all just calm down for a second."

My mother shook her head as she grabbed her jacket from the

back of her chair. "No. You had your chance. Good luck getting justice for your mother."

"Marlow, please." I reached out, meaning to grasp her hand, but she pulled away from me. "They just—"

"I'm out of here, Malin," she said and slid around me on her way to the door.

"Marlow—" I repeated and started to get up, but Teodora held out her hand to me.

"No, stay. I'll go after her." She sighed as she slowly rose to her feet and grabbed her sunglasses from the table. "I can make nice if it means that I can avenge my Adela."

Asher turned to watch Teodora follow after my mother. Through the window blinds, I could see Marlow standing on the sidewalk, smoking a new cigarillo. When Teodora reached her, she didn't immediately punch her, so that was a good sign.

"I'm sorry about that," I said to Asher once it seemed like Marlow and Teodora were talking.

"No, I'm sorry. My grandmother said she just wanted to come for support. . . ."

"It's a very complicated situation," I said.

I spread jam on the flatbread, mostly so I'd have something to do, and Asher reached for the small butter knife at the same time I was putting it back, so our hands bumped against each other. His skin felt rough brushing against mine.

"Sorry," I said.

"Don't be," he said gently, his dark eyes meeting mine, before he roughly spread the marmalade on his own bread, but like me, he never actually took a bite of it.

After a stretch of silence, Asher cleared his throat and asked, "So, you call your mom by her name?"

I nodded. "Yeah. Marlow told me that most Valkyries call their moms by their first names."

"Well, it's starting to sound like Marlow has a bit of a skewed view on what it means to be a Valkyrie," Asher said, and the truth of his words stung hard—harder than he'd intended them to, based on the apologetic expression on his face.

"It seems that way," I agreed with a heavy sigh.

"Did she tell you why she didn't kill Tamerlane Fayette?" Asher asked directly.

"She did." I paused, trying to figure out how exactly to word it, but the hopeful look in Asher's eyes underneath his gathered eyebrows compelled me to just tell the truth. He deserved to know. "She said that he was good, and she thought the world would be better with him in it."

He laughed darkly. "Yeah, the world is real great with him in it."

"She knows she made a mistake," I hurried to say, defending my mother even though I really knew there was no defense for her actions. "She wants to make it right."

"How?" Asher asked skeptically.

"She wants to kill Tamerlane," I lied, because I wanted it to be true.

Marlow hadn't shared any of her intentions with me or even why she'd wanted to meet with Asher. I had no idea how she planned to try to make this right, or what she even thought the right thing would be anymore.

"Do you think she really will?" Asher asked honestly.

"I don't know," I admitted. "A few days ago I would've said yes, definitely." I took a deep breath. "But it doesn't matter. If she doesn't kill him, then I will."

He smiled then, crookedly because of a scar he had on the left side of his top lip. It was a small gash, like a comma dropping down from the smooth skin of his face to his full lips. But his smile softened his whole face. Even his eyes seemed lighter.

It wasn't until that moment that I fully appreciated how handsome he was. He had this ruggedness about him—unshaven, with slightly disheveled hair, thick eyebrows, leathery hands—and it clashed wonderfully with the beauty of his other features—high cheekbones, full lips that were almost pouty, eyes that were a disarming shade of blue.

He wasn't much older than me, but he had a world-weariness that made him seem older, like he'd been through things I couldn't even imagine. It was in the rumbling tenor of his voice, and he still somehow managed to be soft-spoken.

Everything about him seemed to be a contradiction—weathered but youthful, gruff but gentle, angry but forgiving. Yet it all seemed to work for him.

"I do appreciate you meeting with us," Asher said finally. "I know this all must be very hard for you. The position that you're in."

"Nobody's in a good position. I mean, I can't imagine what this all has been like for you and your grandmother."

"It hasn't been easy," he admitted.

He looked out the window, at the animated conversation between Teodora and Marlow. Both of them were waving their arms and shouting at one another.

"But I do really want to thank you." Asher turned back to me and reached across the table.

He took my hand in his—strong and rough and warm—and I noticed the paracord bracelet around his wrist. It had a small metal plaque imprinted with the three horns of Odin on an eagle. That was the insignia for the Vörðr—the Evig Riksdag police.

Competition to get into the Vörðr was harsh, and the job itself was renowned for being grueling. Recruits had died going through the relentless boot camp, but the Vörðr had to be the best of the best to protect the Riks from vengeful immortals or rogue Valkyries.

I lifted my gaze, letting his eyes meet mine, and I felt heat flush through me as he smiled at me.

Then Teodora came in like a blizzard, her sarong billowing around her, and Asher pulled his hand back from mine. She walked over and sat down heavily in her seat beside Asher.

"We managed to come to an agreement." Teodora motioned vaguely out the window, where Marlow was still standing on the sidewalk. "She's out there waiting for you when you're ready."

"What's the agreement?" Asher asked.

"She's going to work with you to find Tamerlane Fayette," Teodora explained as she poured herself a cup of black coffee. "And then she's going to kill him."

Asher raised an eyebrow and glanced over at me, before asking her, "That's your agreement?"

"Yes." Teodora sipped her coffee. "Well, that and if she doesn't kill Tamerlane, then I'm going to kill her."

SEVENTEEN

—◆—

Marlow was waiting outside for me, just as Teodora had said. But as soon as she saw me, she turned and started walking back toward her brownstone, and I had to jog to catch up with her. I was actually half an inch taller than my mother, but she'd always had these long strides that I had to struggle to match.

"Teodora said you reached an agreement," I said as I caught up with her.

"If you can call it that," Marlow snorted.

We stopped at a crosswalk, and a woman with a small child at her side glared up at Marlow—more specifically, she was glaring at the cigarillo in her hand.

"That's disgusting, and you're polluting the air for everyone around you that has to breathe in that noxious smoke," the woman reprimanded my mother.

Marlow turned to face her, putting her hand on her hip, and

leaned forward, reminding the woman of her size and strength. "Look around, honey. This whole city is nothing but pollution."

She gestured wildly with her cigarillo, and unfortunately she wasn't wrong. Even on a sunny day like today, a thick haze hung in the air. No matter how many attempts were made to be more environmentally friendly, there were just too many beings living too close together.

The light changed, and the woman huffed on ahead. Marlow laughed to herself, but she tossed her half-finished cigarillo into the gutter anyway.

It was late afternoon, and the sidewalks were full. They usually were, but today had the added benefit of being unseasonably warm for autumn. The air was still brisk, and Marlow pulled her coat more tightly around her as she stalked down the street.

Plus, it was the Friday before a holiday weekend. Sparkling black and purple garlands were wrapped around light poles, while images of skeletons and coffins were pinned up everywhere. All the storefront windows had flyers proclaiming their sales and specials for the Feast of the Dead celebrations.

"You know, I got an assignment from Samael last night," I told Marlow, since she seemed to have no interest in discussing her conversation with Teodora.

"He's got you busy, busy, busy," she said, and I swear she picked up her pace again, so I was nearly jogging to stay at her side.

"I was thinking tonight we should stake her out," I said. "She lives in the Gold Coast, which isn't too far."

"Tonight's no good. I've got to work at the call center."

"Tomorrow—"

"Tomorrow's no good," Marlow cut me off. We'd reached her brownstone, so she stopped and turned to face me. "Honestly, this whole weekend is no good because of that damned feast."

I glanced toward the front door, but apparently she wasn't going to invite me up, so we were going to have this conversation on her front stoop.

"But when we get an assignment, we're supposed to make the return within seventy-two hours if at all possible," I said, reciting the rules I'd been taught.

She shrugged. "Well, I'm telling you it's not possible for me to help you this weekend."

"Should I call Samael?" I asked.

"Why don't you take care of it yourself?" Marlow asked.

"I'm not licensed."

She rolled her eyes. "Can you handle it yourself or not?"

"I can," I replied, trying not to sound as uncertain as I felt.

"Then what do you need me for?"

"You're supposed to go with me," I persisted.

"Who cares? You got it covered."

"I know. I would just feel better if—"

"I'll only drag you down." She rummaged through her purse and pulled out her keys as she walked up the steps toward her place. "I just screw things up, Malin. I ruined everything with Tamerlane, and I don't think I'll be any good to you tonight. Go take care of this yourself."

I stood outside her brownstone for several long minutes after she'd gone inside. Some part of me hoped that she would come back out and apologize, explain that she was all worked up about the meeting with the Värjas, and she didn't mean any of it.

But she didn't, and really, I shouldn't have been surprised. In the nineteen years I'd been alive, I'd never known my mother to apologize. Not even once.

Marlow had left me with very limited options.

Samael had been okay with meeting him on my own, but there was no way he'd be cool with me actually going out on the assignment by myself. If I told him that Marlow was too busy to help me, that would most likely result in some kind of reprimand for her, and if there was an inquiry that went along with it, Tamerlane Fayette's name would almost certainly come up. That would lead to termination for her—and I didn't just mean of her career.

The second option was that I could just wait around for the weekend, and hope that Marlow changed her mind come Sunday or Monday. But that was a long shot, and I would most likely end up back where I was. But by then I'd already be extended past my deadline.

And the final option was just to follow Marlow's advice and take care of it myself. Assuming there were no hiccups in the assignment, then everyone would be none the wiser. The target would be killed, and neither Marlow nor myself would be in trouble.

So I headed back to my apartment to do as much prep work as I could. Samael had sent me all the files on Amaryllis Mori in my drop box.

I told Oona of my plan, so she made supper, which freed me up to spend as much time as I could studying everything I could about Amaryllis and the best ways to fight Jorogumos in general. Oona made tofu meat loaf, which I slathered in hot sauce and ate while hunched over my tablet, with Bowie curled up at my side.

Finally, it was time. According to the information Samael had sent me, Amaryllis should be getting off work in a few hours, and I wanted to be sure that I got there with enough time, in case she got out early.

I geared up—my sword Sigrún was sheathed around my waist, my dagger was in my thigh garter, and I had my asp and acidic pepper spray in my messenger bag.

"I still don't think you should do this," Oona told me for the hundredth time as I dropped my messenger bag over my shoulder. She stood in the center of the living room, cradling Bowie in her arms and frowning at me.

"I know, but it has to be done," I insisted. "I can't just let it go, or I'll end up with another Tamerlane situation on my hands. And we've all seen how that turns out."

"What if something happens to you?" she asked.

I walked closer to her and scratched Bowie between his antlers, and he nuzzled up against my hand. "If I die, you get Bowie, and you have to take care of him, because I said, and that will be my deathbed declaration."

She gave me her I'm-not-kidding-around look. "Mal. I can handle Bowie. He's not what I'm worried about."

"I gave you all the info." I motioned to a note I'd tacked up on the fridge.

Oona looked back over her shoulder at it and read it aloud. "*Amaryllis Mori. The Nysa club in Gold Coast.* That's it?"

"That's all you need to know if you decide to send out a search party," I said. "But don't be premature about it. Wait until at least three A.M. before freaking out. If you're worried, text me first."

"But you have to reply to the text, or I'll panic. You know me."

"I do."

"Be careful, Mal. There's a lot of crazies out tonight because of the holiday tomorrow," Oona cautioned. "I'd go with you, but I'm no good in a fight."

I smiled. "That's true, but I appreciate the sentiment." I bent down and kissed Bowie on his forehead. " 'Bye, Bowie. Be good for Oona."

With that, I left, heading out into the city to commit my first independent kill.

EIGHTEEN

---◆---

Hiding out beside the dumpster in the back alley behind the gentlemen's club, I had to appreciate that at least the garbage smelled better in the Gold Coast than it did around Shibuya. It was still dank, and the air held the putrid stench of stale beer, moldy food, and exhaust fumes.

Even a nice establishment like this—and Nysa was arguably the nicest strip club in the whole city—had a familiar stench to it. Whenever the back door to Nysa opened, the scent of cheap buffalo wings and sweat would waft out, along with the thumping bass of whatever music the women danced to.

The building itself had been styled after the Greek architecture that inspired the name, with Parthenonesque pillars surrounding it. They'd added plenty of gold flourishes and neon lights for good measure.

It was getting late, and while I had seen plenty of women coming out after their shifts—all high heels and body glitter—I had yet to see Amaryllis Mori. I was beginning to fear that tonight might be a bust, but then I began to feel it.

My sword felt heavier and grew warmer on my hip. I glanced down and saw that Sigrún had begun glowing a dull purple in its sheath; soon it would be bright enough to light up the entire alley.

The anxious electricity raced through me, and it was difficult to force myself to stand still. My body wanted to move, to run, to chase anything it could. My breathing grew more shallow as a metallic taste filled my mouth. The buzzing around my heart intensified, sending a heat pulsing through me, and the pressure began to build in the base of my stomach.

The hyperfocus kicked in, and I could barely feel my own body. I was aware of every subtle change in the breeze, every tiny sound that happened in the fifty-foot radius around me. The world slowed down, and I saw everything.

Amaryllis finally stepped out of the club, and she was even more beautiful in real life than she was in pictures. Her skin was like porcelain, with her long slender legs stretching below her short skirt to her stiletto heels. A few gold-leaf extensions had been added to her long silken black hair, glinting as she walked.

She took a few steps in the opposite direction from me, going toward the street where she could catch a taxi, but she stopped short. Warily, she turned back to look at me—she was the first to look at me the entire time I'd been staking out Nysa—and her big doe eyes widened even farther.

"No." She shook her head once, slow and deliberate. "It can't be you. It can't be now."

"Amaryllis Mori, you have been chosen to die," I said, as I walked toward her. "It is my duty to return you to the darkness from whence you came."

She smiled then, a bright red slit spreading out across her face. "Not if I send you first."

In the hours leading up to our confrontation, I had read every single thing I could find about the Jorogumos. But I had never seen one in real life before, and there really isn't anything that can prepare you for watching a beautiful young woman transform into a spider.

Her face changed first—her lips peeled back, revealing a mouthful of sharp teeth, including two fanged incisors, and her eyes multiplied, with bright red eyeballs popping out all across her forehead and cheeks.

Her legs went next—the pale satiny skin ripping open with an audible tearing sound. Her two legs quickly became eight spindly spider legs, covered in venom-filled razor-sharp hairs called setae, and her abdomen filled out and expanded to take on the bulbous shape of a black widow.

Her torso remained mostly unchanged, with her slinky dress clinging to her womanly curves, and human arms. Her willowy neck remained attached to her monstrous half-human, half-spider head, and her long black hair swirled around her.

"You think you can kill me, little Valkyrie?" she cried out at me, smiling through her fangs at me. "Kurnugia is more powerful than you'll ever know."

As she stepped closer to me, her pointed feet pattered on the asphalt. I stood my ground, and I felt no fear. The Valkyrie in me had taken over completely, and the only thing I could think about was ending Amaryllis.

"It gives me no pleasure to end you," I told her as I unsheathed Sigrún, but the pressure was building inside me so much, I could hardly stand it.

"Too bad," Amaryllis said, somehow making a *tsk*ing sound with her awful mouth. "Because I am going to *love* killing you."

She swung at me with her leg, and I narrowly ducked out of the way. In her spider form, she was much taller than me, which made it much harder to cut off her head. I jumped at her, but my sword merely nicked her shoulder before she struck me with her leg and sent me flying back into the building.

It didn't hurt, because I couldn't feel anything other than the anticipation of the kill, but for a moment I couldn't breathe. But everything I read had said she shouldn't have been able to throw me like that. Jorogumos were weak compared to Valkyries.

Amaryllis ran at me, and I tried to scramble out of the way. The sharp end of her foot stabbed through my calf like a knife, and she lifted me up off the ground. I dangled upside down, as she held me up by my left leg, and I could hear the sound of my pants and flesh ripping.

"The tables have begun to turn, little Valkyrie," Amaryllis said, holding me up in front of her. "But don't worry. Soon enough, the underworld will come for you."

She cackled then, and I swung out with Sigrún, slicing off the end of her leg. She howled in pain as I fell to the ground, with the end of her leg still embedded in mine.

I lay motionless on my back, letting her charge at me. She stabbed her foot into my right shoulder, pinning me to the ground, and I allowed her to. I waited until she was hovering right above me, her saliva dripping down onto my forehead, and I drove my sword right into her abdomen.

She screamed like a banshee—her voice echoing through everything and sounding like a thousand voices screaming out at once. Her belly opened up, pouring out thick black blood, and she stepped back from me, unpinning me.

As she lost blood, she stumbled and tried futilely to hold it in. While the injury was severe, it wasn't fatal, and I still needed to finish the job.

"No! *No!*" she screamed as I climbed onto her back. "No, you can't do this! It isn't supposed to happen like this!"

I grabbed her by the hair, yanking her head back, and told her, "This isn't my decision to make." Then I pulled my sword across her throat, easily slicing through her neck and decapitating her.

The air around us began glowing bright purple from Sigrún, and a wind came up, out of Amaryllis, and twisted through the alley. Relief began flowing over me in warm waves, and my muscles quivered.

I climbed off the corpse of the Jorogumo, and I fell to my knees on the ground beside her, breathing in deeply.

The sound of wings flapping pulled me from my moment of relieved euphoria, and I looked up to see a massive black raven standing at the end of the alley. It was roughly the size of a bobcat, larger than any raven I'd ever seen before, and its beady eyes were locked right on me.

Even though the purple light from Sigrún had all but gone out, the light somehow seemed to linger on the bird's black feathers. It tilted its head as it watched me, squawking once.

"What do you want?" I demanded, but the raven had no reply. It just flapped its wings and disappeared into the night sky.

NINETEEN

———————◆———————

W hile I was in full Valkyrie mode I may have felt nothing, but now the pain hit me with the intensity of a thousand suns. I doubled over on the ground, writhing in the thick blood spilling out from Amaryllis's body.

"Malin?" a familiar voice called out, sounding panicked, and suddenly Quinn Devane was at my side, kneeling down beside me. "By the gods, Malin, are you all right?"

"Yeah, I'm great," I lied through gritted teeth.

She frowned at me, brushing back her silver hair from her face. "You are not great. You were attacked by a Jorogumo, and you have poison flowing through your veins."

I wanted to argue with her, but there was an agonizing fire inside me that felt like it was burning me from the inside out, so all I could manage was a grimace.

"It shouldn't be hitting you this hard, though," Quinn said, her husky voice tightening with worry. "Valkyries aren't entirely immune, but the pain shouldn't be so severe."

I squeezed my eyes shut and barely managed to say, "Sorry my pain isn't at the correct levels."

"Wait. Just wait," Quinn commanded, and I heard her rummaging through her purse. A few seconds later, she held a cold vial to my lips. "Drink this."

"What is it?" I asked.

"I'm not a stranger trying to roofie you in a bar. I'm your . . ." Quinn trailed off, then quickly added, "Whatever. Just drink it."

I did as I was told, swallowing down the cold bitter liquid. It tasted exactly how gasoline smelled, and I barely gagged it down.

"Oh, hell, that's terrible," I groaned.

"It's not supposed to *taste* good," Quinn said. "It's an antivenom, not a soda pop. It'll stop the pain."

Sure enough, within moments I felt it running through me like ice, putting out all the fire that had been threatening to burn me alive. I blinked a few times, and stared up into her worried emerald eyes.

"Thanks," I said.

"You're not all healed up yet," Quinn warned me. "You'll still need Oona to stitch you up when you get home."

I groaned as a realization hit me. "That's what you're doing here. Oona sent you to check up on me."

"And you're lucky that she did. It's strange that the venom affected you so powerfully. . . ." She trailed off for a moment, thinking, then she shook her head. "But it did, and you could've died, rolling around in pain, if I hadn't gotten to you."

"I would've been fine," I insisted, even if I wasn't sure that was true. "I'm always fine."

Quinn let out an exasperated sigh, a sound I'd heard quite often during our brief relationship. She would always talk about how much she enjoyed being around me, but the thing I seemed to do most was exasperate her.

"Why do you always have to be like this?" Quinn asked. She sat back on her knees, watching me as I struggled to get up. "There's nothing wrong with accepting help."

"There is if I don't need it," I said and then stumbled and nearly fell over.

I would've actually fallen, if Quinn hadn't gotten up and raced to catch me. Her arm around me felt strong, stronger than I remembered her being, and I allowed myself to lean into her.

"I'm walking you home," Quinn said firmly. "And I don't care what you say. I won't be able to live with myself if I don't make sure you get home safe."

"Fine, if it's what you want. . . ." My voice trailed off.

"It is," she said, and we started walking down the alley toward the street. Her arm securely around my waist, me leaning against her as I limped.

My luft was parked three blocks away, but I was in no condition to drive it. I didn't know if Quinn planned on walking me the entire way home, or if she had a car somewhere nearby. But at the moment I didn't care all that much. I was just relishing the way it felt to be touching her again.

Her skin was so soft, and I remembered the way it felt when she ran her hands over my body. My mind flashed to when she had kissed me for the first time. Her mouth had been so hungry and eager, and she tasted like plums. We had been drinking, but the only thing I was drunk on was her.

I had never felt that way before I met her—so light-headed and excited and nervous and wonderfully sick.

"What were you doing anyway?" I asked, trying to distract myself from my own thoughts. "Before Oona called you to come rescue me."

"A Feast of the Dead pre-party," she replied, and that explained her outfit.

It was a skintight sweater dress with thigh-high boots. The dress was low-cut, so when I happened to look down, I could see the edges of her black lace bra barely covering her chest, and her Vegvisir amulet lay between her breasts.

I pulled my gaze away, forcing myself to look at the sidewalk in front of us. "Were you with anyone?"

"So what if I was?" she asked, not unkindly.

"I was just making conversation," I contended.

She waited a beat before asking, "Are you still seeing that guy you were with the other night?"

"I'm not seeing him."

"That's not what it looked like to me."

"He's just my mechanic," I insisted.

Quinn scoffed. "Uh-huh. My mechanic has never looked at me the way he was looking at you."

"Well, maybe you should wear this outfit, then."

"What is that supposed to mean?" she demanded.

I sighed. "I was just trying to say you look amazing tonight."

"Oh." She paused. "Thank you. I'd say that you look good, but honestly, you look like crap."

I laughed. "I wouldn't expect any less from you."

"Why were you out on your own, anyway? You could've gotten yourself killed, and are you even licensed yet?" Quinn asked, and I involuntarily tensed.

Telling Oona about Marlow had been one thing. She'd been my best friend forever, and I pretty much had to tell her everything. But the more people who knew about Marlow's flagrancies, the more likely it would be that a higher-up would find out, and then she would be done for.

"My mother had stuff to do," I answered cagily. "She couldn't be here, and I had a job, so I did it."

"That's not protocol."

"Please, Quinn," I begged. "I've had a long night. Can you not lecture me, for once?"

"Oh, sorry," she said with exaggerated remorse, her words dripping with sarcasm. "I didn't realize that having a conversation was lecturing you."

And then I remembered exactly why I had ended things with her. Quinn was always pushing and pushing, demanding more from me than I was ready to give. Probably even more than I was capable of. I would never be enough for Quinn, no matter how hard she tried to mold me into being who she needed me to be.

When we'd first met, she'd taken my breath away with her beauty and her quick wit. But by the end I was suffocating under her unmet expectations.

I stopped. "You know what? I'll just get a taxi." I pulled away from her, even though putting the full weight on my leg hurt like hell, but I kept my expression stoic, so she wouldn't know how much it hurt to walk away from her.

Her face instantly fell, and she reached out for me, but I just hobbled back from her. "Malin, no. I didn't mean it like that. I can get you home."

"No, a taxi will be fine." I walked to the edge of the sidewalk, raising my hand to flag down the first thing that came by.

"Malin," Quinn repeated, just as a bright yellow hovercar pulled up beside me.

"It's fine, Quinn," I assured her. "Thanks for all your help. I'll see you around."

TWENTY

—◆—

"Oh, bloody hell!" I cried out, causing Bowie to thump his back foot on the floor in a show of anger.

He'd already taken to hiding under the kitchen table, since I'd been cursing and yelling for the past twenty minutes as Oona attempted to take care of my battle wounds. She had cut off my pants just above the knee so it would be easier to get to my injury.

"Isn't there something you have to make this more painless?" I asked through gritted teeth.

Oona knelt on the floor in front of me, wearing thick vinyl gloves to protect her from the Jorogumo venom inside the setae, and her tackle box of thaumaturgy healing and apothecary tools was open beside her. She'd placed a towel on the floor underneath me to help maintain the mess, since my leg was soaked with blood—red from me and black from the Jorogumo.

"Okay, Mal, you have a giant spider leg jabbed straight through the muscle of your calf," Oona explained as calmly as she could.

"There's only so much I can do to make this painless. You really should go see a doctor."

"No doctors." I shook my head.

While a doctor, with expertise, sterile equipment, and syringes filled with beautiful, beautiful morphine would be ideal, I couldn't risk it. Doctors would ask questions, which could lead to them figuring out that I was working on my own as an unlicensed Valkyrie, and they were legally required to report that to the Evig Riksdag.

So that left Oona as my only option for medical care. And she really wasn't that bad at it. She'd already stitched up the puncture wound in my shoulder that Amaryllis had given me, but pulling a spider leg covered in needlelike hairs out of my leg was a little beyond her usual area of expertise.

"Here." Oona held a thick piece of leather toward me. "I'm gonna pull the leg out now. Bite down on that."

"All right, screw it, let's do this." I took it from her and did as I was told. I bit down as hard as I could and squeezed my eyes shut.

"Here goes nothing," Oona said, more to herself than to me, and pain exploded in my leg.

It already hurt like hell before she even touched it, but now the setae were burrowing deeper into my muscle as she yanked on the spider leg. It felt as if she were trying to pull my leg inside out.

When the pain began to reach the point where I felt I couldn't take it anymore—I screamed against the leather in my mouth as nausea rolled over me, and darkness edged around my thoughts like I was on the verge of blacking out—I heard the wet *thwak* as the spider leg finally came free.

"There!" Oona declared proudly, but I already felt it.

My leg still hurt something fierce, but nowhere near as bad as before. I spit out the leather and relaxed back against the couch, gasping for breath.

"It should be much easier from here on out," Oona assured me. "I'm going to start cleaning it now."

I winced as she started digging around in my leg, getting out any setae that had decided to stay embedded in my muscle, and I stared up at the ceiling.

"This is why you shouldn't have gone alone," Oona said after I cursed under my breath again. "I bet this wouldn't have happened if Marlow was there."

"Maybe not," I allowed. "But it shouldn't have been this bad anyway."

"What do you mean?"

"Valkyries have immunities to this kind of stuff. From everything I know about Jorogumos, their poison should only have a minimal effect on me." I shook my head. "Even Quinn commented on it."

Oona spritzed a pale purple liquid on my leg wound. It stung for a moment, then the pain quickly faded to a dull nothingness. "That should help numb it a bit, and now I'm gonna start stitching you up."

"Thanks for the heads-up." I made sure to keep my eyes on the ceiling so I wouldn't see the needle go in. Oona was right—the spray did numb the pain. I still felt it, the pressure of the needle and thread going through skin, but it wasn't as bad as it could have been.

"Do you think it could be because you're not licensed yet?" Oona asked.

"That's not how it works," I explained. "A piece of paper doesn't give me the antibodies or super-strength. I'm born with it. It's in my blood."

"Could your father have diluted it or something?" she asked.

"No. All Valkyries have mortal fathers, and I've never heard of them having fewer abilities for that reason."

Oona lifted her head and looked up at me. "Who was your father?"

"I don't know. Just some human," I said, then quickly added, "No offense."

She snorted. "None taken."

Valkyries were in an odd place where we weren't immortal, but we weren't exactly human, either. We were a breed all our own, with many of the same weaknesses as humans, like death, aging, and the need for oxygen and sunlight. We were just stronger, more resilient, and had an innate ability to hunt immortals, and while our blood weakened the immortals around us, it had no effect on humans.

"But this is different anyway," I said. "Amaryllis was saying all this weird stuff."

"What do you mean?"

I closed my eyes, trying to remember exactly what Amaryllis had been saying to me through her fangs. "That she was going to kill me, and the underworld is more powerful than I'll know, and the tables are turning."

"That's not normal posturing and threats?"

"Kind of. But it just . . ." I sighed. "I don't know. It didn't feel like an empty threat. It was almost like . . . like she *knew* something."

Oona stopped stitching me for a moment. "I'm doing the best I can with this, but you're still going to need to go to the doctor at some point to make sure this is taken care of for real."

Then I felt the needle going back in, and Oona said very little as she concentrated on finishing the sutures. When she was done, she started washing off my leg and then covered the wound with some kind of anti-infection salve.

"Did Marlow ever get beat up like this?" Oona asked as she wrapped my leg in a bandage.

Marlow had returned with a black eye or a fat lip a dozen or so times. I remember waking up once when she came in late. Her lip was bloody, and her knuckles were all scraped up from punching. She sat in the darkened living room, drinking vodka straight from the bottle, and when I tried to ask her what had happened, she just snapped at me to go back to bed.

But that was probably the worst I'd ever seen her. No broken bones. No puncture wounds. No parts of spiders trapped inside her.

"She came home with a few scrapes and bruises from time to time, but it was never this bad," I admitted.

"So it could be because of your inexperience." Oona had finished bandaging my leg, so she sat back and looked up at me. "Or it could be because something is up." She waited a beat before asking, "Is there any way this could be related to that guy that Marlow didn't kill?"

I groaned, realizing belatedly that it could be. "I don't know."

"You're gonna have to talk to someone, Mal. That's the only way you'll find out what's really going on."

"Who am I gonna talk to?" I asked, sitting up straighter on the couch. "Marlow is stonewalling me, and anyone else I could talk to, like Samael or my teachers, they would just turn me in."

"You could talk to Quinn," Oona proposed.

My heart skipped a beat, as if Oona saying her name would somehow invoke her presence, and I shook my head adamantly. "No, I'm not talking to Quinn."

"She wouldn't turn you in."

"You don't know that, and even if it's true, I can't," I maintained. "It's too complicated."

"First off, I *do* know that," Oona argued. "She cares about you. When I told her what you were doing, she freaked out because she was so worried about you."

I groaned loudly in exasperation.

"And second, I don't even know why you broke up with her," Oona went on, undeterred by my reaction. "You two were crazy about each other, and then you suddenly pulled the Valkyries-can't-fall-in-love card."

I rubbed my hand over my face and regretted ever introducing Oona to Quinn. "I already told you it's complicated."

"Okay, it's not, but let's say that it is," she conceded. "That there's all sorts of complex, unrequited feelings going on between you and Quinn. You know what I say to that? Suck it up, buttercup. If she can help you deal with whatever crap is going on right now, then you need to ask for help. That's the bottom line."

"I know you're right. . . ." My voice trailed off.

"But?" she supplied.

"But the fewer people that know what's going on, the safer it is for both me and Marlow. So let me just try talking to her, and if I can't find out anything, I'll go to Quinn."

"That's all I'm saying," Oona relented finally.

I stood up slowly, careful to not put too much weight on my injured left leg. "Right now I should get some sleep."

Oona scrambled through her thaumaturgy kit, before finding a miniature mason jar. It was filled with tiny ocher crystals, and she dumped out two into the palm of her hand. "Here." She held them out to me. "Take this."

"What is it?" I asked, already taking it from her.

"It's called solamentum, and it's made with ginger and angelic toadstool with just the smallest touch of codeine," she explained. "It should help with the inflammation, pain, and risk of infection."

I threw back my head and tossed them in my mouth, and instantly regretted it. They were tart and acidic, like grapefruit juice mixed with battery acid. "That tastes terrible. Why does everything that's good for me taste so awful?"

"That's just how the world works, Mal."

I smiled down at her. "Thanks again for taking care of me."

"That's what friends are for, right?" Oona smiled back.

"Come on, Bowie." I whistled for him as I hobbled toward my bedroom, and he hopped after me. "Let's hit the sack."

TWENTY-ONE

It wasn't even noon yet as I made my way to Marlow's place, and the city was already bursting with Feast of the Dead celebrations. A parade had traffic blocked up all over, and it took my taxi driver an extra thirty minutes just to get me to where I'd left my luft parked in the Gold Coast.

The streets were dripping with decorations, from black streamers to strings of purple lights. Each light post I went past on my way to Marlow's had a different poster of a figure from the underworld, all of them labeled with:

Patron Saint of Kurnugia

Normally the Feast of the Dead seemed like a fun—albeit obnoxiously traffic-jam-inducing—holiday, but today everything felt strangely unsettling. The patron saints posters—the sage Hades with a thick beard and blue flames rising behind him, the terrifying horned Supay with red eyes and bloody flesh peeling from his body, and the arresting Ereshkigal with lush black skin and an impish grin sitting atop her throne of bones—were particularly unnerving.

Even though they were just pictures on paper—an artist's rendering in exquisite detail—they carried such an imposing presence that I could swear their eyes were following me as I hurried past, making the hair rise on the back of my neck and an icy chill run down my spine.

To get to Marlow's stoop, I had to push my way through a throng of teenage girls and ghouls, all dressed up in couture mourning gowns, several replete with gauzy black veils flowing around them. They all talked and laughed loudly, and if the smell was to be believed, they were already drunk on cheap booze and liliplum.

Marlow hadn't answered her phone when I tried calling this morning, and given the severity of everything that had happened with Amaryllis Mori, I decided I couldn't wait to talk to her, and I was coming over uninvited.

After walking up the four flights of stairs to her apartment, I was really hoping she was home, because I doubted that my leg could handle the trek again. Oona had even given me a couple more of those solamentum crystals to help with the pain, but my wound was still throbbing. I'd smartly worn a flowy skirt with slits down the side, so it wouldn't rub against my leg too much.

I knocked, and though it took a bit for her to answer, I heard Marlow talking inside. The slot for the peephole clanged and she muttered, "Dammit," on the other side of the door. Just what every daughter wants to hear when she visits her mother.

Finally she opened the door a crack. She was wide awake, with hair and makeup properly styled, which was usually a good indicator that she would be less cranky, but based on the irritation in her eyes, I realized that wasn't the case.

"What are you doing here?" Marlow demanded through the gap in the door.

"I just—"

Before I could finish, she shouted back over her shoulder, "Did you tell her you were here?"

"No," Asher said from inside Marlow's apartment. "I didn't talk to her."

"Asher is here?" I asked. "What's going on?"

"Fine, come in." Marlow opened the door all the way and gestured wildly around her. "Let's all just have a big old chat."

The first thing I noticed was that her apartment was significantly less cluttered than it had been when I came over the day before yesterday. All the garbage had been removed from the kitchen, and most of her random military surplus objects seemed to be stowed away somewhere.

The boxes were still stacked up, blocking the only window, and there were still the tubs of rice and lentils, but in general everything felt more orderly and neatly piled up. The only light came from what little spilled around the boxes, several fat candles on the coffee table, and a solitary bulb shining over the sink in the kitchen.

Asher sat on the couch, smiling sheepishly and offering me a small wave as I stepped inside. Marlow had stomped off to the kitchen, pouring herself a cup of coffee with a hefty dash of vodka, so I closed the door behind me.

"Your mother invited me over to discuss things," Asher explained awkwardly, since it seemed like Marlow didn't plan to. "I got here about ten minutes ago."

"Why didn't you tell me?" I asked Marlow.

"Why would I?" She sat down in a slipper chair across from Asher and crossed her long legs, one over the other. She stared up at me with her steel-gray eyes. "This doesn't involve you. This was part of my agreement with Teodora, not you."

"How does this not involve me?" I protested.

"I'm the one that made a mistake, so I'm the one fixing it," she replied coolly. "You don't have anything to do with it."

"Yeah, sure, you're right." I took off my messenger bag from where it hung looped across my chest and walked over to the couch, where I sat down heavily beside Asher. "I almost got killed last night, but you're right. None of this concerns me."

Marlow tilted her head and narrowed her eyes slightly. "What do you mean, you almost got killed?"

"Remember how you were too busy this weekend to help me do a job I'm not ready to do yet?" I clunked my heavy moto boot on her battered coffee table and pulled my skirt to the side to show my leg. Oona had rebandaged it this morning, but it was still bleeding through. My skin above and below it was dark purple from bruising. "Well, I went to take care of it myself, and the Jorogumo almost got the best of me."

My mother looked at my wound and exhaled wearily. "By Odin's ass, Malin, you should've been able to handle that yourself."

I dropped my skirt and tried to ignore the sting I felt in my chest. Asher had gasped when he saw my leg, and he stared at me with wide eyes. Marlow had hardly reacted at all.

I wanted to scream at her, demanding to know how she could take pity on some condemned angel like Tamerlane Fayette but she couldn't manage to care at all about her own daughter.

But I didn't. Instead I just said, "The Jorogumo was stronger than it should've been. The poison wasn't supposed to affect me, but it nearly killed me."

"Are you okay?" Asher asked. His body tilted toward me, and his voice was low with concern.

"Yeah, I'll live." I forced a reassuring smile at him. "Thanks."

"It didn't kill you, and you need to learn to fight better," Marlow interjected.

"No, Marlow, you're not listening. Quinn was there—" I began to argue, but my mother cut me off.

"Quinn Devane?" She snorted. "Since when did she become an expert on all things Valkyrie?"

"At this point, I honestly feel like she knows more than you," I replied defiantly.

Marlow narrowed her eyes. She'd been about to drink from her mug, but she stopped after I mouthed off, her lips hovering a centimeter above her coffee. "Don't even—"

"I mean," I cut her off, "she does know enough to always kill her assignments."

"This is exactly why I didn't invite you over here." Marlow set down her coffee on the stone end table, and opened the wooden humidor resting on it, pulling out a slender cigarillo wrapped in dark brown leaves. "I knew you'd just hold that over me."

"Marlow!" I shouted in exasperation. "I am not browbeating you! I am trying to tell you what's going on and ask for your help."

She scoffed as she lit her cigarillo. Then she took a long drag from it, before licking her lips and eyeing me. "What could you possibly need *my* help with?"

"Figuring out what's going on," I replied simply.

"What's going on is that I need to finish this shit with Tamerlane so he stops wreaking havoc on the world and Asher can get some closure," Marlow said. "That's plenty, isn't it?"

I pursed my lips and nodded. "Yeah, that's plenty."

She cleared her throat. "Now, as I was telling Asher before you interrupted us, I have a contact. She's always made it a point to know everything about everything. I reached out to her last night, and she said she'd be willing to meet with us."

"Does she know anything about Tamerlane Fayette?" Asher asked.

"I didn't ask her anything directly yet," Marlow said. "I didn't want to set off any alarms. But if Tamerlane is still alive somewhere, she'll know about him."

"How can you be so sure?" I pressed.

"It's what she does. She's over six hundred years old, and she's managed to accumulate a lot of knowledge and a lot of friends in that time," she explained.

"Six hundred?" I asked. Most of the assignments had been for immortals that were only a couple hundred years old. I'd never even met anyone over four hundred years old. "Why hasn't she died?"

"She just hasn't been chosen to return yet." Marlow shrugged and cast her annoyed gaze toward her window, which was mostly blocked by her boxes. "Now, with the ridiculous Feast of the Dead today, traffic is going to be murder, so we should get going if we want to meet with her before the sun sets."

"Is that a stipulation?" Asher asked.

"It's what she requested," Marlow replied simply.

"Who is this magical all-knowing person?" I asked.

"Cecily Stavros. She's a gorgon," she replied as if meeting with a gorgon were no big thing, and then she stood up. "Now, if you don't mind, I'm going to go to the bathroom, and then we can head out."

Marlow took her cigarillo with her when she went into the restroom, but the cloud of clove-scented smoke lingered behind. Asher and I sat in the dimly lit living room as silence enveloped us.

He leaned in closer to me, so his knee brushed up against mine, and in a low, conspiratorial tone he said, "I don't want to sound rude, but your mother is kind of a bitch sometimes."

I laughed. "Yeah, she certainly is."

TWENTY-TWO

———◆———

Marlow locked up her car, then started walking. The sidewalk was crowded and cluttered with decorations and garbage, but she kept clomping on ahead, not waiting for either Asher or myself.

"Now, she doesn't know I'm bringing the two of you," Marlow said, once we'd scrambled to catch up to her ridiculous fast pace. "So don't say too much or you'll freak her out. She doesn't like visitors."

"Then how does she find everything out?" I asked.

Marlow waved me off. "It's not my business how she knows her business. I just know that she's helped me track down many of my trickier assignments."

"I thought you hadn't talked to her in a while," Asher said.

"It's been over ten years," Marlow admitted.

"Why has it been so long?" I asked. "If she was so helpful in the past."

"We had a falling-out," Marlow replied vaguely, and then she stopped so short, I almost ran into her. "We're here. Well, she lives down there."

She pointed to the narrow stairwell to her left. It was dark and dank, running so deep underground I thought it might lead us to the sewer. Leaves and trash had piled up at the bottom, blanketing the concrete in front of a keyhole doorway.

"Have either of you ever met a gorgon before?" Marlow asked, turning back to look at Asher and me.

I shook my head, while Asher replied, "I've seen pictures of them."

"She won't turn you to stone," Marlow prepped us. "I mean, she *can* if she wants to, but it doesn't just happen automatically. But don't look directly at the snakes. It's rude."

I was about to ask if there was anything we should know about Cecily Stavros specifically, but Marlow had turned and was already bounding down the steps. Asher and I waited politely in the darkness behind her as she knocked.

It was a few minutes before the door finally creaked open. Her hand on the doorframe was the first thing I saw. Long red fingernails and pale skin with a few iridescent green scales trailing down the back of her hand to underneath her satin dressing gown.

Then her face slowly materialized in the gap from the open door. At first she appeared to be a woman in her sixties—an admittedly attractive woman in her sixties, but on the older side nonetheless. Her skin looked soft and smooth, though wrinkled, with more of the green scales trailing around her hairline and down her neck toward her décolletage.

Her hair was beautiful golden waves, and intertwined with it were five living, breathing snakes. They grew out from her scalp and danced around her head like a halo. The snakes leaned out farther than her, their tongues flitting out, and the light from above the stairwell shimmered off their scales.

"It's been a long time," Cecily said, and her eyes—brilliant green, matching the snakes—were locked on my mother. Her lips twisted into a strange smile.

"It has," Marlow agreed, returning her own uneasy smile.

"You killed my sister," Cecily told my mother.

I sensed Asher's posture grow more rigid, as if readying himself to spring into action if necessary. He was beside me, but he took a half step forward, almost as if to protect me. Which was silly, because I was far more equipped to battle something like a gorgon. Instinctively, I reached for my hip, but I'd left Sigrún at home. The sword was useless when I wasn't on an assignment, anyway, but it gave me comfort just touching it and knowing it was there.

"I did," Marlow admitted calmly. "I was only doing my job. It's not me who decides who lives or who dies."

The peculiar smile remained fixed on Cecily's face as she stared up at Marlow. "Just following orders, were you?" she asked, and Marlow nodded. "I've heard that excuse to explain away all kinds of evil acts in this world."

"I don't expect it to explain away anything I've done," Marlow said. "I'm only telling you that it wasn't personal."

"Well, if you had known Calixta, it would've been personal," Cecily said with a light laugh. "I hated my sister, and I'm glad she's dead." The gorgon stepped back and opened the door wider. "Come on in."

Immediately inside the door was a small foyer that looked about as dark and dank as the stairwell around us, but when Cecily opened the door beyond that, it was a totally different story.

Brightly lit by an opulent chandelier, everything was white marble with gold embellishments and crystals everywhere. Huge mirrors with ornate bronze frames hung on the walls. Every piece of furniture—from the flared bench by the door to the mirrored sideboard cabinet—was all glamorously art deco.

Cecily led the way through the surprisingly spacious apartment, her long blush pink dressing gown flowing on the marble floors behind her, and went down a few steps into her sunken living room. She sat on a sofa near a baby grand piano and gestured widely to the room.

"Please, sit," she said, lounging back on the sofa.

In the center of the room was a large glass coffee table sitting atop a white fur rug, and Marlow sat down on the tufted ottoman beside it. I decided on the velvet settee, and Asher sat down beside me, so close our legs touched when he leaned forward, resting his elbows on his legs. Sitting across from Cecily like this, with Asher at my side, I felt a bit like an uneasy teenager being introduced to her new boyfriend's disapproving parents.

"Aren't you going to introduce me to your guests?" Cecily purred as she lounged back on the sofa, and her gaze lingered on Asher.

"This is my daughter Malin and her friend Asher." Marlow gestured to us.

"And I am Cecily Stavros, one of your mother's oldest and dearest friends," she said, laughing lightly. She rested her head on her arm, and a snake coiled around her wrist. "I understand you've come here asking for a favor."

"It's not a favor, exactly—" Marlow started to explain, but Cecily cut straight through the bullshit.

A snake in her hair began to hiss, and Cecily held up her hand to silence it. She asked, "Do you want something from me, or did you just come for a friendly chat?"

Marlow sat up straighter. "We only wanted information."

Cecily clicked her tongue, then narrowed her eyes. "And what shall I get in return?"

"What do you want?" Marlow asked.

"I want you to tell me when I'll die."

TWENTY-THREE

—◆—

Marlow took a deep breath, looking the gorgon directly in the face, and unemotionally answered, "I don't know. I don't know until the name shows up on my orders."

Cecily got up, walking across the room to a gold and glass serving cart. "But certainly my time must be up soon." She looked back over her shoulder at Marlow. "I can't be the only one that they allow to live forever."

She began pouring herself a drink, a dusty pink liquid from a lavish decanter, into a highball glass. From a small bowl she plucked two small globes that looked like ice cubes, but when she dropped them in her glass, they fizzed and bubbled.

"The math of the gods is a mystery to all of us," Marlow said simply.

"So what do you have to offer me?" Cecily asked. She walked past me and Asher on her way back to the sofa, and she paused in front of Asher to run her hand underneath her chin. "Did you bring me this delicious young man?"

All the snakes in her hair leered toward him, and he continued to stare at her impassively. But a small tick in his jaw made me suspect that it was taking a great deal of fortitude to keep from pulling back from her.

"I'm here because the information is of great benefit to me," Asher said.

Cecily threw back her head and laughed—a cheerful cackling sound—and then she strode back to return to her spot lounging on the sofa. "Don't be so serious, my dear boy. I'm only teasing."

"He's actually the reason I'm here," Marlow interjected, her voice sounding light, probably because Cecily seemed to have taken a liking to Asher.

His gaze turned stormy as he rested his blue eyes on my mother. "Not to argue semantics, but the reason we're here is actually because of *you*."

"Oh, there seems to be contention in the group." Cecily's eyes bounced excitedly between Marlow and Asher, and one of her snakes dipped its head into her glass, drinking. "Do tell all the juicy details."

"There isn't much to tell," Marlow replied, casting an irritated glare toward Asher.

"We're looking for the man that killed Asher's mother," I interjected, because I feared they would go around and around like this all afternoon. "Tamerlane Fayette."

Cecily tilted her head and sipped from her drink. "Name doesn't ring a bell. I've always been better with faces, anyway."

I pulled my phone from my messenger bag and quickly scrolled through until I found the picture of Tamerlane I'd saved to it. Then I walked over to her. Cecily touched the phone, moving it so she could get a better look, but she just shook her head.

"This isn't enough. I'll need more. Is there anything else you can tell me about him?"

Asher looked over at Marlow, and when she didn't say anything, he cleared his throat and said, "He's supposed to be dead."

Cecily's eyes widened with glee and her smile grew so wide, it looked painful. I don't know if I'd ever seen anyone quite as happy as she looked just then.

"Asher," Marlow hissed, with fury in her eyes. If she were any closer to him, she would've smacked him across the head, something I'd experienced firsthand plenty of times.

Asher shrugged. "It's the only other thing we really know about him."

"Did you let someone slip away, Marlow?" Cecily wagged her finger. "You dirty bird."

"It's a complicated issue, and I would like it if you could keep it between us," Marlow said.

"What's a little secret between old friends?" Cecily intimated as she took another drink.

Marlow smiled thinly. "Thank you."

"But now that you mention it, I have heard rumors about draugrs," Cecily said, and when Asher looked quizzical, she followed up with, "The undead."

Asher's brow furrowed. "You mean like a zombie or a vampire?"

"No. Not just immortals like vampires, or myths like zombies. Draugrs are undead in that they are immortals who managed to escape their fate and skipped their date with a Valkyrie," Cecily elaborated.

"So it has happened before?" I asked.

"There's talk of it from time to time, but most of the time it's only gossip and urban legends." Cecily waved her hand and tossed her head. "I've been alive for over half a millennium, and I've only met one draugr. He was a miserable old fool. Their time is up for a reason, and he eventually came to see me and asked me to turn him to stone. So I did."

She nodded toward a statue at the other end of the living room. He was marble perfection, with the chiseled physique of the gods, wearing only a loincloth, and with two large wings coming out of his back.

"Do you know anything about draugrs nowadays?" I asked, and Asher continued staring back over his shoulder at the statue.

"I had assumed it was nothing more than rumors or wishful thinking," Cecily admitted. "We immortals are always looking for stories about cheating death and ways to extend our existence here on earth."

The thing about immortals was that they never really died. There were ways to destroy their earthly bodies—either with the blade of a Valkyrie, or in various difficult tasks, like a vampire with a stake to its chest or a silver bullet for a lobishman. But once their bodies were dead, they merely moved on to the next plane of their existence—down to Kurnugia.

But Kurnugia was alleged to be dark and unpleasant, with several millennia's worth of angry demons and devils jostling for control and tormenting everyone around them. Without the Vanir gods and the Valkyries to intervene, it was chaos, and death wasn't an option anymore, so it was an endless nightmare.

There was a bastion of peace—a solitary fortress known as Zianna that was ruled by angels and other divine immortals. But with the population of immortals growing for all eternity, it was legendary for being nearly impossible to gain entrance. There were far too many immortals, and even discounting the huge swath that were too cruel and malicious to ever be invited in, it would be impossible to house all the saintly beings.

With the prospect of spending the rest of eternity in the cramped hell of Kurnugia, and with the doors of Zianna locked to them, most immortals preferred to live out their days on earth, where the sun was bright and pleasures were easy.

"What rumors have you been hearing?" Marlow asked.

"That there's a whole trio of draugrs stalking about the city," Cecily said.

"At least you're not the only Valkyrie shirking your duties," Asher muttered, causing Marlow to give him another dirty look.

"What is it they say?" Cecily asked. "Trouble always comes in threes?" Then she tilted her head. "Or is that death?"

"What are they doing in the city?" Marlow asked, returning the conversation to the topic at hand.

Cecily answered, "The same thing everyone else does here—get into as much trouble as you can without getting caught."

"Do you know anything about them?" Marlow asked.

"Not much." Cecily let out a dramatic sigh. "Only one of them I've heard of by name—Bram Madichonnen."

"Have you heard if he associates with Tamerlane Fayette?" Asher asked hopefully.

"Honestly, I haven't heard of this Tamerlane fellow at all, and the only thing I know about Bram Madichonnen is that he's allegedly a draugr and likes to hang out at the Red Raven."

"The Red Raven? Of course he does," Marlow groused.

I'd never been to the Red Raven, but the debauchery and sinister clientele there made it infamous around the country. It was a bar and dance club located in the Aizsaule District of the city, which had unofficially become an "impious-only" neighborhood. To top it off, the Red Raven was owned by Velnias—a demon who thought of himself as some kind of mobster.

Cecily leaned forward and set her drink on the coffee table. "Since we're old friends, I would *hate* to see you hurt. So it's as your friend I'm advising you to tread very carefully." The elation in her expression had fallen away, and she spoke gravely to my mother. "Draugrs are dangerous."

Marlow smirked. "I think I can handle an immortal."

"An immortal, sure," Cecily relented, but her gaze only grew more somber. "But draugrs are something different. They can't be killed."

"Of course they can," Marlow said with more conviction than I thought she should have. "Everything dies. One way or another, we all end up in the dirt or down in Kurnugia."

"Why do you think I turned him into a statue?" Cecily pointed sadly to the statue. "Poor dear Armaros had grown weary of this life, but nothing else worked. The Valkyrie blade couldn't cut him."

Asher leaned forward, resting his arms on his knees. "So you're saying that Tamerlane Fayette is immortal *and* unkillable?"

"If death marks you, and it misses you, who knows how long it will be before death comes around to mark you again?" the gorgon asked.

TWENTY-FOUR

———◆———

Once we'd all piled back into Marlow's car and she finally got it started—it was an old Jeep, with actual tires instead of hoverpads, and it always took a few tries before it finally started up—Marlow immediately lit up a cigarillo and let out a frustrated breath.

"So." Asher leaned forward from the backseat. "When are we going to the Red Raven?"

Marlow eyed him in the rearview mirror, looking at him like he was an idiot. "Not tonight. It's going to be a madhouse."

"Doesn't that make it the best time to go?" Asher asked. "It's almost guaranteed that this Bram guy will be there."

"A night like tonight, it's going to be rowdy as all hell," Marlow explained. "It's not worth the risk. If he hangs out there a lot, he'll be there another night when it's quieter."

Asher pressed on, "What if—"

"I said not tonight," Marlow snapped and put the Jeep in gear. "And that's final."

The rest of the car ride across town, none of us said anything, aside from Marlow cursing at other vehicles and pedestrians that she felt were slowing her down. When she parked in her spot by her house, she grunted a quick goodbye, and then headed toward her apartment without another word.

That left Asher and me standing awkwardly on the sidewalk.

"Thanks for coming today." He scratched behind his ear and glanced around. "You were helpful, I think."

"Yeah, no problem," I said, even though I wasn't sure I'd done anything at all. Then I turned to walk away.

"Are you going to the Red Raven tonight?" he called after me, and I turned back to face him.

Under the bright autumn sun, the blue in the darkness of his eyes glimmered. A smile played subtly on his full lips, and he moved closer to me. I couldn't help but notice that when he looked hopeful like this—his eyes both eager and nervous, his smile unsure but bold—he appeared strikingly handsome.

"Are you going?" I asked.

"I was thinking about it." He paused, chewing the inside of his cheek, before asking, "Would you care to join me?"

"Yeah."

"Now?"

I shook my head. "No, it's too early, and we can't go dressed like this anyway."

He glanced down at his jeans and distressed jacket. "Why not?"

"It's the Feast of the Dead. It's like demon New Year for them," I elaborated. "You gotta dress up for it, or you won't even get in the door."

"I guess I'll have to dig out my Sunday best, then," he said.

"Do you wanna meet me at my place at nine, then we can head out?" I suggested.

"That sounds like a plan."

I started to walk away, then stopped and called back to him, "Oh, and this should go without saying, but don't tell Marlow."

He waved in confirmation, and then he disappeared into a crowd of costumed characters. Presumably they were performers from the parade, based on their bright makeup and ornate regalia.

Back at the apartment, Oona interrogated me about visiting Marlow, and I filled her in as best I could, including all the details about meeting Cecily. After that, I enlisted her to help me get ready for the Red Raven. It wasn't the kind of event that I could skimp on.

Oona shaved the left side of my head, because Marlow had been right—it was getting long. Then she pulled out a dress that her mom had designed specifically for me.

This dress was a little black number with cutouts on the side and opaque black fabric laid at angles all over sheer black mesh, so it hinted at more skin than it actually showed. The sleeves were long mesh, hiding the bruises and injuries I'd suffered in the Amaryllis Mori encounter, but the hem was short and only hit my mid-thigh.

As I stood in front of the mirror, fixing my eyeliner and reapplying my Velvet Vampire lipstick, Oona stood behind me with her arms folded over her chest and a self-satisfied grin on her face.

"You're lucky you have me," she said.

I looked at her in the reflection of the mirror and said, "I know."

"You'd be totally lost without me," she reiterated.

"I really would," I agreed with a laugh.

"You could show your appreciation a little more."

I turned back to her. "Hey, I made you breakfast this morning, and I helped you work on your term paper for your Miracles and Visions course."

"That is true." Oona considered this for a second. "But I did stitch you up last night and shave your hair today, and I helped my mom make you that dress that looks amazing on you."

"Fair enough. I'll take you out for drinks this week?" I offered.

"Deal." She held out her hand to me and I shook it. "You really do look great."

"Thank you. You look . . ." I glanced down at her old leggings and oversized Ravenswood Academy T-shirt before deciding on the word, ". . . comfy."

Oona laughed. "Thanks. That's the look I was going for. Bowie's often impressed by this."

"I would invite you to join us, but . . ."

"No. I get it." She sat back on the couch. "I don't wanna get killed or punched in the face. Are you sure it's safe for you to go out tonight? I mean, if Marlow says it's too dangerous . . ."

I pulled my knee-high boots out of the pile of shoes by the door and sat on the couch beside Oona.

"It's not that she thinks it's too dangerous," I explained as I pulled on a boot. "She just doesn't want to deal with all the crowds and traffic. Plus, she really hates the Feast of the Dead."

"How come?" Oona asked.

"Because of everything I just said. Actually, now that I think about it, she hates most holidays."

"She sounds like a real hoot to have grown up with," Oona said dryly.

"You know it."

My right boot had gone on easy, but the left boot was a fight because my calf was still swollen and tender. I had to be careful, but I couldn't go out with a bloody bandage exposed, so I had to hide it under my boots.

"Marlow's anti-holiday rhetoric aside, it is going to be danger-ous out there," Oona said. "The Red Raven isn't exactly known for being civilized."

"I know, but I can handle myself, and I'll have Asher with me."

"Yeah, but you don't really know Asher that well," she pointed out. "Can he even fight?"

"He seemed to handle himself when we scuffled." I'd finally gotten both boots on, so I turned to look over at her. "Plus, he was a Vörðr."

Her eyes widened. "Really?"

"I mean, I think so. He has a paracord bracelet with the Vörðr insignia on it, and I just get this vibe from him. It would also explain how he was able to get some of the classified information he showed me."

Oona thought about it and nodded. "Well, you did describe him as battle-weary before. You'll probably be safe, then."

"I think we can manage it," I said, hoping that I sounded more convincing than I felt.

If Oona noticed my ambivalence, she didn't say anything, and thanks to the knock at the door, she didn't have time to.

I answered the door to discover Asher standing there, clean-shaven and more handsome than ever. He wore a perfectly tailored suit that hugged his broad shoulders and tapered to his narrow waist. It was black on black, and he'd left the top buttons of his shirt undone, revealing just a hint of his chest.

I hurried to pick my jaw up off the floor and managed a smile before teasing, "So you can knock after all?"

"Yeah." He smiled crookedly, and I felt his eyes going up and down over me, causing a warm flush to spread through my body. "You look . . . you look great."

"Thanks. You clean up nice, too."

"I'm Oona Warren, by the way," she interjected, pushing herself between me and the doorframe to extend her hand toward Asher. "Marlow's best friend and roommate."

"Asher Värja." He smiled as he shook her hand.

"Take care of Malin, will you?" Oona asked, and I rolled my eyes.

"Of course." He stepped back and motioned to the hall. "Shall we?"

"Be safe, you two," Oona commanded as I grabbed my bag. "And don't stay out too late. The real trouble always starts after midnight."

TWENTY-FIVE

———◆———

Somehow, the Aizsaule District always seemed darker than the rest of the city. Maybe there was a hex over it, one that sucked up all the light. Even the sky above looked darker, without a single star showing.

The Red Raven was built out of some kind of shiny black stone, with an animated neon red bird above the door, moving up and down as if picking at the patrons. Two red searchlights roamed on either side of the door, but it wasn't as if the place needed help attracting more customers. There was already a line down the block, with all sorts of humans and supernatural beings dressed in their most gothic haute attire.

Fortunately, Asher and I looked good enough that we didn't have to wait very long. We'd been queued up for a little over a half hour, which wouldn't have been so bad if it weren't for the two Aswangs standing right behind us.

The Aswangs were particularly horrifying-looking humanoid creatures. The bottom half of their head was all mouth, filled with many jagged teeth and a long, serpent-like tongue. They also smelled like sulfur and rotten meat, and the two behind us had a particular lack of understanding of personal space.

They kept creeping up toward us, almost pushing Asher and me forward. He put his arm around my waist and moved back a bit, putting himself between me and the Aswang duo. It wasn't necessary, since I didn't need him to protect me, but I still thought it was a nice gesture.

And I especially enjoyed the way his hand felt on the bare flesh of my skin, exposed by the cutaway in the dress.

Periodically, a doorman walked down the line, plucking out those he deemed worthy enough for the Red Raven. He came over and motioned for Asher and me to go on in, and the Aswangs behind us let out an annoyed shriek, so I smiled and flipped them off.

Inside, everything was dim and glowing red, reminding me of an old darkroom for developing camera film. The Red Raven had several rooms—some private and off-limits, others looking far too S&M for my tastes—so we decided to bypass them and head for the largest main room.

It was about half the size of a football stadium, with a large dance floor in the center. A long backlit bar took up one whole wall, while booths and tables were lined up against the far wall and in the balconies that wrapped around the length of the room.

A stage at the end of the room had a band playing. The lead singer was a beautiful siren, accompanied by thrashing guitar players, a drummer, a keyboardist, and a DJ. The music was pulsing techno, with her melodic voice carrying through it.

"So how do we want to do this?" Asher asked, his voice in my ear and his hand around my waist, pulling me close to avoid us getting trampled at the edge of the dance floor.

"Let's go to the bar and start asking around," I suggested.

The bartender immediately came over—a chubby woman with

blue streaks in her jet-black hair. She leaned over on the counter, letting her large chest spill onto the bar from her skintight top. Something in the way she moved, the sultry turn of her lips, and the lure of her pheromones let me know instantly that she was a succubus.

"What can I get you?" she asked through her byzantine lipstick.

"What do you recommend?" I asked, trying not to be enchanted by the look in her eyes. As with the venom of the Jorogumo, I wasn't entirely immune to the charms of the succubus, but I did have a stronger resistance than the average human.

She pointed to a smoky red drink that another patron was drinking. "The Diablo's Dream is the special tonight."

"Two of those," I said.

She smiled wider, and I wanted to melt into a puddle of goo. "You got it."

"We shouldn't get drunk," Asher murmured, and the sound of his voice pulled me from the minor spell that the bartender had put me under.

"Drink slowly, then," I replied.

When the bartender returned, she set the drinks on the bar, and before she could even tell us how much it was, he set a fifty-dollar bill in front of her.

"Thank you." She smiled as she put the money in her bra.

"We were supposed to be meeting someone here." Asher leaned over the bar so she could hear him better. "He's supposed to be a regular. Maybe you know him?"

She shrugged. "I know some people. What's his name?"

"Bram Madichonnen," Asher said, while I tried my drink. It was all cherries and spice, but there was something else in it. Something thicker, warming my skin.

Her smile instantly fell, and the enchantment disappeared from her eyes. "Never heard of him," she replied blankly. She tapped the bar once, then started walking away. "You two have a good night, now."

"That was weird," Asher commented after she'd gone.

He left his drink at the bar, while I continued slowly sipping mine as we wandered around the room. We tried to seem casual, like we were just two people here celebrating the holiday, and we got a few demons and cravens to talk to us.

But as soon as we dropped Bram's name, the conversation would grind to a halt. No matter how much either Asher or I tried to flirt and play it off, it always ended the same.

"This isn't working," Asher commented.

"Maybe we should try loosening up more," I suggested.

I'd just finished my drink and left the empty glass discarded on a nearby table. Between the alcohol and the music thumping through the room, I felt fiery and free. A carnal heat rushed through me, setting my skin ablaze, and desire swelled in the pit of my stomach.

Asher leaned against the bar beside me, and even in the darkly lit room I couldn't help but notice how sexy and strong he looked. His suit fit him to perfection, hugging his muscular frame.

I'd been standing beside him at the bar, but leaned into him now, letting my lips brush against his earlobe as I whispered, "We could dance."

"We could," he murmured, and that was all the encouragement I needed.

I swayed my hips as I danced closer to him, subtly rubbing against him, and I put my hands on the lapels of his jacket. His hand was on my hip again, cool against my warm flesh, and I pressed against him as I danced. He pulled me closer, so close my lips were almost touching his, and I wondered what his full lips would feel like against mine.

Before I could find out, I stepped back from him. The air felt thick and electric, and I needed to put distance between us so I could think clearly again, because thoughts of Asher and what I wanted to do to him were clouding my mind.

Still dancing suggestively, I backed away from him, and he leaned against the bar, watching me with a mixture of bemused desire darkening his eyes.

He mouthed the words *Watch out*, but it was too late. I bumped into someone, their body firm and unyielding behind me, and I turned around to see Arawn—a demon powerful and famous enough that I recognized him immediately.

TWENTY-SIX

———◆———

Under the red light of the club, his long white-blond hair glowed a dull crimson. He wore a suit made of pure white, clashing with the color scheme of nearly everyone else here. He was handsome, the way many demons were, but his smile managed to freeze the heat inside of me.

"Are you having a good time?" Arawn asked in a voice like satin.

"I am," I said, pushing down the chill inside me and managing a flirtatious laugh. "How about you?"

"Always." His smiled widened, looking hungry, and he looped an arm around me, pulling me out to the dance floor with him.

He moved gracefully across the floor, somehow making me a more elegant dancer along with him. I wasn't exactly clumsy, but my movements had never felt so fluid as with his arm around me, guiding me through the steps.

With a hand on my back, he pressed my pelvis against his, then dipped me low. I relaxed against his arm, allowing my hair to drag on the floor, as he supported me and pulled me against him.

"You're a good dancer," Arawn mused, his lips mere inches from mine.

"Thank you," I breathed.

"What's a nice girl like you doing in a place like this?" he asked.

"I'm not so nice," I replied with a coy laugh. "But I was hoping to meet someone here tonight."

He gave me a predatory smile. "Well, you found me."

"Maybe if you play your cards right," I teased, keeping my voice as sultry as possible. "I was actually looking for Bram Madichonnen."

Arawn waited a beat before replying, "Haven't heard of him." His arm was still around me, but his eyes darted behind me. "Your boyfriend is getting jealous. You should probably head back to him."

I glanced back over my shoulder to see Asher standing at the bar watching us. His eyes were dark, and his lips were pressed into a grim line, but I read the expression for what it actually was—not jealous, but cautious and diligent.

"He's not my boyfriend," I said, and when I turned back to Arawn his smile had vanished.

He let go of me and stepped back before commanding, "You should head back to him anyway."

The crowd had parted a bit to make room for us to dance. Arawn was the kind of guy who demanded space. But when he walked away, he left me standing alone in a small circle on the dance floor, with leering eyes surrounding me.

I tried to play it off and walk as calmly as I could to join Asher at the bar.

"Who was that? He looked important," Asher asked when I reached him.

"He is." I ran my hand through my hair and exhaled. "He's a bigwig at the Kurnugia Society."

It had been named for the ancient word for the underworld Kurnugia, and it existed as a counterbalance to the Evig Riksdag. The impious believed that the Riks tended to land on the side of "good" more often than not, and they didn't want the divine inheriting the world.

The Kurnugia Society was basically a demonic version of the FBI, with a strong emphasis on making sure the impious and craven were treated "fairly."

"Did he know anything?" Asher asked.

"Oh, yeah, he definitely knows something," I said. "But he's not talking. As soon as I mentioned Bram, he shut it down."

Across the dance floor, Arawn had settled into a private booth, and he waved over a scruffy bouncer-looking guy. He leaned over as Arawn whispered into his ear, and then he turned toward us—his red eyes scanning the crowd before landing on me.

"They're on to us," Asher said.

"Maybe." I grabbed Asher's hand. "Let's dance and act normal, and then get out of here the second they stop looking."

We tried to get lost in the crowd, moving closer to the stage where the music was louder and the bodies were crammed closer together. There wasn't much room to move, so I pressed my body against Asher's and wrapped my arms around his neck.

His arm was around my waist, but this wasn't like before when we'd been dancing—this was protective and fierce. I'd never been around anyone who tried to protect me, other than Oona's motherly suggestions, but that didn't feel like this. My whole life, I'd always counted on my own strength to get me through anything, and so far, it had.

But for the moment, with Asher's strength enveloping me, it felt . . . nice. A new warmth grew inside me, softer and deeper, making me feel dreamy and romantic. I didn't need Asher's protection, but that's what made it all the more gallant. He knew how strong and capable I was, and he still cared enough to shield me.

He kept looking around, his eyes conspicuously darting, so I put my hand on his face, forcing him to look at me.

"Keep your eyes on me," I told him. "We're trying to look natural."

"Right." He nodded, and his eyes met mine.

I let my hand linger, caressing the scruff of his face, and his expression softened from fear to something else, something like when he'd been watching me while I danced. We swayed together, an island in a sea of people. Alcohol and adrenaline buzzed inside me, but that wasn't why I felt so wonderfully light-headed in his arms.

I imagined him kissing me then. The scruff of his chin scraping against my face and neck as his arms tightened around me. I wanted nothing more than to take him to a dark booth and give in to every urge that had taken hold inside me.

But I couldn't. Not then. Not with demons and monsters lurking around, waiting to pounce.

"Is he still watching?" I asked Asher, trying to break through the fog of my own lust.

"What?" He blinked at me, then looked around. "Oh. No. I don't know where he went."

Then I felt a hand on my shoulder, burning hot through the thin fabric of my dress, and I looked back to see the bouncer Arawn had been talking to. He looked even bigger up close and personal, with veins bulging through his dark skin, and his eyes were blood-red.

He was a Pishacha—a flesh-eating demon—and right now his carnivorous gaze was fixed on me and Asher.

"Mind if I cut in?" he asked.

"Yes, actually. I do," I said firmly.

"Maybe you haven't heard of me. I'm Cormac Kaur," he informed us, grinning like a wolf. "I'm the head of security around here. So why don't we go have a little chat?"

"What's this about?" Asher asked, trying to remain calm.

"It's easier if you just come with me," Cormac commanded, and, based on the look in his eyes, I knew there was no arguing with him.

TWENTY-SEVEN

◆

The back room was lit by a solitary bulb dangling from the ceiling, and the concrete floors were covered in rust-colored stains that looked suspiciously of blood. It even smelled of it in here—metallic and earthy.

The room was the size of an average walk-in freezer, and the steel door looked like it had once belonged to one. The walls were exposed brick, and there was nothing in it except for a single chair.

Cormac had led us off the dance floor, gripping me by the wrist so tightly it would've snapped if my bones hadn't been supernaturally strong from my Valkyrie blood. Asher followed at his heels, demanding to know what this was all about, but Cormac said nothing as he led us through the dark winding halls until finally shoving us into this back room.

"What do you want?" Asher demanded again, his fists balled up at his sides.

Based on everything I knew of Asher—his Valkyrie mother, his muscular physique, his possible experience as a Vörðr, his profes-

sion tracking down his mother's killer—he was a formidable oppo-
nent in his own right. But Cormac was a huge dude, with demonic
strength flowing through him, and he was used to dealing with the
unruliest patrons at the Red Raven.

There would be no way that Asher could win a fight against him.

"You've been annoying our clientele," Cormac informed us, and
he began circling us the way sharks circle their prey.

"How so?" Asher asked, feigning naïveté.

"You've been interrogating them about one of our patrons,"
Cormac said.

"So Bram Madichonnen is a patron?" I asked.

Cormac's self-assured smile faltered. "We don't discuss private
business here. We like to keep to ourselves. And you'd know that if
you were from around here."

"We're just looking for an old family friend," Asher said, trying
futilely to maintain our innocence.

Cormac ignored Asher and closed in on me. His red eyes bulged
out from his skull, and his lips were pulled back into a snarl, revealing multitudes of pointed teeth. The scent of raw meat radiated
from his breath, and I had to swallow back my urge to vomit.

"At first I thought you two were just curious humans, but you're
not. You're something else." Cormac tilted his head. "What are
you?"

"Look, we don't want trouble. We only want to find a friend."
Asher was at my side, but he moved, trying to wedge himself between
me and Cormac.

Annoyed, Cormac glared at Asher, and without warning, he
struck. He punched Asher, knocking him to the floor, and then I
lunged at the Pishacha. I hit him in the face, and a stunned Cormac
stumbled back, his fingers at the blood forming on his lip.

He growled, then charged at me. I dodged his punch, and kicked
him in the stomach. This time he fell back, and I kicked him in the

side again, just to make sure he was really down. Then I walked over and stomped my boot on his neck, pinning him there. My stiletto heel dug into the tender flesh of his throat, and he gulped as he looked up at me.

"Shit. You're a damn Valkyrie," he realized.

"I am," I admitted. "And now you know that I can kill you if you piss me off. Why don't you tell me where Bram Madichonnen is?"

Cormac laughed. "You're not allowed to kill me."

"Try me," I said, pressing my boot harder against his throat.

"Okay, okay," he croaked, and I let up a bit so he could talk more easily. "It's not like I have his home address."

"Tell me what you know!" I commanded.

"He hangs out with this Fallen girl," Cormac said finally, referring to the vernacular for fallen angels. "Eisheth Levanon."

"What do you know about her?" I asked.

"She's an ex-prostitute, but she used to work for some kind of archangel before she fell in with us," Cormac elaborated. "I don't know where she's staying, but if you find her, you'll find him."

"Thank you," I said, and since I knew he wouldn't let us just walk out of here, I pulled back and punched him as hard as I could. It didn't knock him out, not completely, but it would leave him dazed enough that we could get out.

"Come on!" I yelled and grabbed Asher's hand.

I didn't know where we were going, but I had to get out before Cormac alerted all the demons that there was a Valkyrie in their midst stirring up trouble. I darted down the narrow hallways until I finally spotted a door with a bright red Exit sign above it.

I pushed through, still holding Asher's hand, and we ran out into the cold night to a deserted back alley. Despite the chill of the air, my skin was flushed with heat, and my body felt like a live wire, electricity surging through me.

Once we'd gotten outside, I let go of Asher's hand, and we stood under the dark sky, which was glowing red from the lights of the club. We stood together, both of us breathing deeply to catch our breath, and in that moment, the two of us alone in the alley, I couldn't recall a time that I'd ever felt more alive.

When I looked over at Asher, a sly smile played on his lips, and something in his eyes made me think he felt the same way.

"That was badass," he said, his voice a husky rumble, and he stepped closer to me, causing my heart to skip a beat.

I meant to thank him, but the words died on my lips. My pulse raced, and my breath came out shallow and shaky in anticipation—anticipation of what, I didn't know, but I felt it coming, or at least I hoped for it. *Ached* for it, really.

My legs felt weak, like jelly, but I also felt stronger than ever, like I had taken on an army of ogres and still came out on top. Everything was now in hyperfocus, as if time were slowing down. The world felt like it all might pitch to the side, but I wasn't scared at all, because I knew that Asher would catch me if I fell.

I was acutely aware of how close to me Asher was. So close I could reach out and pull him into my arms, if I wanted to. My thoughts raced back to the dance floor, when my body had been pressed against his, and I could still feel his hands, cold and rough on my hips, and I'd only wanted him—

Then he was there, right there against me, with his hand on my face. I sucked in a breath, breathing him, and the scent of his cologne suddenly transported me to a memory of my childhood, when I'd been lost in a dark forest outside of the city during a rainstorm.

It was the most frightening and exhilarating and enchanting memory of my life, and that's exactly what Asher smelled like now—woodsy and dark and crisp and alive. Like terror and happiness.

His eyes searched mine, and his thumb tentatively traced the outline of my lips. When his mouth finally found mine, it was like getting struck by lightning—I could actually feel the electric heat pulsing through me.

He pushed me backward, but I didn't stumble. I just clung to him, letting him lead me until my back pressed against the cold stone of a wall. As he crushed me against it, kissing me ravenously, I realized I'd underestimated his strength.

Asher was raw power and lust, and the intensity of his kisses and the insistence of his hands roaming my body sent shivers all through me. It all terrified me, but I couldn't get enough of it, enough of him, and I held him to me, lifting a leg to wrap around him and pull him closer to me.

He let out a low moan, a soft rumble in my ear, that made my stomach swirl with delicious excitement, and his lips brushed against my neck. His moved down, gripping the bare skin of the thigh that I'd wrapped around him, and his fingers dug into my flesh as he kissed me.

As abruptly as he'd started, he stopped, stepping back and leaving me gasping against the wall. My skin was trembling, and the mixture of pleasure and relief that washed over me reminded me of how I felt after I'd finished a job and had killed an immortal.

Except, of course, that Asher left me unsatisfied and desperate for more.

"Sorry. That probably wasn't appropriate," he breathed.

I shook my head. "No. That was . . . that was good." It was the most perfect, intense kiss of my life, but I didn't want to explain that to him. Not then.

Squawking—a robust cackle, really—from behind Asher finally made me pull my gaze away from him and his stormy blue eyes. A few meters behind him, in the otherwise deserted alley, a massive raven was perched on a dumpster.

The bird's dark, beady eyes were locked on me, and I realized it was the same raven I'd seen before. The one that had watched me kill Amaryllis Mori, the Jorogumo. I wondered dimly how long it had been here, how long it had watched me with Asher.

"We should get out of here," I told Asher, just as the raven cawed and flew off.

TWENTY-EIGHT

———— ◆ ————

I stumbled out of my bedroom, limping because my left leg was killing me, just as Oona was coming in the front door. Despite the overcast skies and rain hammering against the window making it look like night, the alarm clock on my bed assured me it was well after noon.

"Are you just waking up?" she asked, taking off her jacket and kicking off her shoes.

"I had a long night," I reminded her as I hobbled into the kitchen to make myself a cup of coffee. Bowie was hopping around my feet, begging to be fed, and I nearly tripped over him as I dumped a cup of Lagomorph Chow into his bowl.

"I was sleeping when you came in. Did everything go okay?"

"Yeah. As good as it could, I guess," I answered. "Where were you?"

"Brunch with my mom and my cousin Minerva."

"How'd that go?" I asked, pouring myself a huge mug of coffee.

"Fine, except my mom kept getting annoyed that me and Minerva were talking about thaumaturgy and all that." Oona stopped talking to eye me as I hobbled to the couch to sit down. "How is your leg?"

"Awful," I admitted, but I tried to gloss over it by immediately asking her, "Is Minerva the sorceress?"

"She is, and she gave me these cool protection crystals to try out," Oona said, but she was already turning and walking into her room.

A second later, she came out with the ocher-colored solamentum in the palm of her hands. She held them out to me, but when I reached for them, she closed her fist and pulled them back. "I'll give you two more of these, but you have to promise me that you'll go to the doctor tomorrow and get your leg checked out for real. Promise me."

"I promise," I said, but honestly, I would've agreed to most things if it meant I could take something to ease the throbbing of my leg. I downed them quickly before she had a chance to change her mind, and she sat down on the couch beside me.

"So, what all happened? Did you find out anything?" she asked.

I explained to Oona what had happened and what we had found out, deliberately leaving out the part where Asher had kissed me, but just thinking about it made my skin flush. It wasn't that I was ashamed or wanted to keep it a secret—there were just more important things at hand and I didn't want to waste time dissecting what was happening between me and Asher.

Especially since I didn't know what was happening with us. The kiss had been exhilarating and brilliant, albeit very brief, but after that there had been nothing. We left the club and drove around for a bit, partially to cool off and partially because the streets were so crowded it was hard to get anywhere quickly.

But then we'd just parted ways and agreed to meet up later.

"I could probably track her down," Oona commented, once I'd finished explaining that Cormac Kaur had said Bram Madichonnen was staying with Eisheth Levanon. "You could, too."

I shook my head. "I tried searching the Internet. But you know how the impious can be. They're either posting everywhere all over social media, or they're completely silent and working in the background."

"No, I mean, you could use alchemy," she corrected me.

"No, I can't." I groaned and leaned my head back against the couch. "Alchemy is so hard."

"You need to practice it more, Mal. You wanna be a Valkyrie? You wanna track down this guy that's turning the world upside down? Then you gotta get a handle on your alchemy."

"Can you just help me today, and tutor me on alchemy another day?" I asked hopefully.

Oona sighed. "Fine. First, what do you know about Eisheth Levanon?"

"She's a Fallen and Cormac says she's an ex-prostitute."

That made sense, because a lot of Fallen ended up that way. Some angels were allowed to live and love freely, but certain sects were required to be completely "pure" and abstain from all sorts of physical pleasure. If they gave in to their urges, they were booted out of their group and usually lost their jobs. And without any real skills, other than their former purity and goodness, many of them fell onto prostitution.

"She lives in the city?" Oona asked.

"Supposedly. A lot of Fallen live in the Wolf River District, so if she's here, she's probably staying somewhere in that area."

"Great. That narrows it down. I'll get my kit," she said, and she was already up and hurrying to her room.

Oona gathered up her alchemy toolbox and lugged it to the living room. She pulled out a mirrored tray and set it on the coffee table, then began rummaging through her toolkit until she pulled out several different-colored vials.

One of the largest bottles, curved and filled with a glowing lime-green liquid, sat near the top, and she picked it up and pulled out the glass stopper. Slowly, she poured it into the tray, filling it up to the edge of the lip. With deft movements I didn't understand, Oona waved her hand over the liquid, causing a glowing mist to rise above it and dissipate throughout the room.

"This isn't going to hurt Bowie, is it?" I asked.

My wolpertinger was sitting by the window, dutifully cleaning his long ears with his front paws. But at the sound of his name, he perked up and looked over at me.

"I would never do anything to hurt Bowie. He'll be fine just as long as he doesn't drink this."

She added a few more vials, saying a Latin phrase each time she poured one in. Taking a long stick from her box, she stirred the mixture before adding a vial of black crystals. The pool of liquid turned black and became smooth and reflective, appearing more like a television screen than a tray of potions and liquid.

Oona rubbed her hands together and cleared her throat. "*Ostende mihi Wolf River District.*"

"What'd you just say?" I asked, and she held up a finger to silence me.

The liquid began to swirl, changing from black to gray, and slowly an image began to take form. At first I didn't recognize it, but as the streets and old warehouses took shape, I realized it was an aerial view of the Wolf River area.

"*Lumino angelorum lapsus,*" Oona said, and buildings started lighting up, glowing bright green.

"What's happening?" I asked.

She motioned to the tray. "It's showing places where fallen angels live."

"That's like a hundred places or more," I pointed out. "Is there a way to narrow it down?"

"Well, I was hoping there would be fewer spots on here." Oona chewed the inside of her cheek. "What else can you tell me about Eisheth?"

"Um, she's supposedly been hanging around with this Bram guy a lot lately," I said.

"Would you say she was his consort?" Oona asked helpfully.

I shrugged. "Maybe?"

"And what do you know about Bram?"

"Just that he's a draugr. Allegedly."

"Oh, right." Oona thought for a minute, then leaned over the tray and cleared her throat. "*Lumino consorcio immortui.*"

Many of the lights blinked out, but about two dozen still glowed.

"I think that vampires and a few other types of the impious are being lumped in because I had to use the word for 'undead,' since I didn't know the one for draugr," Oona explained. "So I need something else."

"Can you just say Eisheth?" I asked.

Oona shook her head. "It doesn't work like that. Beings go by many different names. You have to describe *who* they are, not *what* they're called."

"Cormac thought she used to work for an archangel, if that's helpful."

"I'll try it." She rubbed her hands together again and incanted, "*Lumino servi archangeli.*"

With that, all the lights went out, except for one.

"*Adducet eam ad me,*" Oona said authoritatively, and the image in the pool zoomed in, bringing us just above the glowing building. "That's where she is."

"So where is that?" I asked, tilting my head.

"What does that look like?" Oona leaned over the pool, squinting at a street sign. "I think that says . . . Lake Street and . . . Canal Avenue." She sat back on her knees, looking proud of herself. "Eisheth lives in a building at the corner of Lake Street and Canal Ave."

I was about to thank her, when something occurred to me. "Why can't we do this with Bram or even Tamerlane Fayette?"

Oona shook her head. "They're way too powerful. This kind of thing only works on low-level supernatural beings, like Manananggals or the Fallen. I doubt it would've even worked on Tamerlane Fayette *before* he became a draugr."

Angels were divine and immortal, but once they became Fallen, they gave up their immortality and all their authority. That would make Eisheth Levanon easier to deal with once we found her, because she wouldn't need a Valkyrie sword or a kill order for me to be able to end her life, if that became necessary.

I leaned back in the couch, exhaling deeply. Bowie came over and hopped onto my lap. He ruffled his feathered wings, and I absently petted him, smoothing them out.

Oona propped her elbows on the table and looked up at me. "What's your next move?"

"Wait for the pain meds to kick in, and then go tell Marlow that we found a link to Bram Madichonnen," I decided.

"Are you gonna contact Asher?" she asked.

I shook my head. "Not today."

Things were already strained enough between Marlow and me right now. I didn't need to add the tension surrounding Asher and all the mixed feelings about his quest. Besides, I was only going to relay some info to my mother. It'd be simple and quick, and nothing exciting should happen. He didn't need to be there for that.

TWENTY-NINE

———◆———

Y ou didn't have to come with me," I told Oona as she huffed up the flight of stairs behind me.

She'd wanted to drive me here because she didn't think I'd properly be able to drive the luft with my injured leg since I'd overdone it last night, even though I'd been coping pretty well the last couple days. But if it made her feel better to tag along, I was happy to let her.

"No, no, I got this," she insisted, jogging up the last few steps to catch up with me. "I do really need to start working out more. It's ridiculous that it's harder for me to go up those sixty steps than it was for you with your injured leg."

"I do train for this kind of thing," I reminded her, pausing at the landing outside Marlow's apartment to give Oona time to catch her breath.

"Maybe I should start training with you." She reached out to touch my bicep, firm and brawny underneath my light jacket. "Wow. Maybe I could start out slower, like with a spin class."

I knocked at the door, and Marlow answered relatively quickly, at least for her. Her hair was still wet from a shower, and she was makeup-less, other than her usual dark red lipstick. She leaned on the doorframe, sighing at me.

"Don't you ever call anymore?" she asked.

"You never answer when I call," I countered, which was true. I'd tried calling her three times before I came over, but she literally never answered her phone.

Marlow raised an eyebrow. "Doesn't that tell you something?"

"That's a real nice way to talk to your daughter," I muttered before plunging into my spiel. "I just came to tell you that we found out something about one of those draugrs, but if you don't wanna talk—"

She instantly straightened up and her eyes narrowed. "What do you mean, you found something out?" Then she glanced over at Oona. "Oh, fine, come in. The both of you."

Marlow walked into her dim apartment, which was still fairly clean from Asher's visit, though there were several empty alcohol bottles piled up around the sink. So either she had cleaned out a closet, or she had gone on a minor drinking binge after parting ways with Asher and me yesterday.

Some exercise equipment—free weights and a stair-stepper—was strewn about the living room, and she had on her stretch pants and a loose muscle shirt. The armholes hung low, exposing the black of her sports bra and a nasty scar that ran along her ribs below it.

Oona and I sat down on the couch, but Marlow remained standing, lighting one of her cigarillos.

"How are you doing, Oona?" Marlow asked. "Is your mom still running that dress shop?"

"I'm good," she said, sounding exaggeratedly chipper. Like most people who had met Marlow, Oona was intimidated by her. "Yes, she is still sewing and tailoring."

Marlow nodded, taking a long drag of her tobacco. "That's good. Tell her hi when you see her."

"Will do," Oona replied.

"So." Marlow cast her gaze on me. "What is this exciting new piece of information you discovered?"

"Last night, Asher and I went to the Red Raven—"

"You did what?" Marlow growled, instantly tensing, and Oona shrank back on the couch beside me.

"It wasn't a big deal," I said, trying to play it off. "We were both fine."

"I specifically told you not to! It's too dangerous!" Marlow shouted at me.

"Well, we were fine, so it wasn't that dangerous," I argued. "And you didn't seem to care that much about my well-being when you sent me out to face Amaryllis Mori on my own."

She shook her head and began pacing slowly across the living room. "That was different."

"How is that different?" I asked.

"You're supposed to handle Amaryllis on your own," Marlow contended. "You trained for it, have a sword for it. Hell, you were born for it! You can't just go taking on the demon underbelly by yourself."

I let out an exasperated groan. "We were fine! I don't even know what you're so mad about."

"Because you didn't wait for me when I asked you to," Marlow said, speaking to me like I was either stupid or a small child, or maybe a particularly stupid small child.

"We're not just going to wait around forever for you," I told her. "Tamerlane Fayette has already killed at least one Valkyrie. We need to stop him before anybody else gets hurt."

Marlow finally stopped pacing. She flicked her cigarillo in a nearby ashtray, and her entire body slackened. Staring down at the floor, she rubbed her temples and exhaled heavily.

"You need to be more careful," she said.

"I am," I insisted.

She looked at me like she wanted to argue, but she took a resigned breath instead. Her normally hard steel eyes were misty when she said, "I know I'm not much of a mother, Malin. But I just want you to be safe."

I opened my mouth, wanting to say some sort of word of comfort, but I couldn't think of anything. I wasn't used to any tenderness from her and didn't know how to react.

But she was still my mother, and I did still love her.

"So what did you find out?" Marlow asked finally.

I explained everything Asher and I had found out at the Red Raven, which caused her to respond with several eye rolls and tongue clicks. Then Oona chimed in to explain the incantations she'd done to track down where Eisheth Levanon lived.

"Well, I suppose we ought to get going, then," Marlow said abruptly when we'd finished.

I glanced over at Oona in surprise before asking, "Right now?"

Marlow put out her cigarillo, then went over to her pantry. That's where most people stored their food, but hers was filled to the brim with weapons. She grabbed several knives, including her sword Mördare.

"You were asking around the Red Raven last night and caught the attention of Arawn," Marlow explained as she laid out her weapons on the kitchen table. "It won't be long before Bram Madichonnen and any other draugrs know that you're looking for them. And then they'll either skip town or go on the offense and come after us."

"So you're saying that we need to get to them first?" I asked.

"Exactly," she replied. "Oona, are you coming with us?"

"I can, in case I might be able to help if you guys get lost," she offered.

Marlow held a jagged knife toward her. "Then you better take this, just to be safe."

Oona did as she was told, while Marlow headed back to her bedroom to finish getting ready. I went over to the weapons cabinet to start picking out a few knives for myself. Oona stared down at the knife with nervous eyes and chewed her lip.

"Stay close to me, and you'll be fine," I promised her.

THIRTY

───────◆───────

The large square brick building before us had once been a warehouse—an old luftfahrrad factory, Marlow thought—but it now housed over a hundred small loft apartments. Or at least that's what the property manager had claimed.

Oona's magic had gotten us to the building, but it was Marlow's old-fashioned detective work that got us to Eisheth's door. She'd gone in to the property manager's office and, using a combination of flirtation and threats, was able to ascertain that Eisheth Levanon lived in apartment 21B, and even got the manager to buzz us into the building.

The lights in the hallway hung below the exposed pipes and kept flickering on and off. In the last few seconds before Eisheth finally opened the door, we were submerged in total darkness.

For a moment the only light came from her loft, and she stood backlit in the open door—a dark shadow with wings towering over her. The silhouette of a demon.

Then the hall lights flicked on and revealed a beautiful young woman standing in the door. Her long dark hair cascaded past her shoulders, and two black leathery wings extended from her back. She wore a white sarong, loosely tied up around her neck, so her ample breasts were all but falling out the sides, and the sarong was sheer enough that her nipples were entirely visible.

She parted her lips slightly and tilted her head. "I didn't buzz you in, did I?"

"No, the manager let us in," Marlow explained. "We just wanted to chat with you."

She laughed hollowly. "I've already met my lord and savior, and I don't have any money to buy anything else you might be selling. Sorry."

Marlow put her hand on the door, stopping Eisheth from closing it. "No, we're not here to convert you or sell anything."

Eisheth narrowed her eyes, but didn't try closing the door farther, so I took that as a good sign and plunged ahead by saying, "We only wanted to know if Bram Madichonnen is around."

Instantly her expression hardened. "I don't know anyone named Bram." She tried to slam the door, but Marlow held strong, and the door wouldn't budge.

"We know you're lying," Marlow warned her.

"How could you possibly know that?" Eisheth demanded.

"I'm a sorceress," Oona piped up confidently. "I know all kinds of things."

Eisheth gave up and sighed. "Fine." She turned and walked back into the loft, her hips swaying subtly under her dress. "You can come in if you want, but Bram's not here. And when he gets here, if he doesn't like you, he'll kill you."

The loft was sparsely furnished, with thick black drapes covering the large windows and blocking out any light—and keeping out any prying eyes. The décor felt very bohemian, with lots of draping, beads, and mandalas. There were no traditional tables or chairs—only cushions and pillows on the floor.

Candles had been set out all over the space. Kitchen counters, the mantel, the floor, nearly ever surface had a candle on it, burning dimly. Melted wax was dripped onto everything.

"I'd offer you something to drink, but I don't want you here, so . . ." Eisheth laughed lightly at her own joke, then fell back onto the "bed," a collection of overstuffed pillows and blankets.

I walked to the center of the room, close to where Eisheth lounged. Oona followed me more slowly, careful not to step on any open flames or freshly melted wax. Marlow began circling the edge of the room, taking slow, deliberate steps.

"We don't mean to intrude, and we don't plan to be here long," I said.

"Mmm-hmm," Eisheth murmured, lounging back on her pillows.

"When do you expect Bram back?" Marlow asked, stopping to admire a large art piece made out of macramé.

"Soon," Eisheth replied indifferently.

"How long have you known Bram?" Marlow tried again.

"I'm not telling you anything about him," she said. "If he wants you to know, he'll tell you himself."

"That sounds fair," Oona said.

Eisheth turned her narrowed eyes on Oona. "Are you really a sorceress?"

Oona nodded. "Yeah."

"Show me something," Eisheth commanded.

Oona smiled nervously. "I'm not a magician. I don't just perform feats for simple entertainment."

Eisheth leaned forward, resting on her arms, and looked up at Oona. "If you show one of your tricks, I'll tell you something about

Bram." Oona glanced back at me, so Eisheth added, "If it's something really good, I'll tell you *three* things."

Oona chewed her lip, thinking. "Okay. I got it." She dug into the pockets of her jacket and pulled out a small satin bag. "My cousin Minerva just gave this to me today, so I'm not entirely sure it will work."

"Show me what you got, Magic Man," Eisheth teased.

Oona dumped the bag into her hand, filling her palm with tiny amethyst crystals, looking like purple grains of salt. She closed her eyes and began slowly rubbing her hands together. Her lips were moving, but I couldn't hear any words.

Finally she opened her eyes and held her hands far apart, up in the air, and all the purple crystals were gone.

"*As ypárchei skotádi*," Oona whispered, and the candles went out—every single one, plunging the loft into near-total darkness.

"*Kai egéneto fos*," she breathed, and all the candles lit up again. Only this time, for a few seconds, they burned bright purple before changing back to their normal amber flame.

Eisheth threw her head back, cackling with glee. "That was great!"

"I held up my end of the deal," Oona said proudly. "Now tell us three things about Bram."

"Okay." Eisheth sat up a bit. "I've known Bram for two years. He hates surprises, and . . ." Her smile widened, growing more seductive. "He's going to kill you when he gets home."

That caused her to burst out laughing again, and Oona looked nervously at me. I was about to tell her that everything would be okay when the door to the apartment opened. Eisheth barely managed to stifle her giggles as a man strode into the room.

His eyes were hard, but his smile was bemused. His dark hair had begun graying at the temples, and though he looked much like a mortal man, he was much taller and more broad-shouldered.

When he caught sight of Marlow standing in front of his fire-place, he let out a warm chuckle.

"You're not Bram Madichonnen," Marlow said, and I could hear the struggle in her voice to keep its tenor even. "You're Tamerlane Fayette."

He grinned more broadly. "You're in luck. I'm both."

THIRTY-ONE

◆

Marlow took slow, deliberate steps away from the fireplace, putting herself between where Oona and I stood and where Tamerlane had entered the room. I did the same, moving so I partially shielded Oona.

As soon as Marlow said his name, I recognized him from the pictures I'd seen, but he did look different. In photos, his skin was tawny and warm, but now it had a dull blue tone to it, making it appear ashy and gray.

And somehow, he seemed bigger. Larger and more imposing.

"You don't look happy to see me," Tamerlane commented. "Or are you just unhappy that I'm still alive?"

"Why would I be unhappy?" Marlow smiled, and very slowly the two of them began circling each other. He would step closer, and she'd step away—keeping the distance between them the same. "I'm the one that let you live."

"Oh, I haven't forgotten." He scratched his head, seeming very nonchalant, and I noticed the ends of his fingertips were scarred—

he'd burned his fingerprints off to help mask his identity. "I've been meaning to thank you for that. But I hadn't been able to find your address. You Valkyries are always so secretive about where you live."

I tensed, even more so than I already was, and Oona gasped softly behind me. While we'd been hunting down the draugrs, it hadn't occurred to me that they'd be hunting *us*.

"You've been looking for me?" Marlow asked calmly.

"How else could I send you a gift of gratitude? Maybe a bouquet of flowers?" Tamerlane mused. "You seem like the kind of woman that would appreciate a few dozen red roses."

"That's very kind but unnecessary," she demurred, opting for flirtatious, even though I knew that she was furious.

"I only recently came back to the city." Tamerlane paused to give her a puzzled look. "How did you know I was here?"

"I didn't," she replied. "It was just serendipity. Why did you come back?"

He smiled slyly. "I thought you might have some regrets about me."

"Now, why would I?" Marlow asked.

"Someone's been looking for me," Tamerlane told her. "I've heard rumors of my name, of people searching for me, and you're about the only ones left alive that knew I hadn't died."

My breath caught in my throat. Asher—in his search to avenge his mother—had brought attention back to us. If he hadn't found me when he did, there was a very good chance Tamerlane would've gotten to us first.

"What about your family?" Marlow asked. "I let you live so you could care for them."

Tamerlane's expression fell, but only for a moment, and he was quick to erase it. "Those are things of the past. I no longer have ties to anything on this earth. My work has become much greater than that."

"And what is your work?" she asked.

"I don't think you'd approve." He grinned. "Or even understand."

Eisheth laughed at that, a hysterical cackle rising deep from within her, as she lay on the bed watching this all unfold with rapt attention.

"Try me," Marlow replied.

"I would really love to catch up with you. Honestly, I would love to hear how you've spent the last four years of your life, while I've been toiling away as a draugr." Tamerlane held his hands up, shrugging helplessly. "But I haven't got the time."

Marlow had moved so she was standing between Tamerlane and the door, blocking his escape, and she was facing me.

"You know I can't let you leave alive," she warned him. "Not again."

"If you really wanted me dead, you had to kill me back then," Tamerlane contradicted her. "Now it's too late."

"We'll see about that."

Sheathed on her hip, my mother's sword began to glow red. It was much duller and muddier than normal, but Marlow reached for it. She pulled it out just as he moved toward her, but it was already too late.

It only took a matter of seconds—Mördare was pointed at Tamerlane, and then he was on Marlow, grabbing her wrist and breaking it with an audible snap. He turned my mother's own sword on her and drove it through her stomach. From where I was standing, I saw her eyes widen with pain and shock, and her mouth hung open.

"No!" I cried out.

Oona wrapped her arms tightly around my waist, trying to hold me back. I began dragging her across the floor as I ran toward Marlow. I screamed as her body started to slip backward, going limp, and I reached for my own sword.

"*Tin prostasía mas me to fos sas!*" Oona shouted as she held on to me with all her might.

Suddenly the candle flames turned dark purple and exploded around us, throwing me and Oona back against the wall. Eisheth screamed as hot purple smoke filled the room, burning my eyes and lungs. The windows exploded outward, and Oona bent over me, trying to shield me from the flames and glass.

"Eisheth, we leave now!" Tamerlane shouted.

I lifted my head just as the fires went out, and tiny bits of glass were still falling to the floor, like the room was raining glitter. Eisheth grabbed on to Tamerlane, and she ran toward the window, her large wings already flapping, and leapt out into the night.

I scrambled away from Oona, crawling through the smoke and melted wax to where Marlow lay on the floor. Her blood had already begun pooling around her, and Mördare left her stomach glowing red.

"Marlow," I said, brushing back the hair from her face.

A line of blood trailed down from her lips as she stared up at me. Her mouth was moving, but no words came. Her body twitched slightly, like she was having subtle convulsions.

"Marlow, it'll be okay. Just hang on," I told her.

Her back arched, and she stopped trembling. Her eyes changed from dark gray to pure white—no pupil, no color. An inhuman voice came from her mouth, sounding twisted and angry, saying, "Remember that we all must die."

Then she gasped once, and her body collapsed back on the floor. She went limp, and her head lolled to the side.

"Marlow!" I wailed, shaking her as if that would help somehow. Oona had crawled over to my side, and she put her hand on my arm.

So I turned to her, screaming, "Help her! Oona, you have to help her!"

"I can't!" Oona said with tears in her eyes. "I'm sorry, Mal. But I can't. I can't bring her back from the dead."

"Why didn't you use that spell sooner?" I demanded. "Why didn't you save her?"

"I couldn't." She shook her head, tears streaming down her cheeks. "It all happened too fast, and I didn't realize until it was too late. I'm sorry."

Then a strange weakness came over me, and I collapsed into her arms, sobbing. Oona stroked my hair, repeating, "I'm so sorry," over and over.

THIRTY-TWO

———◆———

Who do we call?" Oona asked, her voice soft and comforting as she gently rubbed my back. My mother's body lay a few feet away from us, and her blood was staining the knees of my jeans. "Mal? Who do we call?"

"What are you talking about?" I asked.

"I don't know what to do," Oona said simply. "Do I call the police? Or . . . we can't just stay here with Marlow like this. Tamerlane might come back."

I sat up slowly, and I felt like I was waking from a horrible dream. I hadn't been sleeping, but it still felt like none of this could be real. My eyes were raw from crying, and I rubbed at them as I looked around at the disaster that had become of Eisheth's loft.

"Who do we call?" I repeated.

"Do you have a number? I can call, if you need me to," Oona offered.

I stood up, thinking that somehow that would make me feel better, and I stumbled over toward the windows. The wind was blowing in, making the curtains billow into the room and letting the amber glow of the city stream in, along with the icy night air.

"Mal?" Oona called after me, sounding worried.

"Samael," I said thickly.

I dug my cell phone out of my pocket and pulled up his number. Then I stood waiting, rubbing my temple and hoping he answered, because I didn't know what to do if he didn't. This was too much of a mess, and I didn't trust anybody else.

"This is Samael," he answered.

"Samael, it's Malin." I sniffled and closed my eyes. "I need you to come down here, and I think we need . . . we need a cleanup crew."

"What are you talking about?" Samael asked. "What's going on?"

"Everything went to shit," I said. "And Marlow—" My voice cracked on her name.

"What about Marlow?" Samael asked, and I could already hear the panic edging into his voice.

I let out a shaky breath and finally forced myself to say, "She's dead."

There was a long silence on the line, so long I was afraid the call had been disconnected, but I didn't have the strength to say anything. So I just waited, and finally Samael asked, "Where are you?"

I gave him the address, and he promised to be here as soon as he could. I don't know how long it took him to get here. Maybe five minutes. Maybe an hour. All I knew was that by the time he arrived, the loft had gotten very cold, and Oona was worried that I might get sick. She wanted me to step back from the window, but I wouldn't. I couldn't, and I didn't know how to explain it to her.

And then Samael came, and I don't think I'll ever forget his expression when he saw Marlow. His face went white, his eyes widened, and I don't think he breathed or moved for a long time. The cleanup crew—a group of lower-level angels who took care of this kind of thing—stayed outside the door, and when they asked to come in, Samael barked at them to stay put until he called for them.

As he stared down at my mother, fighting back tears, I think that was the first time I really knew that he was in love with her. I'd known for a while that they had some kind of flirtation, but I could see now, as he realized she was gone . . . he was devastated.

When he asked me what had happened, I thought about lying to him. For a moment I really considered hiding the truth to protect my mother. Nobody else needed to know what she'd done, that she'd failed at her job and it had gotten her killed.

But Tamerlane Fayette was still out there, and he wanted to kill everyone who knew he was alive, which now included me, Oona, Asher, and Asher's grandmother. Not to mention any other innocent people who got in his way.

So I told Samael the truth. I told him, and I watched his expression change from shock to horror to disappointment to horror again. I didn't leave out anything, even the parts I wanted to, and he listened patiently.

"We need to keep this quiet," he said once I'd finished, and the air had gotten so cold, I could see his breath when he spoke. "I can do that, and I will. No one outside of this room can know the truth. Not yet. Do you understand?"

I nodded. "Yeah, I do."

"Do you have someone you can go home with?" he asked. "I don't think you should be alone."

I motioned to Oona, who'd been standing beside me the whole time, but Samael looked at her like he'd forgotten she was there. This was all a lot to take in for him, I supposed.

He nodded, then, brusquely, he reached out and hugged me, pulling me close to him. I closed my eyes for a moment. He smelled of autumn leaves and campfires, and his arms were so warm and strong. I realized that I couldn't remember the last time my mother had hugged me, or what she smelled like, other than cigarillos.

"I'll take care of her," he promised me, then he let me go. "You go home and take care of yourself. We'll talk soon, okay?"

I nodded because I didn't think I could talk without crying, not anymore, and I let Oona take me out of the apartment. I don't remember leaving or walking or any of the way home, but I know that eventually we made it home. The first thing I said was that I didn't know if I was an orphan or not, because my mother had never bothered to tell me much about my father. That never seemed like a big deal before, and I was always fine that it was just the two of us, except now it wasn't just the two of us.

It was just me, and it would only be me from here on out.

"That's not true," Oona insisted as I stared out the window at the vast city below us. "You have me. You'll always have me."

"Nobody really has anybody," I told her. "We all must die, and we all die alone."

THIRTY-THREE

———◆———

I lay on the sofa in my living room, staring blankly ahead. Bowie kept nuzzling my hand, trying to get me to pet him, but I couldn't muster the energy.

"You need to eat something," Oona told me, standing before me with a bowl of harira soup. The scent of savory tomatoes, ginger, and lentils was usually enough to whet my appetite, but right now it only made me more nauseated.

"No, I don't," I said.

"Mal." She sighed and set the soup on the kitchen counter. "You've been lying on that couch since we got home yesterday. You can't just stay there forever."

I rolled over, burying my face in a throw pillow, and muttered, "Watch me."

After a long silence, Oona gently said, "I can't even begin to pretend to understand how you feel."

"Then don't try," I snapped.

"Fine. I'll leave you be. But when you want to talk, I'm here."

I heard her footsteps retreating to the other side of the apartment, toward her bedroom, but a knock at the front door halted her progress. I didn't bother to roll over and instead just lay buried in the couch, listening as she answered it.

"Asher," Oona said in surprise.

"I heard about Marlow, and I wanted to see how Malin was doing," he said.

"That's how she's doing. You can try talking to her, but I don't know if she'll talk back," Oona offered bleakly.

I rolled over to see Asher standing in the doorway. His normally handsome face had aged under the burden of remorse. Dark circles under his grave eyes, deep creases of worry on his forehead, and lips pressed into a grim frown.

"How'd you hear about Marlow?" I asked.

He took that as an invitation and stepped into the apartment. Oona closed the door behind him before quietly retreating to her room, giving Asher and me some space to talk alone. There was an awkwardness about him, a tension that hadn't been there before, and it wasn't from Marlow's death.

I could almost feel him wanting to reach out and comfort me, but he managed to suppress the urge, instead restlessly rubbing at his thumb as he stood in front of me.

"I have some friends who are on the Vörðr force," Asher explained. "They said they're keeping it under wraps how she died, but it's still big news on the inside that a Valkyrie was killed."

I sat up on the couch and, without the potency it deserved, I mumbled, "Tamerlane killed her."

For a moment Asher said nothing. Slowly, almost weakly, he sat down on the couch beside me and gaped at the floor. "You found him?"

"Yeah, but only long enough for him to kill Marlow and then escape again."

He grimaced. "I'm sorry I dragged you into this."

"You didn't drag me into anything. This was all Marlow's fault, remember?" I said. "And besides that, Tamerlane admitted he was in search of Marlow, so it was only a matter of time until he found her. Her death was inevitable."

My mind went back to the conversation I'd had with Sloane Kothari, where she admitted that she didn't believe in free will, and that meant the whole world moved in predestination, with someone—or something—controlling everything.

I wondered again if that was true, and if there was anything I could've done to prevent Marlow's death, or if this was the way it was always supposed to be.

Maybe she'd broken free from her track, and her punishment had been death. Because if the whole world exists rotating in a perfect order, there is no room for someone going rogue. Eventually she was bound to be ground up and destroyed inside the machine.

"I'm still sorry it happened," Asher said, pulling me from my thoughts.

I shrugged emptily. "Yeah, well, you know how it goes."

"When my mom died, it was the worst day of my life. I didn't know how I would ever get through it," he said.

I rubbed my eyes and snapped, "But you did, and I know that I will, too." I was in no mood for a pep talk or an inspirational speech about the strength within or how I'd always carry memories of Marlow with me.

"I never doubted that you would," he responded. "You're strong and resourceful."

"Thanks."

"But it does make it easier if you let people help. My grandma—"

"You had a family to help you," I cut him off. "I don't."

"Family doesn't have to just be blood," Asher contended. "You have your friend Oona. You have me. I'm sure you have others you can count on."

"Marlow told me that Valkyries didn't do well with long-lasting relationships," I replied, and even as I was arguing against him, I knew there was truth in Asher's words. Oona had been my best friend for years, and I'd always be able to count on her.

But at the moment I didn't feel like agreeing with him. I wanted to be isolated in my pain. That's what Marlow would do.

"I don't know about all Valkyries, but that is true for some," he admitted.

I laughed hollowly. "Good to know Marlow wasn't wrong about that."

"But you can make your life what you wish. My mom did."

Asher looked at me—really looked at me, for the first time since he'd come over today. Before, his eyes had been focusing just off to the side, as if looking at me directly would spur an awkward conversation about our kiss the other night and how that played into our relationship, which was now further complicated by my mother's murder.

He was now stuck in the terrible position of comforting me over the death of someone who had caused the death of his own mother. But when he looked at me, there was no anger, no sense of justice or retribution. Only compassion and hurt and warmth.

His normally stormy eyes were like a calm sea, inviting me to join him in peace, where the two of us could cling to each other for comfort. So, when he reached over, taking my hand in his, I let him. It made me feel . . . safer and less alone.

"Well, your mom sounds more progressive than mine," I said.

"Marlow seemed like a very complicated, strong-willed, independent woman." He spoke slowly, as if choosing his words carefully.

"She was. She was all those things and so much more," I agreed.

Then, rather abruptly, I said something that had been digging at me since she died, since before then, really, but since her death it had been a sharp dagger twisting inside my chest: "I don't think she loved me."

The realization of that coupled with Asher here, attempting to comfort me and care for me, only compounded the brutal truth that I didn't think anyone had ever really loved me. Maybe Oona had. Probably, actually. But sometimes I needed more than one solitary friend in the whole entire world who really and truly loved me.

"I . . ." Asher took a deep breath. "I honestly didn't know her. I want to tell you that she did love you, in her own way, and I think that's probably true, but I don't know."

"It's okay," I lied as tears welled in my eyes. "I think I always knew that she didn't love me. And I was okay with it, because I thought, *That's normal. Valkyries can't love. This is just what we are.* But deep down, I always knew that was a lie. Because I loved her."

Asher put his arm around me, pulling me close to him and letting me cry into his shoulder. He held me fiercely in a way that I couldn't remember anybody else ever holding me, and he kissed my hair.

"I know nothing I can say will take your pain away," he whispered. "But I promise you that I will do everything in my power to avenge Marlow and my mother. Tamerlane Fayette won't escape death again."

THIRTY-FOUR

———◆———

In the Rosehill Cemetery, bodies were piled on top of each other. The population explosion of the last few centuries had created the need for alternative burials, with cremation and shared graves becoming the top affordable options.

Fortunately for me, that was one thing I didn't have to worry about, thanks to my mother's status as a Valkyrie. All Valkyries—whether they died in the line of duty, by accident, or simply from old age—were buried in the Mausoleum av Veteraner Från Kriget Mot Ödödlighet.

The crypt sat on a large hill in the center of the cemetery, surrounded by rosebushes, which had already begun to wither and die with winter around the corner. It was a large square building made of white marble, with the only decoration being the coat of arms above the door—a shield emblazoned with the three horns of Odin and nine swords fanned out behind it.

Inside the mausoleum were hundreds of white marble drawers, all labeled with simple gold letters stating each name, year of birth, and year of death. Nothing more, nothing less. Near the end of the hall, in a spot four rows from the bottom, was my mother.

MARLOW GRACE KRIGARE

Her letters were brighter and shinier than the others', since they were newer. Fresh flowers stood on a pedestal near her tomb, and an Eralim in a black uniform stood to the side, presiding over the funeral.

It was a sparely attended funeral, the way many Valkryies' funerals were, but Marlow had even fewer connections in life than most, I suspected. There might have been more mourners, but Samael was doing everything in his power to keep the news of her death from spreading.

Valkyrie deaths could be rather public spectacles if allowed to be, but in Marlow's case that would only lead to questions and suspicions and unwanted attention for myself and Asher. So Samael kept it quiet, and only eight people had shown up, including Samael and his two guards, Atlas and Godfrey.

Oona had come with her mother, Rhona, and they stood on one side of me, while Asher and his grandmother Teodora stood on the other. Both Oona and Asher seemed ready to reach out and steady me, should I need it, but I held strong throughout the service, and never shed a tear.

The Eralim presiding spoke of living a life of honor and virtue and dedication, and I wondered if any of those words even applied to Marlow. He finished up by talking about how Marlow was at peace now, and I hoped at least that part was true.

"I'm so sorry about your mother," Rhona said after the service had ended, and she squeezed my hand tightly. "I can't imagine how difficult this must be for you."

Atlas and Godfrey offered similar sentiments, giving me their sympathies for my loss, and I realized that nobody really had said anything about Marlow. I appreciated that. I didn't need them lying to me about how kind or generous she was. She didn't need her memory to be exalted higher than how she lived her life.

Teodora smiled thinly at me, pulling her black cloak around her. "I know your mother and I had our differences, to put it lightly, but I would never wish this upon you. Losing a loved one is never easy."

"Thank you for coming," I mumbled, because I didn't know what else to say.

Asher looked like he wanted to say something, but Samael stepped up, edging his way in.

"Mind if I speak to Malin alone for a moment?" he asked.

Asher looked to me, his gaze protective and warm, and I nodded to let him know it was okay to leave my side. "Sure, of course," he said, squeezing my hand gently before turning to take a few steps away. The other guests had gone outside, leaving the three of us alone in the mausoleum, and Asher lingered nearby with just enough distance between us that he wouldn't be eavesdropping.

Samael's eyes were red-rimmed and his umber skin was unusually pale, and though I don't think he could ever really look bad per se, this was the worst I'd ever seen him. Even his lush curls seemed lifeless today. He fidgeted with his handkerchief and stared down at the floor, which was covered in petals from the dying flowers left on the doors of other tombs.

"What do you want to do?" Samael asked finally.

"What do you mean?" I asked.

He lifted his aquamarine eyes to meet mine. "About Tamerlane."

"I plan to kill him," I replied honestly.

"You don't have to," Samael said, then he hurried to correct himself. "I mean, I can take care of him. I *will*, if that's what you want."

"I appreciate that, but I think I would rather handle it myself," I said.

Samael nodded. "I thought that's how you would feel. But I wanted to let you know that I'm here to help you as much or as little as you need. I want to end this bastard just as much as you do."

"I do need help finding him," I admitted.

I'd spent the twenty-four hours after Marlow died numb and unable to think of anything, really, and then Asher came over and woke up the pain inside me, and it all came tumbling out. Since then, I'd only really been thinking of one thing—how to find Tamerlane and kill him.

The only speed bump in that plan was that I had no idea where to look. Marlow was the one who had connections—she'd introduced us to Cecily Stavros, who was able to point us in the direction of Tamerlane.

But without Marlow, I didn't know where to start.

"I'm already on it," Samael assured me. "I have feelers going out as far and wide as I can, and as inconspicuously as possible, of course. And just so you know, I'm also having a few off-duty Vörðr keep an eye on you and Oona, in case Tamerlane comes looking for you."

"I don't really think that's necessary," I objected.

"I'm not doing it for you," Samael said with a pained smile. "It's what Marlow would've asked me to do. She wanted you safe."

I lowered my eyes, since I couldn't argue with the wishes of a dead woman. "I'll just keep a lookout for them, then."

The clacking of heels echoing through the mausoleum caused me to look up, and I saw Quinn Devane walking slowly toward us. She wore all black, and managed to somehow look beautiful, even on a day when I didn't think I'd be capable of finding beauty in anything.

"I'm not interrupting, am I?" Quinn asked, chewing her lip.

"No." Samael shook his head, then touched my arm gently. "I'll let you know when I found out anything, Malin. Take care."

"Thank you," I said, and I watched him walk away, disappearing outside into the overcast afternoon. Only then did I finally force myself to look back at Quinn.

With her silver hair cascading around her shoulders, she had an extra ethereal quality to her to beauty, and I realized that I couldn't remember the last time I'd seen her in the daylight. So much of our relationship had been done clandestine, with stolen kisses in dark bedrooms, both of us with busy schedules and me afraid of what the higher-ups at Ravenswood would think.

Seeing her here like this reminded me of seeing a teacher outside of class or an actor out of costume. It was disarming, and suddenly I felt uneasy. I looked over at Asher, who still lingered down the hall, reading the plaques on the wall, and just knowing he was nearby gave me the strength to face Quinn.

"What are you doing here?" I asked finally.

Her eyes were filled with sympathy as she softly said, "I heard about Marlow, and I wanted to make sure that you're okay."

"I'm fine."

Her shoulders sagged, and her lips twitched slightly. "Malin, I know you're hurting. Why do you have to shut me out like this?"

I ran my fingers through my hair and tried to think of all the things I wanted to say to her, all the emotions I couldn't form the words for. The contradictions of missing her and being afraid of her. Wishing she hadn't come here and also grateful that she still cared.

Feeling edgy, I glanced from Quinn to Asher, and I realized the key difference between the two of them—Quinn left me breathless and invigorated and pushed me too far so that I never felt safe, and Asher left me breathless and exhilarated and made me feel . . . certain in a way that she never had.

Quinn was always a question, and Asher was the answer.

But right now I couldn't deal with it, so I just looked up at her and asked, "Do you really think now is the best time to do this, Quinn?"

"No, of course not. I'm sorry." She lowered her eyes and shook her head, her fair cheeks reddening subtly with shame. "I only wanted to . . . I wanted to let you know that I'm here for you, if you need me. For anything at all."

"Thank you, but . . ." I began, but then I realized we weren't alone. A man was wandering through the vast halls of the mausoleum, carrying a large bouquet of flowers. It was so big, it looked like he might nearly topple over.

"Sorry," he said as he approached us. "I have a delivery for the Krigare funeral?"

"It's over now," I told him. "But I'll take them."

He apologized profusely as he handed them to me. "Sorry about that. The order just came in, and we rushed as quickly as we could."

He left me, struggling with a heavy vase full of two dozen red roses, the exact same shade as the lipstick Marlow always wore. Hardly anyone had come to Marlow's funeral, and as far as I knew, she didn't have that many friends in the world, so I couldn't imagine who would send them.

"Who are they from?" I asked Quinn, since I was too busy trying to hold them to look at the card.

Quinn moved around the roses and found a small card, matte-black with a message inscribed in gold ink. "It only says, *With all my love, Tamerlane.*"

THIRTY-FIVE

◆

Dead mother or no, Oona had decided that I'd put off going to the doctor long enough, and I was inclined to agree with her. I'd woken up the day after Marlow's funeral with a nasty infection brewing in my leg and all sorts of unpleasant sights and smells going on underneath my bandage.

But after the taunting bouquet of flowers Tamerlane Fayette had sent to the funeral, I didn't feel I could put off plotting to find him, either. Oona and I came to the agreement that while I was at the doctor's, she would gather information and call people, so that when I was done we could have a discussion and figure out what to do about Tamerlane.

A few hours later, I came back from the hospital with a freshly irrigated wound and a bottle of very strong antibiotics to find Asher and Quinn sitting on my couch. That was exactly what I wanted to deal with today. My ex-lover and my maybe-sorta-current-lover together. Discussing things about me. Without me.

Oona had set out a vegetable tray on the coffee table, which

Bowie was sneaking a carrot from. I must've looked as shocked as I felt, because Oona offered me a sheepish smile.

"How'd it go?" Oona asked.

"Great," I said, feigning a smile.

"Why don't you have a seat?" Quinn suggested, patting the spot between her and Asher. He actually scooted to the side a bit, to make room between the two of them, and the thought of that made me feel more claustrophobic than I ever had before.

"Nah, I think I'll be good over here." I went into the kitchenette area of our apartment and dragged an old kitchen chair into the living room, so I could sit across from Quinn and Asher.

"So, I was doing research about Tamerlane and how to handle draugrs, like we talked about," Oona explained as she sat cross-legged on the floor beside me. "And I realized that this is such a vast undertaking, it might be helpful to have more people, so I called over Asher and Quinn."

I scratched the back of my head, doing my best not to look as annoyed as I felt. "Uh-huh. That makes sense."

"And Oona filled me in about everything that's been going on," Quinn said, but she didn't need to. I could already tell by the worry in her eyes and the grim downturn of her mouth. "I really wish you would've come to me sooner. I could've helped."

"I didn't want it getting out," I said. "I was afraid about what would happen to Marlow, but . . . now that doesn't really matter."

"Tamerlane is the one who sent the flowers yesterday?" Quinn asked.

After I'd gotten the roses, I'd thrown them on the floor of the mausoleum. The vase shattered, and I stomped all over the flowers while Quinn kept asking me what was wrong. I was too irate to see straight, so I'd stormed off without explaining anything to her.

Oona groaned in disgust. "I can't believe he did that. That's so messed up."

Angry bile rose in my throat, and I was barely able to swallow it down before muttering, "He did say he ought to thank her by sending her flowers."

"So does anybody know how to kill Tamerlane?" Asher asked, smartly changing the subject before I lost my shit again.

"Back when I was going to Ravenswood, I took an elective on Mythology and Urban Legends," Quinn said. "We briefly discussed zombies and the undead then, but it wasn't anything too in-depth. The only thing I really remember is them saying that the Valkyrie sword would no longer work on them."

"That seems to be as much as I've been able to find, as well," Oona agreed. "Only information on what does *not* kill them, which isn't helpful at all."

Asher leaned forward, resting his arms on his knees. "When we were talking with the gorgon the other day, it got me thinking about things in a way I hadn't before, so I started going through my grandmother's books. She has hundreds of these really old books from our homeland, and in a book filled with fables and stories I found a chapter on draugrs—"

Quinn interjected, "You guys keep mentioning draugrs, but I haven't heard anyone use that word before today. What does it mean, exactly?"

"I just looked it up, actually, and learned it's an old Norse word meaning 'again-walker,'" Asher explained. "They were thought to be like zombies."

"But zombies don't exist," Quinn argued. "'That which is dead cannot rise.' That's Supernatural 101."

She was right. That was one of the first things we were taught about the world we lived in. To maintain order in a world where immortals lived alongside humans, we were all only given one life—with humans lying in their tombs, while the immortals were shuttled down to the underworld.

But both were given the same commandment: The dead must stay dead. That which is dead cannot rise.

"They're not exactly zombies," Asher continued. "Just immortals that found a way around the Valkyrie loophole."

"But those are just old Scandinavian stories," Quinn reminded us.

"Well, me and Oona saw Tamerlane," I pointed out. "He's alive, when he should be dead, and he killed *two* Valkyries, which shouldn't even be possible. We're now in an uncharted world where the impossible has become possible."

Oona frowned as she considered this. Bowie had given up on stealing carrots and hopped over to sit on her lap, where she absently began to stroke his feathered wings.

"Did the book say anything about how to stop them?" Quinn asked, resting her emerald gaze on Asher.

"Not really. But it did have this passage—I wrote it down so I would remember it exactly." He pulled out his phone and scrolled through it. "It says, *From whence the draugr rose, only that will make the draugr fall. If his master waits in Helheim, it is his sword that makes the call.*"

We all sat silently for a minute, thinking about what Asher had read and trying to decipher whatever coded message might be hidden in it. Quinn played with her long hair, something she did when she was agitated, and she grew rougher with it the more she thought.

Finally, she broke the silence and asked, "What does that mean?"

"Helheim was the Norse afterworld, which I get," Asher supplied. "But if we assume that Tamerlane Fayette is a draugr, who is his master?"

I shrugged. "Supposedly he's hanging out with two other draugrs, but I don't know if any one of them is really a 'master,' or who they would answer to."

"Who is the big head honcho around here?" Oona asked, her eyes darting between the three of us.

"Velnias has a lot of sway in the demonic community, and he's the head of the Kurnugia Society," I said. "But I doubt he'd talk to us, after the way everyone at the Red Raven shut us out when Asher and I went there."

"And if Velnias is Tamerlane's master, I seriously doubt he'd help us fell Tamerlane, anyway," Asher added.

I rubbed a hand over my face and slouched back in my chair. "Figuring out how to kill Tamerlane is almost a moot point, since I don't know if we'll ever find him again. I'm sure after all this he's going to burrow even deeper underground."

"Maybe not," Oona argued. "Sending flowers to Marlow's funeral was pretty bold. Not to mention the stuff that happened with Amaryllis Mori."

Asher turned to me, his gaze a mixture of curiosity and concern. "Who's that?"

"She was a Jorogumo that I killed for work, but she almost bested me, and her venom was more powerful than it should've been," I explained. "And she told me that the tables were turning, and the underworld was growing stronger."

"Tamerlane might not feel the need to hide," Quinn pointed out hopefully. That was just like her—trying to look for the bright side in a completely impossible situation.

"Well, he has been staying in the city using the alias of Bram Madichonnen," I countered.

Oona sat up straighter, gently knocking Bowie off her lap, so he hopped angrily to the other side of the room. "So, I've been thinking about that, and I looked into it more, because I was curious as to *why* he chose the name that he did."

I shrugged. "What does it matter?"

"Marlow spared him because she thought he was good and pure, and now he's a megalomaniac who killed the person that saved him," Oona said. "Something changed."

"Yeah, he became a draugr," Asher replied.

Oona shot him a look but continued. "Yes, but the name he chose loosely translates to 'cursed father.'"

"Why would he pick that?" Quinn asked.

"Before being a draugr, by all accounts, he was a happy father who helped run an orphanage," Oona said. "Now his family is dead, brutally murdered, and his orphanage is closed. Everything that mattered in his life is gone."

"When he became a draugr, he had to give that all up," I said. But that was something we already knew.

"And based on his name, I'm thinking that might not have been his choice," Oona reasoned.

I thought back to the confrontation I'd witnessed between Marlow and Tamerlane. He'd been cool and casual right up until the moment Marlow mentioned his family. That was the only time his mask of nonchalance slipped—only for a moment—and then right after that everything had fallen apart.

"He did seem really touchy when Marlow mentioned his family," I remembered.

"So, he begged Marlow to spare him so he could take care of his family and be with them because he loved them and all that," Oona went on, sounding more excited as her idea came together. "Then he became a draugr, and . . . then what? Did he kill his family? Did he have a change of heart? Or did someone else make him do it? Or did someone else do it to send him a message?"

"Maybe all of the above?" I said. "If what Amaryllis Mori was saying is true, there is something brewing in the underworld."

"But you can't return from Kurnugia," Quinn maintained. "That's one of the rules. When humans and mortals die, we're just dead. When immortals die, they get to go to Kurnugia, but they can't return."

"Well, we all know they've never been too thrilled about the Valkyrie and Kurnugia arrangement," Asher pointed out dismally.

"If they're working together to form some kind of underworld uprising—which is scary as hell—then they must have some kind of leader," I said. "And now all we have to do is figure out who that is to either kill them or get them to kill Tamerlane, and then we'll be all set."

"And we should probably also work on quelling that uprising in Kurnugia," Oona added.

Quinn smiled, trying to remain optimistic, but the twitch at the corner of her crooked lips gave away her unease. "Well, if anyone can handle all that, it ought to be the four of us, right?"

THIRTY-SIX

---◆---

After hours of going over who might be Tamerlane's master—throwing out names from Velnias to Odin, and even delving deeper into the underworld with figures like Ereshkigal, Hai-uri, and Erlik—we were no closer to figuring out who it might be, even assuming there was a master. There was even a chance that Tamerlane was his own master, but I wasn't exactly sure how that would work.

As the conversation went late into the night, Oona grew tired and eventually fell asleep. She lay on the floor with a throw pillow under her head and Bowie curled up beside her. When she started snoring softly, I woke her up and helped her get to bed.

After Oona mumbled a sleepy good night, Asher excused himself to use the restroom, and Quinn stood up and stretched. Her shirt rose up, revealing her taut stomach, and I noticed a collection of black stars tattooed just above her hip.

"New ink?" I asked, motioning to her hip. It had been only six months since we'd last been together, and I vividly remembered tracing my hands over every inch of her. I could still remember every freckle and scar that marked her skin, so I definitely would've recalled a tattoo.

"Yeah." She smiled demurely and ran her fingers seductively over her hip. "It's the constellation for Capricorn."

"Capricorn?" I asked in surprise. "But you were born in August. Aren't you a Virgo?"

Her smile deepened, looking pleased that I still remembered her birthday.

"I did, but I was officially sworn in as Valkyrie on a cold day in January two years ago," Quinn explained. "I just finally got around to getting a tattoo to commemorate that."

My mind flashed to a time when we'd been lying in my bed together, our arms intertwined, with the early morning light spilling in through my bedroom window. Her head had been resting on my chest, and I curled up close to her. Her hair had been dyed lavender then, and I remembered breathing her in and thinking it fitting that she smelled like lilacs and summer.

We'd been sharing war stories from our childhood. While I had plenty of anecdotes about Marlow, Quinn had very little to say about her own mother, and instead focused most of her stories on school bullies and ex-girlfriends. She had pulled herself closer to me, her arm wrapped around my waist and her cheek pressed against my bare skin.

"But that's all behind us now," she'd told me in her husky voice, as rich and sweet as honey. "We've come out of it and we're on the other side, stronger and braver for it."

"You really think that?" I had asked her, and she tilted her head to stare up at me with her wide green eyes.

"I do. Sometimes I think of my existence as two lives," she had explained. "There was the time before, when I had no control and I was dragged around the world, feeling unloved and un-wanted.

"And then there's the life when I became a Valkyrie," Quinn had gone on. "The day my life became my own. Sure, I have orders to obey and responsibilities, but my fate is in my own hands. Some-times I feel like my real life didn't begin until then."

"Well, I'm glad that I'm a part of your real life," I'd teased her.

"Of course you are." She moved, propping herself up so she hov-ered above me, smiling down at me. "You're the main reason that I know this is my real life, that everything before this was just prac-tice for what was to come. Because you're here, and the way I feel about you is the truest thing I've ever known."

She'd leaned down and kissed me then, and while her kisses felt wonderful and left me dizzy, this one had been different. This one had filled me with an urgent panic that I couldn't explain, and I couldn't breathe.

I was overwhelmed by her—she'd always overwhelmed me, but before, it had felt exciting. But in that moment, it just felt terrifying and heavy and too much.

Though Quinn had begged me to stay in bed with her, I had made some excuse about why I had to go. Two weeks later, I had broken up with her.

Now, standing in my living room, Quinn's smile faded, maybe because she was thinking of the same memory, or maybe she was just tired, as she suppressed a yawn.

"It is getting late," she said. "I should probably head home."

"Thank you for helping," I told her as I stood up and walked her out.

She lingered in the doorway, toying with her Vegvisir amulet hanging around her neck.

"You're a very good friend," I added, trying to reaffirm that distance I'd put between us.

"I know." She nodded once, smiling sadly at me, and then started backing away. "I'll see you around."

Once she had gone, I closed the door and leaned back against it, breathing in deeply. I closed my eyes, trying desperately to push down all the confusing feelings that whirled inside me.

THIRTY-SEVEN

———— •◆• ————

Is everything okay?" Asher asked quietly, and I opened my eyes in surprise. For a moment I'd actually forgotten that he was still here, and I hadn't heard him come out of the bathroom.

"Yeah." I forced a smile. "Everything's fine."

"I should probably leave you be," he offered.

But even though I'd sent Quinn away out of fear of the complexities of our past, I didn't really feel like being alone. I knew sleep wouldn't come easy for me—it hadn't since Marlow died—and I didn't want to sit up alone all night, thinking my horrible thoughts and worrying my terrible worries about what may come of the world.

"No, you don't have to," I said, which was as close as I could get to asking him to stay, and walked toward the kitchen. "Do you want a drink?"

"Uh, sure. What are we drinking?" he asked.

"Oona's got an old bottle of wine in the fridge she said I could finish off." I pulled out a large black bottle, simply labeled with BOAL MADEIRA in big white letters.

"Sounds good."

Oona and I didn't have much in the way of dishes, since we ate a lot of takeout, and I grabbed a large beer mug and a glass decorated with the logo for the Ravenswood Academy soccer team, the Raging Raptors. Oona had gone on a mini-shopping spree after getting accepted into the academy, so we had all kinds of random stuff with school logos.

"So," I said, as I filled up both the glasses. "Tell me about yourself."

"There's not much to tell." He shrugged.

"Oh, I doubt that." I took a big gulp of my wine, then walked back to the living room to get more comfortable on the couch. "Especially since I know next to nothing about you."

"My childhood was mostly normal and uneventful," Asher elaborated disinterestedly. "I was born twenty-one and a half years ago to a Valkyrie who loved me very much, and a mercenary. My mom raised me on her own, because my father was off doing his own thing, and I grew up just south of the city. My first job was as a bike messenger, but that didn't last long."

"Why not?" I asked.

He took a long drink, then stared down at his cup. "Because my mom died."

I grimaced. "Sorry."

"After that, I basically threw myself into finding her killer, and now here I am with you." He smiled crookedly at that.

"You can't just brush over the last three years," I persisted. "I know you had adventures. You told me you searched all over the country."

"I did," he admitted, scratching his cheek. "I became a private investigator, to help fund my own investigations, but mostly I was hired to look for spurned lovers."

He turned to look at me. "The other night with you, at the Red Raven. Now, *that* was an adventure."

"That wasn't much of an adventure. It didn't last very long." I was leaning my head against the back of the couch. My knees were pulled up nearly to my chest, my glass of wine cradled between them, and my feet pointed toward him.

"Yeah, but you were badass," he said, sounding wistful.

His eyes were the darkest shade of blue I'd ever seen, like the sky just before it completely gave way to the black of night. Whenever he grinned, it drew attention to the scar on his lip, a tiny blemish on his otherwise flawless skin that somehow made him even sexier, and that felt like the perfect analogy for Asher himself.

Then, rather abruptly, he turned bashful—lowering his gaze and smoothing out nonexistent wrinkles in his pants. His cheeks flushed slightly, and his dark lashes landed on them heavily.

Asher cleared his throat. "I wanted to, um, apologize."

"For breaking in? I thought you already had," I said with a laugh.

"No." He licked his lips. "For kissing you the other night. I shouldn't have done that."

"Why not?" I asked, then added, "I wanted you to."

He lifted his head, his eyes filled with an unexpected eagerness and hope that made him appear more youthful. "You did?"

"Do you think I would've kissed you back if I didn't like it?"

"No, I don't suppose you would," he admitted with a small laugh. "But you just seemed too cool for it."

I raised an eyebrow. "Too cool for kissing?"

"Too cool for kissing *me*," he amended.

I laughed again. "I don't even know what that means."

"I don't know." He furrowed his brow, like he couldn't think of just the right words to say. "You seem above everything, sometimes."

I frowned. "I'm not." I took another drink. "But I think I know why I seem that way. Sometimes—well, most of the time, really—I'm afraid to feel things."

"What do you mean?" Asher asked.

My mind went back to a memory, a time when I couldn't have been more than five or six. I had a crush on this girl at school, and when I told her, she made fun of me in front of all her friends.

I came home bawling, and Marlow knelt down and looked me square in the eye, and told me, "Don't be a crybaby. You're a Valkyrie. Valkyries don't cry over petty shit like this, and they don't fall in love. You're stronger than this."

She meant it to be encouraging, but all I learned was that I should suck it up and shove down any feeling I had.

I took a deep breath and stared down at the wine in my cup. "I don't think I know how to have feelings, real ones like passion and anger and sadness and all that. Marlow always taught me that real Valkyries don't feel like that. That those emotions are just for humans. But I do feel them, and I always have, even when I tried not to."

Asher moved closer to me, putting his hand soothingly on my leg. "Real Valkyries do feel. My mother was emotional and passionate, and she was damn good at her job."

Suddenly tears were forming in my eyes. I didn't know why, and I hurried to wipe them away. "I know. I've only just begun to realize that this was another thing that Marlow was wrong about."

"I didn't mean to make you sad," he said, his voice low and soft.

"I'm not. It's okay," I insisted, sniffling a little. "These last couple weeks have just been so very long."

"I'm sorry. I shouldn't be here bothering you and taking up your time." He started to move away from me, but I reached out, putting my hand on his forearm to stop him.

"No, don't go," I said, and even I could hear the desperation in my own voice. It wasn't something I normally felt, but right now with Asher, that's exactly how I felt. Desperate to feel close to someone. For someone else to care about me and worry about me, so that, even just for a little bit, I didn't have to take care of myself.

He glanced at the doorway, as if having an internal debate, and he bit his lip before asking, "You sure?"

"Yeah. Right now, I really want you to stay."

"Okay," he said, and there was something about the way he said it—the weight of his words, the depth of his voice—that made me certain he knew exactly what I was asking.

He set his glass on the table and moved closer to me on the couch. I slid into him, so he wrapped his arm around me, pulling me to him. I curled up in his arms like that, relishing how strong and safe and warm I felt.

And he held me in a way that no one ever had before, not even Quinn. She would get feisty sitting still too long. But Asher seemed to have boundless patience inside him. He didn't try talking or kissing me or moving. He never asked a single thing from me—he just held me as long as I needed him to.

But eventually I realized I needed something more. I tilted my head up toward him, and his lips found mine, and all I wanted was to lose myself in him. I pressed my body against him, kissing him more deeply, and his hands were all over me, tracing the contours of my body.

It was less electric and insistent than our first kiss had been, but that didn't make it any less wonderful. It was gentler. Deeper. More intimate. This wasn't lust and adrenaline. It was something else.

His hand was on my cheek, and when we stopped kissing, he was looking me right in the eyes. He was right there with me, so close, and I felt a familiar panic inside my chest. I wondered painfully why it hurt so much to feel close to someone.

But at that moment, I thought it would've hurt more to be away from him. All I wanted to think and feel and be was with him, in the safety of his arms, until everything else just fell away and it was only me and only him and only us.

"Let's go back to my room," I told him breathlessly.

He lifted me up, and I wrapped my legs around him, allowing him to carry me to my bed before we both collapsed onto the mattress, ditching our clothes in a flurry.

THIRTY-EIGHT

❧

The blinds in my room were open slightly, letting in the blue light from the billboard across the street, and I lay in Asher's arms in the sapphire afterglow. My head was on his chest, and his hand ran down my bare back.

In the dim light, I noticed a few jagged scars across his chest— all small and curved, dotting his smooth skin like angry bits of punctuation. I traced my fingers along the bumps, and Asher shivered involuntarily, but he didn't ask me to stop.

"What happened there?" I asked.

"It was from when I was a Vörðr," he said.

I tugged at the paracord bracelet he still had around his wrist, the one with the Vörðr emblem. "I was wondering when you were going to get around to telling me about that."

"Yeah, I was a Vörðr," he admitted with a sigh. "But it didn't last long."

"Why not?" I asked.

"It's hard to explain."

I tilted my head to get a better look at him. "Try me."

"I'd always wanted to be a Vörðr, ever since I was a little kid," he explained. "I couldn't be a Valkyrie, so I thought this was the next best thing. Proving my mettle, protecting and serving, saving the world. It all sounded so appealing."

"But it wasn't what you thought?" I asked.

"I don't even think it was that," he said. "After my mother died, everything changed. *I* changed." He paused. "I went after it anyway, because I didn't know what else to do, but my heart was never really in it. All that fighting and anger and death . . . it just didn't seem worth it anymore.

"No offense to you," he added in a hurry. "I know how important your job is, better than most people, actually. It just . . . it wasn't for me anymore."

"No, I understand," I assured him, pressing myself deeper into his arms, but something about his words hurt in a way I couldn't explain.

Maybe it was because he'd been able to get tired, to decide that violence wasn't for him, to leave it all behind, but for me it was in the very core of my being.

I had been born with an urge to kill, a calling inside me that intensified as I became a teenager. Getting rid of immortals brought me immense pleasure, and I couldn't imagine ever giving it up.

It was a strange, cold thing to realize I was born to be a murderer.

"Hey," Asher said softly, sensing the tension in my body. He reached down, putting his hand under my chin and gently forcing me to look up at him. "You are strong, and you are good. You are more than your job, and you're not your mother."

"You don't know that," I whispered around the lump in my throat, desperate for his words to be true even though some deep, dark part of my heart was certain that he was wrong.

"No, I do know that," he insisted with a gentle smile. He must've seen I was about to protest because he explained, "My grandmother said that sometimes our ancestors—those that died before us and love us—leave us truths when we most need them."

"How?" I asked, staring up at him skeptically.

"It's a thought that comes in, but it's truer and brighter, and it becomes branded across my heart." He brushed back the hair from my face as he looked down into my eyes. "And when I met you, I just knew," he said as his fingers trailed down my temple. "I *knew* you were good, and I knew you were who I was looking for."

Somehow, he'd known how to say exactly what I needed to hear at the moment, so I kissed him gratefully and wrapped my arms around him. I wanted to stay like that forever, with him.

When I was with Asher like this—in the quiet moments between plotting to fight a demonic draugr—he made me feel like a girl, in a strangely wonderful ordinary way. I wasn't some monster or machine or tool of the gods. I was just someone he cared about, and for a little while, that was all that mattered.

Eventually Asher drifted off to sleep beside me. I lay awake, thinking about everything and listening to him breathe. But the sound of flapping outside my bedroom window drew me from my thoughts.

It was actually more than flapping—something was pecking at the glass. I sat up and peered through the blinds to see the large black raven, stalking me. It stared right at me, unblinking, and I swear it could see straight into my soul.

"What do you want?" I whispered, but it only squawked in reply, then flew off into the night.

THIRTY-NINE

oming into class three minutes before it was set to start seemed like a good move on my part, but when I entered Professor Wu's class for the first time since my mother's death, I instantly regretted it.

Almost all the other students were already in class, and they had been talking among themselves. When they spotted me, there was hushed murmuring before the class fell silent, and I could practically feel their eyes burning into me.

Samael, I was certain, had done his best to keep the news of my mother's death and the circumstances surrounding it as secret as possible. But even within the Riks, hot gossip and rumors had a way of making its way through the city—and nothing was more scandalous than anything that happened with Marlow.

"Malin," Professor Wu said, and even his tone sounded off—more unsure and tight. He didn't seem to want to look directly at me, his eyes landing in the general area around me as I slowly took my seat. "We didn't expect you back so soon."

He had definitely heard something. How much he really knew—and how much of it was misinformed conjecture—I couldn't say, and I wasn't about to ask him. There was no point in explaining Marlow's actions, because the truth was damning enough, so I just had to keep my head down and barrel my way through the whispers and the stares.

"Getting behind in school wouldn't help anything," I said, dreadfully aware of all the ears hanging on my every word.

"If you need more time, you should take it," he persisted.

"I'll be fine," I maintained.

"Well, all right, then." He smiled cheerlessly, then turned to the whiteboard at the front of the class. "Since everyone seems to be here, we might as well get started. As we were talking about on Monday, there is one way for immortals to willingly return to Kurnugia, and that is through the Gates of Kurnugia—a city under impious control located just north of the equator, created by Ereshkigal a millennium ago."

As he began writing on the board, his demeanor returning to his usual dapper intellectual self, I heard two nearby students whispering. They meant to keep their voices down, but they were just loud enough that I could overhear them.

"I heard they killed her mother because she wouldn't do her job," one of them, a moody vampire, was whispering.

My heart pounded in my chest, causing my ears to flush with heat, and I bit my lip to keep from shouting out. The vampire wasn't wrong, not exactly, but I still didn't need to hear him gossiping about my mother so soon after her death.

"That's so weird, because she was just asking about what would happen if Valkyries didn't do their job last week," his friend agreed. "Do you think they were in on it together?"

"Hey," Sloane Kothari snapped at them. "Can you keep it down? Some of us are actually trying to learn here."

Professor Wu glanced back over his shoulder. "Thank you, Miss Kothari. If you don't want to be here, you don't have to be, but please don't distract the other students."

Sloane turned back to look at me, and instead of the usual disdain in her eyes there was sympathy, and something else. Worry, maybe? Her lips pressed into a thin smile, and I realized with some dismay that she might be the closest thing I had to a friend in this class. And as word got out about the suspicions regarding Marlow, I wondered how many friends I would have in the future.

For the rest of class, I kept my head down and dutifully copied the notes that Professor Wu told us to write and listed the chapters he told us to read. But otherwise I couldn't remember a single thing he said. My heart kept racing so loud I could hardly hear my own thoughts.

The second he told us we were excused, I bolted out the door, with no intention to try to stick it through any more of my classes. I hurried down the long halls, my footsteps echoing off the marble floors, when I spotted something that made me freeze in my tracks.

On one of the sterile white walls there was a large rectangle of white, even brighter and more stark than the surrounding area. Beneath it was a smaller rectangle where a plaque had been taken off, leaving an unpatched blemish in the plasterboard.

I looked around the hall, suddenly feeling disoriented and dizzy, and noted that all the other art pieces were still in place. All the paintings and sculptures created by former students remained exactly as they had been since I had started going to Ravenswood Academy.

All of them, except for one. The one titled *The Desire of the Valkyrie* had been removed, leaving only the white space behind it. Marlow's painting.

The school was already distancing itself from her. In life, she had been a hero, a mentor, someone to aspire to be, but now, in death, she would become a villain to be ostracized, to be hidden away.

"Malin," Sloane said, pulling me back to reality.

I turned to look at her, blinking a few times to assure me this was all real. Sloane stared at me, appearing as prim as she always did. Her black curls were pulled back in a tight ponytail, and her lips were pressed together in a thin line.

"I just wanted to say that I'm sorry about your mom," she said, and it sounded like she really meant it.

"Thanks . . . I think," I replied, narrowing my eyes. "Why are you being so nice to me?"

She glanced around, confirming that we were alone. This part of the hall was just far enough from the classrooms that it was generally deserted, and today was no exception.

"Most people here know that my dad is a Deva," she said. "That's fairly common knowledge, because I've worked really hard to keep it hidden that my mom was an Apsara."

I hadn't known that, but I also didn't know why it mattered. Apsaras were immortals, known for their beauty, their love of nature, and their lack of inhibitions. They were sort of like muses, in that they often inspired people to do more and create more.

"There's no shame in being an Apsara," I told Sloane in confusion.

"Just as there is no shame in being a Valkyrie," she agreed. "But your mother wasn't just any Valkyrie, nor was my mother just any Apsara."

Glancing back at the blank space on the wall where Marlow's painting should be, I realized bleakly that I was going to have to get used to feeling shame when I thought of her. Before, it had only been pride and fear. But never shame.

"Because of the very nature of the Valkyries' existence, my

mother did not believe she had free will, much like me," Sloane explained. "The fact that a being exists that decides when she should die meant that her life had to be preordained, at least to some degree. But she got it in her head that if she overthrew the Evig Riksdag, we would all be free to live as we wanted. That without the Eralim giving orders and the Valkyries to carry them out, nothing could be preordained or controlled.

"Though she held no vendetta against the Valkyries personally, she couldn't see a way to coexist with them and truly be free," she went on. "So she mounted an attack against the Riksdag, and it failed miserably, so you've probably never heard of it. She was thwarted almost before she began, and she was killed instantly."

I gaped at Sloane for a moment before managing a meek, "I'm sorry. I had no idea."

"I'm not looking for your pity," she replied haughtily. "I am only telling you this because I know what it's like to love someone and also be mortified because of their actions."

I felt a lump growing in my throat. "That is hard to explain or know how to feel. I don't even fully understand it myself."

Sloane went on, "There is also the bitter irony that if my mother was right about free will, it is not her fault that she did the things she did. She did what she was always meant to."

"I know how you feel about predestination, but I just can't believe that this is what my mother was meant to do." I shook my head. "Marlow wasn't perfect by any means, but her greatest mistake was letting someone she believed to be good live.

"But he's not good, not even a little," I said. "He's in bed with something evil, and if left unchecked, he could destroy so much. How could that possibly be the plan?"

"It may have been your mother's destiny to set evil free," Sloane said. "But it may also be yours to stop it."

"How?" I scoffed. "I'm barely even a Valkyrie, and I have no idea how to find who I'm looking for. I don't even know for sure who I am looking for."

She chewed her lip. "If it is your destiny, you'll find a way."

I waited for a minute, expecting her to say something more. There was a look of perplexed uncertainty on her face, pinching her eyebrows together and creasing her forehead. But she didn't say anything else, and while I appreciated her kindness—especially on a day when no one else seemed to want to show me any—I didn't have much use for her platitudes and proverbs.

So I nodded once and said, "Thank you for your support. But I should get out of here, so I can start finding my destiny." I took a few steps backward from her. "I'll probably see you around."

She just stared at me, chewing her lip and looking indecisive. I offered her a small wave and turned around, walking away from her. I'd made it halfway down to the garage when I heard her calling after me.

"Malin! Wait!" Sloane jogged over to me, and when she reached me, she was out of breath, and her tawny skin had paled some. "I don't know if I'm doing the right thing, but my father says it's impossible for any mortal to know for sure what is right."

"And what exactly are you doing?" I asked.

She started digging through her bag as she spoke. "Since I heard about what happened to your mom, I got to thinking about all kinds of things, and I felt compelled to go through my mom's stuff, and when I found this—"

Sloane pulled out a rectangular stone. Twice the size of a matchbox, it looked like an ice cube with imperfections mottling its transparency. It sat flat on the palm of her hand as she held it out toward me.

"—I took it as a sign," she said. "And then you just happened to be in class today, the day after I found this, and you're saying you're looking, and . . . and I just feel like you should have it."

I stared down at the stone, trying to figure out what it was, since Sloane was treating it with such reverence, but I had no clue.

"What is it?" I asked finally.

"A sólarsteinn," Sloane said. "It's a sunstone."

But she hadn't needed to add the explanation. As soon as she said sólarsteinn, I realized exactly what it was. The sólarsteinn was a fabled stone that worked similarly to a magic compass, in that it could show you exactly where to find whatever it is you're looking for.

"I thought these were only in legends," I gasped.

"Well, they're real, apparently," Sloane said. "My mom planned to use it in her failed attack on the Riksdag, but she got caught before she even got in and got to use it."

"How does it work?" I asked.

"You have to be close to your target, and you have to *really* want to find it, like it has to be your heart's strongest desire," she elaborated. "Then you just hold the stone up to the light, and whatever you're really looking for will show."

"How close to my target do I have to be?" I asked.

Sloane shrugged. "I don't know for sure. I would guess at least within the same city."

Gingerly, I picked up the stone and held it so it would catch the light from the bright chandeliers in the halls. "So you think I can use this to complete my destiny?"

"I think it's the only chance you've got."

FORTY

——◆——

After Sloane gave me the sólarsteinn, I spent every moment finding out everything I could about it. As soon as Oona got done with class, I enlisted her help, since she knew more about talismans and enchanted objects than I did.

We tried all sorts of different things, but no matter what I felt or how I held it up, I never got the damned thing to glow, or whatever the heck it was supposed to do to show me where Tamerlane Fayette was hiding.

"Maybe he left town," Oona said, coming out of her bedroom wearing her green polo with the name DILLINGER'S CORNER MARKET & APOTHECARY embroidered on the chest.

I lay on the floor of the kitchen, holding the stone up toward the window where the setting sun streamed in. Bowie lay sprawled out beside me, sunbathing as much as he could with what little light filtered in through the smog.

"But he sent flowers to the funeral just the other day," I reminded her.

"He could've called from anywhere in the world," Oona pointed out. "Or he could've left right after the funeral. It doesn't make sense for him to stick around here, not when he knows that you and other Valkyries are probably coming after him."

"That assumes he considers us a threat," I muttered. "Or maybe this damned thing doesn't work. Do you think Sloane could be screwing with me?"

"Maybe, but I doubt it." Oona stood over me, with her hands on her hips. "Are you going to be okay while I'm at work?"

I set the stone down on my stomach so I could look up at her. "Yeah, why wouldn't I be?"

She shrugged. "This is the first time I'm leaving you alone since . . . you know."

"I'll be fine, Oona. I'm just in mourning—I'm not suddenly a toddler."

She rolled her eyes, and she started walking toward the door. "Just don't do anything stupid while I'm gone, okay? And I'll be home in five hours."

"I never do anything stupid," I insisted, but she just laughed as she left.

If Oona was right, and the reason the sólarsteinn wasn't working was because Tamerlane was out of range, then I didn't know if the stone would ever really be of help. How could I ever get close enough to Tamerlane to find him, if I didn't know where he was? I'd be stuck in cyclical reasoning forever.

But if I couldn't get to Tamerlane, maybe I could get to someone close to him. I closed my eyes and tried to redefine my greatest want. I'd been trying to focus directly on Tamerlane, but now I broadened it to include anyone I felt was responsible for my mother's death, which included Eisheth Levanon.

If Eisheth hadn't been abetting Tamerlane, he wouldn't have gotten away so quickly, and maybe Oona and I could've stopped him.

Or at the very least held him until Samael got there, and he could've done something.

I squeezed my eyes shut tighter, focusing on her face and her name, and since I wasn't entirely sure how the sólarsteinn worked, I started chanting inside my head, *Show me where the fallen angel Eisheth Levanon is. Bring me to her.*

Then I took a deep breath and opened my eyes. Bowie had sat up beside me and leaned forward, sniffing the stone with his big ears cocked at odd angles below his antlers.

"Here goes nothing, Bo," I said as I picked up the stone and held it toward the window. My wolpertinger sat up on his hind legs, sniffing the air, which I decided to take as a good sign that something magical would happen.

A sliver of sun broke through the clouds and passed through the skyscrapers that surrounded us, perfectly striking the sólarsteinn. For a moment nothing happened, but then slowly a prism of color began to grow inside it.

I closed one eye, so I could see it better, and very clearly a rainbow of light was cast out from it, pointing back toward the inner city. It was pointing me where to go.

I leapt to my feet, panicking that the stone might change its mind and stop working. I ran around the apartment in a flurry, scribbling a note for Oona so she wouldn't worry, dumping a cup of food in Bowie's bowl, and filling my messenger bag with knives and my baton.

"I'll be back as soon as I can," I told Bowie as I pulled on my boots. "Stay out of trouble, and if I don't come back, be good for Oona."

With the sólarsteinn in my pocket, I raced down to the street and hopped on my luft. Every few blocks, whenever I was stopped at a red light, I'd pull out my stone and check it. The prism of light remained pointed in the same direction.

It led me deep into the heart of the city, a few blocks away from the Evig Riksdag. The light began to glow brighter, and I decided to finish the journey on foot, so I could keep my eye on the stone. I parked my luft and hurried along the sidewalk.

Downtown was buried in darkness, since the sun had dipped low enough past the horizon that the buildings blocked out its last rays. But the city was never truly dark—buildings and streetlights and traffic kept it twinkling at all hours.

Then I spotted her. Her big leathery wings stood out on the crowded street. She was waiting at a crosswalk, and I pushed through the other pedestrians, running as fast as I could to reach her.

Eisheth's gaze was focused on light across the street, waiting for the walk signal to flash green, and she didn't even notice me at first.

"Can we talk?" I asked.

She looked over, and when she realized it was me, she sneered and shook her head. "We've got nothing to talk about."

"We've got lots to discuss."

"Well, I don't agree, so get lost," she replied dismissively, and started across the street, a split second before the light turned green.

I reached into my pocket, holding on to the dagger I had stashed there, and ran across the street after her. As soon as I caught up to her, I grabbed her by the arm and threw her against the plate glass of the storefront beside her.

Through the window I could see people getting their hair and nails done, and they all gasped when Eisheth's big wings were splayed out against the glass, but I didn't care.

"Ow!" Eisheth winced as I held her pressed against the salon window. "What the hell are you doing, you little freak?"

I don't know why she called me "little," since I was bigger and stronger than her, and I slammed her again to remind her of that.

Then I pressed the dagger against her ribs, which were exposed underneath her cropped shirt. Angels had hearts that were larger and lower in their chest cavity than humans, and it would be easy to drive the knife between her ribs, into her massive heart.

Before she had fallen, I would've needed my Valkyrie sword to slay her (along with specific orders from an Eralim to do so), but now all it took was a dagger made of forged iron, which I just happened to have in my hand. The blade was ancient and dull, but I would easily be able to slide it through her flesh and into her oversized black heart.

"You think I won't I kill you, right here and right now?" I asked. "But I don't care anymore. You can scream for help, but you'll be dead the second the words escape your lips."

Her eyes darted around at the people passing by. Some had slowed, but nobody stopped. That was the wonderful and terrible thing about living in a city as crowded as this—you were often alone and unnoticed on the busiest of streets.

Eisheth finally relented and glared at me. "What do you want?"

"Where is Tamerlane?" I demanded.

She scoffed. "How the hell should I know? After you showed up, he ditched me and skipped town. I haven't heard from him since."

I pressed the blade harder against her skin, enough to draw blood, and she cringed back against the glass. "I don't believe you."

"You think I like admitting to you that he used me and threw me away like some piece of trash?" Her lip curled in disgust, trembling slightly, and it looked like tears were forming in her brown eyes.

I might've felt bad for her, if she hadn't been laughing while she watched her boyfriend kill my mother.

"Did he have you convinced that you were some special snowflake?" I mocked her.

Eisheth blinked back tears as she confessed, "He told me he loved me. He promised me that when the new world was established, I would be by his side. He would make all the humans and useless immortals bow before the one true queen."

I smirked. "You thought he was going to make you queen?"

Now she laughed, that same unstable giggling she'd done in her loft. "No, not me. We would serve *her*."

Out of the corner of my eye I saw a woman come out of the salon. She leaned against the open door and held out her phone toward me, as if threatening me with it. "What's going on out there?" she asked in an authoritative voice.

"Mind your own business!" I barked at her.

"I'm calling the cops!" she announced.

"Stop talking about it and call them, then!" I yelled. The woman huffed at me, then went back into the salon, presumably calling the police as she did, and I turned my attention back to Eisheth, whose full lips had twisted into a bitter smile.

The buzzing had started growing around my heart, and electricity raged through my veins as my pulse quickened. The urge to kill her was growing inside me by the second.

"Her who? Who are you going to serve?" I asked, barely able to restrain myself.

"You don't know anything, do you?" Eisheth asked.

"I know that I'll kill you if you keep playing these games with me," I warned her, digging my knife deeper into her skin, and I could feel her blood warm on my fingers.

Eisheth pulled her shoulders back and stared at me defiantly. "Go ahead and kill me. You think I even care if I live or die? This life means nothing to me anymore."

"If that's as you wish," I said, twisting the knife, and Eisheth grimaced in pain.

"Don't," a woman commanded beside me.

"I already told you to mind—" I began, but it wasn't the woman from the salon.

Quinn had somehow snuck up, and she was standing right beside me. Her eyes were grave, and she put her hand on my arm, strong and unyielding.

"Don't," Quinn repeated. "This isn't your job. This is murder. And there's a ton of witnesses."

I stared at Eisheth, into her dark eyes, knowing that I could take the light from them with the simple push of my wrist. But, using all my willpower, I lowered the knife and stepped back from her. "Go on. Get lost."

Eisheth put one hand over her wound and used the other to flick me off before disappearing into the crowded street. I wiped the blood off on my black shirt, and then put the knife back into my messenger bag.

It would only be a matter of time before the cops arrived, so I started walking quickly in the opposite direction that Eisheth had gone. Besides that, walking fast helped lessen the buzzing around my heart, so I didn't feel quite as much like I would explode if I didn't kill Eisheth.

"What are you doing here? How did you find me?" I asked as Quinn easily kept pace beside me.

"I've been trying to keep tabs on you," Quinn said. "I wanted to make sure you were safe."

I raised an eyebrow at her. "You mean you've been following me?"

She raised a shoulder, shrugging it coolly. "On and off. I lost you a few blocks back, but I'm glad I found you when I did."

"I guess it was probably for the best," I reluctantly agreed.

The world would most likely be a better place without Eisheth

Levanon in it, but one of the main tenets of being a Valkyrie was that that kind of thing wasn't my call to make. I didn't get to decide who lived or died.

"Actually, I was going to come get you around now anyway," Quinn said. "I just needed to wait for the sun to go down."

I stopped walking so I could look at her directly. "What for?"

"Come on." She smiled and took my hand. "I'll show you."

FORTY-ONE

The alley led to a dilapidated stairway leading underground, then to an old subway system that had long since been shut down. The awning above was rusted, and most of the glass had been broken out.

Quinn let go of my hand to hang on to the rail as she led the way down the steps, explaining as she went, "I couldn't stop thinking about that thing that Asher read yesterday: *From whence the draugr rose, only that will make the draugr fall. If his master waits in Helheim, it is his sword that makes the call.*"

"Right, but we have no idea who his master is," I said. "Eisheth did just say something about a queen."

We'd reached the platform underground, which was filthy and full of leaves, trash, and presumably any number of vermin. Even though the subway had been closed for decades, it was brightly lit by kerosene torches hung up on the wall.

"A queen?" Quinn asked, stopping just before the turnstiles to look back at me.

"Yeah. She said she and Tamerlane serve one true queen, who- ever that is."

She scowled. "Oh."

"What? Why do you seem so disappointed?" I asked.

I mean, I wasn't exactly thrilled about the idea of tracking down this one true queen who had some sort of plan for world domina- tion, but I didn't know how that specific piece of information could put a wrench in any of Quinn's plans.

She shook her head and jumped over the turnstile, apparently deciding that her disappointment wasn't enough to halt our travels.

"Because I was looking into things, and I discovered who I thought was Tamerlane's master," she explained as I jumped over the turnstiles behind her. "But he's male."

"Who's his master?" I asked.

Quinn reached the edge of the platform and jumped down onto the tracks. When I got to the edge, I hesitated, so she held her hand out to me.

"You'll be okay," she promised me. "I'm here."

I took her hand, then leapt down. I stumbled in my landing, but Quinn was there to catch me, pulling me into her arms. For a mo- ment I was pressed against her, with her arms wrapped around me, and heat flushed over me before I managed to untangle myself from her. I cleared my throat and started walking slowly down the tracks.

"As for Tamerlane's master," Quinn said, "I was thinking more of who created him in the first place, and less of who he works for since he's become a draugr. *From whence he rose* to me implied at first that it was your mother—who didn't kill him, thus making him a draugr—but since she wasn't able to kill him when she tried, I was thinking that line was referencing something further back."

"You mean like going back into the Petro Loa lineage?" I asked.

She nodded, and the flames from the kerosene lamps made her silver hair glow like a halo. "Exactly. And I discovered this guy Kalfu was the first true Petro Loa, and he spawned all the other Petro Loas that exist today."

"Great. So where is this Kalfu?" I asked.

"Well, he died," she replied matter-of-factly. "A Valkyrie returned him around seven hundred years ago."

"So you're saying that there's no one alive that can kill Tamerlane? This all seems like terrible news." I glanced over at Quinn, who was stepping carefully along the tracks while smiling her lopsided grin. "I don't understand why you look so happy."

She waved me off. "No, I'm not saying that. I started putting out feelers, and I contacted this old friend of mine, Gable Tawfik."

Ahead of us, the subway tunnel descended into total darkness, but there was a well-lit hole in the side of the tunnel, with another set of cement stairs leading even farther down. Quinn started going down them, but I stopped short.

"Where are we going, by the way?" I asked, for the third time since I'd started following her away from my confrontation with Eisheth Levanon. So far, Quinn had avoided answering me, but it was getting to the point where I wouldn't keep following her without an answer.

She must've realized that, because she stopped and told me, "To the Avondmarkt."

"You mean the black market?" I asked.

"It's not the *black* market. It's a night market," Quinn corrected me. "Where they just happen to sell illicit and difficult-to-find antiquities, potions, and other various properties."

"Uh-huh. And why exactly are you dragging me there?" I asked.

"To meet Gable. He found something."

With that, she turned and jogged down the stairs, and I hurried to keep up with her. As I reached the bottom, I could already hear the noise—talking, laughing, movement, the sounds of a marketplace.

At the bottom of the stairs, a narrow hallway opened into a spacious underground bazaar. The high ceilings were two stories above us, and they were covered in backlit glass that gave the airy impression of having a skylight for a roof.

It was as busy as any marketplace I'd ever seen, with people crowding the walkways and vendors with stands taking up every available inch. As Quinn descended into the crowd, I reached out and grabbed her hand so I wouldn't lose her.

Every booth was overflowing with exotic and strange wares, like dragon's breath in a bottle, bones that allegedly belonged to Hercules, and the quills of a thunderbird. Someone was selling a smelly paste that they claimed was made from the liver of the Batutut, a Bigfoot-like creature that was protected under the Endangered Cryptids Act by the Evig Riksdag.

There was even a living Kting Voar calf for sale. It was a small, fluffy baby cow with a mouthful of angry-looking fangs. The man selling the calf had it on a leash as he proclaimed, "Get your Kting Voar, and all your snake and vermin problems will be gone forever! This Kting Voar will eat anything pestering your household!"

Quinn took us to a table covered in antiquities, with weapons and jewelry that appeared to be hundreds of years old. The jinn standing behind the table had his back to us when we approached, but when he saw us, he broke out in a wide smile.

He was very striking, with thick lashes and deep olive skin. In another realm, he probably would've been a model, if it wasn't for his height. He couldn't have been more than five feet tall, if that.

"Hello, Quinn Devane!" He grinned broadly at her, his dark eyes sparkling. "You are looking especially lovely today."

"Thank you, Gable. You're as handsome as ever," she said with her smile that could charm anyone, and his cheeks reddened a bit as she motioned to me. "This is my friend Malin."

"Any friend of Quinn's is a friend of mine," Gable assured me.

"It's nice to meet you," I said.

"I think I have found what you are looking for." He bent down and pulled a small trunk out from underneath the table. He set the box on the table, then opened it, revealing an oblong object wrapped in a burgundy satin cloth.

"Can we see it?" Quinn asked.

He gestured toward it. "But of course."

She carefully pulled back the cloth, and there sat a dagger with a jagged blade of black tourmaline. It looked like it had been broken from a chunk of stone, with sharp angular edges. The hilt was a deep red, with a symbol carved into it, right in the center of the quillons.

I wasn't sure if I had seen this exact symbol before, but in researching Tamerlane and Petro Loas, I'd learned enough to know that this appeared to be a Vévé symbol. This sword had definitely belonged to a Loa of some kind.

"You're certain this was Kalfu's dagger?" Quinn asked.

"I am as certain as you are beautiful," Gable told her, making Quinn smile.

"This does look real," I agreed.

"You will be taking it, then?" Gable asked hopefully.

"How much is it?" I asked.

"We already discussed the price," Quinn told me as she dug through her bag and pulled out a fat stack of cash wrapped in rubber bands that she handed to Gable. "Here you go. It's all there."

"Thank you." Gable bowed slightly to her, then wrapped the dagger back up in the satin cloth before handing it to her. "It is always a pleasure to do business with you, Quinn, as I do love making your every wish come to fruition. Please do not hesitate to contact me if you are in search of something in the future."

She handed me the dagger, which I placed deep in the bottom of my messenger bag, hiding it as best I could. Quinn said her goodbyes to Gable, then took my hand to lead me through the crowded marketplace.

"How much did you pay for that?" I asked as we climbed the stairs up away from the Avondmarkt toward the subway tunnel.

"It doesn't matter."

"It seemed like a whole lot of cash," I pressed, following her. "How could you afford it?"

"You remember my Vegvisir amulet?" she asked, and I realized with dismay that for the first time since I'd known Quinn, she wasn't wearing it around her neck.

"The one that had been in your family for generations?" I asked.

"I sold it."

"You sold it?" I stopped so I could yell at her incredulously. "Quinn! Why would you do that?"

She stopped and took a step back down, so we'd be at eye level. "Look, Malin, Tamerlane Fayette is bad. He's a draugr who might be able to bring about the end of the world. And this weapon might be the only thing that can kill him. An old amulet seems like an easy price to pay."

I shook my head. "Quinn. I have to pay you back. That's too much."

"No, you don't. I wanted to do this. I want to protect you. Why can't you just let me?" She moved closer to me, so her breasts were nearly touching mine, and the light from the lamps danced in her emerald eyes.

"I don't need—"

"Don't tell me you don't need it," she cut me off. Her voice was low and husky as she brushed back my hair from my forehead. "I don't know why you have to be so stubborn all the damned time."

"If I were perfect, it would be too much," I replied, trying to make a joke, but the air suddenly felt thick and I couldn't even muster a smile.

With her eyes still on mine, she leaned down and kissed me. Her mouth felt soft and eager against mine, and her tongue parted my lips, hesitant, tentative at first. But then I was kissing her back, and her hand moved, her fingers knotting in my hair as she pulled me to her.

It was strange, because I expected her to taste different, but she didn't—her lips were cool and sweet, and she smelled of fresh lilacs, the way she always had. Everything felt the way it was before.

My heart pounded erratically in my chest. There was an ache inside me, a familiar mixture of pain and longing, because I had missed her desperately. Since we'd been apart, hardly a day had gone by that I didn't think about her.

But being with her still petrified me, and my stomach didn't know whether to twist into horrified knots or leap in elation, so it did both, until I couldn't take it anymore. As amazing as it felt kissing Quinn, I was terrified that I might throw up, so I used what was left of my willpower to pull away from her.

As I stepped back, both of us gasping for breath, we stood staring at each other in the poorly lit stairwell for a few seconds. I could see the conflict in her eyes—she wasn't sure whether to kiss me again or not, and if she did kiss me, I wasn't sure that I'd have the strength to say no again.

Finally, she said, "We should go. This isn't a safe place to loiter."

She turned her back and started running up the stairs without waiting for me as I struggled to catch my breath and slow the racing of my heart.

FORTY-TWO

◆

So this is what we've got," I told Oona, setting the sólarsteinn and Kalfu's dagger down on the table in front her.

She sat at the kitchen table, with one knee pulled up to her chest and a bowl of cereal in front of her. She'd been awake for all of twenty minutes this morning, and I was already pestering her.

After the Avondmarkt last night, Quinn and I had parted ways. She had been distant since the kiss, probably because she didn't know how I'd react, which was just as well, because I didn't know how I'd react, either.

Then I had come home with the full intention of looking up everything I could on Kalfu and his dagger and how to stop draugrs like Tamerlane, and I did manage to, for a little bit. But then the exhaustion of the past week came crashing down on me, and I passed out before Oona had gotten home from work.

Now Oona sat half awake at the kitchen table as I laid out my plan.

"Where'd you get that knife?" she asked, eyeing it suspiciously.

"Quinn gave it to me," I said, deciding to abbreviate what had happened to avoid a lecture. I summarized everything I knew about the dagger and Kalfu, and assured her that Quinn had gotten it from a reliable source.

"So this"—she tapped the stone—"will show you where Tamerlane is, assuming you know the general area he's in and get close enough to him, and this"—she touched the dagger—"should kill him, assuming that you can find him and that he doesn't overpower you the way he did Marlow."

Oona said that last part gently, since she wasn't trying to be cruel about Marlow's death. She was merely pointing out that a Valkyrie with much more experience than me hadn't been able to stop Tamerlane.

"You sound skeptical," I said flatly.

"No, that's not it." She set her spoon in the bowl and pushed it away from her. She pursed her lips as she thought, making the studs above her lips twist and sparkle. "I'm just worried we're getting in over our heads."

I took a step back and folded my arms over my chest. "Quinn and I are both Valkyries, and Asher's had tons of training as a Vörðr, not to mention he has Valkyrie blood from his mom. And you know all kinds of potions and tricks because of your familiarity with alchemy and thaumaturgy."

"All that may be true, but Tamerlane is a draugr. Don't you think that's beyond our skill set?" Oona stared up at me helplessly.

"No one has experience with draugrs," I reminded her. "And individually we wouldn't be able to handle him, but together I think we can."

She sighed and ran her hand through her short black hair. "It's just early in the morning, and I'm worried. We don't even know where Tamerlane is. How are we going to find him?"

"Well, we—"

The ringing of my phone interrupted me. I was planning to let it go to voice mail, but the screen was face-up on the counter, with the name SAMAEL on it in big bold letters, so I rushed to answer it.

"Malin, it's Samael," he said when I answered. "How have you been holding up?"

"Okay, I guess." I had my back to Oona, but I could feel her eyes watching me expectantly. "How are you?"

There was a long pause before he finally said, "I've been better. But I was wondering if you could come in and talk?"

I shifted my weight from one foot to the other, balancing on my noninjured leg. "Do you have another assignment?" I asked, hoping that he didn't, because I had no idea how I would fit one in with everything else that was going on.

"No, you won't be getting any more assignments. Not until we find you someone new to apprentice under," Samael told me, and my heart plummeted.

I hadn't wanted to deal with a new assignment right now, but I had been so busy mourning Marlow's death and attempting to avenge her that I hadn't really considered what her death meant for my career. She was my mentor, my teacher, and without her—and with her name now tarnished—I didn't know if I'd ever be able to find someone else willing to apprentice me.

So, on top of everything else, I was just coming to the bitter conclusion that my career as a Valkyrie might be over before it even started.

"Okay," I said once I managed to find my voice again. "What's this about, then?"

"It's about Marlow," he said. "When can you come in?"

"I can be there in a half hour."

"Good. I'll see you then," he said, and hung up the phone.

"Was that Samael?" Oona asked, right behind me. "What'd he want?"

"I don't know. He said it's about Marlow." I turned back to face her.

She was standing with her hands on her hips, nodding as her eyes darted around. Whenever she was working something out, she'd play with her piercings, pushing the studs with her tongue so they bobbed as she thought. I could almost see the wheels turning inside her head.

"Okay, so you wanna do this? You wanna track down Tamerlane?" she asked.

"Of course."

"Samael will help, right?" Oona asked, looking at me hopefully.

I nodded. "He told me he wanted to catch Tamerlane as badly as I did."

"Great." She exhaled, looking relieved. "He works for the Riks, so he has all kinds of access to information and weaponry. You need to get everything you can from him."

"I can do that," I said.

Oona started walking, pacing the kitchen as she spoke. "While you're gone, I'll do my best to gather what I need for protection spells, and I'll see if I can do anything for tracking. But you have to get Samael to give you as much as possible."

"I will," I assured her.

I hurried to get dressed, and Oona was already flying around the apartment, digging through her thaumaturgy kit, and pulling out old grimoires that had belonged to her ancestors. I promised her I'd be back as soon as I could, but she barely mumbled a goodbye and kept her head buried in a book.

FORTY-THREE

◆

Godfrey and Atlas were posted on either side of Samael's door, as usual, but they'd added black armbands wrapped around their massive biceps. The same way they did whenever a comrade had fallen.

It was a simple gesture, a common one, but it wasn't something I expected to see done for Marlow, and I felt a pain in my chest as I tried to swallow back unwelcome tears.

"He's waiting for you," Atlas told me, forgoing his usual small talk to offer me a sympathetic smile.

"Thank you," I said.

Godfrey reached for the bronze door to open it for me, but he paused, his solitary eye resting solemnly on me. "Your mother was a very intimidating woman," Godfrey said, his voice a low rumbling bass. "I liked her."

I smiled gratefully up at him. "I think that's the truest thing anyone's ever said about her."

Inside Samael's office, he was sitting behind his long black desk, but he stood when he saw me. "Malin. It's good to see you."

Samael strode across his office with quick strides, and before I could say anything, he pulled me into a hug. Then he released me, looking directly into my eyes in a way that made me nervous that he could read my mind. "Are you sure you're holding up all right?"

"I'm all right." I rubbed the back of my neck and avoided his gaze. "What did you want to see me about? Did you find out anything?"

"I did, actually. But let's start at the beginning." He gestured toward his sofa. "Shall we sit and talk?"

I sat down on the couch, and he sat beside me. His usual boyish face seemed to have aged even more since I last saw him, and I wondered if sadness affected him more greatly than time.

"Did you know that Tamerlane Fayette is a draugr?" he asked me directly.

I wavered a second before nodding. "I suspected as much, yes."

He leaned back on the couch, his aqua eyes appraising me. "How long have you known?"

"Not long," I admitted. "Marlow had told me a few days before she died that she hadn't killed Tamerlane as she was instructed to, and it was only after that I really even learned what a draugr was."

"I've had feelers going out about any news on draugrs, and I've been getting word back that they're heading to the Gates," Samael said.

"You mean the Gates of Kurnugia? The city in Central America?" I asked, and the knot in stomach only twisted harder.

"Yes, and as you may know, it's under impious control."

I rubbed my forehead. "Are they trying to enter Kurnugia?"

"Possibly, but it's not something they can just go in and out of. The doors exist the same way a door exists on a safe or even to this building." He motioned vaguely toward his office doors. "But not just anyone can walk in. And in the case of the Kurnugia, the doors to it are very rarely allowed to open, and no one is ever allowed back out."

"Do you know why they're all heading down there?" I asked. "They must be planning something."

"I agree, but I'm not sure what." He shook his head sadly. "I talked to the higher-ups about sending help down to investigate, but they said this was not a matter for us to interfere. They believe that we need to let the mortals and immortals handle whatever conflict may be brewing themselves."

"But draugrs aren't even supposed to exist," I argued. "And by the Rikdag's own decree, Tamerlane Fayette is supposed to be dead. Don't they just want to take care of him themselves?"

Samael frowned. "I tried to reason with them, but they are unfortunately rather orthodox, and they like to live to the very letter of the law, which means being as hands-off as possible in this case, even if it's to the whole world's detriment."

"So Tamerlane Fayette is headed down to the Gates?" I asked.

"Yes, assuming he isn't already there."

I chewed the inside of my cheek, mulling over everything I knew about Tamerlane that might give me some hint as to what he was up to. The only things I really had were Amaryllis Mori's claims that the underworld was planning an uprising, and Eisheth Levanon's certainty that they were following a queen.

"Do you know of anyone that the draugrs might be serving?" I asked Samael. "I heard that Tamerlane says he's working for the one true queen."

He raised his eyebrows. "A queen?"

"Yeah. If they're planning to get through the city and into Kurnugia, I'm guessing she's connected to the underworld. Maybe a spurned goddess?" I suggested.

"An underworld goddess?" He exhaled deeply before he began

listing them off. "Mictecacihuatl, Laverna, Ereshkigal, Sedna, Nyx, Hine-nui-te-pō, Dewi Sri, Nephthys, Hel, Maman Brigitte, Marzanna . . . And those are just the ones I can think of off the top of my head."

I groaned. "So that doesn't exactly narrow it down."

"Unfortunately, no," he agreed pessimistically. "Not unless you have more information."

"None yet," I said, slouching back on the couch.

"Do you want me to go with you to the Gates?" Samael offered.

I considered this a moment before asking, "Can you do it without attracting attention?"

"No," he admitted. "Eralim are very rarely granted any kind of leave of absence."

"Then it'll probably be best if I go without you. I don't want anyone stopping us from going after Tamerlane simply because you're with us and they don't want you interfering."

Samael leaned forward, resting his arms on his knees, his forehead pinched with worry. "You're not going alone, are you?"

"No, I have friends that are fighting with me." I looked at him hopefully, remembering Oona's request for more weapons. "Do you have any weapons that might be good for fighting a goddess or draugrs or whatever other demonic jerks we might go up against?"

He smiled at that and stood up. "I do, actually, have just the thing."

Samael went over to the wall that was lined with shelves. On a lower shelf that came to his waist, he moved an antique totem to the side, revealing a small touch screen. He tapped in a few numbers, then put his hand down to scan his print.

The screen let out a happy bing of recognition, and a second later a thin concealed drawer slid open, revealing a hidden cache of ancient weapons, carefully cushioned on black velvet.

"This is Tyrfing." Samael pointed to the first sword, one with a long blade with a golden hilt. In the center of the pommel, a triquetra symbol had been engraved. "This sword has been endowed with a power so that it never misses a target, no matter who swings it."

He moved down the line, pointing to the next sword. It was shorter than the first, with a beveled blade, and both the blade and the hilt appeared to be made out of a singular piece of a black obsidian-like material.

"This is Kusanagi," he went on. "This is a very powerful sword, forged inside a dragon, and it's believed to control the wind."

The next sword also had a black blade, but the hilt was a deep red, and the cross guards were shaped to look like flames coming out of the grip.

"This is Dyrnwyn, and legend has it that if whoever wields this sword has a quest that is pure, the blade will burn," Samael said. "The user will remain unburned, but the flames will destroy the enemy."

"But what if their quest isn't pure?" I asked, since I really had no idea how this particular sword might feel about what I was planning to do to Tamerlane.

"Then it's just a regular sword, albeit with a very powerful blade," Samael said, then moved on to the next weapon.

Unlike the first three, this was not a sword. It was a mace with a long bronze staff with a rather gruesome-looking spiked head made of iron attached by a chain.

"And this is Sharur," he said. "It's enchanted so that it will fly great distances to its owner, should its owner need it to, and it has a very precise aim."

"You think these will be able to kill whatever the hell is brewing down in Kurnugia?" I asked.

"If any weapons on earth can help, these will be the ones to do it," Samael said. "They're all enchanted, and most were gifts from the Vanir gods, back in times when they still deigned to interfere with mortal matters."

"So it's all right if take them?" I asked, glancing down at the cache of invaluable weaponry before looking back at Samael. "I can't guarantee that I'll be able to return them, though I'll try as hard as I can."

His eyes were grave. "I told you that I'd do whatever it took to bring that bastard down. If that means losing a few ancient trinkets in the process, that is a price I am more than happy to pay."

"Thank you."

Samael went to retrieve something to carry the weapons in, so I wouldn't be walking down the street with an armload of swords like some kind of maniac. He came back a few moments later with a long black case with padded cloth sides, so it appeared similar to a duffel bag, only longer and more rectangular. Then he helped me carefully load up the weapons.

"Is there anything more I can do for you?" he asked.

I shook my head. "You've given me weapons and a direction to head in. That's more than enough."

"Let me know if there's anything more I can do, anything at all."

He walked me to the door, but when I was about to leave, I hesitated. The bag of weapons weighed heavy on my shoulder, but there was something nagging at me that I couldn't let go of, no matter how hard I tried.

"Can I ask you something?" I asked. "It's not about the weapons or Tamerlane."

He spread his arms wide. "You can ask me anything."

"Was Marlow kind to you?" I asked him awkwardly.

He thought for a second before answering. "I believe that she was, but I suppose it depends on your definition of *kind*. Are you asking was she soft and affectionate with me? As much as she could be, but honestly, that wasn't nearly enough."

"But you still cared about her."

"That's the funny thing about love," he said. "It doesn't wait for perfection—the heart loves who it loves, exactly as they are, faults and all."

"Do you . . ." I hesitated, since it felt uncomfortable to ask, but I had to know, so I pressed on. "Do you think she loved you?"

He smiled then, but there was a pained edge to it, so it didn't quite reach his eyes. "I don't think any of us could ever truly know what was in Marlow's heart, not even her."

FORTY-FOUR

What on the good green earth is that?" Quinn asked, wrinkling her nose at me. Her long silver hair was pulled back into a ponytail as she stood outside the Tannhauser Towers, leaning against her black hovercraft. It was rebuilt from a vintage sedan, replete with suicide doors, rounded fins, and a heart-shaped grille.

Oona had come out ahead of me, and she was already loading up Quinn's trunk with all her thaumaturgy gear, along with an over-night bag crammed with as much clothes and necessities as she could fit into it.

I hobbled out of the apartment complex with a backpack filled with my personal stuff, the padded case of weapons, and a pet carrier containing my twenty-plus-pound wolpertinger, along with a bag of his food.

"This is Bowie," I said, setting a few things down on the curb before I accidentally dropped everything into the canal.

"I know who Bowie is, but you can't possibly think it's a good idea to bring a rabbit along," Quinn said, picking up my bags so she could put them in the trunk.

"First off, he's not a rabbit," I corrected her. "He's a wolpertinger. Second, we're not bringing him with, but I can't exactly leave him at home by himself when we don't know if or when I'll ever be back."

"So where is he going?" she asked.

"We have to make a pit stop."

Once we had the car loaded up, I hopped into the backseat so I could sit with Bowie, while Oona took shotgun. Bowie had never been fond of traveling, and I calmed him down by sticking my fingers through his cage and stroking his nose as I directed Quinn on how to get to Galel's Garage.

She parked in the tiny parking lot beside the auto body shop and offered to help me carry everything, but I didn't want to deal with the awkward interactions between Quinn and Jude, so I told her that I could handle it myself as I hurried to gather Bowie and his things together.

When I got out of the car, Jude Locklear was just coming out of the garage. His coveralls were unbuttoned at the top, revealing a thick black tattoo across his chest. His dark hair hung down in waves behind his ram's horns.

"Malin." He smiled at me as I approached. "I haven't seen you in a while. How have you been?"

"I've been better, honestly," I said as I set Bowie's carrier down near his feet. "My mom's dead, and I have to leave town to take care of some business."

His face fell. "Oh, no. I'm sorry to hear that. Is there anything I can do for you?"

"Well, believe it or not, you're one of the few people in the world that I actually feel like I can trust, so I'm going to ask you a really huge favor," I said.

Jude eyed me warily as he asked, "What is that?"

"Can you take care of my wolpertinger, Bowie?"

He puffed out his cheeks before exhaling and put a hand on his chin. "I've never taken care of a wolpertinger. I don't really know anything about them."

"It's a lot like taking care of a cat," I assured him. "Bowie's nice, and he's litter-box-trained. I brought a bag of his food, but he also enjoys carrots and cucumbers. I have the emergency number for his vet on his carrier, so you can call them if you have any problems. And you can look up anything else you might need to know about wolpertingers online."

Jude crouched down so he could get a better look, and Bowie sniffed the door. "He is mighty cute."

"He is," I agreed as Jude scratched his nose.

"All right," he relented and straightened back up. "If it will help you and make you feel better, I'll take care of him."

"Thank you. It really will." I was so grateful I almost hugged him, but I was all too aware of Quinn's prying eyes behind me in the car.

"How long are you going to be gone for?" Jude asked.

"It should only be a few days. But if I don't come back . . ." I stared down at Bowie's cage and cleared my throat. "Maybe try to find him a good home, if you can't care for him."

"If you don't come back?" Jude's voice was tight with worry, and he stepped closer to me. "What's going on? Do you need me to come with you?"

"No, I think I've got this covered." I flashed him my most reassuring smile. "Just take care of Bowie."

"Okay," he said reluctantly, and I turned to walk away. "Hey, Malin, you always were my favorite customer."

"I know." I smiled back at him. "Goodbye, Jude."

With that, I jogged back to the hovercar and jumped into the backseat. Quinn drove off, while I sat staring out the window, wondering if I'd ever see Jude or Bowie again.

"So that guy's not your boyfriend?" Quinn asked, and I looked up to see her watching me in the rearview mirror.

Her eyebrows were slightly pinched, and her slender lips were pursed together. No doubt her mind was on the kiss she and I had shared last night, the one that conspicuously neither of us had addressed.

"Nope. He's just a friend," I said as I settled back into my seat.

"Now where to?" Quinn asked.

"Down to Hegewisch to pick up Asher," I informed her.

Before I had left the Evig Riksdag, I had texted both Quinn and Asher to see if they were up for a revenge trip down to the Gates of Kurnugia, and when they'd both given me their enthusiastic yeses, I told them to be ready ASAP. Quinn agreed to pick us all up, since she had a car while I just had a luft, and Asher texted me his address.

"Oh, so Ash is coming with?" Quinn asked, and the tension lines deepened across her forehead.

"Yeah, why wouldn't he? Tamerlane killed his mother, too," I reminded her.

"I just thought . . . I don't know." She sighed, and there was an unmistakable sadness in her voice. "No, it makes sense. We need all the help we can get."

My heart skipped a beat. I didn't know what Quinn had figured out, but she definitely knew there was something between Asher and me. Which was just great. I didn't even know exactly how I felt about my ex-girlfriend or my current sorta-beau, and now we were all going on a road trip together to avenge our mothers and save the world.

FORTY-FIVE

—◆—

When Quinn pulled up in front of the tiny, cozy little house that Asher shared with his grandmother, Asher was already sitting on the front steps, waiting with a duffel bag beside him. It was warm, almost exceptionally so for October, and he wore a pair of jeans with an old T-shirt that pulled taut over his arms and chest.

"Hey," he said as I walked over to greet him.

Behind me, Quinn and Oona were waiting in the car, arguing about what music we were going to listen to, and it suddenly hit me as Asher stood up, smiling sheepishly at me, that this was my first time I'd seen him since we'd slept together.

His hands were shoved in his pockets, and he stared down at me with a look in his eyes, one filled with such warmth and affection, it actually made me feel strangely gooey inside, and I wondered if anyone had ever looked at me like that before.

Quinn's amorous gazes tended to be hungry and demanding, but Asher's were soft and gentle. Quinn wanted to throw me up against a wall, and Asher wanted to pull me into his arms. The problem was that I wanted both at different times.

"How are you doing?" Asher asked.

"Excited. Terrified. Nauseous."

He laughed softly. "Yeah, me, too."

I was about to ask him if he was ready to go when the front door to his house opened behind him. His grandmother, Teodora, strode out with her arms folded over her chest and a rather severe expression on her face.

"Is that it?" she asked as she slowly descended the steps toward us, her white hair ruffling in the wind.

"Is what it?" Asher asked, glancing around.

"That's your whole team?" Teodora motioned vaguely toward the car, where Quinn and Oona were bickering loudly about what constituted rock music. "Your whole plan to defeat this draugr?"

"*Amma*, we already talked about this," he said.

She shook her head adamantly. "No, I talked about how I didn't want you to die at the hands of the same madman that killed your mother, and you didn't listen to me!"

"This isn't just about Mom, not anymore," Asher said, trying to keep his cool in the face of her distress. "If an immortal is allowed to escape and live on, everything could fall apart. The whole world could be undone."

Teodora gestured wildly. "So let it be undone, then."

"That doesn't even make sense," he said. "If the world ends, that includes me and you, *Amma*. I'm going to die either way."

"Maybe, but maybe not. And if you do die, you'll be here with me." She reached up, touching her grandson's face with tears in her eyes. "We'll be together."

"I have to do this," Asher insisted. "But I'll come back. I promise you."

She exhaled a shaky breath, then turned her attention toward me. "I don't hold your mother's actions against you. Asher has told me that you're kind and you share his strong sense of justice. I hope that he is right, and I am asking you to succeed in protecting him, where your mother failed with my daughter."

I swallowed hard and somehow managed to speak around the growing lump in my throat. "I will do my best."

"Wait here one moment." She held up a finger toward Asher and me, then started back toward the house. "I'm going to get something."

"What's the holdup here?" Quinn asked, leaning over Oona to yell out the car window.

"Seriously?" Oona asked. "He's saying goodbye to his grandma. Give him a second."

Quinn sat back down in the driver's seat, but I could still hear her arguing with Oona. "We've only got thirty minutes to make it to the Overland station, so if we're gonna catch it, we gotta go."

"I've always liked you, Quinn, but you can be very pushy," Oona commented.

A moment later, Teodora came rushing out of her house carrying a large shield. It appeared to be made of a heavy dark iron with a Norse symbol of protection engraved in the center.

"Here," she said, handing it to Asher. "This was my grandmother's shield, and her grandmother's before her, and so on. We call it Rök, and it can withstand most any supernatural attack. Since I'm too old to be going with you, this is the only way I can still protect you."

"Thanks, *Amma*," he said, and she kissed his cheek before he grabbed his bag and dropped it in the trunk.

Asher got in the backseat beside me and looked out the window at the receding figure of his grandmother, all of us knowing that this might very well be the last time he ever saw her. I reached over and took his hand, and when he looked back at me, he seemed a bit relieved.

"Let's do this, then," he said.

We arrived at the station for the NorAm Overland Express with only seven minutes to spare, which led to a frantic run through the depot and up to the raised platform. The Overland was neither a train nor a bus, but rather an odd hybrid that made travel much faster and easier.

The double-decker carriage straddled several lanes of the highway, with a three-meter gap underneath large enough to accommodate the average hovercraft. It ran on rails located on either side of the highway, with a fixed route similar to that of a train, and it could reach speeds as high as 125 miles per hour.

Quinn led the way, up to the second story of the double-decker carriage, which was slightly less crowded than the main-level cabin had been. Fortunately, there were several rows of seats still open, so we would all be able to sit together.

Quinn put her bags up in the overhead bins that ran between large skylights in the roof. I took a seat by the window, and Oona, in her infinite wisdom, took the seat next to me, thus sparing me from the awkward situation of being stuck directly between Quinn and Asher.

Asher finished loading up the bags, while Quinn excused herself to use the restroom located at the back of the carriage.

"You know, there's a saying," Oona said, giving me a knowing look. "You don't shit where you eat."

I gaped at her for a moment, since I hadn't told her anything about my recent romantic entanglements with either Asher or Quinn. She'd known about my previous relationship with Quinn, obviously, but when she asked anything about my feelings toward her now, I always denied them.

But Oona knew, and really, it had only been a matter of time. Somehow, Oona always managed to figure things out. Maybe that was one of the consequences of being best friends with someone for over a decade. She knew me better than I knew myself, and I couldn't hide anything from her.

"I don't know what you mean by that." I feigned ignorance, since now didn't seem like the best time to be having this conversation.

"It means," she said, lowering her voice, "don't go hooking up with *both* of the people you need to help you complete your mission."

"I didn't," I insisted, which wasn't exactly a lie, but it wasn't entirely the truth, either. "It's over with one, basically, kind of, and . . . okay, so I accidentally maybe started something with the other. But this is important. We're all focused on what we need to do, so nothing else matters. Not even who is sleeping with who."

"What are you talking about?" Asher asked, taking the seat on the other side of Oona.

"Nothing," Oona and I replied in unison.

FORTY-SIX

◆

The Overland horn let out two long bleats as a final warning that we were about to take off, and I settled into my seat for the long ride south. Just as the express lurched away from the station, a hulking figure with a familiar face lumbered up the stairs—Atlas Malosi, one of Samael's personal guards.

As soon as he saw me, a relieved grin spread out on his face, and he walked down the aisle toward us. He hurriedly shoved his suitcase in the overhead bin, then rather clumsily slid past the other passengers in the row so he could take the seat directly in front of mine, right by the window.

"What are you doing here?" I asked him.

"You know this guy?" Oona tilted her head as she looked up at him, kneeling awkwardly on the seat in front of me so he could look at me, but his large frame hardly fit in the seats to begin with. "I thought I knew everyone you knew."

"This is Atlas, he works for Samael." I gestured vaguely toward him.

"I'm Oona." She leaned forward so she could shake his hand, and his hand was like a massive bear paw enveloping hers.

I returned to the question at hand that he still hadn't answered: "What are you doing here?"

"Since Samael would draw too much attention if he attended to this personally, he sent me along in his stead," Atlas explained, smiling sheepishly at me. "He thought you needed as much help as you could get, and he told me that I was the best he could send."

"That's very generous of him, and you." I smiled as gratefully as I could, since it was a nice gesture—and probably a necessary one, given what we were up against.

It still felt vaguely awkward having Atlas tagging along, knowing that he'd most likely be reporting everything that happened back to Samael, and it was also kind of embarrassing having my boss/my mom's-sorta-boyfriend checking up on me.

"Welcome aboard the Revenge Express to Hell," Quinn replied cheerily and leaned over Asher to shake Atlas's hand. "I'm Quinn, and we're happy to have another body with us."

Asher squished back in his seat to avoid getting Quinn's breasts shoved directly in his face, and he was still leaning back a bit even after she sat back down.

"That's all well and good, and we really do appreciate your help," Asher said carefully. "But how did you know where we were? On this exact Overland at this exact time?"

"Samael told me where you'd be, but that I'd have to hurry if I was going to catch you," Atlas said with a shrug. "I don't know how he got the information, but he has his ways of finding out most anything he wants to."

"Good to know," I said under my breath.

"Do you guys wanna go over a plan or anything?" Atlas asked.

Quinn motioned to the people sitting around us. "I think it's best if we wait until we get where we're going."

"Right. Of course." Atlas turned back and sat down in his seat, but a few moments later, he craned his head back around to look at us. "I have snacks up here, if any of you guys want any."

"We're good for now, but thanks," Oona told him with a smile.

Atlas finally settled into his seat, and Oona pulled out a thick, heavy book that smelled of dust and burnt sage, with the title *Sorcellerie Grimoire* embossed on the front. It had been a gift from her cousin Minerva, and she was studying up on it to prepare for what lay ahead for us.

Meanwhile, Asher was on his tablet and looking up maps of the labyrinthine city of the Gates of Kurnugia. It had been deliberately designed to be confusing and maddening, to keep immortals from escaping and to keep mortals from invading their space.

And at the far end of the row, Quinn had put her earbuds in and stared down at her phone, presumably watching a movie.

With everyone otherwise occupied, I was finally able to relax for a bit in my seat, knowing these might be some of the last truly peaceful moments of my life. I looked out the window at the decrepit, overcrowded landscape of the city as the Overland whizzed through the south-end slums.

Eventually we escaped the shadows of the skyscrapers, and as the buildings started thinning out, so did the smog that shrouded the city. The darkness of the metropolis gave way to deserted plains, cracked dry earth that had been overfarmed and underwatered.

The vast wastelands that stretched between the various megacities were virtually uninhabitable, leaving the several billion mortals, immortals, and various creatures that lived in the United States to overcrowd the cities.

Through the skylights above, I watched as the dark clouds moved in, blotting out the orange sun, and they rumbled loudly with the threat of an oncoming storm. I closed my eyes against the world and tried to get some sleep while I still could.

I awoke sometime later with stars twinkling above. I yawned and lifted my head, blinking to focus, and I was startled to find that I had been sleeping with my head resting on Asher's shoulder.

"What's going on?" I asked, glancing around the dim carriage of the Overland Express. "Where are we?"

"You were out for a while," Asher explained in a hushed voice. "We all kind of moved around so we could get more comfortable."

He motioned to a row over, which had been filled with passengers when I passed out, but now only had Quinn. She had lifted up the armrests and spread out, napping with her coat bunched under her head as a pillow.

In the seats right in front of me, I could hear Oona—her voice soft and excited as she argued with Atlas about the proper ways to fight a demon.

"Where are we?" I asked, since it was dark and the carriage had obviously emptied out quite a bit.

"We're almost to our stop."

I sat up sharply and looked out my window, at the night landscape and the dark desert outside that had subtly begun to shift to waving fields of grass under a full moon. "This is Mexico? How long was I asleep?"

"No, our express stops just short of the border, so we're spending the night in Sugarland, and we'll catch the next express down to the Gates first thing in the morning," he told me.

"So tomorrow." I took a deep breath and settled back in my seat. "Tomorrow we'll get there, and hopefully, soon, this will all be over."

Asher took my hand in his, sharing his quiet comfort with me. I cuddled up next to him, resting my head against his shoulder, and he kissed my temple.

I relished the brief moment of affection before turning my attention back to avenging our mothers. "What were you working on?" I asked, gesturing to the tablet resting on his lap.

The screen had gone black, but he tapped it to reveal detailed floor plans of a building that reminded me of a cathedral, almost, except the entire structure appeared to be made out of bones, if the designs were to be believed.

"This is the Bararu Mutanu Ossuary," Asher explained, and he swiped away from the blueprints to show me a full-color picture of the exterior.

"It blocks the entrance of Kurnugia," I said. I'd learned about it in school, but I didn't think I'd ever really seen pictures of it, not like the ones that Asher was looking at.

"Right." He started scrolling through the pictures, flipping past one skeletal room after another. "It's rumored to be impossible to get through, but if Tamerlane is trying to get into Kurnugia, he'll have to go through here."

"But I thought he was just hiding out nearby. Why would he want to get in?" I asked. "I mean, he could've just let my mother kill him, then."

"Maybe he didn't think she could kill him and he just wants to find a way in on his own," Asher offered, then paused. "Or maybe he's not trying to get *in*—maybe he's trying to let someone *out*."

FORTY-SEVEN

———— ◆ ————

The view from the motel window was of a crowded parking lot. We were on the fourth floor, and it felt too close to the ground, the skyline too short without towering skyscrapers surrounding us. Sugarland looked as if the mega-cities I was used to had been squished down and compacted, with a thinner layer of smog allowing the stars to shine through.

We were in an older motel, with paint chipping off the stucco sides and an outdoor walkway to the rooms. Our room was on the highest floor. The walkway outside was lined with a rust-covered railing. The doors, at least, had microchipped keys, so it would be harder for anyone to break in. Hopefully.

"That sure is a weird-ass painting for such a small-ass room," Atlas commented behind me, and I turned back to survey the room.

The hotel room was two narrow queen-sized beds jammed against the wall with a door in the corner leading to an economy-sized toilet/shower combo. Above the beds was a massive drawing of a woman, framed with ornate obsidian.

We'd gotten another room as well, one door over, but we were all packed in this one like sardines now. I'd wanted to pace—my legs were restless from the long ride and anxiety was kicking in, electrifying my skin. But there wasn't enough room.

Atlas's hulking frame blocked the door, while Oona sat cross-legged on one bed with Quinn sprawled out beside her, letting her shirt ride up and her jeans hang low on her hips.

"So what now?" Oona asked.

"We could sleep," Asher suggested, barely suppressing a yawn, from where he leaned against the slim dresser beside me.

Quinn took her hair down, slowly shaking her head to set her long silver locks free. "We shouldn't have slept so much on the train."

The large framed drawing above the beds was photorealistic and managed to be both completely captivating and totally unnerving. It showed a gorgeous woman with dark brown skin lying back, with her hair shaved on either side of her head, leaving her with a short curly Mohawk. She was naked except for the fur blanket that swathed her.

At the bottom, larger and more centered than the artist's signature scribbled in the corner, was the title:

Ereshkigal in Repose

The air in the room began to feel thinner, and my breath came out shallow. I had the strangest sense of vertigo, like the entire room had pitched to the side, only my gaze fixed on the painting keeping me upright.

Suddenly I felt hot—not just flushed with warmth, but *burnt*. The heat rose from the soles of my feet, scorching my skin as it traveled painfully up my thighs, and the scent of fire and smoke filled my nostrils. My mouth tasted of fresh blood—metallic and warm— as panic surged through me.

I was terrified and in pain, but I couldn't move or scream or do anything. I stayed totally frozen, my eyes locked on the woman in the painting.

Then I heard a voice like satin in my ear: "Remember that we all must die."

"Mal?" Oona was saying—almost yelling, sounding afraid—and rather abruptly everything stopped.

The heat. The fear. The taste of blood. It all fell away. I was just standing in the hotel room with four concerned faces staring at me. Asher touched my arm, meaning to comfort me, I was sure, but I nearly jumped out of my skin.

"Malin?" he asked. "Are you okay?"

I shook my head, trying to clear it. "Yeah, I'm fine. I just . . . I think I need to get some fresh air."

"We could grab something to eat, maybe?" Atlas suggested, and his voice was cheery, but his dark eyes were anxious. "It might be good to get out and move around for a while."

I motioned to all our bags and gear piled up on one bed, including the one from Samael filled with irreplaceable weaponry. "But we can't just go out and leave all the stuff here."

"I'll stay and watch the stuff, if you're worried," Asher offered; he was still close to my side, in case I might need him to steady me or pull me from another trance.

"You sure?" I asked, but really I didn't want to wait to hear his answer. I didn't want to stay inside a second longer. I needed to get out, to move, to breathe.

"Yeah," he assured me with a smile. "I'll be fine."

I wanted to look at him directly, to see if there was any hesitation in his eyes, but I didn't trust myself to look at anybody. Everything still felt strangely off-kilter, and so I just nodded, taking his word for it, and stepped out to the hallway balcony.

A few moments later, Quinn, Oona, and Atlas followed suit.

Quinn said she considered staying behind to help Asher, but she felt as pent-up as I did. Oona didn't want to leave me on my own, and it sounded as if Atlas was essentially my bodyguard at this point, even though I did not need a bodyguard.

"What happened in there?" Oona asked me, her voice low as we descended the stairs toward the street below, with Atlas and Quinn a few steps ahead.

"Just exhaustion and stress, I think," I replied vaguely.

I shook my head, and I wasn't trying to brush her off, but the truth was that I didn't really remember, not exactly. It was like, waking from a vivid dream, when you tried to tell someone about it, you only had a few fragmented images to hang on to.

So I had to chalk it up to my own mind playing stress-induced tricks on me, because what else could it be?

The weather in Sugarland was cool, but it lacked the crispness of back home that I so wanted right now. At least the streets were less crowded here—you could take three or four steps before bumping into another person. But it was still busier than I expected for an outskirt town like this.

We'd only walked a couple blocks when Quinn stopped short. She'd been leading our small group, since the rest of us didn't feel like taking charge. After she stopped, I could see why.

Across the street from us was a large adobe building, where a small crowd had amassed trying to get in. They looked much like the clientele I would see at the Carpe Noctem bar back home, but with more cowboy boots and hats.

The bright pink and green neon sign in the front read DEL SUDOR Y PECADO, and it featured an animated demon with horns and a forked tail taking off his hat and saluting the patrons as they entered the bar below him.

"How about this place?" Quinn suggested, hooking her thumb at it.

"This doesn't exactly look like a restaurant," Atlas said.

"Yeah, well, I don't need food to help me sleep," Quinn muttered, and without waiting for the rest of us to respond, she walked ahead into the bar.

FORTY-EIGHT

◆

Shots?" Quinn suggested with a raised eyebrow, her eyes darting between the three of us.

We stood at a high-top table next to a table full of squealing Nephilim celebrating a bachelorette party, and discarded peanut shells and sawdust crunched underneath our feet. A strange fusion of country and death metal blasted out from a high-tech jukebox that glowed red in the corner, and everything smelled vaguely of sweat and wood chips.

"Hunting a demon with a hangover doesn't sound ideal," I said, nearly shouting to be heard over the music.

"He's not a demon—he's a draugr," Oona corrected me as her gaze followed a waitress walking by with a tray of brightly colored drinks, and I could almost see her salivating.

"That changes everything, then," I said with a sigh.

"Nobody's getting drunk. Just one shot," Quinn promised, holding up her index finger. "Just to take the edge off."

Oona was staring at me hopefully, and I knew her belief that alcohol made everything better was very skewed, to say the least, but something to calm my nerves did sound necessary at this point. Especially after my weird freak-out at the hotel.

"Fine," I said, and the words had barely escaped my lips before Quinn was off, flagging down a waitress to procure the shots.

A few minutes later she returned, carefully carrying our tiny cups of red liquid with bright orange flames dancing out of the tops.

Atlas took a shot from her and wrinkled his nose. "What is this?"

"Who knows? The waitress says it's the best, so blow out your drink and swallow it down." Quinn raised her glass and waited for the rest of us to do the same. "To saving the world!"

We clinked our glasses, blew out the flames, and I tossed my head back, gulping down the sour liquid as fast as I could.

"There," Quinn said, smiling at me as I grimaced. "Isn't that better?"

"Maybe. Give it a second to kick in."

While I waited for the liquid to do its job and soothe my frayed nerves, I noticed Oona eying a guy at the bar. He was shirtless, which actually didn't appear to be out of the ordinary for this bar, and he looked like he'd been chiseled out of marble. He leaned against the bar, casually sipping a beer with his cowboy hat cock-eyed on his head.

"Wow." Oona leaned forward, resting her arms on the high tabletop as she ogled him.

"He's an immortal. Maybe a demigod?" Quinn guessed.

I shook my head. "No. I don't recognize his lineage, so he's something lower-level. Maybe a warlock?"

"I didn't realize you guys read people that easy," Atlas said, looking at us both with bemused amazement. "I usually don't get to hang out with Valkyries outside of work."

"It's something we just . . . know." Quinn shrugged, because there really wasn't a better way to explain it.

"Can you tell if he's gay?" Atlas asked with a raised eyebrow.

"Or straight?" Oona chimed in hopefully.

"Nope," Quinn said. "You'll have to figure that one out on your own."

Oona and Atlas exchanged a look, and apparently decided to give it a go. Oona grabbed one of the brightly colored drinks from a waitress as she and Atlas made their way over to the ripped immortal, presumably hoping to come back with a better understanding of which one of them had the best chance with him.

"You wanna dance?" Quinn asked, looking at me with that crooked smile of hers.

"I don't know if I should." I tried to decline, but the drink was finally starting to kick in, making my muscles feel loose and easy.

A warm relaxation had settled in over me. My smile came easier, and saying the word *no* suddenly felt so much more arduous than it had a few moments ago. Even the music that had seemed so grating when we first came in actually made sense, and I found myself swaying with it involuntarily.

"Will another shot get you to dance?" Quinn arched her dark eyebrow.

"Maybe, but I definitely won't be doing that," I said, using all my willpower to refuse. "I need to be clearheaded for tomorrow."

"A dance it is, then."

She took my hand, leading me through the bar to a clearing in the center. I wasn't sure if it was really a dance floor, exactly, but several folks were dancing there—a few drunk young ladies on their own, and a few couples grinding against each other.

At first Quinn and I danced much like the drunk girls—our only connection being where our fingers were linked loosely together as we moved and swayed. But when the song switched to something melodic, less angry and more electronic, Quinn pulled me to her.

She looped one arm around my waist, pulling us together, and

I wrapped my arm around her neck. And I didn't know if it was her or the shot, but it all hit me at once. Her skin was so soft against mine—how was her skin so soft, how was it even possible?—and she smelled of lilacs and alcohol in a way that seemed to be so perfectly Quinn.

Then her fingers were on my face, gently caressing my cheek and jawline, and I looked at her. I wanted her to kiss me, and she *knew* it, so she didn't. Not right away. She just held me to her, letting her hand trail over my skin underneath my shirt.

I couldn't take it anymore, and I pulled away a bit. "I'm not drunk enough for this."

Hurt flashed through her eyes like lightning, darkening her face, and she stepped back from me. "What is that supposed to mean?"

"I just meant dancing," I said lamely, and the fog of the drink and her touch was making it hard for me to argue.

"Did you? Or did you mean you're not drunk enough for me?"

"Come on, Quinn." I ran my hand through my hair. "When we were together, you were the only thing that I was ever really drunk on."

"Is that why you ended things with me? You didn't like the hangover the next day?" Her husky voice was quiet, barely loud enough to be heard over the music, and pain made it tremble slightly.

"It's not like that," I said, because I didn't know what else to say, but the truth was that she wasn't far off the mark.

Being with her was wonderful and exciting, but she never gave me space to breathe, and after we'd spend a weekend together I'd end up feeling exhausted and drained. She cared too deeply, too fiercely, and I could never keep up. I could never be who she needed me to be.

"Why did you end things? You never explained it. Everything was so good. *We* were so good."

"Were we?" I asked, almost plaintively. "It wasn't all roses."

"Even roses have thorns, Malin. We were *good.*" She reached out, brushing back my hair from my face.

Then she was pressed up to me again, her mouth on mine, kissing me fiercely the way she always did, and as much as I wanted to give in and kiss her back, I just couldn't. I pulled away and put my hand on her shoulder, pushing her from me.

"This just isn't the right time," I insisted.

"I know the timing is terrible, but this might be it, Malin. You do realize that, right? What we're going up against, there's no way we can all make it out alive. So the time is now or never." She stared at me. "Do you want me or not?"

"That's not fair."

"I'll take that as a no, then." She started walking away, so I grabbed her hand, stopping her.

"Quinn, it's not that simple."

She whirled on me. "No, for me it is that simple! I've wanted to be with you since the day we met, and I knew it. You've never been able to figure out what you really want. I kept waiting for you to know and I was certain that one day you'd come to your senses, but . . ."

"I never asked you to wait!" I shot back, and her face fell, like I had punched her in the stomach.

"You're right. You're absolutely right," she replied thickly. "I will always care about you, and I will gladly follow you into whatever battle may come tomorrow. I won't let you die and I won't let the whole world come crashing down because of what's happening between us. But I can't keep doing this dance with you. I know it's my fault. I know I kept hanging on long after I should, but . . . I'm done now."

"Quinn . . ." I tried to argue, but there was nothing I could say. Especially since she was just saying what I'd been trying to say for the past six months, but somehow hearing it aloud, and seeing the look on her face . . . it hurt so much more than I expected.

Without saying anything more, she turned and walked away, disappearing into the crowd, and suddenly I didn't feel like being there anymore. I pushed my way out into the night air, which was much cooler and cleaner than inside the bar.

I'd only taken a few steps when I heard Oona calling my name.

"Mal, wait!" she shouted, so I turned to look at her. "What's wrong?"

I shook my head. "Nothing. I'm going back to the hotel to get some sleep. Stay. Have fun. Don't get too drunk, and I'll see you in the morning."

Her eyes were narrowed in concern, but I didn't wait for her to say more. I just turned and practically ran back to the hotel. I wasn't in a hurry, really, it just felt better to run. When I made it back, my legs felt like jelly and my skin was flushed, both from the booze and the jog.

We'd quickly discussed sleeping arrangements when we got here, so I went to the room that I would share with Oona and Asher, while Atlas and Quinn would take the other one farther down the hall.

Asher lay on the bed farthest from the door, shirtless, with his back to me. In the moonlight streaming through a gap in the curtains, he looked so serene and peaceful.

Wordlessly, I took off my shoes and pants before sliding under the covers beside him. We hadn't talked about whether I would be sleeping in his bed or bunking with Oona in hers, and I hoped he didn't mind. I wrapped my arm around him and pressed my head against his back.

For a few moments we lay that way, with me trying to quiet the anxiety raging in my head, until finally he said, "Are you okay?"

"I just don't want to be alone tonight," I admitted.

He took a deep breath, then put his arm over mine. "Okay."

FORTY-NINE

———◆———

The next day the NorAm Overland Express took us as far as Belmopan in Belize, and from there we had to take a cab. We all piled into an old van. I sat in the seat farthest back, squished between our luggage with Oona, while the others made do with the seats in front.

Everyone else had slept on the express down from Sugarland, except for me. But I was glad I was awake. Halfway through the long ride, the desert scenery had given way to the most beautiful, lush landscape I'd ever seen. Tall vibrant trees lined our path, and I'd even spotted a few howler monkeys hiding in the branches as we zoomed past.

When we had finally gotten off, everyone had commented on how strangely gorgeous it was here. It was like being transported into another realm, a fairy-tale land. The air was thick and humid, and it smelled sweetly of flowers. Even the sun seemed to shine brighter here, so Oona had bought a pair of oversized sunglasses at the station. It was so unlike the city back home.

During the cab ride, I leaned out the window, staring in awe at all the green that surrounded us, and at a flock of bright red birds taking flight.

Among the greenery were stunning homes and buildings made of limestone with ornate architecture, and massive stone temples looming in the distance. Eventually the trees thinned out and high-rises replaced the rain forest.

Farther on, the buildings began to look rougher and older and became smaller and were crammed closer together. The air became drier and hotter, like sitting too close to a fire, as the paved roads gave way to bumpy dirt. The area lost all pretense of being stable and devolved fully into a shantytown.

"El Noveno Anillo," the cabdriver explained to us, motioning to the homes made of mismatched plywood and sheets of corrugated metal. "This is, uh, how you say—*afueras*?"

"The suburbs," Oona translated for him, and he snapped his fingers in excitement.

"*Si, si*." He nodded, and with a push of a button, he rolled up all the windows of the van, sealing out the growing stench of sewage and decay. Then he blasted the AC to keep the heat at bay. "This is the suburbs of the Gates."

"Why is it called El Noveno Anillo?" I asked, but he couldn't hear me over the racket the air-conditioning was making.

"It means 'the Ninth Ring,'" Oona answered. "I imagine it's a reference to Dante's *Inferno*, with the ninth circle of hell being the final one before the devil."

The cab moved slowly through the town, since the narrow winding roadway was filled with potholes and pedestrians who paid no mind to any kind of traffic laws. The inhabitants appeared to be an even mixture of humans and immortals, but they were all ragged and dirty, and they stared at me through the window with angry glares.

Not that I blamed them. Living in a place like this had to be awful.

Finally the van rolled to a stop just where the dilapidated homes were buttressed against a tall adobe wall. Directly before us was a large archway, with the view inside only revealing more rust-colored walls.

The driver hit the meter and turned back to us. "This is as far as I go."

Oona stepped out, taking off her sunglasses, while I paid the driver and the others started unloading our gear.

"So this is it?" She looked back over her shoulder at me. "I just expected there to be actual gates, or something. But this is just a big open entryway."

"It's actually a poor translation," Quinn explained, referencing something we'd both been taught at the academy. "Originally, when it was first settled thousands of years ago, it was called *In Sabatu Kurnugia*, but someone mislabeled it on a map as *Baba Kurnugia*, and Baba meant Gates. Eventually that took hold, and whenever English became the standard language around here instead of Sumerian, it officially became the Gates of Kurnugia."

"Well what does *In Sabatu* mean?" Atlas asked.

"Rings," I said and pointed to the walls. "They didn't have a word for 'labyrinth' back then, so it was referring to the maze of walls that encircle it, making it difficult for anyone to find their way through."

Oona considered this for a moment as she looked ahead. "So it's really the Rings Around Kurnugia."

Just as she said that, a creature walked by the entrance, on the inside of the Gates. It was a massive reptile, with dark emerald scales and four long legs. With a long snout filled with jagged teeth, it looked like a cross between a crocodile and a velociraptor.

I'd never seen one in real life before, but based on the pictures I'd seen in textbooks, I guessed it was a mahamba.

"What is inside there"—the cabdriver motioned toward the Gates—"the physical world cannot hold it. A gate would do nothing. It is the *brujería* that keeps them inside."

The mahamba stared at us a moment longer—its large green eyes with slit-black pupils locked on us. Then it blinked and turned to walk away, disappearing behind the adobe wall that separated us.

The very second the van was empty, the driver turned around and sped off down the road, going much faster on the way out than he had on the way here.

While most of El Noveno Anillo had seemed heavily populated, the area just around the wall seemed deserted, but that was just as well, because I preferred to get ready with some modicum of privacy.

Oona's large backpack of thaumaturgy gear was almost toppling her over, so Atlas traded his much smaller backpack for hers. She kept a few protection and healing potions in his bag, in case we needed them on short notice.

I crouched down over the bag I'd gotten from Samael, preparing to dole out weapons before we entered the Gates. We'd already discussed who would get what, trying our best to align the best weapon for each person's skill sets.

Tyrfing—the Norse sword that never missed its target—went to Oona; Kusanagi—the sword forged inside a dragon—went to Quinn; Dyrnwyn—the flaming sword—went to Asher; and Sharur—the enchanted mace—went to Atlas.

I kept Kalfu's dagger—the smallest weapon but the one that could hopefully kill Tamerlane Fayette—for myself, sheathing it on my right side, while my Valkyrie sword Sigrún was sheathed on my left, and the rest of my belongings were in my knapsack on my back, aside from the sólarsteinn, which I put in my pocket.

"You should have this." Asher held his grandmother's shield Rök out to me, but his eyes were downcast.

This morning, when I awoke, he'd already been out of bed, and he'd hardly spoken to me, other than a few monosyllabic replies to questions I asked. On the express and in the van, he seemed to avoid sitting by me.

Something was definitely up with him, but I didn't know what it was, and I didn't have time to deal with it. Not now.

"Thanks, but I don't—" I began, but he cut me off.

"You need this more than I do." He cast me a slanted look. "Just take it."

"Thank you," I said, because I didn't want to argue, and I hooked it onto the bag on my back.

"Should we do this, then?" Quinn asked, which was also about the first time she'd spoken to me today. But the encouraging look in her eyes let me know that she'd put our fight last night behind her.

I glanced over at my other friends and saw a similar look in their eyes, even Asher's. Supportive. Nervous. Brave. Whatever had happened between us before didn't matter now. We had a mission—arguably the most important mission any of us had ever been on—and we were going to complete it to the best of our abilities.

The heat was already getting to me, so I pulled my hair up in a ponytail, and then took the sólarsteinn out of my pocket. Holding it tightly between my hands, I closed my eyes and began chanting inside my head: *Show me where the draugr Tamerlane Fayette is. Show me how to find him.*

Then I took a deep breath and opened my eyes.

At first there was nothing, and my heart pounded in my chest.

But slowly I saw it grow—a prism of color and light shining through, pointing straight ahead, toward the very center of the demon-controlled city.

"He's in there," I said, feeling both relieved and completely terrified. "Let's go get him."

FIFTY

———◆———

As we passed under the archway, a strange tingling sensation ran through me. It wasn't exactly unpleasant—sort of like the pins-and-needles feelings I got when my foot fell asleep.

"Did you feel that?" Quinn asked.

"Feel what?" Asher asked, instantly on high alert.

Oona's eyes darted around. "I didn't feel anything."

I felt it, too, and exchanged a look with Quinn. "It must be because we're Valkyries."

"What was it?" Oona pressed.

"It doesn't matter. Let's just keep going." I held the sunstone on the palm of my hand, with the prism of light pointing directly toward a solid wall in front of us. "The sólarsteinn is pointing straight ahead, but we can only go left or right. Where do you think we should go?"

"The ossuary is supposed to be due north, but to get there, we needed to start going east, I believe," Asher said as he pulled out his tablet.

From where I was standing, I could see the screen as he pulled up the plans, but the image started blinking out and the screen went black. Asher kept tapping it and tried to reopen it, but the tablet remained lifeless.

"Shit. This damn thing is acting up," he growled.

"The city is interfering with your reception?" Oona asked.

"Mine, too." Quinn had pulled out her phone when she saw Asher was having trouble with his tablet. "It's not the reception—it's just not working."

Asher let out a frustrated sigh. "Looks like we'll be working from memory."

"So which way?" Atlas asked.

"I guess we go left," Asher replied.

The outer edge of the Gates was a long corridor, with bare adobe walls towering over it, and the ground a dark crimson-red clay. A putrid odor of sulfur and rotten meat filled the hot air.

Eventually, after a few turns, the hallway widened and opened up into an actual city. Not modernized, like the city outside of the slums or the one we lived in, but more like a bustling Bronze Age civilization.

Small stone shops were set up, with wares hanging from their awnings. They were admittedly disgusting-looking wares, like entrails and bloodied ram's horns, but the setup was similar to that of the street vendors at home.

The shop owners appeared to be entirely demonic, most of them overtly so, with horrific appearances, but some were more human-oid. There did appear to be human tourists here as well, haggling with the demons over the price of their merchandise. A man was shouting that he'd come all the way from Papua New Guinea for some magical elixir, and they were fresh out.

The demon selling the ram's horns had dark crimson skin, reptilian eyes, and cloven hooves. He walked beside us a few steps, narrowing his eyes at us, then he leaned over and actually sniffed Quinn. She didn't protest, because the demons outnumbered us, but the demon recoiled in disgust.

"Move along," he simpered with a forked tongue and shooed us away. He hopped back to his stand and started shouting, "Fresh Cambion horn! Perfect for any dysfunction you might be suffering in your nethers! Make your lovers happy tonight!"

I glanced back at him and realized that those hadn't come from a ram—they had come from Cambions like Jude. They were killing each other here, and then selling their parts in an open market.

"Oh, come on." An Aswang with its gaping mouth of angry teeth was arguing with a woman who looked relatively ordinary, except that she was selling necklaces made of tiny human toes. "Don't pull a fast one on me, Lamia."

"That's the price," Lamia replied, snatching the toe-jewelry from the clutches of the Aswang. "Take them or leave them."

"This way," Asher ordered, touching my arm, and it wasn't until that moment that I realized I'd stopped and had been gaping at Lamia.

"We shouldn't linger here," Atlas suggested, but he didn't need to. The market was not a place I wanted to stay for a moment longer than I had to.

Asher led the way through the crowded bazaar, and I tried to keep my head down. I didn't want to see who was selling what. This whole place was a nightmare come to life.

But by trying to keep my eyes off any of the horrors that surrounded me, I wasn't exactly looking where I was going. I stumbled over my feet and tumbled forward, falling right into the wide-open arms of an iron statue.

The strap to my bag got caught on the statue's hand, and it took a few seconds to pull myself free. But when I finally looked up, I instantly recognized who the statue had been made in honor of—the short curly hair, the high cheekbones, the powerful femininity. Ereshkigal.

"I feel like you're following me everywhere I go," I mumbled, staring up into the dark, cold eyes of the statue.

"Mal?" Oona asked. "Are you okay?"

I shook it off and hurried on ahead, and soon enough we found the exit out the back of the market. Here, there were more narrow hallways, winding toward the ossuary at the center of the Gates. We just had to make sure that we chose the right ones.

FIFTY-ONE

◆

As we walked in the stifling heat, I fell in step with Asher, while Atlas, Quinn, and Oona trailed a few steps behind us. The sólarsteinn worked almost like a compass. The light always pointed to the center of the city, and it didn't take walls or buildings into account, so Asher used what he remembered to tell us where to turn.

An olitau flew above, its large red leathery wings blasting hot wind over us, and we all crouched down to avoid getting scraped by its razor-sharp claws. The olitau was essentially a giant demonic bat, and it let out an angry cry as it flew off over the walls.

"This way," Asher directed when we hit a T-intersection, pointing us to the left, and we rounded the corner to bump right into a dead end. "Okay, let's go right, then."

We turned around and walked maybe ten or twenty feet before the corridor turned into another dead end.

"Shit." He ran a hand through his short hair and turned around in circles, as if that would somehow make sense of the dead ends we encountered.

"Maybe we just took a wrong turn," Oona suggested rather unhelpfully.

"Well, obviously, we did," Asher muttered. "I just don't know where." He pulled out his tablet, angrily tapping at it as if that would suddenly make it work.

"There's no one around here." Quinn gestured to the empty space surrounding us. "Why don't you guys see if you can figure something out, and Atlas and I can go back and see if maybe we can find a sign or something?"

Oona was already a step ahead of her. Atlas had set her heavy bag on the ground, and she knelt beside it and pulled out several of her books. "There's gotta be something in one of these."

"Just don't go too far away," I told Quinn. "I don't want you getting lost or separated from us."

She saluted me, then she and Atlas disappeared around the corner in search of some sign of the correct path.

Asher dropped his bag to the ground and began pacing, cursing as he did. Sweat beaded on his temples, and he rubbed the back of his neck. "I can't believe this."

"It's okay. The sólarsteinn says he's still there." I held it flat on the palm of my hand, and the rainbow prism of light still pointed to the same spot it had been aiming at since we got here. "We'll find him."

Asher shook his head. "But we shouldn't be here for nightfall, and it's getting late. I made us waste the whole day."

I stared up at the cloudless sky, and I was surprised by how different it looked here. When we'd reached the entrance to the Gates it had been early afternoon, with a yellow sun shining brightly. But now the sun appeared to be setting, casting everything in dark oranges and reds, and we hadn't been here all that long.

Did time move differently in the Gates?

I squinted up at the sky, trying to make sense of it. "Is it, though?"

"It'll be dark soon," he persisted, and I didn't bother arguing with that. He might be right, and the Gates was definitely someplace I wouldn't want to be after dark.

"We'll find him. It's not your fault." I put my hand on his arm to comfort him, but he shrugged it off and took a few steps away from me.

"How is it not my fault? The task I was assigned was navigation, and I clearly failed." His voice trembled with barely contained anger.

"None of us knew that technology doesn't work here in the Gates. We're almost there, Asher. We're going to find him."

He exhaled deeply and avoided my gaze, the way he had been all day. "I wish I could be so sure."

"Are you okay? You've seemed . . . off all day."

"It's been a weird day."

I moved closer to him. "Is that all?"

Finally, after a long pause, he lifted his head, and his dark eyes were stormy, as he quietly said, "I saw you last night."

"What?"

He licked his lips. "I saw you dancing with Quinn and kissing her."

My jaw dropped. This was not what I was expecting him to say, and I had no idea how to respond. Definitely not now, but probably not ever.

"You were back at the hotel," I managed.

"I left. I found a safe under the bed for the weapons, and I wanted to see how you were doing . . . and then I saw."

"Oh. I . . . I don't know what to say."

"I was just starting to really care about you, and I thought . . ." His mouth twisted into a grimace, and he looked away from me. "I don't know."

"This isn't the time to talk about this, Asher."

"I know. I just . . ." He rubbed the back of his neck, then looked at me again.

"Hey, guys!" Oona shouted, breaking through the tension. She turned her head to yell down the corridor to the others. "Quinn, Atlas, I may have found something!"

"What?" I asked, going back over to where she knelt in the dirt just as Quinn and Atlas came jogging back over to us.

"What'd you find?" Atlas asked, wiping away the sweat on his brow with the back of his arm.

Oona tapped the page in the old book splayed open before her. "It says here that all roads lead from the Merchants of Death, which is the name of that awful market back there, so we just have to go back there and try again."

Asher cursed under his breath again, and Quinn groaned. None of us was looking forward to heading back to the market. The path from there had been wonderfully uneventful—we'd seen hardly a creature or a demon along the way, and that had suited us all just fine.

"Maybe we should just head out and find a place outside of the Gates to camp for the night, and try again tomorrow," Atlas suggested.

"But I don't really think it's that late. I think we—" I began, but the sound of wings flapping and a familiar squawking interrupted me.

There, perched on the edge of the wall, was a huge raven, with the setting sun shimmering off its black feathers. The bird tilted its head at me, and somehow I knew this was the same raven I'd seen before. The one that had been following me around.

"That raven." I pointed up at it. "I know that raven."

"What do you mean, you know that raven? How do you know that raven?" Oona asked, incredulous.

"I just do," I replied as the bird started hopping down the wall away from us. "I think we should follow it."

"What are you talking about?" Quinn asked.

"I'm gonna follow it," I decided just as the bird took flight.

"Malin, that doesn't make sense," Quinn said, trying to reason with me, but there wasn't time to argue before I lost sight of the bird. The raven was flying on ahead, so I took off after it, and I didn't wait to see if anyone else was following.

FIFTY-TWO

───◆───

As the raven flew overhead, guiding me through the winding paths, the walls around me grew higher and higher, until I realized that they weren't actually walls at all. They were large pyramidesque structures that soared toward the reddening sky above, and homes were carved into the sides, like cliffside pueblos.

My focus was on the raven and making sure I didn't lose sight of it, but I heard the others running behind me. I quickly looked back over my shoulder and saw that all four of them were behind me.

When I glanced over at the homes built into the towering pyramids, I saw that demons were leering at us from their windows and doorways and narrow balconies. I could almost feel their eyes burrowing into me, and I ran faster, afraid of what would happen if all the inhabitants decided to descend the long staircases after us.

While all of the Gates had a putrid stench, as I neared the end of the stretch of pyramids I noticed the smell growing more intense.

It wasn't just sulfuric anymore—it was moldy and earthy. And beneath that was a pronounced sweetness, sickeningly so, like apples and berries left to rot in the sun.

It was the scent of death and decay.

The raven cawed loudly, soaring ahead of me, and I raced around a corner and stopped in my tracks. I was in front of the Bararu Mutanu Ossuary.

At first glance, it looked like an average chapel built centuries ago, except all the flourishes, every single detail of them, from the archway to the seal of Kurnugia on the wall, were made entirely out of bones. Skulls and femurs—both from mortals and immortals—decorated every inch. The architecture was impeccable, and it would've been rather beautiful if it wasn't so macabre.

"Holy shit," Quinn said breathlessly as she and the others caught up with me. "What is this place?"

"It's the ossuary," Asher explained. "It's the heart of the Gates, and below it is the entrance to Kurnugia."

We were all so enamored with the skeletal edifice that none of us noticed the beautiful woman standing in front of it—not until the hulking albino wolf at her side let out a guttural growl.

"Easy, Surma," she commanded the beast gently, her voice lilting with an unfamiliar accent, and her blue eyes settled on us. "You look lost. Perhaps I can help you?"

Her gown—made of gauzy, half-decayed rags—ruffled in a light breeze, and part of it had slid down off her shoulder. Her pale skin was mottled gray and blue in places, with the dark lines of her veins visible underneath.

As she walked toward us, taking slow steps, she brushed her fine blond hair out of her face, and I realized that scent of death was coming directly from her. Oona and Asher recoiled from her stench.

"You're Kalma," I said to her, remembering what I'd learned

from textbooks. The demigoddess who guarded the passage to the underworld was renowned for her odor.

"I am." She batted her lashes, unfazed. "Why are you here?"

"Are you sure this is the right place?" Oona asked, sounding almost desperately hopeful that we wouldn't have to travel past a goddess of death into a building made of bones.

But the raven had perched on a skull sitting just above the doorway, so I knew this was exactly where we were supposed to be.

"We need to go inside," I said firmly.

"I can't grant you passage in there," Kalma replied, sounding disinterested in the whole affair. "Kurnugia is no place for mortals."

"We're not going to Kurnugia," I explained, hoping to avoid a confrontation if I could. "We only want to go inside the ossuary. There's a draugr inside there that we need to find."

"Those that are inside are allowed in by invitation only, and I am certain that no one invited you."

I stood my ground, holding my head high. "You can let us in, or we will go in by force."

Kalma offered me an amused smile. "I have no fear of you."

The wolf charged first, lunging toward us, and Atlas moved quickly, swinging at it with his mace. The spiked ball collided with Surma, who let out an angry growl as he flew into the building.

Kalma may have looked young and harmless, but when she threw a punch, Quinn went flying backward and landed heavily in the dirt. I barely ducked out of the way of her next attack.

While Atlas dealt with the demon wolf, Oona crouched beside Quinn, making sure she was okay, but Quinn was up in a flash, wiping the blood from her lip and charging in to help Atlas. Oona began rummaging through her knapsack for anything that could help in the fight, leaving me and Asher to handle Kalma.

I didn't want to use the dagger and risk breaking it, not before

I used it on Tamerlane, and I wasn't sure how well Sigrún would work against a goddess of death, so that left me fighting hand-to-hand. When I swung at her, Kalma grabbed my fist and stopped it, grinning at me as she squeezed my hand. She was bending my wrist backward, making me kneel before her. My bones were hard to break, but it wouldn't take much more from her before my arm snapped.

Asher pulled Dyrnwyn from its sheath, the black blade glinting under the crimson sky, and swung at Kalma. He connected with her arm, and I could see he was using all his might, but the blade barely even broke her skin, sending dark gray blood dripping down her flesh.

She let go of my fist and turned her attention to Asher, letting out an ethereal laugh. "You cannot kill me. I am of death."

I wasn't sure if Kalma was telling the truth or not, but in my experience nothing was completely immortal—it was just that some were harder to kill than others.

"Use the power of the weapon!" I shouted at Asher. "Aim for her head or heart!"

He held the sword with both hands. Asher closed his eyes as Kalma approached—presumably channeling the purity of his intentions into the weapon.

Finally, just when she was upon him, the blade burst into white-hot flames, and Asher swung with all his might. Her dress went up in flames immediately, the fire blackening her skin as it burned. Kalma let out an agonized scream that died almost instantly as Asher sliced through her neck.

Her head toppled to the ground, her blue eyes still staring upward and her mouth open in an angry scream as her dark blood poured into the dirt.

Surma—her once-faithful companion—saw his mistress dead

and the sword on fire, and let out a confused yelp before turning tail and running off to hide in the labyrinth.

"You okay?" Asher asked, helping me to my feet.

I nodded. "Let's just get going before somebody else tries to stop us."

FIFTY-THREE

——◆——

"This damned thing won't budge," Quinn grunted as she slammed into the massive arched door that blocked the entrance to the ossuary.

Atlas joined her, and together they hit the door so hard that they knocked a door knocker made of human bones loose and it tumbled to the ground.

"It's enchanted." Oona knelt down in front of the three steps that led up to the door, with her grimoire open. "Like the cabdriver said, the inhabitants are too powerful for anything in the physical world to keep them out, so there has to be magic and spells in place."

"Can you break it and get us in?" Quinn asked, rubbing her shoulder where she'd been crashing into the door.

"Maybe, but you have to shut up and let me read," Oona said.

I stepped back, giving her space, and stared out at the darkening world around me. Kalma's body lay a few feet away, still reeking horribly of death, and I wondered dismally if we'd make it out of here alive. Assuming that we could get into the ossuary, and that we could stop Tamerlane, would the demons that populated the Gates really let us get out unscathed?

"We can do this," Asher said, his voice soft and reassuring beside me, as if reading my thoughts. "We made it this far, we can make it all the way."

I swallowed back my fear. "I hope so."

"How's your wrist?" He gently took my hand in his, as if his touch could heal any broken bones, and the gesture did make me feel a bit better, easing some of my anxiety.

"I can't feel it, really, not now, but I'm sure it'll hurt like hell later," I admitted. The Valkyrie adrenaline had kicked in, so I didn't feel pain the way I usually would.

"I'm sorry about fighting with you earlier. Now's not the time for any of this."

"It's fine," I said hurriedly.

His dark blue eyes met mine. "I just want you to know that, no matter what happens here today, I truly care for you, and everything will be all right."

"Everything will be all right?" I smiled bitterly. "Asher, the world might end."

"It might, but it won't. And you'll be all right."

"How can you say that?" I asked, not understanding where this newfound certainty was coming from.

He shrugged. "It's just something I know."

"How?"

"Remember when I told you about how our ancestors can leave truths in our hearts when we need them most? It's how I knew about you, and as soon as I saw the ossuary, I knew about this. I can feel it, right here." He took my hand, putting it on his chest, right over where his heart pounded steadily. "*You* will be all right, and I need you to remember that."

I shook my head. "Why?" Then the implication of his words hit me. "What about everyone else?"

"I think I got it!" Oona shouted excitedly.

"Malin, Ash, get over here! Let's get this shit done!" Quinn barked.

Asher let go of my hand and jogged back over to them, so I did the same, although I felt more dazed than I had a few moments ago.

When I reached the door, Oona was already pouring vials of a dark liquid around the edge of the door and repeating something in a low voice that I didn't understand.

"What's she saying?" Asher asked.

"I think it's Akkadian, but I don't really know it," Atlas replied, quietly so as not to disturb Oona. "I've just heard Samael speak it around the office from time to time."

"Okay." Oona straightened up and rubbed her hands together. "Let's see if that works."

She took a deep breath and grabbed the door handle—made of bones, just like everything else—and, slowly, the door opened.

FIFTY-FOUR

———◆———

Inside, the ossuary smelled like an old root cellar—all earth and must. The doorway opened into a grand front room, replete with several chandeliers made of bones lighting the large space.

The air was cold, strikingly so after the oppressive heat outside, and it was totally silent. I hadn't really expected this to be a bustling hub of activity, given Kalma's warnings about it being invitation-only and the enchantment on the door. But it appeared totally devoid of life in here.

Off the spacious main hall there were six doorways—all arched with bone.

"Which way?" Oona asked.

The raven flew in through the open door, but this time it didn't appear to plan to direct me where to go. Instead, it landed in the center of the main room and picked indifferently at pebbles on the concrete floor.

Fortunately, I still had the sólarsteinn, so I pulled it out of my pocket. The dim candlelight from the chandeliers managed to do the trick, and after a few moments the prism of light shone through the stone, pointing directly toward the fourth door.

I led the way, and while I was surprised when the raven didn't follow, I didn't let that deter me. The sólarsteinn knew who I was looking for, and I wouldn't stop until I found him.

The corridor was narrow but tall, with bones curving over us on the ceiling. Occasionally a skeletal arm would be hanging down, as if reaching out for us.

Softly—almost eerily—the sound of a piano playing began echoing through the hall. The music grew louder, until finally we came upon a large open door that led into what appeared to be a small bar.

At the far end of the room was a piano, and like everything else in the ossuary, it, too, had been created with bones. The pianist himself was a skeleton, with a few bits of flesh still clinging to his bones, and a large pair of dirty white wings sprouting from his back. As he played, feathers would come free and flutter slowly to the floor.

The bartender appeared to be the same kind of creature as the pianist—all bones with just a few bits of flesh, and the decaying wings on his back. He was pouring a glass for the only patron in the place, who sat at the bar with his back to us.

Though I'd only seen him once in real life, I recognized him. The salt-and-pepper hair. The odd bluish tone of his tawny skin. The hunch of his broad shoulders.

"Stay here," I whispered to my friends as we lingered just outside the entrance to the bar.

"What if you need us?" Oona asked, her dark eyes wide and fearful.

"Just stay right here," I insisted. "If I need you, you'll know. But this is my battle to fight."

Asher put his hand on my arm, stopping me just as I was about to enter the bar. "He killed my mother, too. I'm going in there with you."

I nodded. "Let's finish this."

I walked into the bar first, Asher a step behind me. The pianist continued playing, and the bartender wiped the wooden bar with an old rag, either not noticing or not caring about my or Asher's presence.

"Tamerlane Fayette," I said loudly; neither of the angels of death paid us any mind.

Still with his back to us, Tamerlane took a long drink of red wine from a crystal goblet. "I must admit I'm surprised that you haven't given up by now." Slowly, he turned the barstool around so he faced us. "You know this is pointless, don't you?"

My hand hovered above the dagger on my hip. "You don't know what I'm capable of."

He smirked. "You traveled all this way for nothing. You can't kill me."

"Is that why you're hiding out here?" Asher shot back, his voice dripping with venom.

"I'm not hiding—I'm waiting," Tamerlane corrected him.

I raised an eyebrow. "For us?"

Tamerlane let out a low, joyless laugh. "Don't be so arrogant. For *her*."

"Her who?" I asked.

"The only true queen." Tamerlane gestured vaguely around, to the air, to the floor, as if she were everywhere. "The one who I serve. The one who took me under her wing after your mother left me to live in a world that I no longer belonged in."

"The one who killed your family?" I asked sharply, hoping to hit the same nerve my mother had, just before Tamerlane killed her.

It worked. His smile fell away and he stood up, stepping away from the bar and closer to where Asher and I stood in the center of the room.

"Why do you even want to avenge your mother?" he asked, looking at me directly. "You should hate her for what she did. She's the one that brought this all on."

"I do hate her." It was the first time I'd ever said this aloud, but that didn't make it any less true. I hated Marlow, and I loved her. She had good in her, buried beneath so much bad. But in spite of everything, she was my mother and I was grateful to have called her mine. "But it wasn't for you to decide whether she lived or died."

"Just as it isn't for you to decide who lives and dies, and yet you do it all the time," Tamerlane countered.

"No, I am only following my orders," I insisted.

"As was I!" Tamerlane said, almost jovially, and he motioned between himself and me. "The two of us, all of us, really, we're only pawns in the games of the gods."

"Maybe," I allowed. "But I'm not about to let you win."

"It's already too late. Haven't you been listening?" Tamerlane asked.

"It's never too late," Asher replied with more conviction than I felt.

"I can help you," Tamerlane offered, then motioned toward the door, where Oona, Quinn, and Atlas were waiting just around the corner. "And I can help your friends. Let me put you out of your misery before my queen arrives. Humans won't survive long with what she has planned for this earth."

"We won't let her," Asher said.

Tamerlane looked at the two of us. "Do you think that if she could be stopped I would've let her slaughter my entire family?" Then his dark eyes settled on me. "When your mother failed to slay me, I became a draugr, one of the most powerful beings on earth. And yet, I could not stop the queen. I could only fall in line."

"Everything can be stopped," I told him as I pulled Kalfu's dagger from its sheath. "Even death dies."

"That's how you plan to stop me?" Tamerlane chuckled at the sight of it. "With that tiny little knife?"

"We'll see," I said.

"Let's dance, then, shall we?" He motioned for me to come at him. "I'll make it easy for you."

He spread his arms wide, leaving himself exposed, and while I couldn't be certain that it wasn't a trap, I had to take my chance. I walked right up to him, taking careful deliberate steps, and he merely smiled down at me as I drove the dagger straight into his heart.

Tamerlane laughed again, more boisterously this time. "I barely even felt it." He reached down to pull the dagger out, but his expression faltered. "I told you I couldn't . . ." He stumbled back, his skin growing more ashen. "I couldn't . . ."

Then he fell to the floor, slumped back against the bar, and his black eyes met mine, filled with confused indignation. "I can't die," he whispered, and then his head lolled to the side and he fell silent.

The raven suddenly flew into the room, cawing like mad, and Quinn, Oona, and Atlas raced in after it. The entire bar began to rumble. Dirt pushed up from the floor, like giant gophers were pushing their way to the surface, but the reality was much worse.

Skeletal hands broke free, followed by entire bodies. A dozen or more reanimated skeletons came up through the floor, each one of them brandishing a rusty sword.

FIFTY-FIVE

❖

You really thought you could just waltz in here and kill him, and it would be that easy?" Quinn asked, standing behind me as the skeletons circled around us.

"No," I admitted. "But I had hoped."

The five of us stood with our backs together, and once the skeletons finally stopped pouring out of the earth, they charged at us. Sigrún, my sword, began glowing dull purple, and I felt the surge of Valkyrie rushing through me.

I knocked them back just as quickly as they came at me, slicing through their bones like they were made of ash. For every one I killed, two more rose up in their place, but I kept fighting, moving on instinct, as I dodged and sliced until their numbers finally seemed to be dwindling.

Behind me, I heard Oona cry out in pain, but I couldn't let that distract me—if I wanted her to survive this, I needed to stop the skeletons from overtaking us. From the corner of my eye, I saw

Quinn taking three skeletons down in one fell swoop, and I heard Atlas grunting as he fought.

Finally, the skeletons lay in a pile of bones around us, with mounds of freshly overturned dirt beneath them. And still, the bartender kept wiping down the bar, and the pianist kept on playing, undisturbed by the battle for life and death that had been raging around them.

Oona was crouched down in the skeletal pile with a bloodied arm, so I rushed over to her.

"Are you okay?" I asked.

"What?" She glanced at her arm, as if she hadn't even noticed she was wounded. "Yeah, I'm fine." And then she immediately turned her attention back to the rusted sword she was holding. "There's an inscription on their weapons, and I know I've seen it somewhere."

As Oona studied the blade, I unzipped her bag and pulled out a gauze bandage.

"Well, Tamerlane's dead, so we should probably just get out of here before more terrible things happen," I suggested as I wrapped up her arm.

"Atlas?" Oona asked, too preoccupied to listen to me. "You said you knew some Akkadian?"

"Not really," he said, but he bent over to inspect the sword. "But that definitely looks like the Akkadian writing I've seen."

The room began rumbling again, harder this time, and the bones around us rattled.

"Oona, can we do this later?" I asked, getting to my feet. "We should get out of here."

"I know, I know." She ran her hands over the encryption on the blade. "This just doesn't feel over to me."

"Okay, we need to get out of here," Quinn commanded as the quaking intensified, and the raven squawked again before taking off down the hall in the opposite direction from which we'd come, away from the ossuary. "*Now!*"

I grabbed Oona's good arm and yanked her to her feet. She carried the sword with her as we ran out to the hallway just in time to see the ceiling collapsing. Our path back the way we'd come was blocked, so the only way out now was to keep following the long hallway to wherever it might lead.

"Hurry!" Atlas shouted, not that he needed to. We were already running, and the tremors stopped as soon as the ceiling caved in.

The hallway quickly stopped feeling like any kind of formal structure but rather like a cave. Bones were still scattered about, but less in a decorative way. Complete skeletons lay sprawled, as if someone had lain bodies out for everyone to see—as a sacrifice, maybe—and that's as they had been ever since. They had become calcified, which made them look thicker and glittery, like they were made of crystal.

Opaque stalactites hung from the ceiling, like icy teeth reaching out for us, and still we walked deeper into the cave. Somewhere ahead of us, light was shining, casting light down the tunnel. The cold air—which had gotten frigid—started to warm as we walked.

Finally, we saw the mouth of the cave, opening to a large pond filled with bright aquamarine water. Above it, the cave opened to the sun, which shone brightly on us. Not red or dark the way it had been before we entered the ossuary, but like full daylight.

Quinn walked to the edge of the lake first and stared up. The walls surrounding it weren't that high, and the far wall on the other side of the water even had a mossy staircase carved into the side.

"Well, it looks like we're going for a swim," she said. "Assuming we all want to get out of here."

"Do you have any idea where this will lead?" I asked Asher.

He shook his head, crouching down to inspect water. "I'm not sure. The maps I looked at never showed this place." He cupped some water in his hand, smelling it. "I think this is fresh water."

"We should rest for a moment," Atlas said. "But then we should leave as fast as we can."

Oona sat cross-legged on the ground, still running her fingers over the rusty sword as if it could channel all the answers to her, when she excitedly yelled, "I got it! It's a name!"

"A name?" Quinn asked. "Of who?"

Oona rubbed her forehead, concentrating. "One of the underworld goddesses. It's something. . . . Shush? Or Rash? Something?"

"Ereshkigal?" I whispered, as if saying her name louder would somehow summon her.

Oona snapped her fingers. "Yes! That's it!"

The hair on the back of my neck stood up, and I realized dismally that I should've known sooner. The past few days, I had been seeing her face everywhere—her eyes following me from posters on the street, entrancing me at the hotel, even waiting for me with open arms at the Merchants of Death.

It had all seemed like coincidence, like nothing to pay any mind to, but she'd slowly been raising herself in the consciousness of everyone as she gained power. She was an obscure underworld goddess, banished to Kurnugia centuries ago. Why should her name be on everyone's tongue?

Because she wanted it there. Because her underlings were working to prepare the world for her, to ready us all to bow down and say her name, so they plastered her face everywhere, her name on everything, for us all to see and remember.

The water in the lake began to ripple and quake before us. Everyone moved backward, hurrying away from the edge and into the cave, except for me. Because I knew it was already too late.

The crystal-clear lake, which seemed like an oasis in the harsh world of the Gates, was actually something far more sinister. It was the mouth to Kurnugia, a watery portal through which immortals could pass from one world to the next.

FIFTY-SIX

———— ✦ ————

A man arose slowly, breathing in deeply as his head first broke through the water. He had two massive horns from the sides of his head, but beyond that he was handsome, if not slightly unremarkable, with dark waves of hair dripping down his back. When he shook his head, droplets of water flew around him like a halo.

He smiled as he moved forward, and the dark patch of hair on his chest trailed down his bronze skin . . . and that's when I saw he was no man at all. From his waist down, he was all bull, with four muscular legs covered in thick black fur, and hefty cloven hooves trudging through the water toward us.

"I didn't expect a welcoming party to greet me when I finally arrived," he said, running a hand through his thick hair.

"Who are you?" Quinn demanded from behind me, but I already knew the answer.

I recognized him from paintings and textbooks. Often depicted in the background behind Ereshkigal or sometimes seated at her side, he was her consort, her lover, her partner in crime. Gugalanna, the Bull of Hell.

"I have been called many, many names over the centuries," he admitted. "But the one I am most known by is Gugalanna, and since we are going to be friends . . ."

He paused in his own introduction to give his most winning smile and motion toward us all as he towered over us. In a conspiratorial tone, he leaned down and said, "I can already tell we're going to be bonded together for a long time. I mean, this is a special moment, isn't it?"

Then he straightened up, still grinning, and finished with, "Well, since we'll be friends, you can call me Guga."

"Guga?" Quinn asked with an arched eyebrow.

"I know, I know," he said with a sigh. "It's a terrible name, but my parents were so last millennium, so what are you gonna do?"

"What do you want with us?" I asked.

"Right now I'm just checking out this ragtag group we've got here." With his hands on his hips, Gugalanna looked from one to the other of us. "So what have we got here? Valkyrie, Valkyrie, mortal but . . . powerful? Yes? Sorceress, maybe?"

"Sorceress-in-training," Oona corrected him, standing a bit taller.

"Son of a Valkyrie, son of a Valkyrie," he continued down the line, looking rather impressed. "Wow. We've really got a lot of great blood here. I feel like I won the lottery, I truly do, and I cannot thank you all enough for making this so much easier for me. I was afraid I was going to have to go traipsing off into your world, knocking on everyone's doors and asking if they have any old Valkyries just lying around.

"But see, Resh—that's what I call my wife, Ereshkigal—she got this great idea," he went on. "She said we could just bait a trap for some Valkyries, and it would be far easier than fighting them on their own turf, where it would be nearly impossible for us to take them all on at once, and we just had to wait for one to screw up. All we needed was a little mistake, one tiny crack in the wall of perfect order that surrounds your world—like, say, a Valkyrie creating a draugr."

My mouth felt dry, and a familiar tension grew around my heart. He was talking about Marlow, and Tamerlane. Tamerlane had warned me that we were all pawns, and I had believed him, but I hadn't realized the full extent of it, and I don't think he had, either.

Somehow, they'd gotten Marlow to spare Tamerlane, upsetting the balance so they could get an upper hand and grow more powerful as things began to unravel on earth. And then they had used Tamerlane himself as bait to bring us here.

FIFTY-SEVEN

And you know, I'll be honest," Gugalanna was going on. "It took so long, I started to doubt that it was even going to happen. I was just saying to her, 'Resh, my darling, you are the smartest woman I know, but this just isn't happening.' But then, it did! And boy, do I feel foolish.

"So who was it that screwed up?" he asked, his eyes bouncing over us. "It wasn't any of you, was it? No. It was one of your mothers." Then his gaze settled on me. "Yours, I'm guessing, based on that pissed-off but guilty look on your face."

I could hear my blood pounding in my ears, and my muscles ached to fight, but I kept myself in check. I forced myself to stay calm, to wait, even as Gugalanna admitted that everything terrible, everything that threatened to end the world, was his and Ereshki-gal's doing.

"You made my mother do that? How?" I asked, barely keeping my voice even.

"We didn't make her, exactly, but . . ." He waved his hands.

"You know what, I'm already saying too much. I can't give away all the secrets about how Resh works, because her plan is still in action. Don't get me wrong—it's almost done. She's almost ready to come back up here, but not quite. So I better not spoil things just yet."

"What are you doing here?" Oona asked. "What exactly do you want with us?"

"I want nothing with you, actually," he said, gesturing to Oona. "I'm just getting one of the last things on Resh's list. The blood of a child of a Valkyrie."

He let that sink in for a beat before continuing. "It can be from either a son or a daughter, but in our experience, the daughters are harder to control, and I've already had a long day, so I think I'll go with one of you two boys. I don't care which. You can fight among yourselves, if you'd like."

I drew Sigrún and moved, blocking Asher. "You're not taking any of us!"

"Really? You're going to try to fight me on this?" Gugalanna pretended to pout. "I thought we could all be friends."

"You really thought we'd just let you kill one of us without a fight?" Quinn asked, drawing her own sword.

"Whoa, whoa! Who said anything about killing?" He shook his head. "I'm just taking him down to Kurnugia, and, well, we've got some stuff planned for him that I'm really not at liberty to discuss right now."

The cave began to rumble, making the stalactites above us tremble and the water in the lake ripple around Gugalanna's hooves.

"All right, all right," Gugalanna shouted toward the water, as if someone down below could hear him. "The missus says I'm taking too long, so I better get back down there. These portals don't stay open forever, you know."

I charged at him first, but he kicked me back with his powerful legs like I was nothing. He was much larger than us, and too strong—even for a Valkyrie like me. We didn't stand a chance.

As I scrambled to my feet again, he'd already sent Quinn and Atlas flying into the cave walls. Asher was standing his ground, attempting to fight him off with his flaming sword, while Oona pulled a potion out of her bag.

She'd just started reciting an incantation when Gugalanna clicked his tongue at her before turning to kick her with his back legs. I yelled for her to get out of the way, but his massive hoof was already colliding with her chest.

Oona went soaring through the air before crashing down at the edge of the shore, her head lolling to the side in the water.

I wanted to go to her, but Gugalanna had just picked up Asher, and he looked like a rag doll in Guga's massive arms. With Sigrún in my right hand and Rök the shield in my other, I ran at the bull centaur.

I managed to get in one good hit—my blade slid across his leg hard enough to draw blood—and he let out a howl of pain. He knocked me down, and stomped on the shield with all his might. It bent and groaned, but it didn't give.

Then he let out an irritated snort, with Asher held prisoner in his arms, and turned and ran out into the lake.

"*No!*" I screamed, running into the water after them. "Asher!"

The water began swirling, like a whirlpool rising up into a tornado, and Quinn chased after me, grabbing me before I got sucked into it, too.

"Malin, stop!" she shouted. "They're gone! You can't go after them! They're gone!"

FIFTY-EIGHT

———◆———

Oona lay on the lakeshore with water lapping onto her, and her breath came out in loud, shaky rasps. Atlas knelt beside her, rummaging through her giant bag.

"The blue vial," Oona whispered, pointing weakly at her bag.

"Oona!" I rushed to her side. She looked at me through half-closed lids.

"I'm getting her something for the pain." Atlas momentarily glanced up at me from his task. "How are you doing? Can you make it out of here?"

I was bruised and scraped, but otherwise fine. Atlas and Quinn looked about the same—dirty and bloody in a few spots, but they would survive. Oona, on the other hand, wasn't looking good.

Atlas finally found the vial Oona was asking for, and carefully he held it to her lips. As she drank it down eagerly, he looked at me with worried eyes.

"We need to get out of here, fast, if we want her to make it," Atlas said in a hushed voice.

Quinn was already loading up her gear and adding Atlas's smaller knapsack on top of hers. "We'll have to swim across and use those stairs over there." She nodded toward the mossy staircase on the other side of the lake. "Atlas, will you be able to carry Oona?"

He got to his feet, holding Oona's limp body in his arms. Her head lolled against his chest as she let out another painful breath. He waded out into the lake, and when it became too deep for him to walk, he floated on his back, with Oona lying on his chest, and swam backward toward the stairs.

Quinn went after them, but I waited at the edge, staring down at the water where Asher had disappeared with Gugalanna. Only moments ago the water had been swirling and rising upward in a supernatural tornado, but now the water was still, aside from the ripples Atlas caused as he made his escape.

"Malin, we have to go." Quinn stopped, with the water up to her waist, and looked back at me. "Oona needs medical attention, and you can't go to Kurnugia. Gugalanna said the portal doesn't stay open forever, and even if it did, there's no way you would survive down there on your own."

I swallowed back my sadness and followed Quinn out into the water. I hated that she was right, that there was nothing I could do for Asher right now, but my only chance at rescuing him was getting out of here and finding help.

The trek up the stairs was more arduous than I had expected because the moss made them slippery, but we all managed to make it. At the top was an amazing view of the Gates of Kurnugia—we could see how the maze stretched out around us, bending and winding around pyramids and dead ends.

Quinn ripped a page from one of Oona's books and hurriedly drew a map, sketching what we could see around us with a stick of charcoal Oona had in her bag. From where we were, we could see the fastest route to the plaza, and from the plaza it was a relatively straight shot to the entrance.

It was a rather sheer descent down the outside of the cavern to the land below, but sliding down on our backs made for quick travel. Once we were all on level ground, Quinn got her map ready, and we raced toward the exit with the sun slowly setting behind us.

FIFTY-NINE

◆

As I sat on the bench outside the hospital in nearby Caana City, I watched as a steady stream of patients came in. Somehow, even with head wounds and cardiac arrests ambling in past me, the night air felt strangely still. Above me the stars twinkled, shining brighter here than they did back home in the city.

"Mind if I join you?" Quinn asked quietly.

She was backlit by the bright fluorescent glow from the hospital doors, giving her an ethereal glow as she stared down uncertainly at me. She had a few stitches above her left eye and a bandage around her forearm, but otherwise she'd made it out of the Gates okay.

I motioned to the bench beside me. "Go ahead."

"It sounds like Oona is going to pull through," she said once she sat down, close enough to me that our thighs were brushing up against each other.

"Yeah, the doctors said she needed to rest now, but I should be able to see her soon. So that's good news, at least."

"You don't look happy about it."

I breathed in deeply. "I'm happy about Oona. I really am."

"But you're thinking about him."

The lump in my throat grew, and the tears I'd been fighting off since we had left the Gates stung my eyes. "I feel like I let him down. I should've fought harder or done more."

"Gugalanna was too powerful."

"Then I shouldn't have let him come with us," I insisted.

"He had every right to be there, same as you."

"No, I should've—"

"Malin, stop," Quinn said sharply, so I looked up at her. "You couldn't have saved him, okay?"

Part of me knew that was true, but I just kept replaying all the moments over and over again. How when he kissed me, he made everything feel better, and when he put my hand to his chest, promising me I would be all right but knowing that he wouldn't.

I hadn't realized it right away, but that's what he was doing. He'd been given the horrific truth that he wasn't going to make it out, maybe so he could prepare himself or leave, but instead of worrying about himself, he only tried to make sure I would be okay with it.

"He knew I couldn't save him, and he went anyway," I said in a shaky voice.

"What are you talking about?"

"Something he said. . . ." I trailed off as tears spilled down my cheeks.

"Wow." Quinn sounded awestruck. "I didn't realize. . . . Were you in love with him?"

"No." I wiped roughly at my tears with the palm of my hand. "Don't be ridiculous. Valkyries can't fall in love."

"What are you talking about? Of course they can."

I shook my head. "No, we can care about stuff, yeah, and we can love things, but we can't be *in love*. It's not possible."

"Are you serious?" Quinn asked, and I looked over to see her gaping at me.

"Yeah. That's what Marlow always told me, and I've never known of any Valkyries in any kind of serious relationship, so . . . it makes sense."

She leaned back on the bench, looking in shock. "Damn, Malin. Is this why you broke up with me?"

"No. I mean . . . I guess, maybe, it was part of it. I just didn't see the point if we . . ."

"Malin, I loved you." A pained smile had spread across her face. "I was absolutely completely in love with you. So I *know* that Valkyries can fall in love."

I lowered my eyes and swallowed hard. "I . . . I don't know what to say to that."

Quinn sighed and then stood. "You don't have to say anything. I'm gonna go see how Atlas is doing."

SIXTY

---◆---

I stayed out on the bench a few minutes longer, planning to get myself under control before going back inside to check on Oona.

All night patients had been heading into the hospital, but for a few minutes there was a lapse. The entrance was quiet. But quickly I realized it was too silent. I couldn't hear any cars or anyone talking.

Far off in the distance I heard crickets and howler monkeys, but that was it. Everything had gone away.

I stood, preparing to go see if the hospital was the hive of activity I knew it should be, or see if perhaps I had head trauma that was blocking out sounds. Then I heard a bird—the flapping of wings and a loud caw.

The raven appeared out of the night sky and landed on a light post in front of me.

"What do you want with me?" I shouted up at it. "Why are you following me? I thought you were helping me, but you disappeared when I needed you back there! Why are you doing this to me?"

"I'm sorry I couldn't be of more help," a deep voice, thick with a British accent, came from the left of me, and I jumped back in surprise.

While I had been focused on the raven, I hadn't noticed a man materializing outside with me. He was tall and broad-shouldered, larger than Atlas, even, with dark skin, and his left eyelid was withered shut. He wore an impeccably tailored suit with a charcoal-gray duster over it, and he stepped slowly toward me.

"That's my raven, Muninn." He gestured to the bird. "I sent him to watch over you and help you, but unfortunately there was only so much I could do to intervene. My hands are tied in a lot of this."

"Who are you?" I asked, taking a step back from him. "And what do you want?"

"I'm your boss," he said with a smile. "Odin."

I gasped. "Holy hell." I ran my hand through my hair and tried to figure out if I should bow or kneel or what was the proper protocol when meeting with a god of his caliber. I'd never met a Vanir god, and from everything I had learned, they almost never came to earth anymore.

"I can help you get your friend back," he said, drawing me out of my panic to look up at him. "All is not lost for him, not yet. But I need you to do something for me."

Even though I knew I would do whatever it took to get Asher back, I waited a beat before asking, "What?"

"I need you to help me take on Ereshkigal. We must stop her before the entire world belongs to Kurnugia."

Since there didn't seem to be much of a choice—I couldn't exactly let the world end, and I wanted to save Asher—I nodded once. "What do you need from me?"

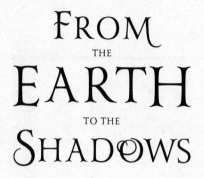

FROM
THE
EARTH
TO THE
SHADOWS

This book is dedicated to my cat, Squeak—
for without her insistence on sleeping on my keyboard
while I worked I would've written this book twice as fast,
but it would've been half as much fun.

Kurnugia: *noun / kər-noo-gē-uh/ from Sumerian, literally "earth of no return," referring to the underworld where immortals exist after death.*

THE VALKYRIE PROCLAMATION

Baldur, the Prince of Men, My Shining Son—
The unrest in Vanaheimr[1] has grown tenfold since last we spoke.
Much has been made of the recent bloodshed between humans,
led into battle[2] against each other by the Great Bull[3] against
the Assaku. Thousands of lives have been lost—innocent babes
ripped from their mothers' breasts and slaughtered in the name of
immortals who care so little for those that follow them.
  It has been many long days since I created the Valkyries, and

---

1 Vanaheimr is the location of the gods; it is generally considered to exist on a plane beyond ours.

2 The battle here is believed to be in the former city of Nawar, now known as the burial site in Tell Brak. This is one of only two written accounts referencing this particular battle, so not much is known, but thousands of bodies have been unearthed in recent history, concurring with Odin's story of a bloody fight. Some historians think this might be the first ever recorded war, but more evidence is needed for this author to confidently state that.

3 "The Great Bull" is the common name for the bull centaur Gugalanna.

aided by your Mother's[4] gift of Sight,[5] the earth seemed as if it had been eased into an order; a wary but stable peace among men and the immortals that live beside them.

But now it seems that all my effort has been in vain, since the humans have proved all too willing to follow any god[6] that asks them to. Many of my fellow Vanir gods have become fearful that our laws favor the mortals too much.

Are they correct? Am I too blind and stubborn to see? Tell me, my dear son, what do you make of the rules?

The laws that govern the land are simple but clear:[7]

— *All immortals of enough reverence and age to be given the title of Vanir gods are allowed access into Vanaheimr.*
— *All other immortals are allowed to walk the earth until their time has come.*
— *Their time is to be decided by the Vanir gods and the Eralim, and the Eralim will pass the orders down to the Valkyries.*
— *The Valkyries are endowed with specific gifts granted by the gods, but they must only use them as directed by the Eralim. They are to end the immortals' life on earth since time itself cannot.*
— *The Valkyries are mortals, so they live and die as humans do.*
— *Once an immortal's time has been decided, they are sent to Kurnugia, where they will stay until they cease to exist.*

---

4 Frigg is the mother of Baldur and the wife of Odin; this letter was written over a thousand years before her long slumber.

5 "Sight" here refers to precognition and Frigg's ability to see all of time.

6 The actual word Odin used here was *mar ilu*, which means "sons of the gods," but I and the other scholars at Ravenswood Academy thought the word *god* without the modifier of either *demi* or *Vanir* would be more appropriate.

7 This is the first known writing of the official tenets of the Valkyries' role with the gods and Eralim.

— *Once mortals die, they are put in the earth, from which they will never rise again.*

— *The dead must remain dead, and the Vanir gods must remain in Vanaheimr.*

I know my beloved Frigg can see far into the future, long past the time when even she and I are both gone, but she cannot tell me what to do or what is to become of the earth if this continues. Many of the Vanir gods believe it is time to let the humans go. They may be but frail and mortal, but they more than make up for these deficits in numbers and determination; why, a man spawned over a dozen children in a single year's time, while your mother has only borne one in the past three centuries.

Their rapid procreation and zealous allegiance have become a matter of grave concern here in Vanaheimr. Hades,[8] in particular, seems to fear the humans banding together, but he is not the only one to propose that we do away with Valkyries and let mankind fall into extinction, the way the kirin and the dinosaurs[9] have. The rallying cry against mortals has begun, and I fear that soon it will be deafening.

I have come up with a plan, one that I am certain you won't approve of. All the years you've walked the earth have given you a profound love for the humans and all living creatures. Your kindness and love are what I am most proud to see that your mother has passed on to you. Of the many gifts she has, those are her most wonderful.

But this latest attack, with Gugalanna leading so many humans to their deaths, has led me to one conclusion: we must create an

---

8 Before becoming a prominent figure in Kurnugia, Hades lived in Vanaheimr with the other Vanir gods.

9 Odin only specifies a "giant scaled beast," but other contextual clues suggest this is a reference to dinosaurs, although other extinct reptilian-like beasts cannot be ruled out.

indisputable way to stop any man or god in their tracks. With the help of the other gods, I have nearly completed a most perfect weapon (if a weapon can be referred to as perfection). With one prick, it snuffs the light from any living thing, and there is no life beyond it—no respite in Vanaheimr or Kurnugia.

My dear, sweet son, I know you will not approve. But it is my hope that the mere existence of such a weapon will be enough to hold them in place. These young gods have no fear of us, the elders watching it all from above. Without fear, we cannot control them, and to allow humans and immortals to collude together, running all over this earth, can only lead to more death and destruction.

Worse still, I worry that Vanaheimr would not be far behind, if both the earth and Kurnugia were to fall.

I am doing what I feel that I must to do. The only thing I can do to protect you, your mother, all the gods, and even the humans from themselves. I hope that you understand, and if you do not, I hope that you can forgive me.

Your father,
Odin

—ODIN, THE VANIR GOD,
IN A LETTER TO HIS SON, WHICH WOULD BECOME KNOWN
AS THE VALKYRIE PROCLAMATION, WRITTEN CIRCA 3750 BCE

NOTE ON LETTER

———◆———

This letter has been modified for clarity and translated from the Olde Language of the gods into English. The letterpress edition of *The Proclamations of the Gods*, edited by Professor Cashel Wu, is available through the Evig Riksdag and Ravenswood Academy. Copyright © 2133 by Riksdag/Ravenswood Press. All rights reserved. Printed in the United States of America.

Because I could not stop for Death—
He kindly stopped for me—
The Carriage held but just Ourselves—
And Immortality.

—EMILY DICKINSON

ONE

———— ◆ ————

The air that fogged around me was thick enough that I could taste it—earthy and wet, with a trace of salt. It stuck to my skin, which was already slick with sweat, and that only seemed to attract more insects. They buzzed around me, leaving burning little bites in my flesh. I wanted to swat them off, but I couldn't. I had to stay perfectly still, or the Kalanoro would spot me too soon.

The oversaturation of green in the jungles of Panama had been a strange adjustment from the smog and bright lights of the city. Out here, it was an endless emerald sea: the plants and trees, the rivers, were all varying shades of green—even the sky was blotted out by a thick canopy of leaves.

This wasn't where I wanted to be, crouched motionless in the mud with a giant millipede crawling over my foot. Not when Asher was still gone, held captive in Kurnugia by the underworld goddess Ereshkigal and her mad centaur boyfriend, Gugalanna. Not when the fate of the world felt heavy on my shoulders, with Ereshkigal attempting an uprising that would unleash the underworld on earth.

It had only been three days since I'd gone to the Gates of Kurnugia, along with Oona, Quinn, Asher, and Atlas to aid me. I'd wanted to avenge my mother—and I had killed the draugr that had killed her—but all of that may have set off a chain of events that would bring about the end of days.

And I had lost the guy I . . . well, not loved. Not yet. But I cared about him. All I wanted to do was rescue him. But I couldn't. There was too much at stake. I couldn't let my heart get the best of me. I had to hold it together, and follow my orders.

After Gugalanna had pulled Asher down into the underworld where I could not follow, the rest of us had gone to Caana City in Belize. It was the safest city near the Gates of Kurnugia, and Oona needed medical intervention to survive. She was on the mend now, and that's why I had left her behind, with Quinn and Atlas.

I didn't want to risk losing them the way I had Asher, and I was on a special assignment, coming directly from the Valkyries' highest authority—Odin.

Odin had found me outside of the hospital where Oona was being treated. I had never met him before, and, like most of the Vanir gods, he changed his appearance to suit his needs, so I hadn't recognized him.

He towered over me in his tailored suit, with his left eyelid withered shut. He had a deep rumble of a voice, with a softly lilting accent, and a grim expression. His large raven, Muninn, had been watching over me, but when I tried to press him for a reason why, he had told me that there wasn't time to explain.

"I need you to go deep into the heart of the jungle, where no man dares to live," Odin explained, as we had stood in the eerily silent parking lot in Caana City. "You must retrieve something for me."

"Why can't you retrieve it yourself?" I asked bluntly. I wasn't being rude, but the reality was that Odin was a powerful god, and I was just a young mortal Valkyrie-in-training. He had far more knowledge and power than I could ever hope to have.

"I'm not allowed to meddle in the affairs of humans or any of the other earthly beings," Odin clarified.

"But . . ." I trailed off, gathering the courage to ask, "What is this *you're doing now, then? Isn't directing me to get something for you the same as meddling?"*

A sly smile played on his lips, and he replied, "There are a few loopholes, and I think it's best if I take advantage of one now. If you want to save your friend, and everyone else that matters to you, you need to act quickly."

"What is it that you need me to get?" I asked, since I didn't seem to have a choice.

"The Valhallan cloak," he explained. "It was stolen centuries ago by a trickster god—I honestly can't remember which one anymore—and he hid it with the Kalanoro of Panama."

"The Kalanoro?" I groaned reflexively. Having dealt with them before, I already knew how horrible they were.

If piranhas lived on land, they would behave a lot like the Kalanoro. They were small primate-like creatures, standing no more than two feet tall, and they vaguely resembled the aye-aye lemur. The biggest differences were that the Kalanoro were tailless, since they lived mostly on the ground, and they had razor-sharp claws on their elongated fingers and a mouth of jagged teeth they used to tear apart the flesh of their prey.

"What is the Valhallan cloak, and how will I find it?" I asked Odin.

"You'll know when you see it. It's an oversized cloak, but the fabric looks like the heavens. The rumors are that the Kalanoro were attracted to the magic of the cloak, though they didn't understand it, so they took it back to their cave," Odin elaborated. "They apparently have been guarding it like a treasure."

"So I have to go into the treacherous jungle, find the man-eating Kalanoro, and steal their favorite possession?" I asked dryly. "No problem."

Which was how I ended up in the jungle, alone, in the heart of Kalanoro country—at least, that's what the nearest locals had purported. In front of me, on the other side of a very shallow but rapidly moving stream, was the mouth of a cave. The cave I hoped was the home of the Kalanoro, but I was waiting to see one for official confirmation.

Sweat slid down my temples, and a large dragonfly flew overhead. The trees around me were a cacophony of sounds—monkeys and frogs and birds and insects of all kinds, talking to one another, warning of danger, and shouting out mating calls.

Back in the city, beings and creatures of all kinds lived among each other, but there were rules. The jungle was not bound by any laws. I was not welcome, and I was not safe here.

I heard the crunch of a branch—too loud and too close to be another insect. I turned my head slowly toward the sound, and I saw movement in the bushes right beside me. Tall dark quills, poking out above the leaves, and I tried to remember if the Kalanoro had any quill-like fur.

I didn't have to wonder for very long because a head poked out of the bushes, appearing to grin at me through a mouthful of jagged fangs and a face like an alien hyena. The leathery green skin, mottled with darker speckles, blended in perfectly with the surroundings, with a mohawk-like row of sharp quills running down its back.

It wasn't a Kalanoro—it was something much worse. I found myself face-to-face with a Chupacabra.

TWO

———◆———

The Chupacabra—much like dolphins, dogs, and quokkas—had the uncanny ability to appear to be smiling. Unlike those contemporaries, there was nothing adorable or friendly about this Chupacabra's smile. It was all serrated teeth, with bits of rotten meat stuck between them, and a black tongue lolling around his mouth.

"You don't want do this," I told the beast softly, even though he probably didn't understand English.

I kept my gaze locked on the Chupacabra, but my hand was at my hip, slowly unsheathing my sword Sigrún. The name came from my ancestors, as had the blade itself. It had been passed down from Valkyrie to daughter for centuries.

Sigrún was a thick blade made of dark purple crystal, so dark it appeared black, but it would glow bright brilliant purple when I was working. It was short and angled, like it had been broken off in battle. Maybe it had—the full history of my blade was unknown to me.

But the handle was a black utilitarian replacement. It had been my mother's gift to me on my eighteenth birthday. Her final gift to me, well over a year ago.

The Chupacabra stared at me with oversized teardrop-shaped eyes and took a step closer to me, letting out a soft rumble of a growl.

Valkyries weren't supposed to kill anyone or anything they were not specifically ordered to kill. The one exception was self-defense. Since I was on an unsanctioned mission into territory I had no business being in, this would all get very messy if I had to kill a Chupacabra.

But the hard truth was that I was beyond worrying about my career as a Valkyrie. I would do whatever I needed to do.

When the Chupacabra lunged at me, I drew my sword without hesitation. Since this wasn't an official "job," my blade didn't glow purple, but it sliced through the leathery hide as easily as I knew it would.

I didn't want to kill the creature if I didn't have to—after all, he was merely going about his life in the jungle. So my first blow was only a warning that left him with a painful but shallow cut across his shoulder.

He let out an enraged howl, causing birds to take flight and all sorts of smaller animals to go rushing deeper into the underbrush. From the corner of my eye, I spotted several Kalanoro darting across the stream back toward their cave. They had been watching me.

The Chupacabra had stepped back from me, but by the determined grin on his face I didn't think he was ready to give up yet. He circled around me, and I turned with him, stepping carefully to keep from slipping in the mud.

"This is stupid," I said, reasoning with the animal. "We should both go our separate ways, and you can go back to eating . . . well, I think you mostly eat the Kalanoro and birds."

Apparently growing tired of my attempts at talking, the Chupacabra snarled and jumped at me again. I dodged out of the way, but he kicked off of the tree behind and instantly dove at me. I didn't move quick enough this time, and he knocked me to the ground.

Fortunately, I fell on my back, with one of his feet pinning me and his claws digging into my shoulder. I put one hand around his long, slender throat, barely managing to hold him back as he gnashed his teeth.

With one of my arms pinned, he was too strong for me, and I

wouldn't be able to throw him off. As his thick saliva dripped down onto me, I knew there was only one thing I could do if I wanted to survive.

I drove my sword up through his breastbone, using all my might. He howled in pain, but only for a second, before falling silent and slumping forward onto me. I crawled out from underneath him, now covered in mud and his thick green blood, along with my own fresh red blood springing from the wounds on my bare arms and shoulder.

In the mouth of the cave across from me, two dozen or so beady little green eyes glowed. The Kalanoro were crouched down, watching me. So much for the element of surprise.

My hair had come free from the braid I'd been wearing, and it stuck to my forehead. I reached up to brush it back, and the Kalanoro let out a squawk of surprise, and one darted off into the woods.

That's when I realized the Kalanoro were afraid of me. I glanced over at the Chupacabra—the Kalanoro's number-one predator, and I had left it dead and bleeding into the stream. They were right to fear me.

I tested my new hypothesis and stepped closer to the mouth of the cave, and the Kalanoro screeched and scattered. Most of them ran into the woods, but a few went deeper into the cave. My fight with the Chupacabra had left them far more skittish than I had anticipated, and I doubted that I would need my sword for them, so I sheathed Sigrún.

I unhooked my asp baton from my hip and pulled my flashlight out from my gear bag. I took a deep breath and walked toward the cave, hoping that this wasn't a trap where they would all pounce and devour me the second I stepped inside.

As I walked into the cave, I heard them chittering and scurrying, but it reminded me more of a rat infestation than man-eating primates. Once my eyes had adjusted to the darkness, I shone the flashlight around the narrow cavern. The beam of light flashed on a few pairs of eyes, but they quickly disappeared into the darkness.

The entrance of the cave stood well over eight feet, but as I walked, the ceiling height dropped considerably. Very soon I had to crouch down to venture farther.

The ground was slick with Kalanoro droppings and bat guano, and it smelled like a musty cellar that doubled as a litter box. Tiny bones of partially digested meals crunched underneath the heavy soles of my boots.

My flashlight glinted on something, and I crouched down to inspect it. It was an old pocket watch, the face broken and the gears rusted, but it had once definitely belonged to a human. Near the watch was another trinket—an old walkie-talkie.

That's when I realized it was a trail of treasures, piling up more as I went deeper into the cave. Old car parts, a titanium hip replacement, and even what appeared to be a wedding band. The Kalanoro apparently loved hoarding shiny things.

On the ground a few feet ahead of me, I spotted something particularly sparkly. It looked like stars, shimmering and glowing from a puddle on the floor. By now I had to crawl on my knees, since the ceiling was so low.

As I reached for those stars, a Kalanoro leapt out from the darkness. Its rows of teeth dug painfully into my right arm, and I beat it back with my asp baton. It took three hits before it finally let go and ran off screaming.

I grabbed at the stars, picking up a satiny fabric. The way it glimmered, it looked exactly like the night sky, and I now understood what Odin meant by looking "like the heavens." This had to be the Valhallan cloak. I hurriedly shoved it into my gear bag. The Kalanoro couldn't be happy about me stealing their treasure, so I had to get out fast.

I raced out of the cave and gulped down the fresh air. Around me, the trees had changed their tune, from the normal song of the jungle to something far more shrill and angry. I could hear the Kalanoro growling and screeching at each other, sounding like high-pitched howler monkeys. They were enraged, and they were chasing after me.

It was a ten-kilometer hike downhill, through thick forests, to the nearest village. There I would be able to clean up and catch the hyperbus back to Caana City. Back to meet Odin. The Kalanoro were now alerting the entire jungle to my presence, and even as I hurried ahead, deftly moving through the trees, I could hear them following me.

I ran down the hill, skittering through the mud and branches, swatting back giant bugs and the occasional surprised snake. My legs ached and my lungs burned but I pressed on, running as fast as I could. I had to make it to the town before dark, because I doubted the Kalanoro would let me out alive.

THREE

❖

The sign above the driver on the hyperbus read *AFORO MÁXIMO 100 PERSONAS*, but there had to be at least twice as many people cramped on the old bus as it lumbered through Central America. A hyperbus was like a regular bus except slightly larger, and it hovered, so it could go much faster than a regular bus, especially through the uneven, wild terrain here.

Since this one serviced primarily rural areas, its passengers included humans, immortals, more than a few chickens, and even a very pregnant goat. For the first three hours of my journey I was forced to stand, holding on to the grip bar and squished between a woman and large Cambion.

There were fewer immortals here than there were back in the city, which was a great big melting pot, with people and beings from all over the world living side by side. Nearer to the Gates of Kurnugia the population was ostensibly diverse and overwhelmingly supernatural. But out here there weren't many immortals that weren't indigenous to the area.

The Kalanoro themselves had been an exception. They'd actually become somewhat of an invasive species after being brought over on a boat from Madagascar, and if it weren't for the native Chupacabra and jaguars, they could have devastated the Panamanian rain forests.

Because of this, and other stories about humans and immortals like this, locals around here tended to distrust outsiders. For once, that worked in my favor, since they gave me a bit of a wider berth than they did for everyone else, which meant I had an extra inch or so to breathe.

Eventually I managed to get a window seat all to myself. I rested my head on the window and clung to my gear bag on my lap. It contained my one chance at stopping the underworld uprising and getting Asher back.

If there even was an Asher to still get back.

I'd been trying not to think about it, but the bus ride was too long, with nothing to keep my mind busy except the blur of the rain forest as we sped by it. I closed my eyes, willing the exhaustion of the last few days to overtake me, and finally, thankfully, I fell asleep.

My dreams were filled with images of a cloak made of the stars. I wrapped it tightly around me, but it couldn't keep the cold out. There was something chasing after me, but I could never quite see it, and I knew that I could never get away from it.

I awoke with a start, gasping, and immediately put my hand to my chest, over my heart. My seatmate—who had apparently joined me while I was sleeping—glanced over at me.

She appeared to be an older woman, possibly in her late sixties, and she managed to distract me from whatever strange dread had awoken me. Based on the symbol of triple goddesses hanging around her neck, along with several black tattoos on her temples trailing down her hairline, I guessed that she was a bruja.

Her salt-and-pepper hair hung down in a long braid, and she eyed me with an irritated scowl, since I'd momentarily interrupted her knitting. She was furiously knitting away, with a strange vibrant black yarn and two long needles—their mottled ivory and the sound of their *clack* when they struck each other made me think they were bone.

"Sorry," I mumbled as she glared at me from under her thick eye-

brows. *"Lo siento."* Since I didn't know much Spanish and she continued
to stare at me, I added vaguely, "It was a bad dream. A nightmare."

"No, *pesadilla*," she told me ominously with a thick accent. Even as
she spoke, her dark mahogany eyes locked on me, her wrinkled hands
working feverishly, the knitting needles continuously clacking away.
"No dream. *Es un mensaje.*"

I stared at her in disbelief, gulping back the rising dread. *"¿Qué?*
What do you mean?"

"He is loud, even I *oír.*" She finally stopped knitting and motioned
to her ear with one hand. Then, using the long bony needle, she poked
gently at my chest, right above my heart. *"¡Escucha!* He is speaking."

I was about to ask her again what she meant, but then I heard it . . .
or maybe felt it. Whatever had woken me up. It was still here, sitting in
my chest, burning inside me. It wasn't like hearing words, not like someone speaking in my ear, but it was something different than my own
voice or thoughts. But it was strangely crystal-clear.

The bruja nodded and smiled, then went back to her manic knitting.
But I barely even registered that. I was lost in a memory.

*In bed, only a week ago, with Asher's arms around me. My bedroom
was lit by the blue lights of the billboards across the river, and Asher was
brushing back the hair from my face, letting his rough fingers trail down
my temple as he looked into my eyes.*

*"My grandmother said that sometimes our ancestors—those that died
before us and love us—leave us truths when we most need them," he
had told me with a soft smile. "It's a thought that comes in, but it's truer
and brighter, and it becomes branded across my heart."*

And now in the hyperbus, alone, I realized it was just as Asher had
said.

His words searing my heart were as clear as if he were speaking in
my ear, telling me, *"You must not worry about me. Forget me. Save the
world."* Somehow, from wherever he was now, he'd gotten his message
to me.

He was still alive, but he didn't want me to go after him.

FOUR

———— ◆ ————

It was early when I made it to Caana City, barely after five in the morning. The sky above the city had begun to change, shifting slowly from indigo to a soft amethyst. Here it wasn't as big or as bustling as it was back home in Chicago, not quite, but the streets were slowly waking up as the residents began their daily routine.

When I finally got to the Caana City Extended Stay Inn & Suites where I had left my friends, the sun had almost fully risen. Before I'd gone off to Panama, we'd decided to check into one of the cheaper motels we could find, since we didn't know how long we'd be staying here. That's why we were staying in the more-distant Canaa City anyway—the capital city of Belmopan was just too expensive on our shoestring budget.

Hopefully, we wouldn't be here for much longer. Although it was gorgeous in Belize and the clean air and bright stars were a nice change of pace from the smog of the city, I was eager to get back home. Mostly because I was hoping that being home meant that the underworld uprising would end before it really started. That Asher would be safe, and life could return to normal.

I'd only just climbed the outdoor stairs up to the hallway balcony when Quinn Devane rushed out of our room and ran toward me. I must've been more exhausted from my travels than I'd thought, because I totally misread her expression for excitement, when in reality it turned out to be fierce anger.

"Hey," I began tiredly as she reached me, but before I could say anything more, Quinn slapped me across the face. Hard. "What the hell?"

"Don't you 'what the hell' me," Quinn growled at me, as I glared at her and rubbed my already throbbing jaw. Her nostrils flared in anger, and her usual lopsided smile was instead a sharp scowl. "Where were you? How could you leave without telling anybody?"

"I left a note," I insisted.

She scoffed. "You snuck out in the middle of the night and left a scrap of paper taped to the mirror that said, 'I'll be back in a few days. Stay safe.—Malin.'"

"I wanted to make sure you saw it," I argued feebly.

"That doesn't explain why you didn't reply to any of our texts or calls, or why you felt the need to sneak out in the first place," she shot back and folded her arms firmly over her chest. Above the low scoop of her tank top, a dark red scar ran between her collarbones, and soon the healing cut above her eye from our recent fights in the Gates of Kurnugia would match.

"At first I was ignoring you," I admitted. "I didn't want to argue about it until I was long gone, but then I didn't get any signal at all in Panama."

"You were in *Panama*?"

"I went to get the thing that the guy told us about," I said, deliberately being vague because we were outside, and I didn't know who could overhear us.

After Odin had talked with me, I had told everyone about it. I had just left out the part about the location, and then once Oona had made up her potions, I'd gone after it on my own.

"Why couldn't you have told me?" Quinn demanded. "What if something had happened to you? I should've gone with you."

"Oona was hurt, and I knew she wasn't up for the journey." I pointed at the door behind Quinn, where Oona was presumably hiding out with Atlas Malosi.

Quinn shrugged. "What does that have to do with me?"

"Because. If I told you, you'd want to come with, and then Atlas would have to come with because Samael tasked him to protect me, and then who would be here helping Oona while she healed?" I asked. "Not that she would be willing to stay behind if everybody else was going, anyway."

Quinn continued glaring at me, and then finally she exhaled and her shoulders relaxed slightly. "You still should've told us."

Now that she was softening, the rage in her eyes was replaced with concern and worry. The line of her jaw tensed, and her lips twisted ever so slightly, so she pressed them into a grim line. The early morning sunlight shimmered off her silver hair, giving her an almost angelic glow, and the air was filled with all the things that neither of us could say.

A few days ago Quinn had made it perfectly clear that she was done pursuing me romantically, which was what I'd been asking her to do since we'd broken up six months ago. But she wouldn't leave me to fight alone, and I knew all too well that emotions weren't something that you could flip off like a switch.

The brutal truth of the pain in my chest and the lump in my throat was that I cared for her still, that I always would. I wished desperately that I'd been able to love her the way she needed to be. The way she claimed she loved me.

But I couldn't. Not when we had been together. And definitely not now, when the world was falling apart, and I had feelings growing for someone else. Someone who may or may not be dead and trapped in the underworld.

I swallowed that thought back and tried to keep my cool.

"I was just getting something from the Kalanoro," I said as casually as I could manage. "It's the kind of thing I was trained to do, and I knew I could handle it on my own. And I did."

That finally registered with her, and an eyebrow arched above her brilliant green eyes. "You got it, then?"

I nodded. "Let's go back into the room and we'll talk about it."

She stepped to the side, allowing me to pass her, but she didn't move over enough, so I brushed up against her muscular bicep. Neither of us commented on this, and I kept walking toward the room, with Quinn following a step behind.

No sooner had I opened the motel room door than Oona leapt off the couch. With her hands on her hips, she shouted at me like an angry matriarch, "Malin Rose Krigare!"

Even though Oona was actually a month and a half younger than me, not to mention significantly shorter and more petite, she had skewed toward a maternal role with me for most of our friendship. Which worked for me, because most of the time I felt like she was the only one who really cared about me.

"I already yelled at her," Quinn said, preempting a lecture from Oona.

I rubbed my jaw, where it still ached from her slap. "Yeah, she really laid into me."

Oona deflated, and I imagined that she'd been practicing what she wanted to say to me since I'd been gone. But the good news was that she already looked a lot better than she had when I'd seen her last. Even jumping up from the couch was an improvement on her weakened state from before.

Her skin had been sallow and almost gray, but it was once again creamy brown and flawless, and her dark eyes were bright. Before, her short black hair had been listless, but the usual luster had almost completely returned.

"You shouldn't have gone like that," Atlas said, chiming in from where he stood leaning against the wall. "Samael called, and he was very upset when he found out what you'd done."

I cringed but quickly shook it off.

Samael was technically my boss—assuming that I was still a Valkyrie and I still had a job, which seemed less and less likely every day—but his investment in me currently had more to do with his relationship with my mother. He'd been in love with her, I think, and protecting me was a way of honoring her, now that she was dead.

"It was worth it," I assured them all and slipped my gear bag off my shoulder.

I set it down on the coffee table and pulled out the mounds of fabric that had left my knapsack bulging at the seams. There'd been hardly any room for my provisions, and I'd actually had to ditch some along the way to keep the cloak from spilling out.

Oona gasped when she saw it, which was a perfectly reasonable response. The bulk of the fabric was a strange matte black. It had this velvety black-hole appearance to it, but it was cool and satiny to the touch.

Interspersed throughout the fabric were twinkling stars and pale purple swirls of galaxies, all of which actually moved and glowed. It was as if someone had cut a chunk of the night sky out and turned it into a long, flowing cloak.

"Holy crap," Oona said and crouched down in front of it to get a better look. Her metal-stud angel bites—piercings on either side of her philtrum, just above her lips—glinted from the starry light as she wrinkled her nose. "What's that smell?"

"Yeah, it still stinks of the Kalanoro cave where it's been for hundreds of years, but I don't have a lot of experience washing mystical fabric," I explained.

"So this is it?" Oona looked up at me in wonderment. "This is the Valhallan cloak?"

I nodded. "It was just like Odin said it would be."

"Now we need to figure out what we're supposed to do with it," Quinn said.

"I couldn't find very much written about it, but I did research while you were gone, and it allegedly has concealing and protective properties." Oona reached out, tentatively touching it. "Wow. It's colder and smoother than I thought it would be."

"I don't think *we* need to do anything with it," I said. "We need to get it to Odin, and then—"

A loud knock at the door interrupted me, and I glanced around.

"Are you expecting someone?" Quinn asked me, her voice just above a whisper, and I shook my head. Her gaze hardened as she looked toward the door. "No one's supposed to know where we are."

Another knock, this time louder and more urgent, followed by a woman forcefully saying, "Open up. I know you're in there, so let's stop wasting each other's time."

FIVE

———— ◆ ————

My hand hovered above my sword holstered on my hip, and I bent down so I could peer through the peephole on the door. Through the tiny lens I saw a swarthy young woman standing outside, with large black feathered wings growing out from her back.

Her dark brown hair landed above her shoulders, falling in frizzy waves. Several black feathers ran along her hairline, blending between her olive skin and wild hair. There were a few more feathers on her bare shoulders, under the straps of her tank top, but other than the subtle plumage and wings, she appeared human.

She stared into the peephole, biting her lip in irritation, while her eyes settled on the door. Her eyes were wide and subtly protruding, so that they looked too large above her high cheekbones and rosebud lips. Shrouded by heavy lids and dark lashes, this gave her an oddly glamorous look that clashed with her unkempt hair and industrial black apparel.

"Who are you?" I asked without opening the door.

She let out a relieved sigh and replied, "Samael sent me."

I looked back over my shoulder at Atlas, who shrugged his broad shoulders. "I don't recognize her, but Samael is probably the only one that has any idea where we are."

Since she clearly knew who we were, and she seemed to be alone, there wasn't any point leaving her out on the balcony to shout through the door. I opened it and stepped back to allow her to come in.

She pulled in her sizable wings, folding them tightly against her back so she could fit through the doorframe, and set a duffel bag on the floor as I shut the door. Behind me, Quinn and Atlas were doing their best to look fierce and imposing, while Oona offered our new visitor a friendly smile.

"I am Valeska Voronin," she said, in a voice that was somehow both sultry and husky at once, with a subtle Slavic accent adding a heft to her words. Then she turned her gaze to me. "I assume you are Malin Krigare."

"That's me," I said dryly.

Her eyes traveled around the room, which had a general "bland motel" vibe going on. We were standing in the small living room with a "kitchenette" on the far wall that consisted of a sink, a mini-fridge, and an ancient microwave resting on a stainless steel counter. Avocado-green walls, worn stone flooring, and a convertible sofa with several mysterious stains were the highlights of the main room, along with a window view of a parking lot, and two full-sized beds were in the adjoining bedroom.

The one thing I could say for this room was that at least it lacked disturbing paintings of Ereshkigal or any other underworld beings on the wall. Here there were only nondescript paintings of abstract neon colors, vibrant lines of blue and green over a black background.

Our stuff was strewn throughout the rooms, although there had been attempts to keep it clean. It was difficult with four people staying in such a small space.

"I was not told there would be so many of you." Valeska looked over at the others, but her gaze seemed to linger a bit on Quinn.

"This is Quinn Devane, a Valkyrie," Oona said, apparently deciding to do the introductions. "That's Atlas Malosi, he's Samael's guard. And I'm Oona Warren, a sorceress-in-training."

"What are you doing here?" I asked, before Oona started asking everyone to go around the room and share interesting facts about ourselves.

"Samael thought I could be of help to you," Valeska explained, settling her wide eyes back on me. "My mother was an Alkonost, and my father is the son of a Valkyrie."

I'd heard of Alkonosts, though I'd never met one personally before. They were immortal cousins of the sirens, with more attributes of a bird, and while they had beautiful singing voices, they didn't have the same ability to cast spells the way sirens did.

"We all have powerful bloodlines." I gestured around the room. Quinn, Atlas, and I were all actually taller and broader than Valeska, and I assumed that we were stronger, too. The only obvious thing she had on us were her wings. "So, no offense, why do we need you? Why would Samael send you?"

"I don't know what it is exactly you're doing here," Valeska said, seemingly ignoring my question. "Samael was short on details. The one thing he made clear is that you were on a quest that had taken you to the Gates of Kurnugia, and he feared that you would need to venture below to Kurnugia. Into the underworld."

I lowered my gaze and shifted my weight from one foot to the other, so I wouldn't have to think about Asher's words burned on my heart. His request for me to forget him, to leave him in Kurnugia.

"I don't know where the quest is taking us," I said and cleared my throat. "But I doubt we will end up in Kurnugia, since it doesn't exactly have an open-door policy. I don't think any mortal has ever gone to the underworld."

"That's where you're wrong." Valeska's mouth turned with the faintest hint of a smile. "I am mortal, and I have been to Kurnugia and back."

SIX

———— ◆ ————

Well, that's a good reason for Samael to send you," Quinn said, breaking the silence, then she looked over at Oona. "I don't know about the rest of you, but I could go for a drink."

"Oh! I'll open the soursop wine I bought last night," Oona announced, and she was already walking over to the mini-fridge.

While Oona went to fetch the alcohol, Quinn sat back on the couch and rested her severe gaze on Valeska. "What were you doing in Kurnugia?"

"It's a simple story, really," Valeska said, causing Quinn to smirk and laugh derisively.

Oona returned with five plastic cups and a bottle of pale wine. She set the cups on the onyx coffee table and proceeded to fill them all to the brim.

"Help yourself," she said, gesturing toward the cups, and then sat down beside Quinn.

There weren't that many places to sit, with Quinn and Oona taking the couch and Atlas sitting in the only chair in the room. Valeska took a cup of wine off the table, then sat down on the table itself, but I preferred to stand. At least for the time being.

"So, what is this simple story?" I pressed, since Valeska still hadn't elaborated on her trip to Kurnugia.

She took a long drink of her wine, then wiped her mouth with her hand. "As I told you, my mother was an Alkonost. She died when I was twelve, and I wanted to see her again. I needed to talk to her."

I understood that urge completely. I would kill for a chance to see my mother and talk to her again. There were so, so many questions I had for Marlow about what she knew and what she'd done—and what she hadn't done.

But beyond that, I just wanted to see her again. To hear her voice, to tell her I loved her. Even if she didn't say it back. Even if she didn't feel it. She was my mom, and I still loved her and missed her.

Unlike Valeska, I knew that I would never have a chance to see my mother again. Alkonosts were immortal, so they went to Kurnugia when their time on this earth was done. Valkyries were mortal, like humans and canaries and a whole host of animals. When they died, they were dead. There was nothing left for them except to rot and decay.

I cleared my throat to suppress the painful lump that was forming and said, "A lot of people miss their mothers. They don't break into the underworld to see them."

"I believed my mother was wrongfully taken from this earth," Valeska told us, matching my gaze evenly. "My grandmother—a Valkyrie—had never approved of the relationship between my mother and father, and one day, she snapped. Using her Valkyrie sword, she killed my mother."

Atlas snapped his fingers and said, "Oh, yeah, yeah. I remember that. It was all over the news that spring."

"Your grandmother was Freya Andvaranaut?" Quinn asked in a strange awed tone.

Valeska nodded once. "She was."

Vague memories of the story clicked in my head, and I realized that Valeska must be a few years older than me. I was only around ten when the story broke, too young to care much about the news, but the sensational nature of the case made it impossible to avoid entirely as the trial went on.

Freya Andvaranaut had been convicted of defying her duty as a

Valkyrie by killing an immortal without orders or just cause, and she was sentenced to death. Before they executed her, Freya had been allowed to give a statement. I didn't remember her exact words, but I knew that she said she would do it all again, exactly the same, if given the chance.

"It wasn't fair, and it wasn't right," Valeska insisted. "It wasn't my mother's time to die. Not yet." She lowered her eyes and exhaled deeply. "I didn't have enough time with her."

"And that's why you wanted to go to Kurnugia," Oona said gently, since Valeska seemed lost in a memory.

"Yes." Valeska blinked several times, then looked up at us. "I thought I could break her free. But first I had to get in there. I began researching, and I learned that nowhere does it state that mortals aren't allowed in the underworld—only that they do not pass there *naturally*."

We already knew there was entrance to Kurnugia. That was what the Gates were, how Gugalanna had been able to pull Asher into the water, through a vortex into the netherworld.

But neither Gugalanna nor his mistress Ereshkigal had been able to keep that door open for very long. There was strong magic that kept it sealed shut so that even the most powerful inhabitant would not be able to simply open it and walk out.

"But if powerful beings like Ereshkigal, Hades, and Anubis can't get out, how did a young mortal like you get in?" I asked, and I did nothing to mask the skepticism in my voice.

"Think of it this way." Valeska turned, folding her knees underneath her to face me more fully. "Kurnugia was designed to be a giant room to lock away the immortals so they weren't wreaking havoc on earth or annoying the gods. They locked the doors, but they left a key."

A leather strap hung around her neck, slipping underneath her tank top, so whatever pendant it held was hidden under the fabric. She reached for it now, pulling out a crudely formed crescent-shaped stone. It had rough, mottled edges, as if it had been made by hammering stone against stone.

The front of it appeared to be a pale sandstone, but the back side was a more jagged crystal quartz. When the light hit just right, it cast splatters of rainbow throughout the room.

Oona leaned forward, resting her arms on her knees, and narrowed her eyes. "What is that?"

"It's the Sibudu Key," Valeska replied with a proud smile, and Oona gasped. "It allows passage into Kurnugia."

"But that isn't . . ." Oona's dark eyes widened in disbelief. "I thought those were only things of legend. People scoured the earth for those, but they'd never been recovered."

"There used to be seven of them, but almost all of them were destroyed centuries ago," Valeska said as she dropped the key back down her shirt.

"How could you have gotten your hands on one?" Oona asked.

"Samael was my grandmother's Eralim, and he felt guilty about what happened with my mother," Valeska explained. "He took pity on me and arranged a meeting between me the Arch Seraph."

I had never seen the Arch Seraph, but I knew he worked on the highest level of the Evig Riksdag—the eternal parliament where Valkyries got all their orders. The Arch Seraph operated as a direct intermediary between those who lived on earth and those who resided in the gods' home of Vanaheimr. He was rarely seen and almost never interacted with mortals. So Samael had to have pulled some serious strings to get a meeting between the Arch Seraph and Valeska.

"What did he look like?" Quinn asked. "The Arch Seraph. I've never even seen pictures of him."

"It's hard to describe." Valeska paused and her brow furrowed as she thought. "It's impossible to look directly at him, because he's made of light. He's both tangible and entirely ethereal. I don't think you can fully appreciate it unless you meet him yourself."

"And the Arch Seraph just gave it to you?" Quinn tilted her head, as if she couldn't quite decide if she wanted to believe Valeska or not.

"No, of course not," Valeska admitted. "I stole it."

Both Quinn and Oona leaned back in their seats, and I took a step back, as if we all expected an angel to burst into the room with a fiery sword and slay us for consorting with Valeska.

When none of us were immediately smote, I thought it was safe to ask, "You stole it?"

"Yes," Valeska replied, looking at us all impassively. "I knew he would never give it to me, and Samael had gotten me into his office, which was by far the difficult part. There's hardly any security inside, because they expect that anyone who makes it through the door must have pure intentions, and I think they suspected me even less because I was only a child."

"How could . . . how is that even possible?" I asked.

"Samael called him out into the hall to speak to him privately," Valeska said. "The Arch Seraph had a glass case that ran floor-to-ceiling along an entire wall. That's where he stored his relics—I knew that from the research I'd done, and I thought if a key still existed, this is where it would be. I was terrified I would be caught, but it was the only chance I had. I had to climb a ladder, and I finally spotted the key in the middle of the tenth shelf. I snatched it and shoved it in my pocket."

"Are you saying that Samael helped you steal that?" I asked.

"Samael asked what he could do for me, promising that he would do anything that he could, and all I asked for was a moment alone in the Arch Seraph's office," Valeska said. "He never asked what for, but I think he didn't want to know. Not really. But he helped me anyway."

"So you got the key, then what?" I asked. "You just strode through the Gates of Kurnugia, past Kalma and her devil dog? All as a twelve-year-old girl without any training? Because we did that journey, and it was hard as hell for us."

"You misunderstand me," Valeska said. "My mother died when I was twelve, and I spent over two years studying and searching. Others had gotten close to getting into Kurnugia before, but they'd always gotten stuck because they had been unable to find the Sibudu Key. But I could still learn from them and study their plans."

"And that's how you got in?" I asked skeptically, since she hadn't really explained anything.

She smiled up at me. "I went through the back door."

SEVEN

———◆———

Valeska stood and hunched over slightly as she carefully peeled up the back of her shirt, revealing badly scarred flesh. Her feathers grew out from her wings down her back, but it was patchy and balding where the skin appeared red and rippled. The scarring covered her entire torso, trailing down below the waistband of her jeans and twisting around her sides, but her back had clearly gotten the worst of it.

"Holy shit," Quinn said, echoing my sentiments exactly. "What happened?"

"My protection spell wasn't strong enough," she said as she pulled her shirt back down.

Valeska explained the "back door" to us. It was the Eshik Mitu—a hot spring that spewed sulfurous water and occasional magma out of the ground. That sounded less like a door than an opportunity to get boiled alive.

The only benefit the geyser had was that it was located right behind the Merchants of Death market, so we wouldn't have to fight our way through the bone-covered ossuary and underworld guardian Kalma again—who most likely respawned after we'd "killed" her last week because it was her eternal duty to guard the entrance to Kurnugia.

"This is what going through the Eshik Mitu did to me," Valeska elaborated. "It was worse at the time. My back and wings were scalded, so most of my feathers fell out. For weeks after, I was in excruciating pain."

I grimaced. "To get into Kurnugia, we'll risk that burn?"

"No, it'll be worse," Valeska replied matter-of-factly. "The magic was barely enough for me, and this time around I won't be going alone."

"Why do you even need to go?" I countered. "Can't you lend me the key?"

"Never," she said fiercely and put her hand over her shirt, covering the crescent of the pendant underneath the thin fabric. "The key stays with me. Always."

"Couldn't you make a stronger protection spell?" Quinn asked, turning her attention on Oona.

"I can try," Oona said, sounding far less confident than I would've liked. "If Valeska already knows it and we worked together, we could come up with something more powerful, but I still don't know how good it'll be." She rested her chin on her hand and thought for a moment. "Really, I should start gathering ingredients now."

"What happened with your mother?" I asked Valeska, as Oona worked through potions and magic in her mind. "Did you find her?"

She lowered her eyes and nodded once. "Yes. She said that she couldn't come with me, and that I should never come back to Kurnugia again."

"You're willing to disobey your mother over this?" Quinn asked.

"Samael told me that he believes the fate of the world hangs in the balance," Valeska said. "I will do whatever needs to be done."

I laughed dryly. "Except give me the key."

Valeska met my sarcastic smile. "Except for that."

"Samael doesn't know everything that's going on, but I don't know that we'll even need your help." I rubbed the back of my neck, easing my growing anxiety. "I don't think we'll be going to Kurnugia."

"What?" Quinn asked, sounding alarmed. "Why not?"

"What about Asher?" Oona chimed in, and it honestly wouldn't have hurt more if she had stabbed me right in the heart.

I swallowed back the bitter pain and replied as evenly as I could, "Odin promised he'd help me. He said . . ." I choked on the words for a moment, so I pushed through them. "He said he'd help get Asher back."

"You're working with Odin?" Valeska asked, sounding more awed than I expected from someone who had stolen a key from the Arch Seraph and then broken into the underworld.

"*Working with* isn't exactly the right term," I clarified, since I didn't fully understand what Odin wanted or needed with me yet. "I am supposed to meet with him later tonight, though."

Odin had told me to meet him at the top of the Caana Temple when the moon was the highest in the sky on the night I returned. When I asked him how he'd know what night I would return, he only smiled and changed the subject.

"Can Odin get into Kurnugia?" Oona asked. "I thought they kept it blocked from everything."

I shrugged. "Odin's one of the highest gods. He can go anywhere." Then I looked around the room, hoping for confirmation, but I was only meant with uncertain stares. "Right?"

"I should go with you to meet Odin," Valeska said firmly.

"Why?" I asked, incredulous.

"Because, if I am to help you get into Kurnugia, and he's helping you, too, we should all be on the same page," she said.

I replied carefully, "Like I said, we don't need to go to Kurnugia, so we don't need your help."

"Malin, why don't we talk for a moment?" Quinn asked, standing up and motioning to herself, Oona, and me, leaving Atlas to entertain our guest. "Can you excuse us, Valeska?"

"Yes, of course." She smiled thinly. "I need to use the restroom anyway."

Even though Valeska had slipped into the small washroom off the main room, Quinn ushered Oona and me into the adjacent bedroom and closed the door behind us. The bed was unmade, and based on the ripped jeans and swords strewn across it, I guessed that it was Quinn's.

"Why are you so opposed to her?" Quinn asked me bluntly. Her arms were folded over her chest as she stared at me.

I shook my head. "I'm not. I don't want us all getting killed."

"If Odin can handle this by himself here on out, great. Then we're done." Oona wiped her hands together, symbolizing that we could wash our hands of this whole mess. "But if not, we have to take her up on her offer. Don't we? I mean, she's the only chance we have to get into Kurnugia."

"Why do we have to go to Kurnugia?" I argued.

"To stop the underworld goddess from escaping and to rescue Asher?" Quinn asked, speaking to me as if I were a moron.

Reflexively, my hand went to my heart, hovering just above where his words were still branded on me. *Don't worry about me.*

Using all my willpower, I managed to keep my voice even as I said, "I don't even know if he's still alive."

Oona's jaw dropped and her eyes widened, and Quinn's breath caught in her throat and she took a step back from me, as if she suddenly realized I was infected with a contagious disease.

"You're saying you don't even want to try?" Oona asked once she'd recovered from her shock.

"You're even more heartless than I thought," Quinn said, and her voice had taken on a forlorn, defeated quality that cut deep through me. "You really don't care about anyone but yourself."

"Quinn!" Oona snapped, rushing to my defense.

"No, it's not like that," I insisted, and though I tried to hide it, the pain and confusion found its way into my words, making them shrill. "You don't think it doesn't kill me that I can't run down and save him right now? Of course it does. But . . ." I paused, and when I spoke again, my voice cracked. "I don't think he wants me to save him."

"How do you know?" Oona asked.

I rubbed my neck and let out a shaky breath. "It's hard to explain. It's just something . . . I *know*."

"Okay." Oona glanced over at Quinn, then asked me, "What do you want to do, then? What's our game plan?"

"Let's meet with Odin and see what he says, and maybe this will be over soon," I said, sounding more discouraged than hopeful.

"Well, then I think Valeska should go with us to meet Odin," Quinn said firmly. "She knows more about Kurnugia than the rest of us, and if that's where Odin sends us next, then it would be best if she was there to find out exactly what he needs from us."

"I was planning to meet him alone, but yeah, sure," I relented, since there was no point in fighting. "Whatever you guys think is best."

EIGHT

———◆———

hen Quinn and I reached the top of the Caana temple, winded and tired from the long trek up the stairs, Valeska was already there. She had flown up using her large, elegant wings, and now leaned back against a mossy stone wall as she waited.

"Maybe next time you meet with Odin you could pick a place a little lower to the ground," Quinn suggested as she slumped against the wall beside Valeska, sitting on the soft grass that covered the mezzanine. There were more levels above us, but they were only small platforms, so this seemed close enough to the top.

"I didn't choose the place," I reminded her. "When a Vanir god tells you to meet him somewhere, you go where he tells you."

The Caana temple was an ancient pyramidesque stone building made by the Maya thousands of years ago, which they eventually abandoned. Over the centuries it fell into ruin, before being rediscovered and becoming a tourist attraction.

This particular one was known as the Sky Palace, because it was the tallest one in Belize, and it towered above everything around it. Even the nearby trees, with their broad leaves reaching toward the sky, were dwarfed by the temple. The only thing above was the full moon, illuminating the darkness.

Technically, we weren't even supposed to be here. The ruins were part of a national park, and they were closed, but it hadn't been all that hard to sneak in through the forest. Immediately surrounding the ruins was a dense jungle, filled with chattering and flitting animal life that we could hear but could not see.

Caana City had sprawled out enough that it had begun swallowing up the rain forest, and from the top of the temple it was easy to see the buildings and high-rises of the city, twinkling in the near distance.

"You know, I could've carried you up here," Valeska told Quinn.

"No, it's okay," Quinn insisted, smiling crookedly at her. "I could manage, and I didn't want to hassle you."

Valeska laughed lightly. "I'm stronger than I look." She then flexed her sinewy arm, forming only the smallest of bumps on her bicep, and Quinn joined in laughing with her.

While those two bantered and joked, I walked along the edge of the mossy half-wall that ran along the front. The grassy mezzanine was surrounded on the other three sides by stairs that led up to higher, more narrow landings, but the steps appeared more like seats in an outdoor amphitheater.

Despite the ache in my legs, I couldn't sit and rest the way Quinn and Valeska were doing. An electric unease ran through me, similar to how I felt before hunting down an immortal to return. Only this time I wouldn't have a release.

In my black bag holstered to my thigh, the Valhallan cloak was stored, filling the bag to the maximum capacity. I'd bound the cloak up as small as I could to make it fit, because I wanted to keep it close to me. The strap strained on my aching thigh, but the pain was a welcomed distraction.

As I paced, I glanced up at the night sky, and I couldn't help but notice how eerily the vibrant Valhallan cloak matched the sky above us. The stars here were brighter than they were back home, even with Caana City as large as it was becoming. From my apartment window back on the canal, I could barely even make out the brightest stars over the blinding lights of the billboards and traffic and lampposts.

"When is Odin supposed to get here anyway?" Quinn asked.

"He said to meet him at the top of the Caana temple when the moon is the highest in the sky," I explained and glanced down at the clock on my phone.

I hadn't known what that meant exactly, but Oona's thaumaturgy studies had left her with an expertise on the phases and cycles of the moon. She'd informed me that the moon would be at its absolute peak over the meridian at 11:46 P.M. And the time had just ticked to 11:55.

Quinn looked up at the moon, fat and almost sunnily bright. "It looks pretty high to me."

"I know," I said with a sigh. "I think he's late."

"Aren't we the impatient ones?" a voice asked jovially. It was deep, almost thunderous, with a thick British accent adding a playful lilt to it.

I turned around to see Odin striding down the stairs from the higher altar, with his long gray duster billowing out around him. Despite the humid heat of the tropical night, he wore a jacket over his tailored suit. Behind him, his enormous raven, Muninn, had landed on one of the stone walls and began preening its inky black feathers.

Odin looked much the same as he had the last time I'd seen him. He was tall and broad, not quite a giant, but with the imposing presence that was far more fitting of a god than a man. With a strong jaw, full lips, and rich dark skin, he was ruggedly handsome, although not overly so in the ethereal way that angels and Eralim could be. Which was better, really, because they could be practically painful to look at.

The only thing that muddled his otherwise impeccable appearance was that his left eyelid was withered shut, but his right eye was bright and wide as he approached us.

"No, of course not," I answered, hoping to match his spirited tone but instead only managing a strained formality. "I was only afraid that we'd missed you."

"And who exactly is this *we*?" Odin asked, and he narrowed his good eye as he appraised Quinn and Valeska.

They had been lingering back, but I glanced over my shoulder when Odin addressed them, just in time to see them walking closer to us.

Quinn's mouth hung slightly open, and her eyes had taken on a wide, awed quality that I wasn't used to seeing on her. Valeska, for her part, appeared as stoic as she had when she arrived at our motel room door, but I wouldn't expect any less from a girl who tricked angels.

"They're here to help," I explained. Valeska politely greeted him, but Quinn did a curtsy before announcing a little too loudly that she was pleased to meet him.

"I suppose you'll need all the help you can get," Odin mused reasonably. "I presume you were able to retrieve the Valhallan cloak?"

"Yes, I have it here for you—" I began as I reached for the bag holstered on my leg.

"Oh, no, the cloak isn't for me," Odin corrected me. "It's for *you*."

I'd been unzipping my bag, but I stopped to gape up at him. "What? What are you talking about?"

"Valhalla is often incorrectly referred to as a place, but in reality it's more of a state of protection. A spell or an aura cast around the gods to protect us," Odin elaborated. "And that cloak you have is imbued with that same protection spell. If you have it wrapped around you, you cannot be harmed by or stopped by any other spells."

"And why do I need that?" I asked, but already my heart was hammering in my chest.

"Because I have another errand for you," he said with a sly grin. "I need you to retrieve my spear, Gungnir."

"I thought that was destroyed," I said, referencing the slim knowledge I had learned about the legendary weaponry in school.

"That's not exactly true," Odin replied carefully.

"What's Gungnir?" Valeska asked. "What's so special about this spear?"

"Back when the world was still young, the Vanir gods became nervous about an uprising among the lesser gods that walked the earth, and they feared that Kurnugia wouldn't be enough to hold them," he explained, with a prescient understanding.

"I offered to forge a weapon, something that would destroy immortals completely. No underworld, no next life, no trips to Vanaheimr," Odin said. "They would just be gone.

"The other Vanir gods were very excited about this, so they helped me craft the perfect spear," he elaborated. "Auchimalgen killed the rare camahueto to bring me his unbreakable horn for the shaft, and Poseidon ventured down to Atlantis to give me the powerful orichalcum for the tip.

"Finally, Brahma gave me Halāhala, the most vicious poison ever created, and I dipped the tip into it," Odin said. "Thus, a weapon capable of obliterating even the mightiest immortal was created.

"Gungnir was so powerful, it was locked away, only to be used as an absolute fail-safe," he went on. "But my son Baldur, always the most thoughtful and compassionate of my children, did not think any such weapon should exist. He tried to destroy it, but he could only snap it in half, leaving the deadly tip intact.

"With no way to break it further, he thought the best course of action was to hide it from the Vanir gods so we could never be tempted to use it," Odin said. "He voluntarily went into Kurnugia, taking the spear with him."

"Why did he go to Kurnugia?" Valeska asked, but I feared I already knew the answer.

"He knew it was the one place I could not travel," Odin replied, and for a moment I couldn't breathe.

"That's what kicked off Frigg's long slumber," Quinn said, slightly misremembering what we had been taught in school about the absence of Odin's wife. "She tried to get into Kurnugia to visit Baldur."

His mood darkened for a moment, but his voice was even when he said, "It was all a bit more complicated than that."

My heart hammered in my chest, making Asher's words throb and burn. Going to the underworld meant I had to either deny those words and save him, or heed his wishes and let him die. And I didn't know how I could do either.

"I need you to go to Kurnugia and retrieve the spear from my son Baldur," Odin said. "Last I heard, he was in Zianna. That cloak will shield you so you will be able to get into Kurnugia and leave with the spear."

I ran a hand through my hair as a wave of nausea rolled over me, and I felt the familiar restless electricity I experienced before a kill. But it was only intensifying, and I had no way of quieting the urges.

"But . . . why me?" I asked, hating how plaintive my voice sounded. "Why can't someone else? Another god, maybe?"

"It's precisely because you aren't a god," he explained, his voice warming to reassure me. "You are a Valkyrie—created with strength and power beyond your humanity, but without the curse and limitations that immortality brings. You can go where I cannot.

"And you must go," he said. "That spear is our only chance of stopping Ereshkigal. If she finds a way to open the door from Kurnugia, all the evil and power that has been locked up for centuries will be unleashed on the earth."

NINE

———— ◆ ————

I sat on the stainless-steel countertop of our kitchenette, the metal feeling cold through the thin fabric of my jeans, and I watched as my friends tried to wrap themselves in the night sky. Or at least that's what it looked like they were doing.

The Valhallan cloak looked massive when spread out across the floor. It was a full circle that took up almost the entirety of the living room/kitchenette. Unfortunately, it was an entirely different thing when squeezing a six-foot-tall Valkyrie, a demi-Alkonost with a fifteen-foot wingspan, and a petite sorceress-in-training under it.

Originally, Atlas had tried jamming himself under it, too, but it very quickly became apparent that his bulky frame would not fit comfortably under there with them. Now he leaned against the counter beside me, sipping Oona's soursop wine while watching Quinn, Valeska, and Oona scramble around.

So far they had tried a dozen different positions, their arms and legs and wings poking out of the satiny fabric as they moved.

Since Quinn was the tallest, she had the long hood draped over her head, and she peered down at the cloak with silver locks of hair sticking to her forehead. Valeska's wings bulged out the fabric where she stood pressed against her side, and Oona was a bump near her knees as she crouched down on the other side.

"Okay, I think we got it," she announced.

"We're all covered?" Oona asked, her voice slightly muffled through the fabric.

"Yeah, we are," Quinn said, then she looked over at me. "Okay, Malin, come on. You try to fit under."

I didn't move. "It's not going to work."

"What?" Oona poked her head out of the front seam of the cloak. One of Valeska's black feathers had gotten stuck in Oona's short hair, and she exhaled hard to blow it free. "There's still extra fabric."

She was technically right, in that there were a few inches pooling at their feet. But last time I checked, I was bigger than four inches around, so there was no way that I was going to wedge myself in there enough to be covered from head to toe.

"Four of us aren't going to be able to fit under there," I insisted. "One of us has to stay behind."

Quinn lowered her gaze, and I could see her jaw tensing under her flushed skin. Her lopsided mouth twitched as she struggled to come up with something, an impassioned protest that would ensure that she would travel with us.

But there wasn't any.

Oona insisted she was well enough to go—and as far as I could tell, she was—and she was the only one who knew protection charms and health potions, which would definitely come in handy in a realm of un-stoppable monsters. Valeska was going because she was the only one who had any experience inside Kurnugia. And I was going because Odin had tasked me with the mission.

Slowly, Quinn untied the cloak from around her neck and let it slip off her shoulders. The stars and galaxies rippled as they fell and landed in a puddle around the three of them. Valeska and Oona straightened up, both of them appearing red and sweaty from hiding out under the cloak.

"Maybe we don't have to be fully covered," Oona suggested, but Quinn strode over to the counter.

"I do not think that is a risk we should take," Valeska said, brushing her damp hair off her forehead, and she didn't need to remind us of the burns that covered her back.

"No," Quinn replied firmly and poured herself a plastic cup of wine, emptying the bottle. "I'll stay behind."

"Hey, at least you'll be safer here," I said, trying to assuage her disappointment, but I realized belatedly that I was probably making it worse. There were many things that Quinn valued in this life, but safety wasn't one of them.

We were going somewhere that we'd only been told about, where no other Valkyrie had gone. Even as dangerous as it most certainly would be, I was sure that, for Quinn, the risk would be worth it, to see things that no mortals were allowed to see.

She looked over at me, her eyes hard, and then knocked back the glass, swallowing the wine in one big gulp.

"I'm assuming we should pack light, so I need to be judicious about what I bring," Oona said, breaking the tension with the practicality of our trip.

The last time we had gone to the Gates of Kurnugia, Atlas had carried her massive thaumaturgy kit, but since he wouldn't be going this time, Oona would have to pare it down to something more manageable. She went over and knelt beside her case to start sifting through it.

"Is there anything we definitely should or shouldn't bring?" I asked.

"Electronics will break down there, so leave all that behind," Valeska said. "And leave your Valkyrie sword. It won't work down there and would only draw unwanted attention." She cleared her throat. "I brought my grandmother's sword when I went down before, and it did not go well."

"So we have no weapons to protect ourselves?" I asked.

"No, other swords are fine. It's only the Valkyrie ones that are no good in Kurnugia," Valeska replied.

Oona groaned as she held up two identical-looking cylinders of bright blue liquid. "How much time do I have?" She looked back over at us. "When are we leaving for Kurnugia?"

"The sooner the better, I suppose," I said. "Does it matter what time we go there? Like, is night more dangerous?"

"There isn't really a true night or day in Kurnugia," Valeska replied flatly. "So it doesn't matter in that regard, and time moves differently."

I sat up straighter. "Time moves differently? How?"

"It's much faster," she said. "In the time that we've lived one lifetime, they've lived five. It makes eternity stretch on for even longer."

"Well, that's nice and freaky," I muttered.

"If time doesn't matter, does that mean we're leaving soon?" Oona asked dismally.

Valeska shrugged and looked to me for the answer. I glanced at the clock, and it was slowly ticking toward one-thirty in the morning.

"We haven't slept yet, and it doesn't do us any good to take on the underworld exhausted," I said. "But we still have to go through the Gates to get there, and I know that's no place for us after dark. So let's plan on being ready by noon."

Valeska nodded once. "At noon, we go to hell."

TEN

———— ◆ ————

Quinn had been kind enough to let Oona and me take the bedroom, since she didn't need rest as much as we did. Not that either Oona or I had gotten much sleep. I managed to get maybe an hour of fitful shut-eye, and when I woke, Oona was already up, sitting on her bed with a large book splayed open in front of her and a dim reading light in her hand.

I recognized it instantly, in part because of the dusty sage fragrance it emitted every time Oona opened its yellowing pages, but it was also undeniably distinct in appearance. It was about a foot long and nearly as wide, and several inches thick, which meant it had to weigh ten pounds or more.

The book was bound with in impenetrable black leather with a lustrous sheen. Inlaid in the dead center was a long spearpoint-shaped bornite crystal that shimmered in iridescent shades of purple and dark blue. There was no title or any wording on the cover or spine, but I knew it as the *Sorcellerie Grimoire*—a book of magic that had been a gift to Oona from her sorceress cousin Minerva.

"I've been narrowing down what potions and charms to bring," Oona said, with her eyes still glued to the pages of the book, as I sat up and stretched. "It's so hard because Kurnugia is a whole other plane. I have no way of knowing how casting a spell really works down there."

"Valeska's protection spell worked," I said, then corrected myself as I recalled the painful-looking red burns that covered her back. "At least partially. And I imagine that it didn't work as well as it could've because she didn't fully know what she was doing."

"That's true." Oona agreed with me, but she didn't sound completely convinced.

I got out of bed and opened the heavy drapes, letting in the bright morning sunlight. The parking lot behind the motel was filled to the brim, mostly with tiny little hatchbacks and rusted hovercars. The black asphalt shimmered with an inferior mirage from baking under the sun.

Facing Oona, I folded my arms over my chest and leaned back against the wall air conditioner, which rumbled and rattled as it attempted to keep the heat at bay with blasts of tepid, stale air. Oona had begun chewing her lip, making her silver studs above her lip twist and turn.

"What are you thinking?" I asked.

"Just . . ." She squinted at me. "Can we die in Kurnugia?"

"I'm hoping we make it out of there alive," I replied carefully. "But if you're asking if it's possible for us to be killed, then yes, I think so. Everything I've ever learned in school only points to one thing—when mortals die, they're dead. There's no afterlife or other plane for us."

"That's what I thought," she grumbled, sounding disappointed. "But I was hoping you might have known of some sort of cosmic loophole."

"If I knew how to cheat death, that would make my life so much easier," I said with a dry laugh. Oona smiled, but it quickly faded.

"Well, I suppose I ought to get gathering my stuff, then." She flipped the book closed with a heavy thud and stood up. "I'll do my best to pack everything we need to keep us alive."

Oona went back out to the main room to get the magic aspect covered, while I decided to focus on the practical things—namely, weapons. I pulled out the long black duffel bag from where I'd stashed it underneath the bed, then set it on the mattress. I unzipped the bag to reveal our small cache of armaments and make my picks about what to bring down with us.

The majority of the weapons had come from Samael, who had gone into his private collection to give me the most powerful, supernaturally endowed defenses he had in his arsenal. Of the two that I had procured without Samael, I had to immediately disregard my Valkyrie sword Sigrún, because it wouldn't work down in Kurnugia.

The special constraints of sneaking down under the cloak meant that despite their obvious power, I wouldn't be able to take all the weapons. The long swords—Tyrfing and Dyrnwyn—would be particularly cumbersome, so I set them aside.

That left me with the jagged black tourmaline dagger that once belonged to Kalfu, the iron-spiked flail chain mace Sharur, and the sword made from a solitary piece of obsidian-like stone, Kusanagi. Three weapons. I hoped that Valeska brought her own, because there really wasn't much to share.

I grabbed the rest of my gear—my hip sheath, my hooded vest with dagger sheath, and my heavy-duty knapsack—and spread it out on the bed so I could account for everything as I packed up. My knapsack was already preloaded with essentials, like bandages, bottled water, and jackfruit seeds to eat, and I added Sharur, the Valhallan cloak, and my sólarsteinn to it. The sunstone had come in handy before, and it might be the best tool for finding Odin's spear.

I pulled off my loose T-shirt, preparing to change and get dressed for the mission, when the door to the bedroom opened. Quinn came into the room, smiling sheepishly when she saw me topless. I thought about covering up, since I was only wearing a black bra and mismatched pair of striped panties, but it wasn't like she hadn't seen me naked plenty of times already.

"I wanted to talk to you before you left," she said. Her voice was low as she stepped closer to the bed, but she appeared completely undeterred by my semi-nudity.

"Well, let's talk, then." I grabbed my ribbed leggings out of my suitcase and pulled them on. They were tattered in a few places, but they were still the most durable pair of pants I had.

Quinn pushed her silver hair behind her ears. "I don't want you to go," she said, then quickly added, "I know that you have to. But it kills me that I can't go with you."

"I'll be fine," I insisted without looking at her.

"I know that you probably will be," she agreed.

I pulled a tank top on over my head, all too aware of how her eyes felt on me. My skin felt flushed, but I hoped she didn't notice as I went back to loading up my gear bag.

"Is that what you came to tell me?" I asked. "That you want to go with, and you hope I don't die? I mean, I appreciate that, but it was already implied, I think."

"Malin." She groaned as I picked up my black hooded vest. I'd just pulled it on and started doing up the sheath buckle when she grabbed my arm. "Can you stop for one second and talk to me?"

Her hand was soft and strong, and I finally lifted my eyes to meet hers. She stared at me with a pleading desperation in her eyes, but I'd already heard that in her voice. Even though I was looking at her now, she let her hand linger on my arm, and I didn't push it away.

"I don't want to leave things like we did," she said. "The things I said back in Sugarland—"

I looked away. "No, you were right. You should've said that stuff a long time ago, honestly."

"I don't know what the future holds. Not for us, not for the world," Quinn admitted softly. "But I know that you're going somewhere that you might not come back from, and I can't go with you." She paused, taking a fortifying breath. "I don't want the last thing I said to you to be hurtful. I still care about you. I always will."

"I . . ." I swallowed hard, struggling to find the words that always wanted to escape me when I was around Quinn. "I still care about you, too."

She'd moved closer to me, somehow, without me noticing. As if she'd been able to materialize in the space right next to me. Her hand moved down from my arm, holding on to my hip, and her other hand went to my chin, gently pushing it up so I'd look at her.

"You have to come back, Malin," she said in a voice that was low and husky.

"I plan to," I whispered, and she closed her eyes as she leaned down to me.

Her lips had barely touched mine when the bedroom door opened.

"Why doesn't anyone knock?" I groaned, but I was already stepping back from Quinn, putting the necessary distance between us.

"Sorry," Valeska said, leaning on the open doorframe. "I was checking to see if you were ready. It's about time to go."

"Yeah, almost," I told her. "Give me like five minutes."

"Okay. Just be quick." Valeska went back to the living room, but she left the door open behind her.

I finished buckling my vest harness, and Quinn moved back toward me, like she meant to pick up where we'd left off. But for me the moment was broken, and I knew that we didn't have time to waste.

"Is there anything else you needed to say?" I asked her as I slid the dagger into its sheath.

"No," she said, but her words were filled with heavy regret. "I think I said it all."

"Mal?" Oona called from the other room, and a second later she was in the room. Quinn finally started backing away from me to let me finish what I needed to do.

"Yeah?" I asked without looking up at her.

"Did Odin say anything else?" Oona asked. "Is there anything else we should know?"

"I don't think so."

"Well, what happened?" she persisted. "I mean, *exactly*. Be specific."

"I already told you like fifty times."

"And if telling me fifty more times could help us, then I'll keep asking you." She had the sharp tone that let me know there was no point in arguing with her.

"We waited at the temple, and Odin arrived a few minutes late—"

"How did he arrive?" Oona asked.

I shrugged. "I didn't see him *arrive*. He was just there, walking down the steps. His raven was there, too, so maybe that's how he travels."

"A raven?" she brightened. "You didn't mention that before."

"I didn't think it was that important," I said. "Odin has a pet raven, Muninn, that he hangs around with a lot."

"Only one?" Oona asked.

I snapped the clips shut on my knapsack and looked at her. "What?"

"Doesn't Odin have two ravens?"

It hadn't occurred to me before, but in at least half the pictures I had seen of Odin he was accompanied by his two black giant ravens, Muninn and Huginn. I'd been too preoccupied by meeting with a Vanir god to really think about it.

"Yeah." I nodded slowly, remembering what I'd learned in school when we'd covered Odin. "Yeah. A teacher told me that they each represent something. Muninn was . . . heart, and Huginn was mind."

"So, Odin is bringing Muninn around with him?" Oona asked. "But where's the other one?"

I slipped my knapsack on my back. "I don't know. Maybe when we get back from Kurnugia you can ask Odin yourself."

ELEVEN

———————◆———————

We took a bus from our motel, traveling through the lush greenery of Belize. When we'd first arrived here, it was like being transported into a fairy tale. It was such a disorienting contrast from the dark claustrophobia of the city back home. Here all the colors were bolder, and even the sun shone brighter.

It only took the hyperbus fifteen minutes to speed north through thirty miles of jungle before dropping us in the middle of El Noveno Anillo, with the driver telling us we'd have to make the rest of the way on our own.

Last time I had come to the run-down suburb that ran around the Gates of Kurnugia—only five days ago, though it felt like a lifetime—we had come to the north side of the city, traveling down from the affluent metropolitan area of Belmopan. We had seen the luxury condos and historic architecture blot out the trees before giving way to the slums of El Noveno.

But this time we'd come up from Caana City, ending up on the south side of El Noveno, and it was even worse than what I'd first been introduced to. The "homes"—if they could really be called that—were almost entirely made of rusted corrugated metal patched together with card-board and mud.

The dirt roads were narrow and uneven, with plenty of holes, dips, and large rocks marring the path. But the area was crowded, with humans and immortals alike, all of them looking ragged and malnour-ished. The instant Oona, Valeska, and I got out of the van, looking all healthy and clean, the locals approached us with outstretched hands, begging for spare change or fresh water or something to eat.

We began walking slowly toward the Gates of Kurnugia, slow not so much by choice but because of everyone crowding around us. Valeska firmly and repeatedly told everyone no and pushed her way ahead, carefully stepping over garbage and moving to the side to avoid a motorbike that bounced carelessly past us.

The stench was undeniable, like a rotting corpse covered in two-month-old trash and left to bake and ferment under the hot sun. Which was exactly what I suspected was happening. Somehow, it was hotter here than in the rest of the country. There was no humidity, but a dry heat, like flames lapping up from a bonfire and threatening to engulf all of us.

Sweat slid down the shaved side of my head, running down to the nape of my neck. I already had my long hair up in a ponytail, but it would do little to combat the sheer intensity of the heat.

Finally, the humans and immortals had begun dispersing, after realizing that we weren't easy marks for begging. It was still crowded, because there were far too many individuals living in too small an area, but they had begun ignoring us and going about their business.

"How much farther?" Valeska asked.

"There is still a ways to go," I admitted, then motioned to the terra-cotta wall that loomed in the distance. "That's how we get in."

A little boy came up to me, with a mop of brown curls. He stared up at me with eyes too big for his face and sallow cheeks. His lips were chapped, with a fresh scab on the corner of his mouth, and he held his dirty hand out to me.

"*Bonjou, fraulein,*" he said in a clear voice, clearer than I expected for a child of his age. Then I realized he was probably around six or seven, maybe even older, but severe malnourishment had impeded his growth, making him appear much younger. "*Ayuadame. Souple, Wasser.* I'm *sehr sediento.* Please, *fraulein.*"

He spoke in a hodgepodge of several different languages. From what I could tell, it sounded like a blend of German, Spanish, French, and English. I didn't know all the words he said, but I was fairly certain that *Wasser* meant "water."

I knew I would probably regret it later, but I didn't know how I could deny a wide-eyed, dehydrated little boy. I slid off my knapsack, carefully keeping it close so the others surrounding us didn't get any ideas, and I grabbed my bottle of water.

As I handed it to him, his eyes lit up like fireworks.

"*Mesi!*" he exclaimed. "*Mesi anpil!*"

He ran off, laughing in delight in between guzzling down the water.

Valeska looked at me, her gaze suspicious under her heavy lids. "How do you know that wasn't a trick? That he isn't a shape-shifter trying to trick you or mug you?"

"I don't," I admitted with a shrug as I slid my bag back onto my shoulders.

My Valkyrie blood usually gave me a sense of immortals, and all my training in school and at the academy meant I was pretty good at recognizing them, but I wasn't 100 percent accurate. Especially given how overpacked the area was and the supernatural vibes that the Gates of Kurnugia gave off.

"I would've done the same thing if he'd asked me," Oona assured me with a smile, but she hadn't needed to. Of course Oona would've helped him. By the pained expression in her eyes every time she denied a beggar I guessed it was taking all her willpower not to give them everything she had.

I couldn't read Valeska's expression well enough to tell if she was disapproving or approving, but what was done was done, so we moved on. As we walked closer to the city, the crowds began to finally give way.

Even the dilapidated homes were more spread out, and I noticed a few eyes peering out at us.

We followed along the wall, heading around to the entrance to the Gates, and our trek had become eerily silent. Every now and again I spotted a rat or other small vermin skittering across our path, and once an olitau flew off over us. Its leathery red wings spread wide above us, momentarily granting us a reprieve from the sun, and the bat-like beast let out an angry screech before disappearing over the walls into the Gates of Kurnugia.

But beyond that, we were alone. Knowing how populated the area was around us, I felt strangely isolated as we made the long trek under the bright sun.

Valeska stretched her wings, flapping them lightly, which caused a wonderful, brief breeze. It also wafted the hot stench around me, but it was worth it for even the slightest of reprieves from the heat.

"This is taking a lot longer than last time," Oona commented.

Since her legs were so much shorter than mine and she was less athletic, she had a tendency to fall a few steps behind, but she would never complain or ask me to slow down. Instead, she'd push herself harder, and I didn't want her to end up exhausted, so I slowed to match her pace.

"Last time we took a taxi, but this is the closest a bus would drop us off to the Gates," I said. "I didn't realize it would be quite this long a walk or I would've sprung for a taxi again."

I said that as if we had unlimited funds, but realistically I had no idea how Oona and I would be paying our rent next month, not to mention getting groceries or any other expenses. We'd both run through our very limited savings, and I hoped that Atlas could get money from Samael so we'd be able to buy Overland tickets back home when we were done here.

"We're almost there," Valeska said and pointed toward the glimpse of the arch rising above the wall. "I think the entrance is right around this bend."

"Finally," Oona muttered.

Then Valeska stopped short, causing Oona to bump right into her wings. Her sharp gaze was fixed on a piece of rusted metal leaning against a pile of trash, buzzing with flies. Oona started to ask what was going on, but I held up my hand to silence her.

Over the swarming insects, I heard it, too. A guttural rumbling and tearing, like a rabid dog attacking roadkill. I saw the snout first, poking out from under the garbage, and then it pushed forward, knocking the sheet of metal to the ground with a clatter.

It was a hulking beast, with trash sticking to its mottled orange and black fur. The head was like a wolf's—albeit much larger—but the body was much broader, with a sloping back that went down to a stubby tail and short hind legs. With its head low, baring its long yellowed teeth, the beast had a hunchbacked appearance.

When it growled, it wasn't like a normal wolf. It was higher-pitched, with a cackling edge to it, but with a throaty depth, so it sounded like a cross between a bear and a hyena. And that's when I knew exactly what was it was—a shunka warakin.

Then I heard another growl behind us, and I glanced over my shoulder to see that two other shunka warakins had appeared. We were surrounded.

TWELVE

———————◆———————

Aren't these things supposed to be on the other side of the wall?" Oona asked quietly as the snarling beast stared us down, with thick drool dripping from its gaping maw onto the dusty road.

"It doesn't really matter," Valeska said, her hand slowly going for the dagger she had sheathed on her hip. "They're here now, and we have to deal with them."

Sharur the mace was in my knapsack, too far back for me to reach, but legend claimed it had the power to fly to its owner if they truly needed it. I had yet to try it out, so I had no idea if this was true or even if I was technically the mace's owner, but there was no time for much else.

Just as the shunka warakin crouched down, preparing to pounce, I raised my hand in the air, high above my head, and shouted, "*Sharur, I need you!*"

Within seconds it all happened. My bag suddenly felt warm on my back, like it was on fire, and I heard the clips explode off of it. The shunka warakin looked at me with startled yellow eyes, and Valeska lunged at it with her dagger drawn.

The bronze handle slammed into the palm of my hand, and I gripped it tightly. I pushed Oona to the ground as I whirled around, facing the two shunkas behind us, and I began swinging the mace. The heavy iron spiked ball was attached to the staff by a thick chain, and it collided with the nearest shunka warakin with a thick squelching sound.

The beast yelped in surprise and jumped back. I yanked the mace back, taking a chunk of the shunka warakin's fur and skin with it. Behind me, I heard the shunka warakin that Valeska was fighting let out a similar pained cackling yelp.

The two in front of me looked at each other, with the non-injured one nipping at the other, and they both apparently decided we weren't worth the fight. There was probably more than enough garbage for them to scavenge anyway, so they turned tail and ran off.

When I turned back around, I saw the first shunka warakin hobbling off, leaving a trail of blood from its wounded leg. There were a few tufts of fur and feathers on the ground from the scuffle. Valeska let out a relieved sigh and pushed her wild hair back from her face, and that's when I noticed the scratch on her arm.

"Are you okay?" Oona asked, already digging into her pack for first aid.

"What?" Valeska glanced down at her arm as if she hadn't even noticed it. "Oh, I'm fine. I just need something to mask the scent of blood. That won't do us any favors inside the Gates."

"I have just the thing!" Oona sounded excited as she pulled out a small vial. She wiped the wound with gauze, then spread a thick amber salve over it.

While she patched up Valeska, I cleaned my mace and put it back in my bag. The bag's clips had broken, so I rigged them shut with a bit of Kevlar cord I'd brought with me. As I did, I thought back to what Oona had said about how the shunka warakins weren't supposed to be here.

"I thought the area around the Gates is usually deserted," Valeska said, echoing my thoughts. "The spell on the walls usually keeps everything at bay."

"Everything ignored us when we were here a few days ago," Oona agreed.

I glanced up at the sky, remembering the olitau. It had passed right over the wall, and I hadn't thought anything of it at the time. Birds were commonly passing over us. But the olitau wasn't a bird—it was a demonic bat. Shouldn't it belong on the other side? Or at least be unable to pass easily through the *brujeria* that held beings inside the Gates and kept them shut?

"Do you think something is up?" Oona asked me, and her dark eyes were filled with worry. "Like the walls are weakening?"

"I think . . . we should be happy that the shunka warakins gave up so easily," I said finally, and I straightened up and put my bag back on. "And we should hurry and get inside the Gates."

We didn't have time to discuss the implications of a weakening wall or worrying that we might already be too late.

THIRTEEN

———◆———

We entered the Gates with little fanfare, going under the arch with ease. I felt the same pins and needles I'd had last time—the odd tingling from the mystical protection created by the Vanir gods, reinforcing the walls for centuries—but this time I didn't comment on it. I just kept moving.

I followed the path from memory, walking along the winding corridor. The high walls were covered in dark red clay, and already they seemed to be blocking out the sun. It had been bright afternoon a few moments ago, but now the sky looked as if the sun was beginning to set.

Finally, the pathway widened as it opened into the Merchants of Death. It was a large open-court bazaar, full of small shops manned by mostly frightening-appearing demons, and I could smell it long before we reached it. Putrid and sulfuric odors mixed with the smell of fresh meat and the metallic scent of blood, thanks to the horrific and taboo goods they sold here.

Bright red entrails, freshly cut Cambion horns, and jars of pickled eyeballs were the types of wares on display. From what I could tell, many of the customers appeared to be humans, coming from places far and wide to buy black market items to help them with every problem known to man.

"Where do we go from here?" I asked Valeska, since she was the one who had promised a backdoor entrance to Kurnugia.

"This way." She headed toward the right, staying as close to the edge of the courtyard as she could.

As we walked, she had to duck out of the way of a serpent-like demon trying to sell her the talons of a griffin, promising they would help her become more fertile.

"I'm not really in the market for a baby," she replied dismissively.

"If you need a baby right now and don't care about the condition, Lamia can set you up," the demon assured her, and motioned to a small stand across the way.

A rather ordinary human-looking woman was standing in front of it, holding up necklaces covered in dozens of tiny little toes. I didn't want to think about where she might have gotten them, so I quickened my pace and hurried after Valeska.

Valeska led us back behind the stalls, underneath a covered alleyway that ran along the adobe walls. The narrow walkway was covered in blood, leaving it a slick, muddy mess that squished underneath my boots.

This was where the butchering took place, with several hulking demons hacking away at the mutilated corpses. I tried not to think about this or even really look at it, but it was hard to ignore. Right beside us, a large slug-like demon was hacking off the wings of a small Pegasus corpse.

He looked at us, with snot dripping from the two holes that protruded beneath his beady eyes, and wiped at his face with the back of his hand—smearing fresh Pegasus blood into the snot.

"You're not supposed to be back here," he barked at us in a thick voice.

"We're taking a shortcut," I told him, and I grabbed Oona's hand to pull her along. I didn't want to risk getting into it with a bunch of demons armed with hatchets.

Fortunately, he was too lazy to chase after us, instead muttering about how much he hated mortals. Valeska continued on ahead, with her head high, her shoulders back, and her wings spread slightly to accentuate her supernatural status, and she strutted around like she belonged here, so no one hassled her.

We hurried on, following the slow stream of blood and water that trickled down the path, and doing our best to avoid getting hit with any splatter from the butchers.

Valeska rounded a sharp corner, but that's where the path ended. It was only an alcove, framed by dark crimson clay where the rusty bloodstains blended into the walls. The stream of blood and guts flowed right into the center, to the rancid geyser that gurgled with mud and red water.

"What are we doing here?" Oona asked, wrinkling her nose in disgust at the rotten stench wafting around us.

"That's Eshik Mitu." Valeska pointed to the steaming, bubbling mess. "That's how we get in."

"What?" I stepped back. I'd never considered myself the squeamish type, but the thought of crawling into that mush and mess made my stomach roll.

"No, no." Oona shook her head. "You only told us that it was hot and could scald us. You didn't say anything about it being a disgusting pit of blood and death."

"Well, it is that, too, but honestly, I thought potentially getting boiled alive was the worst part," Valeska replied.

"You thought wrong," Oona muttered as she stared at it. "And it doesn't even look like much of a geyser. It's just a festering puddle."

"It erupts every fifteen minutes, so if we wait long enough—" Valeska stopped, glancing over at Eshik Mitu as it began to rumble.

Sulphuric smoke and steam began to thicken and rise up as the puddle bubbled. Within seconds, a putrid stream of water shot out from the earth. At least, presumably it was water, but it was a dark brown color and was surprisingly chunky, with globs of mud and boiled organs splatting on the ground. All three of us stepped back, huddling under the protection of the covered alleyway as we watched the gruesome spectacle.

"We only have about fifteen minutes until the next one, maybe less," Valeska said as the eruption subsided and the surface returned to a bubbling puddle. "This is the only way I know how to get us in there. So you can put on your big girl pants and the Valhallan cloak and we can get on with it, or we can turn around and head home with our tails between our legs. Which is it?"

"We're going," I replied without hesitation.

It had never really been a question as to whether we would or not. No matter how disgusting or perilous the path was that lay ahead of us, I would do whatever I needed to do to get down to Kurnugia and save Ash. *(You must not worry about me. Forget me. Save the world.)* I would do what I needed to do.

I ignored the burning in my chest, and I asked Oona, "What do we need to be safe enough to pass through that geyser?"

"But Odin said the cloak would protect us," Valeska said.

"It's not really meant for three people, and we're taking it where it was never meant to go," I said. "Oona's got a protection spell to help cover any places the cloak can't."

Oona took off her backpack and carefully set it on the driest spot she could find, then she crouched beside it. She rummaged quickly through her bag, pulling out a couple stones and a vial, and turned back to face Valeska and me.

"Hold out your hand," she commanded us, and we did as we were told. In the palm of each of our hands, she placed a cool, jagged spear of a stone with a mirrored black sheen to it. "You need to hang on to the hematite crystal as we travel through the geyser. No matter what happens, you can't let go of it."

"What happens if we do let go?" Valeska asked.

Oona shot her a look. "Just don't do it, okay?"

"Okay, jeez," she muttered and closed her hand around the crystal.

"For the next part, I need to put this on your heart." Oona held up a vial of clear liquid. It had an odd opaque quality to it, and small flecks of green leaves and glittering black and white crystals floated inside it. "So, if you could pull down your shirt a bit."

Valeska did as she was told, pulling her tank top down far enough to reveal her cleavage. When Oona uncorked the vial, I could faintly smell it over the fetid stench around us, so it must've been rather potent. It had an herbal scent, almost like fresh-cut parsley or cilantro, mixed with fresh rain, and something else. Something tangy.

"What is that?" Valeska asked.

"It's an armarria potion, so it has mugwort, obsidian flakes, water from the Bidasoa River—" Oona began, then she stopped and looked up at Valeska. "Do you know what any of that stuff is?"

"Not really," Valeska admitted with a shrug.

Oona sighed. "It doesn't really matter what's in it. It's a protection potion, and when I put it on you, I need to say an incantation, and you can't interrupt me."

Valeska nodded once. "Got it."

Oona stared up at her for a second, as if to ascertain that Valeska did in fact get it. Apparently satisfied, she dipped her finger in the potion, and then drew an *X* over Valeska's heart while reciting, *"Ez geala, ba geala, kalte seguru, geala."*

When she was done, she moved on to me and did the same thing. The potion felt icy and tingly on my chest, reminding me a bit of a mentholated ointment I'd used when I had a bad cold as a child. Not bad, exactly, but strange and a little intense.

While Oona made an *X* on her own chest, I pulled the Valhallan cloak out of my bag. At first I tried to be careful and keep the satiny fabric out of the filth on the ground, but then I realized it was going to have to travel through that geyser, so cleanliness was a moot point.

Odin had assured us that the cloak had strong enough properties to protect and shield us from the magic that was designed to destroy any immortal that tried to escape.

"I'm done with my part," Oona said once she'd put the vial back and put her backpack on again. She looked over at Valeska. "What's next?"

"We get under the cloak," Valeska said. "That should help us pass through the supernatural barrier between our world and Kurnugia, and hopefully protect us from the scalding water and the disgusting filth of the geyser."

"What about the key?" I asked. "When does that come into play?"

Valeska pulled the crescent-shaped Sibudu Key from around her neck. "Once we're ready, we stand over the geyser, and I set it on top. Then it opens up, and we slide through."

"And the key doesn't get lost that way?" I asked.

"No, it goes with us," she said unequivocally.

"Let's do this, then," I said.

Valeska and Oona stood on either side of me, squeezing in close, and I draped the cloak around us. I pulled it tight, so that every inch of us was covered. I had the hood draped over my head, because I was the tallest, and I wrapped an arm around Valeska and Oona.

"I'm walking over to the entrance," I told them, since they couldn't see, and the three of us carefully shuffled over to it.

The hot water sloshed up through the cloak, over our feet. It was hot, though not as blistering as I had imagined it would be. Still, it stung my bare skin exposed between my pants and boots.

"I'm dropping the key," Valeska said, and a second later I heard the splash as it hit the water.

Then we waited. Maybe five seconds, maybe ten, but it felt like an eternity during which I worried that we'd done it all wrong or we'd forgotten an important step.

Finally, the ground started to give way, as we slowly sank down into the muck. I tightened my grip around both Valeska and Oona, and for her part, Oona clung to my waist.

I pulled the hood down, covering my face, and that blotted out any light, so we were submerged completely in darkness. For a moment the only sound was that of our ragged breath and rapid beating of my heart.

The earth began to constrict around us, expanding and contracting like it was swallowing us, and I dimly wondered if this was what it felt like being eaten alive by a large snake. Accompanying the movement was the sloshing sound as the water encircled us.

As we went down, the constriction was making it hard to breathe. We were all pressed together, with Valeska's and Oona's knees and elbows digging painfully into me, and Valeska's feathers cut into my back, poking through the fabric of my shirt.

Softly, in a voice that she could barely eke out, Oona had begun repeating the earlier incantation over and over again, and I squeezed the crystal more securely in my fist.

Then suddenly it was like the floor had given out, and we dropped rapidly. There was this strange wooshing sensation, as we were sucked down into the nether realm.

FOURTEEN

———◆———

I woke up in my bedroom back in New Edgewater. Blue light from the billboard across the canal spilled in through the blinds, giving the room a beautiful ethereal glow.

A strange panic made my heart pound. I didn't know where I had thought I would be, but I knew this wasn't the right place. I breathed in deeply and noticed an unfamiliar musty scent permeating my room.

The sheets felt damp beneath me, but when I looked down at them, they appeared perfectly dry. I sat up, sorting out the foggy confusion that filled my mind.

"Is everything all right?" Asher asked, and I looked over at him with a start.

At the sight of him lying shirtless in bed beside me, relief rushed over me like a tidal wave, and a surprised sob escaped my lips. It was over, and he was here with me, and he would pull me into his arms, and I would feel safe and loved in a way that no one else had ever made me feel.

His blue eyes—normally so dark, like the ocean during a storm—almost seemed to glow in the light from the billboard.

I had the most intense urge to memorize every detail, as if part of me was terrified that this might be the last time that I saw him. So I took it all in, savoring the wonderful contradiction of him. The rugged roughness of his face mixed with the soft features of his full lips and high cheekbones, his black hair disheveled and his thick eyebrows pinched with worry.

I reached out, unable to stop myself, and put my hand on his cheek. I had to feel him, to know he was real, that he was here with me. His stubble scraped deliciously against the palm of my hand, and I let my thumb linger on the small scar at the top of his lip, like a soft comma.

"I had the worst dream," I told him, barely able to speak around the lump in my throat. "I dreamt that you were gone."

His expression turned sad and apologetic, and he put his hand over mine, the one lingering on his face. His skin felt rough and cold, and . . . somehow not quite right. Not how I remembered his hand feeling when he touched me.

"Oh, Malin," he said thickly. "It wasn't a dream."

"What?" I asked, my voice trembling, and then I felt it in my chest. My heart breaking all over again, and his words burning into it. "No, but you're here. You're here with me now."

"I'm not really here," Asher replied forlornly. "And you can't find me."

He started slipping away from me. The bed began to lengthen, pulling him away, and putting distance between us. I reached out, grabbing his hand, meaning to cling to him forever if I had to.

"Why can't I find you?" I asked. "Why won't you let me?"

"There are far more important things in this world than me," he said as his hand slid out of mine. "But I need you to know that no matter what happens, you will be all right, and I cherished every moment we spent together."

"No, Asher, wait!" I started crawling across the bed, scrambling through the sheets, but no matter how quickly I moved, he only got farther away from me.

And then I was falling, plummeting into the darkness and through trees with pine-needle branches stinging against my skin, until finally I hit the bottom. My head smacked painfully against a rock, and a bright white light blinded me for a moment.

Cold raindrops splashed on my face, and I could only smell the exhilarating delicious scent of pine and earth and rain. I opened my eyes, staring up at the trees towering over me.

Then someone stepped into my view, blocking the dim light, and the rain falling on my face blurred my vision, so I couldn't see who it was—only a shadow standing over me.

"Don't be afraid," he said, his voice deep and warm, and he held out his hand to me. "You need to wake up." A raindrop splashed into my eyes, so I closed them tightly. "Wake up, Mal."

Then I realized it wasn't his voice, but Oona's. And it wasn't far away, it was right above me, speaking in a panicked whisper.

"Mal, you have to wake up," Oona insisted, and I opened my eyes.

For some reason, I expected it to be dark, but I clearly saw Oona—her short black hair disheveled and damp, apprehension hardening the soft edges of her features and creasing her smooth skin. When she realized I was alive and awake, her taut expression changed to a relieved smile, although her dark eyes were still tinged with worry.

Beneath me, the ground was damp and uneven, and the air had a thick musty smell, like a root cellar or deep cavern. Despite the moisture, the air was oddly acrid, burning my lungs and throat and causing me to cough.

"Valeska says you'll adjust to the air," Oona assured me once the coughing fit had passed.

I tried to shake off the dream and the gnawing ache inside my chest. I could still feel Asher, slipping through my fingers as I cried out for him, and it left me with a longing so intense that it felt like my heart had literally been split in two.

I blinked back tears, gulping down the bitter air, and tried to take in my surroundings. I was in a whole new realm, seeing things that no Valkyrie had ever seen before, and I tried to focus on that and push down the pain.

The ceiling of the cavern we were in was hundreds of feet above us, and the trees surrounding us reached higher than the tallest skyscraper. There was no sun, at least not that I could see, but there seemed to be an ambient light, so it was as bright as the earth on a cloudy day. I lay in a tangle of thick roots gnarled up from the dirt around me, and cool water from the nearby river formed tributaries between them.

"We're here, then?" I asked as I slowly sat up. "We made it?"

"So far," Oona said with a grim smile.

A stone was digging into the palm of my hand, and I realized that I still had my fist clenched around the hematite crystal.

"Do you want this back?" I asked.

"No. Put it in your pocket. We need all the help we can get here."

I did as she suggested. We appeared to be in the middle of a forest, with thick towering tree trunks with no branches or leaves. At least none until it got to the ceiling, where the branches appeared to be mixing with the dirt and holding it above us.

Valeska crouched a few feet away, on the banks of the river, and she was rinsing all the muck off the Valhallan cloak. The mouth of the river came from under the trees, and it widened as it flowed away from us.

"How long was I out?" I asked as I got to my feet.

"Not much longer than us," Oona said. "We were all knocked unconscious when we came through, but we're all okay."

I stepped carefully over the roots to meet Valeska at the banks of the river. Up close, I could see the river had a dark cobalt color to it, like the night sky. She stood up and shook the cloak, drying it off some.

"Do you know where to go from here?" I asked.

"This is the Huber River," she said as she began rolling up the fabric. "It runs straight through Kurnugia, and Zianna is the heart of it. So if we follow this river it should eventually take us to Zianna."

"Are you sure about that?" I asked.

She gave a rather dramatic eye roll as she handed me the damp, smelly cloak. "No. I'm not sure about anything, but that is my educated guess."

I looked back over my shoulder at Oona, who gave a helpless shrug. We were alone in the forest, at least as far as I could tell, but there was no telling how long we would be or what might be lurking around the trees.

"Are we all ready to go?" I asked as I shoved the cloak into my bag, and I glanced up at Oona and Valeska.

They were all geared up, with their packs on, and I could just make out the crescent outline of the Sibudu Key under Valeska's tank top. Their clothes were wet and muddy, with dark smudges of earth smeared on their skin, and Valeska's already untamed hair appeared even wilder than normal. I suspected that I looked about as filthy as they did, but there was no sense in wasting time washing up, especially since the underworld wasn't exactly renowned for its cleanliness.

"Let's get on with it, then," I said.

"So what's the plan?" Valeska asked as we made our way along the river, carefully stepping over thick roots. "I mean, we follow the river to Zianna, then what?"

"Odin said that Baldur took the spear into Zianna, so that's the first goal." I paused to help Oona step over a particularly tall bramble. Then I continued, "Once we get there, I'll use the sólarsteinn to lead us to the exact location."

Even though Valeska wasn't much taller than Oona, she didn't need my help. When she stumbled or lost her footing, she merely flapped her wings and elegantly righted herself.

"But how are we going to get into Zianna?" Valeska asked. "It's not like they just let anyone waltz in and out. That's the whole point of the city."

"I doubt there's a lot of spells to keep mortals at bay, since we aren't even supposed to be here," I pointed out, crossing my fingers. "But that's also why we brought Oona along."

"When we get close enough I can get a sense of what kind of magic is protecting Zianna, and I can tailor a spell or potion to get us through," Oona elaborated.

In front of us was a steep embankment several meters high, but fortunately the twisting roots worked as a makeshift ladder. Valeska bypassed it all and flew up to the top, while Oona and I followed more slowly.

As we made the climb, Valeska looked down at us and asked

pointedly, "You really think you're powerful enough to do that? No offense, but didn't you say you're just a sorceress-in-training?"

"I'm not *just* anything," Oona snapped, giving her an icy glare. "I've been training for a long time, and I know a lot, and I'm actually at the top of my class. Besides that, I got us through that geyser safe and sound. You didn't get any burns this time, did you?"

"Fair enough," Valeska said.

She bent down and extended a hand toward Oona, who seemed to debate a second before accepting it and letting Valeska help pull her up onto the top of the embankment.

The trees had thinned considerably, and the roots were no longer protruding through the dirt to trip us up, leaving a relatively smooth path alongside the river for us to follow.

"I'd expected there to be more creatures and whatnot down here," Oona commented. "There has to be thousands of years of beings. I didn't think we'd ever really be alone."

"We're out at the fringes of Kurnugia," Valeska explained. "But we'll run into immortals soon enough."

No sooner had the words escaped her lips than we heard a man let out a bloodcurdling scream, following by growling and the gnashing of teeth.

FIFTEEN

———◆———

Instinctively, I crouched down, grabbing Oona's arm to pull her down with me, and whirled around to see a rather disturbing scene unfolding about fifty feet away from us.

A body went hurling through the air before crashing into a thick tree trunk. When it landed, I realized it looked human, with delicate, androgynous features. Two small antlers poked through the long bright crimson hair on its head, the antlers being the only visible supernatural part.

But I only had a few seconds to look at the fallen body, because a large reptilian monster—a sirrush—was tearing through the trees toward it. While shiny emerald scales covered the majority of the creature's body, running all down its long neck and torso, its legs were covered in a thick dark fur, appearing more like they belonged to a large jungle cat than a dragon. The talons were long and razor-sharp, and a solitary horn protruded from the center of the beast's head.

I had seen pictures of a sirrush in books, but I'd never encountered one before in real life, and as it lunged toward its prey, I found myself immensely grateful that I'd never been tasked with returning one of these things.

While the red-haired victim wailed—screaming in agony, really—the sirrush reached out and sliced it open with a sharp talon, disembowel-ing it.

Without thinking, I stood up and shouted, "Hey!"

"Malin," Valeska hissed, but it was too late. The sirrush turned back to look at me, flicking its forked tongue at me while blood and intestines oozed out of its victim.

It was stupid, and I knew that instantly, but I couldn't stand by and let this dragon eviscerate somebody. Not when they were screaming and begging for mercy.

"Get out of here!" I shouted, hoping to intimidate a monster that very clearly would not be intimidated, and I unsheathed my dagger.

The sirrush stepped toward me with its solitary horn pointed right at me, and I dismally recalled the conversation I'd recently had with Oona in which I'd reminded her that because we were mortal, we could die in Kurnugia. And there would be no coming back for us.

"Lux splendida!" Oona shouted, and a bright white light flashed, more intense than a lightning bolt, and momentarily blinded me.

The sirrush cried out in surprise and pain, clawing at its eyes. Ap-parently deciding that whatever made that light wasn't worth the trou-ble, it ran off into the woods, back to where it had come from.

"You're so lucky that worked," Valeska said.

"I should work on a cloaking potion," Oona said. "I doubt very many of the monsters we encounter will be so easily frightened off by parlor tricks, so it'd be best if they didn't notice us."

"Good idea. And thank you for saving my life," I told her, and though I meant it, my attention was fixed on the victim, who was still groaning and bleeding.

I walked over, meaning to help if I could, and as I got closer, I saw a looped square branded on the victim's shoulder, where the shirt had been torn. It was the Hannunvaakuna—a Finnish symbol of good luck—and I realized that the red-haired victim was most likely Lempo, a trickster god.

"Are you okay?" I asked, extending my hand toward him.

He didn't say anything and barely even glanced at me as he pushed himself to his feet. His intestines were literally tumbling out of him, leaking all kinds of grotesque fluids everywhere. He cradled them in his arms as he began to walk off into the woods, but a long loop dragged behind, collecting dirt.

"A thank-you would've been nice," I muttered as he walked away, but he never turned back or said anything.

"Why would he thank you?" Valeska asked, and I turned to face her. "It's going to happen again in a few days, maybe even tomorrow. Over and over, he's going to be eaten alive by that sirrush or some other monster."

"Holy shit." I stared down at the trail of blood he'd left on the ground as my stomach twisted in knots.

I'd learned about this in school. Kurnugia was where immortals went when their time on earth was done. There was nowhere else for them to go, and they couldn't die, they were immortal. They would just heal up and do it all over again.

One of the first stories we'd been taught in high school about Kurnugia was the tale of Prometheus. He'd angered Zeus, so he'd been chained to a rock, where his liver was eaten daily by an eagle, and every night it grew back, only to be eaten again the next day.

The teacher told us that when he was finally marked for death and the Valkyrie came for him, Prometheus had been grateful and thanked her for setting him free. Eternity in Kurnugia was a reprieve from his torturous life on earth.

That lesson was supposed to teach us that Valkyries were necessary, and not even a necessary evil, but something good. Something that spared immortals from the pain of living forever on earth.

Even then, I had known that wasn't true. They still had eternity to live somewhere—it was only the humans that had been spared sharing it with them. And now, seeing the bright red blood of a repeat victim, I realized that the Valkyrie had not saved Prometheus.

There was no reprieve for him. He'd merely been shuttled somewhere else. It was the same eternal punishment, only with a different wrapping.

SIXTEEN

———◆———

On the ground in front of us sat a squat black candle in a votive holder. All sorts of symbols were etched into the rhodium metal, creating a lattice effect that the light could shine through. Or at least the light normally would shine, except this flame was dark blue and cast little light.

Despite the small size of the candle, it produced a considerable amount of indigo smoke, but I guessed that was the point, based on the way Oona was fanning it toward us. It wouldn't have been so bad, except the smoke had a pungent odor. Like fermenting blue cheese that had begun to rot in the sun.

"Ugh." Valeska groaned in disgust and held her nose. "Is this really necessary?"

Honestly, I would've complained as well, but the combination of the putrid scent mixing with the acrid air caused me to have a bit of a coughing fit.

"It is if you want us to go unseen." Oona remained undaunted as the smoke billowed over us, and she began chanting, *"Omnium visibilium et invisibilium omnium manemus."*

When she had finished, she picked up the candle and blew it out.

"I know the valerian root candle reeks something fierce," Oona said. "But it'll help with our concealment."

"So now we'll be invisible?" Valeska asked.

"Not exactly," Oona said and carefully placed the still-warm candle in the side pocket of her backpack. "But we will be less visible. Others can still see us, but they have to be looking for us."

"Let's move on so I don't have to smell that awful candle anymore," Valeska muttered, and started walking ahead without waiting for either of us.

As we walked along the river, none of us said anything. I tried to take in the sights, but there wasn't much to see. It was mostly various shades of brown. The dirt ground leading into clay walls, with the occasional tree holding up the ceiling.

For a while we were alone. At least as far as we could tell. But eventually we started coming across some immortals. Several large griffins were drinking from the river, and we gave them a wide berth, but they never even glanced in our direction.

As we went on, the river became busier, with more immortals walking alongside it. Some were drinking from it, while others appeared to be swimming or socializing. It wasn't all that different than going to a lake on a summer day, and there was something oddly disquieting about that. How normal and ordinary the immortals seemed to be existing here in the underworld.

"Your enchantment seems to be working," Valeska told Oona, since none of the beings around seemed to notice us. We'd moved away from the flowing water to give them more space, and no one reacted to us at all.

"We still have to be careful," Oona said. "I imagine it'll be easier for the more powerful immortals to see through the spell."

Valeska nodded, as if that had already occurred to her. "We should try to avoid the cities, then, if we can. The demons of destruction tend to run them, and they would love to get their hands on the Sibudu Key. They're always looking for any way to break out of here."

"The demons of destruction?" Oona asked, looking at Valeska as we walked along.

"Yeah, like Abaddon, Vanth, and Nirriti," Valeska explained, and she pointed up ahead, to where the river was hidden behind a thicket of trees. "The city up ahead around the bend is Tartarus, and when I was here last, it was under the rule of Perses."

"There's just like regular cities here?" Oona asked, sounding shocked. "Immortals going about their business?"

Twenty feet away from us, a very human-looking woman was singing to herself in a lovely voice. She crouched on the banks of the water and used a bristled brush to scrub her clothes against a rock. Beside her was a wicker basket filled with her dirty laundry.

None of this was how I had imagined it. Before we'd gotten here, I would've been shocked by the idea of cities in the underworld. But now, seeing the woman washing her dirty clothes, it made perfect sense.

They were just living their lives. Or deaths, as it were.

The only real sign that this all wasn't a normal place on earth—other than the total lack of sky, with the dark umber of dirt entwined with the branches soaring above us—was what lined the path we walked. Near the river, it had been mostly smooth, presumably worn that way by centuries of travelers venturing to the water.

But now we had ventured out farther, giving the immortal residents space. There wasn't grass, exactly, but there were plants. A few were taller, about knee-high, with burnt-orange leaves and sharp thistles, along with some flowering plants with blood-red blossoms that smelled of death when I grazed them.

Mostly, though, the dirt was blanketed with a ground ivy with deep olive-green leaves and long tendrils that moved out of the way as we walked by. Occasionally I felt them tickling against the backs of my ankles as they reached out after me, attempting to grab me.

Through the plants, sharp white bones jutted out here and there. When I looked closely, I could see that the ground was littered with fragmented bones, fractured skulls, and the odd fang or broken talon. Oona stumbled over some of them, and I caught her arm before she fell.

"Of course," Valeska replied matter-of-factly to Oona's question about cities. "They have eternity to build their own civilizations."

"How do you know so much? Most of what you've told us isn't common knowledge up on earth," I said.

I'd spent most of my life training and studying to return immortals to Kurnugia, and I hadn't heard of half the things that Valeska was explaining to me. It was beyond the scope of any course I'd taken at Ravenswood Academy.

"How could it be?" Valeska retorted. "No one comes back up to tell the tale of what they've seen. The only things we really know about Kurnugia are what the Vanir gods have told us."

"So you learned it all from your mom?" Oona asked.

Valeska lowered her gaze, and she was slow to reply. But eventually she said, "She told me some, but not very much. I mostly learned it through trial and error."

"What do you mean?" Oona asked.

"When I was here before, I was here for a month before I finally found my mom," Valeska answered, causing Oona to gasp. "Kurnugia is a massive place. I don't know how vast it is, even. Maybe as big as a continent, maybe as big as the galaxy."

"How did you survive that long?" Oona asked, echoing my thoughts.

Valeska lifted her head, staring straight before her as we walked, and there was a hardness to her expression. Her jaw was set, and her large eyes had darkened. "I snuck around and hid a lot. Having wings definitely helped me avoid a lot of bad situations."

"Did you make friends?" Oona asked, sounding hopeful.

"I kept to myself as much as I could," Valeska answered flatly. "You never know who you can trust down here."

From the corner of my eye, I saw someone looking at us. I tried to just keep walking, but she was staring at us intensely.

She stood ahead of us, standing between where we walked and the river. I couldn't tell what she might be, but she appeared to be a beautiful woman in her forties, with long black hair and tawny skin. Her face was slightly long but was not unattractive, and her arms and legs were sinewy. The sari she wore was dirty and faded, but the way it draped across her shoulders had an elegance about it. Around her neck she wore a gold chain with a large locket. It actually reminded me more of a golden bell jar, with an exquisite engraving on it.

"What about her?" I asked Valeska, motioning toward the woman. "Is she a friend of yours?"

Valeska paused and furrowed her brow. "No, I don't think I've ever seen her before in my life."

"Well, she definitely sees us," I said, since she'd started walking over to us.

"Is the enchantment wearing off?" Valeska asked.

"No, it shouldn't be. Not yet." Oona glanced around. "And no one else seems to be looking at us."

We'd stopped walking, since this woman was coming straight for us and it might cause more of a scene if we tried to run away. It wasn't until she got closer that I realized she wasn't looking at *us*, or even at Valeska, the way I'd assumed she was.

No, her dark chestnut eyes were locked on me.

"Do I know you?" she asked, sounding as confused as I felt, and my hand hovered above the dagger sheathed at my side.

"I . . . I really doubt it," I stammered, unsure of how to respond.

She tilted her head and narrowed her eyes. "There's something familiar about you. We must've met."

I knew for certain that I hadn't returned her. I remembered the faces of everyone that I had killed. But I couldn't say the same about who my mother had killed. No one had ever told me that I looked a lot like Marlow, but there had to be some family resemblance.

And if Marlow had killed this woman, and hers was the last face she'd seen on earth, I imagine that it would be etched in her mind forever. That she could see the similarities I shared with my mother.

"I really don't think so," I insisted and started walking, afraid of what this confrontation might uncover.

"Tell me your name, at least," she persisted, following after me. "Let me put my mind to rest."

I tried to brush her off, but she was right at my side, and others had begun to look at us. I had to do something. "Malin. My name is Malin."

"Malin?" she repeated, and then suddenly she was in front of me, blocking my path, and her eyes had taken on a frantic intensity. "Do you know my daughter?"

"Your daughter?" I asked.

"I'm Lyra," she said, speaking rapidly. "My daughter is Sloane."

"Sloane?" I asked, barely able to hear my own voice over the sound of my pounding heart.

Sloane Kothari, my classmate who had given me the sólarsteinn. The same sólarsteinn that had once belonged to her mother, an Apsara who had been killed years ago during an attempted uprising against the Valkyries.

For a moment I was frozen, unable to respond. My fingers lingered on my dagger, and I cleared my throat.

"How do you . . ." I began, then started over. "When you died, I didn't even know Sloane. How could you possibly know of me?"

"I hear from her in her prayers." Lyra smiled sadly at me. "She's mentioned you a lot recently." Then her smile fell abruptly, and her eyebrows arched in suspicion. "But you . . . I know what you are, and you shouldn't be here."

SEVENTEEN

———◆———

My mouth had gone dry, and I wanted to take a deep breath to help clear my head of the electric panic that coursed through me, but the air only burned, feeling as if flames were lapping down my throat and into my lungs.

The handle of the dagger felt cool and comforting against my skin, but that did little to combat my tension. I glanced around, looking for an out. All around me were immortal creatures—ranging from small peaceful goblins to violent lumbering giants—and the one thing that united them all was that they had been put here by a Valkyrie.

If Lyra decided to out us, there would be nothing I could do. I couldn't possibly defeat all of them. The only thing I could do was tell Valeska to grab Oona and fly off, leaving the two of them to complete the mission.

I swallowed hard and looked at Lyra, preparing to say just that, but before I could, she put her hand on my arm. The gentleness of her touch startled me. It was almost . . . comforting.

"We shouldn't talk here," Lyra said, lowering her voice as she glanced around. "There are too many prying ears."

"Do we need to talk at all?" Valeska asked, with an edge to her words that let me know she'd been playing out the same scenario that I had, with dozens of immortals descending upon me and tearing me apart.

"Yes," Lyra replied firmly. "I have somewhere we can go."

She let go of my arm and readjusted her sari, then motioned for us to walk on. I looked to Valeska, but she only shook her head grimly. What choice did we have but to do as Lyra asked?

We continued on the way we had been going, following Lyra around the bend past a thicket of trees. Beyond the trees the ground sloped down in a hill before coming to a vast canyon. A bridge extended over it, carved from the same sienna-colored stone that made up the chasm itself.

Across the bridge was a large city carved into the rocky mountain that extended miles above the canyon and bridge. Despite the sheerness of it—it rose at nearly a ninety-degree angle—hundreds of square buildings had been carved into it, with narrow winding paths running between them.

Based on the dozens of immortals going back and forth across the bridge, it appeared to be a bustling city. With all the music and chatter, barking animals, and even clotheslines draped between the homes, it reminded me so much of my neighborhood back in New Edgewater.

"That's Tartarus," Lyra said, motioning to the city. "My home is at the bottom, across the Acheron Gorge."

"We're going to your house?" I asked.

"It is the best place for us to talk," she replied simply and kept walking.

Oona leaned in close to me and whispered, "Do you really think this is safe?"

"No," I said honestly. "But I can't see what choice we have."

Lyra led the way across the bridge, while I followed behind a bit more slowly. I wasn't afraid of heights, but this definitely made me nervous. It was only about ten feet wide, and it had no railing. There was nothing preventing us from tumbling over the side, or any of the beings passing us from pushing us over the side.

I made the mistake of looking over the edge, at the darkness that fell far below us. Through the shadows I saw hints of gray hands and arms reaching out, clawing futilely at the air. Under the murmur of the urban life and the chatter of the population, I could hear the faint sound of wailing echoing off the walls of the canyon.

Once we crossed the bridge, I expected us to head into the city, but Lyra turned sharply. At first I thought she was about to walk off the edge of the cliff and fall down to the grasping clutches of the damned souls below.

But then I realized there was a very narrow path, maybe a foot or two wide, that ran down the sheer wall of the canyon. The walkway was so narrow that Valeska had trouble navigating with her wings, and eventually settled for flying along beside us. From the path, the wailing seemed louder, and the acrid air smelled of death and decay.

Finally Lyra stopped in front of a small door crudely carved into the cliff face, and motioned toward it. "This is my home."

I went in eagerly, happy to be away from the edge, and entered the quaint little cave home of the Apsara. It was one small room, with a lumpy daybed next to a makeshift wood-burning stove, its small chimney disappearing into the wall. A table sat in the center of the room, with two chairs, but several overstuffed cushions were on the floor, resting on a threadbare rug. On one wall was an antique armoire, with intricate mandala-like designs carved into it.

Once we were all inside, Lyra closed the thick wooden door and bolted it shut. She walked around, lighting a few candles and a stick of incense before closing the shades over the only two windows.

She turned to us, wringing her hands as her eyes darted among the three of us. The dim light from the candles made her skin glow, adding to her ethereal beauty, and I understood exactly how she had been a muse for humans in her life on earth.

"I presume none of you are dead," Lyra said finally. "So what is it exactly that you are doing here?"

"We're on a mission," I answered evasively, but she only raised an eyebrow, waiting for me to explain. "From Odin."

She let out a joyless laugh. "Of course. Only a Vanir god would be arrogant enough to tamper with the underworld."

"We're not trying to tamper with anything," I insisted. "We only want to make things right."

"I'm certain you do." She smiled at me. "But nothing is ever that simple, now, is it?" Her smile filled with pity. "Maybe you're too young to understand."

"We understand plenty," Valeska interjected haughtily.

"Are you all friends of Sloane?" Lyra asked.

"No. Only I am," I said, then corrected myself. "I mean, we're sorta friends. I guess. We're classmates."

"Is she well?" Lyra asked with a hopefulness that was almost painful to hear. "Is she happy?"

"I think she is," I said as honestly as I could. "But she's troubled by the same things that I am."

"She helped Malin on our quest," Oona piped in, referring to the sólarsteinn. "She believes that what we're doing is the right thing."

"I know. She hopes so, anyway." Lyra looked at me pensively for a moment, before nodding, as if deciding something. "I suppose that's settled, then, isn't it? I will help you. That's what Sloane would want, and I can do so little for her from here. But I can do this. I can help her friends."

EIGHTEEN

———◆———

Oona and I sat across from each other at the table on the wobbly old chairs, while Valeska had taken a cushion on the floor. Lyra was at the armoire, pouring a syrupy pale peach-pink liquid from a crystal decanter. We'd tried to refuse, but Lyra insisted that we drink while we talk.

When she set the brass cups of what appeared to be lassi in front of us, a sweet scent wafted to us—like honey and fresh-cut flowers.

"What is it?" Oona asked, as she admired the liquid swirling in her cup.

"Amritā," she explained. "Some call it the 'nectar of the gods.' It will give you strength and courage for what lies ahead."

I drank first, while Valeska stared down at her cup as if she expected a monster to leap out and bite off her face. It was almost overly sweet, but not quite. Despite the viscosity, there was a lightness to it, almost reminiscent of cucumber lemonade, but with an earthy undertone, like it had been left to age for a very long time.

"Did Sloane tell you how I died?" Lyra asked as I sipped my beverage.

Already I could feel the liquid coursing through me. It was soft but heady, like the exhilaration right after a first kiss, without all the heart-pounding and butterflies. Just a good, strange intoxication. But unlike alcohol, which muddied my thoughts, this made me feel more clear-headed and alert.

When I breathed in, the air no longer burned my lungs.

"She told me some," I answered carefully. "An uprising against the Evig Riksdag."

"Against Valkyries," Lyra amended. She stood, leaning back against the armoire, with her gaze resting heavily on me. "But I want you to know I never held any hatred toward you or your ilk personally. You were merely the weapons. You were as exploited as the rest of us."

"I wouldn't really say I'm exploited," I argued, but without as much conviction as I would've had a few weeks ago. "I was born a Valkyrie, but I didn't have to be one. Not if I didn't want to."

"I used to think like you," she said with a bemused smile. "Then everything changed. I went my whole life believing I had a choice, that I had free will. Then one day I realized I was wrong."

Oona had gulped down her Amritā, and she wiped her mouth with the back of her hand before asking, "What changed?"

Lyra sighed and then began. "I lived for a hundred years before getting married, and then Sloane's father and I waited another fifty years to have her. As immortals, we were always very conscious about having a mortal child."

Lyra and her husband were immortals, but they were different species. She was an Apsara, he was a Devi, and while there were many similarities between the two, they were not the same. The child of any mixed parentage—even of two immortals—will be mortal. Since both of Sloane's parents were divine immortals of different species, she was a mortal Nephilim.

"I didn't think I'd ever have children after I fell in love with a Devi, knowing that meant that we'd most likely outlive any child we had," she went on. "But we both had so much love, and we wanted to share it with our own baby.

"So." Lyra paused, thinking for a moment before continuing. "We had Sloane, and I loved her with all my heart. I still love her with every part of my being.

"When she was still very small, she fell off a changing table. I ran and barely caught her. If I had arrived a moment later, she would've fallen to the floor. She could've been hurt or even killed. Mortal babies are so fragile, and that's why I had never wanted to have a child."

Lyra held her arms out, miming as if she were cradling a baby, and she stared down into them, lost in her memory. "Then, as I held my beautiful baby girl, worrying about all the ways she might be maimed or killed, I realized that I had never wanted her."

She looked up sharply then, her voice strong. "Don't mistake that for me saying that I didn't love her—I do. I did. Always. But I *never* made a conscious decision to have her.

"I remembered the conversations I'd had with her father, where we talked at length," she went on. "I could hear my own words coming out of my mouth, saying, 'Let's have a baby.' But in my heart, deep within me, that's not what I wanted." Her smile turned bitter as she spoke. "But I had been compelled to say it."

A chill ran over me, and I wondered painfully if Marlow had felt the same way about me. If she had never wanted me, but had been compelled. Unlike Lyra, she'd never mustered the ability to love me the way Lyra loved Sloane.

"Many women experience things like that," Oona countered gently. "Having children is life-changing. It's easy to have regrets and fears."

"No, this was different," Lyra insisted, with a finality in her words. "And the more I thought about it, the more I realized that so many things in my life I did, I hadn't wanted to do. Part of that was my nature. Because I'm an Apsara, I had a duty to be good and kind and to motivate others to do the same. It's instinctual, the same way a robin knows how to make a nest. I knew how to inspire."

"Because you're immortal, you have stronger instincts," I said. "But I have them, too."

"Of course," Lyra agreed. "It's only the humans who were favored by the gods that were truly given free will." She rolled her eyes at that. "But I had come to realize that it was stronger than that for me.

"Like having Sloane," she went on. "It was as if something else was controlling me. I investigated more, and it occurred to me that would be the only way that Valkyries make sense: If there is someone else writing our destiny, controlling our fate. Making us do things that we don't want to do."

"So you think you don't have free will. What about me?" I asked, then motioned to Oona. "Or Oona?" Then I pointed to Valeska, who responded with a groan of annoyance that I was bringing her into the argument. "Or children of mixed parentage, like Valeska here or Sloane?"

"How can any of us truly have free will if the entire immortal population is controlled by someone—*something*—else?" Lyra persisted. "They're behaving as they are made, behaving around you without choice, so all your interactions have become choreographed. None of us can be free. That's why I wanted an uprising. I wanted to liberate Sloane.

"But then I realized the truth far too late, not until after I had been down here for some time," she said with a weary sigh. "I can't break free. I can't do anything I wasn't destined to do. To go against destiny would be to tear at the very fabric of our existence, causing the magic that traps all of us into our respective worlds to fail, and it would only be a matter of time before all the immortals here found a way back to earth. There are so many here who want only to reclaim what they believe was stolen from them—their time up in the sun—and they will do anything to get it back, even if it means destroying everything."

Her eyes were downcast as the weight of her words settled in around us.

"So I stay here," she said finally. "I will toil away for as long as my daughter is alive. She has such a short time on the earth, and I want her to enjoy it as much as she can. I want her to be happy and alive."

Valeska broke the ensuing silence with, "That's very admirable of you."

"What choice do I have?" Lyra asked with a bitter smile. Then she straightened and clasped her hands together. "I'm certain you didn't come down here to listen to the ramblings of an old woman. What is it that I can help you with?"

"We are—" I began, but Valeska cut me off, clearing her throat loudly.

"No offense, but after everything you've told us, I don't know how we can trust you," Valeska said, and I cast her a look, but she just stared impassively at Lyra.

"Sloane helped you because she believes your mission is good, and I want only to keep my daughter safe," Lyra replied evenly. "But if you don't want my help, I can't force you."

"I think we need as much help as we can get," I clarified, still glaring at Valeska, but then I turned to Lyra. "For your safety and ours, it's for the best that you don't know the details of our mission. But I don't think it would hurt, and it would help us a great deal, if you could assist us in getting to Zianna."

Lyra arched a dark eyebrow. "You're going to Zianna? You won't be able to get in without the help of a divine immortal like myself. They won't let just anybody wander in."

"But you think you could get us in?" I asked.

"Yes. But you'll need to get cleaned up first." She motioned to our dirty skin and tangled hair. "I'm not sure what we'll do about your clothes. I have things you can wear, but they might be too ragged for strangers like you to be let through the door."

"I think I can help with that," Oona said with a hopeful grin. "But we'll be happy to take whatever you can spare."

NINETEEN

———◆———

Valeska gave another irritated grumble, and I looked at her from the corner of my eye, since Lyra held my head still as she carefully plaited my long black hair.

"Is this *really* necessary?" Valeska asked, her husky voice almost pleading, as she motioned to her changed look.

Her wild hair had been tamed into loose curls thanks to a combination of Lyra and Oona's expertise, and a bejeweled ribbon headband ran across the back of her head to keep it all in place.

Her new outfit consisted of off-white trousers paired with a snug, embellished vest that had to be modified to accommodate Valeska's wings. Both the top and the pants had seen better days, with fraying and loose strings everywhere.

My outfit was only a little better, made of a gold fabric that had long since lost its sheen. The top was cropped, revealing my midriff, and the long skirt hung low on my hips.

"I feel like we're wasting time," Valeska lamented. "And these don't even look that good." Then she gave Lyra an apologetic smile as she quickly amended, "No offense. We appreciate the effort, but is all of this even going to matter?"

"I can polish us up once we're just outside Zianna," Oona reminded her. "We have to wait until we're closer, because the effects won't last that long."

Oona was bent over the table, peering into a warped mirror as she applied a swab of gold dust across her eyelids. While the dress she wore was rather ill-fitting, with mounds of fabric draping over her petite frame, the burgundy color looked wonderful against her skin.

"I know this isn't the best, but I hope it's enough to get you through the door." Lyra tied off my hair and stepped back, pursing her lips as she looked over the three of us. "It may not work, but it certainly has a better chance than the filthy rags you came in."

Those rags had all been tucked away safely into our bags, which sat packed by the door, ready to go.

"But you're right," Lyra said, resting her eyes on Valeska, who stood by the door with her arms folded over her chest. "We shouldn't waste time. Let's be on our way."

"How long will it take to get to Zianna?" I asked as we gathered up our things.

"Too long," Valeska snorted.

"It is long, but I have ways to make it quicker," Lyra assured us, and held the door open for us. "I know a shortcut, and we won't be going on foot."

"How will we get there, then?" Oona asked, exchanging a look with me, as Lyra closed the door to her home.

Instead of answering us, Lyra turned and walked ahead on the narrow path. Once again, Valeska decided to forgo the whole walking thing and flew up ahead, waiting for us at the end. I clung to the side of the wall, moving slowly, with Oona constantly glancing back at me.

"Do you want me to come and get you?" Valeska called to me when I'd almost reached the end.

"No, I got it," I insisted, and it took all my willpower not to look down at the black abyss of the canyon and the wailing death it contained.

Finally I made it off the path, but instead of crossing the bridge back the way we had come, Lyra headed into the city of Tartarus. I scampered to catch up to her, but it wasn't exactly easy.

Oona's cloaking spell was still in full effect, which meant the other immortals around kept bumping into me, since they didn't notice me. Even in the overpopulated city back home I wasn't used to seeing this many immortals cramped together like this.

Many of them were quite large and powerful, while some were almost tiny, like the hobgoblin who ran into my shins as he tried to dash ahead. While a few were humanoid in appearance, the majority of them appeared more monstrous, like demons with red scaly flesh or the werewolf-like Lobishomen.

But no matter how they appeared, all of them had the same expression—blank, almost lifeless, with eyes that stared right through me. I wondered how many times they had made their commute across the bridge, leaving Tartarus to do whatever it was that filled their existence here in Kurnugia.

A wendigo was walking straight toward me, its dead black eyes staring out from beneath its large antlers. The ashy gray skin hung off its bones, exposing throbbing red organs underneath. I tried to move out of the way as much as I could, but the wendigo slammed into my shoulder anyway, knocking me back.

"Easy, there," Valeska said, catching me before I fell to the ground. For a second I leaned back in her arms, my head resting against her chest, and she grinned down at me before pushing me back up onto my feet again.

"Thanks," I mumbled, preparing to hurry to catch up to Oona and Lyra, only to see that they had somehow disappeared into the crowd. I'd only looked away for a second, but now, as I scanned around me with a growing sense of panic, I couldn't see them.

A few yards away, lined up in front of awnings attached to the wall that ran around the city, was a row of massive Kting Voar bulls. They were built like yaks, with large humps behind their big heads, and smooth brown fur mottled with white spots. A pair of two-foot-long horns protruded on either side of their heads, the thick bones twirling and twisting asymmetrically like a serpent, which was ironic given the creatures' reputation for eating snakes.

To assist with their reptilian appetites, they had rows of sharp teeth that looked like they belonged more in a wolf than a bovine animal. They also had two large saber-like fangs extending down a good six inches.

The one in front let out a braying grunt, then shook his massive head. Because of his horns, the immortals around him moved out of the way, giving a brief opening in the crowd, and in that moment I caught a glimpse of Oona and her burgundy dress.

"This way!" I shouted and grabbed Valeska's hand to pull her along after me.

As I rushed through, narrowly dodging all sorts of creatures and ducking underneath a bull's horns, I saw that Oona didn't appear to even notice we weren't with her. She was smiling as she petted a bull, while he ate large pellets out of her hand, carefully as to be mindful of his massive incisors.

The yoke around the bull's neck was attached to a large covered buggy, and Lyra stood beside it, haggling with an ogre in Sumerian.

"Thanks for waiting for us," I said to Oona breathlessly as I reached her.

"I knew you'd catch up. You always do," she said with a knowing smile, then motioned to the bull. "Meet Kalbi. He's going to take us on the rest of our journey."

"We're riding with this?" I asked, staring up at the monstrosity that nuzzled my best friend.

My experience with Kting Voars on earth had been rather limited, as their large size and fiery temperament made them dangerous, despite their big doe eyes. Besides that, I didn't know how much I wanted to put my life in the hands of a giant beast confined to the underworld.

"Greedy ogre," Lyra muttered as she walked back to us. "I booked the Voar Cabriolet."

"Is this the best way?" I asked skeptically, but then, when I glanced down the line of bulls, I realized exactly what this was—it was a line for taxis.

Electricity didn't work here, so for all intents and purposes Kurnugia had become a medieval society populated only by immortals. It was the supernatural Dark Ages.

"Of course," Lyra replied. "Kting Voars are the quickest and safest way to travel around here. They're big and fast, and trained to protect the carriage at all costs."

"He'll take good care of us," Oona said, patting him one last time.

Lyra climbed into the buggy, then turned back to face me. "Come on. Let's go."

TWENTY

———— ◆ ————

$\mathcal{L}$yra was right. Kalbi had lumbered through the crowded city and over the bridge, but once he got out into the open land, he took off like a bullet. When we began running at full-spring, I clung to the seat of the bouncing carriage, more than a little afraid that the whole thing might fall apart in a dramatic explosion of wood and wheels.

Lyra sat up front in the footman's seat holding the reins, since she'd paid extra to drive the cabriolet herself. It would be best if no outsiders went along with us.

Valeska, Oona, and I sat in the back, under the black fabric hood that covered the four-wheeled carriage. The exterior of the carriage had been stained black, but inside, the floorboards were bare and warped. There were two benches, one in the front and one in the back, each covered with a burlap-like material and the thinnest of padding.

Above each bench was a window. The back one was covered in a murky glass, but the front was just a dark curtain that could be pulled back to talk to the driver. On either side of the carriage were half doors, with the top left open, letting the wind and air rush in from the outside.

Once I felt comfortable that the cart was stable enough to handle our speed, I settled back in beside Oona. She sat with her legs crossed underneath her, a stack of notes on her lap. Her spell book was far too large and important to sneak down here, so she'd copied important spells down and bound the pages together with weighted string so they couldn't easily blow away.

Valeska had spread out on the other bench. Her legs stretched the length of the bench, and her wings propped her up slightly, so her head rested against the side of the carriage.

I leaned back, futilely attempting to relax myself, when I noticed how strangely the cover over the carriage had been sewn together. The pieces of the cover were haphazard and patchwork, with thick thread binding them. It reminded me of the cover of a Necronomicon I had seen back at the Ravenswood Academy, where the cover had been made with human flesh.

"Is this real leather?" I asked, running my fingers along the thick jagged seams of the cover.

Valeska looked up at it, then shrugged. "Probably."

"But where would they get it from?"

"Same place they get it on earth," she replied disinterestedly. "Kting Voars are basically cattle, so I'm sure they can get some leather from them."

"But they can't die . . ." I trailed off as a horrific realization hit me. They were skinned, they were eaten, they were tortured while they were alive, and eventually their skin and their meat would grow back, so it could happen all over again.

"That only means the Voars are an endless supply of leather." Valeska closed her eyes again and settled back on the bench.

"What are you guys talking about?" Oona asked, looking up from her notes.

"Nothing," I answered quickly, since finding out about Kalbi's life would devastate her.

I stared out above the half door on my side, with the musty wind blowing in my face. I tried not to think about the horrors of the realm we were in, or what fresh new hell might await us all up ahead.

It was hard to say how long we had been traveling, bouncing around in the back of the cabriolet, because time didn't feel the same here. There was no sun, no sky, not even a clock. No time, really. Just moving forward, for what felt like hours.

But it had to have been quite a while before the jostling lessened and Kalbi began to slow. From where I sat I couldn't see much outside the opening above the door, but it definitely seemed darker outside. Generally, Kurnugia seemed to be lit like earth on a cloudy day—I couldn't see the sun, but it was still light enough to see.

But now it had darkened, like a heavy storm was moving in.

Valeska sat up and pulled back the curtain so she could ask Lyra, "Why are we stopping?"

"We're not stopping," Lyra assured her. "We're slowing down. It's safer that way. We'll draw less attention."

"Less attention from what?" I asked, but Valeska had already leaned out the window for a better look.

"She'ol," she said with a heavy sigh, then settled back into the seat.

Both Oona and I scrambled to look out at the bleak landscape around us. The grassy plains had shifted to waves of hardened black magma and jagged rock formations that protruded from the ground.

In the center of this, surrounded by a moat of flowing red magma, was a giant castle that appeared to have been carved out of a volcano. A few of the crude windows had smoldering red lava pouring out of them, making the castle look like it was bleeding.

Many smaller buildings dotted the immediate landscape around it. But from this distance it was difficult to get a good look.

The place reminded me of the Aizsaule District back on earth—the area of the city that was under demon control. Somehow it was always darker than the rest of the city, as if that small part sucked the light out of everything.

"She'ol?" Oona asked, sitting back in the seat. Even though we were moving slower, it wasn't exactly stable back here.

"It's a city ruled by Abaddon, the self-proclaimed Lord of Destruction," Valeska explained as she stared down at the floor with a bitter twist of a smile. "The good news is that we're getting close to Zianna."

I sat up and asked, "What's the bad news?"

"That we're this close to Abaddon and She'ol," Valeska replied. "Abaddon is powerful, cruel, and somehow deceptively charming. And like most demons he's power-hungry, and he's always looking for ways to take over Zianna, break out of Kurnugia, and ultimately destroy the world.

"He's not that original, I know," Valeska said, sounding exhausted by the whole conversation. "But like I said, he's charming, so he has tons of minions lurking around, always ready to take on anyone that will further their master's cause."

"Good thing we're not going there," Oona commented. Then, more tensely: "We're not going there, are we?"

"I don't know why we'd need to," I said, swallowing back my own fear, and I pulled my gaze away from the darkness out the window and back to Valeska. "How do you know so much about Abaddon and She'ol?"

"Because," she answered with downcast eyes, "that's where my mother is."

Oona gasped. "What? Why? Isn't your mother an Alkonost? I thought they were divine, or at least neutral. Why would she have to live there?"

"She doesn't *have* to stay in She'ol," Valeska said. "But Zianna is full, with all kinds of divine beings on a waiting list to move in, but there are rarely any openings, since the divine don't slip up enough to get kicked out.

"Most of the cities in Kurnugia are demon-owned and -operated, and while She'ol may be one of the worst, most of them aren't that great." She looked outside with a pensive expression. "Abaddon has a way of getting his tendrils into everyone, including my mom."

"I'm sorry about your mom," Oona said gently.

"Don't be." Valeska settled back on the bench and closed her eyes. "Everybody makes their own choices. My mom made hers, and I'll make mine."

A heavy silence fell over us, and none of us seemed eager to disturb it. I took a cue from Valeska, leaning back and closing my eyes, since I didn't know when I'd be able to rest again.

My thoughts went back to Asher—the way they seemed to every time I closed my eyes since he'd been taken from me. But, being here in Kurnugia, the pain felt even more raw. The remnants of the dream I'd had still lingered, and I could feel him slipping away from my hand.

I squeezed my eyes more tightly shut, as if that would somehow stop the pain and the wave of sadness that rolled over me.

Eventually the sound of Kalbi's hooves pounding against the ground picked up as we moved away from She'ol.

"We're almost there," Lyra announced sometime later.

The instant I opened my eyes, the bright white light hit me, and I realized the air even smelled fresher. Less musty, more clean and floral. I got up and looked, careful to hold on to the sides of the carriage so I didn't tumble out.

And there it was, in the valley below us. It was surrounded by seven tall, glittering walls, and from our vantage I could see over them. A bright grassy field, with flowers and animals flourishing, and sparkling streams rolling through.

In the very center was a tall castle, but from our distance it looked more like a diamond shard—all sparkly and clear, with rough raw edges. It was from that palace that the light shone, bathing everything around it in its bright warmth.

"There it is," Lyra said, sounding as awed as I felt. "Zianna."

TWENTY-ONE

———— ◆ ————

We waited in the long line of hopefuls who wanted to visit Zianna. It was one of the nicest cities in the underworld—with nice shops, delicious food, and a strict policy of no violence. Everyone wanted to get in. But there was also a definite limit on how many beings Zianna could comfortably hold, so the city had adopted a rigid entrance process.

The ones enforcing it were two hulking cherubim. They each stood with a fiery staff and four sets of wings sprouting from their backs. Their bronze skin glowed subtly, and despite their youthful, handsome features, their expressions were hard.

Before coming to Kurnugia, cherubim served the gods, and their number-one skill was spotting sin. Their vision was vastly different than that of humans. They could see auras so clearly that any stains left by evil actions or darkness in your heart would be visible to them.

All they had to do was look at us, and they would know whether or not our auras were pure enough for us to enter Zianna. Even for a visit.

"Why do you still look like that?" Lyra asked, joining us in line after returning Kalbi to a cabriolet waiting area along the wall.

"Like what?" I asked.

"I thought you had a way to brighten yourself up more." Lyra motioned toward us, but she was already eyeing up the beings that stood ahead of us in line—angels, a fertility goddess, even a cuddly rainbow-colored bear of some sort. "It's busy here today, and we're going against some steep competition."

"I have it," Oona assured her. "I wanted to wait until the last possible second, because I'm not sure how long the effects will last."

"We're at that moment now," Lyra told her.

Oona dug in the front pocket of her bag and pulled out three small tablets. They were heart-shaped and barely thicker than a piece of paper. Carefully, she handed one to me and one to Valeska.

"So, you put them on your tongue, and then we take each other's hands and close our eyes while we wait for them to dissolve," Oona instructed.

Valeska raised up her tablet in a faux-cheer and muttered, "Bottoms up," before dropping it on her tongue.

I did the same, closing my eyes as Oona had instructed, and then I felt their hands taking mine. Already the tab fizzed on my tongue, tingling as a sugary sour taste spread through my mouth. A warm breeze swirled around me, lightly ruffling my hair.

Quickly, it was gone, and the only thing that remained was a slight bitter taste.

"That's it?" I opened my eyes, preparing to ask if it hadn't worked, but I instantly saw the answer. *"Wow."*

Valeska and Oona looked like themselves, and even their clothes were basically the same, but there was this dramatic refinement and luxuriousness added, like they had been styled and dressed for a couture runway. Their clothes—which had been somewhat ill-fitting—now were impeccably tailored to their physiques.

The deep merlot of Oona's dress had a sheen to it, and the embellishments glittered with diamonds. Her hair had an extra luster, and the stain on her lips matched perfectly with her ensemble.

Even our bags had changed. They were roughly the same size and shape, but they no longer appeared as practical black gear and instead had become stylish but more handmade, like they could've actually been made here in Kurnugia.

I glanced down at my clothes, the gold now glimmering against my skin, but I didn't have much time to admire myself because Lyra was pushing us along, closer to the entrance.

"Yes, yes, you all look amazing," Lyra said as she herded us forward. "When we get to the entrance, don't say anything. I'll do all the talking."

We fell in behind her, and I did my best to look good and meek. When we finally reached a cherub, my stomach was twisted in knots.

"Purpose of visit?" he barked, unmoved by Lyra's smile. I could barely even stand to look at him—he glowed too bright, shining off the diamond wall behind him, so it was painful.

"My friends haven't been here long, and I wanted to show them Zianna," Lyra replied as honestly as she could. Lying to the cherubim would only get her dismissed.

The cherub looked over at us, his eyes blazing under arched eyebrows, and I held my breath as I forced a smile up at him.

"They must be really new," he said finally. "Their aura is so faint. Go on in. Enjoy the city."

"Thank you," Lyra said, but we were already hurrying ahead, afraid he might change his mind.

The dirt path changed to smooth, opalescent cobblestones that led under the archways going through the seven walls, and went downward toward the valley of Zianna.

As we walked under the first arch, I felt a sensation similar to the one I'd felt when we'd first gone into the Gates of Kurnugia. A pins-and-needles sensation that went through my entire body. Based on the startled expression on Oona's face, I guessed she felt it, too. In the Gates, only Quinn and I had been able to feel the mystical wall that shrouded it with protection—just us Valkyries.

"What was that?" Valeska asked, her voice low but her eyes wide.

"It's the protection from the walls that keeps the undesirables out," Lyra replied simply as we headed toward the next archway—this one gleaming gold—several yards ahead of us.

"Undesirables?" Oona asked. "What qualities are considered undesirable?"

"You mustn't have any darkness or evil in you," Lyra said without slowing her steps.

Valeska faltered, and both of us stopped short. Technically, Valkyries were supposed to be neutral—neither impious nor divine, the same as humans. But I didn't know how it was weighted, if my own personal character and actions could deem me as "undesirable."

Based on what Lyra had told me, the cherubs scanning our auras had been our main obstacle to overcome. The arches and walls worked as both a magical and literal reinforcement to keep anyone from being able to break through.

I'd thought the seven walls were merely a fail-safe, not a further test. But with the tingling I felt—the cold sensation of an enchantment running through me, checking my blood and my heart for anything to deny my entrance into the city of the pure—combined with Lyra's vague assertion about *darkness,* I got the sense that it might be harder for me to get in than I'd thought.

Lyra paused and looked back at us. "Why are you stopping?"

"How do we know if we have any darkness?" Valeska asked. "What happens if we do?"

"You wouldn't make it through." She arched an eyebrow as she eyed Valeska. "Shall we continue?"

Valeska nodded. "Sure. Why not?"

I looked back, beyond the line outside the archway and the cherubim standing guard. At the shadow of She'ol way off in the distance, over the ridge behind us. My thoughts turned to Asher, and my hand instinctively went to my chest, over my heart, where the last words he'd said to me lingered.

I hoped that he wasn't in She'ol. I hoped that he was safe. That he was still alive. That he could wait for me a little bit longer.

Once I was done with this current mission, once we had Gungnir, I would send it back to the earth above, and I would find Asher. If I had to fight every monster in the entire underworld to save him, I would. There was nothing in this world or any other that could stop me from bringing him back to me.

TWENTY-TWO

⸺◆⸺

We went under the golden arch, and the next three, with relative ease. The tingly sensation grew stronger, growing more painful with each arch. It was like being zapped with an electrical current, one that shot through me and left a burning ache in my bones.

Passing through the wall made of glittering blue garnet, I had to grit my teeth, but I made it. I took a deep breath and pressed on, heading toward the ruby archway in front of us.

"Are you okay?" Oona asked softly and touched my arm.

"I'm fine," I lied and looked at her.

She stared at me, her black walnut eyes filled with concern, but with no hint of pain. No sign of the residual shock that had begun to make my eyes water.

"You don't feel anything," I realized and glanced over at Valeska, who appeared similarly unruffled.

"I feel a tingle, but nothing bad," Oona admitted.

Suddenly, a few feet in front of us, under the shimmering red glow of the ruby arch, a man fell to the cobblestones, writhing in pain. I didn't know what kind of immortal he was, since he had a basic human appearance, but we had been following behind him all through the gates.

It wasn't until this one that it had become too much. He convulsed and let out guttural cries of agony, his face contorting with pain as his muscles contracted.

Finally, a cherub flew down and picked him up, pulling him away from the arch and its magic that was causing him so much pain. Then the cherub carried him away, back out of Zianna, back to where we'd come in.

"What happened to him?" Valeska asked.

"The magic grows stronger through the walls," Lyra explained. "It must detect even the smallest impurities in your heart and blood to keep those who do not belong in Zianna out."

Oona loosened her grip on my arm and let her hand slip down so she was holding my hand, and she whispered, "I will pull you through. No matter what. I'll make sure you get through. We got this."

I squeezed her hand gratefully, and we walked forward. The pain was much worse this time—an excruciating jolt that momentarily blinded me—but I made it through.

The final wall was made of black opal, and it was by far the most dazzling. The rich black stone was mottled with brilliant specks of gold, blue, copper, and red. The spatters of color against the darkness made it look like the stars in a clear night sky.

Lyra tried to pause, probably wanting to give me a moment to catch my breath, but dragging it out would only make it worse, so I trudged on ahead.

I walked under the arch side by side with Oona, but as soon as I was under the arch, I froze. The pain hit me so intensely and so suddenly my knees buckled and my stomach lurched. I could feel my teeth grinding as my muscles contracted, and I couldn't breathe.

Then, dimly—almost as if it were happening somewhere else, like I was dreaming—I felt tugging on my arm, and my legs managed to take a couple lumbering steps.

But that was all I needed. As soon as I stepped out from under the arch, the pain stopped, and air filled my lungs. There was still lingering soreness, but it was nothing compared to the agony of before.

"You did it," Oona said, squeezing my hand again, and I realized that she must've pulled me through before I collapsed.

"How was that possible?" I asked, looking over at Lyra.

"You have more goodness in you than bad," she explained with a sympathetic smile. "There's just more darkness in you than the rulers of Zianna would prefer, but they're snobs. You made it through, so you're worthy of being here."

I rubbed my arms, which were stiff from the last arch, and muttered, "I don't feel all that worthy right now."

"You made it, and that's what counts." Lyra's smile deepened, and she stepped to the side and spread her arms expansively. "Welcome to Zianna."

And there it was, spread out before us. The rolling green hills of grass, so green and soft, with streams of crystal-clear water. Flowers of every color dotted the landscape, and I swear colors existed here that I'd never seen before. Shades of blue and pink and purple and white that seemed to change and shift and exist out of any spectrum I'd ever seen.

The impossible beauty of it all had a strange dizzying effect, because I couldn't fully comprehend it. The lushness and loveliness went beyond my senses.

While I tried to take it all in, a herd of kirin ran toward us. They looked like white horses, but they were more a mixture of unicorn and dragon. Two dark gray antlers grew out before their ears, and one smaller horn grew in the center, lower on their forehead.

Dotted along their cheeks, foreheads, and all along their backs were iridescent scales that shimmered in the bright light. While their fur was white, their manes and tails had the slightest bit of color, tinged with pastel pink or blue. The tails were long and prehensile, like that of a spider monkey, but with long fur at the end, similar to a normal horse. As they ran, their tails curled up.

"They're stunning," Valeska intoned in awe.

The three of us had never seen a live kirin before. Because of their exquisite beauty, their horns and scales had been prized, and they had been hunted to extinction on earth thousands of years ago.

When they had been wiped out, that was when Odin called for Valkyries, saying that immortals were too powerful to be left unfettered and that they would ravage the earth for all living things. If even other immortals like kirin could be obliterated, what chance would mortals and other less aggressive immortals do with dragons, demons, and vampires controlling the world?

It's because the kirin were gone, enduring only in the underworld, that I even existed.

The herd of kirin turned just before they reached us and ran across the cobblestone in front of us. Up close they were even more beautiful, and Oona let out an awestruck laugh.

Once they'd gone, she turned back with a broad smile. "This is all too much," she said with another laugh that teetered on an overwhelmed mania.

"You really can get lost in the majesty of it all," Lyra admitted, but her tone had an admonishing quality. "But you don't really have time for that, do you?"

"No, of course not." I shook my head, attempting to clear it of the overstimulation and regain my wits. "We don't have much time at all."

"So, where do we go from here?" Lyra asked.

"We need to find Baldur," I said. "He has what we're looking for."

"Baldur?" Lyra thought for a moment. "I believe he lives in the palace, but that's really a city unto itself. I can get you as far as the palace, but beyond that you'll be on your own tracking him."

"That will be good enough," I said.

"You mean it'll *have* to be good enough," Valeska corrected me dryly.

TWENTY-THREE

———◆———

t wasn't until we got closer to the palace that I could fully appreciate its size. The central area of the building seemed to be a vast rotunda with a glittering dome in the center. Seven glass towers of varying heights rose up from it, and any of them would dwarf even the tallest building I'd seen on earth.

The palace sprawled out far beyond that, with white marble buildings extending out for miles. That didn't even count the hundreds of acres of greenery that surrounded it. Vaulted terraces of all types of flowers, trees, and fruits created a pyramidesque garden encircling the palace.

We climbed stone stairs that passed over waterfalls and aqueducts, with wisteria dripping around us and vines climbing up the support walls of the terraces beside us. The air smelled even sweeter as we went higher, like peonies and roses and fresh-cut grass and rain.

When we finally reached the top of the steps, we all should've been winded. We'd ascended hundreds of stairs, but I could breathe easier than I ever had before. My legs didn't hurt, and even the ache from passing under the arches had passed. Just being here, so near to the citadel, had a restorative effect.

The mezzanine was the highest level of the gardens. It was a lush plateau that extended the length of several city blocks. Pearlescent slabs lined the pathway, and marble benches and fountains dotted the periphery. Many beings—most of them beautiful or pleasing to the eye, all of them impeccably dressed—milled around the lawn, talking, laughing, reading, eating fruit. It all seemed so peaceful and happy.

"That's the entrance." Lyra pointed to the far side of the mezzanine, to the last few steps that led into the round central hub of the palace.

"Is this where you leave us, then?" Oona asked, her small voice sounding uneasy.

"Yes, this is as far as I go." Lyra nodded solemnly. "There are several orisha that work helping everyone navigate the citadel. They can help you the rest of your way."

"Thank you again for all your help," I told her, wishing that I had a more meaningful way to show her how grateful I truly was.

"It was no trouble." She moved closer to me and took my hand in both of hers, holding it warmly but firmly. Her rich brown eyes locked on mine, and though she was smiling, there were tears swimming in her eyes. "Tell Sloane that I think of her every day, and that I love her so much." She swallowed back her emotion. "Tell her that I'm sorry for what I did. Please."

"I will," I promised her.

She let go of my hand and wiped her eyes. "Thank you. I wish you only good fortune on the rest of your travels." Lyra turned and started walking away, but Valeska called after her.

"What are you going to do now?" Valeska asked.

Lyra smiled demurely. "We all have business to attend to."

I watched her retreating figure for a few moments—her silken black hair swaying behind her as she headed back down the steps. But we had much to do, so I followed the pearlescent paths that wound around the benches.

"Are you going to ask those orisha for help or whatever?" Valeska asked as she fell in step beside me.

"No."

The orisha were helpful spirits, but I didn't know how eager they would be to help us disturb the order of their world. In reality, we were only hoping to maintain it, but seeking out Odin's son to get the spear he'd hidden would most probably seem like an intrusive disturbance to them.

"What's the plan, then?" Oona asked. "How are we going to find him?"

I stopped beside rosebushes near the steps up to the palace for a bit of privacy. Valeska must've known what I was about, because she spread out her large black wings, shrouding us even further from any prying eyes.

I quickly rummaged through my bag and pulled out the sólarsteinn.

"There's no sun here," Oona pointed out, her voice tight with anxiety. "Is that a problem?"

As I stared down at the translucent stone in the palm of my hand, I answered, "I think it only needs light, and there's plenty of light around here."

Valeska stared at it with her arms folded over her chest, scrutinizing it before asking, "What does it do?"

"You have to focus on what you want to find most, and this stone will show you where it is," I explained.

"And what is it that we want to find?" Valeska asked. "Are we going after Baldur, or straight for the spear?"

"I'm afraid that the spear will be locked up or inaccessible to us, since Baldur took it to hide it from his father," I said. "If we find Baldur, we can reason with him and tell him what Odin said and what's happening up on earth."

Valeska scoffed. "You think he'll hand it over?"

"Odin said that Baldur was the most compassionate of his children," I reasoned. "He'll have to be sympathetic to our cause."

"And what if he's not?" Valeska asked.

"We'll use the stone to find it," I said firmly. "And then we'll do whatever we have to do to get it. I'm not leaving Zianna without it."

Valeska smiled then. "What are you waiting for? Let's get to it."

The sólarsteinn had worked for me before, so I tried to remember what I had done earlier. I closed my eyes and focused on Baldur, on every detail I knew about him. Then I started chanting in my head, *Show me where Odin's son Baldur is. Bring me to him.*

Then I opened my eyes and held up my palm, so the stone could catch the light. And we waited.

I held my hand up even higher, as if I were offering the sólarsteinn to the gods. I could see the light hitting it—a bright beam shining through. Just when I thought all hope was lost, a prism of color shifted inside the stone.

A rainbow of light shone out from it, pointing right toward the palace.

TWENTY-FOUR

———◆———

I t was busy inside the palace, and that worked both for and against us. We were easily lost in the crowd, but that left us with no privacy to use the stone.

Inside the lavish rotunda, underneath the glittering glass dome, was a grand open room. At the edge, where the extremely high ceiling ended, was a stoa encircling the space. Thick columns surrounded the walkway, creating a semi-open hallway, which had dozens of ornate archways leading out of the main room.

Despite the rather monochromatic color scheme—a great deal of white marble and granite, with only the occasional splash of copper or gold, and even most of the guests inside seemed to be wearing white or gold—it all had an air of sophistication and elegance.

This also made the place stunningly bright, so I quickly palmed the sólarsteinn. With this much light, the stone would be liable to cast a giant rainbow over everyone, and I did not want to draw any attention.

As Lyra had predicted, orisha were waiting around the entrance, happily asking if anyone needed help finding their way around the cita- del. I declined as politely as I could and scanned the room for even the smallest hint of seclusion.

The space was filled with breathtaking architectural flourishes, and it was impossible to take them all in. Oona had become mesmerized by an elaborate rose gold mandala inlaid in the white marble floor, and I had to take her hand to get her moving again.

"I wish I could take pictures," she moaned, gazing around the grand room as I led her to the far side, to hide in the shadows behind a pillar.

A trio of immortals were walking toward us, chatting, but once they passed, it looked like I have might have a few seconds when I could take a peek at the sólarsteinn. I leaned back against a column and waited.

"This isn't a vacation," Valeska chastised Oona, but I saw the way she looked around the room—she was as enamored with it as Oona and I.

That was the point, after all. Zianna had been created, by some of the most powerful divine beings that ever lived, to be a magnificent sanctuary. It was the culmination of millennia of talent and magic, so obviously the result would be the most beautiful thing that us mere mortals had ever laid eyes on.

"I know," Oona said as she looked around wistfully. "I'll never see this again. Do you think we'll remember it all? When we go back?"

Valeska's expression hardened, and her thick lashes laid heavily on her cheeks as she nodded once. "I remember everything from my time here before."

I didn't have time to ask her more. I opened my hand, just enough to let the light hit the stone, and instantly a rainbow prism appeared, shining right toward a door before the wall curved out of site behind the pillars.

"That way," I commanded as I closed my hand around the sólarsteinn again.

Fighting the urge to run, I walked as briskly yet casually as I could and smiled politely at anyone we passed. When I turned under the archway, ahead was a long corridor with all sorts of marble busts lining the walls. They sat on pedestals of rose gold, four feet off the ground, and the heads themselves towered another two to six feet, depending on who they depicted.

Some I recognized, like Anubis, Venus, Ishtar, and Moai, but there were far too many for me to know them all just by glancing at them as we hurried by. Once the coast was relatively clear, I hid beside the bust of Anubis, leaning back against the wall behind his large jackal head, and pulled out the sólarsteinn again.

The light directed us farther down the hall, until we turned off onto another smaller and darker one. We turned twice more, following wherever the stone indicated, until we took a long winding staircase, going down deep below the palace.

I heard the running water before we reached the bottom of the stairs, but I was still surprised to see that we had come to a stream that ran underneath—or, rather, through—the palace. A small stone walkway ran on either side, and the tiled walls curved up and around us. If it wasn't for the opening at either end of the stream, letting bright light in, or the fact that the water itself was crystal-clear and large koi-like fish were swimming in it, I would've guessed this was a sewer.

The stone pointed far to the left of us and across the brook, to a door on the other side. Fortunately, there were a few stones protruding up above the water, so we were able to cross them like stepping-stones.

"Have you noticed that there aren't any guards around?" Oona asked as we carefully stepped across the stones. We hadn't spoken much so far, but now it appeared we were alone. "No one to stop us or tell us not to go in."

"Why would there be?" Valeska countered when we reached the other side. "The arches we passed through are intended to keep out any evil. Zianna is home to the divine, who are incapable of doing anything wrong. Even if they were to sneak into any area that they weren't technically supposed to be in, the fact that they did it means that it wasn't wrong. Whatever they do is the good and just thing to do, so why would anyone here want to stop them?"

"But . . ." The crease in Oona's brow deepened as she considered Valeska's answer. "Does that mean that we're the most wicked beings in all of Zianna? Or that the only things we can do here are good and right?"

"I think it means that we have free will, unlike everyone else that lives here," Valeska said. "We can make choices that they can't."

The conversation reminded me of one I'd had with Sloane before, when I had first learned that my mother might not have done her duty as a Valkyrie and instead had let a targeted immortal live. Sloane had posited that there were only two choices: either everybody has free will, or nobody has free will.

"But hopefully we're exactly where we're supposed to be anyway, so it's all a moot point," Valeska amended.

When we reached the archway the sólarsteinn had pointed to, we encountered our first real door. It was wooden, with an iron support bar running across it secured with a padlock, and it wouldn't budge.

"Dammit," I muttered, and I crouched down in front of the door to pull my lockpick set out of my bag.

"What's wrong?" Oona asked.

"It's locked." I took the heavy padlock in one hand and slid a pick in with the other. Valkyries were well trained in the art of picking locks, because sometimes immortals liked to hole up and lock themselves in when they realized their time was up.

"Oona jinxed us by pointing out the lax security in Zianna," Valeska said.

Oona cast her a glare. "That's not how jinxing works."

Finally the lock clicked and I slipped the padlock off.

I opened the door slowly and realized this had to be the end of our journey. It was one room, with no exits or doors other than the one I was standing in. The walls and ceiling were made of solid slabs of gray marble, and a bronze sink and toilet sat on one side of the wall.

Directly across from the door was a small brass bed. A man was lying on it, with his back to us, unmoving. I timidly took a few steps into the room, gathering all my courage.

"Baldur?" I asked hopefully.

Then he sat up and turned around, and the air caught in my throat.

It wasn't Baldur at all.

It was Asher.

TWENTY-FIVE

———◆———

He stood in front of me, looking just as I had seen him last. His clothes were different—traded in for white linen—but everything else was the same: a broad-shouldered walking contradiction of beauty and softness, strength and vulnerability. His full lips parted slightly as he looked at me in disbelief, and his entire posture was rigid.

Then, I couldn't help myself, I ran to him. I had to touch him, to feel him, to know he was here. As soon as I reached him, he pulled me into his arms, hugging me to him. The weight and warmth of his body pressed against me, his heart pounding in his chest.

"Is it really you?" he asked breathlessly as he brushed a lock of hair back from my forehead.

"It's me," I promised as I gazed up into the indigo of his eyes. "Is it really you?"

He smiled crookedly then, making the scar on his upper lip more pronounced. "It's me." Then the smile faltered. "What are you doing here? I told you not to come and find me."

"I didn't, actually," I admitted.

I wanted to linger in his arms forever, but that wasn't the best way to have a conversation, so I moved back. But I still kept my hand on him, touching his arm, afraid that he would slip away if I let go even for a second.

"Odin sent us here to look for a spear, and I was using my sólarsteinn," I explained as I realized the error. The sunstone always takes you to what you most want to find in the world, and I couldn't make myself want anything more than Asher. "I was looking for Baldur, but it led me to you."

He expression softened. "I know I shouldn't be, but I'm glad you're here."

"I was so worried that . . ." I trailed off and narrowed my eyes. "What are you doing here? Did Gugalanna bring you here?"

He shook his head emphatically. "No. He brought me to She'ol."

I winced, and now that I had stepped back and was really looking at him, I could see fresh wounds, still red and puffy, visible along the hems of his shirt. Just above the V-neck of his shirt, the blotched edges of a purplish bruise were visible.

"They wanted my blood, so most of my time there I spent fading in and out of consciousness as they drained me of it as much as they could without killing me." His jaw tightened under his rough stubble. "They only kept me alive so that I could make more blood, and they used all sorts of strange incantations to help with the process. They wouldn't tell me what they planned to do with it all, but they were definitely draining me as much as they could."

"How did you end up here?" I asked, mostly because I wanted to know, but also because I didn't want to think about Asher being tortured in She'ol.

"A scout from Zianna found me, and a team of exousia rescued me and brought me here," he explained.

Exousia had once been angelic warriors that protected the gods that roamed the earth. But after the Valkyrie Proclamation, they had all gone down to Kurnugia, to protect the divine from being overrun by evil.

"They didn't know what to do with me, so they locked me up to keep me safe, and to keep themselves safe," Asher said.

"Well, we're breaking you out." I squeezed his hand and smiled wanly. "Any chance that you know where Baldur or a spear are hidden?"

He shook his head sadly. "I'm sorry. The only ones I know by name that I've met are Gugalanna, Abaddon, and Sedna."

"You were in contact with Abaddon?" Valeska grimaced.

He looked over at her, noticing the newest addition to our group for the first time. "Who are you?"

"Valeska Voronin," she replied, hooking her thumb at us. "I'm with them."

"Samael sent her to help us," I elaborated. "She's good."

"As touching as this reunion is, we should get moving," Valeska said dryly. "We still have a lot to do before we can get out of here."

"Do you think you can get the sólarsteinn to work now?" Oona asked. "That it will focus on Baldur?"

I was about to answer, but the sound of footsteps stopped me. They were pounding on the path outside, echoing through the tunnel. Before we had a chance to make a move or plan, they were here.

A trio of exousia—clad in golden armor with white-feathered wings extending out from their muscular torsos—stood in front of the doorway, blocking our escape.

TWENTY-SIX

❖

I knelt on the floor, the stone feeling cold and hard through the fabric of my skirt. The exousia had walked us down the length of a long room and directed us to kneel before the throne at the end.

Directly before me was a semicircle pattern inlaid in the floor using various shades of gold and copper to create the sun. Just beyond that were half a dozen marble stairs that led up to an elegant veranda, where a tall, empty throne sat in the middle.

Above the throne, the ceiling curved down to ornately carved arches and low half walls. Other than the arches, the throne was entirely open to the outside. A crimson phoenix flew by, letting out a solitary despondent squawk.

As Asher, Oona, Valeska, and I waited—for who or what, the exousia would not tell us—I studied the carvings. They appeared to depict all sorts of great battles among the Vanir gods and other immortals.

Finally a door off the side of the veranda opened and an exousia walked in, followed by a serene woman in an elegant gown of white suede and fur. She was tall and poised, with tawny bronze skin, and her long black hair fell like a satin curtain around her. Her dark brown eyes were narrow but large and captivating under sharp eyebrows. On her forehead two black inverted triangles were tattooed, and five dots were tattooed across the fullness of the apple of her cheek.

As she walked to the throne, her movements were so smooth and graceful, as if she were floating. Instead of sitting, she stood at the top step, looking down at us.

"I am Sedna," she said in a strong, cool voice. "I am the hundred and third ruler of Zianna, and I have been chosen by all the beings that dwell here to handle the matters that concern our citadel. As such, I need to know exactly who you are and why there are so many mortals where they are not meant to be."

I glanced to the side, half expecting/half hoping that Oona or Valeska would take the lead on this, but they both stared up Sedna, with lips tightly sealed. I sat up as straight as I could.

"It's a pleasure to meet you, Your . . . Majesty?" I said uncertainly. "I'm not sure what I should call you."

"Sedna will suffice," she replied coolly. "And I can do without the pleasantries. I simply want you to tell me why you're here so I can decide whether or not to have you executed."

"We're here to see Baldur," I answered quickly, since Sedna was clearly not screwing around. "We were sent on a mission from Odin."

Sedna arched an eyebrow. "You didn't come to rescue your companion?"

"No," I admitted. "I had hoped we could find him while we were here, but we were sent here by Odin to speak with his son Baldur."

Sedna's composure slipped for a split second as shock slackened her expression, but she hurried to smooth it over by narrowing her eyes as she stared down her nose at me. "Why did Odin send you on an errand of such importance? You are mortal, are you not?"

"We are," I said.

"That's why he sent us," Valeska elaborated. "It's easier for us to pass through the entrance of Kurnugia than it is for immortals."

"But the risk is so great," Sedna persisted, sounding dubious. "Eresh-kigal and Abaddon were using the blood of the child of a Valkyrie to open the door so all of Kurnugia can be unleashed on the earth above."

She motioned toward Asher, who was kneeling beside me. "They bled your friend quite a bit, but fortunately we found him before they had enough. With you three here in the underworld, there's a much greater risk of Ereshkigal or her Bull finding you and completing the ritual."

Unrelenting guilt throbbed in my chest, like a splinter lodged in my heart. I had listened to Asher and left him. I did what I thought was needed, but it destroyed me that any of this had happened, that I hadn't been able to save him from this.

"We don't want to stay here long," Oona told Sedna. "We need to talk with Baldur, and then we'll be out of your hair."

"Why do you wish to speak with Baldur so badly?" Sedna asked.

"Odin tasked me with finding Baldur and retrieving Odin's spear," I said.

A puzzled crease deepened in the smooth skin of Sedna's forehead as she asked, "Odin wishes to have Gungnir returned to his possession?"

"Yes," I said. "He thinks it's the only way to stop the uprising that Ereshkigal is planning."

"Vanir gods have no bearing on our world down here." Sedna spread her hands wide, gesturing to the underworld around us. "They have total control over Vanaheimr, and more influence than they should on earth.

"But we have Kurnugia," she continued emphatically. "This is our domain to rule as we see fit. Just by sending you here, Odin has broken the agreement and weakened the magic that seals off the underworld from the realms above. He's made it even easier for Ereshkigal and her followers to escape."

"He might not have known that—" I began, but Sedna interrupted.

"Of course he knew it," she said with a humorless smile. "Who do you think authored the agreement in the first place?"

I cleared my throat and tried again, saying, "Well, I can only assume that he thought our mission was more important and worth the risk."

"Or he's very reckless," Sedna countered.

"Can't it be both?" Valeska suggested wryly, causing the ruler to cast an annoyed glare at her.

"We have heard rumblings of what Ereshkigal and Gugalanna are attempting, but we have been handling it all ourselves, before they are even able to break through to the surface," Sedna said and turned her gaze to Asher. "You were with them for some time. How far along are they?"

"I can't say with any certainty, since they weren't very big on telling me anything," Asher said. "But from what I overheard, Ereshkigal and Abaddon think they're very close, but they're definitely overeager, especially Gugalanna. There's a chance that he might pull the trigger before they're ready. But I would say even if they are premature, our side needs to be ready. Ereshkigal still seems to have a lot of power behind her."

Sedna clasped her hands in front of her. "You have given me much to consider. I will consult with my advisers, and Baldur, of course. Until then, you must stay with us—both for our protection and yours." She looked to the exousia standing behind us. "You may take them away now."

"Shall we return them to the dungeon?" an exousia asked—the one pointing his bronze spear at my neck.

"No, that won't be necessary," Sedna said. "The tower will be adequate, but be sure to keep the doors bolted."

"Yes, of course," the exousia said. Then to me, as he grabbed my arm, he ordered, "On your feet."

"I'm working on it," I muttered, since by yanking me up he'd only succeeded in throwing me off balance and slowing down the whole process.

Once we were standing again, the exousia began directing us down the length of the throne room. We hadn't made it that far when Sedna called after us, and I turned back to her.

"Before you go—what other gods is Odin working with?" she asked.

"He didn't mention any," I said.

"He's acting on his own?" Sedna asked.

"He didn't say," I said blankly.

"That is something more I must consider." She motioned for the exousia to take us away, then she turned in such a hurry that her long white train billowed out behind her.

TWENTY-SEVEN

◆

The four of us were taken up to a round room high in the tower. Or at least the height was what I gathered based on the amount of steps we went up, but there were no windows for me to gauge for certain.

The room itself had been set up as a studio apartment: a chaise lounge with a few wing chairs and end tables created a parlor, a quartz table with matching chairs under a candlelit chandelier formed a dining area, a queen-sized bed next to an armoire was a bedroom, and a door off the side led to a rather grand bathroom, replete with a claw-foot tub and rose-gold sinks.

It was all styled much the same as the rest of the palace—plenty of white marble and rose-gold flourishes. The furnishings were covered in plush pewter velvet, while the bedding was topped with a luxurious Siberian gray fur. Despite the lack of windows, all the lighting made the room feel surprisingly airy and light, and that was further helped along by the strategic placement of large bouquets of white and blush-pink flowers.

The first thing Valeska did when we got in the room—after futilely searching all over for a way to escape—was change out of her clothes.

Oona's spell had worn off, and we no longer had that glamourous sheen we had when we'd first entered Zianna. That was just as well, since the sheen only helped us to blend in so we could get through the city unnoticed, but we'd been caught, so that didn't matter anymore.

One by one, we took turns going into the bathroom to freshen up and change back into our regular clothes, while debating how long we would be here and if Sedna would decide to help us. (Valeska was firmly in the they're-going-to-execute-us camp, while Oona was far more optimistic.)

Asher was the last one into the bathroom, and he'd been in there for a little while when an exousia came in pushing a dinner cart made of gold and glass. It had been piled high with all sorts of exotic fruits and delicious-smelling pastries, as well as several decanters of brightly colored juices and wines.

"Sedna has sent you this feast for you to enjoy," the exousia told us, speaking in clipped tones.

He motioned stiffly to the food, keeping his eyes downcast the entire time, while Valeska sat perched on a chair with her hand hovering above the dagger she had in her ankle sheath.

"Enjoy" was the final word from the exousia before he turned and marched out the door.

"Thanks for bringing it in," Oona called after him as she walked over to the cart. "And tell Sedna thank you for sending it up."

The exousia gave no indication that he'd heard her or would pass along the message. He just went outside and locked the door loudly behind him.

Once he had gone, Valeska immediately rushed over to inspect the wares. She eyed the food the exact same way she had the exousia that had brought it in—warily and tensely, as if she were ready to fight for her life. Oona, on the other hand, had already begun loading up her plate.

Valeska held up a crescent-shaped slice of pale pink fruit and sniffed. "Is this some kind of mango?"

"I don't know what that is." Oona picked up a similar slice and took a bite, then groaned happily. "But it is delicious!"

"What's this?" Valeska asked as she held up a flat, peachy-golden fruit covered in a soft fuzz. "Is this like a mango donut?"

"It's a pan-tao," Oona replied as she walked over to the chaise with a plateful of various fruits and pastries. "Why do you keep asking if everything is a mango? Have you ever even had one?"

Valeska shrugged. "Everything looks like mangoes to me."

"Oh, my gosh!" Oona moaned after she took a bite of a pan-tao and wiped the juice off her chin. "This is the best thing I've ever eaten. You should try it."

"Sure, if I wanna die in agony of poisoning," Valeska muttered, and she left the food cart behind to go back to pacing the length of the room.

"If they were going to kill us, they would come out and do it," I said. "They don't need to sneak it in and wait around for poison to kick in."

"Mal, you should get some of this," Oona told me through a mouthful of food. "Seriously. It's *sooo* good."

"I'm gonna check on Asher first and see if he wants to come out and eat," I said, ignoring the rumbling of my stomach.

I didn't know how long we'd been here or the last time I'd eaten. It felt like somewhere between ten hours and eternity. But Asher had definitely been in the bathroom long enough that I'd begun to worry.

I knocked softly on the bathroom door and said, "Asher? Are you okay?"

"Yeah, I'm fine," he replied, his words slightly muffled through the door. "It's open, if you wanna come in."

I opened the door cautiously at first, peeking in, but when I saw Asher standing in front of the sink, I came in and shut the door behind me. He was shirtless, wearing only his white linen pants, and his hair was still wet from his bath. Based on the dabs of white cream on his now-smooth face, I guessed he'd just finished shaving.

"A good bath and a good shave do wonders to make you feel like a normal person," he mused, wiping at his face with a towel, and then he turned to me.

In another time, seeing Asher's chiseled abs and broad chest would only send flutters of happiness and lust through me. But this was my first real chance getting a look at him since we'd found him.

There were half a dozen slits going down either side of his torso, below his pecs and down his ribs. Each cut was about six inches long, and though the wounds had already begun to heal, they were red, with raised, jagged edges, like he had been cut in the same place over and over to keep the wounds open.

On both his forearms he had another six matching cuts, making it look like he had badly but desperately attempted suicide multiple times. I knew that wasn't what had happened, that it was a way for them to drain his blood, but it was still a shocking and disturbing thing to see.

But the marks I found most horrifying were the ones carved on his chest, just to the left of his heart. They were less jagged than the others, but the skin around them was much darker, like a blood-red shifting to black where the incisions had been made. They were two symbols, ones I didn't recognize.

Asher stood before me, looking better than he had before—his body was more relaxed, his eyes brighter, even a smile played on the edge of his lips. But, looking at his skin all torn up like that, I could barely fight the urge to throw up or sob. He turned to inspect his shave in the mirror again, and I couldn't take it anymore.

"I'm sorry," I said, my voice cracking on the word.

He looked over at me, startled by the emotion in my voice, and asked, "Why?"

"I should've come for you. I should've been here sooner. I shouldn't have let him take you." I swallowed back tears as he stepped closer to me.

"No, no." He put a hand on each of my shoulders and bent down slightly so he was eye level with me. "Listen to me, Malin. You did exactly the right thing. You did what I wanted you to do, what I *asked* you to do, and, more importantly, what you needed to do. You have nothing to apologize for."

"But look at what they did to you." I motioned to the jagged red marks on his arms and the bruises all over his torso.

"Yeah, okay, Abaddon was a real bastard," Asher allowed. "But honestly, I don't remember much of it. I was unconscious most of the time. So, yeah, I have some new battle scars, and I'm honestly a bit sore, but it wasn't that bad. At least not nearly as bad as it could've been, being held captive by the evil lords of the underworld."

"Yeah?" I asked hopefully. "So you promise you don't hate me?"

He laughed, warmly but softly. "I'll never hate you, Malin."

"Never say never," I replied, which only made him laugh harder, so he moved away from me and leaned back against the bathroom counter.

When he'd finished laughing, his expression shifted—his eyes were still light, the smile still curled his lips ever so slightly, but there was a new seriousness hardening the edges of his happiness. His words had a certain gravity when he asked, "You wanna know the truth?"

"Always."

He reached out, taking my hands and pulling me closer to him. His voice was low and husky as he stared into my eyes and said, "When they brought me here, they showed me the unimaginable enchantment of the world outside these walls. I have seen beauty beyond anything I could've dreamed, the full breadth and majesty of everything their heavens have to offer."

He smiled softly and cradled my face in his hand. "And still, I've never seen anything as wonderful and beautiful as you walking through that door in the dungeon."

Then I couldn't wait any longer. I leaned close and kissed him—intensely, passionately. With all that I had, with all that I wanted from him. My hand was on the back of his neck, my fingers in his hair, and his hand was pressed on the small of my back, holding me to him.

TWENTY-EIGHT

——— ◆ ———

Asher lay beside me in the bed, sleeping soundly. We didn't know how long we'd be here or what would come after this, so we decided to rest and eat while we had our chance. Even Valeska had finally caved in and eaten some of the food, since the rest of us hadn't shown any signs of poisoning.

Now everyone else was asleep—Oona on the chaise under a fur blanket, and Valeska perched barefoot on the back of a chair with her wings folded over, reminding me of an overgrown chicken.

But I couldn't sleep. I'd been dozing off when a terrible thought had occurred to me: the Valhallan cloak wouldn't be big enough for the four of us.

Even if the mission was a success and Baldur gave us Odin's spear, I didn't know how all of us could get out of the underworld and back to earth.

I lay on my back with an arm under my head, staring at the dark ceiling, running a hundred different scenarios through my head. I couldn't leave any of them behind here, and I didn't want to stay here myself. I would, if I had to. Without hesitation, I would sacrifice myself for them if need be.

But there had to be a better way.

Or at least I hoped desperately that there was a better way.

Asher moaned softly, and I glanced over at him. When we'd decided to sleep, Oona had gone around blowing out most of the candles, but she left a few burning so we would find our way around in the dark. The lamp on the nightstand burned low, but I could still easily see the outline of Asher beneath the sheets beside me and the darkness spreading out over his chest.

I sat up and scrambled to turn up the kerosene lamp, and as the warm light brightened, I saw the dark blotches were bright red. Asher moaned again, louder this time, as he stained the sheets like a bloody Rorschach test.

"Asher," I whispered and touched his shoulder. His skin felt cool as I shook him. "Ash, wake up."

He twitched—a violent quick jerk—but it only lasted for a second, then he lay motionless. I was about to shake him again, but then he turned his head toward me, and, slowly, his eyes fluttered open.

When he saw me, a groggy smile lit up his face. "Good. You're still here. I didn't dream you."

"Asher, you're bleeding."

"What?" He sat up and the sheet slid down, revealing the deep cuts on his chest, the ones that didn't look like all the rest.

"They stop for a while, but eventually they always start up again," he complained as he dabbed at them with the sheet, and the bright red blood appeared to be darkening as it slowly scabbed. "When they brought me here, they gave me a salve for my wounds, and most of them healed up over the last few days. But these ones . . . at least they seem to be done bleeding now."

"A few days?" I echoed. "You've only been in Kurnugia for five or six days." But even as I was saying it, I couldn't be certain. How long had I been here? A day maybe, it felt like, but how much time had passed on earth? Hours?

"What? No . . ." He looked up at me, shaking his head. "I've been here for . . . weeks."

I gently told him, "Time moves differently here."

He leaned back, resting his head against the headboard as he stared forward. "I'd heard that, but I didn't realize it would be so drastic."

"You were with Abaddon and Gugalanna for *weeks*?" I asked, still keeping my voice hushed so we wouldn't wake Oona or Valeska.

"It felt like that. I think. I don't know." He shook his head again. "My time in She'ol was such a strange, painful blur."

"Do you know what those marks mean?" I pointed to the drying wounds on his chest.

He looked down at them. "No. Abaddon made them when we were alone together. He gave me something to drink first, said it was to help me get my strength. And then he used a dagger to carve into my chest, and he laughed as he finished and said, 'Now no one else can have you.'"

"He was branding you as his property?" I asked thickly.

"Probably." Asher looked over at me again and took my hand, gently squeezing it. "But I'm not his property anymore. I'm here, with you, and that's what matters."

A knock at the door interrupted us before I could reply. Valeska leapt off the chair, sending it clattering to the floor, and she flew up toward the ceiling, while Oona sat up with a start. A moment later, an exousia entered the room.

"Ready yourself," the exousia commanded. "Sedna and her court are ready to see you."

TWENTY-NINE

On the marble platform, in front of the open balcony, a dozen chairs had been set out. All of them were the same elegant gold design as the throne, only smaller versions with lower backs. Six of them were on either side of the throne to create a semicircle facing us.

Seated in each one of the chairs were what appeared to be a dozen divine immortals of great stature. A few of them I recognized—like Bastet, a humanoid goddess with the head of a cat, and Tsukiyomi, a stoic god with silvery lavender hair—but many of them I could only guess based on their imposing presence and particular features, like a goddess with navy-blue skin or a god with brightly colored feathers and the feet of an emu.

Standing at the side, wearing a fitted white tunic with loose trousers, was a tall but slender man, and his cranium was totally smooth. He was plain but not unattractive, with a broad nose and full lips, but his dark eyes were anxious as he looked down at us.

We knelt before them, as we had before, as the exousia directed. They stood behind us, armed with golden spears, should we decide to charge the gods. Not that we would.

"Thank you for your patience as I consulted with my court," Sedna announced in her cool, clear voice. "I trust you have been comfortable."

"Yes, thank you," I replied, keeping my voice as cool and strong as hers. "We truly appreciate all your hospitality."

"Yes, yes, we're all giant bowls of gratitude," Bastet said with an exaggerated roll of her bright green eyes. "Let's move on with it, shall we?"

Sedna cast her a look, then continued. "Our main concern is what you plan to do with the spear once you have it."

"I plan to give it to Odin," I answered honestly, which was met with a few scoffs, eye rolls, and irritated muttering.

"That's exactly what he wants!" one of the other gods shouted in protest.

"We're playing into his hands," another agreed with a scowl. Her expression now matched the rest of the court's—save for Sedna, who continued to look impassive.

Tsukiyomi folded his arms over his chest and shook his head. "The spear shouldn't even exist. It goes against everything this world was built upon."

"Yes, but so does immortals kidnapping the child of a Valkyrie," Sedna countered. "The impious have drawn the first blood, and we cannot let them rise up to the earth."

"We all want to stop an uprising before it's too late, but I don't trust that spear in the hands of a Vanir god," Tsukiyomi said. "Especially not Odin."

"Agreed," Bastet added. "Baldur took the spear from him for a reason." She looked over at the man in the tunic standing off to the side. "Didn't you?"

"Of course," he replied, sounding uneasy. Baldur stood tall, with his hands clasped behind his back. "The ability to snuff *any* living thing entirely out of existence, with no consequence or resistance, is unparalleled. It's too much power for any one god to wield."

Sedna finally said, "I'm not sure how we can resolve this."

"You haven't let them speak," Bastet argued, motioning toward us.

"There has to be an agreement that can be reached. Baldur, tell her directly what you want, and let the girl tell you what she needs."

Baldur cleared his throat and looked down at me. "I cannot let the spear go back into the hands of my father. I took it to protect all the beings on earth, and below, so I can't let that all be destroyed."

He paused and licked his lips before continuing. "Many centuries ago, my own mother Frigg came to the Gates of Kurnugia. We could not and would not open the doors for her then, and had she asked, I would never have given the spear to her. That is how strongly I feel."

"The problem seems to be that you don't want the spear left in the hands of a Vanir god," Oona interjected.

Baldur nodded. "Precisely."

"Then we won't do that," I said, with far more confidence than I actually felt. "I will return the spear to you when this is all over."

I had no clue how I could possibly get the spear back from Odin if I brought it to him as he asked, but if Odin believed it was important, I would do whatever it took to get the spear back on earth. Returning the spear afterwards would be a problem for another day.

"You'll return to Kurnugia?" Sedna asked, raising her eyebrow.

"There isn't an open door here," Tsukiyomi contended. "You can't just come and go as you please."

"I got in here once," I persisted. "I can do it again."

"It's actually much easier for a mortal than you immortals might imagine," Valeska added.

"Frankly, that does little to address Baldur's concerns, and mine, for that matter," Sedna said. "Yes, the Vanir gods are particularly dangerous with a weapon like that, but you are a mere mortal. What's to stop Odin from simply keeping it once you give it to him? Or another immortal might take it, or even another human."

Suddenly there was a loud sound—like an avalanche and a lion roar—and the whole palace began to tremble. The floor rumbled beneath us, like an earthquake.

"Stay calm!" Sedna commanded, even as the room swayed and the immortals let out gasps and yelps of surprise.

The shaking began to lessen, but the deafening sound of a hundred salpinx erupted. It was a brassy, sad note that reverberated through me.

Sedna stood up and looked behind her at the world outside, beyond the balcony. "They've broken through the first wall."

"How is that possible?" a goddess wailed.

"We should've killed them all," another god said, almost to himself. He was the only one still sitting, and his eyes were downcast and his shoulders slumped. "That was our only chance. We should've killed all the mortals that came into a realm where they don't belong."

"It was already too late," Sedna insisted. "As soon as they had a Valkyrie bloodline, they had what they needed to unseal—"

The word died on her lips as another wall came crashing down, echoing through the palace as it shook.

"Go!" Sedna ordered. "All of you! Arm yourselves if you can fight, and get to safety if you can't. Gugalanna is leading an army on Zianna, and they will be here soon."

As everyone began to scramble, doing as their ruler had ordered, I got to my feet and raced up the stairs toward Baldur. I grabbed his arm, stopping him before he escaped the room.

"Please," I begged him.

All around me, I could hear things crashing as statues fell over and paintings clattered to the floor. The cries of the immortals throughout the citadel came in through the balcony, interrupted by the bleat of the salpinx horns.

Baldur put his hand on the marble rail that ran around the veranda, bracing himself as the floor shook beneath us. He met my gaze with an intense uncertainty—his dark eyes flitting around the chaos that had enveloped the room, before landing back on me—and then he reached under his tunic and pulled out a spear.

It was only about a foot long, with the shaft ending in a jagged break. The head appeared to be made of a near-translucent red glass with a razor-sharp tip, while the rod was twisty metallic dark blue.

"Here." He held out the spear toward me. "Take this."

I took it quickly, afraid he might change his mind if given more time, and I was surprised by the weight of it. Not only was it heavy, but there was a strangeness in the density, with an underlying heat. It reminded me of a thermos filled with hot liquid sloshing around inside and warming through the outside.

"Tell my father that I warned him about this," Baldur said as the palace quaked around us. "He cannot keep everything trapped down here forever. Eventually it will all come to the surface."

THIRTY

———•◆•———

I hid the spear way down deep in my bag, beneath the Valhallan cloak. The throne room had been deserted—Baldur was the last one to go, while Valeska, Oona, and Asher waited behind with me as I got the spear safely tucked away.

In the time it took me to put it away, another wall had come down. Oona and Valeska stood on the veranda, watching it fall.

"There's only four walls left," Oona announced morosely as she surveyed Zianna. "They're almost halfway through."

"Let's try to make it out before they make it all the way," I said as I secured my bag on my shoulders.

Asher glanced around the massive, empty throne room. "Do you know how to leave? Because I haven't a clue."

"Not off the top of my head," I admitted. "But the sólarsteinn got us here, so hopefully it can get us out."

"*Or*—" Valeska said loudly, and I looked back to see her smiling slyly as she stood on the railing that ran around the veranda. "If we wanted to go faster, I could give you a ride."

Without looking, she jumped backward off the railing, only to come flying back up a second later. She hovered above us, her large black wings flapping languidly behind her.

"Can you carry all of us?" I asked cautiously as I walked over to her.

"I don't think I could carry all three of you at once," she admitted. "And I couldn't take two of you higher, but if I had you and Oona, I'd be able to glide you down to the ground."

The loud *wooshing* noise of another wall falling rumbled through the palace, and I looked out at the chaos below for the first time. Many of the divine immortals inside Zianna had run toward the next remaining wall, attempting to support it with their strength and boulders, while others were armed, waiting for a battle if the impious broke through.

Gugalanna was leading the charge—kicking at the wall with his massive bull legs. But he wasn't the only one, nor was he the largest. He had an army of giants and monsters beside him, attacking the wall with everything they had.

The exousia and other flying immortals were diving at the impious, but they appeared to have little effect on them. Gugalanna punched an exousia out of the sky, then threw his head back and laughed.

Beyond the fighting and destruction, back far enough so as not to risk any injury, a woman in black sat on a throne of bones. The throne was part of a sedan chair, with a dozen ghoulish carriers holding the poles on their shoulders. Even when they weren't moving, her servants still held her up, so she could see her work unfolding from a slightly higher vantage.

The distance was so great that I couldn't really make out her features—I couldn't see her toying with the gold rings on her fingers, or the impish smile on her lips, or the glimmer in her black eyes—but I knew it just the same. What seemed possible or impossible was irrelevant to her.

Ereshkigal looked up at me—her eyes piercing through me—and her smile deepened.

"All right, let's do this," I said and turned back to Valeska.

Valeska instructed me to give Asher my bag, since she didn't want the extra weight. She'd paired me and Oona together because we were the two lightest ones, and we didn't have time to waste for her to make three trips.

I hated leaving Asher again, even for a second, and I kissed him brusquely before whispering, "Hurry down to me."

Then I ran over to where Valeska waited, standing on the railing of the veranda. Oona was already at Valeska's left side, with her arms wrapped tightly around Valeska's waist as she clung to her.

"What happens if we get too heavy?" Oona asked as I climbed onto the rail to take my place.

"You won't," Valeska assured her.

I looked down at the ground below, and I felt a dizzying nausea roll over me. I gripped tightly on to both Oona and Valeska—I had no intention of letting either of them go.

"But what if we do?" Oona persisted.

"Then we fall," Valeska replied matter-of-factly. "Hang on."

"Wait—" Oona began, but it was too late. Valeska had already jumped off.

I squeezed my eyes shut so I wouldn't see how quickly the ground was rising up to meet us, and the wind blew through my hair. Her wings beat above my head, and I tried to focus on the sound of that and not the feeling of my stomach rising into my throat.

It wasn't until she finally set us down, with the ground firmly beneath my feet, that I realized I'd been holding my breath.

"Told you I could do it." Valeska grinned as she stretched her wings, then she stared up at the towering palace. "Be right back. I'm gonna go rescue your boyfriend."

I thought about correcting her, that Asher wasn't my boyfriend—I mean, at least not officially, yet—but she was already flying off again. And honestly, did it really matter? I cared about Asher, he cared about me, and with the world literally falling down around us, labels no longer really seemed to matter.

As I looked out at the walls trembling beyond the valley, the sound of crashing rocks mixed with battle cries. A lot of things I'd worried about up on earth didn't seem to matter anymore. Time really did move differently—an entire lifetime had gone by in a matter of hours. So much was changing, so quickly.

Oona stared at the incoming carnage with wide, fearful eyes and her mouth agape. It was still far away, at the very edges of Zianna, but it was only a matter of time before Gugalanna and his crew broke through.

"How are they doing this?" she asked. "Haven't these walls been up for centuries?"

"I think so, but they used Asher's blood to unseal the protective spells," I said, explaining as best as I understood it. "They'd never been able to get their hands on the child of a Valkyrie before."

When she looked back at me, her eyebrows were drawn together, and her skin had paled. "Did we do this? Is this our fault?"

"I don't know," I admitted around the growing lump in my throat. "But we're going to do everything we can to make it right."

Valeska returned a moment later with Asher, along with my bag of gear and Oona's. Oona blinked back her sadness and took a deep breath, easing her anxiety by focusing on the task at hand.

The familiar anxious electricity churned through me, warming my muscles, and I felt the buzzing growing around my heart. The urge to fight, to kill, was growing inside me, but this wasn't my usual Valkyrie mode: the angry ache in my stomach was because I wanted to protect Asher, to avenge him and my mother.

"Let's go while we still have a chance," I said. "We'll deal with everything else later."

THIRTY-ONE

———— ◆ ————

The only entrance—and exit—of Zianna was right by the melee, so that would be no good for escape. Gugalanna and his army couldn't walk under the arches—they had to tear down the walls to fully break the spell that kept them out. But they were blocking the pathway of anyone else who might want to get out.

The final wall—the starry black opal one—was still standing, but it had begun to weaken. So our only way out that we could see was to find a crack in that wall. We started as far as we could get from the fighting, but the wall held too strong. We had to get closer to the battle.

I ran alongside the wall, my legs humming with delighted electricity at finally getting a chance to move. I was racing toward the fighting, and my vision shifted subtly to hyperfocus.

My wounded leg should've been throbbing. It still wasn't completely healed from when I tangled with a spider woman I had been sent to kill. But running like this helped my instincts kick in enough, as my body prepared for its job. The edge of my vision darkened, tunnel vision that allowed me to focus on a single immortal at a time, so I forced myself to slow my breathing.

The others trailed behind me, since they couldn't run as fast. Walking now, I ran my hand along the smooth cool stone, until I finally spotted a break. It was much closer to the fighting than I would've liked—only a few yards separated the crack from where Gugalanna kicked at the wall—but it was the first gap I had seen that was large enough for us to fit through.

I motioned for them to hurry, my eyes darting between them and the trouble at the wall. Valeska went first, deftly sliding through the growing crack in the trembling wall, and Oona and Asher hastily followed.

Valeska was still leading the way, climbing over the red crystal rubble of the sixth wall, by the time I squeezed through the crack after them. Oona stumbled on a stone, and Asher grabbed her arm, helping her across, and I hurried after them.

We all moved as swiftly and as quietly as we could to avoid detection, and fortunately everyone else seemed to have their hands full, so they didn't notice us climbing over the remains of the wall.

I made it to the fifth wall when I realized that Valeska wasn't leading the way anymore. I stopped and looked past Oona and Asher, who stayed a step or two behind me, and I saw Valeska standing on a tall chunk of blue garnet, staring intently at where the impious pounded at the final wall.

"Valeska?" I called her in a hushed voice, but she didn't move.

I followed her gaze and instantly realized what she was looking at—a swarthy woman standing at the edge of the fighting. Her large black wings were outstretched behind her, and with her dusky skin and wild hair, her similarities to Valeska were striking. She even had the same wide, prominent eyes.

"Valeska," I repeated, slightly louder this time.

She continued staring for another second, then jumped down off the garnet.

"Was that your mother?" Oona asked softly, falling into step beside her, as the four of us headed back on our way.

"It was," she replied curtly.

"Why didn't you say anything to her?" I asked.

"She's helping to take down Zianna," Valeska said. "She's working with everything I'm fighting against. What's there to say?"

I felt a rush of air behind me as the final wall began to fall, and the loud cheers of celebration from the impious nearly drowned out the roar of its collapse. Valeska never looked back. She just kept walking.

Unlike most of the walls, which were gems or stone, the one directly in front of us was made of platinum, so it didn't fall the same way the others did. It was torn in some places and bent down in others, making it resemble shredded paper. That's how strong Gugalanna and his monsters were. They made metal crumple like nothing.

Because parts of the platinum wall were still standing, we had to walk farther down to find a gap to slip through. I kept glancing back over my shoulder as we walked, at the flood of impious streaming into Zianna.

"Hello again, little Valkyrie," a familiar voice purred, and I looked ahead to see a beautiful woman stepping out from the shadows behind the metal wall. I blame the stress of everything for not recognizing her, not immediately. It took a second, but when she smiled at me—her smooth skin peeling back to reveal a mouthful of growing fangs—I knew exactly who she was.

It was Amaryllis Mori, the Jorogumo. The spider woman who tore a hole in my calf before I killed her.

THIRTY-TWO

———— ◆ ————

Remember me?" Amaryllis asked as her voice distorted from something lyrical into a deep monstrous growl.

Her transformation was already well under way. The delicate features of her face tore open as multiple red eyes sprouted across her forehead and cheeks. Her legs ripped, shedding blood and skin, to make room for her long spider legs.

Seeing the venomous setae on her, sticking out of her legs like a thousand deadly needles, gave me flashbacks of the agonizing pain she had left me in.

"Who is this *cýka*?" Valeska asked, sounding disgusted over the audible sound of Amaryllis's stomach distending until it tore open, to allow for her bulbous arachnid abdomen.

"Oh, just an old friend," I said as I reached for the dagger on my hip.

Amaryllis took a step toward me, her long spindly legs moving lightly over the crumpled wall. "You should've let me go when we were on earth. You could be making your escape right now."

"There's still time," I replied, taking a step back from her.

I definitely did not want her setae getting anywhere near me, but my fear had actually begun to abate. That was the thing that happened when instinct took over—I lost any real sense of my body or normal mortal fears and emotions. And I became a weapon. As the buzzing intensified around my heart and a pressure built at the base of my stomach, it calmed me some to know that all of my dread and panic would be gone in a few seconds.

"Valeska, get them out of here," I said, wanting them to get clear before things got really bad.

"Um . . ." Oona sounded uncertain, so I looked at her from the corner of my eye. "Valeska already flew off."

"What?" I asked, and Amaryllis threw back her head and began to cackle.

I suddenly became all too aware of the fact that I couldn't see either Asher or Valeska from where I stood, with the monstrous spider woman encompassing most of my vision. Oona was the only one lagging beside me, and it didn't really matter where the others were, as long as they were out of the long reach of Amaryllis's venomous legs.

"Get out of here," I told Oona without looking away from the Jorogumo. Then, more emphatically, because I knew Oona wouldn't want to listen: "*Go!*"

"Your friends are already deserting you?" the spider woman asked. "You're going to die alone."

"Well, I did kill you once before by myself," I reasoned. "I think I can defeat you again."

Her smile fell away, as her skin twisted around her fangs into a ragged scowl. "You had an unfair advantage. But down here, this is my turf, little Valkyrie. We're all growing more powerful than you can imagine."

"You should be thanking me!" I argued, taking a step back every time she stepped forward. "Because I returned you, you got a spot fighting right next to Ereshkigal. Isn't that what you wanted?"

I kept talking because I didn't have a plan, not yet. Without Sigrún I felt naked, and I wasn't sure how effective my Valkyrie abilities would be at tempering Amaryllis's otherwise superior strength and venom.

My only goal was to keep everyone safe until I saw an opening, and then I would take her down. Waiting for the right time, unfortunately, was at odds with everything else I was feeling. My entire body was longing to fight. I felt like a coiled spring, the pressure becoming almost unbearable.

But I couldn't kill her—she couldn't die here—so I had to wait until I had the best chance of landing the most damaging blow possible. I had to get her down long enough that I could make a run for it.

"I was fighting for Ereshkigal up there!" she bellowed, and as she leaned toward me, saliva dripped off her fangs. "I wanted to stay free, instead of being trapped in a dank, dark cellar!"

Then she straightened up so she towered above me. Her beady red eyes blinked in unison, pulling her pale flesh into eyelids and stretching her already taut skin even more. When she smiled, blood dripped down from her lips onto her fangs.

I crouched, making myself into a tripod with one hand, a knee, and a foot. In my right hand I gripped the dagger at my side, and if she took a step closer, and I kept myself low enough to the ground, I could run underneath her and slice her open from end to end.

"But I won't be here for much longer," Amaryllis said, almost bragging as she took one small step forward. "It's already begun. The dead won't stay dead for much longer."

I needed a little more from her—one full step—and I would be close enough that I could dive between her legs before she had a chance to stab me with them.

"I'm going to leave soon, go back to the surface and the sun," I taunted her. "You'll still be down here, and I'm going to see to it that you never escape."

Amaryllis snarled and lunged at me. I dove forward—tucking and rolling under her legs—and then I was directly underneath her. The red hourglass marking on her black exoskeleton was like a bull's-eye, inviting me to take a jab.

So I did. I drove the blade into her abdomen, breaking through the skin like it was a thick eggshell. Her black gooey insides started to spill out like a demonic yolk, and she howled and bucked backward.

Unfortunately, my dagger went with her—stuck in her as she staggered back, crying out in anger and pain. It was all I could do to scramble out from under her without getting trampled.

"How dare you!" Amaryllis yelled. She was weakened, swaying from side to side as she hobbled toward me, but she was relentless.

She had backed me into a corner—literally. I was trapped between a pile of rubble and the platinum wall. There was nowhere for me to go.

"Incoming!" Valeska shouted, and I looked up in time to see her flying high above us as a giant chunk of black opal fell in our direction.

Amaryllis was looking up, too, her many eyes locking onto the massive gemstone before it smashed into her. I held up my arm, shielding myself from the splatter as her abdomen exploded into a mess of disgusting goo and guts.

She cried out in pain, because she was still alive. There was no release of death here for her, which meant that her plans for vengeance hadn't stopped yet, either. Slowly, she began crawling toward me, tearing her humanoid torso off her spider body and using those arms to pull herself forward. The sound coming from her mouth was completely inhuman. A guttural mutation of a scream.

I stood up, preparing to stomp her into submission if I had to, when Asher appeared on top of the rubble holding a sword made of bones. The blade itself appeared to be made from a gigantic femur—maybe a centaur's—with one edge sharpened to a razor-thin blade.

When Asher walked over to her, she hissed and tried to spit her venom at him, but she only succeeded in causing herself to cough up black blood. He raised the sword, and with one fell swoop, he sliced off her head.

"That oughta keep her immobile for a while, right?" he asked, looking over at me.

"I hope so, but I don't know how long it takes for her body to regather itself."

Asher wiped her blood off his brow with the back of his arm and said, "Let's go, then."

"Where'd you get the sword?" I asked him as we walked away from

Amaryllis's squished body, toward where Valeska and Oona were waiting outside the walls of Zianna.

"One of the skeleton soldiers lost it when an exousia ripped off his arm." He gestured toward where the impious and divine were colliding. "I figured I ought to have a weapon."

"Sorry it took me so long," Valeska said as we reached them. "I was looking for a rock big enough to squish her that I could lift while flying."

I rubbed the back of my neck, trying to ease the growing tension inside me, and I told her, "Thank you." My words came out flatter than I meant them to, so I forced a smile at her.

As grateful as I was for her help, my body still craved the release of a kill. And my fight with Amaryllis had done nothing to alleviate that.

"We should hurry, before anyone else recognizes you," Valeska said.

"How many immortals have you returned?" Asher asked, cocking an eyebrow at me as he wiped the Jorogumo's blood off his new sword. "Do we have many more of your fan club that we'll need to face off?"

"I don't think any of the rest of them should give us any trouble . . ." I trailed off as my attention was diverted by the sound of pounding hooves.

The herd of unicorn-like kirin was running toward us, bounding over the fallen walls to escape the escalating conflict. An ogre reached out, grabbing for one, but the kirin narrowly dove out of his grasp.

"I think I know how we can get away quickly," I said, watching them come toward us. "But we're going to have to move very fast."

THIRTY-THREE

———— ◆ ————

The kirin, like everything else that was allowed to live in Zianna, were instinctively good and kind, and after centuries of living among the immortals here, they had become semi-domesticated. Or at least that's what I hoped as I stepped in front of the stampeding herd.

At first they only slowed, then parted so they could run around me. But one of them stopped right in front of me. He was a large stallion, with hints of blue in his long mane that parted around his smoky gray antlers. His long tail twitched behind him, like a cat about to pounce, and he leaned down and chuffed at me.

"We only want to get away, just like you," I told him calmly, and I slowly reached out to pet his nose. His fur felt soft, and the iridescent scales mixed in with it were warm and smooth, like a snake that had been lying out in the sun.

While most of the herd continued running, a few other kirin had stopped with the stallion, inspecting us. Oona was the first to move closer to them, gently petting them and cooing words of encouragement.

"I know it's been a rough day for all of us," I said as I went around to the side of him, running my hand along him as I walked. "But we need to go."

The stallion hadn't moved yet, so I took that as a good sign. With the sounds of fighting raging on, I cautiously reached up and took hold of his mane to steady myself, and I put my other hand on his back. Then I jumped up.

It wasn't elegant, as I lay on my stomach, splayed across the kirin, but I was up, and he wasn't freaking out. He brayed, but didn't move as I sat up and swung my leg over. I had successfully mounted a kirin, and he didn't seem to mind.

Asher climbed onto a kirin beside me, using the same inelegant technique that I had, while Valeska was able to fly up and land gracefully on a kirin's back. She could fly all the way, but hitching a ride on a kirin would save her energy for what lay ahead.

Since Oona was so short, she didn't even try to get up on her own. She came over to me and I grabbed her hand and pulled her up. She got situated behind me and held on to my bag for stability.

"Where do we go from here?" I asked, looking at Valeska.

"Follow the herd." She pointed to where the herd of kirin were racing on ahead so the worst of the fighting and the army from She'ol lay behind them.

"But that's the opposite of where we came in through the Eshik Mitu geyser," I said. "Shouldn't we go back?"

Valeska shook her head. "No, that was only an entrance. We can't get out that way. We have to exit through the Gates."

"I don't understand," Oona said. "How do we get out?"

"It's hard to explain," Valeska said with a sigh. "We'll end up in a lake outside of the ossuary."

"That's where Gugalanna pulled me through," Asher said wearily. "I only remember the water as we went through, but the first thing I remember of Kurnugia is being bound and carried by skeletons, then we followed Gugalanna through a dark, hungry forest. The kirin are going in the general direction of that forest, so we can follow them for now."

"That can't be right," Oona argued. "We've gone so far from the entrance. The geyser and the ossuary have to be what . . . half a mile from each other? Without all the twisting maze, they may be even closer. But we've traveled for hours, covering miles and miles away from the geyser already, and you're saying that we still have a lot to go until we're underneath the ossuary?"

"Kurnugia isn't like a vast cave that exists just below the surface of the earth," Valeska reminded her. "This is another realm. Distance and time move on a separate plane here."

The stallion I was on brayed again and stomped his foot, growing restless.

"So you're saying we should follow the other kirin?" I asked.

"For now," Valeska said. "But I don't know where they're going."

I rolled my eyes. "I didn't think you had a psychic connection with the kirin. I was just saying that we should leave."

"Let's go, then." Valeska barely had the words out before she was spurring her mare on, and she bolted ahead, racing after the rest of the herd.

Without waiting for me to signal him, my stallion took off. I gripped his mane tightly to keep from flying off. Even though I had watched them run—I had felt the wind as they rushed past me—I still was not prepared for how fast the kirin could go. I leaned into the stallion, to keep from blowing off, and my bag strained at my shoulders from Oona hanging on to it.

Soon we had caught up with the herd, and soon after we actually passed them. My kirin was leading the way now, bounding over fallen logs and gulleys like they were nothing. He never seemed to tire, and he didn't even slow, not until we got to a clearing alongside the Huber River.

We seemed far enough away from Zianna, and the kirin clearly needed a break, so we dismounted. There were a few trees on our side of the river, but mostly around here it was drab green grass that the kirin began to graze on. A few taller, angrier plants were dispersed among the clearing with bright red flowers that snapped at anything that moved by, like a Venus flytrap on steroids.

The ankle-grabbing ground ivy was here, too, with its olive-green leaves and long tendrils that tried to wrap around my feet, but fortunately the kirin seemed to scare it away. I watched as long vines started winding around their hooves, only to be mercilessly stomped into the dirt, and the ivy began to retreat back into the ground.

I went over to the river to wash off the black blood from my run-in with Amaryllis Mori, and also because the riverbank was free of any plants that wanted to eat me. I figured there were probably plenty of monstrous creatures that lived in the water that would happily take a bite out of me, so I went to the shallow narrow bend in the river.

On the other side of the river was a dark forest, filled with thick, tall tree trunks with black vines wound tightly around them. Dark green moss and hornworts appeared to blanket every surface, but it was hard to see under the heavy fog that hung over the forest.

As I crouched down, rinsing my hands in the dark blue water, Asher sat down next to me, resting his bone sword in the dirt beside him. His arms hung loosely around his knees as he watched the water coursing by, but his expression was unreadable.

"Ash?" I asked. "Are you okay?"

He blinked, then looked over at me. "What?" Then he shook his head and his brow furrowed. "Sorry. I was lost in thought."

Behind me, Oona was stretching her legs and pacing the shore, and she asked, "Should I make a cloaking spell?"

"Probably," Valeska said. She stood a bit farther down on the riverbank, her arms folded over her chest as she stared into the dark forest. "I mean, we're going to have to go through that."

"What?" I looked sharply at her. "We have to go through *there*?"

Valeska nodded. "Yeah, that's the Cryptomerian Forest. It surrounds the portal out, but it extends for miles, and it's full of all kinds of horrible crap to dissuade anyone from going through."

I should've known when Asher said he'd traveled through "a dark, hungry forest" to get to She'ol, but I had been hoping for an easier path anyway. Not that any of this had been easy. I sat back on the bank and let out an irritated sigh. "Great."

"We made it this far." Oona set her bag down beside me, then knelt next to it so she could begin pulling out what she needed for the cloaking spell. "We can make it a little bit farther. Once we get to the exit, we're practically home free."

"Practically," I said under my breath and steeled myself to tell them my realization about the cloak: that I didn't know how all of us would escape. "There's something that we need to—"

"Do you hear that?" Asher interrupted, tilting his head.

"What?" I asked, but then I heard it, too.

A high-pitched chirping sound, like a cross between a tiny alarm clock and baby bird. And it was growing louder.

"What is that?" I stood up and turned around, scanning for any sign of it.

Oona looked up at me with wide eyes. "Mal, I think it's coming from your bag."

She was right. I still had my gear bag on and I hurried to slip it off and threw it on the ground.

Behind me, I was vaguely aware that the kirin sounded agitated— stomping their feet, moving around, and chuffing a lot. But for the moment, I was more focused on finding what was chirping inside my bag.

I opened the main pocket first, digging around, but when I leaned in closer, I realized the chirping was coming from an outer pocket.

"Hey, Malin," Valeska said.

"Hold on," I told her absently. I unzipped a few pockets—which turned up empty—before I finally spotted something. An oblong lump that didn't belong.

"But Malin—" Valeska repeated.

"I think I got it!" I shouted excitedly.

I reached in and pulled out a big scarab beetle, chirping loudly in my hand. It was beautiful—for a giant bug, anyway—with an iridescent shell of bright purples and blues.

Asher peered down at it, sitting calmly on the palm of my hand, and he asked, "What is it?"

"I don't know," I admitted. "Do you think it's dangerous? Like, should we kill it?"

"I would rather you didn't," a woman said from behind me. "Since she's mine and I would like her back, safe and sound."

I turned to see a simurgh standing a few feet behind me. The simurgh was a massive feathered beast with the body of a white lion, the crimson head of a dog, two gigantic brightly colored wings of emerald and violet, and a tail made of long, vibrant peacock-esque plumages.

The sight of such a colorful, large creature so near to me, with the herd of kirin parting around it, took all my attention, so I didn't immediately notice a woman standing beside it. Not until she stepped away from it, pushing back the hood of her dark cloak so I could see her better.

It was Lyra Kothari.

She had followed us.

THIRTY-FOUR

She's a homing beetle," Lyra said as she plucked the little creature from my hand.

She held it up and made a soothing chittering sound, which quieted the beetle. With her other hand she opened the large locket around her neck—the one shaped like a golden bell jar. Inside, in one half of the locket, was another beetle, this one bluer but just as beautiful and bright.

"She's angry about being separated from her mate," Lyra explained as she put the beetle back in the locket, and the two of them nestled next to each other before Lyra shut it again. "But she stays wherever I put her, sending out a psychic signal to her love, and he chirps whenever I move closer to her, directing me where to go."

"You tracked us?" Valeska was incredulous.

She'd moved closer to us, scowling and casting angry glares at Lyra. Her black wings had extended slightly in her anger, the feathers spreading and puffing up to make her appear larger and more menacing.

"It was the only way I knew I'd be able to find you again." Lyra offered Valeska an apologetic smile, but Valeska remained unmoved.

"Why did you need to find us again?" I asked. "Did you come to stop us?"

"No, of course not!" Lyra insisted, her eyes wide as she shook her head emphatically. "I only wanted to help."

Valeska snorted. "Help us or help yourself?"

Oona shot Valeska a look, and then gently but firmly told Lyra, "You can't come with us. You know that, right?"

"I do," Lyra replied with a sad smile. "I know that better than you, I'm sure. I don't plan to leave here, but I did want to ask a favor of you."

"I knew it!" Valeska shouted triumphantly, startling the kirin, who were already on edge with the simurgh loitering about.

For his part, the simurgh seemed content to lie down in the clearing, but the kirin weren't taking any chances and started galloping off, heading farther down the river.

"It was why I had to leave you before. I had to get something for my daughter." Lyra's dark eyes were imploring as she looked at me. "Can you give it to her?"

"No," Valeska replied instantly, before I had a chance to answer.

I hesitated before cautiously saying, "It depends on what it is."

"It's only this—" Lyra reached into a deep pocket and pulled out a heart-shaped stone of crystallized pink tourmaline. "An itayakkal."

"What is that?" I asked as she handed it to me.

"It's an enchanted stone," Oona answered, leaning over to look at the gemstone in my hand. "Whoever it's given to will be able to feel how much the enchanter cares for them."

Lyra's eyes were moist as she smiled nervously. "I want Sloane to know how much I still love her."

I looked to Oona, who seemed to know plenty about this stone, but she just shrugged.

"Sure," I decided, since I owed both Lyra and Sloane for helping me so much. "I can do that."

"Thank you," Lyra said, looking relieved and elated. "In repayment, I can help you navigate the forest quickly and safely."

"Are we going to ride on that through the forest?" Oona asked hopefully, motioning to the simurgh, who was busy preening its feathers.

"The trees are too close together, and it's much too dangerous," Lyra said. "She won't go in there."

"But we're going in there?" Asher asked.

Throughout the conversation, he'd been standing to my side, with his arms folded, taking in the situation. He'd said nothing and hardly reacted to any of her claims, but now he looked at her with pinched eyebrows and dark eyes.

"We're much smaller, and I know the way through," Lyra said.

"How and why would you possibly know that?" Valeska asked, apparently taking turns with Asher on being suspicious of everything Lyra said and did.

"I told you that when I first came down here I still wanted to be free," she explained. "I wanted to liberate Sloane and everyone else on earth and below. So I planned an escape. I learned everything I could, including how to get through the Cryptomerian Forest, and I practiced it until I had it down."

"But then you decided not to escape?" Asher asked.

"I will admit that initially it wasn't so much a decision as it was an impossibility," Lyra said. "I couldn't get through. But eventually I came to the bitter conclusion that escape came at a very high price. If I got through, I risked creating a tear between our two worlds that would allow every vile monster in here to escape onto earth.

"My mortal daughter would almost certainly be killed, perhaps even the whole world would be destroyed. I would not and I could not do that to Sloane," Lyra finished, with enough conviction that Asher relaxed his stance.

We'd already taken a long enough break, and with Lyra here to lead the way, it seemed like as good a time as any to get going. We packed our things—with me safely tucking the itayakkal in my bag—and Lyra began to describe what we could expect in the forest.

"Stay close to me, and never stray off course," Lyra warned. "Don't touch anything, not unless you absolutely have to. And don't respond to anything, either. Say and do as little as possible."

"What about breathing?" Valeska asked dryly. "Can we do that?"

Lyra only gave her a hard look before continuing her explanation, telling us we wouldn't always be able to trust our eyes or ears in the forest. Finally, after warning us once again to stay close, she started leading the way, lifting her long skirt to walk across the shallowest part of the river toward the forest.

"Who is she?" Asher asked in a hushed voice as he fell in step beside me.

"She's a friend of a friend, I guess," I said, since that was the easiest way to explain her.

"And you trust her?"

"Maybe. A little," I admitted. "But we have to leave as soon as we can, so I don't see what choice we have."

He licked his lips and stared ahead at the dark, twisting forest. "I guess we follow her into that, then."

THIRTY-FIVE

———◆———

W e're getting close," Lyra said, after we had wound our way through the dark and twisted forest.

But she hadn't really needed to say anything. I could already hear it—a whooshing roar, like a plane taking off mixed with the rush of a waterfall.

We were close enough that I could smell it. I remembered it clearly from when we had been in the ossuary. Unlike everywhere else in the underworld outside of Zianna, which smelled vaguely of mustiness and death, this was clean water and sunlight and dirt. Not the stale scent of decay around us, but like the freshly tilled soil of a garden during a summer rain shower.

It smelled like *life*.

I wanted to tear through the forest and race on ahead. I couldn't wait to get out of here and feel the sunlight and breathe air that hadn't been bottled up for centuries. But I kept my pace slow, following Lyra's steps exactly.

Even though we were close enough to hear and smell what was ahead, the fog and the branches were still too thick for us to see it. A light mist fell over me, dampening my hair, and I looked up, searching for a source, but it was only trees soaring into the darkness above us.

"Is it raining?" Oona asked, sounding as confused as I felt.

"No, it's the portal," Valeska replied.

It was so loud now, I could almost feel it rumbling through me. Wind rustled through the trees.

An overgrown thicket of brambles blocked our path, and Lyra crouched down, carefully lifting up the branches to make a narrow opening for us to squeeze under. Pools of water sat underneath, rippling from a gust of wind that blew in through the gap.

I crawled on my hands and knees, with fresh mud soaking through my pants, but I barely even noticed.

And then there it was, right in front of me—a cyclone of water that stretched all the way up toward the ceiling, as far as I could see. Closer to the top, it looked like it stretched a mile across, but it slowly narrowed until it came to a point where it hovered a mere six feet above the ground.

We had found it. We were going home.

Or at least some of us were.

THIRTY-SIX

The cloak isn't big enough for four," Valeska said in a hushed voice, barely audible over the sounds of the rushing wind and water.

My gear bag was open, sitting by my feet, with the cloak still tucked inside. It was all ready to go. I just couldn't bring myself to pull it out yet.

I'd been standing and watching the cyclone while Oona got ready. Asher stood directly under the cyclone, with his eyes closed and his head back, letting the mist and wind blow over him.

Oona was a few feet away from us, mixing up a fresh batch of her protection armarria potion before we went through. Lyra crouched beside her, helping some, but mostly watching her and talking.

"I know," I told Valeska finally, as I watched the sublime relief on Asher's face as he breathed in deeply. He'd been here for so much longer than me—especially in Kurnugia time—and I imagined he had to be relishing the feel of the clean air and water.

I swallowed hard then turned to look at Valeska. "But you made it through without one. Your biggest injuries were from the geyser, going into Kurnugia. This shouldn't burn me." I paused, pushing back my fear. "Right?"

"No, this one won't burn you. If anything, it's cold." As she spoke, she tilted her head back, letting her eyes follow the full length of the water cyclone up to the ceiling. "But it takes a long-ass time."

"Well, that doesn't sound so bad. I can handle being cold for a while."

"Yeah, but how long can you hold your breath?" Valeska asked.

"A couple minutes?" I chewed the side of my cheek. "How long does it take?"

She shrugged. "Ten minutes? Maybe twenty? I just know that my protection spell ran out halfway through, taking all my oxygen with it. I almost blacked out by the time I surfaced, and I was coughing up water."

I glanced over to where Oona was hard at work. "Her potion is more powerful."

"Is it?" Valeska asked. "Or was it the cloak that protected us earlier?"

"Are you trying to freak me out?" I asked her directly.

"No." She scoffed. "I just don't want you to kill yourself. If you die on the way up, I'm the one stuck getting that spear to Odin."

"What else would you have me do?" I asked, lowering my voice in case Asher or Oona might be able to hear. "I'm not leaving any of you behind, and I won't stay here by myself. So what else can I do but hope that everything is enough?"

Valeska didn't say anything for a moment, and then she looked at me. Her wide eyes were solemn under her heavy lashes, and her small mouth was pressed into a thin line.

Oona had finally finished her potion, so we all gathered together to get ready. We said our goodbyes to Lyra before Oona got started with her incantations, but she lingered at the edge of the forest to watch.

"Leaving requires a few more steps than it did to get in," Oona explained. "But I'm going to start with the protection spell first, and then move on to the next part."

Like she had before we entered Kurnugia, Oona began the protection process. First, she handed us each a mirror-black hematite crystal and warned us to hang on to it. Then she opened the vial of her armarria potion and marked each of us with it in an *X* over our hearts as she recited an incantation.

Asher was wounded above his heart, but Oona insisted the placement was necessary. He pulled down the collar of his shirt, giving her easier access, and he winced as she gently slid her finger across his lacerations.

"Oh, damn, that burns." He grimaced, looking down at his chest. Steam actually came out of the cuts, but only for a second.

"Sorry about that," Oona said. "But I don't want you getting hurt any worse, so I had to do that."

"No, it's okay." He let go of his shirt so that his marks were covered up, and he rubbed his hand over the spot.

"The next part is weird, but at least the Kurtari incantation is quick." She pulled out a vial of thick purple liquid. "So, first I'm going to pour a bit of Eralim blood on your head"—she shook the vial—"then I need you to spin counterclockwise while reciting the incantation."

Valeska wrinkled her nose and said, "I used only the Eralim blood when I did it before."

"Yeah, well, you were alone," Oona countered. "There's four of us going back, so the portal needs to be bigger and open for longer."

Oona ushered us under the cyclone, the wind whipping through our hair and clothes. She smeared purple blood across each of our foreheads, including her own, then shouted to be heard over the noise. "Repeat after me: *At-eh-bah-map ah-dilz ah oh-doh!*"

We all turned counterclockwise, going the opposite of the direction the cyclone was churning in.

"Okay!" Oona yelled when we'd finished. "All we need is the cloak and the key, then we should be home free!"

"But how do we know if it's worked?" Asher asked. "Nothing's changed!"

"If it sucks us up, it works!" Valeska shouted over the roar.

I had the cloak out, but I'd been holding it balled up in my hands. Now I let it unfurl, hanging on to it tightly to keep it from blowing away. Asher was in the center, because he was the tallest, so I put the hood over his head. Oona and Valeska took the spots on either side of him, with me standing in front, so my back was to the open gap in the cloak.

Valeska took the Sibudu Key off from around her neck and raised her hand up high until the key touched the bottom of the waterspout.

"Are you—" I started to ask, but then it sucked us up.

One second I was standing on the ground, and the next I was submerged in icy cold water. I buried my face in Asher's chest, breathing for as long as I could, and I felt Valeska's hand over mine—small but strong as she gripped tightly.

My back felt frozen, and there was an intense pressure, like I was being slowly squished. It was getting harder to breathe—my lungs didn't have enough space. I tried to push back from Asher to get more room, but there wasn't any to be had.

My throat burned and my entire chest ached, and pain and panic set in as I realized I was suffocating. I gasped for air, and the muscles in my abdomen began to spasm painfully. My eyes were closed, but I could see spots dancing across my vision as my mind felt black and foggy. I squeezed Valeska's hand as tightly as I could, but within seconds I was gone.

THIRTY-SEVEN

❖

It was like falling asleep in reverse.

Before I even opened my eyes, I could feel the sun warming my skin and the sandy beach under my back. I looked up through a blur of water and tears, and I could see the blue of the sky.

"She's alive!" Oona shouted excitedly, and she leaned forward, blocking out the sun. "Oh, gosh, I'm so glad you're alive. You are alive, right?"

"I think so," I replied thickly.

"Oona, give her some space, will you?" Valeska said. "I told you she would be fine."

Oona groaned but moved away from me. "Just because you say things doesn't make them true."

I sat up, looking around at the pond in the center of the cave. Above it was the wide opening, letting in the daylight and a beautiful view of the sky. Across the pond was a mossy staircase carved into the wall, which would be our emergency exit out of here. We were back on earth, in the cave beyond the tunnels that stretched below the ossuary in the Gates of Kurnugia.

This was where I'd lost Asher, and now it was where I found him again. Lying beside me, with the sun bathing his face. But his eyes were on me.

"I'm glad you're okay," he said, taking my hand in his. "I don't know what I'd have done if I lost you."

"Well, you'd have to go back to the underworld and get me," I teased.

"I suppose it is only fair that we take turns rescuing each other. So next time, I got you."

"It's a deal."

"You know, we still have the journey back to Caana City," Valeska reminded us. "And I wanna get out of this stinking, festering cesspool and get a shower and eat real food. Not to mention, you've got a meeting with Odin that you can't be late for."

The last time I'd spoken with Odin, he'd left me the same instructions as before: meet him at the top of the Caana Temple on the night of my return, when the moon is highest in the sky. How exactly he knew when I'd return was beyond me, but he'd met me last time on that same directive.

And he was a Vanir god. I was sure he had his ways of finding things out.

I stood up. "Let's go, then."

Last time I'd left here, it had killed me to leave without Asher. But now he was here, by my side, and I couldn't wait to get away from all this.

We swam across the pond and slowly climbed up the slippery steps. Well, Asher, Oona, and I did. Valeska flew up to the top and waited for us to join her. When we finally reached her, we were treated to a stunning view of the Gates of Kurnugia—the winding maze and the tall pyramids—with the sun setting on the horizon.

We slid down the sheer side of the cavern to the ground. Combining Valeska's ability to fly with our own memory of the path we'd taken before, we made quick work of getting out of the Gates of Kurnugia. In fact, we made such good time that we made it to the middle of El Noveno Anillo in time to catch the 5:45 hyperbus back to Caana City.

I sat next to Asher on the bus, giving him the window seat. He looked out the window the entire time at the world racing by. I closed my eyes and rested my head on his shoulder, loving the feel of him next to me.

"It's all so strange," Asher said softly. "Escaping was such a victory, and I want to relish it. But I know there's still so much left to do. The war hasn't even started yet."

"Maybe there won't be one," I suggested. "Maybe when I meet Odin later he'll tell me that's it, and this will all be over."

"No." He said it with such certainty that I looked up at him. "Gugalanna won't stop without a fight. They took down Zianna, and it's only a matter of time before they break through up here. They want a war, and they're going to have one."

I reached up to him, touching his face gently to get him to look at me. "We only have ten minutes left on this bus, then we'll go back to the motel where the real work will start.

"But for now, there's nothing else that we can do, nowhere else we need to be," I went on. "Let's pretend that we're two normal people, just happy to be together."

He smiled then, faintly, so the corners of his mouth barely moved, but there was light playing in his eyes. The weary creases on his forehead smoothed as he relaxed, letting his happiness soften the harder edges of his face.

"Okay." Asher leaned back in his worn bus seat. "I'll play. What would two ordinary people without a care in the world be doing on a hyperbus in Belize?"

"We're on vacation," I replied amiably.

He arched an eyebrow, and his smile deepened. "Our honeymoon?"

"Now you're getting ahead of yourself," I said, causing him to laugh warmly.

It was such a wonderful sound, and I wondered dimly when the last time I'd heard him laugh had been. When was the last time even I had laughed?

"Okay, so just a vacation," Asher agreed. "I assume we've been seeing the sites?"

"Of course! We took a tour of the rain forest and saw the temples."

He managed to look suitably impressed as he said, "Ooh, those were really fantastic, weren't they?"

"They were, but what we really enjoyed was getting some sun."

"Oh, yeah, we don't have sun like this back in the city." Then he looked out the window, at the setting sun splashing on the jungle around us, and there was a wistfulness in his eyes that wasn't just pretend.

For him, it had been weeks that he'd been in Kurnugia, without sun, without fresh air, without anything.

"What do you think we'll do tonight?" I asked, making my words sound extra cheery. I wanted to bring him back here, with me in the moment, and not thinking about whatever he'd endured in Kurnugia.

He waited a beat before turning to look back at me, an easy smile returning. "We could check out that cute little restaurant the concierge recommended."

"What kind of food do they serve?"

"It's a taco/sushi fusion, but what they're really known for is their ice cream," Asher said, totally deadpan, and it was enough to make me burst out laughing.

"That is a very *unusual* menu," I said as I stifled more laughter.

"We wouldn't want this vacation to be ordinary, would we?"

"No, of course not," I agreed. "I can't wait to try the black bean California roll. And maybe tomorrow we'll do some shopping."

"We should really have a relaxing day," he suggested. "Sleep in late, have breakfast in bed, and hit the souvenir shops in the afternoon."

"Oh, yeah, that would be nice! I could get a shirt for Oona, and maybe a shot glass for Mar—" I'd started to say Marlow. I'd gotten so caught up in the fantasy of being carefree, on vacation with my boyfriend, that I allowed myself to forget—just for a second—that my mother was dead.

But now the illusion had been shattered, and real life crashed down on me. The sun didn't seem as bright anymore, and the scenery flying by was nothing but a dark blur.

Asher sensed the shift in my mood, so he put his arm around me and pulled me closer to him. "Right now, with you and me on this old bus, it's honestly the best vacation I've had in a long time."

THIRTY-EIGHT

❖

Quinn hugged me first. I don't know exactly how I had expected her to react, but it definitely caught me off guard when she grabbed me and pulled me into her arms.

There was an intensity that reminded me of when we had still been together. It was a little too tight, almost bone-crushingly tight, but it only hurt because of how fiercely she cared. Sometimes she couldn't help herself.

We were inside of the doorway to the motel suite at the Caana Extended Stay Inn & Suites—I'd barely had a chance to get inside before she pounced on me. Atlas stood behind her in the main room, where the bland motel living room and tiny kitchenette looked immaculate. Quinn must've been stress-cleaning while we were gone.

"I'm so glad you're safe," she said, her breathy voice in my ear.

Then she let me go, just as abruptly and intensely as when she'd first embraced me, so I almost stumbled backward into Asher.

"We weren't even gone that long," I argued lamely, which was true from her perspective. For me, it felt like I'd been gone for almost a full day, but in earth time it had only been four hours we were in the underworld.

Quinn's attention had already moved on to everyone else anyway.

"Asher!" Quinn gasped. She raised her arms like she meant to hug him, but then changed her mind at the last second and let them fall back to her sides. "You're alive!"

"Yeah, it would seem that way." He rubbed an eye with the palm of this hand. "It's been a long . . . week, I guess. And I'd really like to shower and change back into my own clothes and get something to eat."

I showed him where the bathroom was, then got his bag of clothes that we'd carried with us since Gugalanna had taken him. Meanwhile, Quinn made a big show of greeting Oona and Valeska. She hugged Oona, too, and she was about to go in for one with Valeska, but Valeska told her firmly, "I don't hug."

Quinn and Atlas had a thousand questions for us, and fortunately Oona was more than happy to answer them. She sat on the couch, filling in every detail with lots of excited hand movements, while Valeska sat on the stainless steel kitchenette counter eating a day-old plantain sandwich and chasing it with an energy drink called Ādityas Elixir.

Asher came out of the bathroom wearing a threadbare motel robe when Oona had just gotten to the middle of her story. He went into the bedroom to change, so I followed him and quietly closed the door behind me.

"Are you feeling any better?" I asked and sat down on one of the beds.

"Some." He slipped off his robe, leaving him wearing only a pair of boxer briefs.

While most of his wounds seemed to be healing nicely, the marks on his chest continued to look angry and inflamed. The edges were puckered and bright red, and the wound itself was a dark brown gap that only seemed to be widening.

I grimaced and motioned to his chest. "It looks worse."

"What?" He looked down at it. "Yeah, I was scrubbing at in the shower. I was hoping that would help somehow, but I think I only made things worse."

"You should have Oona take a look at it. She has all kinds of potions and salves that would help."

"Maybe." He shrugged noncommittally and pulled a black T-shirt on over his head, hiding the marks. "I don't want to bother her."

"It's not a bother. She likes to help people."

"Maybe," he repeated as he put on a pair of jeans, then changed the subject with, "What's the plan? Now that I'm back and you have the spear. Are you supposed to be meeting Odin?"

"Yeah, but not until late. Like a quarter to midnight," I said, and Asher raised an eyebrow, presumably at the oddly specific time. "He asks to meet when the moon is the highest in the sky. Vanir gods run on different time."

Asher glanced over at an alarm clock with its bright green numbers. "That gives me a few hours to eat and rest up."

"Well, I was thinking that you should stay back," I told him gently. He looked at me sharply, but before he could protest, I went on. "You've already been through so much. You don't need to go out tonight."

"They know you have the spear," he insisted. "And we don't know who Gugalanna and Ereshkigal are communicating with up here or how they're doing it, but they obviously are, since they were working with Tamerlane Fayette and somehow got him to trick your mom into sparing him."

I looked past Asher, out the window behind him, so I wouldn't have to see the conviction in his eyes. Night had fallen, and thick clouds were rolling in, blocking out the moonlight and the stars. In the distance, the clouds lit up with a burst of lightning.

"I know," I said finally. "I won't go alone. Quinn and Atlas can come with me. You and Oona and Valeska should stay here and rest."

"Malin," he said.

"Have you talked to your grandmother?" I asked, and that was enough of an emotional startle to get him to stop arguing about whether or not he should go with me.

"Not yet. Did you talk to her while I was gone?"

I shook my head. "I didn't know how to contact her, and I wouldn't have known what to say even if I had."

"I should call her now."

He dug through his bag looking for his cell phone, and I snuck out while he was distracted, hoping we had put that argument to bed.

THIRTY-NINE

———◆———

The argument was not put to bed, but eventually Atlas and Quinn were able to convince Asher that they would be more than enough protection for me.

Samael had wired Atlas money, so we rented a sturdy little side-by-side ATV. It was basically like if a golf cart and a Humvee had a weird little baby.

The sky was rumbling, and long tendrils of lightning were spidering through the clouds. We didn't want to risk getting caught in the rain, and also, Asher was right: Ereshkigal would be sending someone after the spear as soon as she was able. So I wanted to get it to Odin as quickly as possible.

Quinn and I sat in the two seats of the ATV, with her driving, and Atlas sat on the rear rack, hanging on to the backs of our seats so he didn't bounce off. The forest surrounding the Caana temple was dense, but it wasn't impenetrable. Quinn had to take it slow in several spots, but when we got on a well-worn game trail, it was smooth sailing.

As much as I would've loved to take the vehicle up the many stairs of the temple—and as much as Quinn assured me that the ATV could handle it—I didn't want to risk desecrating an ancient pyramid to make my life a little easier. So we parked at the bottom and made the arduous trek up the stone steps to the grassy mezzanine, and then waited for Odin.

And we waited, and waited some more.

Because of the cloud cover, I couldn't see where the moon was at or how high it might be, but Oona had been certain that it wouldn't be until after midnight this time—12:44 A.M., to be precise. He'd been a little late last time, but he still arrived before midnight, and now it was going on 1:30 in the morning.

"At least we have a show," Atlas commented.

He was sitting on the steps, watching the dazzling array of lights above us. Every few seconds the sky would light up as another burst of lightning shot between the clouds. So far the flashes had yet to hit the ground, instead preferring to leap between clouds. Most of it was bright white, the way it always was, but the occasional burst appeared to be shades of purple and blue.

The strangest part wasn't even the unusually colored lightning—it was the eerie silence that accompanied it. There hadn't been a single clap of thunder or even a faint rumble. It was silent flashes, without a hint of rain or any sign of an incoming storm.

"It is sort of amazing," Quinn agreed tiredly. She sat up a little higher on the steps than Atlas, leaning back on her elbows, with her legs crossed at the ankles. Her gaze was on the sky, but her expression was far more indifferent than amazed. "Any sign of Odin yet?"

"He'll be here soon," I insisted for the tenth time, but with less and less conviction each time I said it.

"Do you have any way to contact him?"

I paced. "No. He just told me to meet him here. So far, he seems to know how to find me when he wants to."

"What do you think the holdup could be?" Quinn asked.

"I don't know," I said, but my mind was racing through a thousand scenarios, all equally horrible.

"I mean . . ." Quinn stopped and ran a hand through her hair. "He couldn't be hurt or anything, could he?"

"I don't know," I repeated.

"Can Vanir gods even be hurt or held captive?" Quinn asked, but it sounded more like she was thinking aloud. "I know they're powerful, but they're not *all*-powerful. They have weaknesses, right?"

"Everyone has weaknesses," Atlas said.

As if to punctuate his statement, a gust of wind suddenly came up, breaking through the stillness. It had been warm since we'd been in Belize, even in the dead of night, but the wind brought a chill with it, dropping the temperature by several digits within a matter of minutes.

"How long are we going to wait here?" Quinn asked.

"As long as it takes," I replied firmly.

"You want to stay here until the sun comes up?" Quinn asked.

"Of course I don't want to, but I will." I stopped pacing to look over at her. "What else am I supposed to do? I don't know how to reach him, and I don't know what to do with the spear."

"I understand the situation," Quinn said, keeping her tone calm and reasonable. "But I'm being realistic here. There's a storm coming, Malin."

"Quinn's right," Atlas agreed, giving me an apologetic smile. "We don't have to go yet, but it won't be safe staying out here all night in a storm. We'll have to go back."

I looked away from them, instead scouring the sky for any signs of Odin or his ravens. "He'll be here," I said, then, more quietly, "He has to be."

We lapsed into a silence after that, and I was fine with it. The wind had picked up, blowing leaves and dust as it roared over the temple. I began pacing again, both to keep the chill at bay and because of the anxious energy coursing through me.

Then I realized that it wasn't exactly anxiety, and I couldn't feel the chill from the breeze anymore. I could still feel the wind rustling through my hair, but it was more like being aware of it and less actually *feeling* it.

My mouth tasted metallic, and a dull buzzing was growing around my heart. My muscles tensed, wanting to charge after everything.

This wasn't anxiety or impatience.

This was my Valkyrie instincts kicking in.

I stopped pacing, forcing myself to stand perfectly still. "Something's wrong."

"What?" Quinn asked, sitting up more.

"Do you feel it?" I looked over at her, and I saw the confusion in her green eyes.

"What do you feel?" Atlas asked, and he was already on his feet walking over to me.

Before I could answer, thunder rumbled. An angry deep roar that echoed throughout the ruins, and the hair on the back of my neck stood up.

"Maybe you sensed the storm?" Quinn suggested as she came down the stairs to join me and Atlas in the center of the mezzanine.

"No, I . . ." I trailed off as the thunder rumbled again, and the pressure grew in the base of my stomach.

I tilted my head, listening closely to the thunder. It was coming from the sky, but there was something beneath it—something closer. A murky growl mixing with it.

"That's not thunder," I said, and my hand went to the sword sheathed on my hip. I'd left Sigrún at the motel, deciding instead to take the dragon sword Kusanagi, and it felt cool and heavy against the palm of my hand.

By then we all heard it—the guttural growl of an enraged big cat. Then there it was, climbing up over the walls that surrounded the mezzanine. A massive beast of a cat, at least the size of a donkey, with paws as big as a bear's, and a brindled coat of dark gray fur.

It was a Mngwa, a violent predator imported from Tanzania centuries ago. It opened its mouth—revealing a mouthful of giant sharp teeth—to let out another short burst of a roar, and this time another Mngwa replied as it came up the stairs toward us.

FORTY

———— ◆ ————

The three of us—two Valkyries and the son of a Valkyrie—should be enough to ward off two hungry giant jungle cats. Or at least that's what I told myself as they circled toward us.

We stood with our backs together, each of us brandishing our own weapon. I had Kusanagi, while Quinn had brought her Valkyrie sword Eir, but it still didn't glow its usual bright blue, despite the fact that we were surrounded. It wouldn't be as powerful, since we weren't assigned to kill these immortals, but it should be effective enough.

"Are we allowed to kill them?" Atlas asked as the Mngwas circled around us, talking to each other in their quick guttural bursts as their stubby tails swished behind them.

"Let's make sure they don't kill us, and we'll take it from there," Quinn said.

One of the Mngwas swatted at her, but Quinn swung her sword right back, and it stepped away. But a second later the other Mngwa swatted at me, and then the first cat moved closer. They were feeling us out, checking for weaknesses.

"Maybe you should use the spear," Quinn said through gritted teeth.

"No, it's not for that," Atlas insisted before I could respond, but it was a moot point. The spear was safely inside my bag, and I wouldn't be able to get to it—not before one of the Mngwas pounced on me.

Thunder rolled overhead, and the cats had apparently tired of testing us. They had made their decision.

The larger of the two leapt at Atlas, going right for his throat. He tried to stab it, but the creature knocked the sword from his hand and had him laid on the ground within seconds.

I dove at the Mngwa, driving my sword between its shoulder blades. It let out an angry yowl and swatted at me. I ducked, but one of its massive claws managed to connect with my forearm, slicing through my skin and muscle.

Quinn was busy taking on the other Mngwa, trying to chase it off the temple, but I barely had a chance to look at her. Atlas was bleeding and making an awful wet bubbling sound when he breathed, and the big cat wasn't keen on letting him go.

I was hoping that after I stabbed it, it would come after me, but both of its back legs were firmly planted on Atlas's torso as it swung at me and hissed. I stayed back just out of its reach and crouched down, waiting.

As soon as the beast turned its attention back on Atlas, I charged at it and dove onto its back. I stabbed it again, this time in the side, and when the cat tried to buck me off, I twisted the knife in deeper, lodging it between the ribs so I could use it as a handle.

The Mngwa ran in a circle, finally getting off of Atlas, and bit at me. To avoid getting a chunk taken out of me, I untwisted the knife, and fell free off the cat.

But now it was pissed and bleeding, and I was lying on the ground. When it stalked toward me, I kicked it in the face as hard as I could—twice in a row—before it let out an angry yowl and stepped back. It pawed its face, and I saw that I had managed to break one of its fangs, and the broken bit had gotten embedded in its lip.

Just then, lightning shot down—striking the top of the temple. A deafening crack of thunder reverberated through the air. Both of the Mngwas shrank back in fear, and then, bloodied and battered, they took off down the temple.

Quinn was still standing, and other than a quartet of claw marks that tore through her pants and into her thigh, she appeared okay. Atlas, on the other hand, was not doing well at all. His torso had been torn up by the Mngwa's back claws, and his shoulder had a bite taken out of it. But his throat—pouring blood onto the ground around him, as he sputtered and tried futilely to hold it in—that was the scariest part.

"We've got to get him out of here," Quinn said.

"Go get the ATV," I told her as I crouched beside Atlas. "Bring it up here. We don't have much time."

But she was already running, racing down the steps. I ripped off part of Atlas's shirt and held it against his neck, pressing it to the wound. With my other hand, I took his hand and held it. His hand was so much bigger, stronger, but his grip was weak, and his eyes were wide and terrified as he stared up at me.

"It's gonna be okay, Atlas," I promised him. "We're gonna get help."

By the time Quinn made it up with the ATV, his hand was barely even holding mine anymore. He'd closed his eyes, but he was struggling. Quinn and I managed to lift his hulking frame and get him in the passenger seat. There were only two seats, so I knelt behind him on the rear rack, leaning forward with one arm around him holding him in the chair and the other hanging on to the metal ATV frame.

"Hang on!" Quinn shouted before throwing the vehicle into gear and bouncing down the stairs.

It was a rough ride, but time was of the essence. Once we were down and out onto the game trail—which was relatively smooth sailing compared to the rest of the jungle—she asked, "What the hell happened up there?"

"I have no idea," I said, narrowly dodging a branch as we drove through the dark forest.

"Do you think Odin sent them?" Quinn asked. "Or Ereshkigal?"

"I can't think right now," I said, which wasn't a total lie. I didn't *want* to think. I didn't want to worry. I wanted to be out of the woods and at the hospital, where a doctor would tell me that Atlas was going to be okay, that everything would be okay.

FORTY-ONE

◆

Everything was not okay.

Quinn and I returned to the motel an hour later, our clothes covered in drying blood. The doctors had stitched us up—her thigh had been worse than I'd thought and took over forty stitches, while my arm only needed a few.

But there hadn't been anything they could do for Atlas. He was gone before we even made it to the hospital.

I was too numb to cry, but Oona wept as we told them what had happened. Asher's face hardened, and I could see his jaw clenching. He stood off to the side of the room, inhaling tensely through his nose and staring out the window at the lightning storm that had yet to produce any rain.

I sat with Oona, rubbing her back gently as she softly cried, since that seemed like the only thing I could do to make anything even a little bit better. Valeska sat on the arm of the couch beside her with downcast eyes.

Quinn, meanwhile, was pacing the room like a caged animal. Her silver hair had been pulled up in a messy bun to keep it out of the blood. Atlas had been bleeding so profusely that our moving him around had left us covered in it. Her left thigh was bandaged in layers of gauze, but that didn't slow her down.

"Where in the hell was Odin?" Quinn asked, demanding an answer she knew I didn't have.

"I don't know," I replied wearily.

"He should've been there," she persisted. "This never should've happened!"

I licked my lips before saying, "No, it shouldn't have."

"Where was he? How could he have left us out there like that?" Quinn ranted, and as she went on, her tone kept getting shriller and more unstable. "Why didn't he help us?"

"I don't know!" I snapped in frustration. "I don't know where he is or what he's doing! I know as much as you do, okay?"

Quinn stopped pacing to look at me. "Well, I know that it really seems like we're all totally fucked right about now." Her eyes were daring me to disagree with her, but I couldn't.

"Maybe we should all take a step back and catch our breath." Oona sniffled and wiped at her eyes. "We've all been through a lot."

"That's true," Valeska agreed wearily. "And we've still got a lot more left to go, I imagine." She lifted her eyes and let her gaze bounce slowly between Quinn and me. "What are we going to do from here?"

I ran my hand through my long tangles of hair and exhaled. "I'll have to contact Samael and let him know about Atlas, so he can make arrangements for getting him back home."

"Well, that's a start," Valeska said.

"Could they have been after the spear?" Asher asked quietly, speaking for the first time in quite a while. He'd been standing with his back to me, staring out the window, but now he turned around, facing me.

"I don't think so. I mean, they're immortal, but they're animals," I reasoned. "I don't think they really follow orders, and they never went anywhere near my bag."

"But this isn't normal behavior," Quinn insisted, as if anyone had been pretending that any of this was normal. "Not for Mngwas or any jungle cat to attack in the middle of a lightning storm on top of a temple."

"The animals have been acting really strangely lately." Oona leaned forward, resting her arms on her legs. "Remember the shunka warakins that went after us outside of the Gates of Kurnugia? And that olitau that flew over the walls?"

Everything about tonight had been bizarre. The storm, Odin's absence, the fact that I sensed the Mngwas before they arrived even though I wasn't assigned to kill them.

"What if they're targeting us? Because we're Valkyries?" Quinn asked, her voice still tilting toward shrill.

She wasn't pacing, but she kept shifting her weight from one foot to the other. She couldn't stand still. Her lips were pursed, her eyes wide, and I realized that for the first time I was seeing what she looked like when she was afraid.

"But the only reason we're still alive is *because* we're Valkyries," I argued. "Atlas is a huge strong dude, and they knocked him down like he was nothing. We could only fight them so well because our blood weakens them."

"*Was,*" Oona corrected me quietly. "Atlas *was* a strong dude."

"It's not logical or rational. You said it yourself—they're *animals,*" Quinn countered, practically talking over Oona. "But a shark doesn't make a conscious decision to chase a wounded animal. It's something instinctual."

"We're not wounded animals," I said. "I mean, we weren't. Not before they attacked us."

"But they can sense weakness," Valeska said as she considered Quinn's theory. "That's probably why they went after Atlas first, and they must think you're getting weaker, too, or they wouldn't have braved attacking him while you were around."

"Oh, hell," Asher muttered and turned to look back out the window.

"That would make sense. The Jorogumo affected you so much worse than it should've," Quinn said, referring to my first run-in with Amaryllis Mori when I sent her to the underworld.

Oona leaned back on the couch, taking it all in. "Whatever is happening in Kurnugia is affecting your Valkyrie powers."

"We can't stay here," Asher said emphatically. "We're too close to the entrance to Kurnugia. The underworld has a stronger hold here."

"I'll call Samael, and we can get things figured out." I rubbed the back of my neck. "But you're right. We should head out in the morning."

There really wasn't anything more for us to do in Caana City. I couldn't keep going to the temple hoping that Odin would show up, especially not after what had happened tonight.

Besides that, he was a Vanir god. He could find me.

"I need some air and something to drink," Quinn announced and started walking toward the door.

"You're covered in blood!" Oona pointed out, sounding alarmed.

But Quinn was totally nonplussed and didn't slow her steps. "That should scare off any riffraff on my way to the liquor store."

"You shouldn't go out alone," Valeska said as she stood up. "I'll go with you."

They were out the door within seconds, leaving Asher, Oona, and me in a tense silence as we all thought about where we'd been and where we were going. After a few minutes of that, I excused myself to go get cleaned up.

It wasn't until I went into the bathroom and I saw my reflection—the blood drying on my ashen cheeks, the leaves from the forest that the frantic ATV ride left tangled in my hair—that I really felt it hit me. I rushed over to the toilet and threw up what little I had eaten that day. Afterward, while washing off my face and hands, I heard a soft knock at the bathroom door.

"Are you okay?" Asher asked, opening the door a crack when I didn't answer.

I turned around and faced him, leaning against the cold metal sink. "Sure. Why not?"

He came into the room and pulled me roughly into his arms. I pressed my face against his chest and leaned fully on him, letting him be my strength when I had none.

FORTY-TWO

———◆———

Quinn was hungover when we boarded the NorAm Overland Express in the afternoon, but Valeska seemed no worse for wear, which was impressive given the fact that I heard them drinking and talking all night long. Somehow, Asher and Oona had managed to sleep through it in the bedroom with me, but I hadn't been so lucky.

We sat on the second story of the double-decker carriage, the same way we had on the way here. But this time we did it for different reasons. The upper story had a big storage area in the back, which was reserved for large pieces of luggage or other oversized personal belongings.

In our case, that included the body of our friend and guard, Atlas Malosi.

Samael had arranged for him to come back with us, which did seem like the most fitting way for him to come home. The conversation I'd had with Samael had been brief, with him sounding rather shell-shocked as he repeatedly asked me if I was all right.

I lied and told him I was. I insisted that everything else was fine, and Samael told me to hop on the first Overland back to the city. I pretended that I could handle this, that I wasn't drowning in my own inability to protect Atlas and Asher and everyone I cared about.

I tried not to think about it as I slouched down in my seat. I put on a pair of oversized sunglasses I'd bought at the terminal. The warm sun that shone through the skylights—the sun that seemed so refreshing and beautiful a day ago—was now just an irritating reminder.

Fortunately, my lack of sleep the last few days finally caught up with me, and I was able to sleep through the majority of the long ride on the express. We had a stop in Texas, but I spent the whole time in the terminal, flipping through a paperback that someone had left on a bench.

Some twenty-eight hours after we first boarded the NorAm in Belize, we finally arrived back in Chicago. The sun was beginning to set as the express pulled into the city, and soon the towering skyscrapers blocked out what little light was left.

We waited on the platform, which was glowing from the bright billboards and flat-screen televisions that played NorAm info on an endless loop. At the end of the concrete platform, a large black hearse was parked in the emergency zone, which was marked by neon orange lights zigzagging through the pavement.

Four members of the Evig Riksdag—all in matching dark gray jumpsuits with copper patches on their shoulders in the shape of the three horns of Odin—unloaded the white rectangular box that the hospital had sent Atlas home in. They wheeled it past us, without looking at us or saying a word, and then loaded it into the hearse.

"Where are they taking him?" Oona asked.

"I don't know," I said. "Probably wherever his family requested he go."

We all stood together on the platform, our bags on shoulders or at our feet, and we watched as the hearse drove off.

"I should be getting home," Asher said. He moved so he was standing in front of me. "You could come with me."

"No, I can't. I have stuff I need to do."

"I understand." He chewed his lip for a moment, debating something, before saying, "We'll talk soon, okay?"

"Of course." I smiled weakly at him. He kept looking at me, like he wanted to say something more, but he never did. He just nodded, picked up his bags, and walked down to the cab line.

"I should get down to the Riks to see Samael," I said.

"I'm going with you, you know," Quinn said matter-of-factly.

"You don't have to," I said.

She scoffed. "Yeah, I do."

"Can I hitch a ride with you guys?" Valeska asked. "I need to see Samael, too."

"Gosh, now I feel left out because I'm the only one going home," Oona said with a weak laugh.

"I'll be home soon," I said, then quickly amended it with, "I hope."

"Do you want me to give you a ride?" Quinn offered Oona. She'd made the same offer to Asher earlier, but he insisted on taking a cab, since his place was the opposite direction of where we needed to be downtown.

"Nah, I can catch a cab." She slung her backpack over shoulder, then turned to face me. To my surprise, she threw her arms around me, hugging me quickly but tightly.

"I love you, Mal," she said, before she released me.

"What . . . why did you say that?" I asked, stumbling over my words in my surprise.

She shrugged. "You looked like you needed to hear it, and I do, so why not say it?"

FORTY-THREE

———— ◆ ————

Being back in the city felt so strange. It had only been just over a week since I'd left, and the city hadn't changed at all. But that week had been so intense and surreal, some part of me had believed that things couldn't be "normal" here. Because *I* was different, the world would be, too.

But the city was exactly as I had left it. A thin layer of smog blanketed everything, and all the lights—from cars, streetlamps, shop windows, and glowing adverts—seemed to be in a competition about which could blind me the most.

Traffic was a nightmare, both on the streets and the sidewalks, with pedestrians squeezing through bumper-to-bumper hovercars without paying us any mind. Last I heard, the population for the metro area had ballooned to over thirty-one million (and climbing), and based on how slowly we were crawling through the city, it seemed like half of them were downtown.

The overcrowding only added to the claustrophobic feel of the buildings soaring hundreds of feet in the air around us, many of them covered with billboards and posters. They lined every narrow street, with a thick layer of pedestrians and pop-up shops and food carts sandwiched between the buildings and the streets.

It was a nice night, at least for Illinois in late October, with an invigorating crispness to the air, so I rolled down the window of Quinn's car. Of course, that meant I was also letting in all the noise that was the song of the city—endless honking, snippets of music, people talking, laughing, cursing, and vendors selling their wares.

(In the eternal question, "Would I like an overpriced statue of the Willis Tower or a tonic made of vampire blood?" the answer was always "No.")

With the open window also came the smell. The scent of a million different beings and a thousand different cuisines mixed with exhaust and garbage created a ghastly but familiar aroma that was oddly comforting.

This—despite all its faults—was home, and I was glad to have made it back.

Eventually, after being caught in traffic long enough that Quinn had started threatening every driver within a twenty-foot radius of her car, we finally made it to the very heart of downtown, where the Evig Riksdag sat.

It was much smaller than all the buildings around it, and much more oddly shaped. While the architecture in downtown generally favored practicality, so that most buildings were slight variations of skyscraping rectangles, the Riks had taken a much different approach and built a concrete mushroom.

The design actually allowed it to be more secure, with the lower twenty floors narrow and nearly windowless. The top ten floors—where all the important celestial work took place—were much wider than the base and held up by metal supports.

Once we parked in the underground garage—passing through three separate security checkpoints on the way—Quinn, Valeska, and I took the elevator up to the twenty-ninth floor. When we got off, a long hallway of black marble floors and copper walls stretched out before us. At the very end was my Eralim Samael's office, but standing between us was a massive bronze door and a solitary guard.

The last time I had been here, there were two. There'd always been two, actually. But now Atlas was gone, leaving only Godfrey Wright to guard Samael.

Godfrey was a hulking cyclops, standing well over seven feet, with a giant bulbous eye that seemed to stare at everything and nothing all at once. His scalp was always shaved smooth, and he had a wide flat nose in the center of his rather square head. He was a man of few words, and I had no way of knowing how he really felt about anything, including myself, Atlas, and the whole world.

"We're here to see Samael," Quinn said when we reached Godfrey, and I was glad that she was the one doing the talking.

He didn't say anything, but he looked down at us with his single eye—unblinking, unmoving. I don't know that I'd ever felt as small as I did when he was appraising me then, so I avoided his gaze and looked at the dual black armbands wrapped around his thick bicep.

They were bands of remembrance for fallen comrades. One was for Marlow, my mother, and the other was for Atlas.

Godfrey reached for the door to open it for us, but he stopped, letting his hand linger on the bronze handle. "Samael has been very worried about you," he said in his rumbling baritone, and that was all. I thought he might say more, but he just opened the door and we went into Samael's office.

I'd never seen any of the other Eralim's offices, so I didn't know how Samael's stacked up against theirs, but it always seemed to me that it had to be one of the nicer ones. Everything was meticulously arranged, like it was set to be photographed for an art deco magazine.

He had little in the way of furniture—a large desk in front of the glass wall, a few chairs and a sofa, and his display shelves that housed art he'd collected over the centuries, as well as a secret cache of ancient weapons.

Samael had been standing at the window looking out at the city below, but when we came in he turned to face us and threw his arms up in his excitement.

Despite the fact that he'd been born over three centuries ago, he still had the appearance and exuberance of someone in his twenties, although his usual glee had been tempered since Marlow's death. He'd even seemed to age some—not a lot, but there were lines in his smooth umber skin that didn't used to be there.

Still, he was handsome, the way all Eralim tended to be. His aquamarine eyes were bright under a strong brow, and natural highlights coursed through his dark curls. Today he wore his thick hair up in a bun, and the sleeves of his white dress shirt were pushed up to the elbows.

"You're here! You're finally here!"

Theoretically, Samael was speaking to all of us, but his eyes were on me, and I was the first—and only—one that he pulled into a hug. He always smelled of autumn leaves, even though I hardly ever saw him leave this building.

He released me, but kept his hands on my shoulders for a moment, inspecting me to make sure that I was all right. Ever since my mom had died, whenever we met he looked at me with this earnest intensity, like I was a damaged puppy that had been abandoned at the shelter and he was the in-over-his-head prospective adopting parent hoping that a few kind words and meaningful hugs could erase all the pain that had come before.

Finally he moved on to Quinn, putting a hand on her shoulder as he said, "Quinn, are you holding up okay? Malin told me you were injured."

"Nothing I can't handle," she said with a shrug, and the scar from an ennedi between her collarbones was proof enough of that.

Valeska had taken a step back from us and folded her arms firmly across her chest, presumably to ward off any hugs or touching Samael might attempt. Usually I didn't find him to be much of a touchy-feely kinda guy, but extreme situations had a way of bringing all kinds of reactions out of people.

"Valeska, it's always good to see you," he said, as she eyed him warily from under her thick lashes. "Thank you for coming in to to help with this. I know you put yourself at great risk, and I don't know how much could've been accomplished without you."

"We didn't accomplish much with me," Valeska replied dryly, then looked over at me and Quinn. "No offense."

"None taken," I said. "I wouldn't exactly call our mission a rousing success."

"I know you filled me in briefly on the phone, but would you want to sit down and talk about it? All of us together?" Samael asked. "What exactly happened?"

We sat down in his sitting area—me in his three-legged chair that had clearly been designed for style and not comfort, and Quinn on the black velvet couch next to Samael. He leaned forward, resting his arm on his knees like he was hanging on every word—and I began telling him everything, from the moment we first arrived in the Gates of Kurnugia.

How we found Tamerlane Fayette and I killed him, but he was only bait for a trap that Ereshkigal had set. How Gugalanna kidnapped Asher, and how Odin found me outside of the hospital in Caana City and sent me to retrieve the Valhallan cloak.

As I spoke, summarizing all the fantastic and horrifying details of entering Kurnugia, running into Lyra, and eventually making our way to Zianna, Valeska never sat down. She stood off to the side, occasionally interjecting when she thought I'd forgotten or misspoke about something.

When I got to the part about Zianna, Samael noticeably blanched. The only time I'd ever seen him look even remotely stricken like that was when he saw my mom right after she'd been murdered.

"They got into Zianna?" he asked in a quiet gasp.

I nodded. "Yeah. We escaped when it was beginning. Gugalanna and Ereshkigal looked intent on taking it over."

"Holy shit." He tented his fingers and stared off into space. "It's really happening."

"Brace yourself, Samael," Valeska said. "Malin hasn't even gotten to the worst part."

FORTY-FOUR

———— ◆ ————

Valeska walked over to Samael's desk, where he kept a crystal bowl stocked with whatever unusual delicacy he was in the mood to snack on. Usually it was something unsettling, but she braved it, scooping up a handful without hesitation.

"And what's the worst part?" Samael asked, looking back over his shoulder at her, and honestly, I was curious about what Valeska might consider the worst.

"Odin's missing." She held up what looked like a jelly bean but with a dark center, inspecting it briefly before popping it in her mouth. She chewed it for a moment, before shrugging and carrying the bowl back with her.

"I mean, losing your friend was the worst part for all of you, and it really does suck about Atlas," Valeska amended her statement as she sat down in the chair next to mine. "He seemed like a nice guy. But I would say that Odin's disappearance is a bigger problem for mankind as a whole."

"We don't know that he's missing," I argued. "He just didn't show up."

"It was a really strange night," Quinn agreed. "We don't know what kept him."

"First off, he's a Vanir god. He can be anywhere at any time," Valeska contended as she munched on the strange jelly beans. "Being omnipresent is one of their coolest abilities. And second, you had his spear. His mega-important enchanted spear that has been hidden for like a million years or whatever. And now he's about to get it back, and he misses his chance to get it?"

She shook her head. "Doesn't add up."

"Are you suggesting that he was kidnapped or held hostage or something?" I asked, then looked over at Samael. "Is that even possible?"

He shook his head. "I don't really know much about what the world of Vanaheimr is like."

"Where do you go when you die?" Valeska asked abruptly.

"Me?" Samael asked, looking taken aback. "When my time is up, I will go to Vanaheimr."

"Is your mom there now?" Valeska asked.

"No." He shook his head. "My mom was a Valkyrie, so she died about two hundred and fifty years ago."

"Your mom was a Valkyrie?" Valeska sat up straighter and her eyes widened. "Wait. How does that work?"

"Every Eralim has two parents, with the mother being a Valkyrie and the father being a Seraph," Samael explained. "The idea is that we are to exist as a bridge between the earthly world and the mystical one. Eralim are immortal, but we are unable to have children."

"Oh, like a mule or a liger," Valeska said.

He smirked. "Something like that."

"But if your dad's a Seraph, isn't he gone by now? Can't you ask him what's up?" Valeska asked. "Seraphim go to Vanaheimr, right?"

"Yes, he has passed onto Vanaheimr, but the Seraphim there can't have any contact with anyone on earth," Samael said. "Very few immortals are allowed into the Vanaheimr—only those that work for the Evig Riksdag, actually—but they have very strict rules in place. If he were to speak to me now, my ears would bleed, my eyes would explode, and I would die a painful death."

"Have you ever met Odin?" I asked Samael, getting the conversation back on track.

"A few times, but not many," Samael replied. "There aren't many occasions for Eralim to interact with him, and they like to keep it that way."

"What about any of the other Vanir gods?" I asked, remembering when Sedna had asked me if Odin was working alone.

He thought for a moment, then said, "Zeus, once, a very long time ago. But that's it. They tend not to grace the earth with their presence."

"Can you ask your boss about Odin?" I suggested. "Maybe see if they've heard anything about what he might be up to?"

"I could . . ." Samael allowed. "But then that would mean I'd have to explain how my Valkyrie-in-training not only had unauthorized contact with a Vanir god, but broke into their underworld prison. And she did it all with my permission."

"But Zianna has fallen." I leaned forward. "Does anybody upstairs have any idea what's going on? What's coming for the world?"

"They're supposed to." He rubbed his chin. "And they might. But I'm not part of the big discussions. I get handed assignments, and then I hand them down to the Valkyries. The bulk of my job is training Valkyries and handling any problems that arise with them. All the decisions and plotting and info, that's all above me."

"So what you're saying is that we're on our own?" Valeska asked.

Samael licked his lips. "For the time being, yes. I would say that we are."

We lapsed into silence for a moment, all of us thinking about what this meant for us and what we were going to do.

Samael broke the silence first, saying, "But that's okay." He nodded, as if to convince himself. "For now, you all should go about living your lives as normally as possible while I try to figure out what our next move should be."

"What about Odin?" I asked. "And the spear?"

"I'll find out as much as I can without raising suspicions." He looked over at me. "And what you do with the spear right now is up to you."

I rubbed my temple and weighed the options. I could keep it, which could draw unwanted attention, and if someone had done something to Odin to get it, they could easily do something to me. I didn't stand a chance against something capable of incapacitating a Vanir god.

Or—

"Could you keep it here?" I asked Samael. "I can't imagine a safer place for it than locked up with your weapons, inside the Evig Riksdag, surrounded by Vörðr and guards."

"Of course," he said. "I'll always help in any way I can."

I took the spear out of my bag and handed it to Samael, who took a moment to admire it. It was beautiful, as far as weapons went. The camahueto horn used for the shaft had an otherworldly sheen twisting through it, and the red glass looked like a glimmering ruby.

"So this is the legendary Gungnir," he mused.

Samael got up and strode over to the shelves that lined his wall. Antiquities and priceless objets d'art were carefully displayed. On a lower shelf he moved aside a totem to reveal a touch screen. After tapping in a few numbers and having his hand scanned, the screen beeped, and a concealed drawer popped open. He cushioned the spear in the black velvet lining, then closed the drawer and locked it.

We all talked for a bit longer, mostly rehashing our plans and him reiterating that we needed to lie low for now. Meanwhile, Valeska had nearly polished off the bowl of jelly-bean-like confections.

Just before we were about to leave, Samael stopped us. "Oh, there is one more thing. It's a bit uncomfortable, given the situation, but I have to ask you a question, Valeska."

"Me?" She glanced back at me and Quinn. "What?"

"With the turmoil in the underworld, and the tragedy that befell Atlas, I've found myself short a guard in a time when I need it most." He was almost sheepish as he spoke, with one hand in his pocket. "You've proven yourself to be intelligent, tough, and resourceful. I would be happy to have you working for me, if you're interested."

Valeska only considered this for a second before shrugging and saying, "Sure, why not? The world's gonna end, I might as well get a front seat to the show."

FORTY-FIVE

———◆———

After the long conversation with Samael, Quinn suggested heading out to Carpe Noctem for drinks and liliplum. But I was eager to pick up my wolpertinger and get back to my own apartment, so I declined.

Not that Quinn or Valeska seemed to notice or mind. I got off the elevator on the lobby level so I could hail a cab, but they were heading below to the garage. They had been talking nonstop the whole ride down, and when I got off the elevator I turned back to wave to them, and they didn't even see me.

They stood so close to each other they were nearly touching, and Valeska leaned over, making a joke about the jelly beans, and Quinn threw her head back, laughing. That's what I saw as the door slid shut.

Good for them, was what I told myself as I tried to ignore the pinch of jealousy. Quinn and I weren't a good fit for each other, and I'd told her as much. She had every right to flirt and find happiness with someone else.

And all that was true, but it still hurt in a strange way. Her happiness made me happy, but part of me was still a little sad that that happiness couldn't be with me. Even if it was my fault and my choice.

Fortunately, I was too exhausted to worry too much. I sank low in the back of the cab and looked out the window at all the mortals and immortals going about their daily life. I wondered if any of them knew what was brewing below the surface. I wondered which side they would be on.

Galel's Garage was closed when I got there, so I went around back, up the stairs to Jude Locklear's apartment. I knocked on the door, hoping he was home, since I hadn't contacted him to let him know I would be there.

But, much to my relief, he was home. He answered the door shirtless, but that was just like him. Not that I was complaining anyway.

His broad chest and abs looked like they had been chiseled from marble, all rippling muscles and smooth dark olive skin. His wavy black hair parted around his two thick ram's horns before landing at his shoulders, and his dark eyebrows arched sharply, giving him a permanent look of suggestive playfulness.

I suspected that he'd gotten his ridiculous good looks from his incubus father, but fortunately Jude's demonic heritage had never put a damper on our friendship. Because he was a Cambion, he was mortal, and that helped, but Jude was always the kinda guy who let stuff slide off his back. Which was why our arrangement as friends-with-benefits had worked out so well with me for so long.

He grinned broadly. "Hey, you made it back alive!"

"I did. And I come bearing gifts." I held up the lime-green T-shirt I'd gotten him, one that would most likely barely fit over his broad shoulders and thick biceps.

"You better Belize it"? He laughed as he read it. "What is this?"

"I picked it up at the Overland terminal."

"Well, thank you." He stepped back, inviting me in. "Wanna have a drink?"

I smiled ruefully. A small part of me would've loved to hang out with Jude and have a drink, just like old times, before all the insanity. But a larger part knew it wouldn't be right, not with Asher in the picture, and, more importantly, while Jude was fun, the times I'd had with him didn't compare to my times with Asher.

"Thanks, but I can't stay long," I said. "I wanted to get Bowie out of your hair and head back home."

At the sound of his name, my chubby little wolpertinger came racing around the corner. He was a peach-colored bunny with two tiny antlers between his big ears and a pair of feathered wings that he was too fat to use.

"Hey, Bunny Bo!" I said, using my nickname for him, and I crouched down so he could dive into my arms. He cooed as he nuzzled up against me, giving me tiny little kisses as his antlers scraped my chin. "How are you doing?"

"He was really good," Jude said. "I actually liked the little fella. I might have to get one myself."

"Yeah, they do make great pets."

Jude leaned against the doorframe beside me. "How are you doing, Malin? Did everything work out okay for you?"

I laughed, focusing on the soft feel of Bowie's fur as he cuddled up to me so I wouldn't cry. "I made it out alive."

"That bad?" he asked, and I looked up to see him grimacing. "You know, if you need a hand, I'm always happy to help."

"I know. I don't want you to get messed up in . . ." I floundered, searching for an innocent way to describe the situation before lamely finishing with, "Whatever it is that I'm messed up in."

"Well, if you ever reconsider or it gets to be too much, you know how to reach me."

Jude began gathering up Bowie's things, putting his food and dishes in a bag. He brought over the carrier, and I put my wolpertinger inside. He was so excited for cuddles, I had to push the door shut and lock it in a hurry.

"Oh, I got the little guy something!" Jude snapped his fingers, then walked across to his small living room to pick up a black canvas contraption sitting on an end table.

"What?" I straightened up. "You didn't have to get him anything."

"No, it was no problem." He smiled. "I could hear him hopping around if I went down to the garage to work, and he sounded so anxious when I left. I thought I could take him down to work with me, but I didn't want him to get run over or anything. So I went out and I picked him up this Babybjörn."

"Wait, wait, wait." I held up my hands, stopping him as I barely contained my giggling. "You got a baby carrier for my wolpertinger? And you wore him around? Like on your back?"

"Yeah." Jude laughed. "I did! And he liked it. It worked out well."

"Oh, I wish I could've seen that." I put a hand over my mouth in an attempt to keep the laughter back. "How much do I owe you?"

"Don't worry about it." He shook his head. "We can settle up the next time you bring your luft in, and let's face it, we both know you're going to bring your luft in again."

"Thank you again." I smiled at him. "With everything going on, it was a really big help that I didn't have to worry about Bowie, because I knew he was in good hands with you."

"Well, you do know how good my hands are," Jude teased.

I gathered up Bowie and his things, thanking Jude again as he walked me to the door. When I left, he leaned against the doorframe and watched me go down the stairs.

"If you need anything, call me," Jude called after me. "And don't be a stranger."

It wasn't until after I'd left and began the long walk back to my apartment building that I realized I shouldn't have let my cab go when I arrived. Jude's place was right at the end of New Edgewater, where the roads changed from pavement to canals, and it was only a few blocks down to my place out on the lake. But they were big city blocks, and Bowie and his food weighed a lot.

I had to make my way along the crowded sidewalks, dodging between everyone with my arms full, while also struggling to avoid both getting splashed with the murky water as hovercars sped by and falling in myself. Both of those scenarios would be disastrous because the water smelled of gasoline and dead fish and the scent would linger for hours, even after a shower.

Finally I reached the Tannhauser Towers in all their faded glory and rode the elevator up to the sixty-seventh floor. As I walked down the long hallway to our apartment, I heard our neighbors—TVs blaring too loud, couples fighting, a baby crying, and some strange dubstep polka that I hoped didn't catch on.

Our little apartment had been billed as a "luxurious two bedroom, one bath" despite the fact that it was essentially a living room/kitchen combo with two closet-sized bedrooms and an even smaller bathroom, and I would definitely not describe the concrete floor or metal walls as luxurious.

The only nice thing was the window that took up the entire exterior wall. It gave us a view of the canal below, but the other buildings and their noxious billboards blocked us from seeing much beyond that.

When I came in, Oona was on the couch with her feet propped up on the coffee table. The little TV affixed to the wall outside our bathroom was on, playing a trashy old slasher flick. On the table in front of her was one of the bottles of soursop wine she'd bought before we left Belize and two large plastic tumblers, and a super-sized bag of delicious fried kibbeh was on her lap. We usually bought them from a vendor down the street from us, because they were the best in the city.

"Hey," Oona said through a mouthful of food, and the second I let Bowie out of his cage he hopped up on the couch to see her. "Bowie!"

I finished unloading all of my and Bowie's stuff while he and Oona greeted each other with lots of cooing and kisses.

"Mal, come join us," Oona suggested. "Putting your stuff away can wait until tomorrow."

She wasn't wrong, and I was exhausted, so I sat down beside her. She nudged the empty tumbler toward me with her foot, and I poured myself a drink before settling back onto the couch.

"What are we watching?" I asked as I pilfered a couple kibbeh croquettes from her bag.

"I don't know, but that girl there is about to get stabbed a bunch," she said.

And that's how we spent the next couple hours. Drinking wine and eating lukewarm kibbeh with Bowie sprawled out between us, snoring softly. I was more than content to spend the rest of the night that way, but a knock came at the door after midnight and interrupted our plans.

FORTY-SIX

———◆———

"Maybe you shouldn't answer that," Oona warned me as she sat up and put her glass on the table. "It could be a murderer."

I was already halfway to the door, so I scoffed. "You've been watching too many scary movies."

"Or maybe you haven't been watching enough," she countered.

I rolled my eyes and opened the door to find Asher. He had a shadow of stubble growing on his face, and there were dark circles under his eyes. But otherwise, he looked better. Much better, actually, than when I had seen him last. His color had returned, and he stood a bit taller, as if a weight had been lifted on his return to the city.

"Hey," I said. "What's going on?"

"My grandma is smothering me, and I couldn't sleep." His eyes landed hopefully on mine. "I thought I'd see if you were still up."

"Yeah, I'm up, come on in." I stepped back, allowing him in, then locked the door securely behind him.

"Hi, Ash," Oona said as she stood up and clicked off the TV. "Don't mind me. I'm heading to bed."

"Oona, you don't have to do that," I said, but she waved me off.

"No, no, I've already drunk too much wine anyway," she insisted as she walked into her room. "I'll see you guys in the morning." She winked at me before closing her bedroom door.

Through the thin cold metal walls I could hear the neighbors arguing about who had done all their drugs (spoiler alert: it was both of them), so I turned on the stereo to drown them out. Since Oona was in bed, I didn't turn it up too loud, just enough to let the mellow instrumental music blanket the room.

I picked up the wine bottle, swirling the pale yellow liquid around before asking Asher, "Do you want anything to drink? We still have a little bit of wine left."

"That'd be nice. Thanks."

"So, your grandma is being a bit much?" I asked as I grabbed a beer mug from the kitchen.

He lingered in the living room, walking slowly around the small space and admiring our décor. We didn't have a great deal, both because we were broke and because we didn't have the space for it.

Our shoes were piled up by the door, under an overflowing coatrack. The end tables were homemade from cinder blocks and metal Jude had given us. On top of them were books piled up, a few candles, and a nice incense burner that had been a gift form Oona's cousin Minerva.

Beyond that, there wasn't much to the place. We had a couple posters—one of lagomorphs with pictures and boxes explaining the differences between jackalopes, wolpertingers, rabbits, pikas, and colugos and a fantasy-inspired one for Oona's favorite band, a dream-pop duo called Eden's Eternity—and a brightly colored tapestry that Oona had hung above our old couch. A couple throw pillows that Oona's mother had made and a threadbare rug on the floor completed the picture.

"That's an understatement," Asher said with a sigh. "I didn't even tell her everything that happened. I toned it down as much as I could, but she was still this awful combination of livid, panic-stricken, and affectionate. She kept yelling at me *while* she was hugging me."

"I'm sorry." I poured wine into the glass and handed it to him. "That sounds uncomfortable, but she's freaked out because she loves you."

An unfortunate apology flashed in his eyes—the one that said he'd just remembered how cold and terrible my mother was, so he shouldn't complain about being loved too much.

"I know," he said, softening his complaints. "And I love her, too. I just needed some space."

"Yeah, I get that, too."

We stood in the middle of the living room, both of us slowly sipping our wine. The lights from the billboards across the way shone through the large window, so shades of red and blue played across the room, giving us a soft, ever-changing mood lighting.

I wondered if I should suggest we sit down, but the truth was I didn't feel like sitting. There was enough alcohol in me to numb the ache in my arms and legs, and while I had been content relaxing with Oona, I'd begun to feel restless when Asher came in through the door.

"I'm not intruding, am I?" he asked, then took a half step back, toward the door. "I can go. I wanted to get out and move and clear my head."

"No, you're not intruding." I put a hand on his arm to stop him. "I'm glad you came over."

He moved closer to me. "Yeah?"

"Believe it or not, I like having you around." I smirked.

"Yeah, I figured that when you braved the underworld to rescue me."

"I didn't go there *for* you," I corrected him, but I felt heat flushing my cheeks.

The sunstone had inadvertently shown everyone exactly how I felt about Asher, and I hated having my feelings out in the open like that. It left me exposed and vulnerable. Even now, standing with him, I wanted to downplay it, pretend I didn't care as much as I did, but I held my tongue and forced myself not to run away.

"Right." He set his glass down on the table and moved even closer to me. "The sólarsteinn brought you to me."

The light that splashed across his face shifted again, changing to pale blue. It did this wonderful thing to his eyes, making them almost glow in the dark room as he looked down at me.

"To be fair, my heart brought me," I admitted.

His voice was low, almost a whisper, when he said, "Finding me was your heart's greatest desire."

"I wanted you safe and I wanted you back," I said as the truth came tumbling out.

I hadn't meant for it to, but something about Asher made it so I didn't want to lie. I didn't want to hide from him, the way I did most everyone else. I stood before him, defenseless and honest and totally unafraid, because the way he looked at me—with such unabashed yearning and warmth—I knew I had nothing to be afraid of. Not from him.

"Do you know what my greatest desire is right now?" he asked.

"What?"

He didn't answer, not right away, and instead he moved even closer, so his lips were mere inches from mine. His eyes were wide open, looking in my eyes—looking *through* me, it felt like.

And then his mouth was on mine, hungry but gentle in a way that only he could be. His hand was on the small of my back, strong and firm as he held me to him, and I wrapped my arms around his neck.

This time, he was restrained, and I was ravenous. I wanted him, almost desperately. It was an ache deep within me—a pounding demand from my heart, and an insistent heat in the base of my stomach.

I was pulling him with me, backward to the bedroom, both of us refusing to stop kissing as we stumbled across the room. I nearly fell over my bag, but he caught me and lifted me up, carrying me to my room.

"I don't think anyone's ever carried me before, not since I was a kid."

"I'm glad I could be your first," he said with a laugh.

Then he was setting me down on the bed, and our clothes were off—not fast enough, it was never fast enough. I wanted to feel him—*needed* it, really—his bare skin against mine, as close as two people could get. I needed to know that he was real, he was really here with me, and as he kissed me I wanted to beg him not to leave me. I wanted to tell him that he could never leave me again, not like he did before, not even if it wasn't his fault, because I couldn't handle losing him again.

Because I loved him.

I'd fallen in love with him, and I wasn't ever letting him go again.

But I didn't say any of that. I couldn't. I was too busy kissing him and touching him and letting his hands roam all over my body, and that was just as good. Maybe even better.

FORTY-SEVEN

— ◆ —

I had been dreaming about a dark forest during a rainstorm, and I awoke in my own bed, with my sheets smelling of Asher—woodsy and dark and crisp. In the early morning light that streamed in through the slats of my blinds—still more of the pale blue before the golden hour—I could clearly see him sleeping beside me, and a rush of adoration and relief swept over me.

I wanted to snuggle up with him, but I was afraid of disturbing him, so I lay on my side, watching for a moment.

Then, abruptly, he twitched. His whole body trembled, then a quick spasm went through him, like he'd gotten a chill or a bad scare. He lay motionless for a second, then he moved again, almost thrashing, and he let out a moan.

I sat up and started shaking him. "Asher."

He calmed a little, but he kept shivering, and his head twitched subtly.

"Asher!" I was nearly shouting by then, and he finally opened his eyes.

"Malin," he said, his voice still thick with sleep, and his eyes closed again. "You shouldn't have rescued me."

"What? Are you okay?"

"You should've left me there," he murmured.

"Asher!" I shook him again, because by now he had totally freaked me out. "I need you to wake up."

"What?" He rubbed his eyes with the palm of his hand and looked up at me. "Malin? Are you okay?" He must've seen the panic on my face, because he sat up, quickly growing more alert. "What's wrong?"

"You tell me." I motioned toward him. "You were shaking and—and moaning."

"I must've been having a bad dream."

"You don't remember it?"

He shook his head. "No. I know I've been having nightmares a lot since She'ol, but I don't usually remember them."

I hesitated before telling him the part that really scared me, but I decided that he should know. So I said, "You told me that I shouldn't have rescued you."

"I don't know why I said that." He reached over and rubbed my arm, comforting me, when he was the one having the nightmares. "I'm sorry. I didn't mean to freak you out."

"Don't apologize. You went through hell—literally." I put my hand over his. "That's not something you can just get over. I only want to make sure you're okay."

"Yeah, I'm okay," he assured me.

"Promise?"

"I promise."

He pulled me into his arms and back onto the bed. I lay with my head on his chest, listening to the steady thud of his heartbeat, and tracing my fingers along the edges of his gauze bandage that covered the marks on his chest. Before we'd finally fallen asleep last night, he'd assured me that the wounds weren't bothering him and were healing well.

But I couldn't tell if he was keeping anything from me. He wanted so badly to protect me from everything, I was afraid he would try to shield me from whatever he was going through.

"You can tell me anything," I said now, looking at him. "You know that, right?"

He reached over, brushing the hair out of my face. "Yeah, of course."

"Okay," I said reluctantly, and cuddled up closer to him.

We lay in bed a little while longer, but sleep never returned for either of us, so we decided to get up. Despite the early hour, Oona was already awake. She was sitting on the couch, watching TV and eating thin pancakes out of a Styrofoam container.

"Morning," she said. "We didn't have any food—well, we had food, but most of it had expired while we were gone. So I ordered takeout for breakfast. There's some in the kitchen if you want any."

On the kitchen counters were several containers with *Jaipur in the Morning* written on the side in big, bold pink letters. When I peered inside them, I quickly deduced that those weren't pancakes Oona was eating but pudla—a crepe-like food made from chickpeas. There were also several little containers of different types of chutney, including one that smelled heavily of cilantro, a syrupy one that I guessed was rhubarb, and a spicy bright orange marmalade.

The television had been on a commercial when we came out of the bedroom, but now it dinged excitedly as the show returned. I glanced at the TV to see a big graphic flying on the screen announcing BREAKING NEWS.

Behind the desk sat a pretty news reporter in her thirties, with perfectly highlighted hair and a pair of stylish glasses that walked the line between sophisticated intellectual and sexy librarian. I recognized her as Ellery Park, one of the top reporters for the twenty-four-hour news network NorNewsNow—the "#1 Station in North America," if their claims were to be believed.

"We've been following today's top stories," Ellery said, speaking in the clean, clipped tones of a seasoned journalist. "The extreme and unusual weather conditions that have been devastating countries worldwide, leaving millions homeless and thousands injured or dead."

"Malin, do you want anything?" Asher asked from behind me, as he made himself a plate, but I barely heard him. My eyes were glued to the television.

"Nah, you go ahead," I said vaguely and sat down on the arm of the couch next to Oona to watch the story unfold.

"First, there was the deadly category five hurricane that has decimated Newfoundland, Canada, an unprecedented storm for the likes of the northern province," Ellery said. "Then there are the raging brush fires that have been sweeping across Australia, which have completely destroyed entire cities and are moving toward heavily populated Sydney. Just this morning a massive earthquake hit Egypt, where the prime minister was reportedly trapped inside the rubble, along with fifty other members of parliament. There are also reports that a tsunami is heading for the coast of Brazil.

"Now, as if all that wasn't enough, we're getting word about sinkholes opening up all across the globe," Ellery went on. "Some of them stretching as far as five miles wide, while most appear to be smaller than that. Scientists are racing to make sense of what could be causing these extreme natural disasters and discover if there is any connection between them."

I slid off the arm of the couch and sank next to Oona. Bowie pushed at my hand with his head, so I absently petted him. My heart had dropped to my stomach, and I suddenly felt light-headed.

"What the hell is going?" I asked breathlessly.

"It's all so crazy. And if you look at the crawl at the bottom of the screen, the weather isn't even the only thing that's going insane."

Sure enough, running across the ticker next to the bright blue NNN logo was even more alarming text:

. . . HAVE BEEN REPORTING SPIKES OF VIOLENT CRIME EVERYWHERE. WITH ATTACKS STRIKING PARIS, HAVANA, MOSCOW, AND JOHANNESBURG. RIOTING AND LOOTING HAVE ALSO BROKEN OUT IN CITIES ACROSS AMERICA, INCLUDING MEMPHIS, ATLANTA, SEATTLE, AND MINNEAPOLIS. SO FAR, NO FATALITIES HAVE BEEN REPORTED IN THE DOMESTIC ATTACKS, BUT MANY INJURIES AND MILLIONS OF DOLLARS OF PROPERTY DAMAGE ARE EXPECTED. . . .

"The sheer magnitude and scale of these weather events combined with their rapid-fire frequency has created a worldwide disaster of epic proportions," Ellery Park was saying. "It is unlike anything we have ever seen before, but now is not the time for despair.

"Now we must pull together and help those in need," she continued emphatically. "If you are displaced, injured, or unable to contact any of your loved ones in the affected areas, please go to our website to find help. And if you are looking to help others, we also have links on how to donate or where to volunteer."

"Do you think this is it?" Oona asked softly. "Is this how the world ends?"

FORTY-EIGHT

———◆———

The three of us—Asher, Oona, and myself—watched the news for longer than we should have.

We watched them talk to reporters on location surrounded by unimaginable destruction and devastation. We watched dozens of scientists, meteorologists, and even a few Eralim discussing what it all meant—if anything at all. We watched official statements from world leaders and dignitaries, from important immortals to former presidents, all expressing their condolences and encouragement that we use this time to come together and help one another.

But mostly we watched them all tiptoe around the words *apocalypse* or *cataclysmic* or *end of days*. The one scientist who did mention anything close to this—a brief mention of dinosaurs and meteors—was quickly cut off, and another, more soft-spoken talking head went back to the narrative that we should help each other.

And I think that was the part I found most unsettling. Twenty-four-hour news networks and the quick-paced news cycle relied on fear, on hype, and on excitable hyperbole to keep people tuning in. But this, if anything, seemed downplayed to me.

Three years ago, the day after New Year's, we got five inches of snow in the evening, and every news station in town was calling it a "Snow-pocalypse." Now the world was literally on fire with holes opening up with no explanation, and it was only "extreme" and "unusual" but "we should all focus on helping our neighbors."

While that was a very nice sentiment, it did nothing to explain to me *why* they weren't calling this what it was. Were they hiding the truth? Were they being directed to keep it as quiet as possible? Or were they attempting to help us through it all, as peacefully as they could, like the band playing on as the *Titanic* sank?

"That's enough," Oona decided, our pudla gone cold and untouched in front of us. She flipped through the channels, finding a soothing old cartoon about a talking dragon.

"What do we do now?" I asked.

"Samael told you to wait for him to contact you, right?" Oona asked. "So, I think that's what you should do."

"But—"

"What, Mal? Are you gonna stop a hurricane?" Oona asked. "You already donated blood last month, and we don't have any money to send anybody."

I hated that she was right when I felt restless and had nothing I could do with it. I sank lower on the couch and folded my arms over my chest.

Asher leaned forward, rubbing his temple. "My head just started pounding. Would you guys happen to have an aspirin or something?"

"You came to the right girl!" Oona said, excited to be of help. She stood. "How bad is it on a scale of one to ten? That will help me decide what to give you."

He winced. "Maybe an eight?"

"Got it." She started walking toward her room, then paused and turned back to him. "Do you have any allergies?"

"Not that I know of," he said, and she continued back to her room.

Once she was gone, I slid closer to him and rubbed his back. "Are you okay?"

"Yeah. I mean, my head hurts, but I think it's because I haven't been sleeping well lately," he said, then yawned as if to accentuate his point. "Would you mind if I lie down for a bit? I could go back home—"

"No, you can take a nap here," I assured him. "You can stay here as long as you want."

"Thanks." He smiled weakly at me, and I leaned over and kissed his temple.

Oona came back a few minutes later with two capsules filled with lime-green liquid that she assured Asher would take away any pains he had. He thanked her, then excused himself to go to my room and lie down for a while.

With Asher otherwise indisposed and Oona insisting that I do something other than stress about the chaos breaking out all over, I had to find something to do with my anxious energy. That meant cleaning.

I did the dishes, scrubbed the grout in the bathroom, put away all my stuff (except for the stuff that went in my room, because I didn't want to disturb Asher), and reorganized our shoes. I had cleaned the apartment top to bottom, and it had only taken an hour.

"You can clean my room, if you want," Oona suggested once I'd finished. She was lying back on the couch, flipping through her grimoire (studying up—just in case, she said).

"Nah, I'm good." I sat down on the floor and wiped the sweat from my brow with the back of my hand. "I need a minute to cool down anyway."

My phone started to buzz from where I'd left it, and when I picked it up and saw the name on the screen, my heart skipped a beat. Samael had texted me.

Malin, I wanted to let you know that Atlas Malosi's family has decided to hold a small ceremony for him today. It will be outside the mausoleum in Rosehill Cemetery today at 3:00 p.m. Sorry about the short notice. They wanted to get it done as quickly as possible.

"Do you think you're up for going to a funeral in a little bit?" I asked Oona.

"What?" She sat up with a start. "Who died?"

"Atlas. They're having his ceremony today."

"Wow. That was fast." She paused, thinking. "He only died like two days ago."

"They're probably moving quickly because the whole world is losing its shit."

"Yeah, that is a good reason. I'd want to get my son buried before everything went to hell," Oona agreed.

FORTY-NINE

---

*L*ess than two weeks ago I had been at the Rosehill Cemetery for my mother's funeral, and I felt a painful sense of déjà vu as I climbed up the large hill in the center. The rosebushes that surrounded the mausoleum appeared even more dead than they had before. With only a few crippled leaves clinging to the brittle branches, their sharp thorns were exposed.

Above us, the sky was overcast, and the app on Oona's phone had warned that today the smog levels were unseasonably high. The air tasted of soot and diesel, and it blanketed the city in gloom. What little sun did get through only managed to make the clouds glow an angry burnt orange.

I was glad that we'd left Asher at our place to continue resting. Breathing in the caustic air definitely wouldn't help him feel any better.

By the time Oona and I arrived, a large crowd had already formed around the entrance of the crypt. The minimalist design of the mausoleum made it look like a large white marble cube looming behind the mourners. The only decoration was the coat of arms—a shield emblazoned with the three horns and nine swords fanned out behind it, the horns for Odin and the swords for the original nine Valkyries.

But other than the fact that Atlas's funeral was held at the Mausoleum av Veteraner Från Kriget Mot Odödlighet—the Mausoleum of the Veterans of the War on Immortality—there was little else that this had in common with Marlow's service.

Hers had been sparsely attended, in part because of Samael's attempts to keep her death under wraps, but mostly because there weren't that many people to mourn her. She'd made few friends in her life.

Atlas, on the other hand, had always had a smile for anyone he met, and based on the amount of crying going on, he had been loved by many. That was part of the reason his ceremony had to be held outside of the crypt. There wouldn't be enough room inside for all who wanted to attend.

The other reason was that since he wasn't a Valkyrie, he could not be buried inside the mausoleum. A few rows away were tall white headstones with as many as five names listed on them. That was where the Vörðr and other guards were buried, stacked on top of each other because there simply wasn't enough room.

Everyone had gathered in a semicircle, with a podium and the coffin sitting front and center. Next to the coffin a large picture of Atlas sat on an easel. In the photo he smiled brightly, the way he had every time I had gone to Samael's office. Scores of flowers had been placed on white pillars and on the ground, so Atlas was completely surrounded by large bouquets of white, red, and black.

Samael went up to the podium once it appeared everyone had arrived, and he cleared his throat before beginning. "I want to thank you all for coming today. We're all gathered here to remember and celebrate Atlas Malosi and his robust love of life and everyone in it. Any who knew him can tell you that the only thing bigger than Atlas himself was his heart."

There were murmurs of agreement as well as plenty of crying. I lingered toward the back of the crowd, feeling a sharp twinge of guilt that I hadn't gotten to know him better.

"I had the honor of working with Atlas for two years, and he was without a doubt the kindest and most enthusiastic guard I had ever employed," Samael went on. "Atlas lived his life with the utmost integrity and generosity, and after meeting his parents today, I can say that Atlas was a true reflection of them."

Samael motioned to a couple in the front of the crowd—a tall blond woman and broad, dark-skinned man, with his arm around her as they both sniffled.

"To both of you, Clymene and Aleki, I can only extend my deepest condolences," Samael said. "Atlas brought a light everywhere he went, and the world will be darker without him."

That's when I realized that I knew Atlas's mother. Well, *knew* was too strong a word, but I had met her before. She was Clymene Herja, a retired Valkyrie. When I had still been in high school, she had come to talk to our class about what being a Valkyrie entailed. She had only just retired then, saying that the work had finally caught up to her, and she wanted to help ensure that up-and-coming Valkyries were more prepared for the strain of the job than she had been.

Clymene had actually been the first Valkyrie I ever met, outside of my mother. Since Marlow had few friends and never bothered to acquaint herself with her coworkers, and Valkyries tended to keep their occupation as secretive as possible to protect themselves, there wasn't much of a way for me to meet any before Ravenswood Academy.

Samael spoke for a few minutes more, then there was a musical interlude during which old Norse folk songs were played on kraviklyras and flutes. Then he stepped aside to allow Atlas's older brother to eulogize him. I didn't even know he had a brother, and I suddenly felt like throwing up.

Eventually the service concluded with the pallbearers taking his coffin to a freshly dug grave nearby. I wanted to leave then, but Oona hissed at me, telling me that would be rude. So we watched as they slowly lowered him into the ground.

Finally I could make my escape. The sorrow here was too much. It felt like I had a cinder block on my chest pressing down on me, making it hard to breathe, and there was a claustrophobic panic edging into my grief.

Oona didn't know how nauseous and uneasy I felt, so she was treating this like any other funeral, and headed toward where Samael was talking with Atlas's parents to offer her condolences.

I grabbed her hand, stopping her, and whispered, "We should go."

When she turned back to me, I could see she was about to argue, but then she saw my expression and just nodded. "Okay. Let's go."

But it was too late. Clymene had looked over at us with her red-rimmed blue eyes, and, clutching tissues in her hand, she stepped away from her husband and Samael, coming toward me.

"Malin?" she said, taking long strides toward me. She was tall and muscular, even for a Valkyrie, which explained where Atlas got his physique from. "You're Malin Krigare, right?"

"Um . . . yeah," I said.

I'd briefly considered lying. Not just because I didn't want to have an intense conversation with a grieving mother, but also because I didn't know if she held me responsible for her son's death. I wouldn't fault her if she did. *I* blamed me.

Even though I knew I deserved every repercussion for my actions that she wanted to dole out, I did not want to get my ass kicked by a woman who appeared significantly stronger than me. I'd been assaulted enough the past few weeks, and I couldn't handle another slap across the face. Even if it was warranted.

But her husband and Samael were following a few steps behind her, so I couldn't lie. Oona was beside me, holding my hand, and she squeezed it, passing me some of her courage. And it worked a little. Not a lot, but enough that I didn't run and hide.

"I'm Clymene Herja," she said as she reached me. "I am—I was Atlas's mother." Atlas's father joined her, once again putting his arm around her in a gesture of comfort. "This is my partner, Aleki Malosi. Atlas's father."

"Hello," I said in a small voice that was thick with fear.

"This is Malin Krigare," Clymene said to her husband. "She's the one that was with Atlas when he died."

Oh, shit, I thought, and I could hear my blood pounding in my ears.

"Samael told me that you stayed by his side until he passed and held his hand the entire time." Clymene sniffled as she spoke, but her words were calm and even, without a hint of anger.

"I—I did." I stumbled over my words, because that wasn't entirely true. I did stay with him, and I did hold his hand as much as I could, but most of the time I was clinging to him to stop him from falling out of the ATV as we raced to the hospital.

She smiled then, even as tears spilled down her cheeks. "Samael already told us that he can't say much about the mission you were on, because of the nature of it, and I know how that goes. How stealth and secrecy can be so important. . . . So I won't ask you any questions about that.

"I only . . ." She took a deep breath. "Atlas loved his job. He loved protecting everyone and keeping them safe. Before he left, he called and let me know how proud he was to be going on the mission. He believed it was important and that what he was doing was essential."

"It was," I said.

"He saved my life," Oona added. "Without him, I don't know if either of us would be here."

Still smiling, Clymene began to cry harder, and then suddenly she hugged me. Tightly.

"Thank you for staying with my son," she said as she embraced me.

I managed to mumble, "You're welcome," and then she released me.

After that, I felt rather dazed, and I couldn't remember what I said, if anything. I think Oona and Samael did most of the talking, and finally we were walking away from the funeral, down the hill to where I'd parked my luft.

I managed to keep everything together until we reached the hoverbike, but then I bent over and threw up. I wiped my mouth with the back of my hand as Oona stared at me with worry in her eyes.

"Are you okay?" she asked.

"Everything Marlow ever told me was bullshit," I said. "That woman loved her son. She loved her boyfriend, who I'm guessing she's been with for nearly thirty years, given Atlas's age. She wasn't angry or filled with hate. She didn't even hate me, and I . . ." My voice cracked, so I stopped.

"What was wrong with my mother, Oona?"

"I don't know. I wish I did." Oona put her hand on my back, rubbing it gently. "Let's go home, Mal."

FIFTY

◆

Asher was still at our place, sleeping off his headache, when we got back from the funeral. I changed out of my formal attire and into a baggy T-shirt, then climbed in bed next to him. He wrapped his arms around me, making me feel safe and complete in a way that only he seemed to be able to, and I fell asleep that way.

Later in the evening, once we were all awake again, he decided to head back home. He needed to see his grandma and do all of the normal human things, like shower and shave. The funeral had taken a lot out of me, so I did as close to nothing as I possibly could for the rest of the day, and Oona kept the TV steered away from the news.

After all that rest, I woke up the next morning determined to get things done. One positive thing about talking to Atlas's mom was that it had reminded me of an important job I had yet to complete.

When I came out of my bedroom bright and early and already fully clothed in a pair of leggings and a loose T-shirt with the name of my favorite Thai restaurant, กินอาหารของเรา, written on it, under a fitted but fraying dark purple knit hooded sweater with my Velvet Vampire lipstick and thick eyeliner—Oona gaped at me over her bowl of oatmeal.

"What's going on? Did something happen?" she asked, once she'd gulped down her mouthful of food.

"No." I smirked a little at the panic induced by me simply getting ready in the morning. "I'm heading over to Ravenswood."

Her eyes widened, almost cartoonishly so, and she leaned forward to set her bowl down on the table. "You're going to class?"

"I hadn't planned on it," I admitted. "There doesn't really seem to be a point in going to school right now, at least not for me."

"Yeah, I get that. I considered going this morning, but since I'm not even sure the world will still be around come graduation day . . ." She trailed off with a solemn expression on her face. "What are you going to the academy for?"

"To see Sloane." I reached into the pocket of my sweater and pulled out the heart-shaped stone of pink tourmaline that Lyra had given me in the underworld. "I promised her mother that I would give her this itayakkal."

"Do you want me to go with you?" Oona asked, and she was already halfway to her feet when I held up my hand to stop her.

"Nah, I think I can handle Sloane on my own. Thanks, though."

I promised Oona that I wouldn't be long, then headed down and hopped on my luft. Despite the warnings of strange weather that the TV kept going on about, the city didn't seem all that different than normal. The air was chilled and the sky was overcast, with the city lights making the dark clouds glow above us. And the streets were as busy as ever, as I dodged around stalled-out cars and meandering pedestrians to get to the academy about twenty minutes away from my apartment.

Ravenswood Academy was located right in the center of the slums. All around it were tall apartment complexes crammed to the max with tenants, and then there was this short—in comparison—mansion that looked like it sprang to life from a Jane Austen novel.

The exterior maintained the original Tudor-style architecture, but inside it had been updated, doing its best to always be state-of-the-art. I parked my luft in the underground garage beneath the school. To get into the building, I had to pass through three separate security checks, ending with a retina scan that finally opened the door.

The corridor from the garage was mostly empty, and like the rest of the academy it was always strangely quiet. As I walked down the hallway I kept my eyes on the floor, as if I were studying the mosaic of black-and-white marble tiles.

But the truth is that I was avoiding looking at the artwork, most of which hung on the stark white walls. Many of the various paintings and sculptures had been done by alumni or current students, showing off what they'd learned or showcasing who they planned to serve.

Some of it was beautiful and most of it was innocuous, so it wasn't the art that I was avoiding so much as the absence of one particular piece. It had been the final painting at the end of the long hall, right before I turned off to head to Intro to Divinity and Immortality, and it had been painted by my mother.

It had hung in the hallway for as long as I'd gone to school here, and I assume it had been there for much longer, since Marlow had painted it in her senior year twenty-some years ago. But now it would be gone, with only a bright white square left on the plasterboard as a reminder that something had been there.

That Marlow had been here.

I kept my head down, and I made it to the classroom just before it let out. Through the small window in the door I watched as Professor Wu finished up his lecture. The name "Osiris" was written on the whiteboard behind him in big letters, along with a dozen or so hieroglyphics, so I guessed they had moved on to the underworld unit.

As the students hurriedly jotted down notes, I thought about how strange it was that a few weeks ago, I was just like them. I'd assumed that I would be here, scrambling to prep for the midterms, but instead I was hiding out in the hallway.

When Professor Wu excused the class, I moved away from the door and hid around the corner. I wouldn't really categorize any of my classmates as friends, especially not after the gossip and leering that happened after Marlow had been killed, and I didn't really want to talk to any of them.

Sloane Kothari was the last one out of the classroom, but that was typical for her. Probably staying behind to ask for extra credit, even though her GPA was already at a 4.2. When she finally made her way out—her perfectly coiled curls bouncing in her ponytail—her head was down, so I had to step right in front of her before she noticed me.

She glanced up in irritation, but then her dark brown eyes widened with shock. For several seconds she just stood there, gaping up at me with her books and tablet pressed to her chest.

"What are you doing here?" she asked finally, then narrowed her eyes. "Who let you in?"

"Nice to see you, too," I muttered dryly. "I am still a student here."

"We all thought you dropped out after . . ." She softened, her weight shifting from one foot to the other. "We didn't think you were coming back."

"I'm not back, not really," I admitted, and before she asked more questions, I hurried on with, "I'm actually here to see you. Can we go somewhere to talk?"

"What do we have to talk about?" she asked, sounding more perplexed than irritated, so at least that was a good sign.

I glanced around the hallway, where a few students passed by on their way to their next class, then turned back to Sloane. "It's probably better if we do this somewhere more private."

Sloane nodded. "I think I know a place."

She led me through the winding corridors of the academy, but about halfway through our journey I realized exactly where we were going: to the Sacrorum Wing, where sacred texts and ancient books were stored. They were all locked up in bomb-shelter-like rooms, each filled to the brim with books, and guarded by knowledge-obsessed Sinaa.

Because of the Sinaa—who looked like jaguars, except many of their spots were eyes, so they could see everything—it wasn't exactly a fun place to hang out, which meant that it was often deserted. But it also wasn't a great place to talk, and I was about to argue that when Sloane turned off before the entrance to the Sacrorum Wing.

She walked down the narrow corridor—here the walls were lined with dark wood, giving it a dark, cavernous feel. The hall ended in a small sitting area, where benches had been built into the wall, with elegantly carved wooden buttresses holding them up.

Above the benches was a large stained-glass window that nearly spanned floor-to-ceiling. Most of the panes of glass were blue and white, depicting a frosty winter scene in which a woman lay on a large stone altar. One of her arms hung off the edge, so her fingers were mere inches above a sword that lay in a shocking red pool of blood.

A plaque on the wall titled it *Dreams of a Queen*. While that was a vague and unhelpful title, I assumed that it was meant to honor Frigg. Although I don't really know why she deserved such esteem, since all she'd done for the past five thousand years was sleep.

"Is this really a great place to talk?" I asked, glancing back toward the Sacrorum Wing, whose entrance was only a few yards away.

"I used to eat my lunch here," Sloane explained as she sat down on the bench, carefully adjusting the hem of her skirt so it covered her knees. "No one ever comes by."

"Good to know." I sat down beside her and reached into my sweater pocket, palming the itayakkal.

"Did the sólarsteinn work?" She leaned toward me expectantly.

"It did. It was immensely helpful, and I think I might need it for a little longer."

She tilted her head. "Well, if you're not here to give it back, then what did you need to see me for?"

"I know this is going to sound crazy, but . . ." I began carefully. "I saw your mom."

Sloane recoiled at that, pulling her whole body back away from me until she was leaning into the wall. The sharp, delicate features of her face twisted up as conflicting emotions passed over her—disgust, incredulity, confusion, hope—before landing on anger and contempt.

"What are you talking about?" she asked with venom lacing her words. "You can't see her. She died thirteen years ago."

"I managed to get into Kurnugia, and your mother helped me," I said as quickly but as calmly as I could. I knew I had to get it all out before Sloane stormed off in anger. "Without her, we couldn't have made it through there or found what I needed to find. And she helped me because of you."

She stared at a spot on the floor, her jaw tensing under her brown skin. "Malin, I don't know what kind of game you're playing, but it's sick." Then she stood up. "I don't want any part of it anymore."

"It's not a game," I insisted and held out the stone toward her. "Look, she asked me to give you this."

"What is it?" she asked, her eyes dark with suspicion.

"It's an itayakkal. Just take it."

The heart-shaped crystallized pink tourmaline sat in the center of my palm, sparkling even in the dim light, and Sloane stared down at it, biting her lip. She reached out for it cautiously, as if she were afraid that it might bite her.

But the second she picked it up, she gasped. Her books fell to the floor, and her other hand went to her mouth as she barely stopped a sob from escaping. She clutched the stone to her chest, and tears filled her eyes.

"I can feel her," she said, sounding awed. "Thank you."

"No need to thank me. I was repaying your mother."

She wiped at her eyes and sat back down beside me. It took several moments, but she managed to compose herself enough to ask me, "What is going on?"

"What do you mean?"

"With everything." She motioned vaguely around us and looked at me. "The weather is out of control, and everything is going mad. You can feel it in the air. *Something* is happening."

"I know that the underworld is trying to rise up and come to the surface," I said finally. "I don't know if they'll be able to, but I do know that it won't be good for humanity or any living thing on earth if they do."

Sloane waited a beat before asking, "How can I help?"

"You want to help me?" I asked, and it was my turn to be skeptical.

"I don't want the world to end, and if you made it to the underworld and back, I can only assume that you know what you're doing." Then she amended with a smile, "At least a little bit."

FIFTY-ONE

———◆———

We stood on the landing outside of the apartment on the fourth floor of a narrow brownstone. Me staring at the door, half expecting to hear the clatter of the peephole cover as Marlow looked out at me, and Oona catching her breath after climbing all the stairs.

Visiting Sloane at Ravenswood and discussing her mother had gotten me thinking about my own mother. How I still didn't understand what Marlow had done or why she'd done it, or how much she really knew about Tamerlane Fayette and Ereshkigal.

In the weeks since Marlow had died, her apartment—the same apartment I'd shared with her growing up, before Oona and I got our own place a year ago—had remained untouched. At least as far as I knew, and based on the bright orange notice from the landlord on the door and the several packages stacked in front, no one else had been in here, either.

Oona pulled the eviction notice off the door and unfolded it. "Marlow's rent is two months past due."

"Great. She hadn't been paying rent even before she died," I said in dismay. "What was she doing with her money?"

"Well, if these packages are to be believed"—Oona bent down to read the address labels—"it looks like she was spending it at an army surplus store and someplace called Lentils Unlimited."

"*More* lentils? How many lentils can one person possibly eat?"

Oona nudged the box with her foot. "I would say quite a lot, apparently."

"Let's get on with it, then." I pulled out my old house key. It slid in the lock, and I waited for the familiar chirp that came after it read the chip in the key, then I turned it and opened the door.

The thing that struck me first wasn't that the place looked exactly the same as it had the last time I had been here—unchanged and frozen on the day Marlow died. It was that it smelled like her here—cloves and vodka and coffee. Add a little red lipstick and a bayonet, and that was my mother exactly.

It was still fairly clean, though, at least by Marlow's standards, since she'd cleaned before inviting Asher over for a visit. Despite the clearing away of the usual boxes and garbage stacked everywhere, there were still quite a few empty alcohol bottles piled up around the sink in the small kitchenette.

I flicked on the light, and at least she must've paid the electric bill, because it worked. The apartment was exceedingly dim, thanks to the boxes stacked up, blocking the only window in the living room. Next to the TV, several tubs of brown rice and lentils were stacked neatly.

Her exercise equipment—free weights and a stair-stepper—sat in the middle of the living room floor, exactly where she'd left them. She'd just finished working out when I'd come over, and then a few hours later she'd been killed.

"What should I do with these packages?" Oona asked from behind me.

"It doesn't matter," I said as I looked around. "I can't afford to pay the rent on this place, and we don't have room for all this. Most of this is gonna end up thrown away or donated to charity." I glanced over at a menacing machete resting on the coffee table. "Not that I think many charity shops have a big need for weapons."

"What's the plan for today?" Oona asked as she shut the apartment door behind her.

"Marlow obviously knew something was up." I motioned to the open pantry door, which held her stockpile of weapons. "I want to try to figure out what she knew. I was hoping we could do this over the course of a couple days, but with that eviction notice, there isn't much time. We're gonna have to start tearing through everything."

And so we began. I left Oona to the kitchen, where she quickly ascertained that the only things in the cupboards were a few cups, plates, coffee, and stale crackers. The pantry was where her attention would really be needed, because that's where Marlow stored a lot of her weapons.

Meanwhile, I went ahead to investigate deeper into the apartment. I checked my room first, or at least I attempted to, but the door only opened a few inches before slamming into boxes. A few of them had writing on the side, scribbled in Marlow's inelegant handwriting, with labels like *Body Armor* or *Ultrasonic Weapons*.

The boxes were stacked precariously on top of one another, with larger boxes sometimes resting on ones that were much smaller, and all of them tilting to the side like they were about to come tumbling down. In between the leaning towers, I caught glimpses of the old posters I'd left up, the only real evidence that I had ever been here.

The sheer enormity of the hoard she'd filled my bedroom with hit me all at once. I literally could not understand how she'd done this. Not just how it was even possible to fill a room with this much junk without getting trapped in it yourself, but *why?*

Before I let myself give in to the overwhelming panic at what appeared to be a cleaning job of Sisyphean proportions, I stepped back and closed the door. There was a lot to unpack in there, so I decided to start somewhere that would hopefully be a bit easier—Marlow's bedroom.

Her bedroom door was slightly ajar, and in the little bit of light that spilled in through the narrow window above her bed, I could see particles of dust floating in the air, like forgotten fairies. I put my hand on the door and began to open it when I was suddenly hit by a memory.

I couldn't have been more than five or six at the time, and I'd woken up from a bad dream and had run across the hall toward Marlow's room. That night her door had been partly open, and I stopped myself before I charged in.

"Malin, I see you skulking around out there." Her voice was like a jolt of lightning breaking through the night.

"I had a bad dream," I replied meekly.

She sighed loudly, dramatically, and then, sounding rueful already, she extended a terse invitation: "Come on in."

Before she had a chance to change her mind, I'd dashed into her room and crawled under the covers beside her, but I didn't dare press my luck and try to snuggle with her.

"You can sleep here tonight, but this isn't going to become a nightly thing," she warned, and as far as I could remember, she'd never let me sleep in her bed again.

When I went into her room now, it was messy, but not as packed as my room was. Her bed was unmade, and her closet door was open, because the closet itself was overflowing with clothing and boots. A large mirror hung above her dresser, flush against the wall. On the dresser itself, beauty products were piled up everywhere, already covered in a thin layer of dust—jewelry, hair gel, brushes, and all kinds of makeup.

But it was the dozen or so half-empty tubes of bright lipstick—all of them the same exact shade of Sanguine Lust—that gave me pause. Each tube was designed to look like a silver bullet casing, with the lid clear to show the color. Gingerly, I picked up a lipstick, one where the makeup was worn down halfway.

"Why would you keep this?" I asked softly as I stared down at the lipstick in my hand, one of many that Marlow hadn't thrown away.

Had she ever finished a tube of lipstick? Was she attempting to hoard them so she would still be a bombshell even in a postapocalyptic world?

That tube of blood-red lipstick had become the tipping point for me. I knew her favorite color of lipstick. I knew about her penchant for black clothing and weapons, that she hated most things, but especially anything involving other people, and she smoked like a chimney, loved a good dash of coffee with her vodka, and had sworn at children playing on more than one occasion.

But I couldn't tell you why she did any of it. Her motivations had completely eluded me my entire life. The end of her life had really matched perfectly with every other moment.

"Who the hell were you, Marlow?" I asked as tears formed in my eyes.

"What was that?" Oona called from the kitchenette, and a moment later she poked her head in the bedroom. "Is everything okay, Mal?"

"Why would she keep these?" I asked Oona, my words thick and trembling as I motioned toward the makeup on her dresser. "Why did she keep any of this?"

But Oona could only shake her head sadly. "I didn't really know her."

I laughed—a short staccato burst. "No one did." I chewed the inside of my cheek as I tried to hold back tears. "She was a Valkyrie for twenty-five years, but it wasn't until she explained to me why she didn't kill Tamerlane Fayette that I learned that she really fucking hated it. And she hated being a mom. So why didn't she quit? Why did she have me? Why didn't she retire and move to an island somewhere?"

"Maybe she thought she couldn't?" Oona suggested as helpfully as she could. "Maybe she did what she thought was the right thing to do, even though she didn't always want to do it."

"The right thing to do, if you hate kids, is not to have them," I said bitterly, and my voice was growing shriller and louder as I spoke. "The right thing to do if you want to be a Valkyrie is to do your job and not let anyone go. The right thing to do if you're worried about the end of the world is tell other people so that they can do something about it or at least have a chance to defend themselves!

"But you know what's *never* the right thing to do?" I asked, nearly shouting by now. "Leaving your daughter behind to deal with this mess without any explanation of why."

I stared down at the lipstick in my hand, with a lump in my throat and anger setting my muscles on edge. Then, softly, almost whispering, I said, "I wish that she'd loved me even a fraction as much as she loved this damn lipstick."

And then, because I had to do something with the anger and sadness surging through me, I pulled my arm back and chucked the lipstick at the mirror.

Instead of shattering or even wobbling, the mirror beeped at me. Chirping, actually, the way the front locks had. Bright green text popped up in the middle of the mirror—which was really a screen, apparently— reading ENTER PASSCODE NOW, with a spacer flashing behind it.

Oona walked over to join me in gaping at the mirror. "Well, I think you stumbled onto another one of Marlow's secrets."

FIFTY-TWO

———◆———

Together, Oona and I pushed the dresser to the side of the bedroom, so we had better access to the touchscreen mirror. There were six glowing green squares after the flashing spacer, and right below that was the keypad of 0-9.

First I tried her birthday 030390, and the screen came back with an angry beep and the words INCORRECT PASSWORD flashed.

I cursed at myself under my breath. "I should've known her birthday wouldn't work. It's too obvious."

"What's something more obscure that you know?" Oona asked. "Her Valkyrie number, maybe?"

"No, that's letters and numbers."

"Your birthday?" Oona suggested, and I gave her a hard look. "You could try it, if you can't think of anything better."

After going through many different options and trying a few—including her phone number and Samael's birthday—I was running out of ideas. I was about to type in my birth date when something else occurred to me.

I pulled out my phone, hurriedly scrolling through the images to a screenshot that Asher had sent me when we started working together to find Tamerlane Fayette. It was of the form that he'd managed to get his hands on, the one where Marlow had been assigned to kill Tamerlane.

"What are you looking for?" Oona asked, and I zoomed in on the picture and tilted the phone toward her so she could get a better look.

"There." I pointed to it. "That's Tamerlane's immortal ID number. They're run together here, but usually on forms it would be written out like PL87-653422."

"You think that could be it?" Oona asked.

"It's worth a shot." I carefully punched in the code. I steeled myself for the inevitable angry beep, but this time it chirped happily at me.

The mirror-screen swung slowly out about an inch, and then I opened it all the way, revealing a rather large wall safe. Despite the large size of the safe, there wasn't much in it. Four swords, a fat stack of cash, and an old mobile phone.

The swords, with their stubby blades and jagged edges, were unmistakably Valkyrie swords, and when my fingers skimmed across them, a dull warmth spread through me, assuring me that these were in fact the real deal.

Meanwhile, the cash looked so freshly printed I could only assume that Marlow was taking the money that Samael paid her directly and putting it in here.

"Holy crap!" Oona gasped as she eyed the stack of cash. "She had all this money, but she wasn't paying her rent?"

"Maybe she knew she wouldn't live here for much longer."

Then Asher's words burned on my heart again, and I remembered how he'd known that he wasn't going to leave the Gates of Kurnugia that day when Gugalanna had taken him down. Had one of Marlow's ancestors left a painful truth on her heart, too? Did she know she was going to die?

"Are those Valkyrie swords?" Oona asked as she tentatively reached out and touched one. "Where would somebody get these? You can't buy them off the street."

"Yeah, they're real, and I have no idea how Marlow got her hands on that many."

But I had turned my attention to the phone, the only thing that could be used to store info. It wasn't like my phone, which was a slick touchscreen with all kinds of apps and features. This was an old hunk of plastic with a tiny screen, like a handheld transreceiver with a touch screen.

I clicked the power button, and several agonizing seconds later the screen lit up, though the flashing red battery icon in the corner warned me that it might not be for very long. The date and time flashed onto the screen, and they were both accurate, which implied that Marlow had used the phone recently.

I started to scroll through it, looking for any info it might have, but it was almost entirely empty. No games, no pictures, no text messages, no records of incoming or outgoing calls. In fact, there was only one thing I could find—a solitary contact listed only as "AZ" with a phone number.

"AZ?" Oona leaned over my shoulder. "Is that like *A* to *Z*? Or maybe it could be a reference to alpha and omega? Or maybe it's a nickname? Do you know anyone named Az?"

"Not that I can think of."

"It could also be random letters she used," Oona contended.

"Well, there really is only one way to find out," I said.

Call me, I wrote with trembling hands, and before I could talk myself out of it, I hit send.

"Do you think it'll work?" Oona asked.

"I don't know what else to try, and it's not like Marlow left us a bunch of clues or instructions about what the hell is going on."

"Yeah, she was always—"

The phone ringing cut her off, startling me so badly I nearly dropped the phone. I took a fortifying breath, then I answered with the strongest voice I could muster: "Hello?"

"Marlow?" a man asked, his voice a mixture of shock and anger. "What the hell? I thought you were dead."

"This . . ." I stopped and cleared my throat, deciding that it would be easier if I didn't pretend to be my dead mother. "She is dead."

That confession was met by a silence that lasted so long I was terrified that he had hung up. But then he asked, "Who is this?"

I glanced over at Oona, who stood beside me literally wringing her hands. I wasn't sure how to answer, but I decided this was too important to play games. I had to find out what Marlow knew.

"I'm her daughter," I replied evenly, and Oona gasped and put her hand to her mouth. "Who is this?"

He waited a beat before saying, "I'm her lover. I didn't know she had a daughter."

"Well, I didn't know she had a lover," I admitted.

He actually chuckled at that, apparently relaxing. "Marlow did love her secrets."

"Maybe we should get together and compare notes," I said as I attempted to adopt the coy, flirtatious voice that Marlow would pull out on special occasions.

"Marlow wanted her secrets kept," he countered evenly. "Who are we to expose them?"

"*We* are what's left. She's not here. Who are we protecting her secrets from?" I asked.

He laughed again, but it had the rumble of something deeper and darker. "Everyone needs protection every now and then. Don't you, little girl?"

"I found your number on a phone hidden in a wall safe, with a few other things that my recently murdered mother had hidden away," I said. "She was hiding you for a reason, and I'm going to find out what that reason is. Now, you and I can get together and have a nice talk, or I can contact my friends among the Eralim and the Vörðr. I may not have much, but I'm certain that I have enough that they could find you, but not without causing a big stink first."

I was only half bluffing. If I couldn't get the answers from this guy on the phone, I knew that Samael would not stop until he found out exactly who this was and why Marlow was hiding him from everyone.

The bluffing part came because I could only assume that he had something to hide, that there was a reason Marlow had stashed this phone with Valkyrie swords and wads of cash.

So I bluffed, and I chewed my lip, waiting for him to answer.

"There's a place called Sup D'yavola," he said ruefully. "It's a restaurant in the Aizsaule District. They have the best soup you'll ever
taste. I'll be there at one tomorrow for lunch, if you want to join me."

"How will I know it's you?" I asked.

"My name's Azarias," he said simply. "And I'll know you."

I was about to ask him how he'd know me, when he never even knew
that Marlow had a daughter or asked me my name. But the phone beeped
loudly in my ear before shutting down and going dead completely.

FIFTY-THREE

———◆———

One of the great things about my luft was that it made conversation very difficult. The engine was loud, the wind was in your face, and traffic blared around you. Ever since I'd spoken to Azarias, Oona had been a nonstop worrying, question machine, asking all sorts of things that I didn't have the answers for.

Like: *How will he know who you are? Why would Marlow have kept him from you? Who is he? How can you be sure he's not lying? What if it's a trap?*

As if I hadn't already been worrying about all that myself. As if I had any choice.

I was happy for the reprieve as Oona wrapped her arms tightly around my waist and buried her head in my jacket as I darted through a traffic jam. But that all came to a halt when I couldn't find a break between the vehicles packed together on the road. Bumper-to-bumper across the lanes of asphalt.

Trapped, with only the sounds of honking horns and a street vendor demanding too much money for burnt vegetable kebabs, I felt Oona's grip loosen around my waist. The smog in the city felt thicker, heavy with the acrid stench of chemicals. Even the curses and accusations that the drivers lobbed at one another had a sharper edge, with extra venom lacing their words.

"Do you think he was someone that Marlow was assigned to kill?" Oona asked, so apparently the drive had given her more time to ruminate and come up with new questions that I couldn't answer.

"I don't know," I answered for what felt like the hundredth time. "But the only way I will find out is if I meet with him."

"Mal," Oona said with a heavy sigh, and I could already hear her gearing up for a long speech about how I needed to be more careful and me getting myself killed wasn't going to help anybody.

But then a delivery truck edged closer to the red light, allowing enough room for my luft between it and the neighboring vehicle, and I saw my chance.

"Hold on," I told Oona as I revved up the luft. "I'm taking a short-cut on Foster."

"Foster's not a—" Oona started to argue that it wasn't a shortcut so much as it was a scenic route, but traffic was actually moving on it, so it was worth the risk.

Her arms tightened around me as I twisted the throttle, and the luft lurched forward. We narrowly squeezed between the vehicles, and I took a sharp left on Foster Avenue.

The thing about Foster Avenue was it should've been a relatively straight shot between my mother's brownstone and my apartment build-ing on the lake, but right smack in the middle was the twenty-five-acre Skarpåker Park. So now the straight shot had to wrap around this massive park near the center of the city.

Skarpåker Park had been another fanciful idea the city had under-taken, back before it stretched out into New Edgewater. It was meant to be a place of peace and beauty, where everyone from all walks of life could come together. That was the idea, but in practice it had become a strange combination of tourist trap and crime-ridden violence.

In the very center of the park was its namesake—a large stone in-scribed with an eschatological verse in the old language of the gods. It had been unearthed in a freak earthquake centuries ago, with jagged etches poking out from the middle of the empty field, which was how it had earned its name—Skarpåker meant "sharp field."

I took the luft up onto the bike path in an illegal but desperate attempt to get home. That brought me close enough to the park that I could make out glimpses of the landmarks through the burnt orange and sharp reds of the autumn leaves.

The Petrillo Pavilion, with its interwoven trellis of steel beams, glass, and bright lights, stretching over the lawn; the Fountain of the Fates, with a black granite reflecting pool and a holographic light show above the fountains, depicting three women spinning a golden loom of thread; the *Window to Forever* art installation, which was little more than a gigantic concave mirror, twisted and curved to reflect the sky above us; and far back in the corner, before the overgrown Emmanuel Wooded Garden, were the rocky outcroppings that stretched and strained beyond the grass. On top of the stone, towering above the rest of the park, was a mossy gazebo, known simply as the Place for the Dreaming.

When I paused to let a giantess walking an unruly pack of mastiffs get by, it was the *Window to Forever* that caught my eye. The smooth shimmering steel perfectly mirrored the sky, letting me see exactly how dark and red the clouds were that rumbled over us.

Thunder cracked, loud enough to make Oona yelp in surprise, and I raced ahead. A storm was coming, quickly, and we were still at least twenty minutes from home. Going as fast as I could, darting around anything in my way, I managed to almost get to the edge of the city, where the asphalt gave way to canals, before the rain began.

They were fat, cold drops splashing down, but I didn't notice anything strange about them. At least, not until I heard the people start screaming. A taxi driver opened his door right in front of me, apparently oblivious to me, and I slammed on my brakes as my headlight shattered against his door handle.

"Dammit!" I cursed at him as I steadied my luft. "Watch what you're doing, man!"

But he didn't seem to notice me. He stared up at the sky, slack-jawed, with his palms out, and in a shaky monotone he said, "It's raining blood."

And that's when I really saw it for the first time. All the city lights, reflecting off of everything, made it hard for me to see at first. But now it was obvious as the bright red drops splattered against the windows and pooled on the ground.

I held out my hand, watching the drops hit it for a few seconds, before bringing it up to my face so I could get a better look. While it may have been bright red, it had a thinner viscosity than blood, and a strange chemical smell to it, like sulfur mixed with diesel.

So it wasn't blood, but I didn't want to stay out in a red rain any longer than I had to. I angled the luft around the taxi door, and I sped down the street half a block until I made it to Galel's Garage.

It sat right on the edge of where dry land met the lake, and I pulled my luft right in front, parking it haphazardly in front of the plate-glass window. It was after six on a weekday, which meant that it was closed, but that didn't stop me from slamming my hand against the door.

"Jude!" I shouted. "Open up!"

"*Jude!*" Oona joined in. She stood beside me, pulling her jacket up over her head in a futile attempt to keep the strange red rain off her skin.

Fortunately, he appeared a second later, with a few crimson splatters on his oil-stained overalls. He hurriedly unlocked the door and stepped to the side, letting us run in past him.

"What the hell is going on out there?" he asked.

He leaned against the front window, so close his massive ram horns nearly touched it, and stared up at the nightmare sky. His expression looked grimmer than I had ever seen it. There was a grave stoicism hardening the rest of his normally open features.

"It's not blood," Oona said as she wiped herself off with an old rag. "But I don't know what it is or why it's happening."

"Everything's so strange lately." Jude turned to face me and ran a hand through his dark hair. "And not just the batshit weather. My dad randomly skipped town on Saturday, and I haven't heard from him since. And he's not the only one. When I went to Carpe Noctem last night, half the regulars were gone."

"Where'd they go?" I asked.

He shrugged, playing it off, but worry darkened his eyes. "Nobody tells us Cambions much of anything." Then he looked back out the window. "But whatever is coming, Malin, you gotta be careful."

FIFTY-FOUR

— ◆ —

Oona stood behind me, watching me pack up my messenger bag, before declaring that she had to get me something. The moment she disappeared into her bedroom, a knock at the front door interrupted my preparations.

Bowie sat on the couch beside my bag, anxiously sniffing it, but he leapt off at the sound of the knock, before taking refuge underneath the couch. He'd been extra jumpy since I got back from Caana City, but I wasn't sure if it was because I was gone or because he sensed danger in the air.

When I answered the door, I discovered Asher, and my heart skipped a beat. He'd been looking over his shoulder when I opened the door, absently scratching at the stubble that darkened his jaw, and he turned back to me with an unconvincing smile. He wore jeans today that were snug in a wonderful way, and he wore a black T-shirt under his distressed jacket.

"What are you doing here?" I asked, but then it hit me, and my shoulders sagged. "You can't talk me out of going to meet Azarias."

"Of course not," he said instantly. "I'm going to go with you."

I glanced over at the clock on the wall, which said it was ten past noon. By my best calculation (or, more accurately, the calculation of my GPS app) it would take me thirty-seven minutes to get to Sup D'yavola. I didn't have time to argue.

"I shouldn't have told you," I said, but I wasn't sure if I meant it.

Last night I'd called Asher, not meaning to tell him much of anything at all, but as soon as I'd heard his voice on the phone—deep but soft, slightly husky, and so utterly calm—it had all come out.

There was something about him that made me not only willing to share my deepest fears and most shameful secrets, but actually unable to stop myself. I had this irresistible urge to pour my heart out to him, to lay myself bare before him, to have him see me, *really* see me, because I knew that if I did, he would still tell me it would be okay. That nothing in the darkest part of my soul could scare him away from me.

"Malin." His voice was barely above a whisper but it was forceful and unapologetic.

He reached out then, taking my hand in his. As soon as he touched me—his warm skin rough against mine—I realized exactly what it was.

He was my ocean. In the calm, he was endless and beautiful, able to wrap me up, taking away all my pain and fear until I was weightless in his arms. In anger, he was relentless and unfathomable, an unstoppable force that would not move for anything.

"I appreciate your concern," I said and stepped back, slipping my hand away from him but allowing him to step inside my apartment. "But I don't want to overwhelm him or scare him off."

"Overwhelm him?" he asked once I'd closed the door behind him. "This guy alleges to have dated your mother. If she didn't overwhelm him, nothing will."

"Fair enough."

"Besides, I don't think it's unreasonable to bring one other person with you." He stepped closer to me, putting a hand on my waist so I wouldn't move away. "Let me go with you. Let me help."

Despite both Oona's and Asher's obvious concerns, I felt pretty good about meeting Azarias, all things considered. Not only would we be meeting in a public place, I was bringing along plenty of weaponry to be safe: my asp, my sword Sigrún, industrial-grade pepper spray, as well as a machete that I'd taken from Marlow's place yesterday.

I had left most of Marlow's stuff at her apartment—including the Valkyrie swords, which I locked back up in her safe since I had nowhere secure to store them—but the rather fierce-looking machete had seemed too useful to leave behind.

Besides the machete, the only other thing I had taken from Marlow's had been the burner phone. We had waited out the red rain—which the news claimed was nothing more than a freak acid rain storm—then we stopped at Dillinger's Corner Market & Apothecary to pick up a charger (which they didn't sell anymore, but thankfully Oona's boss, Mr. Dillinger, kept a box of outdated chargers in his office in case of emergency) on the off chance that Azarias tried to contact me again.

But he hadn't, and our attempts at finding him online had been futile. There were over fifteen hundred people named Azarias in the metro area alone. That meant I was going into this meeting relatively blind, so all my weapons were only a small consolation.

But I would always do what I had to do, whether I liked it or not.

"Okay," I relented, deciding that he was right. Or at least close enough to it.

I expected him to smile, to look relieved or happy, but for a brief moment his expression actually hardened. It was like a shadow had passed over him, and I saw darkness flicker across his eyes.

Before I could ask him about that, Oona came rushing out of her bedroom. He lowered his gaze and moved away from me, walking toward the kitchen and the large window with its view of the flashing billboards and overcast skies.

"Here." Oona held out a small bag made of a burlap-like raffia, and when she dropped it in the palm of my hand it felt like it was filled with sand and pudding. "It's kuepuka mchanga, which should help you escape if you need it."

"Thanks, but I'm meeting him for lunch at a public place," I reminded her, but that only caused her to roll her eyes.

"Yeah, in the Aizsaule District. There's no reason not to take extra precautions."

"So, how do I use this?" I asked as I held up the bag of strange sand Oona had given me.

"Kuepuka mchanga is super-easy to use. You take a handful of it and throw it up in the air, like you're tossing confetti, and it makes an opaque plume of smoke that lingers for a few minutes, so you have a chance to escape," Oona explained. "Assuming you need to escape."

"Thanks." I smiled at her, then added the tiny bag to the rest of my stuff.

"At least you're not going alone now," Oona said. Her arms were folded across her chest as she turned her attention to Asher. "Thanks for talking some sense into her."

"What?" He looked back over his shoulder at her, his brow pinched in confusion, and his eyes had a strange fog over them, like a man just waking from a dream.

"You're going with Malin." She glanced back at me. "It's the sensible thing to do."

"Yeah." He nodded rather vigorously and put his hand on the back of a kitchen chair. "Yeah. Yeah. Yeah."

"Ash? Are you okay?" I asked, as if it weren't obvious that he was not okay.

In the brief seconds I'd been talking with Oona his skin had paled considerably, and I could see beads of sweat forming on his temples. His eyes darted everywhere around the room, and he leaned heavily on the kitchen chair, as if he couldn't support his own weight anymore.

He looked up at me, his eyes wide and startled, and in a shaky voice he said, *"Malin."*

His eyes rolled into the back of his head, and Asher collapsed to the floor, toppling the chair over as he fell, and he landed hard on the concrete floor as tremors took over his body.

FIFTY-FIVE

———◆———

"Asher!" I knelt beside him as his body jerked and thrashed on the floor.

"He's having a seizure." Oona's voice was behind me, sounding shockingly calm.

"What do I do?" I shouted, practically screaming, really, as if that could help, and when I looked back at Oona, she was gone.

So it was only me in the kitchen, tentatively reaching out for Asher's flailing body. I put my hand on his chest in a vain attempt to comfort him. I didn't hold him down—I just let him writhe as terrified tears stung my eyes.

Oona came rushing back in, pushing the chair out of the way so she could kneel on the other side of him. It felt like an eternity that she'd been gone as I watched the man I loved contort and spasm, but it probably had been only a few seconds.

"I'm gonna need your help." She put her hand on his forehead, gently holding his head in place.

"What are we doing?" I asked.

She held up a small vial of inky black liquid. "I need to get three drops of this in his eye."

"Why? What is it?"

"Medicine and magic," she replied quickly. "It'll stop the seizures so we can figure out what the hell is going on."

I trusted Oona, and watching Asher thrash on the floor wasn't going to help him any, so I did what she told me. She commanded me to hold his eye open, and with careful, trembling fingers I lifted up the eyelid. His eyes were still rolled to the back of his head, and the black drops of liquid turned the whites completely black.

"Now what?" I asked.

Oona sat back on her knees, her expression grim as she stared down at Asher. "We wait."

I held my breath, slowly counting down the seconds, until finally his body relaxed. He lay slack on the floor, unmoving, and then he breathed in deeply, and relief washed over me in a violent wave.

"What happened?" he asked groggily, barely opening his eyes to look up at me.

"I don't know."

"I think you had a seizure," Oona clarified. She still knelt beside him and took his hand. "Can you squeeze my hand?" He must've, because she looked relieved when she said, "Good."

"I don't understand . . ." He trailed off as he stared up at the ceiling. "My head is killing me."

"I have something for that," Oona offered, and then turned her attention to me. "If you want to go meet him on time, you have to go."

I swallowed down the fear and panic. "I can't. I can't leave Asher."

"I'll be with him," she insisted. "And you don't know if you'll get a chance to see Azarias again."

"You're going to meet him for lunch," Asher realized, and he looked over at me. "You have to go, Malin."

"Asher—"

"You're trying to figure out if the world is ending. That's more important than me or you," he said simply. "I'll be here when you get back."

He was right, and I hated it. I wanted to stay with him, more than anything I wanted to be sure that he was all right, but I couldn't.

I leaned over and kissed him softly on the cheek. "You have to be okay."

"So do you," he said with a faint smile. "Go. And be safe."

FIFTY-SIX

———◆———

The Aizsaule District was always darker than the rest of the city, even in the early afternoon. The cloud-covered sky was dark enough that the streetlamps were already on as I pulled into the parking lot. Sup D'yavola was a little corner diner, one that looked like it could've been on any corner of the city, except here broken windows were boarded up and covered in graffiti and symbols I didn't recognize.

I had managed to get here a few minutes early, thanks to my panic-induced speeding, so I decided to text Oona before I went in.

How's Asher? I wrote.

A few seconds later her speedy reply came. **Seems okay so far. How is AZ?**

Just going in to meet him. Call me if Asher gets bad again, I texted back.

Will do. Stay safe.

Satisfied that Asher was still alive and kicking, I put my phone away and went into the diner. A sign by the door—wedged between a cigarette machine and a prophylactic dispenser—said to wait to be seated, so that's what I did.

The place wasn't dirty, exactly, but it was worn and old. Faded linoleum on the floor, cracked vinyl in the booths, and water spots on the ceiling. Pictures covered every inch of the walls, mostly in black-and-white. All of them featured rather famous immortals and celebrities, and several even had prominent members of the anti-Riksdag group, the Kurnugia Society.

It was relatively dead here, only a few patrons seated around the dimly let restaurant. Most of the clientele weren't exactly humanoid in appearance, except for one man. He sat near the front window—the one with an intact glass pane—but he was looking toward the kitchen, most likely scanning for the waitress.

His dark blond hair was greasy and long, falling below his shoulders, and he had a few rugged braids starting at his temples to keep his locks out of his face. The top few buttons of his shirt were undone, revealing a patch of hair on his firm chest. He had an aquiline nose and a pronounced chin, almost pointed, but as he leaned back in the booth I could see that he had his own bad-boy appeal to him.

He was definitely Marlow's type.

As I walked toward the booth, he finally looked back at me, and as soon as he saw me, he smiled.

"You look like her," he said as he motioned for me to sit down across from him.

"I don't, but thanks," I replied flatly.

He looked past me, at a waitress walking toward us, and held up his fingers in a V. "Two shots of vodka. The good stuff that you hide behind the bar." Then he looked over at me. "Anything for you?"

"Water is fine." I didn't need the alcohol clouding me up today.

"Do you want to order now?" the waitress asked in a bored tone.

Without checking with me, Azarias said, "I'll have the Okroshka with the žaltys sausage."

"I don't know what you have," I said when the waitress turned to me.

"It's all soups. Nothing else. They're on the board." She pointed behind her to a handwritten menu scrawled on a board behind the register.

"Um . . . Rassolnik," I decided, since it was the only soup I'd had before.

"Good choice," Azarias told me, and once the waitress had gone, he leaned forward, resting his arms on the table. "Malin, right?"

"Should we do proper introductions?" I suggested coolly. "I'm Malin Krigare, daughter of Marlow, student at Ravenswood Academy. And you are?"

His smile deepened. "I'm Azarias Göll, former lover of Marlow, and general jack of all trades. And I couldn't help but notice that you failed to mention your job title. Are you still in training, or are you a full-blown *Valkyrie* yet?"

His tone was almost taunting when he said "Valkyrie," speaking loud enough that others might be able to overhear, and that kind of thing could cause a lot of trouble for me in a neighborhood like Aizsaule.

I remained unfazed by his attempts to fluster or threaten me—I didn't know which he was going for—and replied impassively, "You're not immortal. Cambion?"

He laughed and leaned back. "My mother was a siren."

"A Cambion and Valkyrie make for strange bedfellows," I pointed out.

My friendship with Jude Locklear was definitely an exception among immortals and their children, and it spoke more to Jude's character than it did anything. Most beings didn't want to be friends with somebody who might someday kill their parents.

Before he could reply, the waitress appeared with a tray and roughly set down the shots and large bowls of soup. Azarias's bowl looked less like soup and more like a heaping salad of diced boiled eggs, scallions, potatoes, and fleshy pink chunks of snake, all covered in a brown kvas broth.

He leaned over, breathing in his soup, but I didn't know how he could smell it over the scent of fermented cabbage that permeated the restaurant. Once the waitress had left us alone to enjoy our meal, Azarias tossed his head back and slammed the two shots of vodka without a chaser, causing his face to twist in a grimace.

"Well, then. Shall we get to it?" he asked. "What is it that you want to know?"

"What exactly were you doing with my mother?" I asked pointedly.

"You don't know? You look old enough to understand what it is that a man and woman do together," he said with an exaggerated wink that made my skin crawl.

"How did you meet her?"

"How do any two people find each other in this crazy mixed-up world of ours? Luck and serendipity," he said, and when I rolled my eyes, he elaborated. "We met at a bar. But what is it that you're hoping to find out? What do you want me to illuminate for you?"

"Are you sad that she's dead?" I asked, and he looked caught off guard.

"I'm not happy," he said at length. "I had a certain fondness for Marlow. But I'm also not one to get particularly attached to anyone."

"Why did she keep you secret?"

"You tell me," he countered. "You knew her better than I did. But she seemed to be the type that really guarded her privacy."

"I just don't understand why you were with her," I said, breaking down my argument in the simplest terms as he shoveled spoonfuls of the Okroshka into his mouth.

"Wow." He gulped down his food and arched an eyebrow. "Do you really think so little of your mother that she can't possibly have any qualities that anyone would find attractive?"

I knew she was attractive, beautiful even, but her personality was usually enough to drive any wannabe Lothario away. A cold-hearted fighter with an alcohol problem did not a good girlfriend make.

"Not enough for it to be worth the risk," I said.

"What risk?" he asked, but he didn't deny it.

"You asked to meet in Aizsaule, so I can only assume that you live and work here, which means that you're involved with the more unsavory immortals." I gestured vaguely around to the neighborhood. "Most of them would sooner die than date a Valkyrie, and many would be happy to kill you because of it."

"What if the risk is what attracted me to Marlow?" he asked with a waggle of his eyebrows.

I was tired of his games, so I folded my arms over my chest and asked, "What did attract you to her?"

He set his spoon down and stared out the window, thinking for a moment before saying, "She was beautiful, and she was mean. That doesn't sound like a winning combination to you, I'm sure, but it is to me."

He smirked at some memory that I would never know of, and I wondered if he had seen a side of her that I never would.

"So did you ask her out?" I pressed.

He looked at me and tilted his head. "I doubt you want to know all the details of your mother's sex life, so how about I simplify it for you? I work as a bartender at the Red Raven. My boss—"

"Your boss? Velnias?" I leaned forward on the table, and by the expression on Azarias's face I could tell that he'd given away more than he meant to.

"All orders come from him in one way or another," he allowed. "But it wasn't him that night. Just my manager. He saw Marlow at the bar nursing a drink, and he said he sensed that she was trouble and told me to keep an eye on her. One thing led to another, and here we are."

"What was she doing at the Red Raven? Did she tell you?"

"She was looking for someone. That's all she said," he told me in between spoonfuls of soup. "I have no idea who or what, or if she ever found them."

"When was this?"

"A month ago, maybe?" He shrugged. "Maybe a little longer than that?"

"A month ago," I repeated, trying to remember if she'd said or done anything strange then. Or at least stranger than normal. "Did she say anything that seemed . . . suspicious to you?"

Azarias finished his soup with one heaping spoonful, then he wiped his mouth with the back of his arm before settling back in his seat.

"Look, I don't really have much I can tell you about her," he said. "Not that you wouldn't already know. Most of the time that Marlow and I spent together, well, we didn't do much talking."

I wrinkled my nose. "Gross."

"It is what it is." He stood up and pulled out his wallet. "But I have things I need to get to, and since I don't have anything for you, I think I'll be on my way." He tossed a few bills on the table, more than enough to cover our meal. "You should try your soup. It's delicious."

"Thanks," I muttered, staring down at my bowl of brine and barley.

Before he left, he leaned over and, almost whispering in my ear, said, "Oh, and if I were you, I'd get out back where you belong as soon as you're done. Aizsaule isn't a safe place for Valkyries, especially not anymore."

FIFTY-SEVEN

———◆———

No sooner had I opened the door to my apartment than I heard Asher shout, "Molly!"

By the looks of it, he had been lounging back on the couch petting Bowie, who had nuzzled up to him. Asher stood up so quickly when he saw me that he nearly fell over. I barely had a chance to drop my messenger bag and kick off my boots before he rushed over to embrace me in what I could only describe as a sloppy hug.

"Does anybody ever call you Molly?" he asked, and he put his weight on me as we hugged.

"Not if they want to live," I muttered, looking over his shoulder at Oona smiling sheepishly at me.

She was sitting cross-legged on the floor, with her thick grimoire spread out across her lap. The yellowed pages looked as if they would crumble under her fingertips, but Oona always swore that the book was far stronger than it looked.

"Sorry about him," Oona said as I untangled myself from Asher and helped ease him back down onto the couch. "Some of what I gave him to help with the tremors and the headache have made him a little loopy."

"I missed you so much," Asher said, his words slurring slightly as he pulled me onto the couch beside him. I was afraid he would smother me or try making out in front of Oona, but instead he held my hand and stared down at the floor.

"Have you figured out what caused it yet?" I asked.

"No, but that's in large part because I've been having a hard time getting a straight answer out of him." She frowned at him.

"I try to think, I try to answer." He moved his hand around his head. "But it's like a fog, like . . . like I can't get to certain stuff. I know it's there, but I can't see it." His eyes were dark and glassy, with the whites still stained from the eyedrops Oona had given him.

Before he could say more, bright white light flashed outside, followed immediately by a clap of thunder so loud it rattled the windows. The power faltered, bathing us in total darkness for a fraction of a second before flashing back on with startling bright lights and blasts from the neighbors' stereo.

"What was that?" Asher asked.

Rain began pouring down in torrential sheets that slammed against the window, and thunder rumbled on overhead. Fortunately, none of this really seemed to faze Asher. He blinked sleepily at me and barely suppressed a yawn.

"I've been telling him to lie down and rest," Oona said. "It'll help him work through the side effects of the meds faster so maybe I can find out what's going on. But he wanted to stay awake until you got back."

"I had to see that you were safe," Asher said matter-of-factly. "I couldn't sleep if you weren't here."

"Why don't you go lie down in my bed and get some sleep?" I suggested, but he didn't need any prodding. His body had started wilting the second he sat down. I suspect the seizure had been exhausting enough, not to mention that whatever Oona had given him apparently had an inebriating-like effect, so his will to stay awake had to be mightily strong.

He got up slowly, standing on his own, but his brow furrowed in concentration to make it happen. I followed right behind him, and I could tell by the deliberate way he walked that he was doing everything he could not to lean on me.

Once we got to my room, he practically collapsed back onto my bed. He unbuttoned his jeans and tried taking them off, but it wasn't going well, so I stepped in and slid them off.

"Thank you for helping me," he mumbled as I grabbed my blanket.

"It's no problem." I draped the covers across him, and then leaned over to make sure he was nicely tucked in.

As Asher settled down, his eyes suddenly flashed open, and he stared up at me. "You know I love you, right?"

He knocked the wind right out of me, and I could only stay frozen where I was. My hands trembled instantly, and my throat seemed to close up, robbing me of my voice. The strangest feeling came over me, like I was hovering above my body, someplace separate and far away and wonderful and warm. . . .

And I realized that he was staring up at me, waiting, so I managed to meekly say, "I do."

I didn't know what I'd say until I said it, and I didn't know how I felt, but then I meant it. I did know. I'd never before believed that anyone could love me—I'd always thought that I was an unlovable monster—but when Asher touched me, I knew. I just knew.

He closed his eyes, and within seconds he was asleep.

I sat on the edge of the bed beside him, giving myself a few minutes to catch my breath and slow my heart, and eventually I felt grounded back in my body again. My hands still trembled, and I felt this dizzying happiness.

When I left the room, closing the door behind me, Oona was still sitting on the floor with her spell book open, Bowie taking refuge from the storm beside her, but she'd turned on the TV and her eyes were glued to the screen.

I was about to ask her what all had happened while I'd been gone when my phone beeped loudly in my pocket. I pulled it out to see Samael's name flashing across the screen. It was a text message.

I need to see you at the Evig Riksdag. ASAP.

FIFTY-EIGHT

◆

S hit," I cursed to myself, and Oona managed to pull her eyes away from the television screen long enough to glance over at me.

"Mal, you gotta see this."

"Can't." I went over to where I'd kicked off my boots fifteen minutes before so I could pull them on again. "I have to go."

"What? You can't!"

"Samael texted—"

"No, Mal, come watch the news!" She pointed wildly at the screen. "You *can't* go out there."

"Why not?" I walked back over to see what all the fuss was about, but it became obvious very quickly.

It showed downtown Chicago, pitch-black except for the dancing lights from circling helicopters. Between the towering buildings and through the sheets of rain, I could just make out people running. The camera zoomed in on a burning car. Behind it, a human and cyclops were working together to break into a jewelry store.

The red crawl on the bottom of the screen said the entire State District—home to the Evig Riksdag, along with plenty of other business and government buildings—was in chaos.

"I turned on the news to see if they said anything about the storm we're having, and, well, yeah," Oona explained.

"Are they rioting?" I asked.

"Yeah, the lightning blew out all the power downtown, and I guess everyone went nuts."

"But it's raining!" I insisted incredulously. "Why are they outside in a cold rainstorm? What is wrong with everyone?"

"The world is going mad." She looked up at me. "The news reporter said that everyone should stay inside until the police get everything calmed down."

"I have to go."

"Are you not listening?" Oona shouted. "It's too dangerous!"

I sat down on the coffee table so I could pull on my boots more easily. "Samael said he needs to see me ASAP, and it's probably about whatever the hell is going on out there that is making everyone so insane right now."

Oona exhaled through her nose and thought for a second before deciding, "Fine. But you can't go by yourself."

"Asher is out." I motioned to my bedroom where he lay sleeping. "I need you to stay here with him and Bowie."

She rolled her eyes. "Yeah, obviously I'm not going out in that because I'm not a total psycho."

"Then what do you suggest?" I asked.

"Quinn."

I scoffed and stood up, which was the only argument I really had against Quinn. Oona closed her grimoire and set it on the table.

"Mal, hear me out," Oona persisted as she followed me to the door. "She wants to help with this stuff, she lives nearby-ish, and she has a car, so you don't have to ride your luft in the rain."

"Oona." I licked my lips, unable to think up a compelling argument except that I wasn't ready to deal with all the feelings that came up whenever Quinn and I were around each other. "Things are complicated right now."

"No, things are very simple," Oona said firmly. "You want to save the world and you don't want to die, and you're willing to do anything you need to make that happen."

I rubbed my temple. "Fine. I'll text her. But if she says no, I'm going on my own."

FIFTY-NINE

◆

We agreed to meet at Dillinger's Corner Market & Apothecary, since it was roughly halfway between our two places.
I'd ended up calling Quinn, with Oona hovering beside me
to make sure I went through with it, and to my dismay, she'd actually
answered.

I thought she might be avoiding me, but she knew that if I was calling it had to be important. Once I explained the situation, she immediately agreed to join me, but in that regard, I hadn't expected anything
different.

Fortunately, the rain had lessened in the few minutes it took me to
get downstairs and outside. I would still be soaked by the time I made
it the few blocks to Dillinger's, but at least it wasn't like I was jogging in
a tsunami.

New Edgewater wasn't a nice neighborhood, not by any stretch of
the word, but it was generally relatively quiet compared to the rest of the
city. The dirty canals kept a lot of through traffic out, since not everybody had hovercrafts, and the canals dead-ended in a concrete wall
before the lake.

With the weather and the newscasters' directions to stay indoors, it felt eerily quiet. Even three years ago, when we'd had a blizzard on New Year's Eve, the streets hadn't been this deserted. I swear, every time I stepped outside I heard a baby crying—I suspected it was usually pontianaks, attempting to lure victims by mimicking the sound of an infant crying.

But when I stepped outside tonight, for the very first time, I heard nothing. The water in the canal was oddly still, and the air smelled exceptionally like sewage and filth. A couple was walking on the other side of the canal, huddled together under an umbrella, but otherwise, I was alone.

And no one was ever alone in this city.

I started running, not to get out of the rain so much as to get away from here.

Dillinger's was still a block away, glowing dully with harsh halogen lamps like a lighthouse in a storm. A narrow parking lot sat in front, and Quinn's vintage sedan hovercraft was already parked there.

Hers was the only car in the lot, but as she got out of the driver's side, I saw a group of people coming out from the shadows. There were five of them, and even from my distance they were easy to spot thanks to their attire: lots of neon patches and brightly colored metal spikes adorned their jean jackets, with hair to match styled in mohawks and liberty spikes.

On the back of their jackets each of them had affixed a large flamel—a serpent wrapped around a cross. That was the symbol for their gang, Perenelle's Children, though I was using the term "gang" loosely. They were all Cambions, children of various low-level demons and immortals, and they had little to no power or prospects. So they hung around, played with alchemy, and occasionally caused trouble.

Generally, I considered the Perenelle's Children to be nothing more than a vague nuisance, but tonight was not like other nights.

As soon as I saw them, I felt the buzzing. Familiar and intense, wrapping itself around my heart, as pressure grew in my stomach.

I kept running, watching as they approached Quinn. She'd been walking toward the store, but they interceded. They started to surround her, and now I was close enough that I could see the expression on her face—the shift from polite smile to resolute anger as she realized they were trouble.

A woman with a strip of bright pink hair stepped up to Quinn. Two ragged holes were cut through the back of her jacket to allow for small leathery wings, flapping impotently in the rain. When the winged Perenelle tried to push her back against the car, Quinn pushed back.

After that, everything happened quickly. They closed in around her, and even though it looked like she got in a few good hits, they were unrelenting as they tried to get her to the ground.

As I raced toward them, I pulled my asp baton from my bag, clenching it in my fist. They were so focused on attacking Quinn, they didn't even notice me. Not until I was striking them across their backs with all my might.

One of them collapsed in a puddle with a guttural scream, but another—the winged girl with the pink hair—whirled on me instantly. She hit me hard, her fist colliding with my jaw enough that I heard it crack, and I stumbled backward.

The Valkyrie in me had taken over, so I didn't feel the hit, or at least not the pain. But I tasted the blood coming from the corner of my mouth, and Winged Girl threw her head back and laughed, revealing the few sharp teeth she had left in her mouth.

On any other day, the baton would've been enough. Quinn and I shouldn't have had any problem taking on the Perenelle's Children. But Oona was right—the world had gone mad, and in a world of violent delights, only more violence would be the answer.

I took out my machete, holding it in my right hand while I kept the baton in my left, and I spun the weapons around. It was a cheap trick that I'd learned at Ravenswood, meant to intimidate, but Winged Girl did not look intimidated.

She ran at me, so I swung the machete. She lifted up her arm to block it, and the blade easily slid through the flesh and fabric, getting stuck in her bone.

"What is wrong with you?" I asked.

Once again, she only laughed at me. "Don't you know? You don't have the power anymore. *We* do."

"The fuck you do," I growled and yanked the machete out of her arm before kicking her legs out from under her.

She fell to the ground, and before I had a chance to do anything else, one of her comrades had jumped on my back. He wrapped his arm around my neck, attempting to strangle me, so I jerked my head back to headbutt him.

He didn't let go, and Winged Girl had gotten back to her feet, so I was left warding her off while trying not to be knocked unconscious. I couldn't see how Quinn was doing or really anything else, because I had to focus entirely on whoever was on my back and Winged Girl.

It didn't hurt, I couldn't feel much of anything, but my vision started to feel blotchy. I knew I was gasping for air, but I would keep fighting as long as I could. I didn't have a choice.

SIXTY

◆

Suddenly there was a loud, low sound—like a bass drop mixed with sonar—and a rush of air. It was powerful enough that we all went flying backward, skidding so far on the concrete that we almost landed in the canal.

When I looked up, there stood Fufluns Dillinger—the pudgy, balding immortal who owned the corner market. In his hands he held a stocky black gun with a clear parabolic dish at the end of the muzzle, and based on the sound waves that hit us I guessed it was a very powerful USW—an ultrasonic weapon.

"Don't make me shoot you again!" he warned the Perenelle's Children as they slowly got to their feet.

They looked at him warily, but apparently even they were no match for USWs, so they slunk off into the night. Quinn was standing up, leaning back against her now badly dented car. Blood dripped down her temple, but she was alive and she looked okay.

"Malin?" Fufluns asked, peering down at me as I stood up. "Is that you?"

"Yeah." I cleared my throat. "Yeah, it's me."

"Why don't you come in and get cleaned up?" Fufluns stepped back, aiming the USW more toward the sky than at us, and motioned toward the store. "It's not safe out here."

I looked over at Quinn, who appeared stunningly badass. Her silvery hair disheveled from the fight, green eyes still glowing with fierce intensity. The rain had soaked through her gray long-sleeved shirt, so it clung to her skin. But it was the way she stood—tall, strong, confident—even after getting the shit kicked out of her that was what amazed me the most.

She nodded at Fufluns, almost reluctantly, then said, "If we can't handle the riffraff out here, we won't make it through whatever is going on downtown."

"But Quinn—" I tried to argue, but she turned and followed Fufluns back to the store.

"Let's go inside and talk about it," she said over her shoulder. "We don't need to make this poor man stand out in the rain any longer."

Once we were inside, Fufluns locked the front door before pulling down a metal shutter, sealing off the outside. Quinn and I must've looked a little put off by that because he immediately said, "This is not to keep you in. It's to keep everyone else out. You can go whenever you wish, although I would suggest that you not walk."

"No, I won't be walking anywhere tonight," I said, casting a regretful look out the storefront window.

Even though he was a big man—taller than me and with a big, round belly—his clothes were always a little too big. He reminded me of a slacker, like an overgrown college kid or one of the party gods, who appeared to be about in his forties. According to Oona, he refused to work morning shifts, he had the habit of closing the store when he felt like it, and his books were a mess.

Once I asked him how he got into a business like this, and he shrugged. "The economy did strange things to everybody, and sometimes you gotta do what you gotta do."

"Where is Oona?" Fufluns asked, pulling up his loose-fitting leisure pants.

"She's at home," I said.

"Of course. She is too smart to be out in this." He leaned closer to me and lowered his voice, even though the store was empty except for us. "I don't mean to pry, but she is my best worker, and I was wondering, has she . . . has she gotten done the important work she had to do?"

Before taking off with me a week and a half before to chase after Tamerlane Fayette, Oona had called Fufluns and asked for a leave of absence, citing important matters that she needed to tend to. When we'd stopped in to get a charger yesterday, he'd interrogated her about when she would return, but since she was his best employee, he'd probably keep asking every time he saw one of us.

"Soon." I swallowed. "I hope."

While we'd been talking, Quinn had slowly been drifting to the back of the store. Most of the inventory were basic food and home goods—albeit at jacked-up prices—but several shelves in the back were reserved for apothecary and medicine. There were a few items that Oona assured me actually worked, but mostly they were overpriced knockoff crystals, amulets, and various herbs.

Quinn was crouched down, picking out a salve to treat her scrapes and bruises, when Fufluns waved his hands at her.

"No, no, don't use that. It's crap." Fufluns jerked his thumb toward his office at the back of the store. "Let me grab the good stuff out of the first-aid kit. I'll be right back."

Quinn put the salve down and straightened up. With Fufluns gone, she gave me her this-is-very-serious look. "You're going to call Samael and tell him we can't do it." She waited a beat before adding, "Right?" But it was never really a question.

"Yeah. I don't have a choice." I shifted uneasily as she stared me down. "Sorry about getting you dragged into this."

"No, don't be," she said with a softened tone. "I told you that I wanted to help, and I meant it."

The adrenaline and Valkyrie rush were starting to wear off, and I could feel the aches and pains seeping into my muscles and bones. The Perenelle's Children definitely knew how to fight. So now I was sore, cold, and terrified of how to act around Quinn.

"How have you been?" I asked, almost blurting it out like some secret I'd been dying to tell. "We haven't really talked since we got back to the city."

She lowered her gaze, and I swear I saw her cheeks flush pink for a second. "I've been as good as I can be, given the state of everything."

"Have you had any work?" I asked. I hadn't but there were about a hundred reasons why I wouldn't be getting work anytime soon, so I didn't know what if any assignments were going out at a normal rate for everyone else.

"Nope." She shook her head, but she looked totally nonplussed. "I haven't even talked to Samael since I last saw him with you."

"Well, I imagine he has his hands full right now," I said lamely, so I wouldn't have to stand with Quinn in an awkward silence.

Fufluns returned in the nick of time, carrying a great big canister of a waxy substance, and the sheer size of it made me wonder how often Fufluns got hurt and what exactly was going in his first-aid kit.

"Here, this is the good stuff." He held it out to Quinn, who tentatively took it from him. "Slather that all over anything that hurts you, and you'll be right as rain," he directed vaguely as he stepped back toward his office. "I'm watching the TV in my back office. Someone stole a police car downtown, and they have the chase on NorNewsNow. You can come watch it with me if you want."

"We're okay, thanks," I said to his retreating figure.

"What do you think?" Quinn was talking to me, but she was looking at the canister and wrinkling her nose.

The bright green label on the side called it *Manna of the Gods* but the asterisk next to it explicitly stated they were in no way associated with the real gods, Vanir or otherwise.

"I know that Fufluns wouldn't have given this to us if he didn't really believe it worked," I said with a shrug. "He really loves Oona."

That must've convinced her—probably because everybody loved Oona—and she pulled off the lid and put a big dab of it on her finger. It reminded me of a dollop of whipped cream, but if whipped cream were made from melted candle wax. "Here goes nothing."

As she carefully slathered the salve onto a nasty scrape on her arm, I felt compelled to say something, anything, in a vain attempt to alleviate the tension between us and the guilt I felt about being around her. Not just because of things I'd done or hadn't done, but even how I still felt about her now.

That's how I found myself saying, "I'm happy. I mean, I'm happy that you're good, relatively speaking."

"Thanks." She looked up at me uncertainly. "I hope you are doing well also?"

"No, I . . ." I rubbed the back of my neck, acutely aware of how awkward and random I was sounding. "I've been wanting to talk to you since . . ." I paused and started over. "When we were in Belize, you said some things—"

"We don't have to talk about it," she said, talking over me. "You've made yourself perfectly clear."

"I don't think I have," I persisted. "It's hard for me to say how I feel sometimes."

"Oh, believe me, I know." She'd been focusing on putting the healing salve on her wounds, but she stopped now to look up at me.

"I'm being honest with you here," I said. "Can you cut me some slack?"

"Honest?" Her crooked smile deepened, turning bitter at the edges. "You've always been honest with me. It's yourself that you lied to."

I lowered my eyes and chewed the inside of my cheek, trying to keep myself from reacting the way I wanted to. Not that I even really knew how I wanted to react. With tears? With anger? With acceptance?

She stepped closer to me, and I refused to look up, so I stared down at her wet boots on the dirty floor.

"Malin, we don't need to go over this again," she said gently. "I understand who you are, and I always did. I asked too much of you, and I knew it, but I wanted it so badly I thought maybe I could will it into existence. But that's my fault. You told me who you were."

"Shit, Quinn." I turned away from her, barely able to hold back the tears that stung at my eyes.

"No, Malin, it's not like that." She rushed to correct herself and put her hand on my shoulder so I'd look at her. "I'm saying I didn't listen to you. You've got some hang-ups, but they were right there on display."

She swallowed hard before continuing. "I thought that if I tried hard enough, we could plow right through them to some magical happy land." Quinn shook her head sadly. "But that's not how life works. You put those walls up, and you have to be the one to take them down. I can't do it for you."

I struggled to keep it together, but I finally managed to say, "I'm sorry it took me too long to figure that out."

"Me, too." She dropped her hand and went back to the Manna, turning away and giving me a moment of privacy.

I blinked hard a few times and wiped at my eyes with the palm of my hand.

"You were my first love," I said to her back, my words loud because I had to force them out. I had to fight to say them. "I wanted you to know that."

She didn't say anything at first. She stood with her back to me, her shoulders slightly sagging. When she finally did look back, tears had formed in her eyes.

"I didn't know that," she said softly, with a sad crooked smile. "But if you keep letting people in, I know I won't be your last." Then she turned and walked away. "If you'll excuse me, I have to run to the bathroom."

SIXTY-ONE

—◆—

hile Quinn was in the bathroom, I called Samael to let him know that I wouldn't be able to make it. He understood, as he hadn't realized how batshit everything had gone downtown until after he texted me. I happened to let it slip that I was with Quinn, so he told me to take her back to my place and wait for him to contact me.

"I'll figure out a way to meet up with you," he promised me.

"Why can't you tell me what's going on over the phone?" I asked. "I mean, it's important."

He was silent for a moment, then said, "I'll see you later tonight."

And he hung up the phone.

That's how I ended up back at my apartment, sitting awkwardly at one end of the couch while my ex-girlfriend sat on the other, with my sorta-boyfriend passed out in the next room and my best friend obsessively watching the news. Thankfully, Bowie was more than happy to be a buffer between us, spreading out until he was kicking me with his back feet.

Ellery Park—sitting behind the news desk and speaking in her calm, careful tones—informed us the rioting and looting downtown had been contained, with many of the assailants arrested and only a few injuries reported. Still, she warned us all to stay inside until we were given the all-clear by the National Guard.

Finally, when I couldn't handle another pundit telling us all to keep calm and carry on, my phone rang.

"It's him," I announced when I saw Samael's name flash across the screen, and Oona hurried to turn down the TV as I answered.

"Where are you?" Samael asked before I even had a chance to say hello.

"I'm in my apartment." I stood up, pacing the room as I spoke.

"You still live in the Tannhauser Towers, right?"

"Um, yeah, I do." I went over to the window and looked out, half expecting to see Samael somehow magically waiting for me outside, but it was only rain and adverts and a handful of pedestrians. "I'm in the first tower on the north side of Maneto Canal."

"Excellent," he replied. "Can you get to the roof?"

"What?"

"Can you get up to the roof?" he repeated, more slowly this time.

"The roof? Maybe? I've never tried. Why?"

"Get up there, if you can," Samael said. "I'll meet you up there in twenty minutes."

"What? How are you getting there?"

"Twenty minutes, Malin." That was all he said, and then he hung up.

"Samael *really* needs to work on his phone etiquette," I muttered.

I turned back around to find Quinn and Oona hovering right behind me, and they immediately pounced on me with a series of rapid-fire questions. Since neither waited for the other to stop talking before jumping in, I could hardly understand either of them.

Once their inquisition finally ceased, I was able to tell them what little I knew. Quinn insisted on going up to the roof with me, but Oona was okay with staying behind, in case Asher woke up and needed something.

We took the fire stairs up to the roof, so it really wasn't hard to do. Except there were a lot more stairs than I would've thought, and both

Quinn and I were already tired and sore from our scuffle with the Perenelle's Children.

Quinn leaned back against the door at the top, resting. I walked around the roof, checking behind heating stacks and water tanks, in case Samael beat us here somehow.

It was windy on top of the building, but honestly, not as bad as I had feared given the recent storms. The rain had mostly died down, but now it was icy little drizzles that felt like frozen shards of glass stinging my exposed skin.

I stood at the edge of the building, staring down at the city that surrounded us, and I caught a glimpse of something flying between the buildings. At first I thought it might be Muninn, Odin's massive raven that had been following me around.

But it wasn't a bird. It was a woman with large feathered wings, and she was carrying something in her arms. As they came closer, soaring around the building as they gained altitude, I realized that it was Valeska, carrying Samael.

"Holy shit!" I pointed at them. "There they are!"

"*They?*" Quinn asked as she rushed over to join me, and she gasped when she saw them. "Valeska!"

Within a few minutes, Valeska was carefully setting Samael down on the roof, and then she landed beside him. She was a little out of breath, but she held the same cool, vaguely bored expression she had every time I saw her. She nodded hello, and she might have said more but then Quinn intervened.

"Do you have a death wish or something?" Quinn said.

"It's no big deal. I've done that kinda thing plenty of times," Valeska replied nonchalantly. "I'm much stronger than I look."

"I know." Quinn softened and looked at her with soft, dewy eyes—the same eyes she used to give me when we first started dating. "Be careful."

I didn't need to see that—even if I was happy for them, it was still tied up in a painful knot of jealousy—so I turned my attention to Samael.

His cheeks were flushed from the cold air and perhaps the fear, and his normally boyish aquamarine eyes had a new intensity. He popped the collar on his black peacoat to block out some of the wind.

Valeska noticed and moved behind us, spreading her wings wide to help block the wind. Quinn stood the closest to her, almost huddled up against her, with a wide stance, so Valeska could lean on her for support against the blustering gusts.

"What's so important that you had to risk your life to tell me?" I asked.

"That was honestly quite a bit more terrifying than I imagined," he admitted as he raked his fingers through his tangles of hair.

"Samael." I folded my arms over my chest. "What's going on?"

"I know this was a bit of a dramatic way to go about it, but this is safer than meeting down at the Riks." He shook his head. "There might not be anyone I can trust."

"What? What's going on?"

"The walls have ears, I suspect." He scowled. "I know for certain they've tapped all our phones. I don't know what exactly is going on, but they're definitely paranoid about something."

"Everyone is paranoid?" I echoed in disbelief.

"Right. Because Odin's still missing." He gestured vaguely at the air, as if Odin had just disappeared into the ether. "So they're all on lockdown."

"Is that what you came to tell me? That Odin is gone?" I asked.

He shoved his hands deep into his pockets and hunched over. "Not exactly. I wanted to ask you if you've seen him or talked to him."

"No. I haven't even seen his ravens." It had been before I went to Kurnugia that I'd last heard anything from Odin. "I would've told you."

He smiled grimly at me. "I had to ask."

"Why did you want me here for that?" Quinn asked as her silver tangles of hair whipped around her face. "You know I don't know where Odin is, either."

"The other item is more of a personal nature," Samael said. "I know that things have been intense lately, so it's hard to focus on any of the mundane bureaucracies. But it's been over two weeks since Marlow passed, and if you want any say on what they put out about her in the official Hall of Records, it's important that you get the paperwork all filled out as soon as you have the chance."

The Hall of Records was a long corridor with floor-to-ceiling shelves lining either side, all of them filled with books on the entire history of the Valkyries. Every Valkyrie born had a notation about her—name, birth date, death date, notable ancestors on father's side, descendants, the years worked and who the Valkyrie had slain, and any significant life events.

My mother would be included whether I filled out the paperwork or not, but without input from me, administrative strangers working for the Riks would be the ones deciding what her footnote in history would say. Would they call her a traitor? An unstable monster? Or leave it all blank, so no one would ever have a clue of the complexities of my mother?

"The paperwork can be a bit trying, and ordinarily I would go through it with you, but my hands are full with so many other things," Samael explained. "So I thought Quinn could help you, since she's done this all before."

"Quinn's made a report for the Hall of Records?" I looked from one of them to the other, but Quinn lowered her eyes when my bewildered gaze landed on her.

"Yes," Samael said, and now it was his turn to look confused. "When her mother died."

"What?" I asked, and glanced over to see that Valeska appeared nearly as shocked as I did, which meant that she most likely hadn't known, either. "Your mother is dead? When?"

"I'm sorry." Samael gave Quinn an apologetic smile. "I assumed that Malin knew."

"Eleven years ago," she said quietly.

"*Eleven* years ago?" I was practically yelling in my incredulity. "We were together for six months! How could you never tell me that? How could it possibly never have occurred to you to mention that?"

Quinn had avoided talking about her family as much as possible, and all she'd ever said about her mother was that they hadn't talked in a long time. True enough, I guess, but still a very hefty lie by omission.

"It obviously occurred to me. I just didn't want to." Her lips twisted into a scowl that vacillated between sheepish remorse and indignation. "When my mom died I was only eight years old, and it was this nightmare circus. She was killed by the widower of an immortal she'd returned. He was so angry that she took his wife away from him, he decided to take my mom away from everybody. And as if that wasn't bad enough, then the media got ahold of it."

She hadn't needed to tell me that last part. As soon as she mentioned the widower, I knew exactly who it was. The news had obsessively reported it, and I had become terrified that the same thing would happen to Marlow. But no matter how much I cried or begged her to stay home, she refused to let fear cause her to stop working, and she never missed a day.

"For a long time after, that was the thing that everybody knew about me," Quinn explained. "Other kids at school made fun of me or avoided me. Adults fawned over me and asked me inappropriate questions, like what her body looked like after she died.

"And I didn't want her death to define me anymore," Quinn went on. "I didn't want to spend another minute dissecting my mother's death with intrusive strangers. So finally, as I got older and time passed, people stopped making the connection, and then I stopped telling them.

"Whenever anybody asked me about my family, I always gave vague answers," she said. "And when you and I met, I didn't know that we would . . . I didn't realize that things would get serious, so I lied when I met you, and then I never figured out a good way to correct that. I planned on it, someday, but . . . that day never happened."

I swallowed hard and looked away from her. "I guess it's good to know that I wasn't the only one emotionally closed off during our relationship."

SIXTY-TWO

———◆———

"How are you really doing?" Samael looked at me thoughtfully as we stood on the roof with the wind howling around us.

We'd had a few more awkward minutes of conversation with Quinn and Valeska before the two of them stepped away to say goodbye, Valeska spreading her wings to use as a shield from the wind and from prying eyes. Samael and I were sheltering from the wind near a smokestack.

I shrugged. "I'm fine. As fine as anyone could be, given the circumstances."

"That's understandable."

"I went to Marlow's apartment to start going through her things," I said.

"Oh." His eyes widened, and he cleared his throat. "Did you need help with that?"

"No," I said, then hurried to correct myself. "I mean, maybe. But that's not what I'm asking now. I was wondering if you knew that she was a prepper?"

Samael shook his head. "What's a prepper?"

"You know, someone who is overly obsessed with preparing for a disaster or—" I was going to say *end of the world* but I stopped myself. "Marlow had all kinds of weapons and a seriously ridiculous amount of lentils. Did you know about that or what she was preparing for?"

"No." He furrowed his brow, staring off in thought. "She never really invited me to her place, so I didn't know. She was a very private person."

"Yeah, that's putting it lightly," I muttered. "But she had four Valkyrie swords locked up in a safe."

"She had *four* swords?" he repeated. "That's . . . I mean, there's nothing wrong with owning swords. The Riks still makes swords, and some get lost or stolen and end up at the Avondmarkt."

"What could someone do with four Valkyrie swords?" I asked.

"I don't know." He looked as baffled as I felt. "They don't work unless you're a Valkyrie, and a Valkyrie can only imprint on one sword at a time. So there really isn't a use for them."

Samael hadn't told me anything that I didn't already know, but I'd asked him because his experience and knowledge were so much more vast than mine. Vaster than Marlow's, even. Which meant that if he thought the swords were useless, they probably were, and Marlow would've known that too.

"She did have a lot of weapons," I said, striving to make sense of what my mother could have been thinking. "Maybe she thought a few more swords wouldn't hurt."

"Was there anything else that you found in her apartment?" Samael asked.

I debated not telling him. I considered keeping it to myself, so he'd never have to know, and if it was just between him and my mom, I would have. But with everything that was going on, I had to give Samael all the info I could.

"I found a burner phone," I said carefully. "She was seeing someone."

He frowned, a deep scowl that looked unnatural on his face, but he didn't appear surprised. "I thought she might be. The last few months, she'd been distant. Even by Marlow's standards." He paused before asking, "Do you know who it was?"

"Azarias Göll."

"That sounds a bit familiar. Let me check." He pulled his small tablet out of his jacket pocket and hurriedly tapped away at the screen, all the while muttering to himself. "Hopefully this won't raise any red flags. They're probably watching my search history."

"Who is *they*?" I asked, since he still hadn't given me a clear explanation about any of this. "Are you talking about Ereshkigal?"

"No." He shook his head. "Obviously, she probably has something to do with everything, but I don't know how. She's still trapped in Kurnugia, but that means there have to be people—maybe mortals or immortals or both—working for her and doing her bidding here on earth."

"You don't have any ideas?" I asked.

"I think I found him," Samael said, ignoring my question, and he tilted his screen so that I could have a look.

Sure enough, it was the guy I'd met at Sup D'yavola, scowling in a mug shot.

"Yeah, that's him."

Samael looked sharply at me. "You met him?"

"Yeah, but he didn't say much." I tried to brush this off, since I really didn't have much of note to tell him, but he tilted the tablet away from me, so I'd look up at him. "He said he dated Marlow, but she didn't tell him anything. He didn't seem to know that much about her at all, except that she loved to keep her secrets."

"That's not why I'm upset, Malin," he said. "Everything is very dangerous right now. You've got to be careful."

"I am!" I insisted, but even I wasn't sure if that was true.

He went back to scrolling through his tablet for any info on Azarias. "There isn't much here. Some petty crime. There might be more, but since he's a mortal Cambion, the Evig Riksdag doesn't keep very many records that would relate to him.

"The only thing that is interesting is that his father is a rather notable demon," Samael said. "He's the right-hand man for Velnias. But the sins of the father don't always carry to the son."

"But sometimes they do," I said.

The sky suddenly lit up as a bolt of lightning danced across it, zig-zagging through the dark clouds around us. Before the lightning had even faded, thunder clapped, and the wind picked up.

"I think the rain is coming again." Samael put his tablet away and glanced over at Valeska, who was still huddled with Quinn. "We should go before it gets worse."

"You know, just because Valeska flew you here, over all the chaos downtown, doesn't mean that you had to land on the roof. She could've dropped you at the front door," I pointed out.

"I know, but a lot of these places have security cameras, and I know there's CCTV on the streetlights along the canals."

"You really think someone is watching you that closely or that they'd care that you're visiting me?" I asked dubiously.

"Maybe, maybe not." He shook his head. "I honestly don't know anymore. What's happening at the Riks is unlike anything I've ever seen. All of the Eralim are being kept in the dark. No new missions are going out.

"And before you think, *Oh it's only been a few days*, it adds up *very* quickly," he went on. I knew everything that he was saying, but based on the frantic, irritated tone to his voice, he needed to vent.

"Right now, to keep the balance, we're supposed to ensure that point-zero-one percent of the immortals on the planet die *every day*!" Samael explained. "Whether that be the rare case of suicide or murder or we have to send a Valkyrie in to do it, it needs to be done. When you consider there are over six billion immortals walking on the earth right now, that's a hell of a lot of people in just three days that didn't die."

His expression grew more grave. "Now picture what it will look like in a week. Or a month. This is going to be a population crisis of epic proportions."

"That's why Odin's gone."

"Well, obviously that is the line of thinking," he said. "Immortals got sick of dying."

"Maybe it's more than that," I said, thinking of all the extra immortals that were still on earth, the ones who should've been returned to Kurnugia. "What could they do with all those extra bodies?"

With all those extra immortals still on earth, they could form an army large enough to wipe out humanity or turn us into slaves. I stared out at the city. Each of the lights shining in the windows belonged to someone. A human who could be killed, or an immortal who could be a soldier. Right now we were all neighbors. We were friends. But for how much longer?

"If they're not afraid to go after a Vanir god like Odin, I don't know how they can be stopped," I said.

"*Everything* can be stopped," Samael insisted emphatically. "Even death."

I smiled wanly up at him. "That's the problem, isn't it?"

SIXTY-THREE

After Samael left with Valeska, Quinn headed out as well, insisting that it was safe enough for her to drive the short distance to her place. Oona was waiting up for me, and I briefed her as quickly as I could, since we were both exhausted.

When I went into my bedroom, Asher was still asleep, but he woke up long enough to tell me that he was sorry about everything. He wrapped his arms around me, pulling me close to him, and that was more than enough for me.

In the morning, Asher insisted that he was feeling better, and while I believed him, I was still determined to figure out what was going on with him. Oona had been unable to find anything particular helpful in her own research, so she suggested we go visit her sorceress cousin Minerva Warren.

Asher wanted to come with us, but we managed to convince him to stay behind. I told him that I wanted to take my luft, since it was easier to get around in, and that only seated two. But the truth was that I wanted to be able to talk about everything with Oona and Minerva, without worrying about Asher or his reactions.

Especially if things got difficult and personal.

We waited until midmorning, when the news assured us it was safe to venture out, though they warned us to still use caution. But Minerva didn't live that far away. She was only over in Edison Park, a few blocks away from where Oona and I had grown up.

In this neighborhood, a lot of the brownstones were nearly identical, and the one Minerva lived in looked just like Marlow's, except the bricks had more of a reddish hue.

I had visited her with Oona a few times before, and she had a quaint little basement apartment—or at least as quaint as basement apartments go. Her building was a bit nicer than Marlow's, since we had to be buzzed in, and she raced up the steps from the basement to greet us.

"I'm so glad you're here!" she squealed as she hugged Oona, and even though she didn't know me that well, she hugged me, too. "The circumstances are terrible, I know, but I'm always so glad when you can visit."

"Yeah, me, too," Oona agreed with her easy smile.

Minerva was in her early thirties, with tightly coiled curls of dark auburn hair. Just like Oona, her skin was creamy brown and her eyes were the color of black walnut. There were a few differences between them, Minerva being taller, her limbs longer, and her lips thinner. She looked almost as if someone had taken Oona and stretched her out.

When I'd first met Minerva, back when we were kids, Oona had told me she was a sorceress, and I'd expected her to wear long cloaks or velvet gowns. But Minerva was not that kind of sorceress. Today she was wearing yoga pants with an old band T-shirt for Eden's Eternity.

"Ignore the mess," Minerva told us as we followed her down to her apartment. "I've been working on a few things."

As soon as she opened the door, the scent of sage and old books wafted out. Her place smelled exactly like Oona's grimoire.

The door opened into a small living room styled in a bohemian/ thrift store kinda way that seemed to fit college students, nomads, or anyone on a tight budget. The back wall was exposed brick, with two small windows with a view of the alley. Not that I could see much of that past the potted plants that decorated the sill.

An overflowing bookshelf took up the entire wall that separated the living room from the kitchen. There was a long narrow bar made of reclaimed wood, and a wrought-iron trestle covered with all sorts of vials and herbs and pestles and mortars.

Several blankets were draped across an overstuffed couch, and two fat merle-colored rats were curled up sleeping at one end of it. They each had little pink collars with their names on them, and though I could never keep straight which one was which, their names were Victoria and Gussina, or Vicky and Gussy for short.

"So, you're here because something strange has been going on with your boyfriend?" Minerva asked.

"Yeah. He's been shaking, like he's having seizures, and he's had a lot of nightmares."

"And this all started after you came back from the underworld?" she asked.

Oona had already filled her in on most of our adventures, even before she called Minerva this morning to ask for her help. Oona had often told me that was the biggest difference between the Krigares and the Warrens: we liked our secrets, while they shared everything.

"Yeah." I nodded.

She pursed her lips. "And that's exactly why you shouldn't go down to the underworld."

"You know I wouldn't have gone if I didn't think we had to," Oona said in that irritable way she had when she'd already argued about something a dozen times.

"Anyway," Minevera said with a pained smile. "Why don't you two make yourself comfortable? I made some lavender iced tea, so I'll go pour us a few glasses, and then we can sit and get to the bottom of what's happening with your boyfriend."

Oona offered to help her, leaving me alone in the living room to peruse Minerva's cluttered space on my own. Most of her stuff appeared to be connected to her work in thaumaturgy, and there were several implements that I recognized from Oona's kit. Other than that, there were some rat toys, yarn and needles for knitting, and a few framed pictures on the wall.

The pictures were all of Minerva's family, and I lingered on one that showed Minerva as a young teenager, her very pregnant mother, Oya, and her mother's sister, Rhona. All three smiling, standing together on a beach with their arms wrapped around one another. That was the only family picture of all of them, Minerva had explained on a previous visit.

Truth was that Minerva wasn't really Oona's cousin—she was her half sister. Their mother, Oya, had died in childbirth with Oona, and when her dad very quickly became overwhelmed, Rhona decided to adopt her sister's child. Minerva, meanwhile, had already gone to live with their grandmother.

Oona had always known this, or at least she had as long as I'd known her. But it wasn't something she thought about a lot. Rhona had raised and loved her, so Rhona was her mom. She was sad that she'd never gotten to meet Oya, but Minerva and Rhona told her stories about her. Sometimes that's the best you got in life.

I sat down on the couch, and one of the rats lifted its head long enough to blink at me before curling back up to sleep. A minute later, Minerva returned and set two mason jars of pale purple tea on the table. She grabbed a small pad of paper and a pen, then sat down beside me. The way she sat, with her knees tilted toward me, pen posed in her hand, reminded me of a reporter looking for a big scoop.

"So, tell me everything," Minerva said.

"Um, okay." I glanced over at Oona, who was walking around the room, admiring Minerva's things while sipping her tea. "When we found Asher, he was at Zianna, but he'd only recently been rescued from She'ol. And he'd been tortured pretty bad there, so at first I thought his nightmares might be PTSD or something—"

Minerva held up her hand. "Wait, go back. I want you to be as detailed as possible. Any little detail might help. And start back at the beginning. How did he get there?"

So I started with how Asher had gotten dragged down by Gugalanna, how it took us five days to find him but it had felt like weeks to him, how he'd been held hostage and had been bled by Gugalanna and Abaddon. Asher insisted he didn't remember much about what they had said or done, but I told Minerva everything that he'd shared with me.

When I got to the part where I started describing his wounds—the slowly healing cuts slashed down either side of his torso and arms—Minerva's eyes widened.

"The marks on his chest, though, those were the worst part," I said.

"What marks on his chest?" Oona asked.

"They're not fully healed yet, so he's been wearing a bandage," I explained. "It's these two . . . marks or symbols or something. He told me that Abaddon had done it, and at that time he told Asher, 'No one else can have you.'"

"Can you draw them for me?" Minerva asked, handing me the pen and paper.

They were two simple marks, almost like cursive letters that had been left unfinished, so they were easy to replicate. Once I'd finished, Minerva took the page back, tilting it this way and that as she studied it.

"Do you recognize them?" Oona asked, peering over Minerva's shoulder.

"I can't say." She squinted at them. "They look familiar, but I don't know what they are."

She stared at them a moment longer. "I know I can figure it out, but I'll have to look through my books, which may take a little bit. Why don't we go on and see if there's anything you can tell me that would help?"

I told her everything else I knew, describing the nightmares and shaking that I'd witnessed, but nothing else really seemed to stand out. Minerva took careful notes, writing down everything I said so she could look back at it all later.

"Do you have anything of his?" Minerva asked. "I know it sounds silly, but sometimes it can help me get a read on him and what's happening."

"Oona said you might want something, so I brought this." I reached into my pocket and pulled out his Vörðr bracelet. "That's the only thing he brought into Kurnugia that he managed to get out."

"That should be *very* good, then," Minerva said as she carefully looked it over.

The bracelet itself was made of black paracord with a small metal plaque on one side, like a medical alert bracelet. But instead of allergies or conditions, it had the symbol of the Vörðr on it. Every member of the elite security squad got one.

"This symbol—the three horns and an eagle—that's for the Evig Riksdag guards, right?" Minerva asked, and I nodded. "Are the horns for you? For the original three Valkyries?"

"No, the horns are for Odin," I explained.

"There were nine Valkyries originally," Oona said. She scooped up the chubby rats so she could sit down beside me, then sat them back on her lap, where they were very happy to curl up with her. "I'm surprised you didn't know that."

"Oh, I probably learned it at some point," Minerva admitted. "But now that I deal more with alchemy and thaumaturgy than history, I forget a lot of those things."

In a singsong voice, Oona recited the poem we'd learned in grade school to help us memorize all the names of the original Valkyries:

> Nine Valkyries did Odin make
> And in the darkness he did take
> Blades of ice and dragon claw
> Summer sun and winter thaw
> To create the power and the might
> The maiden protectors of mortal plight
> Eir, Göndul, Hildr, Mist, Ölrún,
> Róta, Skögul, Thrúd, and Sigrún.

Minerva smiled and offered a few golf claps. "I am impressed."

"It's just a nursery rhyme," Oona demurred.

"As for this"—Minerva held up the bracelet—"I think it will be more than sufficient for me to be able to make you a protection potion for Asher, and maybe even a few for the two of you for whatever trouble you're going up against in the coming days."

I offered to help, but for the most part, Minerva and Oona had it covered. I handed them a few things when they asked, but mostly I watched them creating—passing ingredients between each other, flipping through books, sometimes speaking in Latin.

There was a strange beauty and fluidity to their movements, and the occasional puff of glittery smoke or fizzing brightly colored liquid only added to the magic. It was almost like a blend of ballet and science, of emotion and precision.

Not for the first time, I was amazed by Oona and her talent, and I couldn't be more grateful that she was my best friend.

SIXTY-FOUR

———◆———

Oona and I returned to our apartment a few hours later, carrying a few new elixirs and powders and balms. Asher was sitting on the couch, watching television with Bowie sprawled out beside him, and I felt this rush of relief and happiness. He looked over at me, smiling in his cautious way, as if he were waiting for something to come along and ruin it.

"You're still here." I hadn't even realized until we'd gotten back, but I'd been afraid that he'd be gone.

"Of course I am." He laughed. "Where would I have gone?"

"I don't know." I dropped my bag on the floor and went over and sat beside him. I wanted to feel him, touch him, know he was really here. "I . . . I don't know."

"Well, the good news is that we made all kinds of good stuff today." Oona set her bag on the table and pulled out the small vials and tubs she and Minerva had filled. "The bad news is that Minerva doesn't know what's wrong with you."

"Does she have any ideas?" Asher asked.

"She has more research to do, but hopefully she can call me tomorrow and let us know something," Oona said.

"Oona was really, really amazing today," I said, to which she rolled her eyes.

"This one right here is the most important one." Oona held out a round flat tub filled with a bubbly blue gel.

"What is it?" Asher asked as he took it from her.

"Salvari Balm," Oona explained. "It's like an antibiotic mixed with an antidemonic, so bacitracin with a serious edge. You need to put it all over your wounds twice daily, and make sure you really get it in there good. It'll be a little cold and it might sting, but it'll help your wounds heal faster, and it'll fight infections, both bacterial and supernatural."

"Should I . . . should I go put it on now?" he asked, looking at me and Oona.

"It won't hurt to get started," she said. "The rest of this stuff is more for offense than defense, but we can go over that later."

Asher thanked her, then headed off to the bathroom to lather up. I offered to help him, but he said he had it covered. There really wasn't much room in the bathroom, so I didn't push it.

Oona sat down on the far end of the couch and propped her feet up on an ottoman.

"Thanks again for helping me so much," I told her.

Oona shrugged it off the way she always did. "You know you can always count on me."

I settled back into the couch, absently petting Bowie and watching the movie Asher had left on. I didn't know what it was, but little blue men were chasing an orange cat around the house, and the cat seemed quite upset about it.

When the movie went to commercial, a news bulletin cut in, which caused Oona to groan and say, "What fresh hell is this?"

But instead of showing us a death count or telling us about a new terror out to get us, Ellery Park was out on location. She was more dressed up than I usually saw her behind the desk, with large sparkling earrings and her hair pulled back. Her black dress was fairly conservative, but she'd ditched the glasses.

It was hard to tell where she was exactly, because the street was so crowded I couldn't get a good look at any landmarks. Behind her seemed to be all types of mortals and immortals, dressed in flamboyant regalia. The good news was that everyone seemed to be laughing and having a good time, so I hoped that meant they weren't all about to be hit by an asteroid or some other ridiculous catastrophe.

"This is Ellery Park reporting live from downtown," she began, and I heard someone yell, *Whoo*, loudly in the background. "In light of recent events, many citizens are feeling scared and uneasy. Now someone thinks they have a solution.

"I'm outside the Red Raven right now, where a prominent member of the community is calling on everyone to come together," Ellery went on.

The camera panned out farther, so she could motion toward the shiny obsidian-black building that loomed behind, flanked by two red spotlights. The camera pulled back enough that I could see the man standing slightly off to her side, and that's when I leaned forward, sitting on the edge of my seat as I watched the news.

He was handsome, in that weathered, rugged look of a cowboy, with pale, almost ashen skin. His graying black hair had a purposeful messy quality to it, and his black dress shirt was tailored perfectly to his formidable frame.

I recognized him instantly as Velnias, the mobster demon.

"For many years, Velnias has been a major player, not just in the Aizsaule District, but throughout the country," she explained. "His close ties to the controversial Kurnugia Society are well documented, but he insists that his only goal has always been to have a fair, equal world for everyone. With me right now is the man himself to explain what he has in store."

"Thanks, Ellery," he said. "I've been a proud business owner in this fair city of ours for four decades. My goal when I created the Red Raven was to create a fun, safe place where everyone can have a good time.

"Over the years, that has tilted toward a very narrow group, and I'm ashamed to say that I didn't do more to welcome in the rest of you," he continued, sounding appropriately somber, with a touch of hope. After all, he'd had plenty of time to hone his political acumen.

"Tonight that all changes." He motioned with his hand, miming as if wiping a slate clean. "With all these disasters, violence, and social upheaval, I want us to remember that we are all brothers and sisters on this big blue rock of ours, and when we come together, we can overcome *anything*.

"With that in mind, I want to extend an invitation to every person in the city. The doors to the Red Raven are open to you tonight—and every night." He put his hands together, like he was about to pray, but then he linked them together and pointed at the camera with his index fingers. "We have some of the best security in the world, and I promise you that if you come here, no harm will come to you. You are safe within those four walls. The Red Raven has always and will always be a place for anybody who needs it."

He was pointing at the camera. Logically, I knew it was at the camera and he couldn't see me. But the way his eyes met the screen—the burnt orange color glistening in the light—it felt like he was looking right at *me*.

"There you have it," Ellery said with a bright smile. "The hottest—and safest—party on the planet is at the Red Raven."

"Mal, I know what you're thinking, but the answer is no," Oona said, already sensing the plans that were forming in my head.

"He says everybody," I reasoned. "We're all welcome there."

"He doesn't mean us," Oona argued.

Then, before the segment wrapped up, the camera closed in on Velnias again. And no matter what I should've known, I couldn't shake the feeling that he was talking to me personally.

"The doors are open from dusk until dawn every day," Velnias said. "I hope to see you there."

Oona clicked off the TV, probably so I wouldn't get any more ideas, but it was already too late.

"No, he does mean us," I insisted.

"Malin." Oona groaned and leaned her head back against the couch. "Why must you be this way?"

"No, hear me out." I pivoted to look at her better. "By Velnias's own admission, this is probably the safest that the Red Raven will ever be. That makes this the best time—and maybe the *only* time—I will be able to question him about what he knew about my mom and Azarias."

Oona scowled at me, her eyes narrowing as she tried to think of a way to change my mind, and eventually she gave up. "Fine. But I still think it's stupid."

SIXTY-FIVE

⸻ ◆ ⸻

The cab could only get us within three blocks of the Red Raven. A stream of potential clubgoers went by, following everyone else toward the flashing red lights that signified the entrance.

"This is ridiculous," Oona announced as she got out of the hover-taxi, careful not to get her chic minidress caught in the door. "There's no way we'll be able to get in."

"We got in once before. We can do it again," Asher reasoned, and then he looked back behind us in time to see a bus dropping off a whole gaggle of fallen-angels-cum-lingerie-models. "Although it is definitely going to be much harder."

"No, we can do this!" I insisted. "We all look hot, we're all bad-asses, and we're supposed to be here!"

Asher and Oona exchanged a look, which only succeeded in irritating me more. Back at the apartment, when it had been taking me a while to get ready, they'd already started teaming up on me, questioning my motives and the logistics and even my sanity (and they were only half kidding).

Damn the exquisitely made gown and my difficulty putting it on. It was a piece that Rhona had been commissioned to make for an opera, but when the show fell through, no one paid for the costumes, so I'd gotten it.

The floor-length gown was fitted snug across my hips and thighs, but flared out below. Silver thread weaved through the white mesh fabric, giving it a feminine chain-mail look. The look was particularly effective across my chest, where the dress plunged in a low V with only the silver thread crisscrossing over it.

"We're *supposed* to be here?" Asher asked.

"I told you back at home. I just *know* it." And I did. As much as I knew the earth was round and water was wet, I was supposed to be here.

"Neither one of us are doubting your beliefs," Oona said quickly, to soften things. "We just don't understand *how* you know."

"Neither do I!" I threw my hands up in exasperation. "But like I said before we left, you guys don't have to be here. You can go back home. I'll be fine."

"No, we're going with you," Asher said, with a finality that I hoped finally put his argument to rest.

We'd already had a big discussion, wherein we debated the pros and cons of both Asher and Oona (or either one of them) going with me. Asher insisted he'd felt fine all day, and if it was safe for me, it was safe for him. Oona's argument was basically the same as that, except she'd also brought a few thaumaturgy aides in her sequin clutch.

"Great. That's settled. Let's go." I turned and walked away before either of them could say more.

When we finally got close enough that we could see the Red Raven and the animated neon-red bird above the door, we were still a block away from the door, and we'd hit the end of the line.

"I am not trying to start an argument," Asher said carefully as we waited directly behind the throng of scantily clad Fallen. "But there's gotta be at least a thousand people ahead of us. I don't see how any of us are going to make it in."

"Fine," Oona said with a dramatic sigh. "I'll get us in."

She stepped out of line into the street. Traffic was at a total standstill, so walking between the vehicles was no trouble. Her plan was apparently to circumvent the line. I had no idea what would happen, but I trusted her, so I followed her into the street.

"No offense to you or your skills," Asher said to Oona as we weaved through the vehicles. "But if what you want to do is possible, why wouldn't anybody do it?"

"Uh-oh." I winced, knowing the can of worms that Asher had unintentionally opened.

"Everyone has this horrible misconception about thaumaturgy, and they think just anyone can do it!" She was nearly shouting as she walked, without looking back us. "That it's like baking, and all you have to do is follow the recipe. And yeah, some of alchemy is like that. But that's not what I do. Well, I mean, I do that sometimes, but that's not *all* I do."

She stopped short and whirled around so she could face Asher directly. "Magic—*real* magic—is near-impossible for the average person or immortal to do. There has to be something in you that connects to the metaphysical. Minerva says that her mother called it *ẹmí*—your life force.

"It's something you're either born with, or you're not," Oona elaborated. "There are a lot of kick-ass fighters out there, but they can't be a Valkyrie. I was born with an intuition so that I can do something the rest of you can't."

"Sorry, I didn't . . . I didn't realize," Asher said.

"It's fine. Most people don't," she said, but she sounded more exasperated than forgiving. "Compared to angels and dragons, a human that can cast a couple spells isn't that exciting, so people like me get overlooked a lot."

The line directly in front of the Red Raven spilled out into the street. The only things keeping the crowd from rushing in the front door were a dozen bouncers and a red velvet rope, and it seemed to be working—so far.

Oona stopped short, outside the edge of the crowd in the middle of the street, and opened up her clutch. She pulled a small blue tablet out of a mint tin, but the way she placed it delicately under her tongue was unlike how I'd ever seen anyone eat a mint.

She closed her eyes, and though I couldn't hear any words, I saw her lips moving rapidly as she recited an incantation. Since she'd dressed up this evening, she'd replaced her usual metal studs in her angel bites with diamonds that glinted red in the light from the Red Raven.

When she opened her eyes, I gasped and took a step back. I was used to seeing Oona doing magical things, but I still couldn't prepare myself for stuff like this.

Her irises had shifted from nearly black to an intense glowing iridescence. Her eyes weren't bright enough that they really gave off light, not like headlights, but they did have an electric quality to them, like they would be better suited in an android than in a petite sorceress sneaking into a club.

"Holy shit, Oona," I said.

She looked at me, blinking slowly over her new strange glowing eyes. "So I take it that it worked, then?"

Asher leaned forward to get a better look. "Can you see with those?"

"Yeah, but it won't last for long, so if we're gonna do this, we gotta do it now," she said.

She grabbed my hand, yanking me along with her, as she weaved into the throng of hopeful clubgoers demanding entrance. I barely had a chance to take Asher's hand, and I was relieved when I felt his strong grip.

In a rare unmerciful form, Oona charged into people and elbowed them out of the way until she made it to a hulking rock demon. Stony skin covered his entire muscular frame, and his yellow eyes were unsympathetic under his protruding brow.

"We need to get in," Oona declared as she stared up at him. He didn't say anything. He stared ahead with his arms folded over his chest. "Hey! Sir! I need to be in there."

Finally he looked down, glaring directly into Oona's eyes.

"You will let us in," Oona informed him. "We're needed in there, so you will let us pass, and you will not give us any trouble. You will instruct the others to do the same."

He exhaled through his nose, and he still didn't look happy. But he stepped back and, without saying anything, he lifted up the velvet rope so we could get by. The three of us hurried under his arm and into the club. Behind us, the others were protesting that they weren't being let in, but we ran on ahead.

SIXTY-SIX

The Red Raven had clearly latched onto the theme in its name and run with it. All the lights inside were dim red, and most of the accents were either black marble or feathered. Even the chandeliers in the front hall were made of black feathers.

The club itself was divided into multiple rooms surrounding a dance hall in the center, but the way the corridors weaved through the smaller offshoots—like the champagne room, an S&M dungeon, and a vampire-friendly blood bar—gave it an overwhelming labyrinthian feel.

"Where do we go from here?" Oona asked, and when she looked up at me, I could already see the light fading. The spell was wearing off.

The club was packed, all kinds of riffraff bumping into us as they squeezed by, and I knew that the dance floor would be the worst. That would be the last place someone like Velnias would want to be—surrounded by sweaty nobodies.

No, he would be above it all. Somewhere quieter, less crowded, where the elite immortals could rub elbows.

"We have to find a way into the VIP room," I decided.

"Where is that?" Oona asked.

"I don't know. We have to find somewhere they won't let us go."

I went on ahead, pushing through the crowd when I had to, with my eyes constantly scanning for any sign of important immortals or hints of where the more prestigious attendees might be hiding out.

As I walked, I ran my fingers along the cool stone surface of the walls. When my fingertips stumbled upon a subtle seam in the smooth exterior, I stopped short. The seam ran up and around, making a rectangular shape.

It was a door.

I slammed into it with all my might, not stopping even when Oona demanded to know what I was doing. But the door gave much easier than I'd thought, and I tumbled forward into a closet. As I fell on the floor, bottles of cleaning supplies and a mop fell down around me.

"Mal, what are you doing?" Oona repeated as she helped me to my feet and out of the closet.

"I don't know. Secret doors usually lead to secret offices or something," I muttered.

Oona closed the door behind me, as best as she could, considering it didn't have a handle. "We need to come up with a better plan. Right now all we're doing is drawing attention to ourselves."

"Shit." Asher's arm was suddenly on my waist, and he leaned over to whisper in my ear, "We gotta go."

"What? Why?" I asked, but I saw as soon as I looked back over my shoulder.

He was tall enough that he was head and shoulders above most of the other attendees, and the way his long sheet of white-blond hair glowed under the red lights made him a beacon. It was Arawn, a powerful underworld demon who had sicced one of Velnias's top bodyguards after us the last time Asher and I had come to the Red Raven.

And he was looking right at me.

Asher's arm was still around me, attempting to steer me away from Arawn, but I didn't budge.

"What are you doing?" Asher asked, his voice a hushed panic.

"Arawn will know where Velnias is," I said.

"Yeah, and he'll probably send another crazed Pischacha after us," Asher argued. "We don't have time to deal with that."

I looked back at Asher, so he could see how serious I was. "He might be the only shot I have at finding Velnias. I have to risk it."

He let out an exasperated sigh, but he didn't try to stop me as I slipped out from his arm.

Arawn turned away, walking in the opposite direction, and I chased after him. The crowd was fighting me, pushing back against me so I was like a salmon going upstream, but I kept my gaze locked on the glow of his hair.

Behind me I could faintly hear Asher and Oona calling for me, but I didn't want to slow down. I couldn't lose Arawn.

I finally made it so I was almost close enough to touch him, but I got stuck between a squawking Aswang and a reptilian demon. When I finally squeezed through, I dashed ahead, only to slam right into a colossal ogre.

When I tried to go around him, he put his big meaty hand on my shoulder. I'd barely glanced at him before, but now that I really appraised him and took in his uniform—black T-shirt, black jeans, earpiece glowing in his ear—I realized that he was security.

"Velnias wants to see you," he said in a rumbling monotone.

SIXTY-SEVEN

———◆———

Velnias's office wasn't exactly as I had pictured it, but it was very close.

The security guard had rounded up Asher and Oona before taking us to the elevator, and the four of us had ridden up to Velnias's office in a tense silence. The elevator opened right into his office, where he sat behind the desk.

It was a large space, but many of the style choices made it feel very cave-like. The back wall and the ceiling were made of this strange red stone that appeared to be left in its natural shape in one solid chunk. It was coarse and bumpy, and curved over us like a wave.

The furniture was sparse, but all of it appeared comfortable and expensive: black leather chairs, a bar made of marble, a desk of dark mahogany. Across from the desk was a massive window that gave a view of the main dance floor and the bar fifty feet below.

What I was most surprised about in Velnias's office was the big-game-hunter décor. I'd expected him to have more of a cosmopolitan style, but there were zebra-skin rugs on the floor and heads mounted on the wall. Most of them were animals, like the tamanduá chifres, ennedi tiger, and thunderbird, all carefully labeled with their genus and species. But there was one in particular that stopped my heart cold.

Right above Velnias's desk was a humanoid head. Throbbing veins bulged under his dark skin, with the one in the center of his forehead looking like it was about to burst. His blood-red eyes stared straight open, and his mouth was open to show off his rows of pointed teeth.

The plaque underneath read:

Cormac Kaur
Pischacha

He had worked for Velnias. He'd been the one who grabbed Asher and me the last time we were at the Red Raven. He had meant to kill us, I think, but I had managed to get the best of him, and I got him to give up a name that led us to find Tamerlane Fayette.

Cormac was a flesh-eating demon, so I didn't feel too bad about his death, but I couldn't help but wonder if Velnias had killed him as a direct result of my actions.

"Welcome, welcome, have a seat!" Velnias spread his arms wide, then motioned to the three chairs across the desk from him.

The ogre that had brought us up here waited back by the elevator door. A three-headed demon dog with leathery black skin lay sleeping near the desk, but I was certain that it would wake up instantly if Velnias directed it to attack us. So despite Velnias's cheery tone, I knew it was best that we all comply as much as we could.

"Can I get you anything to drink?" Velnias offered as we sat down.

"We're okay," I said, answering for all of us because I didn't trust anything that he would give us to drink.

"Thank you," Oona added, evidence that she was pathologically polite.

"Of course. Let me know if you change your mind. I am many things, but a gracious host is the one I take the most pride in." He leaned back in his chair. "Well, not the most. I have a few other hobbies that I take quite seriously."

As I glanced around at all the taxidermy, my stomach rolled in revulsion. "Yeah, I can tell."

"So, we should probably get the introductions out of the way. I am Velnias, owner of this establishment and head of the Kurnugia Society." Velnias then pointed to me. "And you are Malin Krigare, Valkyrie-in-training, daughter of Marlow, and general troublemaker." He wagged his finger between Oona and Asher. "The other two I'm less familiar with."

"Oona Warren. I'm her friend." She kept it short, deliberately leaving off her sorcery skills in hopes that he would underestimate her.

"Asher Värja." Asher sat in a chair with one leg crossed over his knee, scowling at Velnias. "Do you want me to spell that for you so you can get it right on your plaque?"

Velnias actually threw back his head and laughed. "Oh, no, no, no. There will be no death tonight, not for anyone. I invited you here, and as I said, I'm nothing if not a gracious host."

"When you say 'invited us,' do you mean 'us' as in everyone, or 'us' as in Malin in particular?" Oona asked, referring to my earlier assertion that Velnias wanted me to be here tonight.

"Both, I suppose," he admitted.

"So you did invite me here?" I asked pointedly.

"Yes," Velnias said. "I thought it was time we get everything cleared up about Marlow so you can stop poking around and causing trouble for my men."

"Where is Azarias?" I asked. "Did you kill him?"

"No, he's around here somewhere. He has work to do." Velnias leaned forward, resting his arms on his desk. "We all do, really, which is why I wanted to talk it over with you. So we could all move on and get to the things we have to do."

"Did you send Azarias to seduce my mother?" I asked.

"I did. And when that didn't work fast enough, he employed a love spell, and that finally did the trick," he explained.

I shook my head in disbelief. "Why? What could you possibly gain from that?"

"How often do you think about predestination?" Velnias asked abruptly. "Any of you? I bet it's not very often."

"It comes up from time to time," I replied cagily.

"Good on you." Velnias looked genuinely impressed. "Most beings don't think about it at all. It's like oxygen—it makes all life possible, but since we can't see it, we don't worry about it. That is, of course, unless we don't have any left. Predestination won't run out, but it will kill you in the end."

"So what was your plan?" I asked. "Were you hoping to bribe Marlow into not killing you when your name came up?"

"You're thinking too small," he corrected me. "What life is it, being a draugr on the run? Hiding out and always looking over your shoulder, afraid of the Riks or even other jealous or brainwashed immortals? No, that's not enough."

"Is that why you had Marlow let Tamerlane Fayette go? So you could see what would become of a draugr?" I asked as I tried to understand his motivation.

"Tamerlane? I had nothing to do with that." He held his hands up with the palms out toward me. "Your mother did that all on her own, long before I'd even heard of her or Tamerlane.

"But we're getting ahead of ourselves," he went on. "For a very long time—centuries, I imagine—immortals have bucked at the idea of pre-destination. Call it fate or destiny or whatever you will, but to me it only ever sounded like one thing: a prison. I was trapped in it, unable to get off, caught in an infinite loop of decisions already decided by someone—or something—else."

"So you believe that every choice you've made was written by someone else? And not just your choices, but everyone's?" I asked, not hiding the skepticism in my voice. "Every senseless murder or geno-cide? The abuse of innocent children and animals? The extinction of entire species like the kakapo or the woolly mammoth? *That* was all going according to plan?"

"Every decision made here on earth since the Valkyries were created and the Evig Riksdag started giving out orders has been predetermined," Velnias said firmly. "How long in advance our fates are written, I don't know. But, yes, that is the only way I believe that any of this makes sense."

"Hold on," Oona interjected. "So you think that the Evig Riksdag is in control of the world and you're fighting against them? That doesn't make sense. Why would they let you do that?"

"Let's be clear—the Riks isn't in control of even half as much as they think they are," Velnias said. "They're merely accountants, going over the books of the world to ensure they are always balanced. They are interpreting the data, the equations that they can see. They are not the ones writing them initially."

"Who is?" Asher asked.

"There are theories, but I can't say for certain," Velnias said. "The good news is that it ultimately does not matter."

"For a long time, life was considered to be a tapestry, woven by three fates who saw all," Velnias elaborated. "They were always weaving, always working, and the tapestry would never be complete. Now imagine if one thread got loose, near the end where they weaved and worked. Imagine that someone started tugging on it, pulling and pulling until eventually it came free and the whole tapestry was undone. What would happen next? That's what I aim to find out."

"What exactly does this have to do with Marlow?" I asked.

Velnias smiled at me. "She was the loose thread. I only asked that someone give her a little *pull*."

SIXTY-EIGHT

⸻ ◆ ⸻

The self-satisfied grin on Velnias's face faded some when none of us reacted. Inside, my blood was boiling as I listened to him talk about my mother like she was defective machinery.

Even as the defensive anger grew inside me, wrapped around my own confused love for Marlow, a cold thought hit me: He was right. Valkyries were nothing more than tools for the gods, and she had been broken.

But since Velnias seemed to be in a mood for confession, I didn't want to interrupt him. I kept my expression as impassive as I could, digging my fingers into the arm of the chair for some relief from the nauseating anger.

"It had been clear to me for a while that Valkyries were the key," Velnias went on. "That was one of the main reasons that I campaigned to lead the Kurnugia Society. I knew it would put me in close proximity to the Evig Riksdag, and, in turn, with Valkyries. They were the wielders of the sword of fate. I had to find one with a weakness that I could exploit."

"How did you find Marlow?" I asked in a surprisingly even tone.

"Bram—or Tamerlane, as you knew him—came to me some weeks

ago with her name," Velnias explained. "After doing my own research, I agreed with him. She was desperate to find meaning in her life.

"I sent Azarias in with false prophecies in hopes of getting her more unstable and more trusting of him," he went on. "While the instability wasn't hard to achieve, the trust was near-impossible, not until we implemented the love spell.

"I'd chosen Azarias because his mother was a siren and his father was an incubus. He had a natural appeal to him that most beings couldn't resist, but I must say this for Marlow—she was as strong-willed as they come." For a moment Velnias looked impressed by that.

"How did you break her?" I asked.

"She was broken when I got to her," Velnias said with an indifferent shrug. "And if I'm being honest, the love spell got her to trust Azarias, but it was her own desperation that really drove her over the edge. She so badly wanted to believe she was good and she was a hero that she didn't see how she was becoming a villain."

I swallowed hard, quelling the sadness and nausea that wanted to rise up. Everything he was saying so far sounded true, even the parts I hated to admit about her. It would be easy to blame her shortcomings on Azarias and Velnias, but the alcoholism, her rather abusive opinions on child-rearing, letting Tamerlane Fayette live—those were all things she'd done on her own, long before any demon or his minion got their claws into her.

If I had been hoping for an excuse for her behavior, I knew now that I would never find one.

"How did you get involved with Ereshkigal?" Oona asked, keeping the conversation on track while I struggled to process everything Velnias was telling us.

"Ereshkigal?" Velnias shook his head. "I've never spoken to her. My only part was creating a Valkyrie so unpredictable and off-kilter that she would kill who she wasn't supposed to and wouldn't kill who she'd been told to. I needed to turn her into pure chaos, and that would be enough."

"So you don't know anything about Ereshkigal?" Asher asked, sounding dubious.

"I imagine that I've heard many of the same things you have," he admitted with a vague wave of his hand. "She wants to unleash the underworld, to command everyone to their knees before her, and I applaud her efforts. I hope she's successful in dethroning the Eralim after all these centuries. But I am not working for her. I refuse to bow to anyone."

"How do you know that you're free now?" Oona asked pointedly. "You seem to be going on the assumption that everything you've done since you've gotten involved with Marlow has been veering off the track that destiny put you on. But how do you know that are you aren't behaving exactly as you were always meant to?"

"Because I am destroying the Evig Riksdag and everything the gods have spent all this time building," Velnias said. "Why would the fates weave their own destruction into their tapestry?

"But ultimately, I don't suppose it really matters," he elaborated. "Either I am doing what I was meant to do and I can't veer off course, or I'm destroying the cage that holds me."

"Why are you telling us all this? Why not kill me?" I asked.

"I'm telling you because I wanted to put a stop to you harassing my clientele and my employees. And I'm not killing you because I gave my word tonight that no one would die here, and I might be a demon, but my word is my bond." His smile deepened. "Besides, I want everyone to know when the Evig Riksdag falls that I had a hand in it."

He spoke to us a bit longer, not really saying much beyond bragging about how strong and capable he was for outsmarting everyone and everything. But soon he grew bored and dismissed us, saying he had fun to attend to.

Just before we left, though, he stopped us. "Oh, and if I ever see the three of you in my club again, I will kill you." He smiled broadly. "But tonight, have fun. Live a little before the world ends."

SIXTY-NINE

———— ◆ ————

The sun was beginning to rise, and I couldn't sleep.

Asher lay beside me, sleeping, and I listened to the sound of him breathing as I watched the sky slowly lighten through my window blinds. I counted each breath he took, focusing on that in a vain attempt to keep my thoughts from racing through everything Velnias had told us.

There was a lot that he had said that sounded true, or at least true enough. I didn't think he'd lied, but that didn't mean he couldn't be wrong.

But the thing I kept going back to, poking at it like a fresh bruise I couldn't leave alone, was: Had I ever made a choice myself? Did I really love Asher, or was I just designed to feel that way? What about Quinn? Or Oona?

Was anything I had ever felt real?

Before I fell too deeply down that rabbit hole—trying to define "real" emotions and debating whether a lack of choice negated the validity of love or hate or grief—I tried to distract myself with another horrifying thought: Where the heck was Odin?

I hadn't asked Velnias about him, because if Velnias didn't know about the missing god already, it would be dangerous for me to tell him. But I thought it was a fairly safe bet he had nothing to do with it, or he would've been bragging nonstop.

He was so proud that he'd manipulated a Valkyrie—one that had already proven she could be manipulated, thanks to Tamerlane Fayette—and that wasn't anywhere nearly as impressive as kidnapping a Vanir god.

"Can't sleep?" Asher asked, pulling me from my thoughts.

He lay on his stomach, with my pillow all mashed up under his head, and his dark blue eyes were on me. I reached over and put my hand on his arm, acutely aware of the raised bumps of his healing cuts under my fingertips.

My only comfort was that the balm Oona had prepared for him seemed to be working. He still kept the deepest marks on his chest wrapped under gauze because they still bled on occasion, but he assured me they were healing well.

Most importantly, though, he hadn't had any strange tremors or nightmares or even a headache since his seizure the other day.

"No." I rolled over to face him more fully. "I hope I didn't wake you."

"You didn't. How are you doing with everything?"

"Other than my existential crisis?" I forced a smile, making a lame joke out of my very real discomfort. "I'm okay."

"You can't stop thinking about what Velnias said." It wasn't a question.

"No. I try to, but . . ." I sighed, trying to put into words what exactly was twisting me up. "Without free will, I can't help but feel like my whole life is a lie."

His brows pinched in confusion. "How is it a lie?"

"Because I didn't choose anything."

"Choice is what makes something real?" he asked.

"I mean . . . yeah."

Asher rolled onto his side, facing me directly. He took my hand and placed it on his chest, right next to the gauze bandage that covered his heart. "Do you feel that?"

"Your heartbeat?" I asked as it thudded slowly beneath my hand, his skin warming mine.

"I've never chosen for it to beat," he explained. "Somewhere, deep inside my brain, I know synapses fire every second to make it happen. But I've never had a conscious thought about it. No matter how hard I think about it, I can't make my heart stop beating."

"That's different."

"Is it though?" he argued.

"An involuntary reflex isn't the same thing as an emotion or a life decision."

"I didn't choose to feel the way I do about you," Asher admitted. "And if I'm being honest, if I could've chosen when I met you, I wouldn't have. Now isn't the right time. Neither of us are in the best place. But it doesn't matter how pragmatic I want to be. I still fell for you. And I don't know if that's predestination or because love is an impossible thing that does as it pleases."

"What about now?" I asked.

"What?"

"If you could choose. If you could suddenly decide to stop how you feel right now." I paused, steeling myself for the worst. "Would you?"

"No," he said softly, his eyes searching mine. "Would you?"

"Before I met you, I would've said yes. I would've happily shut myself off from caring about anyone. To spare myself all the pain and confusion . . ." I trailed off.

"And now?"

"Now . . . I love you, and I don't want to stop." A rush of terror and elation and relief washed over me as I realized it was true. Completely, irrevocably true. "Not ever."

Then, without waiting for me to say more, he sat up and pulled me into his arms. He kissed me fully on the mouth, his tongue parting my eager lips, as his hands slid underneath my shirt to the bare skin beneath.

I pulled him closer to me, wanting him closer still, but the sound of someone pounding on the front door interrupted us.

SEVENTY

◆

"It's like five in the morning," Asher realized as I untangled myself from his arms. "Who could that be at this hour?"

"I don't know, but I better go find out."

I got out of bed in a flash, pulling on a pair of loose pants as I opened my bedroom door. Oona poked her head out of her bedroom, waiting for me to investigate, while Bowie preferred to hide under the kitchen table and stomp his back feet.

When I opened the door, Valeska was standing there. Her wide eyes were surprisingly alert under her heavy lashes, but her lips were turned down into a bored scowl.

"Took you long enough," she said, pulling in her wings so she could slip through the narrow apartment doorway past me. This was just as Asher was coming of my bedroom, pulling a T-shirt on over his head. "You have sex hair."

"I—I was sleeping," I fumbled and felt my cheeks flush with embarrassment. "Who are you to judge messy hair, anyway?"

She touched her frizzy bob. "Mine always looks like this. Yours is different."

"Anyway," Oona interrupted, casting a look to me and Valeska. "What's going on? Why are you here?"

"Samael doesn't believe in phones anymore. He thinks everything's being tracked or bugged." She waggled her fingers in the air with faux-spookiness.

"Is it?" I asked.

Valeska shrugged. "How should I know? I just started working for him."

"Well, what's going on?" I asked. "Why did you have to come here and wake us all up?"

"Have you ever heard of the Drawing of the Nine?" Valeska asked, her eyes bouncing between the three of us to gauge our reactions.

"Nine what?" I asked.

"Is it a picture?" Oona asked.

"No, not *drawing*, like an artist making a picture," Valeska clarified. "It's drawing like selecting or choosing. It's an old prophecy."

"An old prophecy about what?" I asked.

"The nine original Valkyries," Valeska said, like it should be obvious.

"The first nine are long since dead," I pointed out.

"Believe it or not, Samael knows that," Valeska said dryly.

"So what is the prophecy?" Oona asked.

"The only thing Samael could find was a brief line from one of the gilded books in the Seraphim Library. He copied it down exactly, so I wouldn't butcher it." She pulled out a scrap of paper, rolled up into a tiny scroll, and handed it to me.

I unrolled it to find Samael's insanely elegant calligraphy scrolled across the parchment in bright gold ink.

And if it comes to the end of time, the world will be freed by the Drawing of the Nine.

"What does that mean?" Asher asked, after he'd read it over my shoulder.

"How does Samael even know that's about Valkyries?" I asked. "Nine seems like an awfully vague correlation."

"I don't know," Valeska said, and she was beginning to sound exasperated. "I didn't see the book. Samael found it, then he came to me and said this was super-important and I needed to go talk to you and tell you to go to Ravenswood Academy and go to the Sanctorum Library for research."

"Why can't he go himself?" Asher asked.

"And don't they have the books he would need at the Seraphim Library?" Oona added.

"An Eralim going to Ravenswood would cause a big scene, since they usually only go there for major events, and Samael is doing this all under the radar," Valeska said. "Which is also why he doesn't want to go snooping around the Seraphim Library. Besides that, he says the Sanctorum actually has more books than they do at the Riks."

"They do, yeah," I agreed with a bitter laugh. "The Sanctorum has thousands upon thousands of books. They have a whole wing dedicated to prophecy, even. And the only thing I have to go on are twenty words vaguely written in a rhyming scheme?"

"Yep," Valeska replied, unmoved by my growing frustration. "Samael thinks it's important, though, so it probably is."

"Is there someone who can help you?" Asher suggested gently. "Maybe a favorite professor or a librarian that could point you in the right direction?"

I thought back to the Sinaa—the leopard-like guardians of knowledge who glared at me every time I entered the Sacrorum Wing—and immediately dismissed them. But there was somebody who spent a lot of time in the wing who knew her way around the books.

"There is someone, actually," I said, and glanced over at the clock on the wall. "But considering it is not even seven, I should probably wait a few hours to reach out."

"That'll give us time to see if we can look online," Asher said. "Maybe we can find something that will narrow down your search a bit more."

"That's the spirit!" Valeska said with faux-enthusiasm.

Oona walked toward the kitchen and pulled a takeout menu off the fridge. "Since we'll be working this morning, I ought to get us food. Jaipur in the Morning delivers this early, I think."

"Oh, awesome. Can you order me some of the pudla?" Valeska asked.

SEVENTY-ONE

———◆———

Sloane Kothari met me outside the Sacrorum Wing. Instead of the usual tight ponytail she wore, she had let her long curls bounce free. She'd also traded in her cute Mary Jane flats for more practical boots that went up to her mid-calf, but she kept her plaid skirt.

She saw me as soon as I came down the stairs, looking up from where she texted rapidly on her phone, and while she didn't look as irritated to see me as she once had, her pursed lips and hard eyes weren't exactly happy, either.

"You were vague in your text, so I wasn't able to narrow anything down beforehand," Sloane said, sidestepping any pleasantries. "What is it that we're looking for?"

I had text-messaged her this morning, asking her to meet me at the library for something important, but I didn't say more than that. Samael thought phones might be tapped—by who or what, I didn't know—but if it made him nervous, I thought it would do me well to be cautious.

"We're looking for something that references this particular passage," I said as I handed her the paper Valeska had given me from Samael.

"Drawing of the Nine," Sloane repeated as she thought. "And this is supposed to be about the nine original Valkyries?"

"That's what he told me. Should we start in the Prophecy Room?" I asked.

She stared down at the slip of paper, rereading the phrase to herself before asking, "Have you heard this before?"

"Not until Samael gave it to me, no."

"You're a Valkyrie, so if they considered this to be a prophecy, you would've heard about it," Sloane reasoned. "Which means that any info there might be on it was probably mislabeled as a limerick or poem."

"So . . . where should we look?"

"We should probably split up so we can cover more ground," she suggested. "My top two suspects would be either the Valkyrie Room or the Songs of Adventure."

"I've already gone through the Valkyrie Room a dozen times, and I think it might be better if I went somewhere that I could approach with fresh eyes," I said.

"Then head down to Et Ingressus Est Praetorium Caneret." Sloane pointed down the hall. "Look for the oldest books you can find and grab them all. If this prophecy exists, it had to have been overlooked, which means that it most likely wasn't reprinted tons of times."

With our destinations in the Sacrorum Wing decided, we walked silently down the hall. The bright white walls bled into the ceiling curving above us, making it feel like a tunnel, with two dozen doorways into bomb-shelter-like vaults. Since it was during school hours, the thick metal doors were open, resting flush against the wall.

A Sinaa passed by us, keeping its head down while the large eyes hidden in the jaguar spots eyed me warily. We reached Sloane's stop first, and she quietly whispered, "Good luck," before turning under the plaque that read ET VIRGINES IN MORTE.

I finally found the room that Sloane told me to investigate, all the way at the end of the hall. Fortunately, it appeared to be smaller than the other rooms, but books were still stacked tightly on shelves floor-to-ceiling.

The Sacrorum Wing always had a hermetic smell to it. Not clean or antiseptic, although it was always spotless here, but more stale and empty. It wasn't until I got up close to the books that I could breathe in their must and paper.

As I perused the books—running my fingers along the spines, searching for those that felt or looked the oldest—I came to understand why this room was so small. The titles seemed random and with topics and deities from every walk of life, and I realized this must be where they stuck everything they couldn't find a place for anywhere else.

But I did as Sloane had suggested, grabbing all the oldest books I could find without worrying about the title, until I had a slight stack of twenty-five. I sat down on the floor, carefully but quickly flipping through the ancient pages, looking for any mentions of Valkyries or their swords.

When I finished those twenty-five books, I put them back, then grabbed twenty-five more. There was one book that I hesitated before finally grabbing it. The brown leather cover felt too new, but I kept coming back to it, so I added *Codex Aeterna* to my pile.

I saved it until last, but as soon as I opened it, I realized the cover had been a trick. The pages were ancient vellum—yellowed but transparent, waxy and delicate under my fingers. Some time ago the book must've been rebound, giving it a slightly newer cover.

Written carefully in thick black calligraphy, the pages contained various poems and songs. The first few were strange tales of immortals I hadn't heard of before, but then it came to one about Frigg, Odin's wife.

While I didn't think I had read this particular poem before, the story was very familiar. It described Frigg's love for her husband and her son Baldur, and her refusal to share her precognition with anyone. When Baldur ran off, hiding in the underworld, Frigg was devastated. She tried to reach him, but as a Vanir goddess she wasn't allowed, and Baldur never even heard her cries.

The normally joyful Frigg fell into a deep depression until one day she hatched a plan. She dressed in beggar's clothes and started a fight with the Valkyrie Brynhilda. To defend herself, the Valkyrie slayed the disguised Frigg.

Except, of course, a Vanir goddess cannot be slayed. Instead, Frigg fell into a deep sleep, promising only to awake when her son Baldur returned to her. And so she slept, for thousands of years, until most had forgotten about her.

The poem after that was called "Friggadraumr," which loosely translated to "The Dream of Frigg." It alleged to have been written when Frigg awoke once, shortly after she had fallen asleep, to describe a dream that she had.

This one began with the whole history of the world, giving a brief overview of some of the major events that had transpired before Frigg had fallen asleep. It wasn't until nearly the end—the fifty-ninth stanza when it only had sixty-two—that things started to take shape, and my fingers trembled as I turned the page.

> From the earth to | the shadows
> Fetters will burst | and the raven flies free
> Much do I know | more can I see
> Of the fates of the gods | the mighty in fight
>
> Sun turns black, | sky sinks to the sea
> Fierce is the flame, | but the raven flies free
> Now do I see | heroes anew
> The motherless children | rise together
>
> And the mighty past | they call to mind
> Bloodied blades of | Odin's maidens fair
> In wondrous beauty | once again
> The sun now shines by | the drawing of the nine
>
> Then goodness shall win | on prophetic raven
> Daughters and sons | can now abide
> And happiness ever | there shall they have
> On an unfettered earth: | would you know yet more?

"Bloodied blades of Odin's maidens fair," I repeated softly to myself. "The sun now shines by the drawing of the nine."

In old texts, Valkyries were often referred to as Odin's maidens. Blood-red blades would be their swords, which were apparently needed for the Drawing of the Nine.

My mind flashed back to Marlow's safe that Oona and I had uncovered. All the Valkyrie swords that made no sense, that Samael didn't know what they could be used for. But Marlow had known.

She'd been preparing for the prophecy, for the Drawing of the Nine.

SEVENTY-TWO

———◆———

Oona sat on the couch with her legs folded underneath her, staring down at my phone and the picture I had taken of the books. Ash sat beside her, leaning forward with his arms resting on his knees as he repeated the lines from "Friggadraumr" about the drawing of the nine.

"They mean the swords, right?" I asked as I paced the living room, with Bowie hopping behind me in hopes of getting treats or petting. "That has to be why Marlow had all those swords in her safe."

"Maybe." Oona ran her hand through her short hair, but she sounded too shocked for me to be able to tell whether or not she was convinced. "But I still don't understand what we're supposed to do with the nine swords. We're just supposed to get them and the sun will shine?"

Asher glanced out the window at the dark clouds hanging low around the towers. "It doesn't look like the sun is going to be shining anytime soon."

"Me and Sloane talked about it, and we think that 'drawing' might be a mediocre translation from the Olde Language, and it could really mean more like 'gathering' or even possibly 'wielding,'" I clarified.

"Where is Sloane?" Oona asked, now realizing that I had returned from Ravenswood Academy alone.

"She's still at the library, seeing if she can find anything else," I said. "I wanted to hurry back here and talk to you guys, and get this info to Samael as soon as possible."

I'd rushed back home to talk over my findings with Oona and Asher. He'd been doing research on my laptop, searching online for anything that referenced the Drawing of the Nine, while Oona had been going through her own books. So I had returned to many books spread out throughout the room, all piled up in between empty take-out containers.

Bowie had been nibbling at the corner of one of the boxes, until I stopped him and tossed him a chew stick to keep him occupied.

"How many swords do we have?" Asher asked. "Out of the nine?"

"Mine is Sigrún, and Quinn has Eir, plus the four in Marlow's safe, so that's six," I said, listing them on my fingers. "We're missing three."

"What about Marlow's personal sword, like the one she used working as a Valkyrie? Was that in the safe?" Oona asked.

"No, it wasn't, but Mördare wasn't one of the original nine Valkyries," I said. "There are currently a lot more than nine Valkyries on earth, so there have to be lots of swords beyond the originals."

"Who were the original nine?" Asher asked.

"Eir, Göndul, Hildr, Mist, Ölrún, Róta, Skögul, Thrúd, and Sigrún," Oona said, reciting the Valkyries' names, her words lilting slightly to the tune we'd been taught to sing it to back in school.

"Hildr?" Asher sat up straighter. "That was the name of my mom's sword."

"Excellent!" I shouted in excitement and snapped my fingers together. "Now we have seven!"

"Not to rain on your parade, but how do you know that any of these are the right swords?" Oona asked carefully. "And I don't even mean the ones that Marlow had hidden—which we honestly have no idea about—but even yours. What if somebody thought it would be funny to call your sword Sigrún, but it's really a random sword?"

"That's not how it works," I insisted, but my opinions were based more on *hope* than actual knowledge. "We don't name the blades. The Eralim name them. But you're right. I don't know how to tell them apart. But Samael should be able to. We have to gather the swords, take them to him, and he should help fill in the blanks for us."

"That all sounds good," Oona said, sounding reluctant. She chewed her lip, making her silver studs twist this way and that.

"But?" I asked, addressing her hesitation.

"I'm being cautious, Mal," she said with a sigh. "The wording is very vague, and we have a lot riding on this."

"I get that, but . . . we're close. I can feel it," I said, and I wasn't exaggerating.

There was something in the air. Like an electricity, and I know I wasn't the only one. On the way back from Ravenswood, everybody seemed to be giving each other an extra-wide berth and walking faster than normal.

"I know," Oona agreed. "Something is definitely happening soon."

Asher stood, rubbing the back of his neck as he did. "I should . . ."

"You should what?" I stopped pacing to look at him more directly.

"I should . . ." he repeated. He stared at the floor with his eyebrows bunched together, and his faced looked flushed.

"Ash?" Oona asked. "Is everything okay?"

He looked up at me finally, and his stormy blue eyes were completely panicked. His mouth hung open slightly, and his hands fell to his sides as he stared ahead in horror.

"Asher?" I asked as the room began to shake.

It was a slow rumble as the walls and floors began to tremble. Bowie fled into the kitchen to hide, while I braced myself against the doorframe to keep from falling over. A few glasses and knickknacks clattered to the floor, and panicked yelling from other apartments echoed through the walls.

The lights flickered on and off during a brief power surge, and I realized how dark it had gotten. It was early afternoon, and the sky outside was black with storm clouds swirling around and glowing red.

Finally the earthquake stopped, and Asher was still standing in front of the couch, the way he had been the entire time—unmoving, despite all the shaking.

"Asher, what's going on?" I demanded.

"Remember that we all must die." Those words came out of Asher's mouth, but it wasn't his voice. It was twisted and inhuman.

And the second the words stopped, his eyes rolled into the back of his head and he started falling to the floor. Oona dove forward, barely managing to get a throw pillow under his head just as he collapsed onto the concrete and began convulsing.

SEVENTY-THREE

—◆—

sher!" I screamed as I ran to his side. He lay on his back, thrashing and shaking, and I tried to hold his hand.

Oona knelt beside him, watching him with the same intense expression she had when she was studying for a final.

"Why is this happening?" I asked her plaintively.

"I don't know," she replied without taking her eyes off him.

Finally he stopped convulsing, though his arms and legs still twitched. His eyes were closed, but the lids kept fluttering.

Suddenly his eyes opened, but they weren't his eyes anymore. They were pure black from the pupil through the iris through the whites.

In the same inhuman baritone he'd spoken in before, he said, *"Ol zir de teloah od oresa."* And then he said it again, and again, like a chant.

"What is he saying?" I asked Oona.

"I know it. I know I should know it," Oona said softly, more to herself than to me.

Then, as abruptly as it had all started, it stopped. The chanting ended, his body relaxed, and his eyes closed.

"Asher?" I said gently. "Ash?"

Oona sat back, muttering the phrase to herself. "*Ol zir de teloah od oresa.* I know I just saw it. It's not . . ." She trailed off as she crawled over to the coffee table and frantically began flipping through one of the books left open on it.

I stayed with Asher, holding his hand and obsessively watching his chest rise and fall. If he was still breathing, he was still alive. There was still hope.

Right above his heart, a dark spot started to form on his gray T-shirt. Small at first, but it rapidly grew into a big wet splotch.

"Oona!" I shouted. "He's bleeding!"

"Let me see," she commanded. "Take off his shirt."

Asher didn't wake as I lifted up his shirt, pulling it over his head. He still wore a bandage over the marks that had been carved in his chest, but it was soaked red with blood. Carefully, I peeled it off, revealing the throbbing wounds underneath.

The rest of the marks on Asher's body had already almost completely healed, thanks to the treatment he'd received in Zianna and Oona's expertise in aftercare. They were little more than raised red scars down his arms and sides. But the ones above his heart were still jagged and raw. The skin was inflamed and puffy, turning dark black right at the edges where the wound gaped open around the symbols that were carved into his flesh.

"They're not healing," I realized in horror.

"It's because they're not cuts, like the others. This is something deeper." Oona bent over, staring at them for a moment, before dashing back to her books. "But I think I recognize them. Hold on!"

With Oona otherwise disposed, I balled up Asher's shirt and pressed against his wounds, stopping the bleeding as best I could.

"Ash?" I whispered, with my lips right up to his ear. "Are you in there? Can you hear me? Come back to me, Asher. *Please.*"

"I got it!" Oona announced. "It's Enochian!"

"Enochian? Isn't that a dead language?" I asked.

"Mostly. It's the original language of the angels, but it's not dead to an orginal angel or demon." Oona scooted back over, so she was sitting closer to Asher with her book splayed open. "The marks on his chest, that first one means *darkness* and the second one means . . . *possession*."

"Are you saying that Asher is possessed?" I asked.

"Not exactly. I don't think. Gimme a minute." She flipped through the pages, frantically reading. "So . . . if I understand it right, he was saying, *Ol zir de teloah od oresa,* which means . . . 'I am of death and destruction.'"

"Why would he say that?" I asked.

Oona looked at me somberly. "Abaddon is the angel of destruction."

"Abaddon marked him," I said with tears in my eyes.

"I think Abaddon marked Asher to be a vessel for him," Oona explained slowly.

"Asher is his way out of Kurnugia," I realized. "That's why they didn't kill him, and that's why they let them take him to Zianna. Abaddon wanted him to escape."

"He didn't want to miss the end of the world," she agreed.

"What do we do?" I asked, overriding the shock that my boyfriend had been marked by the angel of destruction. "Can we perform an exorcism?"

"Maybe?" Oona didn't look very confident. "Abaddon is very powerful."

Outside, there was a loud bang—a metallic crunching mixed with a rushing sound. Like the time I had heard a car crash into a fire hydrant, except multiplied by a thousand. The apartment building trembled again, and it seemed to sway, though it was hard to say because everything felt off-kilter.

Oona set aside her book and went to the window, presumably to investigate whatever had made that loud noise, but my attention was focused on Asher.

"He's still alive, so there has to be something we can do," I persisted.

"Mal, you gotta come here," Oona said.

"You have all these books. There has to be an answer in one of them!"

"Malin! Come here!" Oona demanded. She stood at the window, with her hands on the glass, staring down at the canal.

I let go of Asher's hand and stood up, just as the emergency alert sirens began to wail throughout the city. I'd only ever heard them go off for tornado watches or as a test, and when I looked out the window, I saw exactly what the problem was.

The Maneto Canal that ran past our building had been parted, so tidal waves of the putrid water splashed up onto the sidewalks and buildings. On the canal floor, marching in a perfect formation, were rows and rows of skeletons, looking exactly like the ones we had fought at the Gates of Kurnugia.

Leading the way was the massive bull centaur Gugalanna, and on his back rode his queen, Ereshkigal, wearing her crown of bones.

They had broken free from the underworld.

SEVENTY-FOUR

———◆———

"Are you sure this is going to work?" I asked, hovering over Oona and Asher.

He lay unconscious on the floor, the same way he had been for the past ten minutes, while Oona whipped up a potent tonic. It was a smoky blue that seemed to be continuously shifting between a liquid and a gas.

I hadn't understood much of how she made it, since I hadn't been able to watch her. I'd tried waking Asher at first, while she gathered ingredients, and when that didn't work, I left her to the mixing and muttering in a guttural whisper while I loaded up everything important that I could think of—weapons, bottled water, Oona's spell book, a first-aid kit.

"No, I'm not sure." She bit her lip as she carefully drew two milliliters up into a syringe, and then she eyed me over the sharp point of the needle. "I'm not sure of anything right now, but I don't think we should stay here for any longer than we need to, and you've tried everything else to wake him up."

I went back to the window, watching as the skeletons climbed up the canal support beams to the sidewalk and up the buildings, while still more marched out from the earth in a constant stream of death.

They were climbing up the sides of the Tannhauser Towers, their bony fingers digging into the concrete and metal. While many of the skeletons seemed intent on their mission to get to the top of the buildings, others were breaking in the windows either to crawl inside or pull victims out and throw them to the ground far below.

I didn't know how we were going to get out, but we couldn't stay here.

I looked back over my shoulder, watching apprehensively as Oona injected the potion into Asher's arm. I waited, straining to hear any sound from him over the wailing of the emergency alert sirens.

Finally, after several excruciating seconds, he gasped loudly and sat bolt upright.

"Asher!" I ran over to him and crouched beside him. "Are you okay? Are you still you?"

He blinked at me, his dark eyes stormy and confused. "Who else would I be?"

"Can you stand?" Oona asked. "How are you feeling?"

"Everything hurts, and my heart is racing a mile a minute." He rubbed his temple. "Why is that siren going off? What's happening?"

"Ereshkigal escaped with her army of the dead," I told him as quickly as I could. "We have to go, so you have to get up and walk if you can."

"Let me get my stuff," Oona said, and she was already rushing around to gather all the thaumaturgy gear.

Asher was moving slowly, but he got to his feet. When he took a step, he stumbled a little but caught himself.

"Do you think you can handle carrying this?" I asked Asher as I held out my messenger bag filled with weapons. "If you can't, don't force it."

"No, I got it," he insisted as he took the bag from me and dropped the strap over his shoulder. "What happened to me?"

"I'll explain later. I have to get Bowie."

When this was over—assuming we all lived—I would have to send Jude a big thank-you for getting the carrying pack for Bowie. Once I got him hooked in and on my back, I had my hands free, so I grabbed Sigrún, and left the rest of my weapons with Asher.

Oona was ready a moment later, and Asher was pacing, trying to get his bearings back. We were as ready as we were ever going to be to face an army of skeletons, so we headed out into the hall.

With Bowie chittering on my back, I pushed the elevator call button over and over again as the red lights flashed in the hallway. Asher leaned against Oona, still getting his strength back, and once again it wasn't clear that we were doing the right thing.

But I couldn't see another choice. We couldn't sit here and wait to die, which meant that we had to get out and fight.

Finally the elevator doors opened, and I was surprised to find it empty. The lights were out, but the number pad was still lit up, so that was enough for me. I hit the button for the basement, and Oona and Asher leaned back against the wall as the elevator started its rapid descent.

The speakers in the elevator's ceiling let out a long, painfully loud bleat before a robotic automated voice began reading off a warning:

"A civil authority has issued an alert. The following transmission is being broadcast by the Evig Riksdag in conjunction with the United States government. An immortal attack has been released on the city. Due to the uncertain nature of these attacks, all residents should seek out and take shelter. Stay calm and stay in your own homes. Remember there is nothing to be gained by trying to get away. By leaving your homes you could be exposing yourself to greater danger."

SEVENTY-FIVE

❖

The basement was nearly as dark as the elevator, with only the flashing red light. Oona pulled out her phone to use its flashlight so we could make our way through the maze of storage containers, HVAC tubing and machinery, and various broken equipment and garbage.

Finally we found the concrete stairwell hidden in the side corner, and we raced up. As soon as I pushed open the heavy doors, water came rushing in and poured down the steps around us. The alleyway outside was flooded with a foot or two of the water displaced from Ereshkigal's parting of the canal.

A few skeletons were above us, climbing the building and breaking through windows, and one was a few feet away standing on an overflowing dumpster. It looked down at me—its eyes mere glowing red pinpoints in the center of its dark sockets—and then it opened its mouth and let out a most inhuman scream.

All of the commotion and the chaos of sounds—the blaring, the demonic scream of the skeletons, the rushing water, people crying and screaming—was too much for Bowie. I felt him wriggling on my back as he tried to hide deeper in the carrier.

My sword was already drawn, so I rushed the skeleton, and it dove at me. I swung my blade, and it slid easily through the bones, like a scythe through grass. As the bones fell to the ground, they turned to ash and quickly dissolved in the murky water.

It was killed so fast, and the others were so preoccupied with their mission, that this should've been a relief. But it wasn't. As the skeleton fell, I could only feel a strange panic. It was like a black void had opened inside me, sucking up everything around that made sense, so only I would be left, alone, confused, and terrified.

"What is the fastest way to get downtown?" Oona asked, but I didn't answer her right away. I stared down at the water, which looked dark and red from the reflection of the tumultuous sky, and I watched as every last bit of the skeleton swirled and disappeared into the water.

"Preferably with the fewest number of skeletons," Asher added as he warily looked up at the buildings around us.

"We should go . . ." I trailed off, because the truth was that I had no idea where to go.

I knew the building wasn't safe. I knew that Odin's spear was locked up in Samael's office, and Samael was the only being I knew and trusted who would have any idea how to handle what was happening.

But that was it. Once I'd killed the skeleton, I'd felt paralyzed by intense doubt. I didn't know what to do or where to go, and it left me so stricken with uncertainty that I could not move.

"Mal?" Oona asked, pulling me from my panic. "We have to go. We can't just stand here, or the skeletons will come for us."

"I know. I—" I stopped short when I heard a familiar sound.

Even through all the noise and chaos, I recognized that particular cawing, and I knew it was meant for me.

"This way," I commanded. "And we have to hurry."

I grabbed Asher's hand, in part because he seemed too dazed and I didn't want to lose him, but more because I knew that touching him would ground me back here in reality, with him, where I knew exactly what to do.

The buzzing intensified around my heart, and the world seemed to slow down, falling into hyperfocus as I concentrated on the sound of the bird cawing and the flapping of its wings. I couldn't see it, not yet, not as I raced around the buildings, dodging between skeletons and slicing them down when they got in my way.

It wasn't until we were away from the flooding sewage and attacking skeletons, when Oona was panting at me to stop or slow down, that the raven finally showed itself.

I didn't know how long we'd run, I'd lost all sense of time and place as I chased after the bird. It had stopped cawing after we had followed it into a narrow gap between rundown tenement buildings. The space was barely wide enough for me to stand next to Asher, and Oona leaned against the brick wall as she struggled to catch her breath.

Then the giant black bird settled on the cracked concrete in front of us. It was a massive raven, at least as big as a bobcat, and it held a cloth bag in its beak. Its beak was broken at the tip, a jagged crack that zig-zagged through black keratin, and a scar ran across its eye, leaving it glassy and dull.

This was not the raven that I knew. This wasn't Muninn.

It was his brother, Huginn.

He dropped the bag at my feet and ruffled his feathers.

"Where is Odin?" I asked, but the bird didn't—couldn't—answer. He merely cocked his head so he could look at me with his one good eye. "If Odin can hear you, if he can hear me, he needs to know that we need him. We can't fight this on our own."

The raven nudged the bag toward me. Asher bent down and peered inside.

"It's a sword." He reached in and pulled out a stubby blade of teal, with a handle that appeared to be made of a swirling blown glass. "I think it's a Valkyrie sword."

"The raven was gathering the swords," Oona said softly. "Do you think this is how Marlow got her swords?"

"Why would the raven be helping her?" I asked as my heart thudded coldly in my chest.

Oona looked at me, her dark eyes meeting mine evenly. "Why would the raven be helping us?"

A loud squawk interrupted us, and I looked up to see another large raven landing on the streetlight in front of us. This one was unmarred by scars, and when it looked down at me with its big black eyes, I knew that it was Muninn, the raven I'd met before.

"What is going on?" I demanded. "What do you want from us?"

"Malin, I think we should take the sword and go," Asher suggested uneasily. "The streets aren't safe, and once we get somewhere that is we can spend time debating what this all means."

"Fine," I relented, but there was still one more thing I had to try. I crouched in front of Huginn so that we were at eye level. "Please," I pleaded as I stared into his good eye, hoping that wherever he was, Odin could see me. "Tell Odin that we need him. He needs to return."

The raven blinked, then flapped its wing and took flight, disappearing into the sky.

"Should we go after him?" Oona asked.

"No." I stood up. "He's not the one we follow now." I looked back at Muninn, who squawked loudly before flying off. He went slowly at first, circling around us, before heading toward the heart of the city.

"*That's* the one we follow," I said as Asher hid the new Valkyrie sword in the messenger bag with the rest of the weapons, and then the three of us gave chase, letting Muninn lead us away.

SEVENTY-SIX

——◆——

Despite the fact that the Riks building was on serious
lockdown—one that took far too long for me, Oona, and Asher
to get through all the security checks—we finally made it
inside.

The one thing that I had to say for the Riks security protocols,
though, was that they had piped in soothing classical music through the
speakers instead of the intermittent air raid sirens going on outside. It
gave my eardrums a welcome respite as we rode up the elevator to the
twenty-ninth floor.

When the doors opened, the long hallway spread out before us, and
at the end was the door to Samael's office—unguarded for the first time
that I'd ever seen.

I pushed it open without knocking and found Samael, Godfrey,
Valeska, and Quinn crowded around a large television. It was a massive
screen, usually hidden behind a classical painting, but the artwork slid
up to reveal the TV.

The screen showed frightening images of the city under siege. Skeletons attacking innocent people, cars on fire, rioting in the streets. It

looked like a war zone, with the police and the National Guard ineffective against such an unrelenting supernatural enemy.

An explosion flashed on the screen, and we felt the rumble inside the Riks, causing Oona to let out a surprised yelp.

Everyone had been so glued to the violence and anarchy unfolding on the news that they hadn't noticed us come in, but now they all turned to look at us.

"You're here! Thank the stars above!" Samael rushed over and pulled me into a clumsy hug, made more awkward by the anxious wolpertinger fidgeting on my back.

Over his shoulder, I saw Quinn step toward me, like she meant to greet me the way Samael had, but then she stopped short. She stared at me for a moment longer, then she looked back at the TV, where Ellery Park was futilely attempting to convince everyone to stay calm as the world fell apart.

"Is it safe here?" I asked once Samael had released me.

"It's as safe here as it is anywhere in the city," he replied carefully.

"Good enough." I slid the carrier off my back and set it on the floor before unbuckling Bowie. He immediately scurried off, running under the sofa to hide, but I didn't blame him. He'd had a very terrifying day so far.

Oona and Asher were with the others, standing in a semicircle around the screen and watching NorNewsNow, but I put my hand on Samael's arm, stopping him before he went over to join them.

"Have you heard from Odin?" I asked, keeping my voice low.

He grimaced sadly. "No, nothing yet."

"Really?" I asked in dismay. "I thought for certain he'd return with the ravens."

"You saw his ravens?" Samael asked, doing his best to keep quiet despite the obvious shock in his eyes. "Are you positive they were his?"

"Yeah, I'm positive." I nodded. "They helped me on the way here, but they took off the second I didn't need them anymore."

He furrowed his brow as he considered the implications of the return of Muninn and Huginn.

"There have been many reports—" Ellery stopped short and put her hand to her ear, pressing on the earpiece to hear better. She nodded, then began speaking to the camera. "We're getting word that Gugalanna, the Great Bull and one of the apparent leaders of this invasion, is holding an impromptu press conference in Skarpåker Park. We're joining them live now."

The news immediately cut to the park, where Gugalanna stood on the highest part of the rocky outcroppings. Behind him were a small legion of skeletons, standing in attention in front of the overgrown wooded garden.

To the left of where the bull centaur stood was the old mossy gazebo, covered in dying vines and orange leaves. It was the Place for Dreaming, a popular destination for weddings, but now it housed the throne of bones, where Ereshkigal sat, watching silently.

". . . violence is, unfortunately, the only thing this world will respond to," Gugalanna was saying, his smarmy grin barely hidden under his false solemnity. "This is not how we wanted to do it, but it is the only language that works, as it has been for thousands of years. One thing you learn about living as long as I have is that not much ever *really* changes, not deep down at the core of things."

A dark plate of armor covered his chest, but from the human waist down—where the bull part of his body was—he was naked, save for the black fur that covered his four hulking legs and animal torso. Two horns curved out from his dark curls of hair, and his bronze eyes flashed as he surveyed the crowd of immortals, skeletons, and media that had gathered in the park.

"When last I walked the earth and breathed this air—it was much sweeter then, I will say that has been an unpleasant change—there were those that ruled, and those that were in chains," Gugalanna continued. "It has been that way since the beginning of time. You are either the hunter or the prey, the captor or the captured.

"Right now, because we've had to use violence and force, I know we've been painted as the aggressors. As terrorists," he said with condescension dripping from his words. "Conquerors. And I know you must all be so very afraid, but let me assure you that we are not here to take over your world. On the contrary. We are here to *free* it!"

He raised his arms into the air, and the skeletons followed suit. The camera was fixed on him, so I couldn't see the crowd that gathered, but I heard some of them—too many of them, really—shouting out in agreement.

"Throughout history, the ruling class has gotten even better at enslaving you all," Gugalanna said. "They trick you into believing it's for your own good. They keep you safe, they promise. This is what you need, they guarantee. And now they've done such a wonderful job I doubt most of you even realize that you're caged.

"Those with all the power have always hidden away from those they oppress, and none are as far away or as powerful as those that hide in Vanaheimr, far removed from the mess that they've created." The Bull stopped speaking long enough to cast a disparaging glare toward the sky, toward the legendary home of the Vanir gods and goddesses.

"It wasn't until I was trapped in the underworld that I began to see the earth for what it truly is: a cage," Gugalanna explained. "A place to hold you, to keep you busy, distracted. So you don't realize what they're doing to you and everything around you.

"Look at this!" He gestured wildly around. "Look at the sky and the air and the water! The world is all but destroyed! And to what end? Where will you go next? The doors to Kurnugia and Vanaheimr will not open for most of you, and even if they do, you are only exchanging one cage for another.

"But no more." He motioned back toward Ereshkigal, who finally rose from the throne and with slow, deliberate steps walked toward him as he spoke. "I have brought you a queen and an army to set you free. I invite you to join her, to fight by our side and free yourselves of the shackles."

Gugalanna dropped to his knees—bending his front two legs to bow before her. Ereshkigal wore a long gown of a strange black fabric that seemed to move on its own, swirling around her feet as she took center stage. She stood regal and poised, holding her head high under its intricate crown of bones, and the crowd fell silent.

"We will win this war," Ereshkigal declared. Her words were sharp but quiet, and they carried clear and loud throughout the park. "We will gladly give it all back—your freedom, your lives, your earth—to all of you, to every single one of you. All we ask is that you fight with us."

She paused as she surveyed the crowd, then she issued her order: "We must kill all the Valkyries and the Eralim that control them."

SEVENTY-SEVEN

---◆---

I didn't need to hear the crowd erupt into cheers, many of them already chanting their new queen's name. Nor did I need to hear the pundits on the television telling me what this all might mean or wondering whether or not we should give Ereshkigal a chance. I grabbed the remote and turned off the television.

"Hey!" Valeska shouted in irritation and glared at me. "What'd you do that for?"

"Nothing good ever comes from giving evil a platform, especially when they're advocating genocide," I replied.

"They might have more information," Valeska argued.

"What could they possibly know that we don't?" I shot back. "We know that Ereshkigal and Gugalanna are taking over the city, and they're currently staked out at the park. We know that they want to kill us. And we know about the prophecy that might be able to stop them."

"You found out more about the Drawing of the Nine?" Samael asked.

I took out my phone and quickly pulled up the photos I had taken. As I scrolled through the snaps of the yellowed pages, looking for the best one, I realized with dismay that I had only taken these pictures this morning.

It had only taken a matter of hours for the whole world to go mad.

"This is the best I could find," I said as I handed Samael the phone.

He zoomed into the picture, and his lips moved as he read to himself. Valeska snuck up beside him, leaning over his arm to get a better look.

"Bloodied blades of Odin's maidens fair," Samael repeated to himself.

"The swords of the original nine Valkyries," I said. I took the messenger bag from Asher and walked to the coffee table in the center of Samael's office.

I glanced over at Oona, who dutifully recited the nursery rhyme: *"Eir, Göndul, Hildr, Mist, Ölrún, Róta, Skögul, Thrúd, and Sigrún."*

As she spoke, I pulled out my blade of purple and set it on the table, then beside it I set the one of teal that Huginn had dropped at my feet. "I have Sigrún and Mist."

"And I have Eir." Quinn unsheathed her sword, setting it on the table beside the other two. When her blue blade touched the others, they all glowed dully, but only for a second before returning to their usual darkened state.

"My grandma still has my mother's sword Hildr at home," Asher added.

"And Marlow has four swords in her safe," I said.

Marlow's swords only mattered if they were the right ones that we needed. I couldn't guess now, but I was certain that I would know when I touched them, the same way I had known that the sword Huginn had left for me was Mist. The same way I knew who to kill and how to kill.

It was in my blood.

Valeska did a quick count on her fingers. "That's only eight. We're short one."

"No, we're not." Samael finally looked up. "I have my mother's sword Róta. That's nine."

"But what do we even do with them?" Quinn chewed her lip as she stared down at the swords. "We have nine swords, but then what? We all take turns stabbing Ereshkigal with them?"

"*The sun now shines by the drawing of the nine,*" Samael said, quoting the poem, and cast his eyes toward the ceiling. "I've done enough ceremonies in my time. We need to get the blades together and get them up where the sunlight can hit them."

"So we need the swords?" Valeska asked. "Does it matter who wields them?"

"I've been thinking about it, and I think we're the ones that are supposed to do this," Oona said. "It says, '*Now do I see heroes anew. The motherless children rise together.*'" She motioned around to us. "That's us. We're all powerful in our own rights, most of us with Valkyrie parentage, and all of us have dead mothers."

Oona's birth mother died in childbirth; Valeska's was murdered by her grandmother; Quinn's was executed by a vengeful widower; Samael's mother had died centuries ago; and Asher's mother and my mother had both been killed by Tamerlane Fayette.

Outside of Samael's mother, all of them were relatively young and died in tragic circumstances.

"But there's six of us," Quinn said. "Where do we get the other three?"

"My great-grandma died many years ago, so I think my grandma would qualify," Asher suggested. "I have to go back home to get Róta anyway, and she would want to help."

"Minerva will help us," Oona said, referring to her cousin/sister. "And if I qualify, she qualifies."

"We only need one more. Can any of you think of anybody that might be able to help?" Samael asked, looking heavily at all of us. "We only have eight bodies, and we need one more motherless child to draw in the light."

"I know someone," I realized. "Sloane Kothari."

"Do you really think she'll help?" Oona asked.

I nodded. "What choice does she have? The world's going to end if we don't do something to stop it."

SEVENTY-EIGHT

———◆———

The plan was simple:

Quinn would take Oona in her car to get Minerva as quickly and safely as possible, while Valeska would fly Asher down to his house, where they would pick up his grandmother Teodora, her car, and the sword. Samael would stay behind with Godfrey (and Bowie) in hopes that Odin would finally return.

That left me going on my own, with Samael handing me the keys to his souped-up luft. I would get Sloane, then retrieve Marlow's swords from her safe and return.

While everyone was gearing up and going over possible scenarios and protocols with Samael, Valeska had wandered off to the far side of the room to dig through the candy bowl for something to snack on. I took the opportunity to talk to her for a moment in private—relatively speaking, thanks to Samael holding court with the others.

"Just carbo-loading before the big day," Valeska told me, popping a few strawberry-red kola nuts into her mouth, and she grimaced at the bitter flavor. "Want some?"

"Nah, I'm good." I glanced back over my shoulder to be sure Asher was far enough away that he wouldn't be able to hear me. "Do you think you'll be okay with Asher?"

"Yeah, of course. He doesn't look *that* heavy," Valeska replied with a noncommittal shrug.

"There's something that you need to know." I moved closer to her and lowered my voice to a whisper. "Asher's not okay. I don't have time to explain, and we don't have time to fix it. But he's been marked by Abaddon, and it's affecting him."

"Affecting him how?" She arched her eyebrows in an attempt to look skeptical, but I could see the concern in her wide eyes. "Is he going to try to kill me or something?"

"So far he's only had seizures and said some strange things," I said. "Don't let him drive, and hang on to the weapons."

"Do you really think he should be going, then?" Valeska asked.

"I don't know, but we need his grandma and we need the sword," I reminded her.

Valeska inhaled through her nose and nodded grimly. She carried herself with a tough resignation about her, like she knew she would always do what must be done, even if it was terrible. But she had survived in Kurnugia alone for weeks, and that had to have been harder than dealing with a possibly possessed Asher.

"I'll take care of him for you," she promised just before Quinn announced that we should all get going.

The five of us made a motley group as we walked down the long copper hallway together. The elevator would be where we parted, with Quinn, Oona, and me heading down to the parking garage while Valeska and Asher went up to the roof.

We walked fast, knowing there wasn't any time to waste, but Asher and I lingered at the back. As we walked, I felt his hand sliding around mine—his skin warm and rough, safe and powerful. Neither of us said anything or looked at each other. We held hands as we marched on.

Oona pushed the call button and hummed along with the Chopin playing over the speakers, while we made our goodbyes. The roof was only a few flights up, so Valeska and Asher were going to take the stairs, leaving Quinn, Oona, and me with the faster elevator.

Asher started to step away from me, apparently meaning to leave with a simple " 'Bye" and a sad longing in his eyes. But I didn't let go of his hand, and instead pulled him back in close to me. I put my hand on his face, staring up into his eyes, and there were so many things I wanted to say, so much that I couldn't find the words for.

"Come back to me," I told him fiercely.

He smiled at me then, subtly and a little crookedly. "Don't you know by now, Malin? Nothing in all of the heavens or underworld below can keep me from you."

And then the elevator doors opened, so there was no more time to say goodbye. No more chances to kiss him, to tell him I loved him, to beg him to stay safe.

I stepped into the elevator, and I kept my eyes on Asher until the very last second.

SEVENTY-NINE

---◆---

In the center of the parking garage, underneath a bright halogen bulb, sat the slick silver HBS 1300 XXX Cavalieri. Despite the fact that it was a hoverbike, it was a beast of a machine, at least twice as wide as my luft and longer, with a full quad set of hoverpads.

I didn't even know if these were street legal, but if Samael got around on it, I sincerely doubted that anybody would bother stopping me on it today. I grabbed the helmet from the back of the luft, since this thing could top out at over four hundred miles per hour and it would really put a damper on the whole helping-to-stop-the-end-of-the-world thing if I cracked my skull open on the pavement.

Oona and Quinn had been walking on, toward the back corner where Quinn's car was parked, but they both paused to watch me get on the luft.

"Wow," Quinn said, looking far more impressed about a flashy bike than I expected her to be.

"Now's not the time, I know, but have fun on that thing while you can," Oona said.

"When this is all over, I'll make Samael lend me this thing again, and I'll take you out for a spin on the outskirts of the city," I promised her.

Oona smiled sadly. "I'll hold you to it." Then she turned and walked away, following Quinn.

The luft started up the instant I pressed the ignition, and the engine had a nearly silent purr. Music started playing through the wireless speakers in the helmet, and I used the touchpad in the center to quickly skip through Samael's choices in music (mostly classical and instrumental) until I finally settled on an electronic cover of "Immigrant Song."

Then I sped out of the garage, with the luft gliding on air, and hit the streets of the city. Samael's bike made it almost shockingly easy to get around. It nimbly swerved between deserted cars and a dumpster fire, and when a pesky battalion of skeletons decided to occupy an entire city block, the luft easily mowed them down. Of course, I unsheathed my sword so I could take out a few extra skeletons that lunged at me.

Ravenswood Academy had closed when the emergency sirens went off, so I had to look up Sloane's address using the school directory. She lived at about the halfway mark between the Riks and Marlow's apartment. Her street was thankfully deserted, though there were signs of vandalism and violence in the form of broken windows, smashed-in cars, and a few conspicuous splatters of blood on the sidewalk. Even the relatively quiet borough where the Kotharis lived wasn't safe anymore.

I pulled the luft right up to the front stoop to park it—it was pretty much martial law now, and I was going to do whatever was safest and fastest from here on out. I had just gotten off it when the front door opened, and Sloane was standing there, looking decidedly badass.

She'd forgone her usual prep school look for utilitarian black, including steel-toed boots and industrial-grade pepper spray hanging from a paracord lanyard around her neck.

"I'm ready," Sloane said matter-of-factly and walked down the steps to me.

"What?" I glanced around in confusion. "How did you know I was coming? I didn't call you."

"You came to me this morning for help deciphering a prophecy, and then everything went to shit," Sloane said. "I figured either you'd need my help or I'd need yours. Either way, it was only a matter of time until you ended up at my doorstep."

"Well, I can't argue with that logic," I said and got back on the luft.

"Do you have another helmet?" Sloane asked as she climbed on behind me.

"Nope. So hang on tight."

EIGHTY

———— ◆ ————

"But why does it matter if we're motherless children?" Sloane asked as we passed the third-floor landing on the way up to my mother's fourth-floor walk-up. The entire way up, she'd been asking about parts of the prophecy, as if I were more of an expert than her.

I glanced back over my shoulder at her, genuinely astonished that she wasn't more out of breath from climbing all the stairs. Maybe she worked out a lot, but I wouldn't be surprised if she was just so dogged in her questioning that she refused to let anything slow her down, not even her need for oxygen.

"I don't know," I said. "It's supposedly from Frigg's dream, so maybe it had something to do with the fact that she's been sleeping for so long, and her children have been without a mother that whole time."

"So you're saying that she did it as a form of punishment?" Sloane asked.

"What? No." I shook my head. "I'm saying maybe she instilled her own beliefs in the prophecy."

"You think she wrote it," Sloane realized, and she stopped short.

I turned to look at her. "No. I mean, I don't know. Frigg can supposedly see until the end of time, so it makes sense that she would tran-
scribe what she saw if she thought we needed the help."

"But if you're saying that she instilled herself and her ideals or
punishments or whatever you want to call her need for 'motherless
children,'" Sloane argued, "that's not something that she can do if she's
just reporting the facts or dictating her vision of the future. The prophecy is only personalized to her because she's the one creating it."

"I mean, maybe," I allowed. "That would make sense."

"But then . . ." Her expression slacked as something occurred to
her, and she shook her head slowly, making her curls sway. "This whole
time we thought she could see the future, but what if she was the one
writing it?"

Sloane grew more excited as she spoke, her dark brown eyes widening and her words speeding up. "She knows what's going to happen
because she's the one that preordained it all. I always thought it was like
a whole team of Vanaheimr gods and maybe Eralim pulling the strings.

"But what if it was one woman who wrote out the entire history of
earth from the moment Valkyries were created, and then she went to
sleep?" Sloane said. "That would be an exhausting feat, to be sure,
and I'd probably want to sleep for a thousand years after that."

"Until what?" I asked.

Her conviction faltered, and she furrowed her brow. "What?"

"You're suggesting that Frigg wrote the entire history from when
Valkyries were created . . . until when?" I asked. "There has to be an
end point."

"Why?" Sloane objected. "The Vanir gods and goddesses are eternal."

"Everything has an end, Sloane. You, me, the earth, even the sun will
go out and gods will no longer exist. Someday Frigg will wake from her
slumber. And then what?"

"I don't know," she admitted. "But since I'd like to live long enough
to find out, we should hurry up and get the swords and get on with this."

We had spent more than enough time debating the possibilities,
and while it would be worthwhile going over our theories with Samael

in case they might be of help to us, Sloane was right: we needed to get going.

I ran the rest of the way up the stairs but I stopped the moment I saw the door. It looked the same as it had a few days ago when I'd been here last—with notices and mail piling up—except this time it was ajar. And not a crack, like maybe I'd forgotten to close it all the way, but like it had been intentionally left open.

EIGHTY-ONE

I held my finger up to my lips to silence Sloane before she could ask any questions. I unsheathed Sigrún and crept slowly into the darkened apartment. I heard him before I saw him, breaking down the door to my old bedroom to get the hoard that Marlow had stashed inside there.

His back was to me, so he didn't notice me. Not until I grabbed his long hair and yanked his head back. Before he could do anything, I had the blade pressed against his throat.

"Hey, hey!" Azarias shouted in surprise. "I don't mean nobody any harm! I wanted to get weapons and food to survive in the coming days, and I knew Marlow had a mega-stash."

"So you thought you would break in and help yourself?" I sneered.

"Well, it's not like she's using it," he quipped, and I pressed the blade harder against his throat. "But since you're here, you'll probably want the stuff for yourself, so I'll get out of your hair."

"Do you know this guy?" Sloane asked cautiously from behind me.

"Sorta," I said. "He's my mom's ex."

"And I'm unarmed!" Azarias raised his hands so Sloane could see them. "I don't want to hurt either of you, so if you want to let me go—"

I moved the sword and pushed him away from me, since I didn't want to kill anybody that I didn't have to. Not when there would be so much bloodshed up ahead.

"Why hadn't you been out gathering this crap yourself?" I asked him as he rubbed his throat. "You convinced Marlow to prep for this, but you didn't think to?"

"Hey, I never knew *this* would happen." He pointed to the window, and in the dim light of the apartment I could see the fear running wild in his eyes. "I was told that if I seduced your mother and got her to believe my schemes, that we could be free. And I was promised a nice payday at the end, too, but I mostly did this because I was sick of you and your kind telling me when my friends and family lived and when they died."

"How could you *not* know this would happen?" I asked with a bitter laugh. "You were helping Ereshkigal overthrow the underworld, and you didn't think that when the underworld was unleashed on earth there would be hell to pay?"

"First off, I didn't know any of the bullshit I was spewing to Marlow about the twilight of the gods would actually happen," Azarias clarified. "And second, I wasn't helping Ereshkigal do shit."

"Tamerlane Fayette said he was working for his one true queen, Ereshkigal," I countered, keeping my voice even, but his conviction was beginning to unnerve me.

"Look, I don't really know that guy, and I have no idea what his motivations were." Azarias held his hands out palms up. "I only know that I sat in a meeting once with Velnias where I got my orders, and Ereshkigal wasn't there."

"She couldn't come up from Kurnugia," Sloane pointed out. "I always assumed she had a proxy doing her bidding here on earth."

"If anything, *she* was the proxy," Azarias said with a joyless chuckle. "I mean, it's not like Vanir gods are gonna do the bidding of some long-forgotten underworld goddess."

"Who . . ." My mouth had become so dry I nearly choked on the words. "Who did you take your orders from?"

"All my orders came from the big man himself," he answered and pointed toward the ceiling. "Odin."

EIGHTY-TWO

⸺◆⸺

Once when I'd been a young child, I'd been lost in a forest outside of the city. Marlow had reluctantly let me tag along with her on a mission, but we'd gotten separated when a rainstorm rolled in.

I had been lost in the dark, cold, wet, hungry, and terrified, but there had been a strange magic in the moment. Running through the woods—not knowing where I was going or if I'd make it out alive, my feet slipping with every step—had been exhilarating and wonderful in the most terrifying way.

It was a memory that my mind went back to more often than most. Not only because of the fear and the wild elation, but because of what had happened after that.

I had tripped and fallen, and I smacked my head hard on a rock. There was a blinding white light. My ears were rung, and I couldn't see or think or feel anything. The blood pounded in my ears, and my breath came out shaky, and the whole world felt as if it had tilted, like I wasn't standing on even ground.

That was exactly how I felt now, when Azarias told me that Odin—the one I'd trusted and helped and risked my life for—was the one behind all of this. The one who had gotten my mother killed.

But like when I was a child, eventually the confusion began to clear, and when I had been able to finally look around in the forest, a man had reached out and offered me his hand—

"Think about it," Azarias said, breaking the tense silence and pulling me from my memory. "How else could Ereshkigal have gotten her message out of the underworld? It's not like she could just hop in and out anytime she pleased. She was locked in, and she needed someone more powerful than herself. It would have to be a Vanir god."

"Does she know she was working for Odin?" Sloane asked in a matter-of-fact tone that led me to believe she had already accepted Azarias's claims as truth. Which made sense, because it tied in to her burgeoning theory that Frigg had created this scenario. It wasn't much of a leap to believe that she was working in tandem with her husband.

Azarias shrugged. "Frankly, I don't care. The time for worrying about who did what and who knew what when is over. The shit is happening now, and we all have to fight if we want to survive."

As if to emphasize his point, the earth began to shake again. A much smaller tremor than last time, but still enough to rattle the empty vodka bottles in the sink. And then the emergency sirens began to wail again.

"Get out," I told Azarias, but he stayed where he was—staring dumbly at me. "Get out! We don't have time for this, so *get out!*"

Finally, he did as I commanded, and he scrambled out of the apartment. I slammed the door shut behind him.

"Are you okay?" Sloane asked as she followed me into my mother's bedroom.

"I'm okay enough. But we have to get the swords and get back to the Riks." I tried to ignore her concerned reflection in the mirrored screen that protected Marlow's safe and hurriedly punched in the numbers.

"Can we still trust *anyone* at the Riks?" she asked carefully.

"I don't know." I frowned as I grabbed the Valkyrie swords and put them in my messenger bag. "But I trust Samael, anyway, and nearly everyone I care about will be there, so I want to be there with them. And I can't see another option." I paused, gritting my teeth. "Or if we even have a choice at all."

EIGHTY-THREE

❖

Where's Odin?" I demanded as soon as I stepped into Samael's office.

The ride back to the Evig Riksdag proved more difficult than the ride out, the streets more overwhelmingly full of skeletons. Fortunately, I'd grabbed a USW gun from Marlow's stash, and Sloane used that to shoot at any of them that grabbed at us.

We had made it back relatively unscathed—save for a few torn garments and a couple flesh wounds from where their fingers dug into my arms—but the building was quickly becoming overrun with skeletons. They were crowded around and trying to climb it or otherwise break in. The Vörðr had to shoot them off so we could get into the garage.

I could've, and probably I should've, taken a moment to greet my friends—particularly Asher and Oona, who appeared to have made it back safely. Everyone had managed to beat Sloane and me there, but we'd had to make the additional and protracted pit stop at Marlow's, and the streets had definitely gotten rowdier after that second earthquake. I had a feeling that Ereshkigal had unleashed more of her minions.

Valeska was sitting on the back of the couch, most likely to allow for more room for her wings, munching on kola nuts, and Asher's grandmother Teodora sat nearby on the same sofa. They were watching the news on mute, so it was only images of carnage and chaos flashing across the screen. Somehow, even in an apocalyptic situation, Teodora managed to look regal, with her glacial-white hair meticulously styled, and a black capelet draped over her shoulders.

Samael was standing at his desk, hunched over Minerva's giant grimoire, with Quinn, Oona, and Minerva flanking him so they could read as well, while Asher stood alone at the window. His back was to me when I came in, with his battered jacket stretched taut across his broad shoulders, his arms folded across his chest.

When I came in the room, bursting through the door before Godfrey had a chance to open it for me, everyone turned to look at me. I took a second to meet Asher's gaze and smile briefly at him, which was the fastest way I could convey that I was happy to see him safe, before returning my glare to Samael.

Only Samael appeared to register what I had asked, meeting my insistent rage with mild confusion.

"Mal, we think we've figured out what we're supposed to do." Oona excitedly tapped the page. "There's a chart called *biguol en friia,* and it has nine positions and shows us where to stand."

"That is super-great, and honestly, I don't mean to brush over that right now," I told her, but I kept my eyes locked on Samael, studying him for his reaction. "But I need to know where Odin is."

"I don't know, Malin," Samael replied, sounding calm but concerned in his usual way. "I haven't spoken to him or heard—"

I slammed my hand down on the desk, startling everyone. "Don't bullshit me, Samael."

"Malin!" He straightened up. "I've never lied to you!"

"Did you know Odin was behind all of this?" I demanded.

Something flashed across his aquamarine eyes—it might've been surprise or realization or disbelief—but then it was gone, and he was left staring at me with a slack jaw and his arms hanging at his sides.

"What are you talking about?" Quinn asked. "Odin was help-ing us."

"No." Samael took a deep breath. "I didn't *know* Odin was involved with all of this, but I suspected that it had to be a Vanir god. I didn't know how anyone else could pull this off."

I scowled at him. "You should've told me! If you had any ideas, you should've let me know before I ran around doing his bidding and fol-lowing his damn ravens!"

"I didn't know for sure!" Samael argued. "I couldn't know! I only did what I thought I should to protect you."

"Fuck protection!" I growled. "If you suspected him, you needed to tell me! I deserve to have a choice about who I want to serve!"

He swallowed. "You're right, Malin. I'm sorry. I made a grave mistake, and I know I may have lost your trust for good. But right now there are skeletons taking over the city, and we need to figure out what our next move should be."

"Hold on." Asher held up his hand and walked over so he was stand-ing between Samael and me. "Are you saying that it doesn't matter who we're fighting against? Are you honestly implying that who our enemy is has no bearing on how we'll fight?"

"Does it matter which Vanir god is pulling the strings right now?" Samael asked. "Not particularly, not for our purposes. I already believed it to be someone from Vanaheimr, and I still believe that our best course of action is performing the ceremony of the Drawing of the Nine."

"Frigg wrote the prophecy, and if her husband really is the one behind this underworld uprising, then doesn't that make him the vil-lain?" Sloane asked. "And if it does, how can we trust anything that either of them say?"

"Life very rarely comes down to heroes and villains," Samael said with a wan smile. "It's usually just everyone doing what they can to sur-vive, and the best of us will help more than we hurt.

"I don't entirely know what Odin's intentions were with all of this or where he is now," he went on. "But I know that Frigg loved earth, and she considered us all her children. If she could write down a way to save us all, I know that she would've, and I believe that she did.

"By all means, if you have an alternative idea about how we can combat this never-ending onslaught of death and decay at our door, I will gladly hear it or take you up on it," Samael said. "But if not, we need to get to the roof before they kill us all."

EIGHTY-FOUR

---◆---

S o do you want to see what we found, then?" Oona asked, not bothering to hide the impatience in her voice, or even waiting for my answer.

She immediately went back to the grimoire. This was Minerva's book, and, as she explained on a visit once, it had been her mother's before that. It was larger than Oona's, both in height and width, and by the looks of it, it had to weigh over ten pounds. The pages were old and yellowed but with an iridescent sheen.

I came around the desk and stood beside Oona so I could get a better look at it. She tapped the page with a nine-pointed star in the center.

Directly below that was a list of names:

Þruor
Hildr
Gondul
Skogul
Ailrun
Mistr
Eir
Rothi
Sigrun

Though there were discrepancies in spelling—probably either accidental or due to translations and language barriers—these were clearly the names of the nine original Valkyries.

"The translation is a little rough, but we think this is called 'Encharment of Frigg,'" she explained. "It tells us the order we should stand in and what to say and how to hold the swords."

"And this is just in your grimoire?" I asked, glancing over at Minerva. "Why would it be in a spell book?"

"This is more than a spell book," Minerva answered with a hint of indignation. "This is well over a thousand pages long and filled with ceremonies, incantations, potion recipes, and, yes, spells from immortals and mortals. My great-great-great-great-great-grandmother brought together all the magic that she thought to be most vital for this earth, and she bound them together here. Is it really that surprising that a ceremony to save the world would be included?"

"No, I didn't mean it like that." I lowered my eyes. "I was surprised. Sorry. Go on."

Oona went back to elaborating on what they'd uncovered and how she thought the ceremony would go down, and I listened dutifully.

While she talked, Bowie decided to venture out from where he had been hiding and sat on my feet, which was something he did when he was scared and wanted to be picked up. I happily complied, scooping him up into my arms and burying my fingers in his soft fur.

I focused on Oona and what she and Minerva were explaining because I knew how important it was, but I relished cuddling with my wolpertinger as much as I could because I didn't know when—or even if—I would be able to do it again.

With our plan outlined and time running out, everyone set about gathering what we needed before heading up to the roof. Oona started allocating swords and positions—Quinn and I planned to use our own Valkyrie swords Eir and Sigrún, while Asher and Samael were going to use the swords of their mothers, Hildr and Róta, respectively, but everyone else had to be assigned.

While Oona was divvying out the other five swords, I pulled Samael aside.

"Do you have someplace safe?" I asked him, with Bowie nuzzling up against me as I held him.

Samael looked at me quizzically. "How so?"

"Someplace where I can put Bowie so that he doesn't get hurt. Someplace where he can be okay for a while, in case . . . in case we don't come back, someplace where someone could find him later."

"Yeah." Samael smiled and gently stroked Bowie's useless wings. "I have the perfect place."

I followed him across the room, over to where his display shelves lined the wall. He moved aside a totem to reveal a hidden touchscreen. With a few a quick taps and a palm scan, he was done, and the wall beside him slid open.

There was no evidence of a door. Just a two-by-six-foot section that slowly receded and slid inside the rest of the wall. Beyond it was a short narrow hallway and a hermetic-looking bright white room.

"It's my panic room," Samael said as I peered inside. "It's the safest place that I can offer you right now. Every one of the offices has one, and the Seraphim have a master code so they can get in when this is all over."

"Thank you." I smiled gratefully at him, then carried Bowie into the room.

It was a sterile, futuristic room, with plain walls, aside from several computer screens—all of which were currently flashing news about the current situation. Other than the clear plastic table and chairs in the center, there was no furniture, which meant there was nowhere comfortable for Bowie to hide.

I set him down so I could pull off my hooded sweatshirt. That meant I would be performing the ceremony in a black tank top, but I figured I could handle the cold. I knelt down on the floor beside Bowie and made him a little bed out of my shirt, then I bent down and kissed him between his little antlers.

"You are the best pet I ever had, Bunny Bo," I told him. "I love you, and if I make it back, I promise you're going to get unlimited cuddles and carrots from here on out."

When I stood up, Samael was standing behind me in the panic room, and I nearly screamed in surprise.

"You should take this, too." He held out Gungnir—Odin's beautiful spear that Samael had been storing for safekeeping. "You may need it for what comes next."

"It's needed in the ceremony?" I asked.

He shook his head once. "No. I'm talking about what comes after if the ceremony doesn't work. This can kill *any* immortal, and it might be the only chance we have at surviving this."

"Why me?" I asked.

"Why not you?" he countered. "You retrieved it. You should wield it."

"Okay," I said, because I didn't know how to argue with that. I took it from him and then carefully tucked it into the waistband of my pants.

EIGHTY-FIVE

---◆---

The Evig Riksdag building was significantly shorter than my apartment complex, but the wind seemed much stronger and colder on the roof. Above us, dark clouds of black and red swirled and rumbled with angry thunder.

Oona, Minerva, Sloane, and Samael were carefully drawing the nonagram on the roof's surface. They had a sacred ash-and-herb concoction that Samael had whipped up while I'd been gone getting Sloane and the swords, and when they used it to mark the lines, it left a silvery-white line that left smoke rising a few inches above.

That left the rest of us standing off to the side so we didn't get in the way, and waiting for them to tell us when to take our marks. There was bickering between Minerva and Sloane—both of whom had very strong opinions about which direction the center point should be pointed—and I left Oona and Samael to mediate, since they knew more about it than I did.

I went over to the edge of the building, standing as close as I dared with the wind blowing as strong as it was, and I looked down. The skeleton swarm around the building had grown even more, and it would've been impossible for any of us to make it through on the ground level now. They were covering every inch of the ground, shoulder to shoulder, with others behind them climbing over them, and they stretched out as far as I could see, coming down every road and climbing up all the buildings that surrounded us.

The odd mushroom-like shape of the Riks building made it difficult for the skeletons to scale, but a few of them had started making it up the overhang. They still had about another twenty floors of sheer concrete and glass to scale before they made it to the roof, but at the rate they were going, it wouldn't take them that long. The skyscraper next to us was easier for them to ascend, so many of the skeletons were racing up that and attempting to leap over to us, but so far none had been successful.

As I watched their relentless struggle to reach us, I rubbed my hands over my bare arms, trying to stifle a chill that I knew wouldn't go away.

"Do you want my jacket?" Asher asked, his voice soft but clear over the roar of the wind because he was standing right behind me.

I turned around to face him. "Thank you, but no. I'm okay."

He put his hands on my arms, and they felt like fire compared to my icy skin, so he scowled at me. "You're freezing. This is ridiculous. You have to take it."

"Ash—" I tried to argue, but he took his jacket off anyway.

"I know that you're strong and that you don't need me, but I do wish you'd let me take care of you sometimes," he said with a weary smile. "I make a mean vegetable soup, give killer massages, and my shoulder is world-renowned for being the absolute best one to cry on."

I smiled up at him. "If that's your idea of taking care of me, I would happily let you do that anytime you want."

"It's a date, then." He held out his coat to me. "And put on the damn jacket."

"Thank you, but this really wasn't necessary," I insisted, but I slipped it on anyway. "We shouldn't—"

My arguments died on my lips, because a dark shadow had passed over Asher's face. But it wasn't coming from the sky—it was coming from within him, rippling underneath his skin.

"Asher?" I asked, but his eyes had already gone glassy, and then he fell back onto the roof, his body shaking violently.

EIGHTY-SIX

❖

Asher!" Teodora wailed. "What's wrong with my grandson? What's happening to him?"

Valeska grabbed her, gently but firmly holding her back so she wouldn't get in the way of Minerva and Oona, who knelt beside him. He wasn't shaking anymore, but his body had completely tensed. I could see his veins and muscles bulging in his arms, and his back arched sharply, so his spine was a foot off the roof while his head and feet remained firmly planted.

When he opened his mouth, it was the same distorted voice that had come out before, speaking in that Enochian language that I didn't understand.

"He's possessed?" Minerva asked.

"I think so," Oona replied. She had her hands on his abdomen, trying futilely to push him back down.

"By who?" Minerva asked.

"I AM ABADDON, THE GOD OF DARKNESS AND DE-STRUCTION." Those were the words that came out of Asher's mouth, but it definitely wasn't him saying them.

"Move," Samael commanded, and Minerva quickly complied so he could kneel beside Asher. "How was he possessed?"

"He was marked in Kurnugia," I said, clinging to his jacket, which was still warm from his body heat. "On his chest."

Samael grabbed Asher's T-shirt and tore it in half, as his body strained against the demon inside him. The wounds on his chest were black and festering, the edges curling back as if they were paper being burned.

Samael held his hand above Asher's chest, and he began chanting something in the same Enochian language. As he did, his fingers slowly began to glow a warm yellow, and then he plunged his fingers inside of the open wounds on Asher's chest.

Asher screamed in pain, while the demon howled in anger, and he tried to twist away, but Samael held strong. His right arm was wrapped around Asher's waist, holding him close, while his left hand remained clamped inside the wound.

"Bolape voresa oresa noco! Elasa biab ge de oi goaanu!" Samael chanted as Asher/Abaddon screamed and writhed.

Then it began to happen. Asher arched his back, and his mouth pulled back as he screamed. A torrent of dark locusts began flying out of his mouth, swarming around all of us in a disgusting, wriggling cloud. They buzzed around angrily, biting at us and spewing a sulphuric stench, but finally they were all out, and Asher collapsed back on the roof.

"Thank you," I told Samael as he stood back up, giving Asher space to wake up.

"I'm glad it worked," Samael said as he exhaled. "I've never cast out a demon that powerful before."

"You think you cast me out?" a distorted voice came from behind us, followed by a wicked laugh. "You merely set me free!"

The locusts had come together, coelescing into a dark shadow that soon took the form of a man. Dark gray mist shifted into a relatively human form, and within moments Abaddon stood before us. A tall broad-shouldered man with dark red skin—burnt, like he'd been cooking in the sun for too long—and wild tangles of black hair.

"Thank you for giving me a front-row seat to the end of days," Abaddon continued with a perverse grin that revealed his pointed teeth. "I was truly afraid that I would miss it."

"Well, I hate to break it to you, but you still will," I said and started walking toward him. I heard Oona and Quinn calling for me, telling me not to do anything stupid. But I wasn't.

A familiar metallic taste filled my mouth, reminding me of the electric energy crackling through my veins. The buzzing around my heart had started, sending a welcome heat through me, and I could feel the pressure building inside me.

"Really?" Abaddon asked. "I am the lord of the most vile city in the entire underworld, as I have been for centuries, and you think that you, one angry little girl, can stop me?"

"You might be powerful in the underworld, but we're not down there anymore," I shot back.

He threw back his head and laughed, and that's when I pulled the spear out from my waistband. He only saw it the split second before I drove it into his chest, but by the way his eyes widened, I think he knew exactly what it was.

The instant the tip pierced his skin, I felt it. A fiery heat shot through me, and a blinding light flashed out from inside of Abaddon. The force of the explosion of light and heat was so powerful that I went flying backward.

I held my arm over my face, shielding it from the explosion, and then I waited to land. But when I opened my eyes, I was still falling—plummeting down over the edge of the building toward the skeletons waiting below.

EIGHTY-SEVEN

———————◆———————

The good news was that the skeletons caught me. The bad news was that it was like landing on a trampoline made of broken bones.

I expected them to tear me apart, but they were instantly moving me, passing me backward like I was body-surfing over the dead. I tried to fight them off, but they gripped me from every angle. I managed to get my right hand free long enough to safely tuck the spear into the lining of Asher's jacket, and then I let them carry me away, since I couldn't fight them.

It was like floating on wild river rapids, with them hurriedly pulling me along. The skeletons must've been a hive mind, like ants, because they worked together so quickly and efficiently that they had dragged me all the way to Skarpåker Park in record time.

From what I could see as they carried me, the camera crew was all gone, as were most humans. The crowd in the center of the park appeared to be entirely skeletons and immortals, though I couldn't discern if the immortals had followed Ereshkigal from Kurnugia or if they were residents of the city.

The skeletons lifted me up, pushing me onto the rocky outcrop-

A store credit for the purchase price will be issued (i) for purchases made by check less than 7 days prior to the date of return, (ii) when a gift receipt is presented within 60 days of purchase, (iii) for textbooks, (iv) when the original tender is PayPal, or (v) for products purchased at Barnes & Noble College bookstores that are listed for sale in the Barnes & Noble Booksellers inventory management system.

Opened music CDs, DVDs, vinyl records, audio books may not be returned, and can be exchanged only for the same title and only if defective. NOOKS purchased from other retailers or sellers are returnable only to the retailer or seller from which they are purchased, pursuant to such retailer's or seller's return policy. Magazines, newspapers, eBooks, digital downloads, and used books are not returnable or exchangeable. Defective NOOKS may be exchanged at the store in accordance with the applicable warranty.

Returns or exchanges will not be permitted (i) after 14 days or without receipt or (ii) for product not carried by Barnes & Noble or Barnes & Noble.com.

Policy on receipt may appear in two sections.

Return Policy

With a sales receipt or Barnes & Noble.com packing slip, a full refund in the original form of payment will be issued from any Barnes & Noble Booksellers store for returns of undamaged NOOKs, new and unread books, and unopened and undamaged music CDs, DVDs, vinyl records, toys/games and audio books made within 14 days of purchase from a Barnes & Noble Booksellers store or Barnes & Noble.com.

the original tender is PayPal, or (v) for products purchased at Barnes & Noble College bookstores that are listed for sale in the Barnes & Noble Booksellers inventory management system.

Opened music CDs, DVDs, vinyl records, audio books may not be returned, and can be exchanged only for the same title and only if defective. NOOKs purchased from other retailers or sellers are returnable only to the retailer or seller from which they are purchased, pursuant to such retailer's or seller's return policy. Magazines, newspapers, eBooks, digital downloads, and used books are not returnable or exchangeable. Defective NOOKs may be exchanged at the store in accordance with the applicable warranty.

Returns or exchanges will not be permitted (i) after 14 days or without receipt or (ii) for product not carried by Barnes & Noble or Barnes & Noble.com.

Policy on receipt may appear in two sections.

Return Policy

With a sales receipt or Barnes & Noble.com packing slip, a full refund in the original form of payment will be issued from any Barnes & Noble Booksellers store for returns of undamaged music CDs, DVDs, vinyl records, toys/games and audio books made within 14 days of purchase from a Barnes & Noble Booksellers store or Barnes & Noble.com, and undamaged NOOKs, new and unread books, and unopened and undamaged music CDs, DVDs, vinyl records/games with the below exceptions:

A store credit for the purchase price will be issued (i) for purchases made by check less than 7 days prior to the date of return, (ii) when a gift receipt is presented within 60 days of purchase, (iii) for textbooks, (iv) when the original tender is PayPal, or (v) for products purchased at Barnes & Noble College bookstores that are listed for sale in the Barnes & Noble Booksellers inventory management system.

Opened music CDs, DVDs, vinyl records, audio books may not be returned, and can be exchanged only for the same title and only if defective. NOOKs

Valid through 6/6/2019

Buy 1
Fresh Baked Cookie
Get 1 FREE

USE ON YOUR NEXT VISIT

To redeem: Present this coupon in the Cafe

A8U3L7U

Buy 1 Fresh Baked Cookie Get 1 Free:
1 redemption per coupon, while supplies last.
Valid on Fresh Baked cookies only.
Ask Cafe cashier for full Terms & Conditions

purchased from other retailers or sellers are returnable only to the retailer or seller from which they are purchased, pursuant to such retailer's or seller's return policy. Magazines, newspapers, eBooks, digital downloads, and used books are not returnable or exchangeable. Defective NOOKs may be exchanged at the store in accordance with the applicable warranty.

Returns or exchanges will not be permitted (i) after 14 days or without receipt or (ii) for product not carried by Barnes & Noble or Barnes & Noble.com.

Policy on receipt may appear in two sections.

Return Policy

With a sales receipt or Barnes & Noble.com packing slip, a full refund in the original form of payment will be issued from any Barnes & Noble Booksellers store for returns of undamaged NOOKs, new and unread books, and unopened and undamaged music CDs, DVDs, vinyl records, toys/games and audio books made within 14 days of purchase from a Barnes & Noble Booksellers store or Barnes & Noble.com with the below exceptions:

A store credit for the purchase price will be issued (i) for purchases made by check less than 7 days prior to the date of return, (ii) when a gift receipt is presented within 60 days of purchase, (iii) for textbooks, (iv) when the original tender is PayPal, or (v) for products purchased at Barnes & Noble College bookstores that are listed for sale in the Barnes & Noble Booksellers inventory management system.

Opened music CDs, DVDs, vinyl records, audio books may not be returned, and can be exchanged only for the same title and only if defective. NOOKs purchased from other retailers or sellers are returnable only to the retailer or seller from which they are purchased, pursuant to such retailer's or seller's return policy. Magazines, newspapers, eBooks, digital downloads, and used books are not returnable or exchangeable. Defective NOOKs may be exchanged at the store in accordance with the applicable warranty.

Returns or exchanges will not be permitted (i) after 14 days or without receipt or (ii) for product not carried by Barnes & Noble or Barnes & Noble.com.

Policy on receipt may appear in two sections.

Return Policy

Barnes & Noble Booksellers #2871
1260 Churn Creek Rd.
Redding, CA 96003
530-222-2006

STR:2871 REG:007 TRN:4233 CSHR:Danika A

BARNES & NOBLE MEMBER   EXP: 08/12/2020

Cookie S Caramel
  9780594433828   N*
  (1 @ 2.50) Sell @ Cpn $ (2.50)
  #A8U3L7U
  (1 @ 0.00)   0.00
Cookie Choc Chunk
  9781402826344   N*
  (1 @ 2.50) Member Card 10% (0.25)
  (1 @ 2.25)   2.25

TOTAL   2.25
CASH   20.25
CASH CHANGE   18.00-

MEMBER SAVINGS   0.25

Connect with us on Social

Facebook-   @BNRedding
Instagram-   @bnredding
Twitter-   @BNRedding

050.03A   05/21/2019 02:19PM

CUSTOMER COPY

returnable only to the retailer or seller from which they are purchased, pursuant to such retailer's or seller's return policy. Magazines, newspapers, eBooks, digital downloads, and used books are not returnable or exchangeable. Defective NOOKs may be exchanged at the store in accordance with the applicable warranty.

Returns or exchanges will not be permitted (i) after 14 days or without receipt or (ii) for product not carried by Barnes & Noble or Barnes & Noble.com.

Policy on receipt may appear in two sections.

Return Policy

With a sales receipt or Barnes & Noble.com packing slip, a full refund in the original form of payment will be issued from any Barnes & Noble Booksellers store for returns of undamaged NOOKs, new and unread books, and unopened and undamaged music CDs, DVDs, vinyl records, toys/games and audio books made within 14 days of purchase from a Barnes & Noble Booksellers store or Barnes & Noble.com with the below exceptions:

A store credit for the purchase price will be issued (i) for purchases made by check less than 7 days prior to the date of return, (ii) when a gift receipt is presented within 60 days of purchase, (iii) for textbooks, (iv) when the original tender is PayPal, or (v) for products purchased at Barnes & Noble College bookstores that are listed for sale in the Barnes & Noble Booksellers inventory management system.

Opened music CDs, DVDs, vinyl records, audio books may not be returned, and can be exchanged only for

We want to hear your feedback!

Complete our survey at

www.barnesandnoblefeedback.com

or

Text BN to 345345

Your survey code is 8200102-743270

Enter for a chance to win one of twenty
$25 B&N gift cards drawn monthly.

No purchase necessary. Ends 4/30/2020
Must be legal resident of the 50 US
including DC and 21+.
Void where prohibited.
Visit www.barnesandnoblefeedback.com for
complete details and official rules.

pings, and they tossed me onto them, like ocean waves tossing garbage onto the beach. I scrambled to get up, but then I saw her—the self-appointed queen of the underworld resistance—so I decided to stay back on my knees.

Ereshkigal walked over to me, and I was taken aback by how imposing she was in real life. This was my first time meeting her, and she had an ethereal beauty that was almost painful to look at. Her dress was like a black mist forming around her, perfectly coiling to the parts worth accentuating, and her hands were clasped in front of her.

With a knowing smile, she looked at me and said, "You are the one that has given me so much trouble."

"Right back at you," I said, which actually made her smile deepen. "What do you want with me?"

"Are you not the leader of the Valkyries?" she asked.

"Leader?" I said with a laugh. "I'm not even technically a Valkyrie yet."

"Then why have you been leading the fight against me?" she asked, seeming surprisingly unruffled about having my position so wrong.

"It's a long story, but the short version is: because I saw what you were doing, and I couldn't stand by and let you destroy the world."

"I don't want to destroy the world," she insisted. "I merely want to set it free!"

"But the way you are going about it, you are *destroying* the world!" I shouted at her. "The underworld cannot be unleashed without dramatic disastrous consequences. Even if you weren't plotting to kill us all or overturning millennia's worth of doctrine and binding ecclesiastic law, where do you think you will live? There are nearly twenty-five billion beings living here right now. There are barely enough resources to go around, and you want to add the billions of beings from the underworld?"

Her expression was impassive as she said, "Then so be it. Only the strong will survive."

"But you already had your turn!" I argued. "Let the rest of us get a chance at being alive."

"It is still my turn!" she snarled, and her face contorted with rage. "Do you not understand that? It never stopped being my turn. I am still alive, and I refuse to be locked away any longer."

"I'm not saying that your life was fair or that Kurnugia is the most ethical way to handle immortality," I said carefully. "What I am saying is that the earth cannot hold us all, and if you insist on opening Kurnugia for everyone to escape, you will doom us all. The world will be destroyed, and you and Gugalanna and everyone and everything will be doomed along with it."

Still she stood unmoved by my pleas. "If that is the only way to be free, then so be it. I will not give up until all the Valkyries are dead and the seals to Kurnugia have been completely removed so that everyone can be free."

"There is no other way, then," I said simply. "You and the earth cannot coexist." The whole time we had been talking, I had been palming the spear inside my jacket, so it would be ready at a moment's notice.

She tilted her head then, and I struck. She tried to stop me, but it didn't matter where I stuck the weapon as long as the tip pierced her skin. She howled and her eyes flashed black, and that was the last thing that I remembered.

EIGHTY-EIGHT

◆

The air smelled of pine needles and earth, and the rain felt cold as it landed on my face. My back ached terribly, but it was the dull throbbing in my head that made it hard for me to open my eyes.

When I finally managed to open them, I was staring up at a forest. Trees towering over me, their branches covered in thick needles, with only the smallest gaps through the canopy where I could see the overcast sky.

Then someone stepped in front of me, blocking the dim light, and the rain falling on my face blurred my vision, so I couldn't see who it was—only a shadow standing over me.

I knew I should be afraid, but I felt strangely at peace and resigned to whatever happened next. Like a part deep inside me had always known that it would come to this, that this would be how it ended.

The figure bent over, extending a hand toward me, but I made no move toward it.

"Don't be afraid," he said in a voice like faraway thunder. "Take my hand, Malin."

That's when I realized that I recognized the voice. I *knew* him.

I blinked hard, unable to make sense of the world, but when I opened my eyes again, I wasn't in the forest. I was in Skarpåker Park, lying on a pile of bones that dug painfully into my back, and Odin was standing over me, holding out his hand.

"I don't bite," Odin tried to assure me. He looked down at me with a warm smile, his one good eye shining brightly, while the left was withered shut.

I took his hand, because I needed him to help me to my feet since the bones made for unsteady ground. The sky above us was still dark and angry, and the park was littered with thousands of broken skeletons and piles of ash. Both of Odin's ravens were nearby, picking at the remains, but I couldn't see any signs of Ereshkigal or Gugalanna.

"What happened?" I asked.

"Ereshkigal used her own blood—along with that of your friend Asher—to unseal Kurnugia, but it was only powerful enough to allow for her, her lover, and the most primitive form of death to make it through," he explained. "She wanted to kill all the Valkyries, and the combined power of all your blood would be enough for her to break the seal for everyone.

"But when you killed her—no, *killed* isn't the right word. You annulled her existence." He moved his hand vaguely, as if motioning to the ether. "It's as if she never was, and her power to unbreak the seal was removed."

"What happened to Gugalanna?" I asked.

"He is nothing more than a pile of ash," Odin said, gesturing vaguely around to any number of piles of ash around us.

"Why are you here? Why are you pretending to help me?" I asked, but my words came out sounding more exhausted than accusatory.

"Who says that I'm pretending?" he countered.

"I know that you were behind all of this," I said. "The only reason any of this was possible was because you were putting it together. You gave Ereshkigal the means to escape, and you sent Velnias to set up my mother."

He laughed then, a warm sound that resonated through me. "I had far less to do with all of this than you are imagining. Yes, I gave information to Ereshkigal, to Velnias, to you, that put all of this in motion. But that was all."

"Then who is behind all of this?"

"The same one who has been behind every decision that everyone has ever made." Odin smiled. "My wife, Frigg."

"Sloane was right," I realized. "Frigg wrote out our entire destinies."

"Not entirely," he corrected me. "She wrote everything until this moment."

I narrowed my eyes at him. "What does that mean?"

"When you thought I was the one pulling the strings, getting everyone to do my bidding, were you not angry?" he asked pointedly.

"Of course. I was furious. And I'm still pretty angry about what involvement you did have, to be honest."

"But when I said that Frigg has been controlling everything for centuries, you showed no anger?" Odin questioned. "Why were my small actions more upsetting to you than her constant ones?"

"Because . . ." I paused, trying to understand it myself. "I trusted you. I don't like the idea of anyone controlling me or conspiring against me, but Frigg is just a name to me. You were someone I helped, and I thought you were helping me."

"And now you think I have not been helping you?" he asked, looking down at me directly.

"My mother is dead because of you," I said, letting the venom into my voice for the first time since he'd woken me.

"Your mother was alive because of me, too," he shot back.

"Am I supposed to thank you for that?" I asked with tears stinging my eyes. "Thank you for giving me an angry, severely damaged woman for a mother, who could never love me, and then taking her from me before I had to chance to . . ."

"To what?" Odin pressed when I trailed off.

"I was going to say until . . . I got her to love me. But . . . she was never going to love me, was she?"

"No." He shook his head sadly, and his voice was filled with a soft comfort. "It wasn't in her design, the same way it's not in yours to fly or mine to die. I am sorry that life hurts, and I know it's of no consolation, but there can be no joy without suffering. I have tried too often to protect you all from far too much, and it never ends well. Humans crave chaos, even if it is only the illusion of it."

"Yeah," I said as I looked out over the pile of bones. "It's never boring here on earth, I'll give you that."

"I created the Valkyries to protect humanity," Odin said. "The immortals were too powerful, but the other gods dared not strip them of their immortality. It was a precedent they were terrified would take over until none of us were left, and the Vanir gods were no longer welcome. We have seen it happen in other worlds.

"Myself, Frigg, and some of the other gods thought that predestination would be the key," he went on. "*We* would be the ones keeping the balance, guaranteeing it never tilted in the favor of one side or the other. The Valkyries were merely an illusion of power granted to humans, both to help keep them safe and to put enough fear in the immortals to keep them in line.

"But all too soon it became apparent that we had made a grave mistake." He frowned. "It is impossible for life to flourish without free will. Frigg tried to allow room for creativity, for that inventive spark and curiosity that makes humans so special, but it is near-impossible to infuse when every major event in your lives has already been preordained."

He stared off wistfully before adding, "She tried to give you as much freedom as she could, in your thoughts and emotions, but when your actions and choices are limited—or eliminated entirely—there is no real freedom to be had."

"Where is Frigg?" I asked.

"She yet sleeps, in Vanaheimr, where she has been sleeping for the past five thousand years. She'll be awaking very soon, and I will go to her then. I hope to be able to bring our son with us." He focused his gaze on me. "But that is up to you."

"Me? How is that up to me?" I asked dubiously.

"Frigg only wrote the predestiny until the moment that Ereshkigal was killed," he explained. "We both wanted to give the Valkyries enough time that humanity would have a chance to survive among the immortals. The time also allowed for the Vanir gods to grow complacent, forgetful, and distant from the earth, so they would care little about what happened to it."

"Are you saying that you're going to kill us all?" I asked.

He grinned broadly. "On the contrary. All of this work, all these centuries of planning, it was all done so that one day you could all be free. Not just the Valkyries, but the humans, the immortals, everything on this earth."

And that's when it finally hit me. "The Drawing of the Nine was never about stopping Ereshkigal."

"No. It has always been our secret fail-safe, a back door into free will. The other gods would never allow it, and they would have been furious if they had known what we were doing. So we had to give the power to you," he said. "And, fittingly, this choice cannot be made by me or Frigg or any of the immortals. It must be made by you."

"What choice?" I asked.

"Come." He held out his hand to me again. "We should return to your friends, and you can decide then."

EIGHTY-NINE

$\bullet$

Traveling with a Vanir god was much cooler and easier than any other form of travel. Odin pulled me into his arms, and within moments we'd been transported from the park to the roof of the Evig Riksdag.

We appeared near the edge, off to the side of where everyone else stood gathered in the center. There were a few bones strewn about, which meant they'd had to fight off a few skeletons while I'd been gone, but they all seemed to be okay. Valeska was flying around—I wasn't sure if she was taking in the carnage or if she was looking for me, or both.

It was Oona who spotted me first, letting out a squeal of delight and rushing over to throw her arms around me. I had stowed the spear back in my waistband, so I tilted away from her hug as much she would allow.

"I knew you weren't dead," she insisted, but the ferocity of her hug contradicted that. "You can't die."

Asher was right behind her, and once she finally released me, he pulled me into a much more gentle embrace. "It wasn't until you were gone that I realized that I never made you promise to come back to me."

"I thought you knew," I told him honestly. "I'll always come back."

Valeska returned to the roof just as everyone gathered around me and Odin, demanding to know what had happened. It took a few minutes for me to explain, with only a few contributions from Odin. Everyone still regarded him warily, particularly Valeska and Sloane, and their distrust did nothing to calm my nerves about the situation.

"Why wasn't I told of any of this?" Samael asked Odin, once I'd finished my explanation as best I could.

"Because Frigg and I worked tirelessly to ensure that this would happen, and I have spent five thousand years away from her for this," Odin said. "I could not risk undoing thousands of years' worth of work and loneliness, for if word got to the other gods or the wrong immortal, all this would be for naught."

"We have to do it," Valeska said, speaking up now. "Why would anyone turn down a chance to be free?"

"It sounds too good to be true." Sloane pursed her lips. "You keep saying 'free will' like it's this tangible thing that can be handed to us. What does it mean? How would it work with immortals? What will become of the Valkyries and Eralim?"

"Free will does come with a price," Odin answered. "In order for this to work and be fair and for humanity to have a real chance, immortality will be a thing of the past."

"How?" Quinn asked. "All the immortals will die?"

"No, no, no one will die, not from this," he clarified. "All beings with supernatural powers—Valeska's wings, Malin's strength—and even the magic of this world, like Oona's sorcery—all of that will remain. Only no one will live forever any longer. They will get one lifetime, and that's it.

"There will be no more Kurnugia or Zianna," he said. "Only earth, and the time that you have on it."

"What is one lifetime?" Teodora asked. "What that means for a dragon cannot be the same for a mouse."

"It will vary from being to being, but bodies will deteriorate and grow old in a way comparable to the beings of their kind," Odin explained. "The average immortal will have about a hundred years, either from the day they are born or from today, when their immortality was removed."

"A hundred years," Samael repeated softly. He was the only one among us who had immortality to give up.

"What about you?" Quinn asked Odin. "What becomes of you and the rest of the Vanir gods?"

"I cannot take away immortality from anyone in Vanaheimr, not because I'm unwilling but because I am unable," he said. "But we have free will, and we are already so far removed from you, I don't see it as being an obstacle."

"How long do we have to decide?" Sloane asked. "I mean, the idea is that we currently have free will, because we're being offered a choice. What happens if we do nothing?"

"If the ceremony is not performed by the time the sun sets, everything will revert to how it has always been," Odin said. "I will return to Vanaheimr, where Frigg will awaken to continue writing your destiny, if that is what you wish. There will be a great mess to clean up here because of Ereshkigal, but beyond that, nothing will change."

"So it's up to us?" Asher asked. "The nine of us get to decide if there can be free will for the entire planet?"

Oona folded her arms over her chest. "It doesn't seem right that we have to make such a drastic decision that will affect every living thing."

"How is it any different from how they—we—have already been living?" Valeska argued. "Well, except everything was decided by only two gods."

"Life has never been fair," Teodora said.

I looked to Samael, who had been mostly quiet as we talked.

"Would you give up immortality?" I asked him. "If you got to choose all on your own, which choice would you make?"

He didn't answer right away, instead staring thoughtfully at the roof at his feet. "I have been alive for three hundred and thirty-eight years. I have just learned that in that entire time, I have never made a choice that wasn't predestined, one that was my own. And here I am, being given the first true choice of my entire existence. It seems to me that it would be a travesty if my first and only choice I ever made was to give up the ability to choose."

"It's going to be total chaos," Quinn said, shaking her head. "There will be so much anger. People will die over this."

"People will die anyway," Asher said gently. "This way, they get to *live*."

"Whatever you decide, it must be your choice," Odin said. "For now I will return to Vanaheimr to see my wife, and I will let you do whatever it is you need to do."

NINETY

---◆---

The nine-pointed star had been messed up during the scuffle with the skeletons, so Oona carefully went over it with her ash-and-herb stick until it was fixed. Minerva directed us to each of our points on the star.

Oona stood at the northernmost point in the first position, holding Thrúd with its carnation-pink blade. To her left going around the star was Asher with his blood-red Hildr, Teodora with burnt-orange Göndul, Minerva with lemon-yellow Skögul, Sloane with forest-green Ölrún, Valeska with bright teal Mist, Quinn with sky-blue Eir, Samael with dark indigo Róta, and finally me, with purple Sigrún, standing on the point between Samael and Oona.

Above us, the dark swirling clouds finally parted enough to let the sunlight through. The smallest beam of light landed right in the center of the star.

"So, we're all going to hold up our swords, pointing them toward the sky," Oona said, going over the plan one final time before we began. "Samael will read the incantation in the original language, while I will say it in English, and then you can all repeat after me."

Samael was the only one saying it in the original language, because he was the only one who could pronounce it properly. Oona believed that it didn't matter what language we said the incantation in, as long as we said it, but she also thought it wouldn't hurt to have someone reading the original text in its written language.

Then she took a deep breath. "Is everybody ready?" she asked, and we all nodded.

"Let's get this done," Valeska said and held her sword up high over her head, and we all followed suit.

"Gang ût, ût fana themo margę an that bên," Samael began.

"Get out, away from the marrow to the bone," Oona translated, and when the rest of us echoed her, our swords began to glow.

"Ût fana themo bêne an that flêsg."

"Away from the bone to the flesh."

"Ût fana themo flêsgke an lebēn."

"Away from the flesh to life."

The swords had begun to glow almost blindingly bright, and Sigrún trembled in my hand.

"Ût fana themo lebēn an that tōd."

"Away from life to the death."

"Ût fana that tōd an thesa strâla." Samael was nearly shouting now, to be heard over the rumbling of the sky. The sun still shone through, but the clouds were swirling, and a strong wind had picked up.

"Away from the death and into the atmosphere!" Oona gripped her sword with both hands, as most of us had started to do since they had begun to shake.

"Uuodan, uuerthe so!" Samael yelled the final line.

"Odin, make it so!"

Suddenly beams of light shot out from the swords, meeting in the center of the star in a solid rainbow beam that blasted up to the sky. Wind was blowing from it, pushing us all back, but we held strong and would not be moved.

Lightning crackled across the sky, and a twisted, screaming howl blasted through the wind, sounding as if a million demons were screaming all at once. The loudest thunderclap I had ever heard rattled through us, shaking the earth along with it.

Then I had the strangest sensation, as if something were being pulled from within me. Like wisps of weight and pain, flowing through me, away from me, out into the air.

I had lived my whole life with a vise wrapped around my heart, squeezing it so hard it could barely beat, but I'd never even known that it was there. I thought that was how life felt.

Now it was breaking away, being ripped from me, and my heart pounded harder than ever before. It was really beating, for the first time, entirely on its own.

And then whatever it was, all the invisible shackles inside me were gone. The ceremony was over, and we all collapsed onto the concrete, gasping for breath.

"So that's it?" I asked, looking over at Oona. "We're free."

She smiled tiredly, but the happiness was evident in her eyes. "Yeah, Mal. I think we're actually free."

NINETY-ONE

❖

Classical music was still piping in through the speakers in the elevator as Samael and I rode down alone. Everyone else had gotten off two floors above us, where the Seraphim and head Eralim were scrambling together to figure out what had happened.

An interrogation by the Evig Riksdag was still in store for Samael and myself, but I wanted to check on Bowie, hidden away in Samael's panic room, and we wanted to get Gungnir safely locked up before somebody else could get their hands on it. Plus I could really use a moment or two to breathe before being bombarded with questions and paraded through meetings with officials.

In fact, the very first thing I did after the elevator doors closed on the chaotic scene unfolding on the highest floors of the Riks—one that quickly swallowed up all my friends, who gave me rueful looks over their shoulders—was lean back against the wall and exhale deeply.

"You can say that again," Samael said with a tired laugh.

He leaned against the copper wall beside me, his hands shoved in the pockets of his dirt- and bloodstained pants. His wild curls had come loose from their bun and the wind had wreaked havoc on them. The expression on his face was more weary than anything else, and I didn't know that I'd ever seen him look so disheveled and lost.

"How are you holding up?" I asked him.

"Okay." He thought for a few seconds before elaborating, "It's hard to say. How about you?"

"Same, I think." I shrugged. "Do you feel any different?"

His brow furrowed. "I feel . . . exactly the same and entirely different. My heart feels like it's beating so much harder now."

My hand instinctively went to my chest, where my heart hammered away. "Yeah, I know what you mean." I looked at him, and as the elevators opened to the deserted twenty-ninth floor, I asked, "Did we do the right thing?"

"I think we did." Samael nodded as we walked down the long corridor toward his office. "It's impossible to ever really know for certain. Would the world be safer if there were still no free will?"

He stared down at the black marble floor as he spoke. "Maybe, but it never really felt all that safe to begin with. Immortals will probably be unhappy, but I think trading in an endless lifetime of predestination for a mortal one with choice—that has to be better."

"What do you think is going to happen now?" I asked.

"I don't know," he said with a heavy sigh. "It's going to take a while for everyone to adjust to the new world order, and some won't be happy about it. Especially now that Kurnugia is closed."

"So everyone in Kurnugia is just . . . gone?" I asked. I was surprised by the strange sense of loss and guilt that washed over me at the thought of all the creatures and immortals I'd met in Kurnugia and Zianna being snuffed out in the blink of an eye. Lyra, the kirin, Kalbi the Kting Voar, Sedna and the whole court.

"I can't believe that would be the case." He shook his head. "Odin and Frigg's son is still down there, and I can't see Frigg writing a prophecy that would kill him. But they can't come up to the surface, either. So I assume they'll be allowed to live out their one lifetime down there, only now those who are mortally wounded will die instead of getting up again. Within a hundred years or so, I imagine it will be empty."

"What will happen to the immortals that live on earth?" I asked, even though I wasn't sure if Samael knew any more than I did.

"The same thing will happen to you or me—we'll make our lives, hopefully filling them with loved ones, hobbies, and careers that make us happy, and, eventually, we will die."

"But not today," I said, knowing that I should feel relief and pride in that.

"Not today." He looked at me then, smiling warmly. "You did good. I think your mom would be proud."

"You really think so?"

"I do," Samael said emphatically. "She would've made the same choice, if she'd been able to."

"Do you think . . ." I swallowed hard, gathering the courage to finish my question, delaying hearing an answer I feared I already knew. "If she had free will, do you think she would've loved me?"

"It would be easy for me to say yes, of course, but I've always taken you as the type of person that prefers the truth over kindness," Samael answered carefully. "And the truth is that I don't know. I don't know how much Marlow's personality and dysfunctions were endemic to her or Frigg's predestination. It's impossible for us to ever fully understand where our choices ended and the prophecy began. And sometimes some people make really shitty parents."

"Sometimes life deals you a bad hand," I agreed wearily.

He stopped short then, just before the doors to the office, and he put his hand on my shoulder, so I would look him in the eye. "But Malin, listen to me—you are not the sins of your mother," he said, speaking with conviction. "You cannot let yourself be defined by her or her actions or whether she loved you or not.

"You spent the first nineteen years of your life trying to earn the love of a woman who would never give it to you, and whether that was by her own choice or design, it doesn't matter," Samael went on. "We've done something really spectacular here tonight—*you've* done something. And it would be a shame if you let resentments and transgressions from the past overshadow your future."

Tears were stinging my eyes, so I looked away and wiped at them roughly. "At least we have each other, right?"

"That we do." He put his arm around my shoulders. "And though we'll never understand what went on in Marlow's head, she definitely had her own demons to battle. But despite all that, and even after her death, she still managed to help save the world. If she hadn't gathered those four swords, I don't know if we would be free now."

EPILOGUE

—◆—

I sat on the couch in my apartment, with Bowie lying on his back beside me so I would pet his fat belly. I had promised him plenty of cuddles and carrots if we made it through that whole mess, and we had, so I was more than happy to deliver on that promise.

Right now we were watching NorNewsNow, because it was good to check in and see how everybody was handling all the changes.

"It has been forty-two days since Ereshkigal's failed attempt to open up the underworld," Ellery Park was saying at the news desk. "And while officials still don't understand how her actions led to the end of immortality, most are making the best of the new situation.

"Many feel happier, and most are reporting that they feel like they have more control over their lives, as cleanups continue all over the world. Old regimes are falling, and new ones are being put in their place," Ellery went on. "Some are speculating that this might be the beginning of the twilight of the gods—"

No one knew about our part in it, other than Samael and a few Seraphim at the Riks. They feared immortal retaliation against the nine of us involved, and the reality was that Ereshkigal's actions helped bring about the change.

Oona came out of her bedroom and cast me a disapproving glare. "Are you seriously going to sit in front of the TV all day again?"

"I don't sit in front of the TV *all* day," I corrected her, but I stopped petting Bowie long enough to start picking up some of the take-out boxes that had piled up on the table. "I just don't know what to do with myself now that Valkyries are no longer a thing. And I did get a job at Dillinger's, so it's not like I'm doing *nothing*."

She sat down on the couch beside me and clicked off the TV, so I would give her my full attention. "I really think you should consider going back to Ravenswood. Now that nobody can live forever, there's a bigger demand for supernatural-related careers, especially thaumaturgy and apothecary. I've already got an apprenticeship lined up for sorcery in January. The demand is so high they're fast-tracking me."

"It also helps that you're really good at it," I said, but she brushed off my compliment with a demure smile. "I'm happy that you found a path that speaks to you, but you know that magic and all that has never really been my forte. I haven't figured out what I want to do or who I want to be yet. I am deciding what I'm going to do with my life for the first time, so I want to take my time."

"Fair enough," Oona allowed and stood up. "I just don't want you getting depressed."

"Honestly, I feel happier than I have in a very long time," I said. "Maybe ever. You don't need to worry about me yet."

"I'm always going to worry about you. It's my job. You're my best friend." Oona grabbed her book bag from where she'd left it by the front door. "I have to get to class now, but I should be home around five if you wanna grab some dinner together."

"Yeah, that sounds great." I smiled at her.

As soon as she opened the door, she bumped right into Asher, who had his fist raised like he was about to knock. Once they both apologized to each other, multiple times, about their awkward clumsiness, Asher came in, and Oona left.

"I come bearing gifts." He held up a bag of kibbeh, then sat down on the couch beside me.

"Ooh, thank you!" I leaned over and kissed him quickly on the cheek. "I'm starving."

"So what's your plan for today?" he asked.

"I don't have to work, so I was gonna watch bad movies and hang with Bowie," I said around a mouthful of the delicious fried croquettes. "What about you?"

"There's a recruitment going on downtown at the old Riks building. They're creating a special forces unit with the police to handle the new overflow, now that there aren't Valkyries to help keep order. I thought I might check it out."

"You think you might want to join that?" I asked.

He shrugged. "It's a wide open world, you know?"

"I do."

"Oh, my grandma wanted to know if you want to come over on Friday for supper?" Asher asked.

"We have that double date with Quinn and Valeska that night, remember?" I asked, and recognition flashed across his face. "I think we'll probably end up going to Carpe Noctem or something, but I still don't want to bail on plans with them."

"No, that's fair, I just forgot." He reached over and snagged a kibbeh out of the bag before I ate them all. "I'll tell my grandma another night."

As I munched on my food, we lapsed into a comfortable silence.

"Are you still happy?" he asked finally.

"Why do people keep asking me that today? Yeah, I'm happy."

"I meant, you still think we made the right decision?"

"Yeah, of course." I tilted my head. "Do you?"

He nodded. "I just wanted to know, now that the dust has settled from everything, that . . ." He shifted and cleared this throat. "I wanted to know if you still felt like your choices for, um, life and . . . everything, were still your own. If you still wanted to make them."

"Are you asking me if I still want to be with you?" I asked.

"Yeah." He rubbed the back of his neck. "You told me before that it's the choice that makes something real, and I wanted to know if you would still choose me."

I set down my food and turned to face him more fully. "I don't know if I would've chosen you on my own. But that doesn't matter. Because every day since we did the Drawing of the Nine, I have chosen you. I have wanted to be with you and see you and kiss you and love you. And I will choose you every day from now on, no matter what the gods say."

"Good." He leaned down and kissed me gently but sweetly.

Before we could get too deep into it, my phone began to ring. I thought about letting it go to voice mail, but the ID said it was Samael.

"Sorry, I should grab this," I said as I untangled myself from Asher and answered the phone. "Hello?"

"Are you busy?" Samael asked.

"Why?" I hedged.

"I have something that I want your help with," Samael said. "You were one of the more promising Valkyrie students I've had, and with the upheaval in the world right now, I'd like you to join me."

"Join you in what?"

"Just because Valkyries are out of work and immortals don't live forever anymore doesn't mean that crime or scheming have gone away," Samael explained. "A lot of the new faux-mortals are pretty pissed off. But I think if you and I worked together, we could stop innocent lives from being lost. What do you think? Would you ever consider working with me again?"

I thought for a second, but the truth was, I'd probably decided as soon as I answered the phone. "I'm in."

GLOSSARY

———◆———

ACHERON GORGE—a gorge in Kurnugia. It was once called the "river of woe," but it has long since dried up. It is a home to lost souls, who cry out in agony for all of eternity.

ĀDITYAS ELIXIR—an energy drink from Southeast Asia made with mangoes and caffeine, named after the Sun God in Hinduism.

AIZSAULE DISTRICT—a neighborhood in the northwestern part of Chicago. It's home to many demons and other impious immortals. While it is still within the bounds of both United States law and the Evig Riksdag, the demon Velnias has a large amount of influence. The name comes from the Latvian underworld, where Velnias is revered.

AKKADIAN—an ancient language used prominently by the Akkad people in Mesopotamia, circa 2334–2154 BCE. While it is considered an extinct language, many of the immortals in Kurnugia primarily spoke Akkadian before being sent to the underworld.

ALKONOST—winged immortals, similar to sirens, with the heads of women but also the feathers, wings, and other parts of a bird. They have beautiful singing voices, but unlike sirens, their voices and songs do not have any power over anyone. They most commonly live in Northern Asia.

AMRITĀ—beverage of the gods, believed to grant renewal or peace. It is made from churning the salty river that flows through Kurnugia. Slightly syrupy with a sweet but earthy taste. Also referred to as "nectar" or "ambrosia."

APOTHECARY—originally a person who dispensed medical advice and medicine, the term has shifted to mean a person or place that sells various herbs, potions, and crystals with alleged medicinal value. An apothecary may also dabble in thaumaturgy as well as more alternative medical treatments.

APSARA—beautiful, divine Hindu female spirits of clouds and dancing who often inspire others to create and do good works in the world.

ARMARRIA INCANTATION—a protection and cloaking spell that works best in conjunction with the armarria potion. The incantation is: *"Ez geala, ba geala, kalte seguru, geala"* which means "we aren't, we are indeed, safe from harm, are we," in the old Basque language, derived from the songs and spells of the Sorginak (a Basque witch).

ARMARRIA POTION—a potion made of mugwort, obsidian flakes, and water from the Bidasoa River, among other more mystical ingredients. *Armarria* means "shield" in the Basque language. Used in conjunction with the armarria incantation. It must be applied directly above the heart to be most effective.

ASAKKU—evil demons from ancient Sumeria. According to Odin's letter to Baldur, they fought against Gugalanna in the great battle that left thousands dead, buried in mass graves in the city of Nawar.

Aswang—ghoulish, vampiric immortal demons with huge mouths full of teeth. Originally from the Philippines, there is a growing population living in the Aizsaule District.

Avondmarkt—a large black-market bazaar in Chicago, where any number of supernatural items can be procured—for the right price. From the Danish, literally meaning "night market."

Baba Yaga—an immortal being and birdlike witch from Russia.

Baião de dois—a Brazilian dish made of rice and beans, mixed with curded cheese.

Bararu Mutanu Ossuary—an ossuary is the final resting place for human and immortal remains, similar to a crypt. Unlike a crypt, an ossuary is usually decorated with (if not entirely made out of) bones as a way to honor the dead. The Baruru Mutanu Ossuary is one of the oldest ossuaries in the world, dating back several thousand years, and it is located in the Gates of Kurnugia in Central America. Many of the remains there have been calcified to such a degree that they have an appearance of being crystalized, which is how it was given its name. *Bararu Mutanu* translates to "Crystal Death" in Akkadian (the language of ancient Babylonians). Babylonian historians were determined to mark out all the most mystical places on earth, and this particular ossuary is located right outside the entrance to the underworld. Before the Babylonians named it, it had been used as a place to sacrifice to the gods in Kurnugia or to honor the dead.

bebeyaz panir—a popular Turkish cheese similar to feta.

Belize—an independent coastal country in Central America. It is most well known for being the home of the Gates of Kurnugia, which has led to a diverse, global society. It is particularly popular among immortals, with the densest population of immortals in the western hemisphere. As of the year

2137 CE, the total population was more than 9.3 million on only 8,800 square miles. The official languages are English, Spanish, German, and Sumerian.

BELMOPAN—the second largest and capital city of Belize. It is located 20 miles (31 km) NE of the Gates of Kurnugia, separated from the immortal-controlled city by the shantytown El Noveno Anillo. Belmopan is an affluent and beautiful city with a bustling tourist industry.

BIGUOL EN FRIIA—loosely translates to "encharment of Frigg" in Old Germanic. It is both the name of the ceremony and the incantation. The incantation is as follows: *"Gang ût/ût fana themo margę an that bên,/ ût fana themo bêne an that flêsg,/ût fana themo flêsgke an themo hûd,/ ût fana themo hûd an that lebēn /ût fana themo lebēn an that tōd /ût fan themo tōd an thesa strâla/uuodan, uuerthe so!"* In Old High German, this translates to: *"Get out, away from the marrow to the bone, away from the bone to the flesh, away from the flesh to the hide, away from the hide to life, away from life to the death, away from death and into the atmosphere. Odin, make it so!"*

BOAL MADEIRA—a sweet, fruity wine from Portugal with high alcohol content.

BORNITE—a gemstone with an iridescent finish, which gives it the name "peacock ore." Crystal shards are used to enhance joyfulness and ward off negativity. A bornite crystal is inlaid in the cover of the Sorcellerie Grimoire.

CAANA CITY—a city in Belize, nestled along the Caracol National Park. It gets its name from the nearby Mayan temple of Caana (the name of which means "the Sky Palace"). It is 40 miles (65 km) SW of the Gates of Kurnugia, traveling over jungle roads.

CABRIOLET—light carriages, usually drawn by a horse. In Kurnugia, they are drawn by Kting Voars. The name is often shortened to "cab" in the mortal world.

CACHAÇA—an alcoholic drink distilled from sugar cane, similar to rum.

CAMAHUETO—immortal, unicorn-like calves born with a single platinum horn that lived among the Chilote people in South America. The horn was virtually indestructible and was the strongest material on earth, which led to the camahuetos being hunted to extinction on earth in the 1600s CE.

CAMBION—the mortal children of either a human and a demon, or two demons of differing species (i.e., an incubus and a Pishacha). They inherit some of their parents' characteristics, such as horns or powerful sexuality, but as they are mortal, they are not subject to the law of Valkyries from the Evig Riksdag.

CARPE NOCTEM—a dive bar located on the Chicago mainland, near the edge of Lake Michigan before the water district of New Edgewater. The name means "Seize the Night" in Latin.

CE/BCE—CE stands for Common Era, which is a name for the current calendar era used around the world today. BCE stands for Before Common Era, the era preceding Common Era. The current year 2137 CE goes back two thousand one hundred and thirty-seven years, when time is referred to as BCE and counts back from one, so year 100 BCE is one hundred years after 200 BCE, and so on. The Common Era notation system can be used as an alternative to the Dionysian era system, and both notations refer to the Gregorian calendar.

CHERUBIM—immortal angels with four flaming wings and skin that glows brightly. They are able to read auras for impurities or evilness, and they guard the entrance to Zianna. Singular is "cherub."

CHICAGO—a megacity located on the lake in Illinois. According to the 2135 CE census, the dense city has a population over 31 million. It is divided into many boroughs, such as New Edgewater, Aizsaule District, and the Gold Coast. It is known for its vibrant night life and cuisine, as well as being home to the American headquarters of the Evig Riksdag. However, it is also known for its pollution, overpopulation, and crime.

CHUPACABRA—a medium-sized reptilian immortal animal. Its face has been compared to an "alien hyena." They have leathery green skin, quills all down their backs, and legs like a kangaroo. They are carnivorous, and they primarily live in the forests and jungles of Central America.

CODEX AETERNA—an ancient Norse book made of 50 vellum leaves, each covered in songs and limericks. The name means "The Eternal Book" in Latin. It is thought to have been written in the 1270s CE. The poem "Friggadraumr" is located within it.

THE COURT OF ZIANNA—the court of divine immortals that make decisions for the citadel of Zianna. The leader as well as the members are democratically elected and serve for a hundred years at a time. The current leader is Sedna, and her court consists of Bastet, Aphrodite, Apsu, Yemaya, Tsukiyomi, Altjira, Bochica, Danu, Hi'iaka, and Gersemi.

CRYPTOMERIAN FOREST—a dark underworld forest that surrounds the exit to Kurnugia. It is home to many aggressive cannibalistic plants, most notably the *Cryptomeria vorax* (Latin "hidden parts" + "devouring") trees, a subgenus of the trees known for the Yakushima forest in Japan.

CYCLOPS—a large humanoid immortal with only one eye in the center of their head, typically of Grecian ancestry.

DANTE'S LAGER—cheap terrible beer infused with ghost peppers.

DEVI/DEVA—Hindu celestial immortals that commonly take a human form to do good works on earth. They are divine beings, known for helping others and encouraging compassion and love. "Devi" are female, and "Deva" are male. Their name comes from the Sanskrit word for "shining," referring to the light of goodness that glows within them.

DILLINGER'S CORNER MARKET & APOTHECARY—a corner market in New Edgewater that sells basic groceries and a few supernatural items. Owned and managed by Fufluns Dillinger.

DRAUGR—an immortal that a Valkyrie has failed to return. The name comes from the Old Norse word for "undead." They are a very rare, dangerous occurrence.

DYRNWYN—a magic flaming sword created in fifteenth-century Wales. It only burns when the wielder's quest is true. It is an arming sword with a black blade, deep red hilt, and the cross-guards shaped to look like flames coming out of the grip. Roughly thirty-six inches in length.

EARTH—planet where all known life exists. Immortal and mortal beings have coexisted together for more than ten millennia, and by the year 2137 CE the population will have skyrocketed to 24.28 billion. Approximately 25 percent of that is composed of immortals, or 6.07 billion.

EIR—a Valkyrie sword in the possession of Quinn Devane. It has a black handle and blade of blue. It once belonged to one of the original nine Valkyries, Eir. Name roughly translates to "help" or "mercy" in old Norse.

EL NOVENO ANILLO—a shantytown-like suburb outside the Gates of Kurnugia. The name translates to "the Ninth Ring" in Spanish, alluding to Dante's Inferno. To the NE, it connects the Gates of Kurnugia to Belmopan. To the SW (toward Caana City), it's even more rundown. It is part of the Belmopan metro area population of 2.1 million, with roughly 1 million of those residents living in El Noveno Anillo.

EMÍ—the Yoruba word for "spirit" or "life" or "soul." It is the thing that gives one the ability to execute magic, whether the being is mortal or immortal.

EMMANUEL WOODED GARDEN—a forest and garden in Skarpåker Park. Named after twentieth-century Chicago activist Dr. Fannie Emmanuel.

ENOCHIAN—the original language of angels, based on Dr. John Dee's sixteenth-century occult writings.

ENOCHIAN MAGIC—a system of ceremonial magic with the invocation and commanding of various spirits. It is based on the sixteenth-century occult writings of Dr. John Dee and Edward Kelley, who claimed that their information, including the revealed Enochian language, was delivered to them directly by various angels.

ĒOSTRE'S LAGOMORPH CHOW—a perfectly balanced diet for jackalopes, wolpertingers, rabbits, pikas, and colugos.

ERALIM—the immortal beings that tell the Valkyrie where to go and who to kill. They work as intermediaries between the Vanir gods in Vanaheimr and the Evig Riksdag on earth. They are the offspring of Valkyries and Seraphim, and they cannot have children themselves. Their blood is slightly thinner than human blood and is dark purple in color.

ESHIK MITU—a geyser in the Gates of Kurnugia behind the Merchants of Death. It connects to the underworld, but it is filled with scalding water, sulphuric sludge, and a magic that makes it impossible for immortals to pass through, and nearly impossible for mortals. The name comes from Sumerian. *Eshik* means "door" and *Mitu* means "death."

ET INGRESSUS EST PRAETORIUM CANERET—a room in Sacrorum library devoted to epic poems and songs. The name means "The Hall of Minstrel and Adventure" in Latin. This is where *Codex Aeterna* is stored.

ET VIRGINES IN MORTE—a room in the Sacrorum library devoted to Valkyries. The name means "Death and the Maidens" in Latin.

EVERY FEELING ACT—a federal law in the United States that makes it illegal for any sentient being to consume the flesh of another sentient being. The drafted law frequently quotes eighteenth-century philosopher Jeremy Bentham, particularly the argument "The question is not Can they reason? nor, Can they talk? but, Can they suffer?" This law was acted in the mid-twentieth century, when genetically modified substitutions were created that allowed carnivorous immortals to eat and survive without relying on living flesh. While the consumption of nonsentient flesh is still allowed, rigorous testing is done to ensure that only approved beings are slaughtered. It is a controversial law, with the Kurnugia Society often pushing back against it to no avail.

Evig Riksdag—the global office where the Eralim work. The name means "Eternal Parliament." Of the 215 countries on earth, 172 of them have their own Evig Riksdag office that works in conjunction with their individual governments. Some countries refuse to acknowledge the laws of the Vanir gods, but Valkyries are still sent from other offices to return the immortals. They are often accompanied by armed Vörðr guards for missions in hostile countries. Each office is overseen by an Arch Seraph, who works directly with a Vanir god (each Vanir god oversees a specific country or occasionally several smaller countries). Working beneath the Arch Seraph are other lower-level seraphim who solve the Mortal Equation. Directly beneath them are the Eralim, who train and handle the Valkyries, and the Valkyries themselves are the lowest-level officers of the Evig Riksdag. The United States Evig Riksdag is located near the center of the country, in Chicago, Illinois. It is in the State District, only a few blocks from the Willis Tower.

exousia—warrior angels that make up a divine protection service in the citadel of Zianna in Kurnugia. They venture beyond the walls to help those in dire situations, but only at the behest of the Court of Zianna. They also defend the citadel—and the Court in particular—if there are any attacks on Zianna. Their name comes from the Greek, meaning "authorities" or "powers."

Feast of the Dead—a day to celebrate and remember the many gods and goddesses that have returned to Kurnugia. Over time, it has become a wild party where it's customary to dress up and gorge yourself on libations and food. In North America, it is celebrated on the first Saturday in October.

Fountain of Fates—a fountain in Skarpåker Park that incorporates sculptures of the trio of Greek Fates.

FRIGGADRAUMR—a prophecy that is sometimes quoted in the Norse poem "Völuspá." The name translates to "Frigg's Dream" or "The Dream of Frigg."

GATES OF KURNUGIA—an independent sovereign entity in Belize. It is governed—in a very limited capacity, that is—by demons and other impious immortals. When it was first settled ten millennia ago, it was called In Sabatu Kurnugia, but around 1500 BCE, it was mislabeled on an official record as Baba Kurnugia (*Baba* meant Gates). In the fifteenth century, during the English conquest, the name was officially changed to the English translation. *In Sabatu*—the original name—meant rings, since they didn't have a different word for labyrinth, and was a reference to the maze of walls that surround it. The city itself encircles the Bararu Mutanu Ossuary, which houses the carefully guarded and supernaturally locked entrance to Kurnugia. The walls are instilled with magic to keep in those that cannot leave (many immortals are exiled there as punishment, while some demons choose to give up their freedom willingly to enjoy the more depraved life in the city). It is surrounded by the shantytown El Noveno Anillo. The Gates of Kurnugia is 20 miles (31 km) SW of Belmopan, and 40 miles (65 km) NE of Caana City. It's approximately 2,080 miles SE of Chicago. It is part of the Belmopan metro area population of 2.1 million, with roughly 400,000 of those residents living in the Gates of Kurnugia.

GOLD COAST—an affluent neighborhood in northern Chicago, with high-end commercial and luxury residential properties. It is also home to one of the most prosperous and lavish gentlemen's clubs in the world, Nysa.

GÖNDUL—one of the original nine Valkyries created by Odin; also the name of her amber sword. Name roughly translates to "spear-wielder."

GORGON—immortal women with snake hair and scales on their skin. They can also turn a person to stone just by looking at them, but it is a power that they have control over.

GUNGNIR—Odin's spear that was created as the only true way to destroy an immortal forever. The materials to make it were gifted to Odin by other

Vanir gods: the dark silvery-blue shaft is made of camahueto horn gifted by Auchimalgen, the brassy red tip is made of orichalcum gifted by Poseidon, and the tip was dipped in glowing poison Halāhala gifted by Brahma.

HAKAWAI—large immortal raptors, similar to a Haast's eagle, known for their distinctive call.

HALĀHALA—the most vicious venomous poison in the world. The tip of Gungnir is dipped in it, after it is gifted to Odin by Brahma.

HANNUNVAAKUNA—sometimes referred to as a "looped square." It's an ancient Finnish symbol of good luck.

HARIRA—a Moroccan soup made of tomatoes and tomato concentrate, lentils, chickpeas, onions, rice, herbs (celery, parsley, and coriander), spices (mainly saffron, ginger, and pepper), and a teaspoon or two of olive oil.

HEGEWISCH—an older community on the southside of Chicago. It is almost an hour and a half south of New Edgewater.

HEMATITE—a gemstone with a mirror-like finish. Crystal shards are used in various protection spells, most notably the armarria incantation.

HILDR—one of the original nine Valkyries created by Odin; also the name of her crimson sword. Name roughly translates to "battle."

HUBUR RIVER—a river that flows through Kurnugia, from under the Eshik Mitu geyser, straight through the underworld and past Zianna, before connecting with the Cryptomerian Forest. The width varies, and the water is dark blue and salty.

HYPERBUS—hoverbus that goes faster than a normal bus, with an average speed of 90 to 100 miles per hour. It is also more suitable for rugged terrain than a traditional wheeled bus.

INCUBUS/SUCCUBUS—provocative nightmare demonic immortals, with a male called an incubus and a female called a succubus.

ITAYAKKAL—a heartstone made of pink tourmaline that is enchanted so it enables the receiver of the stone to feel the love and warmth of the giver. The name comes from Tamil (an ancient language still used in Sri Lanka, where the gemstone is naturally found), literally translating to "heart stone." In Hindu, the gem is known for its properties of "love."

JACKFRUIT SEEDS—large nutlike seeds from the jackfruit. Flavor is milky and sweet, similar to Brazil nuts or chestnuts.

JENGLOT—a small doll-like immortal that likes to cause mischief, not unlike a gremlin. They are typically found in Indonesia.

JINN—wish-granting humanoid immortals. They are generally smaller in stature than the average human, but otherwise they are physically indistinguishable. While they can occasionally fall into a trickster role, they are generally well-intentioned and kind. Their vast power to grant wishes is not available at all times to all beings, and in fact, most jinn require that certain ceremonies and rituals be performed before one can access their power.

JOROGUMO—shapeshifting immortals that change from beautiful women to horrific giant spiders. They feast on the lust—and occasionally the literal beating hearts—of men, thus earning them a name that translates to "prostitute spider" in Japanese. In the United States, the Every Feeling Act allows them to feed only on the lust of consenting adults.

KAHVALTI—a Turkish coffee house/breakfast diner.

KALANORO—small, primate immortals with hooked claws, a piranha-esque appetite, and a penchant for hoarding "treasures." They are native to Madagascar, but a substantial population also exists in Panama.

KALFU'S DAGGER—a dagger that belonged to the Haitian creator Petra Loa which has the power to kill other Petra Loas. It has a jagged blade of black tourmaline. The hilt is a deep red with a Vévé symbol carved into it, right in the center of the quillons. It is twelve inches in length.

KATMER—a Turkish flaky golden flatbread.

KIBBEH—a deep-fried croquette stuffed with mushrooms, onions, and pine nuts.

KIRIN—extinct divine immortal creatures, similar to unicorns. They possess two antlers and a horn, and have a pastel mane and prehensile tail. Iridescent scales are scattered along their body. Their extinction was actually the inciting act that caused Odin to create the Valkyries to help purge the powerful immortals before they destroyed the earth.

KTING VOAR—a massive immortal bovine, similar to the gaur bison or the short-haired yak. Their dark fur is speckled with white. They generally stand over eight feet tall at the shoulder and can weigh more than 3,500 lbs. They have two-foot-long horns that curve and twist like snakes. They are reputed to eat snakes, and have a mouthful of sharp teeth, including two saber-tooth incisors. Despite their immortality, the Kting Voars have been hunted nearly to extinction, and they are a protected species in their native countries of Vietnam and Cambodia.

KURNUGIA—the official name of the underworld, so named by the ancient Sumerians who first recorded its existence. It is a physical plane, separated from earth by the powerful magic of the Vanir gods, and it has a nearly unbreakable seal that keeps the immortals trapped in Kurnugia once they are returned by the Valkyries. The literal translation for Kurnugia is "Earth of No Return."

KURTARI INCANTATION—the incantation that must be said in order to leave Kurnugia. The phrase is *"atebamap adilz a odo,"* which is the backwards version of the Enochian phrase *"odo a zlida pamebeta,"* which means "open the water unto me." While the chant is being said, the practitioner must spin counterclockwise, and they must be marked by the blood of an Eralim. The name comes from the Sumerian language, *kurtari* loosely translating to "land of return." The incantation only works if the practitioner is mortal.

KUSANAGI-NO-TSURUGI—a powerful sword that controls the wind. It was created in the first century in Japan. Midsized sword with a beveled blade, and both the blade and the hilt are made of a singular piece of a black obsidian-like material. Roughly twenty-three inches in length. It is not a katana.

LEMPO—a capricious and sometimes evil god/goddess of love. Long wavy red hair, androgynous features, antlers, and a hannunvaakuna tattoo on their face. Originally ruled in Finland before being returned to Kurnugia.

LENTILS UNLIMITED—a company that sells lentils to stock up for doomsday preparedness.

LILIPLUM—chemical derived from the *Lilium plumeria* flower. It is a syrupy liquid that, when inhaled through a vaporizer or hookah, creates an opiate-like euphoria and occasional hallucinations. The smoke it produces is a dark violet, and it smells sweet, like the lily flower it comes from.

LOBISHOMEN—werewolf-like immortal with huge fangs.

LUFT—short for luftfahrrad.

LUFTFAHRRAD—a German-engineered type of hoverbike.

MAHAMBA—large reptilian immortal carnivores from the Congo.

MANANANGGAL—Filipino vampiric demonic immortals.

MANETO CANAL—the road/canal that Malin lives on, from the Native word for river serpent.

Mausoleum av Veteraner Från Kriget Mot Odödlighet—a mausoleum where deceased Valkyries are interred at the Rosehill Cemetery in Chicago. The name translates to "Mausoleum of the Veterans of the War on Immortality" in Swedish. It has a minimalist design in white marble, giving it a very cubic appearance. The coat of arms is carved into the marble above: a shield emblazoned with the three horns of Odin and nine swords fanned out behind it.

Merchants of Death—a market in the Gates of Kurnugia where immortal creatures sell taboo and often illegal items to various tourists—both immortals (who need permission and a shielding potion from the Evig Riksdag for a limited pass that allows them to exit and enter the Gates) and mortals (who can pass freely without permission from the Evig Riksdag). Because the Gates of Kurnugia is its own sovereign entity, it is an almost entirely lawless society, with the only law being enforced by Seraphim-controlled protection spells that don't allow the killing of visiting mortals or immortals. Many of the merchants get around that by paying smugglers to kill outside the walls of the city and then bring the valuable parts inside for the merchants to sell.

Mist—one of the original nine Valkyries created by Odin; also the name of her teal sword. Name means "mist" or "cloud" in old Norse.

Mngwa—immortal felines with brindle coats. They are among the largest of the big cats, at roughly the size of an average donkey. They have elongated fangs, razor-sharp claws, and a spiky mane of fur that extends down the backs like a mohawk. Typically from Tanzania.

Mortal Equation—a complex system handed down by Vanir gods to the Seraphim to calculate when immortals should be returned to Kurnugia. It is impossible for anyone outside of a Vanir god or a Seraph to understand, with infinite symbols, constantly shifting variables, and an occasionally untranslatable dimensional language.

Nawar—an ancient city, now more often known as Tell Brak. It was the site of early human civilization in Mesopotamia.

NEW EDGEWATER—a district in Chicago, built out over Lake Michigan in an attempt to handle the population explosion. When founded a hundred years ago, it was designed as a luxury addition with canals for roads. However, due to pollution and the constant moisture, the neighborhood has sunk into poverty and dilapidation.

NORAM OVERLAND EXPRESS—a mode of transportation that runs from Canada down to Honduras. The Overland is neither a train nor a bus but rather an odd hybrid that makes travel much faster and easier. The double-decker carriage straddles several lanes of the highway with a three-meter gap beneath large enough to accommodate the average hovercraft. It runs on rails located on either side of the highway, with a fixed route similar to a train, and it can reach speeds as high as 125 miles per hour.

NORNEWSNOW—a twenty-four-hour news network, with the main station based in Chicago. Ellery Park is one of their lead reporters.

OKROSHKA—a Russian soup that's essentially a salad of diced boiled eggs, horseradish, scallions, and potatoes covered in a broth made of kvas (a fermented cola-like beverage without carbonation) and served with a dollop of sour cream on top.

OLITAU—large demonic immortal bats, with a twelve-foot wingspan, black fur, and red wings. Though they are originally from Cameroon, the Gates of Kurnugia has a very large population, with many immortals breeding and raising them. The olitau have excretions that can be turned into expensive black-market wares.

ÖLRÚN—one of the original nine Valkyries created by Odin; also the name of her emerald sword. Name roughly translates to "secret" or "rune."

ORESA OZIEN INCANTATION—the name itself means "owned by darkness" in Enochian, and it is used in cases of possession. It only works when spoken by an Eralim or Seraph. It is important to physically touch the suspected possessed person while saying, *"Bolape voresa, oresa noco! Elasa biab ge de oi goaanu!"* Which means "Get out, dark servant! You are not of this creation!" in Enochian.

ORICHALCUM—a metallic substance found only in the Lost City of Atlantis. It is considered to be unbreakable. It is brassy with a red hue.

ORISHA—helpful immortal spirits that guide lost souls around Zianna.

PALMITO FRESCO ASSADO—fresh-baked palm heart. It has a mild flavor with a nutty, creamy center.

PERENELLE'S CHILDREN—a street gang named after Perenelle and Nicolas Flamel, famous alchemists from the 1300s. The gang is known for their neon colors and cyberpunk style, and their emblem is the Flamel symbol. They are all Cambions or lower-level demons, and generally pretend to be interested in alchemy but usually just cause minor trouble. The gang is from New Edgewater.

PETRO LOA—an immortal being that exists in an ageless human form. Loas are considered benign spirits, while Petro indicates a type of loa renowned for being fiery, passionate, and strong-willed.

PINK TOURMALINE—a crystal that is used to connect others with love.

PISHACHA—flesh-eating demonic immortals with a mostly humanoid form, but they also have bulging red eyes and rows of pointed teeth. They struggle to survive in the United States, which bans the consumption of sentient flesh under the Every Feeling Act, and they often rely on black markets and "vegetarian" substitutions.

A PLACE FOR DREAMING—a mossy overgrown gazebo on an outcropping of large rocks in the center of Skarpåker Park in Chicago.

Pontianak—female vampiric immortal ghouls that usually take a beautiful human female form. They are tormented and carnivorous, and they lure their victims by imitating the sound of an infant crying. There is a large population of Indonesian emigrated Pontianaks in the New Edgewater district of Chicago, and despite the fact that they do not kill or hunt because of the Every Feeling Act, they still often call and cry out in the night.

Pudla—an Indian crepe/pancake-like food made with chickpeas. It can be sweet or savory, and it is often served with chutney.

Ra—an immortal god with a human body and a falcon head worshipped in Egypt.

Ramen—Japanese deep-fried noodles that are inexpensive and easy to make.

Rassolnik—a Russian hot soup in a salty-sour cucumber base. Typical rassolnik is made with kidneys, brine, root vegetables, and barley.

Ravenswood Academy—a well-respected post-secondary educational institution. It is operated in conjunction with the Evig Riksdag, and it specializes in training for supernatural and supernatural-adjacent careers for those who lack any abilities themselves, particularly humans and the mortal offspring from mixed parentage.

The Red Raven—a vibrant nightclub where demons hang out located in the Aizsaule District and owned by the demon Velnias.

Rhubarb chutney—a spicy condiment made of rhubarb with vinegar, spices, and sugar.

Róta—one of the original nine Valkyries created by Odin; also the name of her dark indigo sword. Name roughly translates to "sleet and storm."

Sacrorum Wing—a wing in Ravenswood Academy filled with important and sacred books. Its creation and maintenance is a joint effort on the part of the elite board of education and the Evig Riksdag, who both believe that some texts contain information too valuable and dangerous to be distributed en masse, and they fear that digital media is vulnerable to piracy. Many historical texts have been transferred onto digital formats, but the Sacrorum is dedicated to preserving and sharing texts that aren't permitted to ever be digitized. As an added level of security, the ever watchful Sinaa protect the knowledge and contents of the wing fiercely.

SALVARI BALM—an antibiotic and antidemonic supernaturally infused bacitracin. It is bubbly and blue in appearance. The name comes from the Old French word *salvari*, which means to "save" or "defend."

SAMBUSA—a popular Somalian baked dish, it is a fried triangular pastry filled with seasoned lentils and potatoes.

SERAPHIM—the divine immortal beings that work in the highest levels of the Evig Riksdag. While they have a humanoid form, they are difficult for mortals and most immortals to look at. They are described as possessing an ethereal beauty and glowing brightly. Singular is "seraph."

SHARUR—an ancient flail mace, created thousands of years ago in Sumeria. It has a long bronze staff with a gruesome spiked head made of iron attached to it by a chain. Most notably, it has the power to fly to its owner when called.

SHE'OL—a city in Kurnugia controlled by the god of destruction, Abaddon. The nearest city to Zianna, and also one of the largest in Kurnugia. It is surrounded by jagged rocks and a magma moat. It's a very dark city, but large, with lots of noise and red light.

SHUNKA WARAKIN—large hyena–dire wolf carnivorous immortals. They have mottled orange and black fur, sloping backs, stubby tails, and short hind legs, giving them a hunchbacked appearance. Their heads are similar to that of wolves, though much larger and broader.

SIBUDU KEY—an ancient crescent-shaped stone made of sandstone and quartz that allows entrance into Kurnugia. It was discovered with other ancient artifacts in the Sibudu Cave of South Africa. The key was created 60,000 to 65,000 years ago, but the creator is unknown.

SIGRÚN—one of Odin's original nine Valkyries; also the name of her purple sword. Name roughly translates to "victory rune" in old Norse.

SIMURGH—a massive feathered immortal beast with the body of a white lion, the crimson head of dog, two gigantic brightly colored wings of emerald and violet, and a tail made of long, vibrant peacock-esque plumages. Most commonly found in Persia.

SINAA—knowledge-obsessed immortals. They have the appearance of jaguars, with many eyes hidden in their spots. They are most known for guarding the Sacrorum Wing in Ravenswood Academy, although they are originally from Brazil.

SIRRUSH—a scaly immortal dragon with hind legs resembling the talons of an eagle, feline forelegs, a long neck and tail, a horned head, a snake-like tongue, and a crest.

SKARPÅKER PARK—a twenty-five-acre park in Chicago on the edge of the La-Bagh Woods. In the very center of the park is its namesake—a large stone inscribed with an eschatological verse in the old language of the gods. It was unearthed in a freak earthquake centuries ago, with jagged edges poking out from the middle of the empty field, which was how it had earned its name—*Skarpåker* means "sharp field." Also in the park: A Place for Dreaming gazebo, Dene rock outcropping, *Window to Forever* art installation, Portello Pavilion over the Great Lawn, Emmanuel Wooded Garden, Fountain of Fates, and a playground.

SKÖGUL—one of the original nine Valkyries created by Odin; also the name of her honey-colored sword. Name roughly translates to "high-towering."

SOLAMENTUM—ochre-colored crystals made with ginger, angelic toadstool, and codeine to help with pain and inflammation.

SÓLARSTEINN—a sun stone used like a compass. Whoever is holding must focus on what they want most, and the stone uses light to guide them to it. Created by Vikings in the early 1000s BCE.

SORCELLERIE GRIMOIRE—a book of magic and history that has been in the Warren family for generations. *Sorcellerie* roughly translates to "sorcery or witch-craft" in French, and *grimoire* means "spell book or magic text book" from French derivation, so it roughly means "sorcery spell book." It is a thick, heavy book that smells of dust and sage. The cover is leathery black with a lustrous sheen, and an iridescent bornite (Peacock Ore) crystal is inlaid in its cover. It is approximately 9.5 inches wide, 12 inches long, and 2 inches thick.

SOURSOP WINE—white wine made from the soursop plant in Belize. Tart but sweet.

SUGARLAND—a midsized city in Texas, it's the halfway point between Chicago and the Gates of Kurnugia. It's also the final NorAm Overland Express stop in the United States before Mexico.

SUP D'YAVOLA—a Russian restaurant in the Aizsaule District that only serves soup and alcohol. The name literally translates to "The Devil's Soup."

TARTARUS—a city in Kurnugia controlled by Perses. A cliff-face town, across from the Acheron Gorge.

TELL BRAK—a site in Syria where mass graves dating from 3800 to 3600 BCE have been unearthed, suggesting advanced warfare around this period.

THAUMATURGY—the study of magic, and one of the more popular majors at

Ravenswood Academy. Twentieth-century Druid Isaac Bonewits defined it as "the art and science of 'wonder working,' using magic to actually change things in the physical world."

THRÚD—one of the original nine Valkyries created by Odin; also the name of her pink sword. Name roughly translates to "strength."

TRASGU—impish humanoid immortals with horns and a tail. They often walk bowlegged with a limp.

TYRFING—a magical Norse sword that never misses a strike. It's a two-handed long sword, approximately forty-three inches in length, and it has a golden hilt.

UNSEEN ENCHANTMENT—a spell of concealment. *"Omnium visibilium et invisibilium omnium manemus"* means "all things visible and invisible, to all we remain unseen" in Latin. Used in conjunction with the smoke from a Valerian root candle.

USW—stands for "ultrasonic weapon." USWs are considered a nonlethal weapon, using high-powered sound waves to incapacitate opponents.

VALHALLAN CLOAK—a hooded cloak created by Odin that protects the wearer from most physical or magical attacks. It has a very distinct appearance, looking as if the night sky had somehow been turned into a fabric.

VANAHEIMR—the plane beyond earth where the Vanir gods live. Not much is known about it, since the Vanir gods are very private, having retreated from interactions with humans several millennia ago.

VANIR—the highest immortal beings of creation; the ones that create all the laws that govern how life exists on earth. The Vanir gods include: Odin

(Norse), Zeus (Greek), Hunab-Ku (Mayan), Jupiter (Roman), Ra (Egyptian), Bondye (Voodoo), and Buga (Slavic), among many others.

VEGVISIR—an old Norse sigil meant to help those who are lost or need protection.

VÖRÐR—the Evig Riksdag's elite security team. Its officers are entirely mortal, as the Evig Riksdag needs protection from immortals almost exclusively. The Vörðr officers use specialized military equipment and tactics to enforce the laws of Evig Riksdag and to protect the Seraphim, Eralim, and Valkyries who work within it. Their insignia is the three horns of Odin on an eagle.

WAGYL—a rainbow serpent.

WENDIGO—a humanoid immortal being with antlers and skin falling off its bones. Wendigos are known to be cannibalistic and do not adhere to the Every Feeling Act. Because of that, there are very few known to be living outside of prison in the United States, despite the fact that they are native to North America.

WINDOW TO FOREVER—an art installation in Skarpåker Park. It is a large, curved, concave circle of polished stainless steel located next to the lake and near the Dene.

WOLF RIVER DISTRICT—a former warehouse district in Chicago. As industry and manufacturing moved out of the city, the warehouses were vacant and soon converted to a residential neighborhood. It is also home to a large population of Fallen angels and demons.

WOLPERTINGER—a mortal domesticated lagomorph; closely related to rabbits and jackelopes. It has two small fanged teeth, plush fur, feathered wings, two tiny antlers, and two large ears. They make good house pets.

žALTYS—mortal grass snakes. Their blood has been found to be helpful in fertility potions, and their meat is considered a delicacy in Lithuania.

ZIANNA—a peaceful enchanted city in Kurnugia where divine immortals reside. It is surrounded by seven gates.

PREPARE TO BE SWEPT AWAY BY THE MAGIC OF THE
TRYLLE TRILOGY!

SWITCHED
at birth...

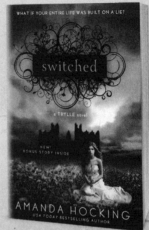

BOOK 1

BOOK 2

TORN
between two worlds

ASCEND
to the magic...

BOOK 3

🐦 St. Martin's Griffin